RUN THE GAUNTLET

Run The Gauntlet

Book 1 of the Blenheim Series

By

Vincent Formosa

2021

Copyright © 2016 by Vincent Formosa.

2nd Edition created 2021.

This is a novel. The characters, situations and military organisations are an invention of the author, except where they can be identified historically. Any other resemblance to actual persons, living or dead is purely coincidental. Likewise, names, dialogue and opinions expressed are products of the author's imagination to fit the story and not to be interpreted as real.

ISBN: 9781520172422

3D Meshes of Bristol Blenheim and Messerschmitt Bf110 created by Mark Rowles and purchased from https://www.cgtrader.com under royalty free commercial licence. Textures for Bristol Blenheim created by Vincent Formosa. Cover layout by Vincent Formosa

All rights reserved under International and Pan-American Copyright Conventions.

No part of this book may be reproduced in any form or by any electronic or mechanical means, ; this includes but is not restricted to information storage and retrieval systems, without written permission from the author or publisher, except by a reviewer who may quote passages in a review.

This book would not exist if it were not for the help and hard work of a number of people. Particular thanks go to Tony Lowe and John Smith of the Blenheim Society for providing much insight and technical knowledge on the aircraft.

Thanks also go to Jon Hayden for spending many hours going over my manuscript, making suggestions and discussing their ideas with me for which I am truly grateful.

Other titles by the same author

The Eagles Of Peenemunde
Maximum Effort
Prototype
Callicoe RNVR

Channel Dash (Book 2 of the Blenheim Series)

Available in both Kindle and paperback formats on Amazon.

Run The Gauntlet

Table of Contents

1939

1.	False Start	1
2.	Foreign Fields	7
3.	In The Cold Light Of Dawn	19
4.	The Grand Tour	25
5.	A Jaunt In The Country	29
6.	Storm In A Teacup	34
7.	This Is The Home Service	39
8.	Baptism	48
9.	He Who Believeth In Me	54
10.	Lay Me Down To Rest	64
11.	Taking Stock	68
12.	Coconut Shy	74
13.	Ten Green Bottles	82
14.	There And Back Again	90
15.	Culottes Et Décolleté et la Vin!	95
16.	Phases	104
17.	Absence Makes	109
18.	Idle Hands	116
19.	Curtains	123
20.	Twice Shy	128
21.	Breaking Bread	135
22.	Ghosts	142
23.	Come What May	150
24.	Attend The List	158
25.	If You Go Down To The Woods Today	164
26.	The Coming Of The King	169
27.	Joyeux Noel	172
28.	Leftovers	186
29.	First Foot	192

1940

1.	Waving The Flag	205
2.	Hard Knocks	212
3.	Picking Up The Pieces	220
4.	Scissors, Paper, Stone	227
5.	Every Dog Has His Day	234
6.	Twilight Blues	242
7.	Café Au Lait	249

8.	A Place In The Sun	258
9.	Whilst The Cat's Away	261
10.	Walking Through Gethsemane	265
11.	Back To Work	276
12	A Moment To Themselves	280
13.	Gearing Up	284
14.	The Vagaries Of Life	296
15.	Do Unto Others	302
16.	From Out Of The East	310
17.	Case Yellow	317
18.	Poised	319
19.	Get Stuck In	322
20.	Taking Stock	333
21.	More Of The Same	343
22.	Once More Unto The Breach Dear Friends	351
23.	Shell Shock	360
24.	The Door Swings Both Ways	366
25.	Forty Pieces Of Silver	368
26.	Today's Fox	373
27.	Fingers In The Dam	380
28.	Bitter Ashes	387
29.	One Fine Day	394
30.	House Of Cards	398
31.	Do What You Can	400
32.	Take What You Can	406
33.	The Sweepings	417
34.	Lost	423
35.	Bread And Circuses	427
36.	The Last Gasp	435

Authors Note   441

1939

1.1 – False Start

In 1939, the world found itself on the actual brink; again. The lessons of the last war were either blithely ignored or conveniently twisted to suit political expediency. European nations drew a line in the sand and dared each other to cross it. *'Peace in our time'* was promised, but after sabres were rattled back and forth, they turned a blind eye to the upstart little Corporal one too many times. Czechoslovakia and Poland bore the first brunt of Blitzkrieg as they were put to the sword.

For the second time in twenty five years, Britain went to war. The Royal Air Force was committed to the offensive almost immediately. Squadrons were moved to France to form the Advanced Air Striking Force. Fighter Command sent four Hurricane squadrons as a show of support for the French. The army sent ten Divisions across the Channel as the British Expeditionary Force and they took up position in the killing fields of northern France. Everyone settled down and waited for the shooting to start, and they waited, and they waited.

At the moment that other units were packing up to head to France, Falcon Squadron, were trading in their Fairey Battles for Bristol Blenheims. While they fell in love with their new aircraft, it felt like they had missed the boat. If they didn't get into the war now, it might all be over before they got their chance.

Left behind, they were kept busy practising their formation flying and increased their training tempo. They crossed the channel a number of times on familiarisation exercises but never saw a whiff of a German aircraft. Morale slumped further when they were told they would form part of the strategic reserve. While friends and colleagues were up at the sharp end, they were at home and hating every minute of it.

As September drew to a close, there was no war, no mass battle, no dogfights and no glory to be won. The days got shorter, it got colder and the papers started to print the age old fantasy that it would all be over by Christmas without a shot being fired. The rush of enthusiasm waned and they settled back down to their usual routines.

As October began, the squadron's world was turned upside down again. Out of the blue, they received movement orders to pack up and move to France. The powers that be had decided to expand the RAF's contribution and form another bomber wing. Falcon squadron were being sent to join two Fairey Battle units to work with the French army and BEF in the north.

The aircrew received forty eight hours embarkation leave. For everyone else, it was one mad rush. RAF Allenby became a hive of activity. There were a thousand and one things to coordinate the movement of a squadron from one place to another. The ground crews slaved to assemble the ground equipment. Admin staff burned the midnight oil to get it all done in time.

Officialdom came to the rescue. As the other units had flown out the previous month, it had all been done before so a lot of the kinks had already been ironed out. In addition, the Air Ministry had made arrangements for bombs, fuel, engines and other spares to be transported to France the previous year. The advance party left on the Wednesday in two lumbering transport aircraft. The squadron Adjutant, Michael Kittinger departed with the engineering officer and a ground crew detachment to get things started. More personnel left in the afternoon in a convoy of trucks for one of the southern ports loaded with spares and supplies.

While all that was going on, the aircrew lined up outside the Medical Officers' hut to get their shots. Nursing hangovers, they presented their arms as instructed. It was like some conveyor belt at a factory. The nurses went down the line, a quick swipe with some antiseptic and cotton wool and then they got jabbed. Rubbing their arms, they went back to their billets to pack. Flying kit and uniform was crammed into bags. They put the finishing touches on their personal affairs and letters to friends and family were put in the mail.

At breakfast the following day, the aircrew listened to news that suddenly made the war far more personal. They sat hunched over their food as they heard snippets of gossip about a clash between a flight from 150 squadron and German fighters.

150's Fairey Battles had been on a recce flight along the border when the 109s had pounced on them from out of the sun. Five Battles were chopped down in a matter of minutes. Two 109s were shot down in return but it was poor consolation. Only the year before they'd shared an aerodrome with the men of 150 on exercise. The news of the losses was a hard blow.

Flight Lieutenant Paul Farmer absently stirred his spoon in his porridge while he thought about the losses. The porridge had gone cold ten minutes before and was stiff and unappetising. His Navigator, William Preddy morosely drank his cup of tea while he digested the news that his roommate from Cranwell was now a wartime statistic.

"Do we know how many made it back?" asked another of the pilots, Sam Arthur. Farmer shook his head.

"I asked, but details are a bit sketchy. I know Tony Hyde-Parker fractured his ankle and Mike Poulton and his crew got pretty badly burned. Only MacDonald actually got back but he went up in flames on landing apparently."

"Jesus." Arthur whistled quietly through his teeth. He ran a hand through his short black hair and rubbed his neck. "The Germans don't muck about do they? It sounds like a massacre."

"Didn't they have an escort?" asked Preddy, his voice plaintive. He had abandoned his cup of tea and started fussily spreading butter on a piece of toast. Farmer shook his head.

"From what I've heard I don't think so. Mac only got away because once he was on his own he made out like some barnstormer apparently."

"Christ, what a mess." Arthur slumped back in his seat and twiddled his thumbs in his lap. "I used to like the Battle but I'm glad we traded them in for the Blenheim." he muttered.

Farmer ate a mouthful of porridge without thinking. Gagging, he washed it down with some tea. He muttered as he wiped his mouth with the back of his hand.

"Careful old man," Preddy teased. He yelped when Farmer hit him where he'd been injected the previous day. He rubbed his arm and pursed his lips in pain.

"It was only a dab old boy," said Farmer casually. Preddy scowled and carried on rubbing his arm, muttering to himself.

"Careful, you might keel over like Fallon," cautioned Arthur. That got a laugh from the surrounding tables and Farmer thumped the table in good humour.

Only the day before when the aircrew had gone to get their jabs, there had been casualties. Pettifer had come out of the MO's office unsteady on his feet. Osbourne had followed him out and leaned against the wall fighting a wave of nausea. It had been Fallon, the runner, the all rounder who was fit as a butcher's dog who'd hit the ground.

While they amused themselves, one of the subjects of their humour came into the mess. Flying Officer Julian Pettifer sat down at the next table and the Steward took his order. Pettifer was tall and painfully thin. It was a running joke that he had pimples rather than muscles and it was some bureaucratic mistake that he'd been accepted for flying training. Most marvelled that he possessed the strength to control any aircraft in the air.

Prissy on the ground, he silenced most of his critics with his flying, being one of the best pilots on the squadron. That was a source of irritation for Farmer and Pettifer's plumby voice and soft manner only served to irritate him more. The feeling was mutual; Pettifer had little love for Farmer and resented the attention of both him and his cronies.

He tugged his uniform jacket down; making sure it was tight across his shoulders. He brushed a piece of lint off his sleeve. Well groomed, he had a penchant for fussing over his nails and making sure his hair stayed in place. He rearranged the cutlery on the table, making sure they were parallel to the place mats, to suit his sense of order.

Farmer leaned back in his chair and turned to glare at Pettifer. The younger man studiously ignored him while he unfolded the day's newspaper and laid it flat on the table next to him. He began reading the lead article.

"Speak of the devil; and he *shall* appear." Farmer rapped his knuckles on the table top and made the quiet man jump. "Pettifer old chap, do join us."

"No thank you," Pettifer replied, doing his best to keep his tone neutral, although his face twisted in distaste. He kept his attention focused as he spread butter on some toast. He frowned when he managed to get some on his fingers. He wiped his thumb on a napkin.

"Ooooooh," said Farmer, giving Preddy a knowing wink. "Too good for us, eh?"

"No," said Pettifer slowly around a mouthful of toast. "I'm just careful who I mix with."

Farmer hitched round on his chair, leaning over the back of it to stare across the table at Pettifer, pitching his voice for Preddy and Arthurs' benefit.

"You know what? I just don't get it boys. Fallon was a rowing blue, stocky, with muscles on muscles. How come he keeled over rather than a long streak of misery like you?"

"Piss off Farmer," said Pettifer, his tone flat. Farmer grinned and leaned lower, trying to catch Pettifer's eye. Every time Pettifer looked in one direction, Farmer matched him to get under his skin. Finally, he succeeded and Pettifer gave in, knowing he would get no peace until he let the older man have his way.

"For heaven's sake, he just collapsed." He spread his fingers wide and placed his hands on the top of the white tablecloth. "We came out of the MO's after getting our jabs. Fallon was rubbing his arm and complaining about a pain in the chest and then he just sort of...went over. Classic Charlie Chaplin, flat on his face. Like he'd been poleaxed." He mimicked a fall, using one forearm as the ground and the other as a body hitting the ground. "I went and got the MO and they ferried him off to the hospital."

"And you didn't touch him?" challenged Farmer, disappointed at such a tame telling.

"I didn't touch him. Ask Osbourne, he was there too."

"I will; believe me, I will."

Farmer turned back to his little group when the Steward brought Pettifer his food.

"We'll pop in and see Fallon later," he said to the rest of them.

"I'm afraid there will be no popping in to see anyone," said a voice from the doorway.

Wallis Dane, the squadron's Intelligence Officer, stood at the door, hands behind his back. Forty two years old, Wallis was a reserve officer who had come from King's College. He'd swapped his seat in advanced mathematics for intelligence work. In some ways, he found life on an operational squadron little different to life at Cambridge. He had merely exchanged one bunch of prima donnas for another.

"Fallon won't be having any visitors for a bit I'm afraid," he said solemnly. That produced murmurs of surprise.

"What got him? The clap?" someone asked from the back of the room. That caused much hilarity but it soon died down when Dane didn't rise to the remark and his face remained set.

"According to the MO, he's had a severe heart attack complicated by some other nasty infection. So we'll be going without him. The doctors have said he needs plenty of rest to recover."

News delivered, he turned on his heel and left the room. As soon as the mess door closed, the men muttered amongst themselves.

"Heart attack? My arse," said Farmer in disgust. He dumped the spoon into the porridge and watched it slowly sink into the unappetizing grey mass. "He was one of the fittest men in the squadron."

"You don't think it was the jabs do you?" said Arthur quietly. His hand involuntarily drifted to his arm.

"Of course not," said Farmer. "They don't need to kill us off with vaccinations. The Germans can do it just as efficiently once we're in the air." He shoved the plate of porridge away from himself. "One down already and we haven't even left yet. Shit!"

That evening, the squadron threw a party. It was a civilised affair with female company present. The CO's wife was in attendance and Kittinger had managed to prevail upon the senior WAAF officer to send along some of her girls. The mess laid on the best plate and silverware. Afterwards there was some dancing and singing around the piano.

Also putting in an appearance were the newlyweds, Mr and Mrs Locke. A tall blonde, Laura Locke had drifted around the room in a pale mint green dress. Locke preened as his wife dazzled them with her smile and her charming manner.

Together for only a short period of time, Locke's looming departure for the front had sharpened their feelings for one another. Using his forty eight, Locke had wangled a special licence and they had two rushed days together at a small Hotel in Filey. Two days wasn't nearly enough, but it was all they had and they'd made the most of it. They ordered room service while Locke did his best to wear out the bed springs and perform his husbandly duties.

Much to the station commander's delight, everyone remained on their best behaviour. The party broke up early around ten. With ladies present and tomorrow looming large in their minds, no one felt much like getting stinking drunk. While they all went to bed, few of them slept. Tomorrow was *the* day, the one they had been training and working towards for years.

1.2 – Foreign Fields

Most of them woke up early, although there was no real rush. It was a short hop over to France so they had plenty of time. Tired faces looked into mirrors as they washed and shaved. Breakfast was eaten with little enthusiasm and mess bills were settled.

They changed into their flying gear and went off to briefing. The station commander, Group Captain Pritchard wished them well. The CO, Wing Commander Winwright took his place on the platform and made it all sound like a jolly Sunday outing. Out for the day and back again for tea and crumpets. He expected them all to arrive at Rouen in good order; he wanted to put on a show for the French.

They took off in groups of three, circling the airfield once before taking up a course for France. Winwright went off first, his bomb bay filled with luggage and bags of spares. Warrant Officer Alistair Burke sat behind the CO in the well above the bomb bay. Burke tried to get comfortable as he folded his tall frame into a small space. His knees bumped the kitbag he held in front of him. He was off to war again.

Every ten minutes, another batch set off. An hour later, Pilot Officer Charles Chandler and his crew led the last group of three away. Pettifer formed up on his left wing and Flying Officer Osbourne on the right. The afternoon sun was high in the sky when they headed for the coast and said goodbye to jolly old England.

Chandler liked the Blenheim. Compared to the tired Fairey Battles the squadron had recently traded in, she was a Rolls Royce. A twin engine light bomber, she had a crew of three and a 1,000lb bomb load. Built as a private venture to challenge the variety of record breaking German aircraft, Lord Rothermere's contender had resulted in an aircraft that was faster than the fighters of the day when it was introduced in 1935.

She was not so fast now; fighters had caught up in the last few years but Chandler didn't care. The Blenheim IV had 9lb of emergency boost to provide an extra burst of power to get him out of trouble. He also liked the safety margin two engines brought him.

Up front in the glazed nose, his navigator, Aaron Morgan was struggling. Twenty eight, he had come into the service via the Reserve. Called up before the start of the war, he had escaped his dreary bank job and thrown himself into service life. He fiddled with his maps as he looked out at the countryside in despair. He'd not seen anything he recognised for the last ten minutes. He checked his watch and hoped their landfall would be vaguely close to what it should be. He glanced over his shoulder back at Chandler.

Sandy haired with dancing blue eyes, his pilot was twenty three years old and had only come out of Cranwell in the spring. Fresh from an Operational

Conversion Unit, he had arrived just before the squadron transitioned from their Fairey Battles to the Blenheim.

Arriving at the squadron at the same time, it was only natural they would be paired up. Coming into an established unit as the new boys brought with it certain burdens. The old sweats viewed newcomers with a certain amount of suspicion until they had proven themselves.

As a crew, they looked after each other and that was fine by Morgan. Unlike some, Chandler would prefer to find the cause of a problem, rather than hang someone out to dry. Morgan needed that catch net sometimes. He fished in his navigator's bag and pulled out a handful of pencils. He started attacking them with a sharpener, making a pile of shavings on his small desk while he wondered where they were, glancing at the maps and hoping something would look familiar.

Leading Aircraftman Mark Griffiths sat nervously behind Chandler in the well. Hugging his knees, he kept trying to catch glimpses of the ground below. His twin brother Martin was the radio operator/air gunner sat in the turret back in the fuselage. He watched quietly as the pilot made small movements with the yoke. He rode the air currents, keeping the flight smooth as silk.

They crossed the channel and the French coast started to slide under the nose. Morgan kept glancing at his maps and could feel the sweat crawling down his neck. He compared the position of the headland and made some rapid calculations. He was off course by miles. The wind must have veered. He wrote a correction down on a slip of paper and passed it up to Chandler.

Pettifer's navigator, Slater, gave a theatrical sigh and passed a slip of paper to his pilot. Pettifer glanced at it and grinned to himself. He looked down into the nose and shared a look with him.

"Even money he doesn't spot the course change for about ten miles skip."

"It wouldn't surprise me," said Pettifer. He called up his gunner. "Willis; get a DF fix will you and pass me the position when you have it."

"Roger, skipper."

Pettifer shook his head as he watched Chandler's Blenheim slightly ahead of him on the right. He liked Chandler. Like himself, the young pilot had come in for some opposition from the more senior cliques on the squadron. He was impressed with the way he had rode out the storm. He also respected Chandler's loyalty to his crew, but he felt that sometimes Chandler took that loyalty too far.

The simple fact was that Morgan was a lousy navigator. His dead reckoning skills were awful and he regularly missed landmarks that might have got him out of trouble. He got lost about as often as he found the way and it was becoming a running joke on the squadron. In peace time, poor navigation might be okay, but in action, things like that could get you killed.

They droned on for another few minutes. Pettifer pondered shouting up on the R/T to advise a course change. The CO had ordered radio silence on the flight over but it would look pretty stupid if they ended up missing their destination and flying over Paris. He was just about to break orders when Chandler's Blenheim wallowed up and down before drunkenly turning left. Chandler kept his turn wide, giving Pettifer room on the inside to keep his position.

As Chandler straightened up, Pettifer checked his reference points and then eased it in slightly, keeping it tight. They headed east, the flight smooth and Slater gave his pilot a thumbs up, happy that the course was good. Give or take another ten minutes or so and they should arrive at their destination. Pettifer turned his thoughts to the task ahead.

While most people on the squadron were naively optimistic that things would be over by Christmas, Pettifer held no such hopes. His family had sacrificed much in the last war and he was under little illusion about his own future. His father had died in 1917 at Cambrai, going forwards with the Rifle Brigade. One uncle had been cut down at the Somme in 1916. The other was killed over Arras in 1917 in the Royal Flying Corps.

He couldn't help remembering his aunts when they gathered together. They talked about the war and all that they had lost, their hopes and fears magnified by the passage of time. He'd grown up in a quiet house, just him and his mother with little male company. He often caught her looking mournfully at his father's photograph in unguarded moments.

Based on his own family's experiences, he knew that blind faith would accomplish little. That was why he devoted himself so much to his flying. He knew that his own skill and that of his crew was the only thing he could rely on.

At Rouen aerodrome, Winwright and Dane stood in the control tower. They peered through binoculars as the aircraft circled the field. The Wing Commander kept checking his watch and scowled. He went back inside the tower, muttering to himself. Dane followed him, skirting past the clerk who fussed over a list and joined the CO by the operations board.

The Blenheims circled the aerodrome twice more before Chandler brought his Blenheim smoothly in to land. He crossed over the perimeter fence and touched down to make a perfect three point landing. He rolled past the control tower, dust swirling behind him. He slowly closed the throttle and gently dabbed the brakes before turning off onto the perimeter track.

"That's the last of them, sir," said Dane as the other two Blenheims came in behind Chandler.

Winwright's eyes roamed up and down the list of aircraft. He grunted and tapped the line marked B-Bertie.

"Any word yet?"

"Only that they'd been picked up, sir. They did confirm that all three of them got out before it sank. They only left the scene when a rescue launch was close to their location."

Winwright grunted. The first day was not even over and he was already an aircraft short. On the way over, the new husband Locke had ditched in the channel after both engines had conked out.

"Chandler's flight was late," Winwright muttered. "Almost half an hour overdue and they didn't have the excuse of Farmer."

"No, sir, they didn't," Dane agreed. He knew Chandler vaguely from his days at King's and the University Air Squadron so he was a little protective of the young officer. "I'm sure he had a good reason, sir," he said, keeping his tone neutral.

Winwright's narrow horse face pinched in disapproval. He looked around the room of the control tower and then made for the stairs. Dane followed him. Winwright did not speak again until they were outside.

"I don't really *care* what the reason was, Wallis; it just doesn't give the right impression to our 'gallant' allies."

"Yessir."

"We can't have our chaps swanning around the French countryside as they please." Winwright stood on the edge of the apron, hands shoved in his pockets, the breeze whipping at his trousers. Chandler's bomber taxied to the end of the row of parked Blenheims and then shut its engines down. The other two were still taxying in across the field.

"The frogs will point fingers. They'll think we don't know what we're doing. Puts up a bit of a black you see." He turned and walked towards a drab green Citroen. He was about to get in when he turned and looked back over the top of the door. "Tell Chandler to report to me at 1800 hours. We'll see what he has to say for himself then."

Dane gave Winwright a crisp salute and held it as the CO drove off. As soon as the Citroen went out of sight round the admin building, he went in the opposite direction, shaking his head. He would have preferred to talk to the Adjutant about this first but he was waiting for them at their destination near Béthenville.

Chandler and Morgan strode into the crew room with their kit bags slung over their shoulders. They looked around the room and were suitably underwhelmed. Paint was peeling from the walls, a fire burned in the grate and patriotic posters hung in frames. A collection of pilots were in various states of repose on sofas and armchairs. The room had the air of some seedy waiting room at a train station. All it needed was the drunken tramp in the corner. Chandler ran his hand through mashed down hair and dropped the heavy bag on the floor. Morgan did the same.

"What a dump," muttered Morgan in his Norfolk drawl.

"Well, we're not staying long," said Chandler. "We'll be off in the morning."

"Not before the CO roasts your behind though," Morgan said, reminding him of his coming summons.

Chandler made a face and tried to catch the eye of one of the Stewards. He picked up a magazine from the side table and idly flicked through the pages before turning back to his navigator.

"Don't worry about it, I'll square it. I'm not worried about *him*."

Morgan heard the sneer in his pilot's voice but chose to make no comment. It was not the first time Chandler had been in Winwright's office and the more he saw of the CO, the less he liked. This was his first operational unit and he'd expected a commander that was a real go-getter, leading from the front with some fire in his belly. Winwright on the other hand was hard and aloof. He expected rigid discipline in the air and often led lectures, preaching the mantra of unit integrity. He'd had them spending hours practising tight formation flying and surprisingly little time on the bomb ranges.

Chandler rolled the magazine into a tube and dabbed Morgan in the chest with it. He pitched his voice low just for his navigators' benefit.

"If anyone asks about where we've been, just tell them some guff about stronger than forecast winds, okay?"

"What if Pettifer or Osbourne say something?"

"They won't. Pettifer's not a snitch and Osbourne's a decent chap. We'll be okay."

Morgan nodded glumly, too embarrassed to say much. It wasn't the first time he'd gotten lost on a cross country flight and Chandler had to cover for him.

Across the room a pair of brown eyes regarded them both. Michael Ashton was a shade under thirty and had a weathered face with sleepy hooded eyes that made a girl's pulse go up a few notches. The South African accent of his youth helped as well and he was never short of female attention on leave.

Ashton had travelled far after university in England. He ended up flying airmail for two years in South America, running the dangerous route between Rio de Janeiro and Buenos Aires. Then one day he'd been in a seedy bar reading yet another story about the rise of National Socialism. There and then he decided it was time to commit his life to something higher. Returning to England, he'd pulled strings with some old university pals and joined the service. Riding the wave of the pre-war expansion, his flight experience soon got him noticed and he was promoted rapidly to Squadron Leader.

He finished his cigarette and stubbed it into the glass ashtray beside him. He glanced sideways at his Observer, William 'Billy' Mitchell. Mitchell rolled his eyes and laughed, because he knew what was coming. Ashton made a show of glancing at his watch before coughing into his hand.

"Mr Chandler, a moment of your time if you will." Chandler drifted over to his Flight Commander. Ashton waited until he was stood in front of him. He folded his paper and laid it across his lap before speaking. "You owe me a pound, Chips."

Chandler's face pinched at the diminutive nickname he had been given. One day he had made the mistake of disclosing that his father was in the wholesale vegetable trade. Amongst his more elite peers, it mattered not a jot that Chandler had gone to a top grammar school and on to King's College. He was from trade and the name had stuck.

"A pound?" queried Chandler. "I already squared the mess bill before we left, didn't I?"

"Yes, yes you did." Ashton agreed, nodding in faux empathy. "This is for today. I had a little bet with Squadron Leader, Graves;" the commander of B Flight nodded, his face serious, "that the one who took the longest to get here between the Flights loses."

Morgan shifted uncomfortably on his feet but stopped when Ashton fixed him with a glare. Farmer shared a look with Preddy and the two of them hitched round in their chairs to get a better view. Chandler fought his corner.

"That hardly seems fair, boss. We were the last to leave to start with; we picked up some strong headwinds."

"I know you weren't the only one who was late," said Ashton, humouring his young charge. "But over twenty minutes was by far the worst performance. You were last, we lost, so you bear responsibility for the honour of the Flight, I'm afraid. So," he stretched out a hand. "Cough up."

Chandler opened his mouth guppy like and then shut it again. He was about to argue but then thought better of it. He already had enough on his plate with the CO; it seemed foolish to piss off his Flight Commander as well. He dug into his pocket and pulled out a tatty pound note and stuck it into Ashton's hand.

"Dankie. Be a good chap and try not to do it again." He turned to Graves and held out the pound note. "Honour is due."

Graves smiled and gave the note an experimental tug. Ashton twisted on the sofa and motioned to the steward in the corner. The man came over.

"Now if you'll follow old Henri here, he'll make sure you get bedded down okay." He lit another cigarette. "Dinners at seven by the way," he said casually, blowing smoke out of the corner of his mouth. Not in the mood to exchange any further pleasantries, Chandler and Morgan gathered their gear and followed the Steward.

Farmer watched the youngster cross the room and then turned back to Preddy. Pitching his voice for the benefit of the room, he said, "Now that we're all here, I really think we should consider court martialling old Locke you know."

"What do you mean?" asked Preddy, amused.

"Well, it all seems highly suspect to me, you know. The only man who got married a week ago is the only one to have a mechanical problem and has to dump his kite in the drink."

The room burst out in sniggers and laughs like kids at school. Farmer arched an eyebrow and Preddy was unable to contain himself.

"He's sabotaging the war effort," he managed to get out between gasps.

"Exactly," said Farmer, leaping on the remark. "It seems some chaps will do anything to get one more night with the bride."

"What *is* the penalty for sabotage these days?" asked Arthur. "Firing squad isn't it?"

"Hmmmm." Preddy nodded. "I imagine the wife would be a bit upset." He rubbed his hands and smiled wickedly. "Pretty little thing she is too," he said, remembering the radiant blonde vision at the mess party. "Yes, it'll be a shame watching old Locke go to the wall," he said in mock regret. He caught the attention of a Steward and ordered another drink. "Of course, the bride will need consoling."

The room descended into mirth.

After a good night's rest, the crews assembled on the pan by the control tower. The Blenheims were all lined up ready to go. The ground crew they had brought with them had spent a good hour checking the aircraft over under the watchful eye of Warrant Officer Burke.

A staff car pulled up and the French station commander got out, followed by Winwright. They made an interesting contrast to each other. Short and stocky, Winwright had his trousers tucked into the tops of his furred flying boots. A slash of red appeared at his throat in the form of a silk scarf tucked inside his shirt with the top button undone. The French officer was immaculately tailored in a uniform that looked like he had been sewn into it. His kepi was tilted at a rakish angle and a small pointed moustache was balanced on his top lip. He slapped a pair of white silk dress gloves from hand to hand as he walked.

Winwright gathered them round. The French officer addressed them in mangled but understakable English. He spoke of British courage, their French brothers, justice and fighting the tyrannical Boche. No one said a word as he warmed to his subject. Winwright's eyes roamed over the group, ready to pounce on any transgression. They behaved, even though the dour rhetoric tempted them to do something.

11

Finally, the speech mercifully drew to a close. Hands were shaken, salutes were exchanged and the station commander withdrew from the field, happy. A collective breath was released once he was out of earshot.

"What a load of old tosh," commented Arthur. There was a general grumble of agreement amongst the men. Give them a good speech about giving the Hun a good thrashing, six of the best and they were happy. Start laying it on thick about being a band of Nelsonian brothers and their patience wore thin.

"Positively ghastly," agreed Preddy. He theatrically shuddered to highlight his displeasure. He pulled on his flying gloves and flexed his fingers in the new soft leather. "There's nothing worse than a frog in love with the sound of his own voice."

"Ah, but what about the women?" asked Farmer.

"That's different," said Preddy. "Froggy women can whisper sweet nothings to me all night if they want."

They were just about to disperse to their individual aircraft when Winwright told them to stay together.

"Just a few snaps for the scrap book chaps. Seeing as we're going to war, I think we should get a few photos for posterity."

A spotty Corporal walked towards them with a camera in his small hands. He suggested getting something in the background and they moved over to the nearest Blenheim.

"Huddle up gentlemen," he told them.

They bunched in close, doubling up the rows. Those in front knelt down. Some chairs were produced and Winwright sat in the middle, arms crossed, with Graves and Ashton either side of him.

The Corporal ran off a few shots, struggling to get everyone into the viewfinder. After that, Winwright asked for a shot just of the pilots. The navigators and gunners shuffled off to get ready.

A more intimate shot, Winwright was more relaxed, and stood with his hands jammed into his pockets. A Flight stood to his left, B Flight to his right. Farmer stood by Graves shoulder, a hulking mountain of a man. Chandler stood next to Pettifer and tried to look earnestly heroic.

There was some jostling into position and Osbourne kept moving. He stood face on to the camera then changed his mind, turning three quarters to the front and squared his shoulders back like he was on the parade square.

"Very pretty," said Farmer. "You ready for your close up?" he asked the Scotsman. Arthur puckered up and blew kisses at Osbourne before Farmer's beefy hand clipped him over the back of the head. "Eyes front, you clot."

"Ready?" asked the Corporal as he looked at them intently through the camera. He took three photos for good luck and then they headed towards their aircraft.

They took off in sections of three, before forming up as a complete squadron and headed east in formation. Only the day before, some German fighters had strayed over the border, spoiling for a fight and the CO preferred to play it safe.

Winwright led the squadron and spent the entire flight haranguing his crews to keep it close. While he was a proponent of Baldwin's theory that the bomber would always get through, he also believed in stacking the odds in his favour. For all its sleek lines and speed, the Blenheim was a bomber like any other.

Fighters were faster and more manoeuvrable than them, so they could neither run, nor dodge the German fighters forever. He knew what they needed to do was keep together and rely on the mutual protection of their own guns. If their turrets could lay down a hedge of fire, then it would be difficult for fighters to press home their attacks. At least, that was the theory.

Flying in formation in the Battle had been relatively easy, but the Blenheim had been giving a few of the pilots some trouble. With engines on either side of the long glazed nose, they had to relearn their reference points. Only with constant practice were they able to get to a standard he was happy with, which was why he had been working them so hard to get it right. Once they went into combat, every flight would be for real and there would be little chance to practice after that.

Winwright took them in a lazy loop towards what would be their new home. Approaching from the east, he flew over the nearest town that would be a place of rest. A bustling place, Béthenville had been virtually flattened during the German offensive in 1918. Stubbornly rebuilt it was hard to tell that had ever happened.

Passing over the town, he pointed out the tall belfry on the church and the large paved square in the centre as landmarks. On the outskirts to the south, there was a large railway station and the railway line running west pointed the way to the airfield.

It was like getting directions when you drove a car. *Go straight west, over the town and then follow the railway line before turning right at the small wood. Keep on going until you come to the large field next to a small hamlet, you can't miss it.*

Bois Fontaine was a large wood on some rising ground about six miles to the west of town. A low hedge and rough wooden fencing surrounded the area on all sides to keep the cows out. A meandering stream came up to the edge of the eastern wood, followed the line of undulating wall and then fell away downhill towards rich farm land. The runway was a grassy, meadow like strip that ran roughly north to south between the two large clumps of trees.

On the southwest corner was a collection of farm buildings. Barns and a rustic looking house surrounded three sides of a cobbled courtyard. Two more stone barns stood on the other side of the wall surrounded by some newly built long wooden huts. A ramshackle wooden barn was in the next field. Next to the huts there were brown scars in the earth where some slit trenches had been dug. A cluster of tents could be seen sheltering under the trees.

A Tiger Moth biplane stood on the grass by the huts. An orange windsock hung limp on a large white pole next to it. It was hardly the comfort of a permanent station, but it was going to be their home for the foreseeable future. They would just have to make the best of it.

Not far away, Winwright saw a large manor house of some kind. It had an impressive facade, a long drive leading up to it and two wings of servant's quarters out back. Nearby was a stable block of some description. Winwright wondered if they would be able to get that as accommodation for the men.

Coming in low, he stayed at one hundred feet and flew the length of the field, noting the contours. The ground crested towards the middle before falling away towards the flat land beyond. That could make things interesting for them if they were not careful.

Satisfied with the layout and approach, he went around again and set up for a landing. He brought the Blenheim down for a neat three pointer. He used bursts of throttle to taxy up close to the huts he had seen from the air. As the propellers windmilled to a stop, the groundcrew rushed in and shoved chocks under the wheels. Falcon Squadron had arrived.

Jaws hit the floor when the crews were shown their lodgings. The assembled officers felt hard done by as they saw the limp and drab tents that awaited them. Dinner was woeful. It was with a grumbling stomach that Chandler settled down for the night. Feeling the cold, he dug through his luggage for spare jumpers. He put one on and then shoved the rest down one side of his sleeping bag.

He'd just about nodded off when Morgan came into their tent and laughed at the pitiful sight in front of him. Chandler's teeth were chattering and he had the sleeping bag gathered up tight around his chin as he tried to keep warm. Breath fogged in front of him. Morgan put on his Sidcot flying suit and wrapped a scarf around his neck.

"You're not cold," Chandler said as a matter of fact.

"Correct," said Morgan, smug, settling into his sleeping bag.

"How come?"

Morgan didn't answer straight away and Chandler looked across the tent. In the gloom he could just make out Morgan's face and thought he'd already fallen asleep when he spoke.

"How come I'm not cold?" He rolled over and the cot creaked with his movement. "I'm naturally warm. Women appreciate it."

Chandler blew a raspberry in reply. "I'm cold," he muttered, feeling sorry for himself. He rummaged around in his sleeping bag and tried rearranging some of his clothes to fight the draught he could feel down the front.

"I'm not getting into bed with you," murmured Morgan.

"Funny." Chandler rubbed his arms. "That's funny."

Morgan lay back, enjoying the warmth while he heard Chandler moving around in the dark. He smiled as he heard his pilot muttering as he tried to get comfortable.

"If you must know, I'm wearing long johns."

"Long johns!" exclaimed Chandler.

"I plan ahead. I checked the weather forecast."

Chandler stopped moving when he finally tugged out a scarf.

"You rotter," he said as he wound it round his neck. "You could have told me."

Morgan blew a raspberry back.

"All's fair, as they say."

A guttural voice from another tent cut in across their conversation.

"If you two lovebirds don't shut up over there, then I really will start a war. Some of us are trying to sleep."

Griffiths settled down under scratchy blankets. He looked out of the window in the barn while he listened to the animal noises below.

He was not surprised when the officers were directed to the tents and the Radio Operator/Air Gunners were steered towards the barns. Rank hath its privileges. The ground crew were packed into the rickety huts and a few had been billeted in the local village.

Each barn was fifty feet long and about twenty across. The walls were stone construction with a wooden slat roof. Down below, the barn was filled with the farmer's livestock and up above was the hay loft. Growing up on a farm with his twin brother, they had mucked about in the barns many times. It felt like he had come full circle. He rolled over slowly, trying not to make much noise as he ignored the bits of straw sticking into his back. His brain was still buzzing from the events of the day.

He peered in the dim light provided by the single lantern hanging from the rafters. His eyes roamed over the bundled bodies lying around him until his eyes rested on Burke. The older man was half sitting, half lying back on the hay, his arm propping his head up. He was reading a book by the light of the lamp but Griffiths could not make out the title.

As far as the enlisted men were concerned, Burke was the nearest thing to god. Older, wiser, there was little he had not seen in his long career. You went to Burke with your problems and he listened and gave you a straight answer and a way ahead. Griffiths had rarely heard him rant. Burke had that quiet manner where you wanted to give him your best and if you messed up, you felt that you'd let him down.

"Sir?"

"Yes, lad?"

"You've done this before?"

There was a pause for a moment while Burke checked his page number before closing the cover.

"I've done this before a lot of times. The last show. On the side of the White Russians against the Communists after that. Jordan fighting against the mad Mullah. On the frontier in India. Afghanistan and lots of other places. Don't worry about it. I was your age when this all happened the last time. In fact, my squadron operated for a time from this very field."

"Really?"

"Yes. I was just an engine fitter on SE5's then. A long time ago." He smiled wistfully at the memory. "I've been lucky enough to do a lot of things since then."

His voice took on a faraway tone as he dipped back into his memory. He could picture the airfield as it used to be. There had been canvas hangars by the barns. The fighters were lined up in a neat row in front of them, the small windsock fluttering on its pole. He closed his eyes as he remembered the smell of leather and castor oil, the tang of the petrol.

He'd come a long way from being a butcher's boy in Halifax. He remembered the fear in his mother's face when he came in that wet Saturday afternoon; his face flushed with excitement to tell her he'd joined up. Not for him the life of his father, six days a week and the early starts down the market.

Life in the RAF suited his restless nature. He'd travelled the world this last twenty years, never in one place too long, always moving and that was how he liked it. He sometimes thought about the people he grew up with, what they were doing now. He'd seen ruins in Mesopotamia, seen action in the cliffs of Waziristan and the snow bound plains of Russia. There weren't many people who could say they'd done the same.

He came out of his introspection to see Griffiths had fallen asleep. He returned to his book.

1.3 – In The Cold Light of Dawn

Chandler was awake long before the sun crept over the horizon. In the end, the cold won and he rolled out of bed. He pulled on another jumper over the one he was already wearing and then scrabbled around on the floor of the tent for his boots. The cold bit into his cheeks and nibbled on the end of his nose as he ventured outside.

Chandler walked slowly, kicking his feet through tufts of grass that were coated in the morning dew. The air was still and aside from the odd cow making the first noises of the day, it was quiet. A few people were starting to stir so he headed off across the field towards the aircraft. Eighteen Blenheims were parked up in a row, their tails towards the woods. He walked past one of the miserable shivering sentries over to his own aircraft, Q-Queenie.

Condensation coated the long glazed nose and beaded down the curves of the fuselage. He walked round the port side and ran his hand along the cold metal. During the night, he'd laid awake shivering, thinking about the possibilities that the day would bring. For the last eighteen months, his one focus had been his flying training; getting to a conversion unit and then on to a squadron. Now it was the real thing.

He strolled around the field, hands jammed in his pockets until he found himself over by the barns. He rounded the corner and found Griffiths sitting on a stool, shaving from a bucket in front of a fire. Chandler stood quietly watching the younger man drag a safety razor up his neck. Griffiths hissed as he nicked the skin. He pushed a rag of material against the cut while he rinsed the razor in the bucket. He dabbed at his neck and then carried on shaving.

Chandler sat down on a log across from him by the fire. He warmed his hands and rubbed them to get some feeling back in his fingers.

"Good morning, Griffiths."

"Morning, sir." The younger man put the razor down and dabbed at his neck again.

"You're up early."

"Not really, sir. You get used to it on a farm." He gestured to the barn. "The cows make pretty good alarm clocks." The wood in the brazier crackled, sparks swirling up into the sky. Griffiths put another bit of wood into it and shoved it with a stick to keep it going. "Good sleep?" he asked his pilot.

"Not a chance," said Chandler. "Far too cold in those tents. And you?"

"Pretty good. It's warm among the hay."

Chandler made a show of leaning forwards and sniffing. He wrinkled his nose.

"I'll pass thanks. I think I'd rather be cold."

Griffiths pulled at his sleeve and sniffed and shrugged.

"You get used to it."

Winwright was gently shaken awake by Osbourne, who was Officer of the Day.

"I'm sorry for waking you, sir," he said, his Scottish accent thick. "A dispatch rider has brought some orders for us."

Winwright rolled over and picked up his watch. He peered bleary eyed at the hands.

"Good god, it's not even six a.m."

"I know, I'm very sorry, sir, but they were quite insistent. It has to be signed for by you."

Winwright swung out of bed and shrugged on his battledress, the material scratching his neck. Still sleepy, he crossed the short distance to the main flight hut. Osbourne handed him a cup of tea as he settled himself behind the desk. Winwright sipped gratefully on the hot drink as he identified himself to the waiting dispatch rider.

"Good morning, sir," the man said as he reached into his leather pouch and handed over a bundle of papers in a manila folder. "Welcome to France."

Winwright took hold of them and signed the proffered pad. His weariness disappeared as he started reading the top sheet. He made notes on a scrap of paper and looked out of the window deep in thought.

He saw Chandler walking across the field. He looked a shambles, hands jammed into his pockets, chin tucked into his chest. Winwright lit his first cigarette of the day. He let the smoke fill his lungs, the heat warming him.

"Osbourne, get the Adjutant, Mr Dane and Mr Ashton for me. After that, find, Chandler will you?"

"Yessir."

Chandler handed Griffiths and Burke another mug of cocoa.

"Thank you, sir."

Burke blew on the steaming mug and tentatively sipped it before looking up at the sky.

"It's going to be another fine day. Give it an hour or so and those clouds will clear up, I think."

"And what have you got planned for today, Mister Burke?"

"Me, sir? Plenty." Burke balanced the mug on his lap and started counting off on his fingers. "I'll rouse this lot out of their pits shortly. There are more tents to put up. I've also got to lay out where the new huts are going to go. Then we need to finish the bomb dump and at some point the rest of the ground crew are due to arrive. There'll be loads of stores to get in. They'll have to be sorted out and that's just for starters."

"I would think the CO will have us up air testing soon," said Chandler.

"And after that, sir?" Griffiths asked.

"Familiarisation trips, I imagine."

They sat in silence as they watched Osbourne striding with purpose across the grass towards them. A short and stocky dark haired Scotsman, his battledress seemed to strain at the seams from his muscular arms. Years ago, a university rugby game had rearranged the nose that was smeared across his face. A dusting of freckles across his cheeks completed the look. When he was not flying, he could often be found running around the perimeter track in his shorts and singlet. Burke offered him a drink but Osbourne declined.

"Morning, chaps. Sleep all right?"

"No. I was freezing," Chandler replied. "You?"

"At least you got some sleep," said Osbourne yawning, his rough brogue plaintive. "I've been up since midnight as OOD." He looked at Chandler and hooked a thumb over his shoulder. "The CO would like to see you, there's a job in. Mister Burke, I imagine you'll have to get an aircraft ready shortly."

"You better start getting your things together," Chandler said, finishing off his cocoa before handing the mug to Griffiths. Burke took the hint and stood up, flicking the dregs from his mug onto the grass.

"And I better get the boys up. It looks like it's going to be a long day."

Things began to move fast once Chandler came out of the hut Winwright was using as his office. Burke had roused the groundcrews and the airfield began to wake up.

He stopped by his tent to pick up his flying gear. He put his Sidcot on over his trousers and shirt. The Sidcot was a one piece overall made from waterproofed green cotton and lined with linen. He double checked his whistle was attached to the left collar and gave it an experimental blow.

Over the Sidcot he shrugged on his lifejacket. More commonly known as the Mae West, some of the pilots had started painting the front of their jackets yellow to make them more visible. Chandler preferred not to do that. The paint was prone to cracking and making a mess. Grabbing his leather flying helmet and goggles, he made his way over to his aircraft.

Morgan was waiting for him and chatting to the groundcrew when Griffiths joined them lugging a box of flare cartridges.

"Are those the colours of the day?" asked Chandler and Griffiths nodded. Every day, the daily identification colours changed. If an aircraft was fired on by friendly forces, they could fire off a series of flares. Griffiths had been to the squadron armourer for that day's colours. Morgan spread a map out on the grass and Chandler started to brief his men.

"There have been reports that some warships are heading for the French coast. The Admiralty doesn't think they're ours. We're being sent out to take a look. We'll be heading north." He described with his fingers a line parallel to the French coast. "We have a fifty mile stretch to patrol off the coast. Other flights are covering other areas so there is some overlap. Just make sure we don't stray across the border into Belgium."

He emphasised the last point and flashed a look at Morgan. Just like the last war, Belgium had decided it was a neutral country. Any aircraft violating their airspace would be liable to challenge or attack. There would be the devil to pay if Morgan got his navigation wrong this time. If they came down in neutral territory, they would be interred and their aircraft confiscated.

"Griffiths, if we see anything you'll need to send a sighting report sharpish." Chandler handed Morgan a pair of binoculars and a book. "You'll need these to keep an eye out. The book has current warships in so if we do spot something, we can say what it is." He stood up and rubbed his hands together, looking more confident than he felt. "Well, let's get cracking."

Griffiths went round and used the hand holds in the left side of the fuselage to climb up onto the wing. At the back of the fuselage he was on his own. Between him and the cockpit were the main spars. There wasn't a lot of space for someone to squeeze through and get to him if he needed help.

He powered up the radio and went through his checks. Satisfied the set was working, he turned to the turret. Powered hydraulically from the starboard engine, the turret was wound up into position after take off. It mounted one Vickers gas operated .303in machine gun and had a one hundred eighty degree field of fire.

Morgan went up next and got into the cockpit using the hatch above the pilot's position. He lowered himself in and one of the ground crew handed him the box of flares. He put the bulky cartridges in their rack and stowed his parachute under the small table in the nose. He opened his canvas navigator's bag and spread the tools of his trade out. He shivered and blew on his hands, trying to keep his fingers warm. The Blenheim was still icy inside from the cold night.

Chandler walked around the aircraft doing his preflight checks. He checked each wheel, giving them a kick. He peered into the undercarriage bays, looking for leaks in the hydraulics. Satisfied that everything was in order, he got on board. Settling himself in the pilot's seat, his nerves started to jangle a little bit.

He took a breath to calm himself and went through the start up routine. As he flicked switches he was reminded of something he did miss about the Battle; the cockpit layout. The Blenheim gave the pilot acres of room but it was poorly laid out. The switches and levers were laid out as if someone had thrown them higgledy piggledy wherever they pleased.

He reached over to the other side of the cockpit and switched the fuel to the inner tanks. He opened the throttles half an inch and set the mixture control to normal. He moved the propeller speed controls fully back before switching the carburettor air intake to cold. For some reason, someone had seen fit to put the controls for the engine cowling gills behind the pilot's seat on the right side. He grunted as he reached round and fed in two turns of the wheel to open them.

The groundcrew stroked the priming pump. Chandler switched on the ignition and booster coils before starting each engine, one after the other. The propellers span, cylinders banged and the engines coughed into life. The last wisps of mist in the grass were torn apart in the slipstream as the sound tore across the field.

Drowsy heads popped into view from various tents to see what was going on and people stopped work as the Blenheim ran up. While the engines purred at a fast tick over, Chandler pulled his gauntlets on. The leather creaked as he flexed his fingers. He could feel the steady thrum of the twin Mercury engines through his seat as they warmed up. His eyes swept the instruments, taking in the details as the needles steadied.

He worked the yoke through the full range of motion. One of the groundcrew gave him a thumbs up that the chocks were clear so he pulled on the brakes and inched the throttle forwards. There was no mag drop and the temperatures were fine. He backed off the throttle, let go of the brakes and edged gingerly forwards.

The Blenheim taxied out from the line and turned left, rumbling over the grass. It trundled down to the far end of the field before turning into the wind. Griffiths checked in over the R/T and Morgan came out of the nose to sit next to Chandler. They were ready to go.

Chandler held the brakes on as he went through the final actions that had been drilled into him time and again. *Double check the hydraulics selector is in the 'down' position. Put the rudder trim tab to neutral. Set the elevator slightly nose heavy, mixture normal, prop speed controls forward.* He selected twenty degrees of flap. He worked the wheel behind his seat to close the engine gills. He opened up the throttle, feeding in the power.

The bomber surged forward with a roar, the engines sucking in the cold morning air. Chandler used a bit of left rudder to counter the tendency to swing right on take off. His eyes roved over the gauges, watching the rev counters and the airspeed indicator closely. The nose came up as they passed seventy knots indicated. He could feel the grass tugging on the wheels and used more rudder to keep the nose straight as they thundered across the field.

As they topped the slight rise, the IAS hit ninety and he slowly and evenly pulled the yoke back into his stomach. Air got under the wings and the Blenheim climbed smoothly away. With no bombs on board she climbed swiftly, the speed picking up fast.

Chandler raised the undercarriage and flaps. He could feel the difference in the controls immediately. The drag of the wheels was no longer there, the ride smoother. He turned the hydraulic selector up to provide power to the turret and told Griffiths he could get his gun ready.

The nineteen year old settled himself in his seat and started working the controls to the turret. He made sure the safety was on before pulling the cocking lever on his Vickers machine gun. He traversed the gun left and right, making sure he had the full range of movement.

Dane watched the Blenheim until it disappeared into the clouds. All being well, they should be back in about two hours.

1.4 – The Grand Tour

A little Miles Magister arrived shortly after Chandler's Blenheim took off. It taxied towards the huts and turned with a flourish, using a quick burst of throttle and the rudder to end up pointing back the way it had come. The pilot got down as the groundcrew chocked the wheels. There was some consternation when he unzipped his white flying suit and revealed the uniform jacket of a Group Captain. Without waiting on ceremony he went into the flight hut and slapped his briefcase down on the desk. Preddy jumped in fright and then stood shakily to attention.

"Good morning, sir."

The Group Captain gave him a very fast up and down appraisal and then the door to Winwright's office opened and the CO appeared.

"It's all right, Preddy. Go and get two cups of tea, there's a good chap."

"Rapidly, boss." Preddy exited as fast as his legs could carry him.

"Good morning, sir."

"Good morning, Winwright. Settling in I trust?"

"We're getting there. There's still a lot to do of course. We only got in last night and a lot of the ground personnel haven't arrived."

"I'll see about that. There have been a few problems moving units around. The French have been lagging a bit in getting organised."

They waited until Preddy reappeared carrying two mugs of tea. Once he'd handed them over, Winwright flicked his head to one side and Preddy took the hint. He made himself scarce.

The Group Captain cupped his hands round the mug, letting the heat penetrate his fingers. His cheeks still stung from flying and the tip of his nose was cold. He let the steam rise into his face as he savoured the tea.

Robert Goddard had only recently been appointed to the staff in France and he was busy doing the rounds of the squadrons to see what they needed. He stood in silence for a few moments, watching the activity around him. He was sharply reminded of the fact that this was now all behind him. He'd had his day commanding a bomber squadron in Iraq a long time ago but he still missed being in the field.

He looked at the shiny new bombers with keen interest. Even though the press had already dubbed this *the phoney war*; you'd never know it at A.A.S.F Headquarters. From the day they'd arrived, the French air staff had been giving everyone a headache, demanding a bigger English contribution. Goddard knew the root cause of this. Months before war had even been declared, Goebbels had written in some natty magazine that England would fight to the last Frenchman. That thought obviously still lingered in the minds of government echelons. After some bleating in the corridors of power, a flurry of signals back and forth across the channel had turned the wires red hot.

21

This Blenheim Squadron and the two other Battle units were a sop to that growing fear. That was why they had been sent to northern France around Béthenville. It was hoped that being based alongside French units would help to bolster morale. All it had done was create a headache in the already strained supply chains.

"When do you think you'll be ready?" he asked.

"By the end of the week I should think, sir. Once the remaining groundcrew arrive we'll be fine. We can make do with what we have until then. I'll have the crews up on familiarisation trips this afternoon."

"Good." Goddard took a sip of his tea. "You've got to drill your chaps between now and when the balloon goes up. You've got to drum into them the idea of fast turn arounds; bombing on a tactical level." He glanced at Winwright who nodded in understanding. "The Lysanders will be the link to the army, giving us information on troop concentrations and then you'll go out to support them." He looked out the doorway. He gestured to the aircraft in one neat line, the sun reflecting on their metal skins. "You'll need to think about getting those aircraft dispersed. This won't be like the first war. I don't want a stick of bombs writing them off all in one go."

"I'm already having that taken care of," Winwright reassured him. "I'm having bays cut into the treeline and we'll drape camouflage nets across. I'll have some sandbag revetments made up as well to give them some protection."

"You seem to have thought of everything."

"I doubt it, sir." Winwright's long face creased in thought. He remembered the effort it had taken just to get the squadron out to France in the first place. "There's always the little things that come up."

Goddard considered that. The last few months had been a whirl of activity for him, working hard to correct the mistakes of peacetime complacency. Even so, there was still a lot of work left to do.

"How are the men settling in?"

"There's been the usual grumbles." Winwright shrugged. "It's a bit of a come down from a permanent station but things will improve."

"Quite." Goddard smiled in good humour. He had seen the tents on the other side of the trees when he had flown over.

"I saw a manor house nearby," Winwright said, fishing for possibilities. Goddard shook his head.

"No go I'm afraid. We did ask when we knew you were coming, but the owners a bit of a tartar, some sort of civil servant by all accounts. Have you been to see the Mayor?"

"Not yet."

"Do, he's a decent man. He was a flier himself in the last show before a crash ended his career. I think you'll get the help you need in that regard."

Goddard put the mug down on the desk.

"Now, let's take the tour, shall we?"

"If you'll follow me, sir."

Winwright led the way towards the aircraft. Goddard watched Burke rush around, haranguing the men to greater efforts. The departure of Chandler's aircraft had stirred the squadron from their slumber and Burke saw no reason to waste an early start. As they had woken up, the aircrew were told to go over their aircraft and make them ready for air testing.

Chaos reigned when six trucks arrived with some of the expected ground staff and missing equipment. The Adjutant, Kittinger, swung into action to get them organised. He lined them up next to the barn. He checked names off a list and then had them dump their kit bags in a pile before they could even catch their breath. Some of them wrestled with putting up more tents while got to work with saws and hammers erecting additional huts.

Gradually, the airfield began to take on more order. A work party dug some extra latrine pits downwind in the woods. Others were hacking at the undergrowth, cutting a path to the tent city that was starting to spring up. Duckboards were dumped in a pile waiting to be laid.

After a walk round, Goddard and Winwright ended up at the northern end of the field. Goddard kicked at a rotten trunk half buried in the grass and stared off across the open countryside. His eyes crinkled under the bright sun and he shaded his face with a hand.

"You know Winwright, no one really knows when this thing is going to start." He lit a cigarette and the air was filled with the pungent smell of the match. "There are some at Headquarters who think it'll all blow over. Some people think Hitler won't dare try and attack the Maginot Line. They think he'll have his army sit on their side of the border and wait for us to come to them."

Winwright thought about that. With all the military might ranged on both sides of the border, he thought it was only a matter of time before the shooting started. Both sides would circle each other like wolves, snarling and snapping at each other's heels.

Goddard flicked the match onto the grass. He fished out a silver hip flask from his jacket pocket. He offered it to Winwright who shook his head.

"I don't pretend to know the future." Goddard kicked at the trunk again, seeing bits of rotten wood splinter off. "I'm not one to read tea leaves and all that rubbish. My job is to make sure we'll be ready, or as ready as we can be. All I can do is keep pushing everyone to their peak." He flicked the stub of cigarette into the long grass and drank from the hip flask. Winwright said nothing, so Goddard continued speaking. "I imagine the SASO will have plenty of work for you. The other squadrons are managing but it's always nice to have the extra capability."

"We'll manage, sir," Winwright said quickly.

Goddard turned and shot him a sharp look, his eyes narrowing.

"It won't be a picnic," he warned. "I hope your chaps realise that."

Winwright glanced back to see the men of his command hard at work. He had a good unit, a good group of men under him. He thought about what lay ahead.

"They know, sir. They may be young, but they know."

Goddard turned on his heel and they began walking back towards the huts. He lit another cigarette and the smoke trailed behind him as they walked along.

Two new huts had been finished and work parties were starting to slap green paint onto the bare wood. The tang of wet paint was in the air.

The Magisters tank had been topped off and its nose was pointed down the field, waiting to go. Goddard retrieved his white flying suit from the cockpit and put it back on. He shrugged on the parachute harness and settled the weight of the pack on his back before getting into the small trainer.

"I'll make sure you get some more ground equipment." He pointed to some trucks which had just pulled up with barrels of aviation fuel on board.

"We can't have your chaps refuelling by hand, so I'll try to whistle up some bowsers." He glanced at the field and noted the ruts on the surface. "We've had to catch up the last few months but we've managed to scrounge up some engineers to help out. Tons of grass seed has been shipped across. I don't know what good that will do at this time of year, but I'll see about getting the ground more level."

"There is the matter of spares, sir," Winwright reminded him.

"Get a list to headquarters and I'll see what I can do."

"Where are you off to next, sir?"

"The Lysanders on the other side of town. If communications break down we'll be relying on them heavily to pass orders." Goddard worked the stick, watching the controls. He settled the goggles on his face and looked back at him. "Make the best use of the time you have, Winwright. If it's anything like the last show, god only knows when it will all end."

He twirled his left hand above his head and Winwright shouted for people to get out of the way. Two erks darted in to pull the chocks clear. The air ripped apart as the engine started.

1.5 – A Jaunt In The Country

Morgan was having a good day. They were on course, he was reading the winds right and the clear weather gave him all the landmarks he needed. He lay off the next course and handed up a piece of paper to Chandler. His pilot nodded and they swung onto the new heading. He checked his watch. Five minutes to the beach.

Slightly off to the left he could clearly see the port town of Dunkirk. The sea was a dull blue, the surface rough from the wind coming off the low lying coastal region. He saw the white painted hulls of some fishing smacks stark against the dark ocean, pitching up and down as they cleared the safety of the breakwater.

There were few clouds out there and visibility was good, at least twenty miles or more. He took an experimental look through the binoculars. He picked out the leading fishing boat and tried to keep it in view while the Blenheim rode the air currents. He found he could just about do it if he braced one elbow on the navigation table and wedged himself against the canopy above his head.

He put the binoculars down and occupied himself thumbing through the recognition book. He turned the pages, glancing at the silhouettes of ships, going back and forth as he compared the shapes of English and German destroyers. He looked up English cruisers and stared at the outline of the battlecruiser *Hood*. He admired the long bow and the sleek lines of her hull. His brother-in-law was aboard her and he wondered where he was now.

Chandler had climbed hard since leaving the airfield. Making the most of the short run to the sea, he'd got up to twelve thousand feet. The drone of the engines drilled into his head and he yawned, working his jaw to make his ears go pop. He was still a little tired from the day before and the bad night's sleep.

In his turret, Griffiths had the best view of all. As far as he could see, the countryside was a patchwork quilt of fields, a mix of yellows and greens. Here and there were little hamlets or clumps of trees and hedges. He saw a car meander along a narrow road below, negotiating its way round a sharp corner.

He looked up and scanned the horizon, quartering the sky around them. He traversed the turret left and right as he sighted along the gun, tracking the clouds, imagining they were a target. Movement off to the left caught his eye. He glanced across and looked up. Something caught the sun and flashed. He squinted and rotated the turret left. A clump of clouds hid his view. He waited. It happened again and finally it came into view. A dark shape emerged from behind the clouds, followed by another one a few seconds later.

He sighted along his Vickers machine gun and followed the target. They angled towards them and began to descend, coming closer. He clicked on his R/T.

"Bandit, coming in about eight o'clock from behind the clouds."

In response, the Blenheim surged forwards as Chandler advanced the throttles. The port wing dipped and they curved to the left, heading towards Dunkirk. It put the approaching aircraft on their tail and turned it into a stern chase. They began to descend, gaining speed.

The two aircraft continued to approach. Griffiths tracked them as they slid out to the right, starting to run parallel to their course. As they got closer, Griffiths was able to identify them and let out a sigh of relief.

"It's alright, skipper. They're French Curtiss 75's. It looks like they're giving us the once over."

Chandler levelled off and closed the throttle in response. Griffiths blanched as the two fighters flicked onto their side and lanced down towards him.

"They're attacking! Break right!"

There was a few seconds delay as Chandler was caught off guard. He pulled the yoke back into his stomach and stamped on the right rudder pedal. The Blenheim reared up and skidded to the right, the wing dropping. Griffiths clung on for dear life.

Up front, Morgan was pinned in his seat by the G-forces of the turn. His arms felt like lead and he had no chance to get to the flare gun and fire off the day's colours.

The French fighters bore in and Griffiths squirmed as they were lined up right on him. He felt like a specimen under the microscope as they drew closer. At the last moment, the trailing Curtiss pulled up and away, but the leading fighter opened fire.

Tracers flashed out towards them and thumped into the Blenheim. Griffiths heard a massive bang behind him in the fuselage. The French fighter roared overhead, rocking its wings in recognition. Griffiths could only mouth a curse as the Blenheim shuddered in its slipstream and levelled off.

He tried the intercom but got no response. He tapped the earpiece of his flying helmet and gave it another try. He ducked down out of the turret to find the fuselage looked like a sieve. Wind whistled through the holes and a panel flapped loose on the starboard side. The radios sparked and little wisps of smoke rose from the casing. He gave them an experimental thump but got nothing in return. He looked down the fuselage towards the cockpit. Chandler was looking back at him, tapping the earpieces of his helmet. Griffiths pointed to himself and gave a thumbs up and then pointed to the radio and gave a thumbs down. He repeated it twice and Chandler nodded his head in understanding before turning back to the controls.

Griffiths returned to his turret and looked around. The two French fighters had reformed on their port wing, slightly back of the tail. The leader edged in closer and pulled his canopy back with his right hand. A bright blue scarf whipped back in the slipstream and flapped down the side of the American built fighter. He pulled his goggles up and Griffiths could make out a long narrow face with a bushy moustache.

He shook his fist at the Frenchman and mouthed an obscenity. The fighter pilot laughed and gave him a Gallic shrug in return, which only made Griffiths even angrier. He waved his arms at the French fighters, blood boiling at the near miss.

"Go on, bugger off!" He shouted into the gale.

The French fighters lingered a few more moments before heeling over and swooping for the ground. Griffiths watched them go, thinking dark thoughts.

Chandler moved the controls around, getting a feel for anything out of the ordinary. It all seemed taut and responsive. He flicked a glance at the gauges and the engines seemed okay too, which left him with one simple dilemma. To carry on or go back.

Without a radio, they couldn't signal back to base if they had a sighting. What worried him more was that with no intercom they had no teamwork. There would be no warning from Griffiths if enemy fighters should bounce them, no warning if he should see the ships. If it was just himself, he would press on, but Chandler had two other lives in his hands.

He looked at Morgan and then glanced over his shoulder back down the fuselage. There were other aircraft out there searching as well; *but one aircraft might make all the difference*, he kept telling himself.

He couldn't face the thought of having to abort and go back. Having no radio was a more than reasonable excuse, but he could imagine the accusing stares in the mess. He had no doubt what Winwright's reaction would be. It was the squadron's first mission, a rush job from Wing. He would be expected to deliver success. No matter the reason, if he turned back now, he would be putting up another black.

Morgan came up into the cockpit from the nose. Chandler lifted the right side of his flying helmet as his navigator leaned in close and shouted above the blare of the engines.

"What are we going to do?"

"Morg, you know the intercoms out. What do you think?"

"Press on, you mean?"

"Yes! Should we chance it? There might be more trigger happy Frenchies about and we'll get no warning next time."

Morgan looked down the length of the fuselage. He could see the young lad constantly moving. His eyes must have been looking in a hundred different directions back there. He glanced forwards again over the nose, the wide expanse of the ocean spread out before them.

"Let's give it a go," he said, his voice sounding more positive than he felt. "I reckon about another five minutes before we turn north east to skirt the Belgian territorial airspace! Heading three zero degrees!"

"Keep your eyes peeled. We're going to need a slice of luck today."

"Roger, skipper."

Chandler took up the new course and scratched off one of his nine lives.

Half an hour later, they were coming towards the end of the first run along their search area. They'd seen nothing other than a few fishing boats and a coastal steamer. The brief was to patrol back and forth along a fifty mile stretch and then run for home. Other aircraft from England were out searching as well. They were just an ant among many ants, but Chandler felt driven to deliver a result. His fears of thirty minutes previous had evaporated with the clouds. He glanced around at a sun chased sky, a blue bowl spread out above him.

It was as if they were all on their own as they cruised along with the Scheldt on their starboard side. Ahead was The Hague, and beyond that, Amsterdam. The coast carried on curving north until the Ijsselmeer before heading east towards Germany. He tried to think himself into the role of the German cruiser. Hugging the coast didn't make much sense to him. Close in shore, the water would be shallow and would restrict their movement. A big ship like that would be further out.

"We're looking in the wrong place," he muttered to himself. Out there, out at sea; that was where they should be. He decided to make one wide sweep before turning for home. He performed a leisurely turn to the left and headed for the open ocean.

In the nose, Morgan glanced at his watch and then looked over his shoulder. His eyes were sore from peering through the binoculars, the reflections off the water burning into his skull. He pressed them to his face again and took another sweep of the horizon. Something off to the left caught his eye, a splash of colour against the dark water, a smudge. He rubbed his face and looked again. Satisfied his eyes weren't playing tricks, he went back to Chandler.

"Something ahead on the water, skipper. It must be a fair size for me to spot it this far out."

"All right Aaron, we'll take a look. Hang on to something, I'm going down fast."

Chandler waited until Morgan was back in the nose and then rocked the wings to give Griffiths an idea something was going to happen. He shoved the nose down and headed for the water. He kept a firm grip on the yoke and felt it bucking in his hands, the controls stiffening as the speed built up. He levelled out at two thousand feet and angled away from the sighting. He kept it about twenty degrees off the nose so he could come in at a more oblique angle.

Chandler could see it was a ship all right. It must have been going at some speed because the surface of the water was all churned up behind it as it headed west. Morgan kept the binoculars glued to his face. He braced his elbows and tried to keep them steady while the Blenheim jolted through the moisture rich air. As it drew closer, Morgan started taking in details.

The hull was long and sleek with a clipped bow and a single mast stuck up jauntily behind the bridge. There were two funnels amidships with three gun mounts at the stern and two up front. He started flicking through the pages for the Kreigsmarine in the Janes book. He found what he was looking for amongst the listings for the destroyers. Happy with his choice, he went up to the cockpit. He shoved the book in front of Chandler and stabbed his finger at the page.

"That's it skipper. A 1936 destroyer I reckon. It's got the clipped bow and shorter funnels, so it doesn't fit the 1934 jobs."

"Not the cruiser we were looking for though," grumbled Chandler.

"I'm not complaining, skipper. They sent us out here to find a tub. We found one. Now can we get out of here please?"

His pilot nodded in response.

"One pass to make sure and then home. Hang on."

Chandler dived for the sea and watched the altimeter unwind.

1.6 – Storm In A Teacup

Chandler flew a sieve back to Bois Fontaine. The Blenheim drew a great deal of interest from the rest of the squadron as it taxied back to dispersal. The whole aircraft was pockmarked with holes and tattered strips of canvas fluttered off the rudder. A crowd gathered round it while Chandler went to the CO's hut to make his report.

Winright had been annoyed that they'd had no signal from Chandler, but his mood soon changed when he was told the whole story. The young pilot pointed out on the map where they had made their sighting. On the way back they'd reported the ships' position by dropping a message cylinder over a satellite airfield near the coast. Chandler smiled when Winwright queried how he could be so certain about the identity of the ship.

They'd come in low, running parallel to their course so as not to alert them. They managed to close to a hair over one thousand yards before they finally spotted him. A solitary machine gun opened up and then a daisy chain of tracer had come flashing in his direction. The ocean erupted in spray as shell after shell was thrown at them. Banking hard to the left, Chandler had pulled the boost toggle and the Blenheim had soared into the sky, opening the range.

Winwright observed his pilot across the table through a cloud of pipe smoke. Chandler sat on the edge of the folding seat, back ramrod straight, his eyes clear; face placid. It had shown great courage pressing home the attack and carrying on without a radio. Some might have argued that he'd risked his crew unnecessarily. The fact he'd succeeded was very often the dividing line between a calculated risk and foolhardiness. Winwright was grudgingly impressed but did not allow his approval to show.

Ashton offered some encouragement and then closed the door behind Chandler as he left. He lit a cigarette before sitting across from Winwright. The CO leaned back in his chair and glanced out of the window at the damaged aircraft. Groundcrew were already swarming over it, making a list of what needed putting right. Winwright reached for the field telephone, which had finally been hooked up.

"Headquarters please."

There was an interminable pause while the operator tried to put the call through. The minutes dragged by and Winwright's temperature rose the longer he waited.

"Yes? Hello? What do you mean the lines down? Well fix it!" Fingers drummed on the desk. "In fact, forget it. I'll sort this out myself." He slammed the receiver down into the cradle.

"If the mountain won't come to Mohammed-" Winwright said in frustration as he pondered the day's events. While their Wing was based around Béthenville, Wing HQ would eventually be located in Arras. The only problem was they hadn't set up shop yet. For the time being, they were miles away at AASF HQ in Rheims.

Making his mind up, Winwright sprang for the door. He snatched his Irvin jacket off the back of the chair and scooped up his helmet and goggles. Blood boiling, he made a beeline for the squadron hack. Kittinger followed him out and caught Burke's eye. He pointed at the Tiger Moth.

"Two six!" Burke shouted.

Immediately, a group of erks rushed towards the small biplane. One jumped into the cockpit while his colleague waited a moment at the nose and then swung the prop. The engine coughed and the prop span once before the engine caught. Two erks draped themselves over the tail as the engine was run up.

The grass flattened behind the aircraft. The slipstream smashed into a hut, making the windows rattle. The blast increased as the erk built up the revs, the stick hauled back into his stomach to stop the Tiger Moth leaping over the chocks. The men draped over the tail huddled against the rush of air, their arms wrapped over their heads, trying to shield their ears from the noise. The airframe shook under their bodies and they could feel it straining against them. The throb of the engine reverberated in their chests as they waited for it to be over, no more useful than sandbags, only because sandbags were not as portable. Finally, the engine note dipped back to idle and they stood up, ears ringing and their noses filled with the petrol and exhaust fumes. The erk exited the cockpit to make way for Winwright. After a quick pre-flight, he took off into the midday sun.

During the one hour flight to Rheims he took a short battlefield tour along his route as Arras, Douai, Cambrai and Saint-Quentin passed below. Just north of Arras was Vimy Ridge, where four Canadian divisions had fought during the Nivelles offensive in 1918. Tanks had been used for the first time at Cambrai. The land still bore the scars of some of the fiercest fighting on the Western Front. Huge swathes of woodland were still threadbare and the ground was torn and shattered from the Great War twenty years before.

He landed at the airfield just outside of Rheims. Taxying over to the English side of the field, he parked next to some Fairey Battles standing in the open. The RAF liaison officer greeted him and after a few quick phone calls, a saloon car spirited him away to the Chateau Polignac.

Winwright saw a town awash with men in uniform as he was driven through Rheims. As they rounded a large building near the centre of town, his chaperone pointed out the Grand Lion d'Or hotel.

"That's where you'll find the war correspondents, sir. The owners Swiss I believe; bit anti-British, but the Champagne is cheap," he offered, trying to take the edge off Winwright's visible anger. Winwright sat in brooding silence, his arms crossed and his chaperone gave up.

Next to the crossroads by Pommery Parc, the car turned and stopped outside the Chateau Polignac. After showing his ID papers to the red cap at the gate, Winwright was allowed into A.A.S.F headquarters. At the reception desk, he asked to see Air Commodore Saundby and was directed to a bench on the other side of the hall. He dumped his flying gear there and stood staring at some propaganda posters on the wall.

One had a stylised Hitler peering round a corner with his hand cupped to

30

his ear. The caption read *"He wants to know your units name; he wants to know from whence you came"*. The other had a charming femme fatale draped over a couch in a barely there negligee saying goodbye to a soldier. Below it said; *"A maiden loved – an idle word. A comrade lost and Hitler served."*

He glanced again at the poster and shook his head. He shuddered to think of what was being said over champagne in the bars in town where anyone could hear it. Having cooled off on the flight over, his temperature was beginning to rise again. Simmering, he sat down on the bench. It creaked under his weight as he shifted position and folded his arms.

"Arthur!" Saundby's voice boomed in the hall. "Good of you to call. You get over okay?"

Winwright had first met Saundby at Cranwell. The older man had been the students mentor and an instructor at the officer training college. Saundby's star had risen fast after Cranwell. He'd gone through a variety of staff positions and Ministry assignments but he crossed paths with Winwright every few years along the way. A tall man, his lithe frame was running to fat in his middle age and his uniform jacket was straining around the waist.

"Got here yesterday," Winwright replied. He gestured around the hall. "But you seem to have secured the better lodgings."

Saundby laughed in good humour and pointed to a door behind him. Winwright followed him down a corridor to a small office. It wasn't much, just a spartan eight foot box with a desk and two chairs. Saundby shoehorned himself behind the desk and folded his hands in his lap.

"That was a good show from your man, spotting the destroyer," he said. A little mollified, Winwright sat in the chair opposite.

"Thank you, sir. Yes, he did well. Better than I expected."

"Well, the nautics were happy at any rate." Saundby tapped a folder on the desk. "I understand they're sending out a fast destroyer group to intercept, but I doubt they'll catch it in time."

Winwright grunted. Saundby had managed to get to the heart of the problem immediately.

"That's what I'm here to see you about, sir. They might have had a better chance if we'd got off the sighting report immediately. My pilot had to drop a message because he had a run in with some French fighters earlier."

"Yes, we've already had the French on the blower about that," said Saundby. He perched a pair of glasses on his nose as he opened another folder. He thumbed through to a signal near the back. "They were quite apologetic about an incident with a Blenheim near Dunkirk." His lips quirked in a smile. "It, ah, didn't take me much to figure out it was your man."

"An incident?" Winwright nearly hit the roof. It was a good few seconds before he managed to regain his composure and speak. "An incident? Is that what they said? It was a bit more than that. The aircraft's practically a write off!" He came down a bit. "No one was hurt though, thank goodness."

"Then it was a very good show indeed, carrying on the mission like that," said Saundby.

"It's simply not good enough sir," complained Winwright. "The Germans already have an advantage of numbers. I can't be losing trained crews to trigger happy Frenchmen."

There was a long pause while the Group Captain thought about the situation. He knew Winwright. He knew him well enough to know that he could be the Devil's own when the mood was on him.

"What do you want to do about it?"

"I'd like to lodge a protest, sir," Winwright replied immediately. Saundby clicked his tongue. Direct as ever.

"You want to lodge a protest?" he said, deadpan.

"Look, Alec," said Winwright, trying to be sensible and not let his anger get in the way. "If their aircraft identification is so shoddy they can shoot up a Blenheim with obvious markings, then something needs to be *done*."

Saundby pursed his lips and twiddled his thumbs for a moment. He sighed. The same old mistakes were happening just like the last war. He could remember diving on a fighter himself, convinced it was a German two seater. He had swooped down, gunsight lined up on the cockpit as the target sailed serenely along. It was only at the last second that he saw the French roundels on the wings and pulled up, scaring hell out of himself and them.

"I wouldn't disagree old boy, but that would create a bit of a situation you see. About the same time your incident happened, two of our Hurricanes tore into some of their Potez bombers and managed to shoot one down. They ah, killed two of the crew. The French have been hopping mad about it."

That was a bit of an understatement. The wires had been red hot between Air Component headquarters and the local French command for most of the morning.

"Ah," said Winwright.

"Ah, indeed, Arthur. It would be a bit rich to point the finger at the Frogs when we've done the same thing, only worse. We've been doing what we can to calm things down. There are a lot of aircraft in these skies of ours. There are bound to be a few mistakes. Temperatures are running a little high. I see no point in fanning the flames by lodging an official protest over your Blenheim."

Saundby paused and let that thought sink in. Winwright sat in silence so he took that as his cue to continue.

"This won't be the only incident to come, I'm sure. Now; we could all go round, thumping tables, demanding heads on platters, but it won't get us very far." Then he delivered the official line. It was one he happened to agree with. His eyes narrowed as he spoke, assessing Winwright's reaction as he said it. "Command's very keen for all of this to just go away. Bad for morale and all that. We can't have our chaps taking potshots at each other; it could only lead to more tragic accidents."

Winwright ruminated on his options and in a fast second decided. The writing was on the wall, writ in letters five feet tall.

"All right, Alec, I hear the message," he grudgingly agreed.

"Write it off to experience, Arthur and let it go. Now, tell me about what happened with your man."

Winwright spent the next ten minutes, giving an outline of what Chandler had done. Saundby thought back to his own war experiences and considered Chandler's actions. The boy had taken a chance and made it home. Courage like that needed some sort of recognition. On impulse, he made a decision. There were enough war correspondents around that needed a good story. Why not feed them a hero, he thought to himself. Good news made for better reading in the papers than a mistake.

"Forward me your man's report along with a recommendation for a decoration on my desk before close of play tomorrow."

Winwright thought about that. Some might question Chandler's judgement, but he had pressed on when many would have cut their losses and quit. Like Saundby said, there were always the political angles and propaganda to consider. Winwright promised to send the report by dispatch rider that evening. As they said their goodbye's Saundby promised to visit the squadron in the near future.

1.7 – This Is The Home Service

After seven days, the squadron's little corner of France became much more comfortable. More huts were erected and grateful personnel had moved in, swapping their draughty tents for four walls and a small stove. Two more huts went up next to the CO's. One was for Dane and his intelligence bumpf. The other was a long hut by the trees. This had become the main ready room and mess rolled into one. The space was filled with beat up sofas, armchairs and two tables they'd managed to scrounge from the locals. A wood burning stove stood in the middle of the room to provide some heat, its flue going up through the ceiling. A large blackboard was hung from one wall. Rows of names were chalked on it, split into A and B Flights.

Osbourne wrinkled his nose as he glanced back over his shoulder. He could still smell the paint which had been slapped on the wooden walls. He preferred standing by the door for some fresh air. He was leaning against the door frame, half in, half out of the hut, feeling the breeze on his face when he saw Ashton and Winwright go to town.

He watched them drive out of the gate in a battered green Citroen that the advance party had *acquired*. It turned left and headed down the lane, dust swirling behind it. He yearned to go to town himself. He was on a promise with a charming brunette but the CO had cancelled all passes in preparation for an exercise.

He let his eyes rove across the field, noting the approach of the leaden skies on the horizon. The wind was stiffening all the time. He could see it in the trees along one side of the field. Their tops swayed and he could smell the rain out there in the air. He grimaced at the thought of flying in rough weather.

He switched his attention to the aircraft and could see Chandler deep in conversation with Burke by his Blenheim. A replacement had been ferried in and he was waiting to air test her before the weather turned.

Waiting for the word on the day's activities, a collection of pilots and observers had gathered in the hut to lounge around like lizards in the sun. Apart from Chandler's reconnaissance mission, they'd not seen any action. Flying kit hung off hooks by the door and a bored pall hung over the room. A few diehards were down the other end of the hut playing cribbage while the remainder were either dozing or reading.

Someone voiced another complaint about having to sleep in a tent but Osbourne ignored them. There had been a lot of bellyaching of late and he was tired of it. Personally, he was quite enjoying living in the field.

There was fresh activity by the Blenheim. Something obviously wasn't right because Chandler left his parachute draped over the tail and stomped towards the crew hut. Osbourne watched him for a moment before casting one more look over his shoulder.

"Bugger this," he muttered.

"Something bothering you old boy?" asked Preddy from behind a well thumbed copy of The Times.

"I'm going for a run," Osbourne announced. "Anyone care to join me?" He went from face to face around the hut but found no takers. Farmer yawned and stretched while he read his newspaper. He was warm and the last thing he wanted to do was trudge around in the wet.

"Don't let us stop you then, toddle on," said Farmer as he made a shooing motion with his hand. Osbourne's lip curled in a sneer and he left to get his gym kit. He might be confined to the airfield, but he was damned if he was going to languish for the rest of the day. As the Scot left, Chandler came in, his boots clomping on the floorboards.

"Much going on?" he asked as he flopped into an empty armchair. He scooped up a random paperback from an upturned wooden crate that was doubling as a table. "They've found a mag drop now." he offered conversationally. Farmer glanced at him but said nothing. He theatrically thumbed to the next page and looked left at Preddy.

"I swear I heard something there, old boy."

"Possibly, possibly," mumbled Preddy in mock boredom.

"You're funny," observed Chandler. "You know, you two could be on *ITMA* as the guest stars," he said, making reference to the Tommy Handley radio comedy.

In the intervening week, Chandler thought the atmosphere had thawed somewhat, but his recommendation for a decoration had divided opinions. While a few of them had seen it as Chandler earning his stripes, Preddy and Farmer saw him as a glory hound and a line shooter. As far as they were concerned, the state of his Blenheim was evidence enough that he'd gone looking for trouble.

Mostly it was just jealousy and Farmer knew it. He glowered at the young pilot over the top of his newspaper. He willed him to look in his direction, but Chandler's attention remained focused on his book. Farmer's father had been awarded the Military Cross in the last show and he felt great pressure to emulate that. Part of him wondered how he would have reacted if it had been him instead of Chandler and he was bothered that he wasn't sure of the answer.

At Wing headquarters, Air Commodore Saundby was in the throes of organising the movement of his staff to Arras. HQ had picked out a nice country pile on the edge of town for them. He was ploughing through some Air Ministry signals when his aide, Squadron Leader Embrey knocked lightly on the door and came in. Saundby glanced up for a moment and then signed his name at the bottom of a file and moved it to the OUT tray. Embrey remained standing, his hands clasped in front of him. Saundby looked up as he noticed his aides flustered air.

"Problem with the move?" he asked.

"It's not that, sir." Embrey moistened his lips.

"Spit it out man," said Saundby, irritated at Embrey's hesitance.

"The Jerries have sunk one of our battleships!"

Saundby's eyes went wide. He put his pen down, the file forgotten. He rubbed his hands together in weary resignation and then pushed himself back from his desk. His chair scraped across the floor as it moved.

"Well, the Navy don't do things by halves, do they?"

"Apparently a U-boat got into Scapa Flow and put some torpedoes into *Royal Oak*."

Saundby glanced at his wristwatch.

"Nearly twelve," he said. "We can catch the news if the set warms up in time."

They left his office together and walked down the corridor to the main operations room in the chateau. Walking past the staff, Saundby turned the radio on. There were hisses and scratches while the valves warmed up. The Duty Officer started to speak but was quickly shushed by Embrey. Saundby strained his ears to hear anything coming from the speaker. The minutes dragged by and then suddenly, the clipped voice of the announcer could be heard.

"-is the BBC Home Service. Here is the news bulletin. As it was reported late this morning, the Secretary of the Admiralty regrets to announce that *HMS Royal Oak* has been sunk, it is believed, by U-boat action. Fifteen survivors have been landed-"

The room exploded in shock and amazement. *Royal Oak* was a battleship with the Home Fleet. For a U-Boat to have penetrated the harbour was unthinkable. Voices rose ever higher until they shushed themselves to silence as the news announcer continued.

"-second attack by torpedo. The battleship capsized shortly after being struck and lies on the bed of the harbour. Hundreds of crew in the water have been picked up and ferried to safety by the tender, *Daisy*. The search continues for survivors."

They remained glued to the radio for the next ten minutes as the news continued. The events of the previous week were recapped, including Chamberlain and Daladier's declining Hitler's offer of peace. Saundby turned the set off when it moved onto an amendment to rationing regulations.

"Well that's one in the eye for the nautics," said the DO with an almost vicious sneer. "They can't even keep house in their own back yard."

That comment brought a few protests. Ignoring the hubbub, a curious Embrey walked over to a sideboard full of identification pamphlets. He picked up a book on ships and thumbed through it until he got to the page for the Royal Sovereign class battleships. He blanched when he saw the crew complement.

"My god, there was over a thousand men on board."

"If the Jerry navy can get into Scapa Flow," whispered an appalled Saundby, leaving the ghastly possibilities hanging. He thought about the radio broadcast describing so many men in the water. Scapa Flow was in the far north of Scotland. He wondered how many would be pulled from the water alive.

"They're not having a very good week are they?" Embrey continued in the same vein. "They couldn't catch that destroyer last week. Now they lose one of their own ships this week."

Back at Bois Fontaine, the mood in the crew room had taken an ugly turn. There was a well trod phrase: *never talk about religion or politics*.

Unfortunately, that line had been crossed with only casual regard for the rules. Arthur and Preddy had started the ball rolling with a few choice remarks about the cause of the war, Chamberlain and the fiasco at Munich. A few others had leaped on board and the thing gathered momentum all by itself.

Flying Officer Mark Hagen, one of the members of B Flight looked askance at Arthur with distaste. Sitting next to him was Martin Wilkes, a Pilot Officer with sandy hair. He hung over the back of a rickety wooden chair.

"What about the Germans?" he mumbled round the end of a pencil he was chewing on.

"They took what everyone else was content to let them take." replied Arthur with some flippancy. "As long as it wasn't us the Germans were coming for, why make a fuss?" He shrugged. "At least, that's how I see it."

Patience strained, Hagen turned on him, eyes blazing.

"That's cold hearted."

"Dash it, I just meant…I mean." Arthur flushed red, embarrassed. His mouth flapped. "Hang it all."

"Don't you think we're just missing the bigger picture here?" said Preddy. "We went to war in the first place to help Poland but that didn't change very much did it?" Wilkes' pulse throbbed in his temple and his eyes widened while Preddy continued. "Germany didn't stop. The French could have done something long before now. The Poles chucked the towel in weeks ago. If Poland was still fighting, then maybe we could justify why we're stuck in the middle of France freezing in some mouldy tents."

"And yet here we are," said Wilkes, disgusted at their attitude.

"I just *knew* you'd say something like that, Preddy," said Pettifer with cool disdain.

"And just what's that supposed to mean?" asked Preddy, shifting his attention from Wilkes to his favourite target.

"I don't get how you think the Nazis will be content with snapping up Poland? They were just the appetizer."

"Well hark at the idealist," sneered Arthur, backing up his pal. Pettifer seemed to grow a few inches as he braced his shoulders and looked at both of them.

"It's nothing to do with idealism. We're in a fight for our survival against an enemy that doesn't abide by the rules. *Peace in our time ring a bell?"* His voice dripped contempt.

"Let 'em come." Arthur pointed towards the door of the hut. "We've got the Maginot Line *and* the BEF has over a hundred thousand soldiers in France. The Germans would be *mad* to take us on."

Farmer had been watching the exchange and seen the temperature slowly rising. Hagen had edged closer to Pettifer and Wilkes was only a few feet away, ready to intercede in case Preddy or Arthur blew up. Farmer got there first. He interposed his big frame between them and kept his voice level. He looked Arthur right in the eye, making sure he had his attention.

"Ease down lads, No need to go to war, we're all supposed to be on the same side, remember?" Arthur and Preddy stiffened. They were used to Farmer taking the lead or being on their side, not taking the part of someone else. His eyes were defiant for a few moments and then Arthur wilted, the steam coming out of him. His voice gabbled in fading bluster.

"But they gave their assurances-"

"Jerry doesn't follow the rules," Farmer said firmly, echoing the point Pettifer had made. "They never have."

"I say; play the game, old boy," responded Preddy, his tone conciliatory. "We dealt with the Hun before, we can do so again."

Instead of defusing the situation, Preddy's throwaway remark touched a nerve where Pettifer was concerned.

"Play the-? Play the game. Is that what you said?" He went pale with rage. "Play the game..." His voice trailed off into a slight hysterical laugh as he struggled to compose himself. "You talk like it's a few overs of cricket or something. My father and my Uncles all died in the last war and you talk about it like it..like it's-"

Realising he had gone too far, Preddy backed off. He held up his hands, palms outward as he took a small step back.

"Take it easy, old boy. Just a turn of phrase, what?" he said with a sheepish smile.

There was a pregnant pause as they faced each other and Farmer looked at each of them, willing them to calm down. Everyone else in the room held their breath, waiting to see what would happen next. Pettifer held up a warning finger and then snarled, stomping from the hut, steam coming out of his ears.

Preddy and Arthur nervously looked at each other. They felt like naughty school children do when they got hauled to the front of the class. Conversation restarted at a lower volume as the aircrews settled down again.

Farmer sank into an armchair. He ignored Preddy and Arthur as they sat across from him, giving them some Coventry time. There was an uncomfortable few minutes before a calm voice over Farmer's shoulder made the hair on his neck stand on end.

"Well that could have been better," said Kittinger quietly as he moved to perch on the right arm of Farmers' seat. Everyone had been so focused on the standoff between Pettifer and Arthur and Preddy, no one had noticed him slide in. Hearing the raised voices, he'd been about to intervene when Farmer had saved him the trouble.

Posted to the squadron not long before going to France, Kittinger was still something of a mystery to most of the aircrew. The previous Adjutant, Beuler, had been a good friend but Kittinger was more distant and tended to keep to himself.

"Far be it from me to be a stick in the mud, but I think it would be prudent to avoid such subjects in the future, don't you?" said Kittinger, his voice distant and almost vague, like a wise grandfather. No one said anything.

"It's interesting how things look from a different perspective." He counselled and hooked a thumb back at his own chest. "I know about duty, but this isn't a game-" he said, echoing Preddy's own phrase.

"-I was only using a figure of speech, sir," said Preddy, quickly protesting his innocence. Kittinger just looked at him, head cocked to one side. He stared at him until Preddy blushed in embarrassment.

"Maybe," he nodded slowly. "Maybe you were, but it wouldn't hurt to think about the fact that we're *supposed* to be a team. Rubbing people up the wrong way is *not* the way to promote harmony amongst one's fellows." He gestured around the room. "Take a careful look around gentlemen, a lot of the faces in this room won't see the end of this war." He paused, letting that little gem sink in. "Maybe *you* won't, maybe me." he said half to himself. He stood and looked down at them for a moment. "Think about that."

Kittinger left the room and Preddy waited a good solid minute before he dared say anything.

"Well, he was full of good cheer," he said. Arthur laughed hard, the solemn mood sloughing away like water off a duck's back.

The green Citroen bowled along the narrow lanes bordered by high hedgerows. Ashton looked at Winwright. The CO's face was lit up with a smile. All the serious lines were gone as he thrilled to the feel of a fast car bowling along. He slowed down as they came up behind a horse drawn cart. He picked his spot, dropping down a gear and floored it to smoothly overtake. In a matter of minutes, they pulled up in the square and walked into the Town Hall.

As they strode across the hall, Ashton patted his pocket once more to make sure he had the list with him. As much as things were starting to take shape at Bois Fontaine, there were still a few things causing discontent at the airfield. The main thing was the food.

The squadron had grudgingly put up with the cold as they slept in tents. They had put up with basic washing facilities but what they could not put up with was awful food. What had been delivered by the French Army commissariat so far was below par. They would tolerate a lot of things but they had drawn the line at horse meat. At Goddard's urging, Winwright had finally decided to take the Group Captain's advice and call on the town Prefect for assistance.

Monsieur Francois Valerie warmly received Ashton and Winwright into his office. Sitting behind a grand desk, the relics of his previous life surrounded him. The hub of a wooden propeller sat on the corner, turned into an ashtray. A glass case contained his medals mounted on green felt. By the side of the desk a brass shell case had a new lease of life as a rubbish bin.

Valerie was a short lithe man with dark brown hair and the keen air of a hunter. His eyes were bright and his hand shake was firm. He ushered the two officers to seats and passed round a box of cigarettes. His secretary brought in a bottle of wine and three glasses. Once they were settled with a drink, he sat down and laced his fingers together on the desk top.

"Good afternoon, gentlemen. I am very glad you're here," he said in a precise, clipped tone. His English was clear with little accent and Ashton watched in fascination as his neat little moustache jinked like a caterpillar as he spoke.

"I don't like to intrude on your time, monsieur," Winwright said in perfect French in return. Valerie gave a little nod of the head and a small smile in appreciation.

"Oh, it is no imposition, Wing Commander. My days are not very full at the moment. You find me at my leisure." He gestured around his office, smiling with bonhomie. "Your arrival caused quite a stir."

"Well, we've tried to fit in. I don't want the men causing any upset," Winwright said earnestly.

"And there has been none so far, I'm thankful to say." His face took on a wistful look and he stared at a photograph of himself in flying gear on the wall.

39

"I remember well how young men can be away from home."

Winwright let Valerie drift into reverie. He swirled the wine glass, watching the deep red liquid circle the bowl. He gave it an experimental sniff and sipped gingerly, trying to process the flavours. Valerie raised his glass in salute to his own portrait and drank deeply. He lavishly refilled the glass and made a face as he did so.

"A not very good '27 from my uncle's vineyard." He dropped the bottle into the shell casing/rubbish bin and nodded as it hit bottom with a satisfying thud. He turned back to the two officers sitting in front of him.

"So, how may I be of service? You have everything you need?"

"Not entirely, that's why I've come. Accommodation is still a problem. I understand some local families have offered to billet the men. I'm afraid the food we've been given-"

"-Is not to your men's liking?"

There was a pause. Winwright shared a look with Ashton. He didn't want to cause offence.

"Well...." He shifted in his seat and shrugged as he tried to phrase it diplomatically. Valerie laughed uproariously and slapped a hand against the top of the table.

"It's quite all right, Wing Commander. I realise the English diet is not the same as the French. I'm sure the army is doing its best but tastes are different, no?" The two RAF officers nodded. Valerie laughed again. "Perhaps there will be something I can do."

He put a finger to his lips and sat back deep in thought. The ticking of the clock intruded into the silence. He cocked an eyebrow at Winwright.

"You have your own cooking facilities?" He asked.

"Of a sort. That's still being organised."

"Bon, that is something. I'll see to it some of the local farms see to your needs. I'm quite sure they'll be grateful for the extra funds."

For the next twenty minutes, Ashton went through the list. Valerie brought in his deputy, Claude Moreau to take notes. A committed bachelor, Moreau muttered as he made notes in tiny cramped handwriting. He glanced sidelong at Valerie, contemplating how much extra work he'd just been saddled with. Winwright arranged to send Kittinger along to finalise things with Monsieur Moreau. Champagne was produced to seal the deal.

After Moreau left the room to start sorting things out, Valerie used his arms to lever himself up out of his chair. He did his level best to walk normally over to the open window but he couldn't disguise the stiffness in his right leg. He pushed the louvred shutter further open and looked across the square. The first spots of rain began coming down as he heard the faint sound of aero engines starting in the distance. Even six or seven miles away, the sound carried on the wind.

"Things have changed quite a bit since I last flew."

"I suppose so," said Winwright. "You would be quite welcome at the airfield whenever you like."

The small Frenchman's face lit up in a beaming smile. Turning, he limped over to Winwright and extended his right hand. Winwright offered his and Valerie shook it warmly.

"Then I will be sure to take you up on your kind offer, Wing

Commander."
"Thank you for your time," said Winwright.
"Au revoir."
"Au revoir."

1.8 – Baptism

The squadron was declared operational five days later. In the intervening days, the weather had improved. The Flights had been worked hard, being sent off in sections to familiarise themselves with the local landmarks. Saundby paid a flying visit and when he was happy all was well, Falcon Squadron were given their first operational order.

It was B Flight's turn on the roster, so Squadron Leader Graves gathered his crews together. There was no shortage of volunteers. The excitement dampened down slightly when they found out it would be a simple patrol. Three Blenheims would fly the flag with the French before ranging up and down the border near the Maginot Line.

Flying along the border didn't sound very exciting, but Chandler's recent experience was still fresh in his mind. Graves believed that any opportunity to show the French what a Blenheim looked like needed to be taken. For this first mission he felt it was only proper to lead his men, so he chose Hagen and Wilkes as his numbers two and three. Striding out to their aircraft, they took off ten minutes later and headed east.

At each French airfield they did the same thing. Graves overflew the runway in a high pass firing the colours of the day to make their presence known. Once they received an answering flare, he brought his flight back around. They made a number of low and slow passes, giving the people on the ground a good look. Job done, they headed for the border.

Graves led with Hagen to port and Wilkes to starboard. As the border approached, his anxiety went up a few notches and he told his wingmen to pull in closer. He wanted them tight on his wing as he turned to the north. He kept the manoeuvre wide and smooth, giving Hagen and Wilkes plenty of room to stay with him.

The sky was a blue bowl with wisps of cloud chasing the breeze. The air was clear but Graves knew that could change very quickly. A number of other squadrons had been attacked recently. That was why operations had changed from singletons to fights of three or more. He thanked his stars that they had converted to the Blenheim before being sent to France.

He'd enjoyed flying the Battle but it was underpowered for the task it was designed to do. With a Merlin engine up front, the new Hurricane and Spitfire were superlative fighters. The Battle had the same engine but had to haul three crew and a ton of bombs and its performance suffered accordingly.

The Luftwaffe had shown up its inadequacies in short order. A number of Battles had been chopped from the sky these last few weeks. The rate of loss was so high that they had been temporarily stood down. This caused Graves some concern as a fair proportion of the air component was made up of Battle squadrons. With them out of the equation, a lot of the workload had fallen onto the shoulders of the Blenheim units.

The press had dubbed this, *'The Phoney War'* and to some degree they were right. The real shooting hadn't started yet. No armies had clashed and aside from the usual propaganda posturing not much had happened. There was a certain air of unreality to everything and Graves had to remind himself that this was all for real. His navigator appeared at his elbow and handed across a steaming thermos cup. He took it and smiled in appreciation. Warm soup was welcome as the temperature dropped. He sipped slowly and felt the warmth of the tomato do its work.

The good thing was that there had been a marked improvement in the food since the CO's visit to town. The Mayor had been as good as his word and between them, Kittinger and Claude Moreau had delivered. The local farms had started providing fresh produce and the cookhouse was turning out some good food at last. Tonight's menu included onion soup. Graves sighed at the thought of fresh baked bread with butter smeared liberally all over it.

"About ten minutes to the next turn, skipper," said Grave's navigator. "Turn to port onto course three five zero and head for the coast."

"Roger. You okay back there, Martin?"

"Fine skip." replied his gunner. "Bit draughty though."

Graves laughed and glanced back down the fuselage. He caught a glimpse of Martin in his turret and knew he wouldn't want to swap places with him.

"Flak off to Starboard." the young man reported.

"I see it; trigger happy French hard at it again." Graves shook his head in resignation. On the earlier familiarisation flights they'd been shot at more than once. Annoying as it was, Graves found it a useful way to blood his pilots. He felt it was better for them to experience it now rather than later. He advanced the throttles and pulled back the yoke to gain some altitude.

Martin watched the small puffs of black with interest in his turret. No matter how many times he saw it, he was fascinated. The explosions crept higher but they soon left them behind as Graves made the turn and ran parallel to the border.

The radio ops on the squadron were a fairly tight knit band. For the princely sum of 1/6d a day on top of their normal pay, they had the privilege of flying. They occupied a strange position in the pecking order. They were not fully groundcrew but not quite seen as aircrew either. A lot of pilots regarded them first and foremost as just a tradesman and they often found themselves excluded from briefings.

He huddled into his jacket and adjusted the scarf around his neck as the air swirled around inside the turret. He flexed his fingers and panned his turret right. He glanced at his friend in Hagen's Blenheim to port and waved.

Wilkes' gunner saw them first and trained his gun on the approaching fighters. Martin picked up the call and traversed to three o'clock and paled. Four, twin engined Me110's were coming in fast. He rummaged around in his head for information on the 110. It was fast; it had a crew of two and had four machine guns and two 20mm cannon.

Graves pulled the boost plug and shoved the nose down. In a straight up run, the 110 was at least 100mph faster than them. The only advantage they had

43

was they were flying light today. With no bombs on board, they could open the taps and pour on the speed, but the 110's were between them and the route home. They could run away, but the Germans would catch them up fast. Right or wrong, Graves elected to go head on at them. It would bring the range down and would be something unexpected.

The Blenheims kept close together and headed into the teeth of the storm. The 110's shook themselves out into line abreast, speeding towards the bombers. It was a very uneven fight, but no one said war was fair. Graves knew they would have to take the first pass.

Guns flashed, he half screwed his eyes shut and braced on the controls. He flicked off the safety and held down the firing button. The controls shook as his paltry single wing mounted gun opened up. He felt *thump*, *thump*, *bang* and then they were past and diving for the ground, throttles wide open, letting the speed build up.

Martin blazed away with his gun as the 110's shot by. He flinched as shrapnel flew in all directions. The leading 110 went head on into Wilkes Blenheim. The wings folded around each other as they hit at over five hundred miles an hour. The engines fell to the earth, trailing a fiery banner behind them, props lazily windmilling. Martin blanched as he realised five men were dead, just like that.

Hagen kept tight on Graves' wing. He could not spare a thought for Wilkes or his crew. They were fighting for their lives and he would have to think about his friend later.

"You okay back there, Guillroy?" he shouted into the intercom.

"Okay, sir," came the piping reply. The twenty one year old winced as he lifted his hand from his arm and paled as it came away dark red. He did not mention he'd been hit. There was nothing anyone could do anyway. He tugged a bandage from his pocket and tied it tight to his jacket while keeping a weather eye on the 110's as they came around.

Graves took them below ten thousand and angled towards a bank of clouds a few miles ahead. Martin called out that the 110's were coming around and were gaining fast from astern. Graves watched the temps like a hawk. They were slowly but surely climbing as he kept the boost pulled well past what was allowed. Hagen knew what Graves was trying to do, all he could do was hope he was right. He stayed tucked in on his leader's port side and watched the clouds creep slowly closer. It was a race. Graves was hoping they could make it to the clouds before the 110's fell on them and blew them to pieces.

The Germans won the race. The faster 110's ate up the distance and fell on the two remaining Blenheims like rabid wolves on sheep. Their guns started chewing lumps out of the bombers as they grimly held formation on each other.

Graves went in first. His starboard engine let go as cannon shells thumped home. A 110 got underneath him and raked the bomber from nose to tail. The canopy starred and fragments cut into his face. The next burst walked through the crew compartment. His navigator doubled up as the bullets tore through his spine and out through his stomach. Graves' feet jerked on the rudder pedals as a round creased his leg. He gritted his teeth while he struggled to maintain control.

Flame burst into life on the starboard wing as fuel spewed out of holed tanks. The engine started to windmill as the prop ran away, the blades thrashing the air.

"Break for it, Tiger Two. I'm finished." he told Hagen. He twisted in his seat and shouted down the fuselage. "Bail out, Martin, bail out!"

The young gunner didn't need telling twice. He ducked down from the turret and clipped on his parachute. He was half out the hatch in the bottom of the fuselage when they attacked again. Bullets tore into the fuselage, impaling Martin even as he was bailing out. His parachute deployed as he fell clear. His lifeless body drifted away under the silk canopy, twisting in the breeze.

Hagen watched in despair as Graves stricken Blenheim went down. Flame streamed back along the entire span of the starboard wing. The control cables let go and the bomber rolled onto its back, wreathed in fire.

On his own, with odds of three to one, Hagen stood the Blenheim on its port wing. Kicking hard on the rudder, he dragged the nose down and round, building up airspeed. Guillroy called out the enemy fighters as they closed in. Hagen used every scrap of his experience and pulled up, skidding into a turn.

The airframe shook as more rounds struck home. He reversed direction again, rolling hard to port. A 110 flashed overhead, missing him by inches. He rolled back once more, chasing the German fighter even as it pulled away. The safety of the clouds was far away. There was nothing but clear skies between them and the three fighters that buzzed around like angry hornets.

It wasn't entirely one sided. Guillroy got in some solid hits as the 110's got overconfident. A 110 took a burst in the canopy and it staggered to the right, out of control. He kept firing his Vickers gun until the barrel grew too hot to touch.

Hagen was running out of tricks as his aircraft was systematically taken apart around him. A burst of fire shredded the rudder and he could feel the controls going slack. Another burst took out the port engine and the temperature went through the roof. He had no choice but to shut it down and he cut the throttle and shut off the fuel. He fought the controls with the loss of thrust and jammed on right rudder, wrestling to keep the wings level.

With the loss of the port engine, they lost hydraulic power to the turret. With no power, Guillroy could only pivot his Vickers gun on a limited arc, but the young gunner knew they were done for.

Hagen knew it too, and he was about to order them to bail out when salvation came from out of the sun. A pair of Hawker Hurricanes came screaming down in a vertical dive, guns hammering into the German fighters. The lead 110 dived away, its engines trailing coolant. The second one broke for home, chased hard by the Hurricanes.

The sky cleared and the ailing Blenheim was on its own. Hagen let out a breath and leaned back in his seat.

"Did anyone see any chutes from Tiger one?" he asked his crew.

"I saw, Martin get it," said Guillroy grimly. "I'm not sure after that. I was too busy blazing away."

Hagen was exhausted. Five minutes of frantic, gut churning action had worn him out and his limbs felt heavy. As the adrenalin began to wear off, the enormity of the engagement began to sink in. Six people from his squadron had been killed and two airplanes had been blown from the sky. He doubted his would be fit for anything if he got her back.

Wind whistled in from the holes in the nose. The controls were sloppy and the remaining engine sounded rough. He backed off the throttle, giving the overworked engine a chance to recover. He played around with the trim tabs to try and give his arms a rest.

He was halfway home when the Hurricanes returned and formed up either side. He waved a thank you and then they broke off, hunting for some more targets. Hagen took his time, letting the Blenheim bimble along, trading height for airspeed.

Ten minutes later, the airfield came into view. He circled for a while, sizing up his approach and judging the conditions. Luckily, there was no crosswind so he went straight in, gently descending. He had to make a final decision when it came to the landing. With the engine out, he had no hydraulic pressure for the flaps, the undercarriage or the brakes. He could blow the wheels down with a backup high pressure air system, but he had no idea if that had been damaged. Even if he did get them down, they may not lock. On balance, Hagen elected to bring her in on her belly. He could cut the switches as soon as he touched down and then coast it in, reducing the risk of fire. His only remaining concern was being on one engine. He would have to keep the speed up to avoid a stall. He worked the controls hard to overcome the offset power differential from the dead engine right up to the end.

Burke was arms deep in an engine when he first heard the drone of the Blenheim. Wiping his hands on a scrap of cotton waste, he shaded his eyes against the sun as he watched it circle. He immediately saw it was in trouble. A thin black wisp of smoke trailed back from the dead engine and it crabbed sideways, rudder hard over. After three more circuits, it came into view from behind the trees shaping up for a landing. He was halfway across to the admin hut when the CO came out and angled towards him.

"It doesn't look good," commented Winwright.

"No, sir." he agreed, grimfaced. He cast his mind back to a long time ago, when his younger self saw planes come back shot up and set down however they could. Now it was happening again.

Hagen did well, he crossed the threshold fence and flared at twenty feet, nose high as he cut the throttle. The prop thrashed for a final time before the tips touched the grass and it was turned into an egg whisk. Divots of grass flew into the air. The Blenheim barrelled across the field, shedding pieces as it went. It came to rest, sat on the grass, steam coming off the starboard engine.

They were running before it even came to a halt. Extinguishers were sprayed into the engines and hot metal cracked and hissed. They stood in hushed awe and watched as Hagen slowly pulled himself out of his seat. He managed a weak smile before he slid back down. Guillroy exited the aircraft and slumped to the ground. His head was ringing and he held a bloodied hand to his temple, but he was alive. He kissed the ground.

1.9 – He Who Believeth In Me

It was a subdued squadron that retired to the hut they were using as the Mess. Hagen sat quietly in the corner, hunched over a table. Concerned glances were thrown in his direction. No one had the nerve to interrupt his introspection. In one hour, the squadron had lost friends they had known for years and three aircraft.

The ease with which the German fighters had blown them from the sky was unnerving. The tight formation flying and speed they'd relied upon seemingly counted for nothing. Two aircraft had fallen to the enemy and the other wasn't fit for scrap. Some of them were amazed Hagen had even managed to get back.

Only a week before, they had stood around and stared in wonder at Chandler's Blenheim. The holes in the fuselage had been a stark reminder of their mortality. What was left of Hagen's aircraft only served to reinforce the reality of their situation.

The bomber shall always get through, was a common enough mantra throughout the 1930's. It had shaped RAF policy and been ingrained into them time and again. Their confidence had remained unshaken when the Fairey Battles were shot from the sky. After all, the Battle was outclassed and underpowered. The day's events had put things in perspective for them.

There were the occasional hushed conversations in the room but they soon petered out. There was little enthusiasm this evening for games and small talk. The door opened. Faces turned hopefully but dropped when they saw Flight Lieutenant Dane come in. Voices hushed as he clasped his hands in front of himself and looked around the room. They had seen that look before back in England.

"The CO has requested that all officers be present for a service tomorrow at ten o'clock. Full turnout please chaps. Meet here at nine to get to the church if you'd be good enough."

An hour later, Kittinger was walking along the borders of the field, skirting the wood. In the fading light of dusk you could just about make out the scar in the ground where Hagen had torn up the turf. It was a cool evening and he shivered as he walked, watching the sky go from dark purple to black. The leaves sighed as a light breeze teased the tops of the trees.

Kittinger took his time crossing the airfield, thinking about the day's events. He tucked his chin into his chest as he thought about the terse description of the engagement from Hagen. He still thought good formation flying could make the difference. It was just unlucky that they had lost Wilkes so early in the engagement. Two aircraft stood little chance no matter how tightly they clung to each other for mutual support.

He knew some of the crews looked on him with suspicion. Coming in to a tight knit unit of men only a few weeks before their departure made them nervous. The faded wings and medal ribbons on his chest raised questions, but it was just something they would have to get used to.

The light was almost gone as he walked back towards his tent on the other side of the trees. He took his time, almost feeling his way. The evening sounds were starting and he listened to the buzz of the insects and the calls of birds up in the trees. He threaded his way through the tents, doing his best to avoid tripping over a guy rope until he came to his own. A lamp dimly illuminated the canvas. He ducked in through the entrance, closing the flap quickly behind himself. His eyes adjusted to the light and he saw Dane sitting on the edge of his camp bed.

"Hullo, Dane. This is a bit cloak and dagger isn't it?"

He pulled a suitcase out from under the bed. He flipped the lid and rummaged around until he pulled out a half full bottle of whisky and two tumblers. Dane held up a hand and shook his head.

"Not for me, thanks. I just wanted to talk to you away from prying eyes. Too much chance for gossip at the moment."

Kittinger grunted to himself and placed the two glasses on an empty ammunition box stood on its side. He poured himself two fingers of whisky and sat down next to Dane.

"What can I do for you, Wallis?"

"What's your view of the men?" Dane asked him, matter of fact.

Kittinger looked hard at the University professor. As the intelligence officer, Dane was the eyes and ears of the squadron. He was the brain that listened to snippets and put the pieces together to come up with a coherent whole. The Adjutant was the mother, clucking round like a hen protecting her chicks.

It seemed that he and Dane had spent the last few hours doing the same thing, trying to gauge the mood of the squadron. Kittinger found it hard to quantify as he thought Dane's question through.

In itself, the idea of casualties was nothing new. Men were lost to all sorts of training accidents and there was an ever pervading feeling that life could be cut short. It was an accepted occupational hazard. For weeks the men had been talking off and on about hitting the silk. Once in the Mess, he'd overheard Osbourne and Farmer talking very matter of fact about getting the chop.

Statistics were unemotional, a cold reality. Today's event was something else, a special case almost. Graves had been a fixture on the squadron for a long time. He looked after his men so it was only natural they should feel his loss keenly.

"I think-" He downed the whisky and poured himself some more. "I think the best way to describe it would be...delicate."

Dane gave him a wry smile. He picked up the other tumbler and Kittinger poured him a drink. Dane sipped at it and made a face. It needed water but it was good whisky.

"Quiet, introspective certainly," he murmured. "Almost like how one feels when their favourite dog gets hit by a car."

Kittinger laughed derisively.

"I hope so," he said. He slopped more Whisky into Dane's glass and told him to drink up. "They better toughen up when the real shooting starts. If they're going to be like this every time we lose someone, they'll crack up."

"They'll be all right," Dane said with assurance.

"How about young Gardner?" With the loss of Graves, Winwright had bumped Flight Lieutenant Alan Gardner up to acting Squadron Leader to fill the gap.

"He'll cope. He'll have to. He was due a promotion anyway, but I think he would have preferred to get it another way."

"Maybe this run to town will help them relax?" Kittinger thought aloud. The CO had seen the mood the men were in and given B Flight the following day off. Kittinger had scrounged up some transport to take them into town when they were ready.

"I'm sure." Dane frowned as he thought about that. His eyes almost disappeared under his brows. "At least, I hope so. A chance to let their hair down and drown their sorrows should be good." He took another pull on Kittinger's whisky and winced as it went down. "It's been a bad day."

Kittinger laughed and poured some more whisky into the older man's tumbler.

"My dear, Dane. You always seem to have the perfect way of understating something."

Squashed into a flatbed truck, B Flight rode into town. After the evening meal, the last thing they wanted to do was hang around the airfield. They sat in silence; each man lost in his own thoughts. The truck squealed to a halt in the town square and they piled out, jamming hats on their heads as they looked around. The driver stuck his head out of the cab.

"The CO told me to pick you up later, Sir. I'll be back at eleven. Anyone not here has to walk back."

Farmer nodded and banged his open palm on the door twice. With a wave and a crash of gears, the truck pulled away, turning in a circle and going back along the Rue du Carillon. Farmer pointed across the town square to the nearest bar and things got a little hazy after that.

Parking themselves at the bar in the Hotel de Ville, they reminisced about Graves and Wilkes. After three hours and some heavy drinking to drown their sorrows, the group began to break up. A few headed back to get the transport. Osbourne and Hagen's Navigators, Woods and Jones were lured by a pair of beautiful brunettes. Dark eyes, a smile and a hint of stocking was enough to tempt them away with the promise of far more to come. That left Farmer in the company of Preddy, Arthur, the dour Osbourne and a subdued Hagen. Long after the pickup time, they were tottering down a grubby little side street in the dark. They leaned on each other for support as they staggered along the cobbles.

They collapsed in a heap at the base of a fountain, their pockets bulging with wine bottles. Preddy lay on his back, staring up at the stars. Farmer's head nearly rested in his lap while he cradled a bottle of red wine. Arthur nuzzled into Farmers shoulder, half asleep. Osbourne perched on a bench seat across from the fountain.

Enjoying the night air, he was glad he'd avoided too much drink that evening. He'd seen the mood of the others and sensed that at least one person needed to keep a level head on their shoulders. So he had elected himself to be the mother hen and shepherd them home.

Hagen's stomach finally rebelled against all the alcohol and he retched his guts up. His head exploded with pain and nausea and he choked back a sob as he threw up again and again. Feeling weak as a kitten, he rested his head on the stone lintel of the fountain, listening to the swirling water. He spat, trying to clear his mouth of the bile. He could feel sweat cooling on his back and his arms felt light. Retching for a final time, he sagged down next to Farmer and ran a shaking hand over his face.

"God forbid we have another day like today," he got out between retches and sobs. "I've never been so scared."

His voice cracked slightly and he snatched the bottle of wine from Farmer's lap. He swallowed it down in big gulps until he choked. Osbourne clicked his tongue in annoyance.

"You don't mean that," Osbourne said. Hagen turned on the Scotsman. His cheeks were flushed but his eyes were bright and unnervingly steady.

"I do you know." He hooked an arm over the lintel and hauled himself up so he sat on the cold stone instead of the ground. "Having to sit there knowing they could chop me into meat whenever they felt like it. It gave me the shivers." He closed his eyes and nearly fell back into the fountain, but a firm grip took hold of the front of his shirt and pulled him back. He looked at Osbourne, teeth chattering. "It was like a cat playing with a mouse. Every time they came in shooting, I thought we were dead."

"But *you* made it back," said Osbourne, reminding him that he'd not died. "Your *crew* made it back, thanks to you."

"Did you see my kite?" Hagen laughed, hysteria lingering on the edges of his voice. He drank greedily, finishing off the bottle of wine. When it was empty, he threw the green bottle across the square. He watched it arc before shattering to pieces on the cobbles. "I came back in a sieve. She'll never fly again."

"Burke thinks she will."

"Bollocks," said Hagen, his voice angry and bitter. "Burke can dream as much as he wants." He walked over to Osbourne and jabbed a finger in the Scotsman's chest. "And I tell you another thing, if it wasn't for the Hurricanes turning up I'd have got the chop. We need an escort if we're going to go up against their fighters." He shuddered and rubbed his hands up and down his arms. He walked around the fountain on shaky legs.

"Guillroy, poor little bastard. The poor kid must have shit himself every time those 110's came in. Staring down the barrel with that shitty little popgun to fire back with. Poor little bastard," he said again as his voice trailed off.

Osbourne helped Farmer to his feet. With the sudden removal of his cushion, Arhur slid to the ground, his face smacking into the cobbles.

"I was speaking to a friend of mine over at 73," said Osbourne. He tried to make casual conversation while they put Arthur to rights. 73 Squadron was one of two Hurricane units that had come over as part of the Air Component. "He said the 109s very inferior to our stuff. He said they're money for jam. Bits of wings fall off 109s in a dive and it's got less guns than a 110."

"That's gratifying," said Hagen, his voice dripping in sarcasm. "That makes me feel so much better when it was 110's that shot us to pieces."

Hagen pulled another bottle of wine out of his pocket and tugged out the cork jammed into the neck. He put away half of it before coming back up for air.

"We're all dead men," he said, pointing at the bottle for emphasis, spilling red wine as he waved it around. "The sooner you all start realising it, the better."

"Wheesht man, stop that," said Osbourne in genuine concern, crossing himself. "Don't tempt fate."

"You and me, we're all on borrowed time." Hagen pointed to himself before taking another swig from the bottle. "Believe it."

"Oh you're full of good cheer," said Farmer, the subject matter under discussion sobering him fast.

"Leave me alone," said Hagen sullenly. He slumped down on the bench and polished off the bottle before slinging it casually over his shoulder. He had thought that drinking himself to oblivion would help, but he'd been wrong. It just terrified him more.

Hagen had been in the RAF for seven years. Most of that time had been spent flying Westland Wapiti's in Iraq. He'd sat in the mess, reading out of date newspapers, craving action and the thrill of combat. Fighting Johnny Arab had not been anything like this.

Flying from RAF Hinaidi, you tolerated the heat, swatted the flies and made the best of things. When the natives got out of line, you might drop some bombs on them. There wasn't much danger. The natives fired at you with single shot rifles, not heavy cannon.

He passed out and sank into a heap. He slowly slid down the bench until he hit the ground and his head was rested at an unnatural angle against the seat. Osbourne roused Preddy and Arthur while Farmer grabbed Hagen under the armpits.

"Come on you dozy bugger. One scrape and you're all doom and gloom." Hagen's head lolled from side to side, drool and wine spilling from his lips.

"Doesn't matter." He half choked and brought up some more wine. "We're all gonna die."

Once they were all upright again, they staggered in the general direction of the airfield. They were doing well until they passed an alleyway and a black cat on top of a garbage can hissed at them. Without warning, Hagen lurched from underneath Farmer's grip. They crashed to the ground while Hagen shuffled on his hands and knees towards the alley. His eyes were locked on the black cat.

Big and fat, it sat on the dustbin lid, paws gathered underneath. Its dark yellow eyes regarded him and then it hissed again, maw wide open. Its teeth caught the light and the ripping sound of its howl shuddered through him. Mustering the energy from somewhere, Hagen grabbed hold of a lump of roof slate on the ground and lofted it at the cat. The slate clattered off the metal bin and the cat sprinted off. Hagen crawled after it, shouting obscenities.

"Go on, get out of here! Little furry bastard!" The cat hissed at him again from the safety of the dark, a malevolent whine that curled through the air. "Get out of here!"

He reached for something else to throw when Osbourne's hand closed around his wrist.

"That's enough. That's not right; the poor animal didn't do anything to you."

Hagen tried shaking him off but Osbourne kept a tight hold and lifted the drunken pilot upright.

"Bloody moggie."

"Steady on, Hagen," Osbourne said.

"Black cats give me the willies," muttered Hagen, "they always have." He half turned and looked back towards the alley. "Bastard!" he shouted.

His voice bounced off the walls of the street but this time he did not receive an answering hiss. Satisfied he'd seen off the cat, he shrugged off Osbourne and held his hands out to keep his balance.

"Bollocks, I need a drink." His hands flexed, claw like for a bottle, anything containing alcohol. Arthur fished a bottle from his tunic and handed it over.

"Here, have this one."

Hagen grasped it like a drowning man and put it to his lips. He spat.

"You stupid git, Arthur. It's still got the cork in." Arthur rummaged in his trousers for a corkscrew but before he could offer it up, Hagen smashed the neck off against a street lamp. "That's better."

He carried on drinking and Farmer just watched in morbid fascination. Normally, Hagen drank sparingly, but tonight he was packing it away. Hagen belched loudly when he came up for air. Farmer was about to say something but thought better of it. He didn't feel much like a fight and he'd seen the belligerent glint in Hagen's eye.

"Did you hear the Frogs found, Martin?" said Hagen aloud. Farmer nodded, letting him get it off his chest. Just before they'd left for town, a phone call from Wing had relayed the news that Martin's body had been found in a wood.

"Poor kid was all mangled, hanging upside down in his chute. He was just about to bail out." He aimed along the body of the wine bottle and juddered his hands like a child does with an imaginary gun. Wine slopped unnoticed out of the bottle and spattered on the ground. "He was hanging half out of the hatch and they skewered him."

"Did they have any news about Graves or Simpson?" asked Arthur. He'd been outside helping with the transport to town when the news had come in and only heard the story second hand. Hagen shook his head.

"Nothing so far but I doubt they'll find much more than a few charred stumps. He was a flamer all the way."

They walked on in silence while they thought about that. Arthur was starting to sober up thinking about what had happened. He'd always thought that he would be able to bail out. Today's engagement had brought home the very real possibility that he might not be given the chance.

Farmer kicked a piece of stone and watched it skitter down the street. He tucked his chin into his chest and jammed his hands into his pockets, shoulders forward. He kicked the stone again and then cursed aloud.

"Shit! Graves was the one person I thought would get through all this."

"How did you figure that out?" asked Osbourne. Farmer shrugged and kept walking, talking over his shoulder.

"I dunno. I just had one of those feelings? Like he'd always be there, you know, like he was the one person you could always count on."

Osbourne's eyes went wide and when no one said anything right away, Farmer turned to find them staring at him.

"Get lost, Paul," muttered Arthur.

"I never took you to be a sentimentalist," said his navigator. Farmer shot Preddy a brooding look but Preddy didn't flinch. "Careful old boy, you'll go soft."

"Everyone needs something to believe in I suppose," Farmer replied simply. He waited for the group to catch up to him and then carried on walking.

"Anyway, don't you dare point the finger at me," he accused Preddy. "You fly with your little stuffed teddy bear. Gibson has a bible in his breast pocket whenever he goes up. I know for a fact that, Maurice has his father's medal from the first war every time he flies."

Hagen cackled with malice. His voice hard edged.

"What a load-" He started cursing and wrenched loose his tie and unbuttoned his shirt. He took hold of something around his neck and pulled roughly. He held up a coin or charm of some kind and a gold cross hanging on a fine chain between his fingers. "I'll show you lot how much good things like that are."

The other four stood mortified. Their faces were frozen as Hagen took careful aim at a drain by the gutter. He lofted the Saint Christopher medal towards them. Horrified, they watched as it bounced on the cobbles and came to rest on the ground. Satisfied, Hagen buttoned his shirt back up and carried on walking.

"There. Better now?" he said in smug satisfaction, his eyes daring them to disagree and provoke an argument. Almost immediately, Farmer bounded forwards, scooping them up off the road.

"Gawd, you can't do that," he said. He held out the medal and cross. "Here."

"Don't need it old man."

Farmer was angry now. He took rough hold of Hagen's left hand and thrust them into his palm, closing his fingers around them.

"Don't be a silly bugger, take it."

Hagen tried to shake Farmer off, but the bigger man kept his hand closed, the edges of the cross and metal disc dug into his palm.

"I don't want it," he said with venom.

"Take it!" Farmer said with more force. "TAKE IT!" he shouted.

There was a long pause while they faced off against each other. Preddy, Arthur and Osbourne stood off to one side in hushed silence, watching the confrontation play out. Hagen gave in.

"All right. Fine," he said in resignation. Muttering to himself, he moved his hand slowly and Farmer let him go. Hagen put them into his pocket. "There! Happy now?"

Farmer smiled.

"Yes, actually."

They carried on walking and Farmer clapped Hagen on the shoulder, trying to lighten the mood.

"Look, I'll have a word with, Gardner. You take a spot of leave, get a woman. It'll help you get things in perspective."

Hagen walked on in silence and simmered. Get a woman, Farmer had said. He could go on leave tomorrow. He could shag half the women in Béthenville but it would do little to change the conclusion he had come to. His number was up. He was a walking dead man and nothing was going to change that. It was just a matter of time.

"God I need to sleep," muttered Arthur.

"That makes two of us," said Farmer. "Come on; let's get back to our warm beds."

It took them an hour to cover the few miles back to the field. In the cool night air they had sobered up and Preddy nursed a buzzing head. Hagen had said little since his outburst in the street and he stared off into the night. Farmer glanced at Hagen's back and then shared a look with Osbourne. Neither of them said anything, but Farmer was concerned.

They rounded a corner in the road and came across two navigators. Pearson was having trouble trying to drag Marsden backwards out of a hedge he had fallen into. Farmer was amazed they had even made it out of town the condition they were in. Taking them under their wing they half carried, half walked them along.

Slowed to a crawl, it took them another half hour to make it to the airfield. As they staggered to the main gate, a little black Citroen with its headlamps blacked out drove past them. It stopped by the sentry and the rear door opened. The car disgorged a figure carrying a large bundle. The group stopped in its tracks and stood, mouths open in shock.

"Bugger me," said Arthur. He blinked again but the apparition was still there. Farmer went very pale. He could hear his blood pounding in his ears and his mouth went very dry.

"I don't believe it," whispered Hagen, eyes wide like saucers.

Graves turned towards them when he heard Arthur and his face split into a smile. He stood there in a stained and blackened Sidcot flying suit with his right arm in a dirty sling. Blood marked the right sleeve and the material was ripped open at the shoulder. His neck was an angry raw pink and a bandage was wrapped around his head.

"Well, don't just stand there, give a man a hand will you?"

The spell broken, they rushed forward, all talking at once; full of questions. Graves grimaced when someone bumped him and he fended them off with his good hand. Hagen smiled and shook his head in disbelief.

"Jesus Christ, you must be the luckiest bastard on the planet." He patted him on the left shoulder and Graves' face creased in pain.

"Careful," he warned.

"But how did you get out? I saw you going down like a Roman candle," said Hagen.

Graves breathed deeply and stared off into the middle distance. His body ached and his neck felt like it was on fire. His shoulder was a constant burning throb even with the sling taking the weight off it. He could still feel the heat of the flames, the screech as his Blenheim went in.

"I honestly don't know. The last thing I remember is reaching for the hatch and when I woke up I was on my back in a muddy field with my parachute dragging me along."

It had taken him ten minutes to struggle out of his harness and another hour trudging across fields before he found help. A farmer had brought him to his house and given him some basic first aid. Luckily for him, the shoulder wound was a through and through, but there was little the farmer could do about his burns. Graves let some good Cognac provide a buffer against the pain.

"Did Martin make it?" he asked.

Farmer gave a little shake of the head.

"Sorry, no. Just you."

Arthur and Preddy gathered up his parachute and walked towards the gate. They shouted at the sentry to get it open.

Graves thanked the driver profusely for going out of his way to bring him to the airfield. The man said it was no trouble and reversed, turning to go back towards the road.

Farmer could not stop smiling and his mood lifted for the first time that day. Without thinking, he clapped Graves on the back and immediately apologised.

"It's good to see you, old man. God, it's good to see you."

Graves laughed. He was only three years older than Farmer, but after the day's events he felt a lifetime older than when he got up that morning. "But what are you doing here?

"Well, I was damned if they were going to stick me in a hospital." They laughed and headed towards the growing crowd. Farmer cupped his hands and shouted.

"Get some drinks! We've got something to celebrate after all!"

1.10 – Lay Me Down To Rest

"We bring nothing into this world; neither may we carry anything out of this world. The Lord giveth, and the Lord taketh away. Even as it hath pleased the Lord, so cometh things to pass: blessed be the name of the Lord."

Father Astley, the Wing Chaplain spoke without looking at the open Bible in front of him. His rich voice echoed within the Norman church. It rose and fell almost like a chant as he went through the service.

They had come together that morning under a moody sky at a small church just down the road from the field. There was a neat little graveyard around it surrounded by a low stone wall. The holes in the ground were ready. A wreath of poppies from the town was leaning against a neighbouring gravestone. A rifle party of ten airmen were arrayed in two ranks of five by the graveside. They stood at ease, their Lee Enfield rifles held at rest. After spending an evening to press trousers and bull their boots, they kept half an eye on the approaching clouds with some trepidation.

Squadron Leader Graves sat with the rest of the command staff at the end of the front pew, his head swathed in bandages. The MO watched his patient like a hawk. With his return from the dead, the morale of the squadron had lifted immeasurably but he wasn't staying for long. As soon as the service was over, an ambulance was waiting outside to take him to the nearest field hospital. The MO had wanted him to go sooner, but Graves had flatly refused until the service was over.

Chandler listened to the Chaplain, his head bowed, hands clasped in front of him. He sat two rows back from the front. Morgan shifted next to him but Chandler did his level best to ignore him.

In their tent the previous evening, Morgan had made his feelings about churches in general pretty clear. He spoke at length about the corruption of the church before Chandler threw a pillow at him and told him to put a sock in it. While Chandler didn't hold himself to be particularly religious, he had a strong respect for church, courtesy of his Aunt Cora.

Farmer, Preddy and Arthur sat opposite Chandler in the other aisle. All of them stood in a half fog, eyes closed as much from self preservation as it was from respect. How Gardner had roused B Flight in time for the service was a mystery. All of them felt like the ceiling was about to fall on them and Farmer had only a hazy notion of exactly when he went to bed. He had vague recollections of the sun creeping over the horizon as his head hit the pillow. His head throbbed and it was not all from alcohol. The smell of incense was strong and the priest had wafted gallons of the stuff into the air earlier when he walked to the front of the church.

He clicked his tongue in impatience when Preddy and Arthur decided to start bumping each other for fun. He turned a withering gaze on the two of them and pointed to the front. They tittered like naughty school children but dutifully resumed a more respectful pose.

Farmer leaned on the pew for support and took strength from the worn wood under his rough hand. He looked around, noting the elaborate frescos on the walls, the marble floor and the silverware on the altar. He was used to his churches being plain and unadorned. No matter where he looked, his eyes always drifted back towards the five coffins on the plinth.

An enlisted forage cap or officer's peaked cap sat on each coffin lid surrounded by a wreath of autumnal flowers and draped in the blue flag of the RAF. An honour guard had carried them into the church and laid them on the plinth in front of the altar. Farmer's lip curled at the nod to decorum. Apart from Martins coffin, there was nothing born of woman in them. Sandbags and a few bricks had been used to bring them up to an appropriate weight.

Father Astley finished his bit and stepped to one side as the CO stood up and walked over to the pulpit. He kept his reading mercifully short and once he was finished they all filed outside to take up position by the grave. Six men carried each coffin on their shoulders, laying them down on the ground outside.

At one end of the hole in the ground, Father Astley spoke again, making the sign of the cross as he did so. A freshening breeze whipped up his vestment.

"Man that is born of a woman hath but a short time to live, and is full of misery. He cometh up and is cut down like a flower; he flieth as it were a shadow, and never continueth in one stay."

Pettifer picked a spot on the horizon and tried to close his ears to the voice of the priest. At the far right of the formation in the rear rank he had no direct line of sight of the grave and he preferred it that way. He was superstitious when it came to funerals. He always avoided going to one whenever possible. This small observance of duty also weighed heavily on him.

Ever since war had been declared, he'd expected to be thrown into action at any moment. Pettifer's expectation had been total war from the word go, but the drag of the Phoney War seemed to have distorted peoples perspective. After all the rush to get to France, he had felt the squadron slipping back into the same stupor they had been in at home. The sudden casualties had brought the squadron back to reality with a jolt, but Pettifer felt they'd not been jolted enough. To his mind, spending a morning on the social niceties of a funeral for fallen comrades and praying over empty coffins was a waste of time. They'd have been better off doing some formation flying or bombing practice as far as he was concerned. The dead didn't care about anything anymore.

Handfuls of earth were thrown into the grave. The rifle party came to attention, shouldered their weapons and pointed to the sky. Birds rose from the trees as the peace of the morning was shattered by the first report. Ten shots were fired in all. As the echoes of the last round faded away, they shouldered arms and then marched off. Burke shouted out the time to keep them in sync. The MO led Graves to the ambulance that was waiting to wisk him away.

Winwright was left alone ruminating on his thoughts. Dane had thought about stopping and saying something but one look at the Wingcos face had convinced him otherwise. Winwright lost track of time until the first drops of rain spotted his shoes. He turned to go when he saw Valerie coming towards him in his odd half limp, half walk, umbrella held up.

The Frenchman joined him and covered them both with the large black

57

umbrella. The rain pattered off the taut material as the heavens opened. Apt, thought Winwright, almost as if the heavens were crying. Valerie stood in respectful silence as Winwright continued to stare at the coffins. Water was starting to turn the handfuls of earth to mud. Drops of rain were beading on the polished wood.

"It does not get any easier," said Valerie, breaking the silence. "I buried many comrades in the last war. Not all of the coffins contained bodies then either."

Winwright felt guilty that someone else knew the secret.

"I'm the Mayor, mon ami." Valerie shrugged. "There is little going on that I do not know about."

Somewhat mollified, Winwright turned back to look at the coffins. He had told Goddard his men were ready but he'd not thought about how he himself might feel. Losing men, *his* men had affected him more deeply than he cared to admit.

"He had a wife, you know." he said, trying to picture Wilkes' wife. Despite meeting her a few times at squadron functions, he could only picture vague details of her. A bright sunny smile, a bob of chestnut hair, he was even struggling to remember her name. "Two children too. Two fine girls by all accounts."

After a final moments' pause, he turned and headed back towards the road. He walked slowly and Valerie hobbled alongside, keeping the umbrella over their heads.

"A bad day to remember such things," said Valerie, his voice sombre. "It is always bad to lose a comrade, but then, c'est la guerre."

"Yes, the war." replied Winwright shortly. "You were a fighter pilot, Francois. You looked after yourself and your Flight. A hunter in the skies," he said, his voice plaintive. "I've got hundreds of men under my command and I've lost some of them already."

Valerie looked out of the corner of his eye but did not reply immediately. Winwright carried on walking, face taut.

"Wing Commander, I've always found that leading men is accomplished with a light touch. You can hound them and you can inspire them. Take it from me; don't punish yourself over things outside of your control."

Valerie stopped by a large gravestone and leaned on it a moment while he rubbed his knee. Standing in the cold during the service had caused some discomfort. Winwright held the umbrella while they stood there. When he had eased the pain, Valerie took the umbrella back as the rain came down heavier. The horizon disappeared into the gathering gloom as a cold gust scudded over the open ground of the church yard.

"Let me tell you a story," said Valerie, as they resumed walking. "It was 1917, my squadron was holding its own against the Boche but we were still hard pressed."

"A new squadron of Boche came into our sector on the other side of the line. In two weeks my escadrille lost eleven men. Not all of them were novices either." Valerie thought of his best friend Georges. He could still picture his bright smiling face and the broken remains when they dug him out of the wreckage of his Spad an hour later.

"The replacements were not much good either. Most had only a few hours of flying experience. They were lambs to the slaughter," he shrugged. "But I sent them up anyway. I had no choice."

They reached the road and Valerie pointed towards their cars. They walked over to them.

"We won in the end, but our losses were fearful. I carry every one of them with me, I still do. But there was one important lesson I learned during that time." He stopped by Winwright's car. "Every single one of them *chose* to be there. They knew the risks and they accepted them."

His blue eyes glittered with an inner steel, a past remembered when life was very different from what it was now. Winwright stood stony faced, his eyes hard and Valerie put a consoling hand on his arm.

"Do not be too hard on yourself, Wing Commander. Do all you can, but leave the judgement to history and better men than us."

Valerie turned and walked the short distance to his own car. Winwright stood in the rain, watching as it pulled away, wheels spinning on the gravel.

1.11 – Taking Stock

After the funeral, Falcon went back to work with their tails up. With Graves' departure they set to with gusto, much happier than they had been the day before. While Graves had survived, he wasn't expected back any time soon. The burns to his neck were worse than they first thought and required more specialist treatment back in England.

Dane read Hagen's after action report again, glasses perched on his nose. What he kept coming back to was the vivid description of Graves Blenheim going down. Roman candle Hagen had said; sheets of flame, he had said. Dane could picture the lads face when he described it, the horror and pain in his eyes as he relived the moment. Dane still found it amazing that Graves had made it out alive. Without doubt the angels had been watching over him.

Dane got up from his desk and leaned against the door jamb, sipping tea from a tin mug. The usual pile of signals and information was beckoning him back inside, but there was nothing that couldn't wait a little longer. Seeing the activity around the aircraft out on the field had given him new enthusiasm after his staid life at university. He watched the groundcrew directing two Blenheims towards bays cut in the trees. With the arrival of these spares, the squadron was back up to its full complement of aircraft but the replacement crews had yet to arrive.

Dane went back into his domain, a small hut eight feet wide and ten feet long next to the flight hut. Settling behind his desk, he warmed his hands by the small stove that sat in one corner. He checked the grate and shoved some more wood in from the wicker basket next to it. He watched the flames lick up the side of the piece of wood before turning back to his work.

The hut had two small windows that provided little light and a stack of candles had been placed on a shelf above the coat hooks. A large map of northern France, Belgium and Germany was tacked to the back wall behind him. Dane had made a number of notations on it, marking up the location of airfields and supply dumps. Areas of known flak concentrations were circled in red. Locked filing cabinets were underneath the map and had piles of books and box files on top of them.

He was still going through the admin when Ellis, the Armaments Officer, came in with Gardner. Gardner stood nervously just inside the hut, still not quite used to his recent promotion. He was short and compact, with brown eyes and a winning smile. Universally popular, Dane approved of Winwright's choice to promote him.

Casting round for something to do, Gardner spotted the kettle on a shelf next to the stove. He gave it an experimental shake and put it on the heat before setting up the mugs. Ellis looked on in amusement as the younger man went through the ritual of making tea. He put the mugs on the corner of the desk nearer the stove. Fussy, he moved one of them so they all had their handles parallel to each other. A tea strainer had been fashioned from a condensed milk tin and Gardner held it by the edge as he poured hot water into the mugs. Soon, the hut was filled with the smell of brewed tea and Ellis nodded gratefully when Gardner handed him one of the mugs.

Naturally nosy, Gardner cradled the mug in his hands and went round the desk to look over Dane's shoulder. He screwed his face up in concentration as he read the movement order and tried to reconcile the name with the location. Ellis tugged a pipe out of his top pocket and asked Dane if he was okay lighting up. Dane smiled and picked up his own from an ashtray on the desk. Within a few minutes the hut filled with smoke from the pipes and Gardner went back to stand by the door. He kept it open slightly with the toe of his boot to let some fresh air in.

Dane carried on going through the papers. His pipe was clamped firmly between his teeth and waggled as he read each one in turn. The pipe stopped moving and his face creased as he handed a signal across to Gardner.

"That might interest you," he said deadpan. Gardner took it and read it twice before laughing and handing it to Ellis. Ellis put on his reading glasses and snorted when he read it.

"Oh Burke will love this. As if we haven't anything better to do."

"Does it really matter?" asked Gardner in tired resignation.

"Not a jot," said Ellis impatiently, "but it doesn't stop the Air Ministry creating work anyway." He looked at the younger man and arched an eyebrow. "There is a war on you know."

"Really?" said Gardner in mock horror, gesturing to the field outside. "I can't see the erks being very happy about it either."

Ellis had to agree. Although their Blenheims were new, they had come from at least two different factories and their paint finishes varied. They sported two different types of underwing roundels and three different fuselage roundels between them. Now they were being told to add a yellow band around the red, white and blue rings on the fuselage markings.

"With everything that's going on, I imagine we'll get round to it at some point, but it's hardly going to be a priority." Ellis rolled the signal up into a ball and lofted it towards the stove. "I'd rather get the armour plate installed behind the mid upper turret before we start buggering about slapping some paint on."

Dane signed an acknowledgement slip and shoved it into the OUT tray.

"Has Burke told you when he can get that done?" he asked. Ellis shrugged, noncommittal.

"There are a few other mods that have come through as well. It's on his list as a priority."

"By the way, 323 is probably going to need an engine change," put in Gardner, piling on the good news. "She had a bad mag drop first thing this morning when the erks were doing the run ups. The fitters were up to their arms in oil the last time I saw them."

"Well, we can always get some spares if it's the engine, as long as we're on top line," said Dane. He tossed a clipboard with a sheaf of papers across the desk. Gardner picked it up and leafed through a few sheets. "Take a look at those. I was discussing some things with the Wingco last night while you lot were in town. He asked me to look at some of the after action reports from other squadrons."

"And what was the conclusion?" asked Ellis.

"That I don't think adding the extra weight of some armour is going to make much of a difference." He stood up and went over to the small window and looked out at the field. "My concern is that our formation flying won't do us any good either." He turned away from the window and looked at Gardner. "That's partly why the CO is going over to Rheims shortly with Ashton, some sort of conference."

"To talk tactics?" asked Gardner.

"Tactics and intentions, plans within plans, I imagine. I can't see much happening before the New Year is out. The Met boys are making noises that the weather could be quite hard before Christmas. I know we have some cameras coming to do some aerial reconnaissance, but er, keep that under your hats."

"I don't like the sound of that," said Gardner. The other Blenheim squadrons had been taking a beating on their flights over Germany. On their first day, 57 Squadron had lost their CO on a recce job.

"You said our flying training wouldn't be any good?" Ellis asked, getting back to the point.

"Matter of simple mathematics old chap." Dane shrugged and sat back down. He picked up a wooden identification model of a 109 on a stick. "Oh, I know we've got powered turrets and a turn of speed, but the German fighters are faster than us and mount cannon. They're in love with the bloody things, unfortunately. The 109s have two mounted in the wings." He pointed to the model, "and the 110's have two under the chin. That's not counting all the other guns they've got. They can just stand off and knock lumps out of us and we won't even be able to fire back with our pop guns."

Gardner shuddered. Hearing it so matter of fact from Dane was disconcerting, but then the man wasn't having to do the flying up there.

"Not very sporting, I must say," said Ellis in contemplation.

"Well, I don't remember seeing the hunting dogs sit round a table and have a conversation with the fox either." Dane put the model back on a shelf behind him. "Could we mount something a bit bigger in the turret?"

Ellis thought about that for a fast second but he knew his equipment, what Dane was asking would not be easy.

"I doubt it. An Oerlikon cannon isn't exactly small. There's no way the fuselage or the turret could cope with the recoil."

"What about beefing up the armament then? Put two Vickers into the turret," suggested Gardner. "It would give them a rude surprise if they *did* come into range."

"Maybe." Ellis' face creased as he contemplated how it could be done, already sketching it out in his head. "We'd have to knock up some kind of mounting from scratch though. That would be a lot of weight for the gunners to move around and reloading would be a problem."

"Can you do it with the tools we have here?" queried Dane. Ellis gave a wan smile.

"In principle, yes. I should be able to figure something out."

"Well, the CO's given it the nod so just get started."

"Done." Ellis pulled a small notepad from his tunic chest pocket and wrote himself a reminder. "I'll get something sketched out later today." He gestured to the paperwork on the table. "Anything else amongst all the bumf that we need to worry about?"

Dane looked down and flicked through a few sheets.

"Hmmm, not much." He tugged out one message that had only just arrived that morning. "There's been a signal from HQ about us being more vigilant with security around the airfield. It seems the Jerries have been dropping spies over our side of the lines. Some black silk parachutes were found caught up in the trees at Verdun. When the Frogs made a search, they found the body of one of their sentries. He'd had his throat slit so have the men keep their eyes open."

There was a knock on the door and they half rose when Winwright poked his head inside the hut. He had his flying jacket on over his uniform jacket.

"Ashton and I are off. Keep the home fires burning; I don't imagine we'll be late."

"Yes, sir. Anything particular you want doing with the boys while you're gone?" asked Gardner.

"Have the erks load up with practice bombs. I want the crews up practising low level bombing. Make sure the replacement aircraft are tested and tell, Mister Burke, I want 323's engine problem sorted out." He was about to go when his head reappeared back around the door. "Have the new crews turned up yet?"

"Not yet, Sir," replied Gardner. "I am assured they're on the way."

"Very well. I'll ask about it when I'm at Wing. If they do arrive while I'm gone, have them report to me this evening."

Leading Aircraftsman Toby Simpson watched the Wingco and Ashton stroll across the field towards the Tiger Moth. He nudged his mate in the ribs and nodded at the CO.

"Must be nice to go for a casual drive whenever you feel like it." He spat on the ground. "Cor, it's like being on holiday."

"Well, I could do with one," said his friend. He stretched like a cat and winced when he rubbed his back. "All we seem to have done since we got here is dig and chop and dig some more. My back is killing me."

"You're right," agreed Simpson. "I've had enough of sleeping in a tent." He leaned on the handle of the shovel and dreamed of sinful pleasures. "Some nice crisp sheets and a nice little French bint I seen in town would sort me out."

"Simpson, Arkwright!" Burke's voice whipped out. "Get your backs into it. Quicker you get that gun pit dug, the sooner you can finish."

Simpson looked up and glowered at Burke as he walked away, shouting at some other men across the field.

"Bleeder," he muttered. "Always shouting."

Burke heard the comment as he walked off. He momentarily slowed as he contemplated hauling Simpson up for that but said nothing. It was not the first complaint he'd heard in the last few days and it would not be the last. He couldn't put every man on a fizzer for that. He knew the cause. Arriving in France to a bleak field meant they had to knuckle down and start from scratch.

Now that the airfield was nearly complete, the tempo should slow down. All work and no play made it difficult to foster team spirit. With the year drawing to a close, he was anxious to get the men settled.

While some of the aircrew were in wooden huts with a modicum of warmth and comfort, most of the ground staff were still in tents. The first group had been found accommodation with some local families. It had not been so easy suddenly finding a billet for over two hundred more men. The Mayor had offered some houses in the town, but Burke wasn't keen to have them located in Béthenville. Aside from the practicalities of getting them transported to and from the airfield every day, he didn't like the idea of having the men out of sight. There was too much potential for trouble.

He thought about a newsreel they had seen the previous evening at the local cinema. The correspondent made light about British troops training along the border. There were numerous scenes of soldiers enjoying themselves in dugouts not far from the Maginot Line. The report had ended with a clip of George Formby entertaining the troops. The men had been cheered watching it, but to Burke, the whole tone seemed wrong and the talk of a Phoney War annoyed him.

The government had been quick to declare war in the support of Poland, but now it seemed like everyone had thrown the brakes on. Apart from the mad rush to get across to France, not much else had happened. Burke had read an Air Ministry directive that German industry should *not* be bombed because they were private property. He shook his head at the absurdity of it all.

He checked on the progress of the other gun pit and then directed the men to start laying the sandbags. The squadron was supposed to be getting some 40mm Bofors guns to put in them but heaven only knew when they would arrive. In the meantime, with Hagen's Blenheim laid up, Burke had been able to scrounge some Vickers guns out of the armaments officer. He had some men knocking up makeshift mounts for them and they would have to do for the time being.

Burke's only concern now was the condition of the field itself. Near to the clay heavy soils of Ypres in Belgium, the field's drainage had always been poor. Even in the last war, it had often been soggy underfoot. For light wood and canvas aircraft that was never a problem. The Blenheims on the other hand were much heavier. The field had already been cut up and rutted from the almost daily flights the CO had them doing. A roller had helped level things off and keep it in reasonable condition, but it was only a temporary measure. Hopefully, Wing could help them out with that too.

1.12 – Coconut Shy

After the CO left for Wing, the squadron got ready for bombing practice. Kittinger went off to find Burke to get the aircraft ready. Gardner gathered the crews in the main hut and delivered the news. There was some grumbling, mainly from his own Flight who were still nursing headaches from their monumental piss up.

As it would be low level bombing, they decided there was no need to ring up the bombing ranges. In the next field was a ramshackle barn that would make a perfect target. West of the flight huts and about five hundred yards from the slit trenches and gun pits, the squadron had been using it for storage. Under Burke's direction, some of the erks quickly dragged boxes out of the barn. Another work party drew some rough circles around it in whitewash on the grass.

Very quickly, a sporting interest took hold and the crews started a book on who would finish top of the leader board. Preddy marked up the blackboard in the flight hut and leaned out of the window shouting for a running order.

"This is money for jam." Chandler said, confident of a good result as he went to get his gear. Morgan's eyebrows shot up and he looked across at his pilot who was striding with more than a little bravado.

"You're confident."

"Not confident, just sure." Chandler smiled. He went into the tent and rummaged around for his gloves and goggles. "Don't even bother using the low level sight."

"Then what are you going to do?"

"Aim the whole plane at the target." Chandler stood up and used his hands to mimic an aircraft and the ground. "Come in about thirty degrees or so and point the nose at the barn. Just as I pull out, you drop a practise bomb. It'll be like shooting fish in a barrel."

"If you say so," Morgan said, unconvinced.

"I'm telling you Morg. I can do this. You should have seen me on Brighton pier one summer on the coconut shy. Three balls, three hits. This'll be a doddle."

Once they'd gathered their kit, they walked back through the woods to find things around the main hut had changed. Some enterprising souls had carried some of the chairs out of the hut and set them up on the grass out back, facing the field. A pair of ladders were propped up against the side of the hut. Osbourne stood on the roof with his binoculars so he could see where the practice bombs landed.

They drew lots for the running order and settled down for the afternoon's entertainment. First up was Gardner himself. They watched while he got himself ready and made his run in. His Blenheim came in from the east at about a thousand feet, angling across the field with the engines going full belt. The bomber bobbed on pockets of air and Gardner worked the rudder to keep the nose pointed at the target.

His first two bombs came in shallow, a good thirty yards short, but his third was spot on. A cloud of splinters went into the air as the bomb went through the side of the barn. The fourth went slightly long, skimming the roof and slamming into the grass beyond.

Gardner finished with an average of just under thirty yards. Next was Arthur who could do no better than a fifty five yard average from four bombs. Pettifer provided the target to beat. Two of his bombs had speared into the wooden walls of the barn and the other two had landed just short. He had an average of just twelve yards.

To make sure everyone got a turn before the light went, they settled into a rhythm. Two aircraft would be up in the air taking turns to drop their practice bombs. A third would be taking off and a fourth would be getting ready to go.

By now, the barn had a visible lean to it and there were a number of new holes in the roof. Chandler doubted it would still be standing by the time they finished. At least they'd get new wood for their stoves in the coming winter.

Osbourne kept track of the results on the blackboard. He called out Farmer's name and told him to take the next Blenheim in line. The big man levered himself up from an armchair and walked with Preddy towards a Blenheim that was being rolled out from the end bay in the trees. He went through a quick pre-flight, signed the form 700 without looking and paid scant attention to the basics before he strapped himself in. He asked Preddy if he was ready and got a thumbs up in return as he started the engines.

Chandler watched as another Blenheim roared across the field. He saw the little practice bomb drop from the aircraft and streak towards the ground. It went long and threw up a chunk of grass as it dug into the ground. Having watched one after another come over in the same old style every time, Chandler was confident he could do better. The others had come in quite shallow on their bombing runs. Keeping straight, they hardly dived at all. A few practise bombs had bounced across the grass and he was sure a steeper dive would get him a better result.

His name was called out next and Osbourne told him to get ready. Chandler grabbed his parachute and slung it over his shoulder. Farmer pulled out of the line, engines roaring and turned right. The tang of the hot exhaust washed over him and Chandler breathed in the heady mix of aviation fuel and oil. He loved that smell and it always took him back to the air pageants he saw at Hendon before the war. Seeing the fighters and bombers whirling over the airfield, he'd always dreamed that one day it would be him up there.

A scruffy looking erk in oil blackened overalls walked towards him while he waited for Morgan to arrive. The erk shouted over the roar of the engines as Farmer went into his take off run.

"You next, sir?"

"Yes!" He jerked a thumb over his shoulder. "I'm just waiting for, Mister Morgan to join me."

"Who's winning, sir?"

"Mister Pettifer at the moment. Is there an aircraft ready?"

The erk nodded and pointed to one of the more worn looking Blenheims on the squadron's inventory. Chandler was not bothered how it looked as long as it flew fine.

"Yes, sir. 389 is yours. She's been warmed up."

Chandler walked round the aircraft checking for defects. He was just signing the form 700 when an armourer ran full tilt out of the woods looking pale.

"What's wrong?" asked Chandler.

The Corporal turned at the question and came running over. He skidded to a stop, braced to attention for a half second and then started talking like a machine gun.

"It's Mister Farmer, sir. He's taken the wrong aircraft." Chandler was mildly amused. *Trust Farmer to cock things up*, he thought to himself. *How was it possible to screw up simple instructions?*

"Well, we don't have a personal aircraft each, Corporal?"

"He took the ready aircraft, sir. It's all bombed up with live bombs."

Chandler had to admit it was a corker.

"He was told to take the last one on the line."

"That's as may be, sir," the panicked Corporal said. "But we'd only just wheeled it out after being loaded up. It's in the ready spot with all the ground equipment." Chandler looked where the Corporal was pointing and he was right. The end slot on the line was reserved for one aircraft for immediate departure and everyone knew that. That aircraft was fully armed and loaded with four GP explosive bombs.

"Gawd," Chandler muttered. "Well, no harm done, we'll just radio him to come back in."

Now it was the erks turn to start sweating.

"You can't, sir."

"Why not?" Chandler snapped.

"Because he didn't take his flying helmet with him. He said because it was a nice day, he wouldn't be needing it."

"Christ." Chandler winced and started massaging his temples. He made a fast decision and pointed to the Corporal. "You; run to Squadron Leader Gardner and tell him what's happened." He pointed to the erk. "You; start me up, now!"

"Start you up, sir?"

Chandler was already running towards his aircraft. He tugged on his flying helmet and stepped up onto the port wing before he answered the question.

"Well, someone's got to stop him. Now start me up."

The erk rushed over to the trolley acc and plugged in the starter cable, while Chandler went through a very fast start up routine.

The Corporal rushed over and leaned in close to Gardner who was sat in a deckchair near to the ladder. His eyes widened when the Corporal finished talking.

"He's what?"

His voice was sharp and a few faces turned in his direction. He looked back down the field in time to see Chandler's Blenheim barrelling over the grass with its tail up. He shot to his feet and told everyone to gather round.

"Okay, listen in. It would appear that Farmer has taken off bombed up. We need to clear out." He turned to Burke who had appeared out of nowhere. "Sound the air raid warning. Everyone get to the slit trenches."

They didn't need telling twice. They ran towards the slit trenches that had been dug at the edge of the field. The wailing keening of a hand wound air raid siren started to fill the air as bodies scattered in all directions. Kittinger stopped in mid run when he saw Gardner heading in the opposite direction towards the flight hut.

"What are you going to do?"

"Fire off some red flares. Hopefully he'll get the message and break off."

"And if he doesn't?"

In all seriousness, Gardner shrugged and smiled. If this didn't work and Farmer dropped his bomb he'd be well within the blast radius.

"Then I've got a grandstand seat, haven't I?"

Chandler kept up a steady stream of cursing as he toggled the boost and begged for every knot of airspeed he could get out of his Blenheim. His only advantage was that Farmers Blenheim was fully loaded, so he had the benefit of a lighter aircraft to try and do something.

Keeping at a thousand feet, he circled around the field with the target markings and craned his neck, trying to keep Farmer in view. As soon as Farmer made his run in, he wanted to come in at an oblique angle to block his approach. It would need some subtle timing and Chandler would have been lying if he said he wasn't scared. If Farmer did something unexpected, if one of them miscalculated, they could very easily collide. He berated himself for not waiting and taking Morgan with him as he could have used the extra pair of eyes. Almost immediately he changed his mind and decided it was better he hadn't come. If it all went wrong, it would be one less casualty.

Gardner saw Chandler circling the field, trying to keep position relative to Farmer's aircraft. Thankfully, Farmer seemed to be in no hurry getting up to height and that had given them time to clear the field and get everyone out of the way. Anxious faces were craned skyward, unable to influence what was about to happen.

Finally, Farmer's Blenheim dipped a wing and came in from about three thousand feet in a shallow dive. Gardner remembered his own bombing runs, trying to gauge what Farmer was doing. Farmer was keeping his aircraft as steady as possible so Preddy could get a good bead on the target through the bomb sight.

Gardner pulled back the hammer on the flare gun and held his left arm high. Screwing his eyes shut, he squeezed the trigger and there was a loud bang as the flare shot into the sky. Palm numb from the kick, he cracked the pistol open and rummaged in his pocket for another flare. Snapping the barrel closed, he held it skywards again and fired off another.

Farmer was pleased with his run in. He was keeping it smooth and was lined up nicely on the target. He continued his shallow descent and juggled the throttles to try and keep the airspeed constant. Preddy kept up a running commentary as he peered at the barn through the sight. As he got closer,

Farmer saw little dots of red popping up from the field. He smiled and half chuckled to himself. Someone on the ground was firing off flares to make it more realistic. It would take more than that to throw him off.

As he approached the airfield boundary he noticed movement out of the corner of his right eye. He did a double take when he realised it was a Blenheim heading right at him.

"What the hell!"

He waggled his wings slightly, trying to warn off the other aircraft, but it continued to head towards him. He held course for a few more seconds, anxiety rising. Maths was not Farmers strong suit, but even he could see if one of them didn't move, there was going to be an almighty crash and a large smoking crater on the ground.

Hauling the yoke back hard, he swore like a trooper and pulled up as the other Blenheim flashed underneath him going the opposite way. With his bombing run ruined, steam was coming out of his ears. His temperature rose further as he saw the offending Blenheim come back around and keep pace with him.

On the second run, the same thing happened. Flares shot into the sky and before he could make the final approach, the other Blenheim cut him off. Cursing, he broke off and circled round again.

His mood now volcanic, Farmer climbed back up to height, his mind spinning. Firing off flares as a distraction was one thing, but he considered it distinctly unsporting for them to send up another Blenheim to mess him about. He looked to his right and saw it circling at a thousand feet, sunlight glinting off its canopy. His lip curled with malevolence as it became personal for Farmer.

All his life he had been stubborn. Playing rugby at university, that trait had served him well. He would get the ball, tuck it under his arm, shove his head down and run. He would keep on running until he was brought down. When he was learning to fly he was like a dog with a bone. While he had a natural touch in the air, he was not the most academically gifted student. That simple bone headed tenacity is what pulled him through ground school. Now, he was becoming consumed by the burning need to succeed, of getting that bomb on the target. He took a few breaths to calm himself and then got ready for his next run.

Chandler cursed under his breath. He wiped the back of his gauntleted hand across his face and got ready for Farmers next approach. He could not believe the man was so dim he didn't think there was something wrong. Going head to head like this was crazy. Sooner or later one of them would make a mistake and it would all be over.

He shot a glance at the gauges and hoped the engines would hold together. The Blenheim he'd jumped into may have looked worn, but the engines had plenty of life left in them. Even so, running them at full power like this, they would crack up eventually. He was backing off as often as he could to give them a rest but he brought the Blenheim back up to full power as he saw Farmer bank to starboard for another go.

He fed in a gentle turn and this time kept in a close circle near the target. When Farmer held it steady on his final approach, he would break out of the circle and close the angle to cut him off. He tightened his turn; his foot jammed on the rudder pedal and flashed across the circle, going right at Farmer, the bit between his teeth.

Four Mercury engines ate up the distance awfully fast. Chandler winced as Farmer flashed overhead and clawed for the sky. He waited a moment and then reversed course, chasing after him while he kept the throttles jammed full on. He came up alongside him on the starboard side at two thousand feet and edged closer. He gestured at the ground and then pointed at Farmer. The man vehemently shook his head and made a rude gesture.

Farmer shot the pilot a baleful glare. His lip curled as he watched them wave frantically at him. He gave them the 'V' sign. He had no idea what was going on but he was determined to get one bomb on the target.

"Bugger off! Bloody idiot! Can't you see I'm trying to do my bomb run?"

"Bloody idiot! Can't you see something must be wrong?" Chandler shouted. They had danced with the devil three times now. That was three of his lives gone and he didn't want to lose any more. Farmer piled on the coals and banked to port, diving for the ground. Chandler groaned.

"Here we go again."

He chased after him and pulled the boost button.

Anxious eyes peered over the lip of the slit trench as the two aircraft continued their dance. Each time they'd expected the worst and now, the twin engine bombers were being flown all over the sky like they were fighters. Farmer tried throwing Chandler a dummy. He side slipped right before flicking his wing over and dropping to the deck. Chandler clung to his tail like a leech, matching every move, not even two aircraft lengths back.

Dane got out of the trench for a better view as he lost sight of them behind the woods. He shaded his eyes and scanned the horizon. Osbourne reached out and tugged on his trouser leg.

"Dane, get back into the trench."

"Oh don't worry, old boy. I'll go, but there's a minute or two before he makes another run."

He carried on peering into the distance, straining to see them. He walked over to Gardner who waved him back. Dane handed him a flare cartridge from a pile on the ground but stayed by his side.

"You know this could all go very wrong," said Dane.

"I don't see any other way," said Gardner. He raised the flare gun and fired again. The air stank of cordite and Dane handed Gardner another flare. "Firing off flares is all I can do."

"We could always just let him bomb the field." said Dane, his voice deadpan. Gardner grinned at the gallows humour.

"Very funny." He fired off another flare.

Arthur idly chewed on a stem of long grass and rested his crossed arms on the lip of the trench.

"Ten bob says they collide," he offered.

There were hoots of derision.

"Twenty bob old Farmer drops one right on the target," suggested Hagen in dour tone.

"I'm not betting," replied Pettifer.

"Misery," chided Hagen.

"On the contrary, old boy. I don't mind an odd flutter on the National or the Gold Cup, but it'll be an almighty bang when they hit the ground."

"Anyone else?" asked Arthur. No one said anything, their attention riveted on the two aircraft coming in low. Farmer streaked down the runway between the trees, Chandler hot on his heels. As they approached the huts, Farmer pulled up hard and half rolled, heading towards Béthenville. Chandler cut the corner of the turn and smoothly followed behind, nipping at his heels as they went out of sight.

Ten minutes later they were back. Farmer thumped it down hard, the landing matching his mood. Chandler landed right behind him. He taxied up fast and was out of his aircraft almost before the airscrews stopped turning. Adrenalin coursed through him as he stomped over, shedding his gauntlets and parachute as he went. Farmer saw him as he rounded the wing and had to be physically restrained from trying to rip Chandler's head off. He jabbed a finger at the younger man.

"You! What the hell were you playing at!" he spat, his voice full of vitriol. When Chandler didn't answer fast enough, he lunged for him again. Arthur and Osbourne had to call in reinforcements to keep him back.

"I asked you a question, *glory boy*."

"Don't call me that."

Chandler swiped Farmer's hand away, which enraged the big man even further.

"Then answer me; *glory* boy! I almost crashed because of you."

Chandler went red in the face, his restraint starting to break down.

"Because of me?" He waved a finger of his own in front of Farmer's face. "I've just saved your miserable career."

Farmer blew up and they were about to come to blows when Gardner's voice cut across the shouting.

"Farmer, that's enough! Flight hut, now!"

In the quiet, all eyes were on Farmer who stood in the middle of the ruck, his chest heaving. His eyes continued to glint and for a moment Arthur kept a tight grip of his friend. He could feel the big man's arms tensing under his leather jacket, the muscles hard. Then the moment passed and the fight went out of him. He shouldered his way through the crowd, snarling in anger, his voice a bark.

It was at this moment they became aware of a small group of people standing by a truck in their blue uniforms, their kit bags piled in front of them. The replacements had arrived.

"This is Falcon Squadron, isn't it?" they asked in confusion.

1.13 – Ten Green Bottles

Winwright and Ashton arrived at Rheims in good time. The same officer who'd met him before was waiting with a staff car. Winwright made the introductions as they drove to A.A.S.F Headquarters. In a much better mood this time, he paid more attention on the drive in, noting the bustle of the town. The hotel was heaving again with a number of pretty girls hanging off the soldiers there.

When they drove past Pommery Parc, Winwright felt they'd made things too easy for the Luftwaffe. Headquarters was always going to be a large building, but choosing one at the end of a long boulevard was asking for trouble in his opinion. As they drove through the entrance gate it felt like he was looking down a bomb sight.

They followed a Squadron Leader into the lobby and they were shown into a large room filling up with other officers. Along one wall were floor to ceiling windows. These had been left open, giving a view of the grounds. Two rows of chairs were laid out in front of a large map board on the far wall. It showed northern France, Belgium and Germany and various airfields were marked with red pins. A table next to it had piles of photographs and folders. An SP corporal stood by the table with a white blancoed web belt and holstered pistol.

Taking an offered cup of tea, Winwwright circled around, taking in the details. He exchanged pleasantries with the CO of the Lysander squadron based on the other side of Béthenville. He went round the chairs and joined Ashton who stood peering at the map.

"Penny for them," said Winwright.

Ashton pointed at the board. He went from pin to pin, ending up at the four that bracketed Béthenville.

"I was just thinking, we look a bit thin on the ground when you see it all laid out on a map."

"I'm sure the Germans are saying the same thing."

"Maybe they are, gentlemen."

They turned to find Air Commodore Saundby standing behind them. Saundby shook Ashton's hand as Winwright did the introductions.

"You were saying about the Germans, Mister Ashton?"

"I just feel we should be more proactive, sir. With the bad weather coming, maybe we need to get our licks in first."

"You're not the only one to have said that recently, but we are instruments of policy." Saundby pointed to a chair. "Take a seat and you'll find out the rest."

Taking the cue, the other officers began to assemble and there was a moment's pause while everyone sat down. Saundby picked up a wooden ruler from the table and stood with it in his hands, holding it as a pointer.

"Gentlemen, now that you're all here, we can begin. Those of you who know me know I'm not one to stand much on ceremony. Now that the last squadron of Battles has arrived the Wing is complete. Our task is to cover the northern sector and fly in co-operation with the French Air Force. In the next few days, Wing Headquarters is going to pack up and move north to Arras. The army has promised to connect the new building into the communications network."

Using the ruler, he pointed out the limit of the main Maginot Line of defensive forts on the German border. He described the forts and how they were equipped.

"The line is defended in depth along here, in some places it's up to twenty five kilometres deep." Saundby then traced the route the expanded line took along the Belgian border. "From Luxembourg going north west in front of us, it's much weaker. Originally, the plan was to cooperate with the Belgians, but ever since they declared neutrality in 1936, the French have been slaving like mad to extend the line to the coast. It's not finished in some areas, but it's better than nothing." He tapped the map and described an arc with his hand around Alsace Lorraine. "The Germans have nineteen divisions in this area. They are facing nearly double that. Here in the northern sector, the French have a good mix of armour and infantry that we will be providing support to."

He perched on the edge of the table by the map and put the ruler down. He looked at each of them in turn and folded his arms.

"Now, thanks to the interference of the Americans, Bomber Command has had its hands tied. It seems the President of the United States finds the prospect of civilian casualties deplorable. So our political lords and masters have decided to adopt what's being called the Roosevelt Rules. From this moment forward, we've been banned from bombing any target where there is a risk of hitting civilians nearby. France has agreed to the same rules as well."

Shocked faces stared back at him, trying to digest the enormity of that. Back home, the Wellingtons would be struggling to find a target. For them it would be less of a problem. Operating at a battlefield tactical level, striking formations in the field would hopefully avoid these restrictions.

"The Germans haven't been very obliging up to this point. The big clash we were all expecting hasn't happened and the French High Command is now planning an offensive in the spring." There was a ripple of interest at this news. Saundby let them settle down before continuing. "I don't have to tell you that's all very hush hush. Of course, this gives us time to build up our forces and plan for the New Year. At the moment, the idea is that we'll move forwards with an advance into Germany, providing battlefield support."

For the next hour they discussed their plans. Saundby outlined some of the secondary airfields that were being prepared closer to the border. The plan was that if the French crossed into Germany, the wing would move with them, keeping pace with their advance. The main question raised was transport. In the mad rush to get over to France, it was one of the things forgotten about. It was easy for the aircraft to get from one airfield to another but they needed the ground staff with them to continue operations. None of the squadrons had much in the way of motor transport. While there was sufficient to run errands, moving whole units would require much more. They'd have to get help from the local army units.

There was some discussion regarding the spares situation and Saundby promised that would be looked at. The aircraft parks in the north were still working up and again, it was a matter of time before the support structure got up to speed. The location of some of the aircraft parks was questioned. Winwright felt they were too far back from the front. It was grudgingly agreed that with the AASF as a whole spread out over such a wide area, there was nowhere closer that would fit the bill.

Tactics came under intense discussion. So far, Winwright's unit was the only one to have seen any action. Faces were grim when Winwright and Ashton relayed the details of Graves engagement with the 110's. Clearly, two Blenheims stood little chance against a concerted attack. It was felt that once a basic formation broke down, aircraft operating individually might stand a better chance.

Winwright favoured level bombing from three to four thousand feet. The CO of one of the Battle squadrons, a Squadron Leader called Bainbridge, questioned its value against an advancing enemy.

"If we're attacking, then defensive concentrations will be easy to spot. Level bombing would give us good results in those circumstances. If we're on the defensive, I'm not sure we'll be able to make the best use of our bombs up high. The Germans use a lot of transport, strung out on the march like that, I'd much rather get down low and pick my targets."

"What did you have in mind?" asked Saundby.

"We go down low in formation, we'll miss a lot of the flak and rubbish that way. I think, keeping it at fifty feet with thirty second intervals, dropping 250lb bombs on a delayed fuse would work best."

Winwright shot Bainbridge a look of concern mixed with respect. Getting down amongst the weeds required a great deal of skill, but it would also make them harder to hit. It would take nerves of steel to press home an attack under those circumstances.

"I'll consider it, Bainbridge," said Saundby, his voice noncommittal. "It's unorthodox, but I see what you're getting at."

The question of increased armament for the bombers was raised. Enemy action had shown how vulnerable the Battles were. As a result, aside from some training flights, most of their offensive action had been curtailed.

Saundby mentioned that a new gun mounting would be coming out to the Battle squadrons. Back in England, a Sergeant at 150 squadron had made a mounting that would allow a third Vickers machine gun to be fitted to the underside. This aircraft had been flown to Rheims and inspected by the AOC and Fairey were in the process of providing mounting kits to be fitted in the field.

Bainbridge harboured little enthusiasm for this idea. The Battles performance was already marginal at best. Loading them up with an extra gun and ammunition would only make things worse in his opinion.

There were no such extras promised for the Blenheims. Regardless, the general agreement was that fighter escorts would be preferable for any raid. Saundby made a note of the general feeling but made few promises. As the Air Components Hurricane squadrons were further south around Rheims, the Wing was going to be dependent on assistance from French fighter units in the north.

Ashton mentioned the friendly fire incident but Saundby had been reassured by the French that this would not happen again. Winwright took a wait and see attitude. He'd seen little to give him much confidence so far. Saundby promised a liaison officer would be based at the Wing headquarters to make cooperation with the French easier. The official line had been delivered, but Saundby knew that it would take some positive action to convince them otherwise.

As the meeting broke up, Saundby asked Winwright and Ashton to stay. Motioning to the open windows, Saundby went outside to the garden. He headed towards an ornamental lawn with some flowerbeds around the border.

"I read the action report. I was sorry to hear of your losses."

Winwright grimaced and looked at his shoes for a moment.

"I was lucky to get Graves back at all. He'll be a while recuperating but it was just bad luck. We'll do better next time."

"I'm quite sure, old boy, but the press have got a hold of it." Ashton cursed and cast an angry glance back at the building, as if the walls had ears. "The Air Ministry has been making some soothing noises but questions are being asked. It would help if you could talk to the press about it."

"Do I have to?" Winwright asked, but he already knew what the answer would be.

"It would help," said Saundby, his voice soothing. "There's a man from the BBC who's quite good, a chap called Charles Cullen. He's been following the Hurricanes quite a bit. He's filed some reports of their recent actions, so he knows more than the average reporter."

"When do you want us to talk to him?"

Saundby beamed and rubbed his hands.

"As it happens, he's here now." Winwright gave Saundby a knowing nod. He'd expected as much. Saundby never changed. He was never one to introduce a subject unless he already had the cards stacked in his favour. "There's going to be a briefing later on the general state of affairs for the press. I should be able to peel him out of the pack for a chat with you before you head back."

"All right, Sir, we'll give it a go."

Saundby patted him on the shoulder.

"Good man. Before I go, there was something else I wanted to talk to you about as well."

Here it comes, thought Winwright. He knew Saundby would not just talk to him outside of the meeting about propaganda. Saundby parked a cigarette between his lips and patted his pockets for a lighter. When none was forthcoming, Ashton got out his own and held it up for the Air Commodore. They waited while Saundby lit his cigarette.

"I know your chaps aren't trained for reconnaissance-"

"No, sir. We're not," Winwright replied sharply. He was almost horrified at the prospect, but Saundby rode over his interruption.

"-but 18 and 57 Squadron have been taking a hammering on their flights over Germany." He took another pull on his cigarette before continuing. "I've argued against it of course. I'd much rather keep you chaps back for the main event, but this comes from the top." He pointed skyward with his free hand. "It's not ideal by any means, but we need the information for the offensives in the spring." Ashton and Winwright reacted in stony silence to the news.

75

"They're long flights, often alone, it's going to take chaps with some guts to get through and make it back."

Winwright did not reply immediately. Flying reconnaissance missions was something new.

"57 are gradually converting to the mark IV, I'll see if I can get a hold of some of their mark I's for you. That should make the job a bit easier, what?"

Winwright brightened slightly at the prospect of getting some dedicated recce aircraft. He bent some thought on who would be suitable.

"It won't be easy, Sir. I can think of a few of my people who could take a good stroke at it. We'll just have to knuckle down and make the best of it, I suppose."

"Good, that's very good. Well, get your chaps up to speed and orders should follow in due course."

"We'll do our best, Sir."

Saundby gave Winwright his best winning smile.

"I don't doubt it." Saundby ground the cigarette under his heel. "Now; I'll get that reporter chap."

Winwright and Ashton watched him walk across the grass back into the chateau. Once Saundby was out of sight, Winwright swore and his eyes blazed as he turned back to Ashton.

"So that's one more thing we have to worry about."

"Ours not to reason why," Ashton mused, he was already thinking about the logistics of this new task. The squadron would need to provision more fuel and he made a note to see the supply section before they left. They'd also have to get maps to cover Germany, all they had at the moment covered the border areas.

"Wing Commander?"

They turned to see a man in Khaki drill uniform and a peaked cap walking towards them. The boots were clean, but the trousers lacked a crease and he looked uncomfortable in the scratchy battledress. The cap badge was a 'C' picked out in gold bullion wire with a rope wire surround on a green backing. On his shoulders were brass flashes.

He was about five foot ten with a rangy build. Brylcreemed hair was combed flat to the sides of his head. His brown eyes hid behind wire rim glasses. He carried a notepad and pencil in his left hand. Winwright and Ashton shook his hand.

"Mr Cullen, a pleasure."

"I understand you've been cleared to talk to me."

"So I believe."

Winwright gave Cullen his best winning smile. It was not his fault Saundby had ambushed them. Besides, it always helped to have a friend at court. Cullen gestured to the back of the chateau.

"Shall we take a stroll? I saw a rather attractive garden round the corner. It's also out of view behind some hedges."

They walked in silence and Ashton did his best to enjoy the surroundings. He had not been to the Headquarters before and he enjoyed looking at the architecture. Built over two storeys, the tan stone was a creamy colour under the late afternoon sun. Cullen led them down a neat gravel path to an ornamental garden at the back of the house. On two sides was a thick belt of tall trees and off in the distance was the high wall that surrounded the Chateau.

"The brass certainly know how to live," said Ashton in good humour.

"It is rather pretty, isn't it?" agreed Cullen. "But I've not been here much, I'm often out and about, trying to see as much as possible."

"Always chasing a story?" asked Ashton pointedly.

"I suppose that would be one way of looking at it, Squadron Leader. Of course," he smiled crookedly. "I could always rely on the official communiqués to report for the folks back home."

"The Air Commodore said you'd been out with the fighter boys," said Winwright, turning the subject slightly. Cullen nodded. "How are they doing?"

"They've got their work cut out for them as you can imagine, but they're not doing too badly I think. They bagged a Dornier a few days ago, coming over on a recce. A few of the chaps are doing terribly well."

Winwright looked off into the distance. He watched a pair of blackbirds weaving in and out of the trees, chasing each other. They made an almighty racket when they perched in the branches of an ash tree. *The chaps are doing terribly well.* The man made it all sound like a jolly outing.

The quiet loomed large and there was that awkward pause you had on a first date, neither party knowing whether to speak or listen. Cullen did his best not to fidget as he looked between the two men in their RAF blue. He'd met quite a few pilots over the last few weeks and he thought he knew what RAF officers were like.

Fighter pilots appeared to have a restrained aggression, like they were straining at the leash. In their airborne steeds they were the hunters of the sky. These men were different. One had that rugged look of a bush flier. The other was almost like a typical bank manager, competent but reserved. They had a subdued air about them, a hidden tension that was simmering just below the surface. It was a marked contrast to the Hurricane pilots he had met.

Winwright turned back from his contemplation of the birds to look at the reporter. He smiled but it didn't reach his eyes and Cullen could see the distrust lurking there.

"I'm not sure what you want to know, Mr Cullen."

"Tell me a bit about the squadron if you like."

Winwright told him about the flight over from England and what they'd found waiting for them. Cullen had been in France since September, so what he heard wasn't anything new, but he was a professional listener. He nodded in the right places to encourage his subject to continue talking. He made the occasional note on his pad as he listened, memorising the main details.

Once Winwright had set the scene, Cullen led him through Graves' engagement. Before talking to Winwright, Saundby had let him read a sanitised version of the combat report. Hearing it aloud was very different from the written word. Even how Winwright talked about it was different to the way fighter pilots told their tales. Their stories were full of action, high speed narrative, closing the target, two second bursts and peeling away. Their hands would describe the engagement as they spoke. Winwright was more measured in his language, his voice slightly edged with strain. Cullen made a note in his pad.

"So the collision made the difference, you would say?"

Winwright thought about that. In his judgement, it had been critical. The safety of three aircraft flying together in tight formation had been removed and all that came afterwards was as a result of the collision.

"It didn't help, I'll go that far," he said in measured tone. Admitting it to Saundby was different to telling a reporter. "Good formation flying and discipline will always make it difficult for the German fighters. Hard put as our aircraft were, we still managed to shoot down one 110."

"And what about the French fighters in your sector?"

"What about them?" Winwright asked sharply, still sensitive about the incident with Chandler.

"Terribly quick on the trigger aren't they?" Cullen challenged. Winwright shot him a look, wondering where he had heard that.

"There's nothing wrong with aggression in a fighter pilot," said Ashton smoothly to cover his superiors' change of mood.

"But that's good, isn't it?" Cullen pressed.

"Not if they're shooting at us it isn't."

There was another pause while Cullen digested that, marrying up their comments with some rumours he'd heard.

"Ah, I see." He made another note on his pad and then looked up. His face scrunched up in confusion. "But they're not all like that are they surely?"

"Probably not," Ashton admitted. "I don't doubt they have good pilots too but I have yet to see them." He kept his tone conversational, playing down the episode. No doubt Cullen had already been sniffing around for scraps of news and their run in with the French was hardly a secret.

"But the Mayor of the local town has been wonderful," Winwright added, hunting for a positive to distract him. He explained about the cooperation they were getting from Valerie and the citizenry of Béthenville. Cullen asked them some detailed questions and then checked the spellings of some names.

He glanced at his pad for a moment. A few scrawled words on a piece of paper contained the life of a squadron over the last few weeks and action that had seen five men killed. It hardly seemed adequate.

"Thank you gentlemen," he said; his voice a little subdued. "I'll try to do it justice."

Winwright shook his hand.

"That's all I ask, Mr Cullen. That's all I ask."

1.14 – There And Back Again

Chandler yawned yet again, trying hard to shake off the feeling of fatigue as they flew along. An early start and lack of sleep were combining to make him sluggish and it was the last thing he needed to be right now. The Third Reich was gliding by underneath his Blenheim as he headed north east in a crystal clear blue sky. At twenty thousand feet, everything below was like a model train set.

His day had really started the previous afternoon when Winwright dropped the bombshell that he was to go on a recce mission over Germany. On paper, it was easy. They were to fly to Auberive, refuel and take off early the following day into the dawn sun. They would head to point X, take the photographs and come home. Of course, if it had been so easy, then 18 and 57 Squadron wouldn't have been taking such a hammering.

Chandler knew something was up when two short nosed Mk I Blenheims had arrived a few days before. Saundby had been as good as his word and arranged for them to be delivered after 57 received their brand new Mk IV's. The erks had wielded paintbrushes and the squadron codes were quickly changed over.

In a foul mood, Chandler had gathered his crew and taken off into the gathering dusk to fly the hundred or so miles to Auberive, east of Rheims. Touching down at 218's airfield, he'd taxied up to dispersal and reported to the CO. He made sure the aircraft was given the once over for the morning before retiring to the mess.

218 was a Battle squadron and a boisterous one at that. He'd spent the evening talking flying with the Battle pilots and gaining some insight into their war. Some of them openly admitted they knew they were flying deathtraps. At the same time, they were quite confident about doing their bit and making a contribution. Chandler couldn't quite reconcile the paradox. They were still carousing hours after Chandler left them to it and had retired to a nearby hayloft.

They'd been roused with the birds and shambled to the Blenheims dispersal as the sun was creeping over the horizon. Chandler had shivered, teeth chattering while he did his walkaround. With no bombs on board, they had almost leapt into the air, as if the angels were pushing them aloft.

For the first few miles, Chandler had circled, climbing to twelve thousand feet before setting course. On their own, they had the luxury of picking their own route and he'd debated with Morgan exactly where to cross the border. They couldn't fly over Luxemburg and they'd picked up a pinpoint at Thionville before flying into 10/10ths cloud cover.

He glanced to his right for a moment to see Morgan fussing over his maps. So far, Morgan had been spot on. The course changes were crisp and he seemed to be on top of things. He checked Griffiths was okay on the intercom and got a cheery response.

Both Morgan and Chandler missed flying the long nosed Blenheim but for different reasons. While it was cramped in the nose, Morgan at least had room to spread his maps and assorted paraphernalia. In the short nosed version of the Blenheim, he was perched on a small seat next to Chandler and he was compelled to keep folding and refolding his maps. For Chandler, it was nothing to do with comfort. While the shorter nose gave him a clearer view, he was feeling the lack of power at Altitude. Twenty thousand feet was high for the mark one and he could feel the aircraft wallowing.

A break in the clouds got them a pinpoint at a bend in the river at Schweich. They headed north, threading round Wiesbaden. Dane had briefed them in the most general terms to look at road and rail movement as far as Bremen. If they could look at any airfield activity as well, that would be appreciated. Chandler wanted to fly over airfields like he wanted a hole in the head. They stuck to following the roads and rail lines.

For a while, he jinked in and out of the clouds, using the cover as long as he dared. He figured the German air defences would be nearer the front line. If he could put some distance between them, then they could operate with less interference. An hour and a half into their journey they popped out of the clouds. Coming into the open, Chandler flinched as he was bathed in sunlight. Blinking away spots, the land was spread out below them under a beautiful cloudless autumn sky.

Morgan glanced at his map, jabbed a finger into it and then pointed ahead of them on the right. Chandler could see the glitter of the sun off water.

"On course, skipper, that's the Biggetalsperre reservoir there. North east of it is Attendorn. Take course zero two zero. It'll be-" he did some fast calculation, "-eighty minutes to Bremen."

"Roger."

Chandler fed in some rudder and watched the compass creep round. Now was the dangerous time. The overcast was behind them and if they were jumped, there were no other clouds to dive into. They followed the roads. Morgan used binoculars to look at traffic and fired up the camera if they saw anything interesting.

The rail line between Dortmund and Kassel was crawling with traffic, so they followed that for a bit. They kept a watchful eye to stay away from the city limits. They knew they'd been spotted when they got to Guttersloh. There was an airfield to the west of town and as they passed near it, Morgan saw fighters scrambling along the runway. The same thing happened at Osnabrück. Chandler warned Griffiths to keep watch after stirring the hornets' nest.

They'd been briefed to go as far as Bremen. As they approached the city, little black puffs of smoke started to dot the sky. It creeped ever higher and soon the Blenheim was rocking from the blast. Chandler opened up the throttles to full power and climbed.

On the approach to the yards, Chandler did his best to keep it steady and Morgan set the camera running. Peering through a clear view panel in the rear escape hatch was a vertically mounted F24 camera. It had a five inch film with a motor driven cartridge that could take two hundred and fifty exposures. They would overlap as their flightpath walked the camera over the terrain below.

Chandler flinched as the flak gunners found their height again. The Blenheim bucked and he fought the controls to get it back level. One burst went off right in front of him and his nostrils filled with the sulphurous stench of explosive. Shrapnel pinged off the airframe and one of the panels in the nose cracked. He looked at Morgan but his navigator had his eyes glued on the ground below. The seconds ticked by, each one feeling like an age as the flak started to close in.

Griffiths called over the intercom that they had some holes in the tail but Morgan ignored him and kept his attention focused on the ground. Chandler heard a rattle in the fuselage and then a loud bang as he fought the controls. He'd heard someone say there was something like four hundred anti aircraft guns around Bremen. It certainly felt like it, the sky was beginning to turn black around them.

"Hurry up, it's getting close up here." he prompted.

"Just a little more, skipper."

"We don't have a little more!" he said tersely.

He counted to ten. It was useless coming all that way and not getting the shots. Gritting his teeth, he hung in there. Finally, Morgan sat back up and patted him on the shoulder.

"That's it, get us out of here."

Chandler didn't need telling twice. As soon as Morgan sat up, they were peeling away. He dipped the nose to build up speed and get under the guns that had them in their sights. He let the speed build up to two hundred and ninety knots before levelling off. As much as he wanted to escape the flak, he didn't want to lose too much height. There could be fighters out there and he'd need every inch of altitude he could get when the time came.

Now they'd done the job, they just had to get back. Their orders gave him discretion to either go back the way they had come or fly to England. It didn't take Chandler a second to decide. They'd already seen the fighters scrambling from Guttersloh and Osnabrück. No doubt there would be more out there lying in wait for them.

"Gimme a course for England, Aaron! We're going out over the top!" he shouted. He reached down to feed in some elevator trim and hauled back on the yoke, getting back up to height.

"Make your course two eight five, head for the coast!"

"You got it."

Ahead of them was the blue line of the coast, just a short distance and then it was a ride across the North Sea and home. More flak burst ahead as they got closer to Emden. He was sorely tempted to photograph the docks on the way out but he felt they'd pushed their luck far enough for one day. He glanced across at the map in Morgan's lap and saw that Emden was right on the Dutch border. He edged a little left and cut the corner, going out over the estuary of the Ems River. The Dutch voiced their disapproval, putting up a shower of flak to rival the Germans. They were hit again as shrapnel nibbled at the wings.

"Bandits! Six o'clock and low!" shouted Griffiths.

"How far back?"

"Quite a bit skipper."

Chandler dipped the nose in response, gaining even more speed as they dove through the maelstrom. He saw surf passing below the nose and kept on diving, passing twelve thousand feet. The yoke shook in his hand and he kept a firm grip on the controls.

In his turret, Griffiths hung on for grim life. The fuselage was shaking around him and he felt every jolt as the air screamed past. When the flak had been going off around them he'd been terrified. A lump of flak as big as his fist had gone through the fuselage and just missed the radios. He could see the fighters behind them; a cluster of 109s trying to close the distance.

The flak stopped as they flattened out over the water. Griffiths kept his gun trained on the pursuing fighters. The 109s followed them for quite a few miles out over the water and then all of a sudden they peeled off back to the mainland.

When Chandler heard the fighters had turned around, he backed off on the throttles and began to relax. They had taken quite a few hits in those few minutes over Emden and Bremen and he checked the instruments. The engine temperatures were a little high but okay. He asked Griffiths to take a look out of his turret.

"We've got some fabric flapping on the tail skipper. There are a few holes in the wings but I can't see anything leaking out."

Happier, Chandler slowly climbed back up to six thousand feet and headed for England. The rest of the flight was uneventful. They fired off the colours of the day as they passed over the coast near Lowestoft. They had an anxious few minutes as they waited to see if the coastal defences would open up at them. Chandler was very conscious they often shot first, and asked questions later.

Morgan gave him a course for Honington, six miles south of Thetford in Suffolk. Chandler hadn't been there before, so he spent a few minutes circling the field when they arrived. Honington had a single runway laid out roughly east to west. Around the perimeter track he could see a number of Vickers Wellingtons at dispersal.

He joined the circuit and the tower gave him a green light on his downwind leg. Coming around, there was a slight crosswind and he used the rudder to keep himself lined up on the runway. Ground crew saw them to a dispersal point near the hangars and Chandler shut the engines down. His ears were ringing and he found it took a few minutes before he could stand up out of his seat. His legs had gone a little numb. When he checked his watch he knew why, they'd been flying for nearly six hours.

Chandler joined Morgan and Griffiths on shaky legs to take a walk around the aircraft. Their tail had been peppered and he stopped counting holes when he got up to twenty. There was a dent in the leading edge on the starboard wing and two clear view panels in the nose were damaged. Morgan whistled when he looked underneath. There was a ragged hole in the port side of the bomb bay. He watched anxiously when an erk removed the camera and took it to a waiting car. It didn't appear to be damaged but they would only find out when the film was developed.

A crew truck picked them up and took them to the operations building for interrogation. They were fed cups of tea and biscuits while the Intelligence Officer took them through their mission. Morgan made reference to his navigation log and showed their track on a map of Germany. He pointed out where had been concentrations of transport on the road and railway tracks.

When he provided details of what he'd seen at Bremen, Chandler was happy to give him the floor. He'd been too busy dodging flak to notice much of anything. They relaxed when they were told the camera was okay.

Assigned some beds in a Nissen hut not far from the Mess, they gratefully stripped off their flying gear for a wash. Borrowing some fresh kit to wear, Chandler and Morgan had shared a table at dinner with some of the aircrew from IX squadron.

They asked him what he thought of Bremen. He listened with interest as they told him about their early attacks over Germany. Chandler winced as they described how effective the 109s cannon had been. He in turn told them about his scouting mission where he'd spotted the German destroyer. He managed a few drinks in the bar before turning in, the long day finally catching up with him.

1.15 – Culottes, Et Décolleté et la Vin!

Preddy shook his razor clean in the warm water. He patted his skin dry and felt around his face for any stray bristles. Satisfied, he put his wash kit back into its bag and fished around for some aftershave. He put a few drops on his hands and steeled himself, taking a deep breath before clapped his hands on his cheeks. His eyes watered and he hissed as the tonic seeped into his pores.

Getting up from the step, he upended the steel helmet he was using as a washbasin. He watched the warm water spill onto the grass, the steam forming in the cold air. He chucked the wash bag across the hut onto his cot bed. He looked at his reflection in a mirror as he went through the rigmarole of fiddling with his necktie. Tonight, he'd decided, was going to be his night. After weeks of working their socks off, tonight was a good chance to let his hair down and have a good blowout. Booze, some antics in town and a bit of skirt would put everything in perspective.

He glanced at his father's letter on his bed and frowned. He read it again and his face twisted the further he went down the page. With a guttural snarl, he ripped the pages into pieces and watched them flutter to the floor. He stood brooding for a few minutes, looking down at the fresh confetti balanced on his toe cap. When they'd been posted to France, he thought he'd left that life behind, but he was only fooling himself. His father had always opposed his joining up. The closer war had loomed, the more he had voiced his opinion. His final leave before coming to France had been a bitter one with many cross words said.

He found it hard to shake off that final memory of walking down the gravel drive to his car. The sounds of his mother's weeping had mingled with the harsh words of his father. If his father thought sending a letter would heal the rift, then he was woefully mistaken. He could picture the old man as he always was, ensconced behind his desk in his office, the reek of cigars in the air. Preddy found it amusing that his father was quick to criticise the war but he was prepared to profit from it. It was a platitude Preddy found distasteful. If his father had his way, England would sit behind the safety of the channel and watch Europe burn.

"The Empire my boy, that's all that matters" his father had said, that final time. "The sun will never set on the Empire. Our strength has always lain in the navy, the Channel and keeping our noses out of foreign affairs. Let the blasted Germans rattle their sabres if they want. You mark my words; it'll all be over by Christmas. Then all you young fools will come home again and drain the state even more."

"I suppose if we had your way we wouldn't even have an air force?" Preddy had asked, his voice dripping in sarcasm. The argument was a well trodden one between father and son. Both of them were obstinate and Preddy had enough of the family's sense of self righteousness to rise to the provocation every time.

His father had slammed his tumbler of whisky down on the sideboard and looked at him hard. His cheeks had flushed; his lips had pulled thin at the temerity of having his opinion challenged in his own house, by his own son of all people.

Shaking off the memories, Preddy stormed from the hut, the door slamming against the frame. He joined the rest of the aircrew by some trucks the CO had rustled up to take them to town. Farmer was talking to Arthur when his navigator joined him. He brushed some lint off Preddy's shoulder and then tugged at his lapels, making the line tight across the neck.

"There. The girls will love you."

Preddy puckered up and blew him a kiss.

"You sweet talker. Girls love that."

Farmer laughed. "We'll see. A couple of *sil vous plaits* and I'll have them eating out of my hand."

Winwright talked to Dane through the open door of the flight hut as he watched the crowd build up. There was a lot of noise around the trucks, and he took note of the groups that were forming. Some of the new boys stood off to one side, uniforms still showing some of the creases of their journey. Pettifer went over to them and started telling a flying story. They listened intently as his hands described an arc through the air.

Milton was a fresh faced alumnus of Oxford, a rowing blue with a torso to match, bulging arms and broad shoulders. His navigator, Michael Shand, looked even younger if that was possible. He'd tried to look older by growing a moustache, but the feeble little wisps of black on his upper lip were a poor attempt.

Stood next to him in sartorial elegance was Ralph, the honourable, Marchland. His father was the Earl of Denby, a loud but ineffectual voice in the House of Lords. Farmer thought Marchland would slot neatly into the social moirés of the squadron. He'd been a few years below the likes of himself and Arthur in the same house at Harrow.

Finally, there was the new money. William Pendleton was talking to Anderson, his braying laugh grating on the ears. Brash and loud, he was loaded to the brim with a generous living allowance over and above his flying pay. His father was a big man in Shell, which he had mentioned at every opportunity since he arrived. His record said he was an excellent pilot, but that remained to be seen.

There was a shout of outrage and Woods came into view, Osbourne's peaked cap clutched to his chest. Woods opened his stride and set off at speed towards the nearest hut, the Scot in hot pursuit. They managed two laps, before Woods broke off to weave through the crowd. Osbourne barged a few people out of the way and managed to get a finger on Woods' collar.

As he was yanked backwards into a heap, the dark haired Welshman palmed the cap off into the crowd. The cap started flying from man to man, with an enraged Osbourne in the middle of the ruck. He flailed his beefy hands and missed as the cap flew across the circle.

"Give it back!" he shouted, the words coming thick and fast as he went red in the face. He whirled as it went over his head and Woods took up the chase again, running off with a comfortable lead. Osbourne went bellowing after him, legs pumping. There was a cheer as they rounded one of the huts.

"Keep going, Timber!" shouted Preddy. "You've got a comfortable lead." Laughing, he turned back to Farmer. "Ossie will kill him if he gets his hands on him."

Nothing happened for a minute or two and they stood with bated breath, waiting for the chase to reappear. Instead, Osbourne walked back around the hut on his own. He dusted off his cap, slapping it against his thigh as he walked.

He was welcomed into the group with some hearty back slapping. He put the cap onto his head and then corrected it to have a slight angle. He waved a warning finger as some brave souls tried swatting it off his head again.

"Blighter chucked it on the roof," said Osbourne. He bent down and brushed some splinters from his trousers. He started grinning when someone handed him a bottle of beer. Woods slid back into the crowd and Osbourne pointed as he spotted him.

"Grab my hat again and I'll chuck you onto the roof stick insect." he warned. Woods held up his hands in defeat.

"Duly noted." Osbourne's navigator, Woods was the opposite of his dour pilot. Tall and rangy, they made an odd pair. Woods more outgoing personality was a good foil to the Scots serious demeanour.

"All aboard the Skylark!" shouted Winwright above the clamour. He came striding out of the flight hut, over to the leading truck. He pulled himself up to the cab and looked back as the squadron loaded up. Someone gave the canvas a thump as the tailgate was shut. There was a crash of gears and the trucks were off, the aircrew singing lustily from the back.

Dane stood nursing a mug of tea as the trucks pulled out. It was good to see them in a good mood, but he was concerned seeing Hagen stood off to one side, sullen and alone. He knew he'd taken a shock, but the man's mood had yet to bounce back since then. Maybe a night on the town would sort him out.

When the trucks dropped them off in the centre of town, they spent a few minutes arguing over where to go. Winwright let them bicker before cutting across the discussion and leading them to a hotel with a welcoming air.

"Is it any good, Sir?" asked Locke's navigator Padgett, a mousy Essex boy with a shock of ginger hair.

"Got to be," put in Morton. "The bigger the hotel, the better the plonk. Line up a few bottles, lay on hot and cold women and everything'll be fine."

They came into the lobby like a bomb going off. The noise level ratcheted up and their footsteps echoed off the vaulted ceiling. They made a beeline for the bar. A cheer went up as they clapped their eyes on a large room with low ceilings, dim lighting and a bevy of women. Farmer spotted a variety of uniforms aside from RAF Blue. French army officers occupied tables at the far end near the stage. Some French aviators lined the bar, nursing their drinks while Gauloises hung from their lips.

As the squadron swarmed into the already overcrowded room, the portly Maitre'de bustled over. Before he could start protesting, Winwright took him forcibly by the arm off to one side and held up a bundle of notes between his forefingers. Any objections melted away and the orders went in thick and fast.

Morton took up station at the piano parked in the corner. Aside from reading pulp fiction, he was also an accomplished pianist. He tapped experimentally on a few keys, ear cocked listening for a bum note. Happy that all was well, he theatrically cracked his knuckles and began crashing out a well known hit. A small group gathered round and joined him in song, knocking back wine with as much gusto as their singing.

Arthur carefully balanced a tray as he threaded his way through the crowd. He deftly dodged a fast moving waiter heading the other way and slid into his seat, plonking the tray down.

"Wine, red, for the drinking of." He draped a napkin over his arm and started bustling round the table, bobbing and saying *Monsieur* a lot. He ruffled their hair, pulled at shirt collars and threatened to pour wine in their lap as he handed out the glasses. Farmer grabbed the bottle off him and pulled the cork out with his teeth, spitting it on the floor.

"Nice," said Marchland. "I always knew you had a lot of class."

"He tries," said Preddy. "You should see him when he puts his feet behind his ears."

"I'd pay to see that," said Arthur, crashing down into a seat next to him. "I can crack my knuckles." He started pulling on his fingers. Farmer made a face and cuffed Arthur across the back of the head.

"You'll have to excuse my friend here," he said with mock gravity. "He never really recovered after getting hit in the head by a cricket ball in his youth."

"Ah, but I threw the ball," said Marchland.

"So you did," said Arthur, remembering it well.

Farmer took an experimental swig of the wine, sloshing it around his mouth before swallowing and making a face.

"Bilge." He drank some more, then topped up his glass.

"I rather like it," said Marchland. He took the bottle off Farmer and peered at the label. "Chateau Grospellier," he mumbled. "Never heard of it."

They ploughed through two bottles of the stuff in short order. Marchland waved his arm, trying to attract the attention of a waiter. A hand clapped him on the shoulder and Winwright leaned into the group.

"I'm off chaps. Dinner with the Mayor."

Arthur turned a horrified expression on the CO.

"Gawd, how dreadful. I'm not sure I could stand an evening of snails, frogs legs and pate."

Winwright tossed his cap up and down, catching it and spinning it at the same time.

"Have to. We need to keep up appearances and the man *has* helped us."

"That is what is called a command decision I think," said Preddy. "But who's going to look after us lot if you hoof it?"

Winwright looked down on them and smiled. It was the kind of smile you give when you wash your hands of something. "Sort yourselves out. You've got plenty of navigators to steer a course for home." As he went he left them with a warning. "Just don't break anything all right?"

They rumbled their assent and Winwright walked out of the bar. He donned his cap as he went outside, the cool night air hitting him after the heat of the bar. Taking note of the street signs, he turned left and went down a wide avenue.

Back in the bar, the energy of the room was ramping up. Musicians had come into the cramped music pit at the foot of the stage and started tuning up. Morton bashed the keys with more gusto and the singers upped the volume in competition. He played *Putting On the Ritz*, his voice carrying a good tune backed up by the other pilots. Some of the diners nearby joined in and gradually the song was taken up across the room. Morton built up to a big finish. His fingers dragged across the keys in a final flourish and he jumped out of his chair to take a bow as the applause started. He made way as a musician came over and took his seat at the piano. Fussing, the man wound the seat back up and flexed his fingers over the ivories.

Morton was half carried by the others across the room in a quick lap. He was dumped into a chair next to Marchland and handed a glass of beer. Without pausing for breath, he upended the glass and downed the pint to much cheering from the others. Foam leapt from the glass as he slammed it down onto the table.

Watching from the safety of a booth, Ashton was tucking into some hearty food. Gardner sat with him, munching his way through a crisp baguette.

"The men seem to be in good spirits," Gardner said round a mouthful of bread. Crumbs spilled onto the tablecloth and he brushed them away.

"Finally," agreed Ashton. "Sometimes they need a good kick up the backside."

Gardner tore off another hunk of bread and dipped it into Ashton's bowl. Sauce dribbled down his chin and he used a napkin to wipe himself clean.

"I say, that's rather good. What is it?"

Ashton shrugged. His knowledge of French didn't extend very far. He saw the French word for chicken, which was good enough for him. The waiter had brought him a rustic dish with a thick stock sauce, rich in butter. It was swimming with shallots, carrots, lardons and peas. A large slab of fondant potato sat on top, surmounted with a chicken breast. It was good hearty food and he tucked in.

"I'll say this for the French," Ashton said around a mouthful of chicken and peas. "They know how to cook." Gardner mumbled agreement and got the waiters attention. Pointing at Ashton's plate he asked for the same.

Pettifer was locked in discussion with the French pilots at the bar. He was offered a Gauloises and he took it, offering one of his Players in return. He lit the yellow cigarette and drew the smoke in deep, choking on the pungent strength of the tobacco. The aroma clung around him as he continued to cough.

"Gad," he said when he could draw breath again. He looked suspiciously at the unfiltered cigarette clenched between his fingers.

"It's good, yes?" asked the Lieutenant next to him. Pettifer nodded diplomatically, still coughing. He took another drag on the cigarette and coughed some more. Laughing, the Frenchman clapped him on the back while Pettifer's lungs continued to protest.

"It's a shame Graves and the others weren't here," said Osbourne. He flicked a glance at Hagen who was slumped over the bar, glass pressed to his forehead. "Absent friends."

"Absent friends," mumbled Marchland awkwardly, conscious he was there because they were gone.

"Speaking of absent friends, does anyone know how Chandler got on today?"

"No, and I don't care either," said Farmer pointedly.

"I say, Farmer, that's a bit off," objected Osbourne.

"Stooging around Germany on his own, I don't give much for his chances," said Preddy gloomily. He closed one eye and took aim along pointed fingers.

"Bloody glory boy," grunted Farmer.

"He saved your tail," said Osbourne.

"I said I don't care!" said Farmer, his temperature rising. He gulped down some wine to stop himself from saying anything else. He scowled and looked at the stage as the lights dimmed.

A spotlight flicked on, a disc of white on the red curtain. A portly little gentleman appeared from behind the velvet dressed in a top hat and tails. His white shirt almost glittered in brilliance under the harsh light. He motioned for quiet as the audience applauded.

"Mesdames et Monsieur, ce soir, nous avons quelque chose de spécial. Madame Ludevine chante Tu Es Partout."

The room quickly hushed. Gardner and Ashton stared at the stage, anticipating what was to come. The curtain twitched and the band started up, a violin at first, its strains haunting. Then the others came in on the next bar, the music building. The curtain twitched again and then it flicked aside as she stepped out onto the stage. She looked around, each person feeling for a moment that she was staring at them.

Preddy and Arthur flinched when they clapped eyes on her. Attractive she was not. If she was a day under forty-five, that was being generous. Her blue dress clung in all the wrong places and her make-up was caked on. The thick eyeliner made her eyes a dark pit. Her black hair was scraped back into a bun, giving her a harsh school mistress look.

Her voice on the other hand was that of an angel. High and pure, it swelled and lilted to the flow of the music, lifting the room and captivating their attention. '*You Are Everywhere*' was, like a lot of French songs, mournful. The lyrics were full of longing and loves lost regrets. Ashton cocked his head and glanced at Gardner.

"What's she saying?" he whispered.

Gardner's head nodded in time to the beat of the song. He leaned closer to Ashton and kept this voice low.

"She's singing about her love that is gone and left her behind. That she sees him everywhere." Her voice began to rise and Gardner quietly mouthed the words in time.

As the last note trailed away, the singer dipped her head, eyes closed. You could have heard a pin drop at that moment, the audience was spellbound. Then an army officer sitting at the front started clapping and the room exploded with applause. People got to their feet shouting *encore* and the singer smiled.

A French officer nudged Morton and pointed at the stage "C'est Formidable, n'est pas?" and Morton just nodded, shouting with everyone else. The band took up a new rhythm and the singer belted out another Edith Piaf song, *Dans Un Bouge Du Vieux Port.* A song about a sailor at sea, she sang of moving waves that spoke of love from yesteryear. Feet tapped along to the beat.

Madame Ludevine moved up and down the stage, gracing the audience with a little twirl. At the end, she bowed to thunderous applause and left the stage. She went over to the bar and the barman gave her a long tortoiseshell cigarette holder with a cigarette attached. She lit it with a match and sipped tentatively on a small glass of Pastis. The hotel owner bustled over, effusive in his praise and played court to her. She smiled, pleased at the attention, and he hung on her every word as they conversed. Locke grimaced when the man theatrically kissed her hand.

"I'm going to be sick," he said.

"Not in my hat you won't, old boy," Preddy moved his cap off the table and shoved it into his lap.

"Look at her," said Locke, gesturing towards the romantic little scene at the bar. "I'd sooner kiss a horse."

"Bit harsh on the horse surely?" replied Arthur. "Anyway, you're married."

"I seem to remember you committing treason to see your lovely wife," put in Preddy.

"Hey, that's not fair," said Padgett, Locke's navigator. "It's not our fault if the engines conked out and dumped us in the drink."

Padgett shivered as he remembered the Channel. When Locke had pancaked into the water, the nose had dug in. Blue green water had washed over the windscreen and they had waited for the Blenheim to tip over and doom them all. The tail had hung in the air for agonising seconds before slapping the waves as it settled back down.

All thoughts of proper ditching drill had fled his brain. Locke had shoved back the hatch and they had spilled out into the frigid waters. The Blenheim had sunk so quickly that the gunner barely made it out alive.

The biting cold had chilled them to the bone. After a few minutes, Padgett couldn't feel his fingers or his arms. The only thing keeping him afloat was his Mae West. If the MTB hadn't pulled them out of the water when they did, he doubted if he would have lasted much longer.

Locke had taken a lot of ribbing from the squadron over the intervening weeks for that episode. The ironic thing was he'd not even got to see Laura when he was dragged back ashore. She'd gone to stay with her family in Norfolk. He'd spent one night in the hospital to warm up and gone straight back to the airfield to pick up a spare Blenheim.

It had been a sad parting, seeing her face at the train station, the smoke swirling on the platform as she left. He was glad she'd gone. It was no life, being in the small cottage by the airfield, seeing aircraft take off every day. Laura was the gregarious sort and she needed people around her. Since then, he had written a number of letters to her but she'd not yet replied. He chewed on his lip with some concern about that.

"You want to get yourself a woman, Locke," Marchland said as he cradled the shapely behind of the female companion on his lap. She laughed coquettishly as his hand strayed along a stockinged thigh.

"Non, pas encore vilain garcon," she said as she waved an admonishing finger at him.

"The little woman's at home. No reason why you can't enjoy all that life has to offer." He whispered in the ear of his girl and pointed to Locke. She smiled and beckoned him over to the bar. A petite blonde sashayed over and blew him a kiss. Horrified, Locke sprang back in his chair and clattered to the floor. He caught a glimpse of shapely ankles before she was swept off her feet into Padgett's arms.

"It's all right skip. I'll take care of her for you." He planted a kiss on her lips and she wriggled in his grasp. "I like France," he said suddenly, shouting "Vive la France!"

Everyone else joined in, raising their glasses high. They snatched kisses from the women around their table as the room took up the Marseillaise, getting to their feet and singing with gusto. No one noticed Hagen strolling out with an attractive Brunette in a purple dress as officers from the Lysander squadron came in.

1.16 – Phases

Mark Hagen slowly rolled over, trying to avoid making the bed creak. Tired, he sat on the edge of the bed and put his feet on the floor. The linoleum was cold and he sat like that for a few minutes, getting used to the room. It had been warmer last night. With the dawning of a new day, the heat had seeped out of the apartment.

He looked around in the gloom. The room was about twenty feet square with a bay window at one end. Hazy daylight filtered through the slats of the closed shutters and lace curtains. A half open door off to his left showed a narrow corridor. He walked around. His fingers brushed along the top of the chair by the dressing table. Everything was neat and tidy and in its place. He'd not noticed that. Pots and jars on the left, brushes and combs on the right. Soft pink silk paper lined the walls and there was the smell of roses in the air.

He looked down at the sleeping figure under the blanket. A wisp of dark chestnut hair peeked out from the covers and lay stark against the ivory silk pillow case. He ran his hand along the line of her body, following the contours. He could feel her warmth through the material and remembered how smooth her skin had been.

When he first saw her, he'd been parked at the bar, drinking fast and not paying much attention to anything else. After the best part of a bottle of wine, he'd started to feel better. He knew that Dane and the others expected him to get blind drunk and magically, everything would be okay. Pettifer had tried bucking him up but threw in the towel after being pointedly ignored. A small part of Hagen felt foolish at behaving like this, but he was still struggling to deal with what had happened. When the replacements had arrived, he'd barely even paid attention to their names. To him they were cannon fodder. Getting to know them would change that view, so he avoided engaging them in conversation.

The warbling singer had grated on him and he was grateful when she had finished torturing some cats. The mood of the room had washed over him but he felt detached from it all. He turned and leaned back against the bar, looking around. He scowled as he saw Farmer hold court at the tables. He knew if he went over there, he would end up getting dragged into an argument. Drawing hard on a cigarette, he saw her down the other end of the bar, perched on the edge of a stool, legs demurely crossed.

She took his breath away. She was stunning. She had a dark cloud of chestnut hair swept back over her shoulders and was wearing a dark purple dress cinched in at the waist. She looked fed up. One hand was balanced under her chin, her elbow on the mirrored bar top as she glanced around slowly. He thought her eyes were wonderful, an iridescent blue with depths. He allowed himself a momentary stirring of emotion before going cold.

For a start, he could think of little reason why she would be interested in him. There was not much a man in his profession could offer a girl. Secondly, he couldn't believe there was any way someone like her was single. He gave the room another glance but could see no obvious suitor hovering around. She spoke to a few of the French aviators nearby, but while they talked to her, none seemed to regard her with any favour. Intrigued, he had tapped the French Lieutenant Pettifer had been talking to on the shoulder and made enquiries. When he pointed her out, the man's eyebrows shot up to the ceiling.

"I would advise against it, Monsieur," he had suggested. "Mademoiselle Janvier is bad luck."

That intrigued Hagen even more, so he pushed for details. He was told of her litany of woes. Her fiancée had died in a flying accident, another lover had been blown up by a minefield and another was missing believed dead.

"We call her the femme fatale, as you say, um....Black Widow?" Hagen nodded, understanding the allegory.

"And she's seeing no one at the moment?" The Lieutenant gave Hagen a sardonic grin, showing his teeth.

"You could not give me all the money in France, Monsieur. I value my life too much."

Hagen's lips pulled together into a grim line. That was a bleak story indeed, but for a man who thought he had little time left on this earth, her reputation was a perfect fit. Against his objections, the Lieutenant had introduced them.

He lit her cigarette and she was coldly polite to him. There was a vulnerable caution in her eyes that Hagen found engaging. They continued to talk and after a while, she had let him escort her home. They left the hotel, walking down narrow streets in the chill night air. He gave her his arm, and she had graciously taken it.

As they walked, she let him talk and he told her what he dared. Avoiding operational matters, they still had plenty to discuss. Subjects ranged from food, the weather and the chances of hostilities starting in earnest. The conversation continued up to her rooms and they'd paused at the door. She opened it and stood with her hand on the frame, her face shadowed.

"Thank you for walking me home."

"It was my pleasure, Mademoiselle Janvier."

He remained standing in front of her, making no effort to go. She looked at him with those limpid blue eyes of hers and he found his reserve slipping. He swallowed hard.

"So now what, Monsieur Hagen?"

"I guess I'll bid you good evening."

Still neither of them made a move.

"Do you want to go?" she asked him.

Hagen paused. He had brought himself to the precipice and now his mind suddenly went blank.

"Well...no, but we can't just stand here all night like this."

She was amused at his sudden reserve. Talking to her in the bar he had been much more confident. Smiling, she pushed off from the frame and slid inside, leaving him standing there. Hagen stood in the corridor, nonplussed to start with. The seconds went by but the door remained open. He heard her bustling about inside. He gently pushed the door open with his hand and went into the apartment. He was standing in the living room, looking around, when her voice came from another doorway.

"I'm in here."

He walked in slowly to find her sitting at the bay window of the bedroom. Her high heels were on the floor, her feet tucked up under her. The shutters were half closed and she was gazing out of the window, watching the night sky. He heard a line of music echoing from somewhere down the street.

"Nice room," he said, making conversation.

"It is adequate," she said listlessly. He sat on a plush chaise longue at the foot of the bed and rested his feet. He fished out a book he had sat on and looked at it. L'Ecole Des Maris, *The School For Husbands*, by Molière. He idly flicked through a few pages and then tossed it onto the bed to this right.

She had closed her eyes and rested her head against the window frame, a few stray hairs moving in the breeze. The tick of a clock filled the room. Hagen took the chance to look at her again. She had long eyelashes and a beauty spot on her left cheek. Her full lips were slightly parted. He followed the line of her neck down to her shoulder and down to the swell of her breasts. Her skin was limned from the slither of light coming in from outside.

She opened her eyes and shifted her head to look directly at him. Her face disappeared into shadow but her voice was clear, the English slightly accented.

"Why are you here?"

The question. He sat up straighter and leaned his elbows on his knees. He picked up his peaked cap and played with it in his hands.

"Well," he said hesitantly. "Because I liked the look of you, and it looked like you needed a friend."

She laughed lightly, amused at such a quaint way of putting it. She had not known many Englishmen. In her experience, they were just boys when it came to matters of the bedchamber.

"It always ends in tears, you know," she said simply, her voice full of sorrow. Hagen knew the regret wasn't for him, but all that had gone before.

"Should it?" he said, trying to carry a certain measure of confidence and self assurance. Her eyes narrowed slightly. His voice did not match his eyes. She could see the nervousness there, the caution. They had both been wounded, in different ways, it seemed.

"Are you not worried about what people will say?" she asked, giving him the out if he wanted to take it.

"I'm not one to let myself be worried by gossip," he said crisply, a military tone creeping back into his voice. His business was his own, bugger what anyone else thought. Gossip was the last thing he was worried about.

After the baptism of fire he'd gone through, he doubted anything like that would worry him again. People could say what they liked; it wouldn't alter what he was inside. He changed the subject.

"I was sorry to hear about your fiancée." Her lips curled down and she looked out the window again.

"Accidents happen," she said sadly.

"I know that all too well." He fished out a packet of cigarettes. He opened the pack and tapped one on the lid before sticking it between his lips.

"Flying's a dangerous business," he said. He held the packet out towards her. "Would you like one?"

There was a moment's hesitation while she considered. Taking it from him was going to the next step. She took a cigarette from the packet.

"Thank you."

He rummaged around in his pocket for a lighter. He flicked it open and held it up. Her face was illuminated by the flame and he watched the shadows dance around her features. Uncoiling from her seat by the window, she sat down next to him. They sat smoking in the quiet, their knees bumping. She looked down and put her stockinged feet next to his shoe. They were tiny.

"You don't want to be with me, Mark," She turned a sad face on him, her eyes bright. "Je suis malheur."

"I was told." He gave her a reassuring smile. "Frankly, anyone who thinks rationally would realise that's a load of old tosh."

"Tosh?" she cocked her head and her brow scrunched up in confusion.

"Guff, balder dash, poppycock," he expanded.

She laughed. It was a nice sound that lifted his spirits. Her face lit up and lost some of its sadness.

"Speak English," she scolded him.

"But I am," he told her, smiling. Feeling bold, he darted forward and kissed her on the lips. "All that stuff about bad luck is nonsense, Lorraine. A fellow makes his own luck."

"But people will say-"

"Let them." He found her hand and meshed his fingers with hers as he leaned in. "I'm not bothered by gossips."

1.17 – Absence Makes

The beauty of the day was torn apart by the snarl of twin Mercury engines as the squadron thundered over the field. Each aircraft went the length of the runway, and then broke right into the circuit. The erks waved as they flew overhead, beating up the field.

Sat in the nose, it was Preddy who saw her first. His keen eyes saw the flash of white on the road by the perimeter wall. A figure was standing next to a small black and red car, waving at the aircraft as they went over their head. He thumbed his intercom.

"That was a woman down there," he said in surprise.

Farmer looked back over his shoulder in reflex.

"How can you possibly know that?"

"I saw her hat and skirt," Preddy assured him.

"If you're right, then I'm standing you a beer tonight."

"I'll take that bet," said Preddy, smugly.

Succeeding aircraft started to go lower to get a better view and the R/T was full of chatter as they circled to land. In the end, Winwright had to tell them to shut up and keep the air clear. Locke's navigator, Padgett, could not stop contemplating the promise of a girl coming to see them. He kept up a commentary on the way round the circuit.

"Did you see her dress, fluttering in the breeze? I'll bet she's a blonde."

"Will you stop?" said Lucas, their gunner. Thirty, he was a rarity among the non commissioned aircrew because he was a Sergeant. He was the shepherd amongst some of the younger men. "All you think about is women."

"That's not true," protested Padgett. "I think about a lot of things. Cars, wine, parties; a good defensive stroke on the field."

"An exhaustive list, to be sure," commented Locke. He followed Pettifer round the circuit, staying high to avoid the turbulence behind his Blenheim. He selected the undercarriage and felt the thump as the wheels went down. He landed light as a feather and let her run, using short bursts of the throttle as they juddered over the rough surface of the field. The erks saw them in and Locke swung her round before killing the engines. The propellers span to a halt.

"Bloody horrible," he announced in the sudden quiet. "Every time we come back, that field gets worse." Padgett grunted his agreement as he stuffed his navigating paraphernalia into his bag.

Locke tugged off his flying helmet and ruffled his flattened hair. His ears rang after two hours in the air. He was rung out, his arms felt like lead and his palms tingled from the vibrations through the yoke.

Winwright had flown them hard, asking for perfection in their formation flying. Each flight flew in three vics of three aircraft. Winwright had floated above them, directing, cajoling and hectoring them to get it right. He had them take it in turns to fly each position. Flying on the far right of A Flight, Locke had a difficult position. On the inside of a turn he was the hub of the wheel. He had to juggle the throttles and pull tighter than everyone else to keep his position. On the outside of a turn, it was the opposite. The throttles went to their stops and he had to race around the outer edge of the circle to keep up.

He dropped down from the wing and did a few knee bends to get some life back into his legs. The weight of the world fell away when he shrugged off his parachute harness. He slung it over his shoulder and started walking. Padgett clapped him on the arm.

"Coming to see the popsy, skip?"

Locke laughed. In the past, he may have done, but not today.

"I'm okay, Pat. I'm just tired. All I need to do is curl up on my bed and sleep."

"What's wrong? Ever since you got married you've become a real killjoy."

Locke stuck out his tongue in response and let that comment pass. He couldn't speak for the replacements, but apart from Winwright, he was one of the few married men amongst the aircrew on the squadron. That meant he was subject to a reasonable amount of humour over his *special* status. Young bucks found it strange to be tied down, they were still too busy enjoying themselves.

He followed the crowd as they strolled across the field. There was a buzz about them as they walked, the worries of the last weeks slipping away. They had flown in good formation, the aircraft were running well and they felt they could take anything on. They gathered around Winwright, laughing and joking.

"Well done today chaps." A small cheer. "I know it's not easy, but nice tight formation flying like that will keep us safe from attack. German fighters will take one look at us and want no part of it and go elsewhere." A bigger cheer went up. "Get some grub; we're stood down this evening, so enjoy yourselves."

Standing at the back of the group, Chandler went back to his tent. His head was buzzing from the formation flying and the concentration it took to fly tight on the leader. He'd only returned from England the previous day. It had taken the groundcrew two days to patch up their Blenheim before they could fly back. Chandler had used the opportunity to go shopping and brought back some home comforts. The hand wound gramophone was gratefully received although his choice of music was poorly regarded. He unzipped his Sidcot and lay on the camp bed, hands clasped behind his head. Morgan ducked into the tent.

"Coming for a drink?"

Chandler yawned and shook his head.

"I'll pass. Too tired. That's just about finished me off after the flying yesterday. It's all right for you, I do all the driving and you're just along for the ride."

"Suit yourself," he said, and his head disappeared again.

Chandler closed his eyes and tried to relax. An engine snarled into life as it was run up. He listened and could hear the dips and swells as the power surged through the range. It ran like that for a few minutes before it spluttered to a finish. Another engine started and then others, as the erks serviced the aircraft and tested their work.

Everyday life on an airfield had beats and silences of its own. In the morning, the aircraft were checked; engines were run up and tested. If the crews were on standby they lolled around. That was the worst of it, the interminable waiting. He opened his eyes and stared at the light filtering through the canvas. The shadows of leaves moved back and forth with the breeze.

The war seemed very remote. There had been such a rush to get out of here he wondered what it was all for. There was no boom of guns on the horizon, no chatter of machine gun fire. Even the everyday pace of operations was missing. The waiting was the strangest thing.

When he had flown that reconnaissance mission he had been scared, but the reaction didn't set in until later. He'd sat perched on the edge of the bed in that room at Honington, trying and failing to light a cigarette. His hands had shaken like mad. Eventually, he gave it up as a bad job and turned in. Sleep had come much later.

During his flying training, death had been a constant companion. Four candidates on his course had died in flying accidents. Another broke his back on the conversion course, but Chandler had always had faith his own skills would see him through. It was the things out of his control that scared him. On the recce; he could choose his own course, fly evasion tactics if he needed to. It was flying straight and level through the flak when he felt helpless.

He had the same feelings every time he went up with the squadron in tight formation. When the fighters came, he would have to hold his position and grit his teeth. That scared him more than anything.

Locke was walking towards the farm buildings the gunners were using as accommodation when he saw the crowd by the gate. He shook his head in amusement as he saw them clustered round the car they had seen earlier.

"Hey, Locke!" someone shouted across the space between them. He stopped and looked at the throng. He caught a glimpse of a white, wide brimmed hat and heard a lilting laugh amongst the babble of voices. Blood hammered in his ears. His heart stopped and he could have sworn his eyes were playing tricks on him. She waved at him.

"Laura?"

The crowd parted and he saw his wife standing at the gate.

"Hello Alex," she said, with a sunny smile.

They made a strange pair as they walked down the path, he in his flying suit and boots, she in her dress and Mulberry overcoat. Winwright had given him permission to leave the airfield and he had driven Laura away in the natty black and red Mathis she had bought. He wanted some privacy for this and he alternated between rage and wonder as he had driven away from the field. Laura had the good sense to keep quiet and she glanced out of the window at the countryside in the afternoon sun. He shot a look across at her as he drove along the country lanes.

Her hair was pulled back into a bun and the hat was perched on her head. The brim hid her face but he followed down the line of her neck to the collar of her Mulberry coat. Little gold drops hung from her ears. Her perfume filled the car.

He picked the first track he could find and followed it until the car was out of sight of the main road. He parked up under the shade of a tree and they went for a walk. Following the path along a stream, they held hands as he marshalled his thoughts. Finally, he came across a large flat boulder in the lee of a hill and sat himself down.

"What are you doing here, Laura?" He picked at a piece of moss on the rock and threw it down the path. "I left you at the train station. You're *supposed* to be in Norfolk."

"It was boring in Norfolk."

"It was a lot safer too," he said with meaning. "You're going back." He stood up suddenly and kicked at a stone. "I mean, how the hell-"

"I took the ferry darling," she soothed "I knew a chap in the army going back to France. He gave me a lift. We got in at Le Havre and I bought the car." She pointed back up to the lane where the roof of the Mathis was just visible. A little four door touring car, it had running boards, a tatty black canvas roof and arched front wings. Her luggage was still in the back. "It was only a few pounds, darling."

"You drove from Le Havre?"

"Yes, some policeman wanted to arrest me near Paris-" It took Locke a few seconds for the penny to drop.

"Paris! But that's not even on the way to Béthenville."

"I know," she giggled. "I took a wrong turn at Amiens. I suppose the fellow thought I was some kind of spy or something."

Locke fumed. Laura's family had money and she was always given to impulsive decisions, but he never imagined she would do something like this.

"Why haven't you written to me?" she demanded. "I haven't heard a word since you left England." Locke sighed and rubbed his face in exasperation.

"I have written to you. Tons of letters. It hasn't exactly been a picnic. There is a war on, you know."

"I was lonely and I missed you," she pouted.

"I suppose you think this is all one big adventure?"

"Darling, you've been to my parent's house. It's in the middle of nowhere, it's dreary and there was no one around except my parents. I thought I'd got away from all of that. Adventure is what I need."

"But you could have gone to London!" he protested. "Lucy works at the Admiralty, she's said more than once you could get a job there."

"I don't need my younger sister getting *me* a job. I don't *want* a job." she said, sniffing with a toss of the head. "Sitting in an office all day, typing letters for some dusty old Admiral. It's *you* I want." She looked at the ground, her voice quiet. "All I *ever* wanted."

He looked at her. She gave him his best winning smile and he knew he would end up giving in. He could never stay angry at her for long; it had always been that way. They had met at a village cricket match. He'd been bowled out for ten off a good wicket and he was angry at missing the opportunity to score more runs. Stomping back to the clubhouse, she'd been coming the other way with a plate of scones when they bumped into each other.

Their eyes had met and that was it for him. She was tall and lithe with a short bob of blonde hair and dancing green eyes that captured him from the first moment. An art student, she had gone to the cricket with her parents for the day. Love was the last thing she had expected to find. After that, it had been a whirlwind romance. The coming war had helped things along and the rush to get to France provided the final impetus to tying the knot.

"Aren't you pleased to see me?" she asked, her bottom lip pouting.

"Of course I am, just...dash it."

She ruffled his dark hair.

"Poor Alex." She leaned in and kissed him on the cheek. "All worried about me."

Locke put his arms around her.

"Laura, I *am* worried about you. This isn't England, you know. This is a shooting war-" She clapped her hands in girlish excitement.

"Oh good, has there been much action so far?"

"Some of the chaps are dead, Laura!" he said sharply. She pulled back, blinking in surprise. He had changed since she'd seen him last. There was a hardness there she'd not seen before.

"Dead?"

"Surely you must have considered the possibility?" He kept his voice rough, riding over her levity. "This isn't a game."

"I never thought-" she said nonplussed, voice quiet. He said nothing, letting her think about it. A change came over her, she stood a little taller. Her eyes were bright. "I'm sorry."

He took her hand and gave it a reassuring squeeze.

"It's all right. It was just a shock seeing you here. How did you know where to find us?"

"I asked at Rheims."

"You asked...at Rheims?" he repeated, guppy like.

She looked surprised.

"Why, of course. I asked where the RAF squadrons were and the locals," she shrugged, "just pointed the way. Then there was an awfully kind staff officer at the Headquarters who told me where to look."

"Told you where to look?" He could not decide if she should be impressed by her ingenuity or appalled at the total lack of security. They'd been warned about femme fatales the Germans may have dropped behind the lines and here was some staff wallah giving out information willy nilly to the first pretty face that came along and batted her eyes.

"Don't worry," she reassured him, "I've got it all arranged. Please don't be annoyed, but I've got us a room in Béthenville." He started to protest but she over rode him. "It's a nice little apartment so I can be near you."

"And what will that cost?" he asked.

"Don't worry, darling. I brought money with me."

"I can't believe your father gave you money for this."

"Alex, it's *my* money. It *is* one of the reasons you married me."

His mouth twitched in good humour. It was a running joke between them. Neither of them were exactly struggling, but by the same token they were not completely independently wealthy. Both of them had generous allowances from trust funds.

"God knows what the CO will make of all this." He brooded on that for a moment. One thing he'd learned over the last few weeks was that there was no point worrying about something outside of his control. "Of course, now you are here, what am I supposed to do with you?"

She cocked her head and gave him an impish smile. Coming close, she ran a finger down the line of his jaw and put it on his lips.

"Let me show you what you can do with me," she breathed into his ear as she led him back to the car.

Locke stood braced at attention in Winwright's office. He picked a point on the wall and stared at it. It was amazing how fascinating a small patch of woodwork could become. He followed the line of the grain up and down the panel while Ashton droned on. He snapped back to attention when Winwright spoke to him directly.

"Yessir."

"I'm not particularly interested in your love life, Locke. What I'm concerned about is how she knew where we were?"

"She was told, Sir," Locke said simply. He started as Winwright's fist slammed the table.

"Goddammit!" He stood quickly, finger pointing into Locke's chest. "By you?"

"No, *Sir,*" said Locke emphatically.

"Because if I find out you breached operational security." He left the threat hanging. Winright was almost incandescent with rage. Locke spoke quickly.

"I've already said I didn't tell her, Sir. Some wallah at Headquarters told her apparently."

"Did they? Did they indeed?" He sat back down again while he pondered that. "Well, I'll make some enquiries in that regard," he murmured. He grimaced at the situation he had before him.

Winwright had no real objections to his men being romantically involved with women. He himself was married and in England, wives and girlfriends were a welcome addition to the social scene of any station. It humanised the mess and wives often accompanied their husbands on postings abroad. Exotic locales like Hong Kong and Singapore were the most popular, but that was in peacetime. He disapproved greatly of women following their men into the field. He considered it an unnecessary distraction when men should be focused on their jobs.

It was like something out of the history books. He remembered reading about Wellington's Peninsular army in Spain, fighting against Napoleon. The women had been as hardy as their men, marching alongside them, cooking their food, salving their wounds. But this was a different day. His own wife and children were back home in Lincolnshire and there they would stay.

"What is she doing here?"

"I wish I knew, Sir. She's *supposed* to be in Norfolk at her parents."

"Did you know she was coming?" Winwright accused.

"No, Sir, I didn't. I'd much rather she hadn't."

The CO fixed him with a narrow stare.

"So do I, Locke. So do I."

101

1.18 – Idle Hands

It started on Tuesday morning. The blue sky turned leaden grey as the clouds rolled in. The heavens opened, slowly at first, building to a downpour. The temperature plummeted and the clouds went with it. Visibility dropped to a few hundred yards and there was a solid overcast overhead. For the first hour, the rain was interesting. After two it became dull. After three, things started getting damp and people lost interest. The airfield started to resemble a swamp as the heavy clay soil struggled to absorb the moisture. Burke put on extra work parties to lay duck boards and dig some drainage ditches, but it made little difference except make the men very dirty.

The squadron was stood down for twenty four hours pending clearer weather. Aircrew huddled against the cold in their tents and huts. A few hardier souls went out but it was heavy going on roads that were inches deep in water.

Kittinger sipped lukewarm whisky from a glass tumbler as he carried on working. He picked up the Lee Enfield rifle and set it across his lap. He ran a hand along the wooden stock, feeling the smooth finish, the cold of the metal breech and bolt. He wiped a rag in a tin of bees wax and started rubbing it into the wooden furniture.

He may have had an old pair of Flying Corps wings on his left breast, but he'd not started in the air. His war had begun as a newly minted Second Lieutenant in the East Surrey regiment at Ypres. Kittinger's war had been far from cosy.

Big shells cratered the ground in massive explosions that pulverised his men into small pieces. Body parts flew into the air and whole platoons were obliterated in a moment. He had very strong memories of mud and wet and rats and mildew and the overriding stench of death. He received a mention in dispatches for carrying one of his wounded men out of the horrors of no-mans land. He stopped rubbing with the rag while he thought about that.

He had been running back to his trench when he jumped into a stinking shell hole full of bodies. He sank into the fetid water and was crawling over dead men when one of them made a sound of pain. He looked off into the distance as he tried to remember his name. He could remember his face clearly. He was just a boy, doing his best to be brave even though his legs were smashed.

Kittinger had hoisted him onto his shoulders and set his feet moving. After that, his world had shrunk into the patch of ground in front of him. He never even remembered the bullets that flew by, tugging at his breeches, tearing up the ground around him.

He got his Military Cross for an assault on a German machine gun nest. He took two bullets in the lungs for that. All he had now was a silver cross with a white and purple ribbon and the scars on his chest to remember it.

He was convalescing in a French field hospital when a DH2 buzzed overhead. He was watching it intently when he saw an old friend from the Guards come down the ward. The man was now an officer in the Royal Flying Corps and it stirred interest in him. As in all things, it was a matter of being in the right place at the right time. When he recovered, he volunteered to be an observer. He soon found himself in a Be2c squadron back on the front line. He made it through the Fokker scourge and ended the war as a pilot, flying high above the carnage he'd started in.

He came back to the present as he watched some erks running full tilt through the trees, trying to dodge the rain. They ran with one hand keeping their forage caps on their heads. One of them tripped over a tree root and fell head first into the mud, much to the mirth of his fellows. The man picked himself up, half dazed and dashed to catch up to his mates. Kittinger refilled the tumbler with some more whisky and put it down on an upturned ammunition box.

"Bloody idiots," he murmured. "Don't know when they're bloody born."

Picking up the oily cloth, he wiped around the chamber and blew away a few flecks of dirt. Checking it was clear; he shouldered the rifle and sighted outside the tent, following a squirrel that darted along the branches.

"Bang!" he shouted, imagining the kick of the rifle. He pulled back the bolt and inserted two clips of five rounds, pushing hard against the magazine spring until they went in. Putting the rifle aside, he drank more whisky and hummed to himself.

Dane heard the humming as he walked gingerly past Kittinger's tent. The duckboards were slick from the wet and he didn't fancy sprawling amongst the dirt like some people had. He huddled under his umbrella and walked to the operations hut. Going inside, he hung the umbrella on a hook and draped his greatcoat over the back of a chair by the stove.

He checked the kettle on top and set about making a mug of tea. Pendleton sat with his feet up on another chair, half awake. He jumped as Dane came in and sat up, yawning like a lion. He scratched and nodded when Dane asked if he wanted tea. He held up two fingers and Dane just nodded, knowing there was no sugar anyway. It was the running joke.

Pendleton was Officer of the Day but as there was no flying, there was nothing to do. The field telephone rang occasionally, but apart from that, he was there to run interference for the CO in the office next door. They chatted for a while, Dane quiet and reserved, Pendleton, loud as always.

A short, compact man, Pendleton had spent most of his youth in boarding school. His father was an executive for Shell and his mother, as a good corporate wife, often travelled with him. As a result, Pendleton had spent many of his summers with an Uncle on the Sussex Downs and it was here he first flew in an aeroplane. His Uncle had a surplus DH9 at a local airfield and those flips were the highlight of his holidays. As absent parents, his mother and father had indulged him with a generous allowance. He'd hoarded it to pay for lessons, getting his pilot's licence when he was nineteen. After university, he considered joining Shell himself, but he enjoyed flying more and had joined the RAF that summer.

His background of going from school to school had left him with a burning need to prove himself, to get noticed. So that is what he did. He drove flash cars, spent money and tried to be the soul of any party, whether he was invited or not. So far he had made a lot of noise and he was itching to get into the air and show everyone what he could do. Now the weather was conspiring against him too.

The door to Winwright's office opened and the CO came out carrying a sheaf of papers.

"Oh, Dane. Good." He dumped the papers onto Pendleton's desk. "Be a good chap and see this mail goes out with the next dispatch rider."

"Yessir."

Winwright beckoned and Dane followed him into his office. He motioned for him to sit and Dane took the seat in front of the desk.

"Wing have been on the line. It seems the rain might last longer than we expected, so I've decided to hand out a few leave passes. Half of each flight can go on a forty eight. I don't want them going too far in case this weather clears up."

"Yes, Sir. I'll speak to Kittinger and get some transport laid on."

Winwright tapped a pencil on the desk. His brow furrowed as he frowned, his face knotting.

"I don't like bad weather, Dane. Idle hands make the Devils work." He stood up and shoved his hands into his pockets and stared brooding out the window. He peered into the gloom, the weather matching his mood. "I've found over the years that aircrew are like cats. They're bone idle, feel entitled to do what they want and need pampering. If they're not flying, they get bored and make trouble."

"In short, I need the men to be kept occupied. We can put on lectures and things, get them out on a few cross country runs." He rubbed his hands with relish. "Nothing wrong with a bit of fresh air. They're all young men. It'll do them good to get out there tramping about the countryside."

"I'll see to it, sir. There's plenty we can get the boys doing." He picked up an Air Ministry pamphlet from the desk and idly thumbed through the pages. "I'm not entirely happy with their knowledge on aircraft recognition, for a start. Some of the French types are very different to ours."

Winwright grunted. He could just imagine the men's reaction when they found out they would be going back to school. Dane sat in thought while he contemplated the long evenings. There was not a lot in the surrounding area to keep the men entertained. Béthenville only held certain attractions and Rheims was too far away for an evening pass.

"Some kind of party perhaps?" he said aloud.

Winwright thought about that. The barn they had used for target practice was no good. It had been peppered by so many practice bombs it was only fit for firewood. Perhaps they could turn a few of the bays in the woods into an impromptu marquee.

"When the rain stops we could get the Battle and Lysander squadrons over. Give the wing a chance to get together? It would be good for the chaps to mix a bit. Get some people over from the French units as well. We're all in this together. I suppose we must try and build some bridges."

"What about entertainment, sir?"

"Are there any concert parties in the area?"

"I don't know, sir. There's bound to be some nearby."

"Good, nothing wrong with a show. Get the chaps in the mood."

Winwright glanced at the newspaper on the desk. The reporter, Cullen had been as good as his word. His story occupied three columns on the front page with the headline *'RAF bombers fight off the Luftwaffe'*. He tossed the paper across to Dane.

Dane fished out his spectacles and glanced at the front page, his eye catching the headline. It described the encounter with the German fighters, the spirited defence of the gunners in the face of mounting odds. It was a sanitised piece. The squadron was not identified. No one was named and their losses were only lightly referred to. He chucked the paper back.

"Very heroic," said Dane. Considering the strictures imposed by the Air Ministry, it wasn't bad at all. "Not a bit like the real thing, but I must confess, it's a riveting read."

"He seems a decent type, if there is such a thing amongst journalists," said Winwright. "Wing are quite keen for the press to get around and report back home. Don't be surprised if a few more correspondents put in an appearance around the field, sniffing for a story." He thumped the desk with sudden energy. "We've *got* to keep the chaps on their toes. The first good bit of weather we get and I can imagine some VIP's doing the rounds with the press men in tow."

They sat in silence for a moment. A fresh squall lashed the glass and they listened to the sound of it hammering off the roof.

"About the weather, sir?" Dane asked.

"What do you mean?"

"Well, it's getting colder. The lads spend a hell of a lot of time out in the open working on the kites. What happened to the order for some winter clothing?"

Winwright nodded. When the squadron had shipped out, most of the groundcrew only had two changes of clothes and no one had thought far enough ahead to the winter season.

"I'll see Wing about that the next time I'm there. I'll raise the issue about accommodation as well. Most of the men are still in tents, we need to do more about that if we can."

Winwright brooded on that final point. Having come from a permanent station in England, conditions at Bois Fontaine were positively primitive. The food was good, hot and plentiful and he was thankful for that, but there were still a lot of things to sort out.

He thought about the field and how long it would take to dry out. Burke had told him what the field had been like during the Great War. He wondered how someone had considered it suitable for bombers to operate from. He would collar Saundby and Goddard and see what could be done.

Hagen propped the bicycle against the wall in the lobby. The concierge had only opened the door after he had knocked hard for five minutes. She muttered disapproval when he came in, soaking wet. He shook off his waterproof poncho and draped it over the handlebars, dripping on the tiled floor. She shook her head as she attacked the puddles with a mop.

As soon as the squadron had been released, he'd half inched a bicycle from the erks and set off for Béthenville. Halfway there he had considered the whole venture quite crazy. His feet were swimming in his shoes and it had only been a matter of time before his wet top half met the wet bottom half. He squelched down the roads until he reached the Rue de Chastain and walked the bike down the narrow alley.

Lorraine let him in and made a fuss of him while he stood dripping in the living room. His wet clothes came off and she threw him a massive blanket as she ushered him in front of the fire. He kissed her as she sat down next to him, a glass of red wine in hand. She handed him a hot cup of coffee and he wrapped his hands round it, letting the heat seep into his numbed fingers. Ever practical, she scolded him while he shivered.

"Mark, you should not have come. Look at you, you're soaking wet."

"Sorry, I came as soon as I could. But I had to see you."

He shuddered and she covered his face in light kisses as she hugged him close. It took him a few moments to realise she had nothing on under her silk shift. In no time at all, they were in bed and she was in his arms. He traced circles on her shoulders while she lay across his chest, listening to his heart.

"I saw your planes flying a few days ago. I was worried about you," she murmured, her voice muffled.

"Don't be. It was just a training exercise. Simple stuff really."

She pulled back and fixed him with her blue eyes.

"Promise me you'll be careful," she said with fierce intensity. He soothed her and promised as she wanted. That seemed to satisfy her and she rested her head back on his chest.

They hovered in that place between sleep, when everything was warm and fuzzy. Hagen dozed as the rain continued to hurl itself against the windows, slapping off the shutters. Thunder rolled in the distance. He listened to the roar of the gods while he held this beautiful woman, the warm line of her body pressed against him, her skin smooth under his hands.

They stayed like that for a while until hunger won out. Lorraine went into the small kitchen and he woke to the sound of a pan being dragged across a hot plate. The smell of toast teased him and he sat up, wiping sleep from his eyes. He looked around but his clothes were still drying, so he slid from the bed and walked naked through to the kitchen.

He found Lorraine crouched down, peering at the bread under the grill, when he crept up behind her. She yelped as he tickled her sides and she spun and wrapped her arms around him, pressing herself against him.

"I thought you were asleep," she got out between kisses.

"I was," he replied. She teasingly ran her nails down his back and then slapped his behind.

"Out!" she ordered. "It'll be ready in a moment."

He grinned and left her to it. He was being nosy in the front room when she came through carrying two plates. He was peering at photographs on a dresser and pointed at them.

"You?"

"Me," she agreed and looked over his shoulder. "Me in Poitiers with my aunt. That one was last year in Normandy." She blushed at the last one. It was a studio shot of her in a Veronica Lake pose, eyes smouldering, long hair over her shoulders as she looked at the camera. "I don't remember about that one," she said, teasing him, her voice husky. "Now," she nudged him back towards the fire with her hip, "vite, vite!"

The flames had burned low in the grate and he stabbed it with the poker, adding a few pieces of wood to get it going again. He pulled a throw off the sofa and sank down onto the rug. She handed him a plate and he attacked the toast and poached eggs with gusto. She watched him eat, picking at her own plate as she did so. The muscles of his chest were taut and defined and she could see the lean strength within him.

They had talked a lot since that first night together and there were few secrets between them. In bed they had lain, holding each other while they talked of their fears, both of them baring their souls to the other. It had created in them a deep bond and she felt bereft when he left to go back to the airfield. With him it was more than just a physical match, they had found each other at the right time, each fulfilling a need in the other that healed their hurts.

The thought of losing him terrified her, far more than the others. She knew she'd made him promise to be careful, but both of them knew it was just words. Flying was dangerous. She knew that better than most. Even the best pilot could fall to an enemies guns; or an accident or just simple carelessness. Nights without him were long and she cherished every moment they spent together.

They made love afterwards by the fire. It was urgent and she clung to him with a burning desire. He looked into her eyes and went into their blue depths like a drowning man, letting her possess him as they crested together. Afterwards, they went back to bed and he held her close while she slept curled up around him, her dreams disturbed.

1.19 – Curtains

The rain that started on Tuesday carried on for the rest of the week. With no let up in the weather, the groundcrew worked hard to keep the aircraft on top line. Extra canvas was rigged over the Blenheims but the damp still got in. Intercoms howled, batteries ran flat and engines ran rough with bad magnetos. Apart from a few ground runs, there had been no flying at all.

Saundby popped by after Wing HQ finally moved to Arras. He was in ill humour. The weather had grounded everything and he was at a loose end. Directives came from the Air Ministry but there was little anyone could do when the airfields resembled boating lakes.

During the day, Dane did his best to lay on activities to keep the men busy but was met with schoolboy resistance. If he'd worn a teaching gown, they would have pinned a 'kick me' sign to his back. They treated the aircraft recognition test as a joke. He was faced with catcalls when he tried to take them through some basic French pronunciation.

They were more interested when Kittinger took them into the woods armed with rifles and boxes of ammunition. He had them charging up and down amongst the trees while throwing thunder flashes at them and firing over their heads. Any illusions they may have had that Kittinger was an old man went out the window when he kicked them to their feet and made them do it again. They were all panting and tired when he took them to the far side of the wood where he'd set up some targets. Bullets flew and anything furry was living on borrowed time. He roundly cursed them when they hit everywhere but the targets.

He kicked Preddy out of the way and took up a firing stance. Wrapping the sling around his arm to help steady his aim, he shouldered his rifle. There was a pause as Kittinger lined up on the target and then he snapped off five rounds rapid. The final cartridge span away as he pulled back the bolt and he dropped prone. He fired again, keeping up a steady rate.

He reloaded smoothly with practised ease and fired off another clip at the most distant target. There was hushed respect when they went to have a look and saw every shot had gone home.

"*That*; is how it is done gentlemen," he'd said, his voice dripping in scorn and disdain. Without another word he stomped back to his tent, disgusted with the dismal show.

Even Burke got in on the act. With Hagen's old Blenheim up on trestles being picked over for spares, he took the opportunity to present some lectures on the engines and hydraulic systems. Their eyes were starting to glaze over when he got Woods up front to change some plugs. There was an excruciating few minutes as they watched the big man stand like a deer in headlights while he fiddled with the engine. Burke finally put him out of his misery and showed them how to do it again. After that, they paid attention and suddenly Dane's lectures didn't seem so bad.

On Saturday, an ENSA show came to Béthenville and took over a local theatre. On Sunday night, transport was laid on for the squadron personnel to get there. Three Bedford trucks stopped outside the theatre and a mix of ranks piled out. The groundcrew had worked hard all week and Winwright felt it was only fair they had a reward just as much as the aircrew. They scampered inside to avoid the rain that still came down in sheets. The huge hall was bustling. Army and RAF uniforms were predominant but a few civilians were scattered here and there.

The red Mathis turned the corner and pulled up in a side street next to the theatre. It lurched forward as Locke put on the handbrake.

"Sorry," he said. "I'm still getting used to the blasted thing."

"Don't worry, it's got its little ways," assured Laura, patting him on the knee. He got out and rushed round to her side of the car, holding up an umbrella. She pecked him on the cheek as she got out and took the umbrella from him. "Thank you darling."

He opened another umbrella and held it up as Lorraine and Hagen got out of the back. Hagen said thanks and huddled under it, his arm around Lorraine's waist. When Locke had offered a lift, Hagen had jumped at the opportunity.

They walked into the theatre and found seats as far from the rest of the squadron as they could. Laura was excited, Lorraine curious. Locke and Hagen were expecting an evening of pure torture. The ENSA shows were not exactly known for their stunning quality. There was a running joke that it stood for *'Every Night Something Awful',* but tonight promised something a cut above the usual. Jack Payne and his band were billed and a number of other acts that sounded halfway decent.

The hall started to fill up and Locke looked around. A Pathé news crew were busy setting up in one of the boxes to the right of the stage. A pilot Locke recognised from his training days sat down next to them. He was stocky with a studied air. His dark hair was cropped short and he had supplemented his uniform with a silk scarf around his neck.

"Tuppy Jones, what a surprise."

"Good lord, Alexander Locke, good to see you." They shook hands and Locke did the introductions.

"Still with 105?" Locke asked casually once they had settled in their seats. Jones shook his head.

"No, I'm an acting Flight Commander now with 295 near Arras." He tapped his shoulder epaulettes and Locke saw the two and a half bars of a Squadron Leader. Jones offered Locke a small cardboard box. "Peanut?" he asked. Locke took a handful. "What bloody horrible weather," Jones observed. "I take it you're as bogged down as we are?"

"The best way I can describe it, is a swamp old boy. God knows when we'll be up once the weather clears."

"If it's any consolation, we're no better. If we have any more rain we'll be able to swim to Berlin."

Locke laughed, Jones hadn't changed.

The lights dimmed and an announcer came on stage to cheers from the crowd. He was a small, dapper chap looking woefully out of place in khaki battledress with a pencil thin moustache.

"Evening all!" he shouted to the throng. He rubbed his hands together with glee. "Tonight, ladies and gentlemen, we have music for you to enjoy. We have the wonderful Jack Payne and his orchestra to entertain. We also have the Alexis troupe of dancers and the lovely voice of Rosalind McAllister." He held up a finger for quiet. "But first, we have some laughs for you from; Arnold Clarke."

He dashed from the stage to applause and was replaced by a stocky man with a big smile and dark framed spectacles.

"Well, well, well. A room full of people just for little old me." He made a show of looking left and right before beckoning everyone to listen. "You know what, the other day I was walking down the street and a man comes up to me. 'Here,' he says, 'wanna buy a watch?' and he opens his coat. I couldn't look, didn't know what way to turn. He's still stood there, and he's got his coat open; so I snatch a peek see?"

The room dissolved into mirth. He kept up the patter, talking like a machine gun. Keeping just that side of the blue line, it was exactly the kind of thing the soldiers liked. He had their attention. He was no Max Miller but he was good.

After ten minutes, his routine was over and he ran off the stage with a cheery wave and applause. The compère came back on and whipped the crowd up some more. The curtains parted and an orchestra started to play a brisk dance number. The applause hit the roof when a line of dancers came on. They wore emerald green dresses that were low cut with acres of leg on display.

They did two numbers and then Jack Payne took centre stage. He was tall, with an easy manner. He was dressed to the nines in a smart suit and had his hair brylcreemed down. He came forward, leading his band in a variety of popular numbers. He finished his segment with '*Underneath the Spanish Stars*' and '*Pagan Serenade*' before the interval.

The rest of the show was more variety performances. The dancers came on again to more cheers and the show finished with Rosalind McAllister. She was the classic English rose, pale skin, dark hair, not amazingly beautiful, but pretty. Backed by the dancers, she closed out the show with a new song, '*We'll Meet Again*'. It was a sad song but nostalgic for home. The audience lapped it up, giving her a standing ovation that nearly brought the house down. She took three encores before exiting off stage.

The lights came up and Locke blinked at the sudden change. He stretched like a cat and stood up, helping Laura to her feet.

"That was wonderful, darling." She kissed him lightly on the cheek. "Absolutely super."

He hooked an arm and she took it as he escorted her out of the theatre through the crowd. They waited in a corner of the lobby until the press of bodies had gone by. Laura leaned in close, nesting in his arms. Her perfume swirled around him and he rested his chin on her head. He saw Hagen and Lorraine come out and waved to attract their attention.

Lorraine took them to a small coffee shop a few streets away. They sat under an awning around a small cast iron table while the rain continued to come down. Locke nursed a coffee while Hagen enjoyed a beer. Lorraine and Laura had a cigarette over a glasss of red. Laura coughed after trying a

Gauloises and handed it back. She rummaged in her little clutch bag for a packet of Wills and lit one to take the edge off the strong tobacco.

"That wasn't a bad show," said Locke.

"I've seen worse," agreed Hagen. He smiled in memory of an entertainment show he had seen in Cairo. That had been an embarrassment with a juggler and a so called comedian being the only highlights. However, when not many entertainers travelled so far, so you took what you could get.

It was a relaxing way to round out what had been a blank of a week. By the time the weekend had rolled around, the troops were thoroughly browned off. Half of them had gone on leave and come back and the other half swapped over. Some went to Rheims, regaling everyone with tales of the Lion D'Or hotel, comfy beds, cheap champagne and willing female company. Others tried their luck elsewhere. Amiens was paid a visit, as was Saint Quentin, but they were dreary in comparison.

Both Locke and Hagen had spent their forty eight hour pass in Béthenville. With it raining so hard, they stayed in their respective apartments. Laura had slowly driven Locke mad, pouting at being stuck indoors. She had visions of quaint little French bistro's, a cafe lifestyle by the river, not biblical floods in a small provincial town.

Hagen on the other hand, had a much more relaxed time of it. Lorraine had laughed in good humour as he mangled Molière, dredging up some very rusty French language lessons from the depths of his memory. She tried introducing him to Pastis but it was not to his taste. He stuck to the bottles of red she seemed to have on tap. Lorraine sketched him while he read and they talked about their past.

Lorraine was a true blue Parisian who had studied art and philosophy. Her father was a baker there and she had two siblings. Her older sister was married to a vigneron in Provence while her brother, Pierre, was an artilleryman on the Maginot Line. Hagen's tale was much shorter. He was an only child and his parents lived near Chester to run the family shipping business in Liverpool. She was fascinated when he told her about his time in Egypt and Mesopotamia. She had never been abroad but she had always dreamed of travelling to Rome and Greece and the Middle East.

The waiter brought a menu and they had dinner. Laura was delighted to talk about art with Lorraine while Locke and Hagen talked shop. Locke studied Hagen carefully while they talked. The change in him had been remarkable and he was glad. It was not nice seeing a good man's life turn into a train wreck of morbid fatalism. He was also glad that Laura had found a friend. His biggest concern with her being in France was what would happen when he was at the airfield and she was on her own.

After the meal, they took the ladies home and then drove back to the airfield. They took their time. The blackout on the headlamps dropped visibility down to nothing and they picked their way along the lanes in the dark.

1.20 – Twice Shy

The new week saw a break in the weather. The skies cleared, a brisk wind came in from the coast to blow the clouds away. The water drained off but it remained distinctly soggy underfoot. Every day, Winwright had a Blenheim wheeled out and run up to see if the field would take it. Every day the erks wheeled it back into the trees.

The temperature dropped like a stone. Everyone went from huddling against the rain, to huddling against the cold. Frost covered the grass and turned the damp tents stiff. A white quilt lay over the surrounding fields and the air turned crisp, making skin tingle. The sentries were given braziers and they sank into their greatcoats. Muffled in scarves, their breath formed great clouds in front of them while they stamped their feet and walked a beat.

Winwright didn't give a damn about the cold. The drop in temperature had turned the ground rock hard, so he had B Flight up at the first opportunity. Gardner took them on a navigation exercise to warmer climes down south. As soon as Wing knew the field was operational again, the squadron was tasked with a new recce job. One aircraft was required to fly along the Siegfried Line immediately. It was Arthur's turn in the rotation but B Flight weren't due back for another hour. Winwright picked Chandler to go in his place.

At first, he thought Kittinger was kidding, but the colour drained from his face when he realised the Adjutant was serious. His knife and fork crashed onto his plate and he clicked his tongue in annoyance.

"Why me? What about Pettifer? He's good."

"I dare say he is."

"But it's not my turn," he protested. Kittinger's face pinched in irritation.

"Oh, I agree entirely, old boy," he said off hand. He suddenly found something interesting on his jacket and buffed his nails against his chest. "But B Flight aren't here, so you're it I'm afraid."

Kittinger looked off to the horizon for a moment, then, in a fluid movement that belied his size, he sat down next to Chandler at the table. He spread his fingers in front of him.

"Look, he's not done one of these trips yet. You have. So there it is, old boy. Get over to the flight hut for a briefing, there's a good lad."

Chandler sat for a few moments, his jaw grinding, but there was not much he could do. He was briefed, gathered his crew and his gear and trailed out to one of the recce Blenheims. The aircraft was like an ice box inside. He wrapped an extra scarf round his neck and went through the start up procedures. The short nosed Blenheim took off into the mid afternoon sun, low on the horizon.

An hour later, they were passing close to Metz at twenty thousand feet.

The countryside was a dirty white patchwork quilt below them. North of the town, the land had flooded and the waterlogged fields glistened as they started to freeze over.

The cockpit was cold and Chandler kept one hand on the controls while he had his other tucked under his armpit. Morgan shivered next to him. At least in the cockpit they were covered. Morgan glanced back down the fuselage where Griffiths sat in his turret.

"The poor kid must be freezing back there," he said to Chandler. His pilot merely nodded and kept glancing at the instruments. His brow knotted as he looked at the temperatures. The port engine was running a little rough. He looked at the spinning disc of the propeller, the blades catching the sunlight. He juggled the throttle and watched the instruments. He gave them an experimental tap and watched the needles jump from the abuse.

The attack when it came was explosive. They came out of the sun, guns blazing. Griffiths caught a glimpse of two fighters as they screamed past, diving almost vertically. He just had time to catch the red, white and blue of the roundels before they were gone.

The first burst slammed into the port wing. The yoke jumped in Chandler's hands as the Blenheim bucked under the impact. It took about five seconds to realise they were flying a coffin that would kill them all if they stayed onboard.

"Bail out! Bail out!" he shouted over the R/T. He fought the controls, trying to keep her level and give them a fighting chance. The Blenhiem pulled to the left and went into a shallow dive as the propeller started to windmill. Chandler stamped on the pedal for full right rudder. He backed off the throttle on the starboard engine and struggled to keep everything on an even keel as they went down.

Morgan dropped everything and clipped on his parachute pack. Reaching down, he tugged on the escape hatch panel in the floor and pulled it into the cockpit. The sudden inrush of icy air hit him like a punch to the chest. He angled the hatch through the opening and threw it out. He was faced with a square opening that gave him a grandstand view of the ground below. He glanced forwards and saw the Blenheim was left wing down and sliding to port. He had to go now.

He braced himself at the edge of the hatch and hesitated for a moment. Less than a foot either side of the fuselage was the spinning disc of the propellors. He had a morbid fear of sliding out the hatch and getting cut into pieces. Chandler saw him pause and thumped him on the back. Morgan swallowed hard, screwed his eyes shut and went feet first through the hatch. He dropped free, tumbling end over end. The tail rushed over his head so close he actually flinched.

Griffiths didn't need telling twice. Even before Chandler told him to bail out he'd dropped down from his seat, clipped on his chute and gone for the hatch. He gave it two bangs and it popped free. A slim lad, he went out the hatch like a slippery eel.

Chandler fought a dying aircraft. The angle of the dive began to steepen even with the yoke pulled back into his stomach. He snatched a glance over his shoulder and saw Griffiths had gone. Keeping one hand on the controls, he reached above his head and yanked back the upper escape hatch. He unclipped his harness and flung the straps over his shoulders.

As soon as he took his feet off the rudder pedals, the Blenheim lurched. When he let go of the yoke, it nosed forwards into its final dive. He kicked off the instrument panel and reached for daylight.

The slipstream battered him and ripped the leather helmet off his head. The air was snatched from his lungs and he was jammed against the rear lip of the hatch. The yoke banged against his legs. He forced one arm free and summoned his strength, a surge of adrenalin coursing through him. His legs flailed, looking for a purchase inside the cockpit. He got one foot against something and shoved hard one last time.

He banged his head off the fuselage and saw stars as he fell towards the ground. He began to tumble as he fell, his view alternating between the sky and the ground. He flailed his arms, trying to steady himself, but that only made it worse. He passed through a cloud. It went dark and the cold moisture shocked him. He flinched when he broke out back into clear air.

He thrashed around, reaching for the ripcord. One finger found the cool metal of the D-ring. His fingers gripped it hard and he pulled for all it was worth. He counted to three and nothing happened. He was starting to think the parachute had failed when there was a loud crack above him. The harness straps dug into his crotch and then his balls were around his neck and he screamed in relief. He looked up and wept to see the parachute canopy deployed above him, a perfect circle of silk.

He looked around as he descended under the silken umbrella. He saw their Blenheim descending in a fast spiral. Tongues of flame started to trail from the port wing, then the main spar let go and she flew apart as she took the final plunge. The nose slammed into a field and the tanks erupted with a hollow thud.

He looked behind and saw two other parachutes higher up, drifting on the breeze just as he was. He waved his arms but they were too far away for him to see if they responded. Below was a wide river and he started tugging on the straps to try to steer away from it. The last thing he wanted was a dunking in the cold water. He got into a swaying motion, pulling on the straps like a kid on a swing. He built up a momentum and started to sweat, his arms tiring from the effort. He was slowly drifting away from the water but he kept it up, pulling and swaying and pulling some more until the river was behind him.

As he got lower he tried to remember the landing drill but his mind went blank. Landing in a ploughed field, the ground came up surprisingly fast and he tensed up. He hit hard, his knees thumping into his chest as he crumpled. Lying in a heap, he stared up at the sky, panting down big gulps of air. He'd heard someone say once that coming down by parachute was like floating with the angels. He disagreed. His groin burned like fire, his head hurt like hell and he was freezing.

A breeze got into the parachute and it dragged him backwards over the frozen ground. His feet flailed, scrabbling for grip until he got stuck in some bramble bushes. The thorns scratched at his face and hands while he struggled to find the harness release. He crawled out on his hands and knees as the branches tugged on his clothes.

Standing up, he looked around. To the east, beyond a small wood, a plume of smoke rose from the grave of the Blenheim. To the west, the two parachutes were low to the ground. Taking a bearing, he gathered up his own parachute and started walking towards them.

It took him an hour of tramping across frozen fields before he came across Griffiths. The young lad had some of his parachute tucked under his arm. The rest of it dragged behind him, like the train of a bride at church. He was pale, his lips blue and he hobbled as he walked, favouring his left leg.

"You okay?" asked Chandler.

"I'm all right, skipper. I just banged my ankle. I don't know if its bust or not." He sat down on his parachute and rubbed his leg. "Bloody hurts though."

He stretched his leg out and eased his boot off. His ankle was swollen, the skin already going purple but he could move it and there were no bones sticking out at a funny angle. His breath hitched in his throat as he tugged the boot back on, the pain shooting up his leg. Chandler helped him to his feet and they wrapped their parachutes around themselves, huddling in them for warmth as they walked.

They found Morgan trying to fish his parachute down from a tree. It was tangled in the upper branches and he was tugging on the lines to free it. A panel ripped and he cursed.

"Leave it, Aaron," suggested Chandler.

"I signed for this thing," muttered Morgan. He jumped up, trying to grab another line. "I'll be damned if my pay is being docked to pay for a new one."

Working together, they got it down but it was ripped to shreds and one or two panels remained in the tree. Morgan was moody as he gathered it into a bundle.

"How come the Jerries got the drop on us?" he asked aloud.

"It wasn't *my* fault," said Griffiths defensively. "They came out of the sun. And it wasn't the Jerries by the way, it was the bloody French."

"French?" said Morgan and Chandler in unison.

"I saw the roundels as they dived past us. I'm not sure of the type, but it was definitely Frog."

They shared a look when they heard that.

"Bastards," said Morgan, kicking at a stone. "That's twice they've done that now."

"This war isn't gonna last long if we're shooting each other down as fast as the Jerries do," mumbled Griffiths. His ankle burned like fire with each step and his boots were not helping much. Flying boots weren't made for trailing around the countryside. The thin leather uppers provided no support for his ankles as he gingerly picked his way over the ground.

They walked along on empty stomachs, cold and shivering. Morgan gave them a course to steer and they carried on walking until they got to a crossroads. The road signs had been removed but Morgan pointed confidently to the right fork. Griffiths and Chandler looked at him.

"You're sure?"

"Totally," Morgan said with conviction. Without waiting for them, he set off along the road.

The light was starting to go when they came across a farmhouse. It was built around a large courtyard with a high brick wall all the way round. A barn was in one corner, the farmhouse was in the other. A few lights could be seen behind the shutters. They got half way round the perimeter when a dog started barking. When they reached the entrance, they found a big German Shepherd in the yard. It was secured to a rope, straining to get free, its front paws waving around.

"Lovely," muttered Chandler.

"I like dogs," said Griffiths. "We've got one just like it on the farm."

"Then by all means go first," said Morgan. The young man hesitated and Morgan and Chandler gave him a shove in the back to put him over the threshold. He dumped his parachute on a cart and walked closer, his boots crunching on the gravel. The dog went nuts, gnashing its teeth, lunging on the rope, almost choking itself in its efforts to get a taste of him.

"Oh he likes you, Griff," shouted Morgan. "Give him a pat."

"Get lost...Sir," replied Griffiths in good humour.

A window in the farmhouse opened with a bang and a head appeared. The business end of a shotgun came into view. Griffiths stopped walking and held up his hands.

"Qui est là. Que voulez-vous?" asked the farmer.

"Bonjour Monsieur," shouted Chandler from the gate. "Pouvez-vous nous aider, nous sommes pilotes anglais."

There was a moment's pause while the farmer thought about that. He pointed the shotgun at Griffiths. He motioned for him to move over to the cart. Griffiths moved with alacrity. Chandler started talking faster.

"Monsieur, nous sommes pilotes Anglais. Nous avons besoin de votre aide."

There was a longer pause and then the farmer disappeared inside. They heard shouting inside the house, then the front door was wrenched open and he came into view again. He was a short, portly man wearing a dirty white shirt with no collar and brown breeches. He held a double barrelled shotgun in his beefy hands.

Chandler and Morgan dropped their parachutes and held up their hands. The shotgun flicked and they shuffled over to stand next to Griffiths. A boy came out of the farmhouse with a torch. He turned it on them. They blinked under its harsh glare but didn't move, they were still looking down the dark end of the shotgun.

There was some muttering between father and son and the boy snapped off the torch. He ran across the yard to the snarling animal and took it in hand. The dog pulled him back in double quick time. The closer it got, the more it snarled. The three of them leaned back, their shoulder blades rubbing against the cart. The boy cuffed the dog and it quietened down. It threw them the occasional growl while it sniffed around their legs, nose buried in their crotch. The torch flicked on again and their arms inched higher.

"Cochon, Boche!"

There was a rapid flurry of 'non' and shaking of heads.

"Anglais, Anglais, Anglais," babbled Griffiths, promptly backed up by Chandler and Morgan.

The shotgun dug into Chandler's chest and shoved his Sidcot open. First one side, then the other was explored. The same happened with Griffiths and then Morgan. Luckily for them, Morgan had his tunic on underneath his flying suit. The brass RAF buttons on his chest convinced the farmer that all was well.

In a moment, his mood changed and he was all smiles. They were hugged in turn and kissed in the European way. He patted them on the back and hustled them towards the farmhouse. His son was instructed to sort out the parachutes. He carried them into the barn while the three fliers were given prime position around the fire. Madame was roused from her parlour and she busied herself in the kitchen. She brought them some cheese and began hacking into a loaf of bread.

"Good job you had your tunic on underneath, sir," whispered Griffiths. He hitched closer to the fire and spread his fingers. They tingled and he rubbed them to get some feeling into them.

"Never travel without it, Griffiths. You never know when it might come in handy."

The young man shot a look at the German Shepherd that lay flat on the floor next to them, its muzzle between its paws. Its ears were flat to its head, happy to be inside in the warm instead of out in the yard.

"Rotten brute," muttered Griffiths. "I thought it was going to have my balls for breakfast."

"I wouldn't worry," Chandler reassured him. "The French are all about equality." He tried stroking the dog's ears but it opened one eye and quietly rumbled at him. He put his hand back in his lap. "It wouldn't go for a working class boy like you; it'll want to take a bite out of me or Aaron here."

The farmer put steaming hot mugs of coffee in front of them. Another log went on the fire and the flames intensified. For the first time that day, they relaxed and the tension eased away.

1.21 – Breaking Bread

Winwright looked at the house for a moment before going in. It stood in its own enclosed garden, a gravel drive leading from the road. A three storey house, it had the sturdy proportions of typical French provincial buildings. The tall windows had their wooden shutters closed and curved stairs with cast iron railings led up to a first floor landing and the front door.

The air was bitingly cold and his cheeks tingled after getting out of the warm interior of the car. He huddled deeper into his greatcoat and retrieved the bottle wrapped in brown paper from the front passenger seat. He walked up the steps and rapped on the door, his gloved hand clattering off the shutter.

There was a moment's pause and then the door opened. Winwright looked down at a young girl, no more than ten years old. He smiled at her and she gave him a slight bob or curtsey before running off to the right. She shouted for her mother as she disappeared through a door into a warmly lit kitchen. Conscious of the blackout, Winwright stepped into the wide hall and closed the door behind him. About fifteen feet wide and thirty or so deep, it had a high ceiling and stairs in front of him. His footsteps echoed off the stone flagged floor while he paced in small circles. A female face appeared momentarily at the doorway to the kitchen and he heard hushed discussion coming from inside the room.

"Wing Commander," said Valerie in greeting as he came through the door to the left. His hands were held out in welcome as he walked towards him, limping as ever, favouring his good leg. "How good to see you again."

Valerie was dressed in casual trousers and a white shirt, open at the neck. He took the bottle from Winwright and pulled it out of its brown paper wrapping. He gave the label on the green bottle an appraising stare. He raised his eyebrows and nodded in appreciation when he saw the name of the vineyard.

"Chateau Sisqueille, 1930. Very nice." He examined the bottle again in pleasure, seeing the dark liquid swirling in the neck under the cork. He put a hand on Winwright's shoulder and led him to the left towards the study. "How was your day?"

On his first visit, Valerie had given Winwright the grand tour of the house, all smiles and bonhomie. They had avoided the kitchen. It was his wife's domain and Valerie explained that if they showed their faces in there, they would only be ordered out anyway. Upstairs were the bedrooms, on the first floor, the kitchen and living room and dining room. The living room led through to a conservatory at the rear of the house and a small room which Valerie used as his office. Downstairs were the storerooms and the garage for his car.

The dinner bell rang and they went through to the dining room to find

Valerie's daughters laying the table. Winwright relaxed in a warm and welcoming house. After weeks with the squadron, it made a pleasant change to see normal family life again. He sat in the middle position of a long mahogany table. Valerie would be at its head, his wife at the other end and his children across from Winwright. It was a splendid table, a long formal dining table in the neoclassical style. The square tapering legs ended in clawed feet. In the centre of the polished top was an olive wreath surrounding an N topped with an eagle inlaid in maple wood.

"I didn't know you were a Bonapartist," he commented.

"Ah, an antique from my grandmother," said Valerie with a flash of recollection. He ran his hand across the top of the table. "A different day. You have your empire, and we had ours." He smiled wistfully as he drank some Cognac. "We would have been on opposite sides of the conflict then. What would you have been, do you think?"

Winwright pondered that for a moment. He thought about his youth, playing with tin soldiers, seeing paintings at the gallery. One hot summer, he'd gone charging around the fields with his friends waving toy swords around.

"I'd have been a cavalryman I think," he said finally. "The Scots Greys, thundering over the ground."

Valerie could understand the sentiment. Cavalry were the fliers of their age, glamorous, wearing flash uniforms. It was far better than being a foot slogger marching from one end of Europe to the other following Napoleon.

"I would have been a cavalryman too," Valerie agreed, "but not a heavy Dragoon, nor a Cuirassier or Carabinier, I think. They were the tanks of the battlefield." He pointed to an etching on the wall in a small frame. "I always wanted to be a Lancer. They were scouts you see, out ahead of the army, looking for the enemy." He rapped his knuckles on his bad leg. "Then I was a scout too, in my little fighter over the lines."

"Pappa?" said his daughter. He glanced across the room and his eldest daughter gestured at the table. Silverware glittered under candlelight and white table cloths and napkins shone bright and clean.

"Bon, Eloise. Bon, Estelle." He gave each of them a kiss on the cheek. "Very good." Laughing, they rushed out, calling for their mother.

"Fine girls," said Winwright, meaning it. The first time he'd dined here, they had been absent. Valerie nodded his thanks.

"Eloise can be wild, you know."

"She takes after her father perhaps?" Winwright offered; his tone light and teasing.

"She wants to learn to fly. And you?"

"Two boys, five and three. They tear around the house, causing mayhem in their wake for their mother and me."

"It gets no better as they get older, let me assure you," said Valerie. He topped up his glass from the bottle in the drinks cabinet. He was about to take another sip when Valerie's wife, Edith, came bustling into the room, wagging her finger at him in admonishment. They sat down and dinner was served by two servants.

The starter was a pork rillette, a classic from the Loire valley where Madame Valerie hailed. Warm fresh bread and great slabs of butter accompanied it and they washed it down with a nice smooth red wine. It might have been expensive. Winwright had no idea; he was no connoisseur when it came to wine.

Chandler broke open another loaf of bread and smothered it in butter. Crumbs fell to the floor and a chicken clucked around his feet, pecking at the offerings that fell around it.

Griffiths slid down his seat, his hunger sated. The warmth of the fire penetrated his bones and his eyelids drooped. The adrenalin of the day was wearing off and fatigue was hitting him hard.

Monsieur Dubreton had been more than hospitable. His wife had opened her larder to them. They didn't have much, but for three hungry fliers it was more than enough. The cheese was good, strong in flavour. Morgan took great delight in crunching on shallots like apples.

They talked amongst themselves for a while, Griffiths telling them again about what he saw falling out of the sky, guns blazing. Morgan shuddered at the thought of copping a packet from their own side. How stupid, how futile it would all have been to earn a clutch of French bullets. He thought about what his epitaph would be; then he thought about the parachute. The torn remains sat in a cart in the barn. He wondered if his pay would get docked after all.

Monsieur Dubreton came over with an earthenware jug and some glasses and sat down beside them. He shooed the dog to one side. It grudgingly moved an inch and settled its muzzle across Griffiths' boots. In the last hour, Griffiths and the dog had come to a better understanding. He stroked its head, running his fingers through the smooth fur.

"Mon amis," Dubreton handed each of them a worn and clouded glass and poured from the jug. Under the flickering light of the fire his eyes glittered with intensity as he looked at each of them. He had seen their like in the newsreels, these brave fliers, but he never imagined he would have them in his parlour. It had been a long time since he'd heard a shot fired in anger.

He gestured to Griffiths' ankle and the young man lifted it out of the water. The bruising had gone a lurid purple and the muscles were swollen. The pain had subsided into a dull throb. He flinched when he tried flexing his ankle and Dubreton laughed uproariously.

He lifted his string vest and pointed to his portly stomach. It was covered in dark swarthy hair but there was a pattern of lurid scars across the skin. He used hand gestures to describe a large explosion. Before they could respond, he lifted one trouser leg to show another scar that ran down his left calf. He pointed to a dust covered photo on the wooden mantelpiece. A thin young man, swamped in his uniform, stared back at the camera, rifle slung over his shoulder. There was a helmet hanging by its strap next to the photo.

"You?" asked Chandler, pointing at the farmer. The older man laughed again and nodded, pointing to himself.

"Oui, moi. Le vaillant guerrier."

They raised their glasses in salute of each other.

The main course was a rich dish of rabbit stew. It was brought into the dining room in a large cast iron pot where it rested on a side table. Steam rose from the pot and Winwright's stomach growled in hunger. The aroma filled the room and got his taste buds going. Big chunks of carrot and potato were surrounded by a thick sauce glossy with butter. The rabbit was done to a turn and Winwright found himself asking Edith for more, much to her delight.

She was younger than Valerie, rosy cheeked and energetic. She wore a dress of blue velvet with her hair pinned up and a string of pearls around her neck. An attractive woman and a good fit for her husband. Winwright was quite jealous when he saw them look with affection for one another across the table.

The daughters asked him questions and he answered as best he could, Valerie translating. Edith asked a question and Winwright looked to Valerie.

"She asks, how long you have been married?"

"Ten years." He fished in his pocket and pulled out his wallet. He held out three small photographs and the family passed them round. The girls cooed over his two sons, James and William.

He looked at his wife's photo as he tucked it back into his wallet. It was an informal photo taken at the beach on the south coast last summer. In the build up to the war, leave had been scarce. He'd managed to snatch a week with the family just before the whole mess at Munich had blown up. They'd gone down to the beach with the children and did their best to ignore the shadows of war looming on the horizon.

Just after she was handing out the sandwiches, he caught her with the camera, a sneaky shot as she called it. He called her name and she turned to look right at the camera, at him. Her eyes were smiling from under the wide brim of her floppy straw hat.

He thought about when they first met all those years ago, in Trafalgar square. Returning from his posting to Egypt, he was visiting London, a city he had always thought about but never seen. He first saw her walking across from the National Portrait Gallery.

Their eyes had met and she saw him, standing by the fountain under Nelsons Column. Tall and bronzed in a linen suit, he was quite out of place amongst all the bowler hats and pin stripes of London. He waved at her impulsively. Thinking she knew him, she stopped and he walked over to introduce himself. He took her to lunch and then walked her back to her office before meeting her again that evening. They married eight months later.

There was a pause while the girls cleared the dishes away. Edith bustled off into the kitchen, issuing instructions for the dessert. It was a strawberry savarin with rhubarb syrup that Winwright found just divine. The savarin was a light sponge soaked in syrup served with strawberries mixed with sugar and framboise. Edith had topped it with thick cream and Winwright's stomach surrendered long after it should have done. He complimented them on the food and Valerie's wife beamed when he asked for the recipe to send to Margaret.

They retired to Valerie's private room after the meal. One wall was floor to ceiling bookshelves. A desk, similar in style to his dining table, was parked in the opposite corner, covered in paperwork. Two plush leather upholstered armchairs stood on an oriental rug in front of a low burning fire.

Winwright got the fire going while Valerie pulled out some cigars from a desk in his drawer. They took one each and lit them from a taper from the fire. Sweet smelling smoke swirled around them and it lacked the harsh bitter edge of some Virginian tobacco. Winwright nodded.

"Good cigar."

"Bon, I'm glad you like it. A Turkish blend. I find they go down well with brandy."

Valerie opened the glass door of the bookshelf in the corner and pulled out a bottle of Napoleon brandy and two crystal glasses. They sat down in the armchairs, cradling the glasses in their lap.

Valerie hitched forwards in the seat and eased his leg, the stump throbbing. It was going to be a harsh winter; he knew that with a certainty. Whenever his leg ached, bad weather was sure to follow.

"Thank you for this evening," said Winwright. "A lovely home and family." Valerie was warmed by the compliment.

"Thank you. I'm a lucky man in many ways. If it wasn't for this," he rapped his knuckles on his false leg, "my life would have been very different."

"How so?"

"Because I swore I was going to leave France, get away from all the filth of the war."

"And what changed?"

"I did, Arthur, I did."

His glance flicked to an aerial photograph of Béthenville over the mantelpiece. It had been taken near the end of the war. The land was a pockmarked ruin, a latticework of destruction.

He cast his mind back to that day in February 1919, limping to the town to find it a ruined shell. Here and there a few pieces of rubble stood, but it was if the gods had come to earth and scoured the surface clean. He'd planned to leave France for the overseas colonies. As he walked, shocked among the ruined streets, a grim determination grew within him. They were his people; his family had lived here for generations. He couldn't turn his back on the place he'd grown up. So he had turned his hand to renewal, to rebuilding rather than destruction.

"How is life at the airfield?"

"Cold," said Winwright lightly. They both laughed. It was a bad joke but it fitted the mood. "But you've made it bearable Francois. I don't know how we would have managed without your help."

"Oh it was nothing. I'm just sorry there was not more we could do."

"Well, it *is* appreciated. Warm food goes a long way to keeping up morale and the people of the town have been very accommodating."

Valerie shrugged. More than one shopkeeper had said similar things in the last few weeks. With the Blenheim unit and the other squadrons based nearby, there was a lot of new money coming into the town. It was a welcome boost to strained finances and high taxes.

Winwright was sombre and he sipped his brandy slowly. Valerie watched him quietly. There was worry there, something he had already seen at the funeral. Valerie reflected on his own experiences of war and he could see what was bothering Winwright without him even saying. He had a crew missing and their fate weighed heavily upon him.

Valerie had seen it take off that lunchtime himself. He had heard it first, the throb of the twin Mercury engines amongst the trees. Then he saw it, climbing into the cold sky. It had not come back. On its own, that meant little. It might have flown to England, it might be at another airfield somewhere, but he did not think so. If that had happened, they would be safe and Winwright's look told him otherwise. They were missing.

It was hard, he knew, sending men up not knowing if any of them would be coming back. Valerie had always thought that war was hard for people with imagination. One more for the slab, fresh meat for the grinder, gone west, they used to say. These were common phrases. Men with imagination used phrases and slang to hide behind, but at night, on their own, they had to face themselves. The cold ones, the killers found it easy, but Francois never had and it was plain Winwright was the same.

"You have a crew missing, yes?" he murmured, breaking the silence.

"How the deuce did you know that?"

Valerie gave him a wan smile.

"Please, Arthur. When aircraft take off and don't return, people gossip, in the towns, the villages." He swirled the brandy around the glass and then drank from it, "People thrive on gossip."

Winwright paused, hesitant. He shot the older man a searching look which was returned with equanimity. He thought he was a good judge of character. You had to be to navigate the politics of the Royal Air Force. To climb the ladder up to squadron level and beyond, you had to know how to play the game. He couldn't talk about this with Saundby; he'd think he had lost his nerve. Ashton or Gardner would have seen it as weakness. He felt he could trust Valerie and he needed someone to share this with.

"You forget, I commanded a squadron too; once upon a time," Valerie murmured.

"I have an aircraft and three men missing."

Monsieur Dubreton bid them goodnight and closed the door of the barn behind him. Griffiths snuggled down amongst the hay. He was warm and dry and there were plenty of other places he could be that night. Come the morning, Chandler was going to find a French army unit nearby and rustle up some transport to take them back to the squadron. It sounded a lot better than walking all the way back.

Winwright shook Valerie's hand warmly as he left. The talk had helped. It felt good to get that off his chest and he looked forward to a new day. He took the country lanes slowly. The black out headlamps provided next to no help and he was glad that the night sky was crystal clear. The thin slither of crescent moon provided a small amount of light as he drove.

His head was buzzing from the brandy and wine and he wound the window down. Mixing drinks was never a good idea but Valerie's wife had laid a good table, it would have been rude to say no. He gasped with the cold rushing into the car but he kept his head near the opening, letting the frigid air work its magic.

123

1.22 – Ghosts

Burke sat by the side of the stream, surrounded by tall grass. He tucked the scarf a little tighter around his neck and picked up the rod. He doubted there were many fish in the water, but you never knew. On the far bank there was a large overhanging clump of bushes low to the water. He saw a few midges dancing on the surface in the shade. He put a chunk of bully beef on the hook and then swung the line into the water. There was a small plop when it landed mid stream so he hauled it in again and cast it further. His wrist flicked on each backward stroke until the bait landed close to the far bank.

His breath frosted on the morning breeze. He liked this time of day, mid morning. All the chaos of the day had subsided, people had their tasks and there was a pause, a small space for contemplation.

The men looked to him to solve their problems. The door is always open he told them and he meant it, but it also meant that he had little time to himself. On Sundays he liked to go a short distance from the field, a chance for quiet reflection. He had no set plan on these days. He would just do as his mood wanted. Today, he wanted some time beside the river.

He remembered fishing as a boy a long time ago. He'd fished in a number of rivers since then, all over the world, but he always remembered the canal at home. It ran along the back of the shops, with the butchers at the end of the row. The water was murky and god knows what had been dumped in it, but it broke up the jungle of houses and back alleys.

A path ran alongside the canal and a bench seat had been put there. He'd go there during his lunch break from the butchers. He'd sit on the bench, having his sandwiches, watching the water flow by. Occasionally, a canal boat would chug by and he sometimes dreamed of what it would be like to just leave on one of them.

Life among those streets was all he ever knew growing up. In his spare time he tinkered with a battered motorbike. He'd spent hours taking the engine apart again and again. He smiled when he remembered its purr, the cylinders firing as smooth as silk. He had a way of keeping it running, knowing its little quirks and foibles. He was always better with machines than people.

When he was old enough, he had gone down to the recruiting office. He knew his parents wanted other things for him, but he refused to just sit, waiting for the conscription notice to come. He didn't want to be called up as an infantryman, just one more life to be fed into the grinder that was the western Front. He wanted to keep control of his own life, so he turned to the Royal Flying Corps. They'd jumped on his mechanical experience and he soon found himself servicing aircraft in France.

When the war ended, he stayed in the service. The thought of going back to Halifax horrified him. His horizons had grown much broader during his time away. His CO pulled some stings and he was packed off to Russia to help the White Russians against the Bolsheviks.

He wound the line back in and looked at the hook. The fish must have been very cunning because the bully beef was gone. He tried a hunk of bread instead and flicked the hook back into the water. The line jerked slightly. Bubbles appeared on the surface. He placed a hand on the rod, making his movements slow and deliberate.

The line jerked again. He watched it carefully, his eyes never straying from the water. He picked up the rod and gripped it in both hands. He tensed, his senses poised. The line jerked again and he struck. He jerked the tip of the rod up and pulled hard. There was a momentary resistance and then it pulled free. The line went slack and he reeled in an empty line. He was a patient man. He put another chunk of bread on the hook and cast the line again.

A short time later, he heard an aero engine and peered into the sky. He shaded his eyes from the sun and saw a Tiger Moth climbing away from the field. It did a few lazy S turns and then headed north, the noise of its engine growing faint.

After an hour, there had been no more nibbles on the line, so he had lunch. He opened his flask to see what the cookhouse had given him. Tomato soup. He poured some into the cup and dug out a hunk of bread from his gas mask bag. He broke the bread into chunks and dipped it into the soup.

A sprightly laugh floated on the breeze and Burke looked around. It seemed to come off to his left and he squinted through the grass.

He saw two people walking along the side of the river. As they got closer, he could see RAF blue on one of them. He was sure of it. Burke twisted his face in annoyance. He'd gone fishing to get away from everyone else.

Flying Officer Locke and a woman appeared over the rise. It took Burke a moment to recognise Locke's wife. They were walking arm in arm. She was wrapped up in a heavy coat with a scarf around her neck.

The wife spotted him first and waved. Face frozen, Burke waved weakly in return. He ground his teeth in anticipation for the social faux pas to come. He got to his feet, brushing crumbs off his greatcoat. When Locke was within a few paces he came to attention and saluted. Locke returned it and they stood in an awkward silence. Locke rubbed his gloved hands together.

"Mister Burke."

"Sir. Going for a walk?"

"We are." Locke glanced at the rod and empty net. "Any bites?"

"Not yet, sir. Weathers a bit cold, I think."

There were some forced smiles as they stood looking at each other. Burke's jaws ached from smiling.

"Oh, Mister Burke, may I present my wife, Laura. Laura, this is Warrant Officer Burke."

She held out a small gloved hand and Burke shook it briefly.

"Charmed," she said; her voice light and cheerful. There was a faint hint of Norfolk in the way she rolled her vowels.

"Not a thing Mister Burke can't fix," said Locke, full of praise. Burke blushed and looked at his shoes.

"Well, maybe not everything, sir, but we do our best."

More silence. Laura Locke looked from one to the other, wondering at the quiet. Burke smiled again. Locke cleared his throat then broke the silence.

"Well, we won't keep you. Enjoy yourself."

There were nods all round, then Locke and his wife carried on walking. Burke watched them go. He stood there, rod in hand and did a full circuit, looking to see if anyone else was coming. Satisfied he was on his own, he sat back down, settling himself on the grass.

The soup in the cup had gone cold. He tipped it onto the grass and poured himself some more while he thought about the happy couple.

She was a pretty young thing, to be sure. Locke had done well there and she had money too, if you believed the gossip doing the rounds. But he couldn't help wondering that having her so near must have been a distraction. Over the years, he had seen a number of long faces when relationships foundered. There were plenty of young men whose heads had been turned by a pair of legs only for it all to end in tears. He wasn't immune, it had happened to him once, and once was enough.

It had been in Iraq in 1928. He was a Sergeant then, servicing Vickers Victories for 70 Squadron. She had been the wife of a civil servant. Angela Rutherford had been her name. Lured by the glamour of the job title, she'd found that the reality of being a civil servant's wife was a pale shadow of the dream. The man she married was not the man she had to live with. Her husband liked brandy, bridge and cricket in that order. He considered it sacred that women were good only for breeding and looking pretty on his arm at the embassy.

Burke had been her salvation and their time together was the great passion of his life. As the relationship had intensified, things began to unravel. Her husband became suspicious and finally, Burke had ended it. A scandal would have ended his career. He wasn't an officer. He didn't have the connections to survive the fallout from something like that. The RAF was his life and he could only serve one master. He wangled himself a posting to Aden to get away. Of course, it wasn't his fault he told her. *Exigencies of the service etc, awfully sorry.* He never saw her again.

Looking back, he often wondered at the what ifs and the might have beens if he'd stayed with her. It was interesting how some decisions had such an impact on the future. Like ripples in a pond, he thought. He picked up a clod of earth and threw it into the stream, watching the ripples in the water radiate outwards.

While the young married couple had gone for a walk, Lorraine had dragged Hagen off the airfield in the Mathis to a small inn a few miles away. They'd arranged to meet Locke and his wife there later. Hagen parked the car while she dashed inside and roused the innkeeper on this cold day.

They had the place to themselves and she took over the seats in a cubby hole near the fire, away from any curious eyes. Hagen positioned the two seat sofa closer to the small table in front of them. The innkeeper brought over a bottle and some glasses and Hagen put some money on the table.

Hagen held up his glass, looking at the swirling red liquid inside. The fire sparkled through it, a kaleidoscope of light.

"To us," he said.

"To us," she agreed.

He leaned back, arranging the pillows to build his nest and she curled up next to him. He put his arm around her shoulders and she leaned in. He stroked up and down her back, his thumb making small circles in a steady rhythm. He dozed for a while, not quite asleep but alert to the slightest change. Lorraine sat peacefully, listening to the beat of his heart.

They never talked about the future when they were together. No hard rule had ever been agreed, it was just an unconscious thing they had settled on. They lived in the now and the other things would have to take a number. She knew the risks that lurked unspoken in the background and tomorrow could take care of itself.

She couldn't remember if it was Henri or Martin who had first shown her this inn. Their faces had blurred into the past along with the heartache. When Henri had died she did not think it was possible to feel such pain, she'd felt numb for a long time. Then Martin had wiped the tears away, but he had died too, in a stupid accident. She felt her eyes glisten and she rubbed her palm across her face, careful not to disturb Mark. That was the past; she had no more space left for regrets.

The small Tiger Moth took off into the brisk wind and clawed into the sky. Getting up to height, Winwright leaned forward and patted Valerie on the shoulder. The Frenchmen nodded and gave him a thumbs up. Winwright sat back, a little nervous and balled his hands in his lap. Valerie had listened intently when he was shown the controls, face screwed up in concentration.

He had turned up as arranged at ten on the dot, his excitement written across his face. For Winwright, a promise made, was a promise kept. He tried not to think about how many regulations he was bending. He had to smile when Valerie had emerged from his car dressed in his old uniform of dark blue tunic and red trousers. Rummaging in the back of his car, he came up with flying gear you saw in Great War photographs. It was almost comical, but Valerie didn't seem to mind.

He boarded the biplane and swung his wooden leg into the cockpit. Groundcrew helped him strap in. He tugged on an old leather flying helmet that could easily have doubled as a teapot cosy. Settling his goggles into place, he gestured to Winwright and pointed to the sky.

They circled once before Winwright handed over control. Grasping the stick with firm assurance, the Frenchman thrilled at the vibration of the airframe. His one fear regarding his leg had proven unfounded. With his false leg fitted below the knee, he still had all the movement he needed to use the rudder and maintain positive control.

He let his senses range. The tang of burnt oil and exhaust was on his tongue and in his nose. His ears were battered by the roar of the engine. If he closed his eyes he could be back over the western Front again.

He advanced the throttle and tried some gentle sweeping turns. He found he needed to use the rudder to counter some adverse yaw. The controls were heavier than he was used to and he missed the hair trigger response of his old Nieuport 17. Now there was a thoroughbred. She had her foibles and you had to watch yourself in a dive with that delicate lower wing, but she would have flown rings around the Tiger Moth.

He tried some more gentle turns, using positive force on the stick to overcome the slow aileron response. Smiling, he levelled off and checked the sky around him before looking down. It was clear out to the horizon and the airfield was behind them.

Turning to port, he let the nose descend below the horizon, letting the speed build up to over a hundred knots. Touching one twenty, he hauled the stick back. Gravity shoved him into his seat and he grunted as the Tiger Moth climbed into the sky. Tensing his legs to help keep the blood in the right place, he kept a firm grip on the jumping stick in his hand. Coming over the top, he strained to lift his head and look over the mainplane at the land below. The countryside was a patchwork quilt underneath him. In his mind's eye he overlaid his memories of the war. The ground had been a puzzle of zigzag lines of the trenches surrounded by a quagmire of mud and shell holes from the relentless artillery.

Dipping the wing to starboard, he saw Béthenville laid out like a street map. In the centre was the square and the tall belfry. Seeing the town from the air made him realise just how much the land had been healed. The town had been a shattered shell when he came back from the war. It had taken a long time to make things right.

France had suffered horribly both during and after the war. Now it was happening again and he wondered what the price would be this time. The country wasn't ready for this; he knew that in his heart. Twenty years of peace had sapped her will and what the war had not accomplished, militant politics and deep social divisions had finished the job.

One of Napoleon's greatest maxims was that attack was the best form of defence, but there was no desire for war this time. Hiding behind the Maginot Line had promoted an almost defeatist air amongst his compatriots and that left him ashamed. They would stand and fight, but he wondered if it would be enough.

His war had ended on a cold autumn day not unlike this one in 1917. With a bullet in his shoulder and riding a damaged airplane down, his engine had quit on him coming in to land. The Nieuport stalled and nosed in just short of the field. The starboard wing had been ripped off and what was left of his fighter had speared into the canal bank. They'd fished him out of the wreckage half drowned and he'd spent the next six months in an army hospital, minus half a leg.

His temper stoked with a cold fury that his leg would keep him from the fighting that was to come. Temperature rising, he rolled the Tiger Moth onto her back and dived for the ground. Winwright clung on to the sides of the cockpit and let Valerie have his head. If he hadn't flown for nearly twenty years, then he would probably have been the same.

Valerie throttled back and eased the nose up slightly, keeping the airspeed below the maximum dive velocity. He began a spin, letting the G forces build up, fighting against the pressure on his chest and head. At one thousand feet he pulled out, the air screeching through the bracing wires.

He topped a rise and then bottomed out over a field. Aiming for some trees running parallel to the river, he banked hard over and squeezed the little trainer down the avenue. Going just over one hundred knots wasn't very fast, but when trees were only a few feet away from your wingtips, it added a whole new dimension to a person's perception.

Winwright leaned left in his seat and looked down the side of the fuselage. They were coming up fast on an army motorbike sidecar combination. The rider was oblivious to their presence but the passenger looked over his shoulder and almost fell out of the sidecar. He thumped the rider on the shoulder and pointed back down the lane at them.

Valerie laughed to himself as the motorbike and sidecar wobbled along the road, the rider frantically looking back. He held the course for a few more seconds to put the fear of god on them and then zoomed into the sky. He rolled off the top and then set course back to the airfield.

Circling round to come into the wind, he set up for a landing. When there was no nudge on the shoulder, he realised Winwright was going to let him bring it in. Coming in a bit high, the Tiger Moth sideslipped and then settled in for a perfect three pointer, running over the grass. Valerie ran the length of the field and then taxied back up to the huts.

When the propeller windmilled to a stop, Valerie levered himself out of the cockpit. He almost floated to the ground, elated from the flight. He turned to face Winwright as the Wing Commander joined him.

"Ma foi!" He breathed deep and patted his chest. "Thank you, Arthur. That was a rare experience, to fly again. It has been a long time, too long I think."

Winwright steered him towards the flight hut.

"That was some good flying," said Winwright. "I think that would be a pass."

Valerie laughed in good humour, warmed by the compliment.

"Ah, if only some senior officers could have heard you say that. After the war, they were not interested in a pilot with one leg. It would have been nice to carry on flying."

"Did you never consider reapplying?"

"Once or twice, but I've had my day, Arthur. If I was to put on a uniform now, they would only put me behind a desk. I already sit behind one." He opened the door to the hut and motioned Winwright through. "I have no interest in being a curio of the past."

Valerie took off his heavy leather jacket and draped it over a chair before sitting down opposite. He propped his false leg up and felt the stiff muscles under his fingers. Winwright watched with some fascination but glanced out of the window when Valerie caught his eye.

Valerie smiled to himself as he continued to massage the cramped muscles. Winwright's reaction was nothing new to him, but he was always intrigued how people would react to his leg. Some were embarrassed; some would stare in morbid curiosity. It was always interesting watching people's curiosity war with their sense of good manners.

"I envy you, you know," said Winwright, taking off his own jacket and unwinding the scarf from round his neck. Screwing it up into a ball, he lofted it towards his office door. Valerie turned a sceptical eye on him. Winwright noticed. "I'm serious."

Valerie considered that and nodded slowly. But then he frowned.

"I believe you. I'm just surprised to hear you say that. I'm afraid the reality failed to measure up to the books and the films." His face pinched with mixed emotions. "Don't get me wrong. I loved my Nieuport. You literally strapped it on to fly amongst the clouds, but they had their vices."

Winwright riffled through a pile of administrative forms on the desk. He picked two out of the pile and reached for a pen.

"I just feel some things were simpler then."

"Maybe," Valerie shrugged. "But all the same, flying was in its infancy. We knew so little about the science of flight. Sometimes you were just as likely to be killed by your aircraft as by the enemy."

His voice was wistful as he thought about the time a wing had folded in a dive, or a freak gust had nearly flipped him on his back. Even flying into certain clouds presented a challenge. He would always have a love for his flying, but he knew he had come close to death many times.

"That's just as likely to happen these days," Winwright said. He finished reading the forms and signed them at the bottom. "Do you miss it?" he asked Valerie, looking out of the window.

"Every day."

1.23 – Come What May

November drew to a close with the Phoney War going full swing and the weather worsening every day. Frost carpeted the land, occasional flurries of snow came and went and Falcon Squadron hunkered down for the duration. Even a blind man could see there was little chance of action until the spring. Armies marched in good weather and they fought in the sun, not when the land was gripped by ice and snow. A tactical air force had little to do when the troops were tucked up nice and cosy in their barracks waiting for brighter days.

Two Bofors guns arrived to beef up the airfield defences but the army personnel to man them did not. A phone call to Wing provided no answer. Never one to stand idly by, Kittinger took a bunch of erks down to the woods. He wanted people who could shoot, so he had them take a pop at the targets he'd set up down there. He kept them at it all day, putting them through their paces. The erks didn't mind, it gave them something to do, but Kittinger took no prisoners. If you couldn't shoot, you were gone. By mid afternoon, the chosen few were shown the Bofors.

He was disappointed when Winwright turned down his request to have a Blenheim tow a target on a rope. The CO was still smarting from losing Chandler's recce Blenheim. He didn't fancy losing another aircraft to friendly fire of their own making. The men would just have to learn on the job. The following morning was spent on firing drills, loading and dealing with stoppages.

After a week of being grounded, Pettifer took advantage of a break in the weather to take his Blenheim up for an air test. His crew grumbled at being roused out of their burrows but he had kicked them into the air and put them through their paces. Pettifer knew that he was next on the roster for a recce trip and he wanted to be ready.

Judging by Chandler's record, Pettifer had a fifty-fifty chance of coming home. He didn't like those odds very much. When you could be shot at by the French just as easily as the Germans, then those odds were probably even lower.

Once they'd seen him off, Burke did the rounds of the ground crew to see how they were getting along. The fitters were doing their best to keep the Blenheims on top line but the bad weather was playing havoc with servicing.

The temperature had gone well south of zero which dulled minds and made hands numb. Simple tasks took longer and tempers were starting to fray. The men fumbled in the cold. They alternated blowing on their hands and tucking them under their armpits to try and get some life into them. Frosted breath rose in clouds around them while they shivered in their uniforms. He spent a few moments with each man, listening to their concerns before moving on, trying to buck up a lot of glum faces.

He was talking to one of the engine mechanics working on 426 when a sharp bang and a yelp came from the tail. Burke went round to see Simpson lifting himself out of the hatch by the gun turret. He sat on the fuselage and ruefully rubbed his head.

"What is it, Simpson?"

The Welshman threw something at Burke's feet. Burke stepped back to see a valve on the ground.

"Damps got into the electrics again. It nearly blew my eardrums before the valve went."

Burke picked up the valve. He held it up between thumb and forefinger as he scrutinised it. The glass dome was blackened on the inside.

"I don't know how they expect us to operate in these conditions," Simpson said aloud.

Burke pursed his lips in exasperation. He was not a shouter. He didn't like it and he didn't encourage it in his NCO's but he dearly felt like dragging Simpson down one side of the airfield and back again. He'd been the most vocal of the malcontents, but not a lot could be said in response because he was basically right. Burke had repeatedly asked for more winter clothing, braziers and other things to help the men, but nothing was coming through very quickly from Wing.

"I hear what you're saying but everyone else is getting on with things, Simpson. We've just got to soldier on." Simpson snorted. Burke pushed his forage cap back on his forehead and rubbed his brow. "Well, I can see you want to complicate the Lord's prayer today laddie." He pointed a finger and dabbed Simpson in the chest.

"You're in the RAF now boyo, not some cosy factory job, see," he said in a mock Welsh accent. His voice hardened. "Correct me if I'm wrong, but you volunteered for all of this, didn't you?" He let the question hang in the air. Simpson glared at him but had the good sense to keep his mouth shut. "So stop moaning about things. Cold?" He clicked his fingers. "Try winter in Russia lad, and then you'll know what cold is."

Without waiting for an answer, he went back round the front of the Blenheim. He hated himself for doing that, but Simpson needed slapping down hard and fast to stop the discontent finding further voice.

"Any luck?" he asked the engine fitter.

The man looked down at him from the step ladder.

"No, sir. She's turning over but not firing."

"Pull the plugs, wrap them in some rags and warm them up over a stove," he suggested. He started to walk off and then stopped. He came back and said, "And drain the oil. Warm it up a bit too. We'll see if that makes a difference."

In a bad mood, Burke stomped off to find Kittinger. He was busy at one of the gun pits, shouting at a hapless LAC who had dropped a clip of Bofors ammunition. Burke caught Kittinger's eye and motioned for him to come over.

"What can I do for you, Mister Burke?"

"More grumbles about the conditions, sir."

"Ah, that." Kittinger pulled a pack of cigarettes out of his pocket and offered one to Burke. Burke said no and watched while Kittinger tried to coax his lighter into life. He kept flicking the flint. There was plenty of spark; but no fire.

"I'm going to talk to the CO about this," said Burke with determination. "It's not good enough, sir. The lads are totally exposed to the elements amongst the trees."

Kittinger gave up and pocketed the lighter. He looked down as he kicked some hoare frost off his boots. He swept the toe of his left foot back and forth and watched it clear an arc through the white.

"I know. I know the chaps are working hard, the boss does too. There is equipment coming-"

"*When*, sir?" Burke interrupted; his patience thin. He'd heard this before.

"Soon," Kittinger said firmly.

"I hope so." Burke gestured to the activity in front of him. "God knows what'll happen if things stay like this."

Kittinger sighed. He held up his hands in surrender.

"All right, Mister Burke. You're quite right. I'll get onto Wing today and get an answer from them."

Burke nodded, but he knew that trying to get a straight answer from Wing was like trying to pin jelly to a wall with a knife.

"Thank you, Sir. But if you're going to call Wing, can you also get onto them about the fuel dump issue? At least a quarter of the tins are leaking and the cold is only making things worse."

Kittinger nodded and mentally added it to the list. Burke stomped off, sniffing out any further problems.

Awkright was pulling plugs from an engine when he heard the throb of Mercury engines on the breeze. He looked up and wiped the back of his hand across his forehead. The sound seemed to be coming off to his right and he craned his neck, trying to see. His partner in crime, Dempster came out from under the wing, his hands and sleeves black with grease and oil. He shaded his eyes from the low hanging sun. He pointed ahead of himself.

"Ey up, Mr Pettifer's back."

Awkright cocked an ear and creased his brow in thought as he listened to the engine note. There was stuttering amongst the thrum of the engines.

"That doesn't sound good," he said, offering his expert opinion. Dempster listened as well and nodded in agreement.

"No it doesn't. What happened this time?

"Sounds like some craps gone up the intake," said Awkright. He pointed as the Blenheim hove into view from the west. "There he is."

The Blenheim came straight at the field, the engine note rough and erratic. As it passed over the trees, a red flare arced into the air. Everyone dropped everything and began rushing around. A red flare meant they had a problem. The Blenheim passed over the field and circled left to shape up for a landing.

"Gawd. It's more than that," said Dempster, horrified.

"Is that a hole in the nose?" asked Awkright, although he could already see the answer. There was a ragged hole up front. The starboard view panel in the nose was punctured and red streaked back along the underside. There was more red on the windscreen too. Dempster started running like the rest of them. He picked up an extinguisher and stood ready.

Pettifer didn't hang around. He was a little fast as he cut the throttle and flared the last few feet. The Blenheim slammed down hard and the ground crew collectively winced. The bomber bucked and bounced as it careered over the frozen ground. The tail wheel came down with a slap and there was a thud and a judder that made them wince again.

They started running even before it came to a stop. The Blenheim looked like it had been pelted with rocks, big ones. There were dents along the leading edge of the port wing and the collector ring on the engine was crumpled. Blood was spattered all over the windscreen and gore was smeared over the paintwork.

Burke was the first man up to the cockpit. With an athleticism that belied his age, he clambered up onto the wing root and pulled back the escape hatch. He shouted for a medic as he saw inside.

Pettifer slumped in his seat, drained of all strength. His cheeks were raw from the frozen air that had blasted in from the nose. His fingers were clenched like claws on the yoke. He listened to the sounds around him. After the barrage of the engines, it was like he was at the bottom of a well. The creak of the airframe, the sound of his navigator moving next to him all came from far away.

He felt the aircraft rock on its oleos as people clambered onto the wing. The hatch above him was pulled back and a face appeared above him.

"Mr Pettifer, sir?"

He slowly moved his head to look up at them. Every movement was an effort and it took him a moment to focus.

"Fine. We're fine."

"Medic, medic!"

Burke disappeared and another face took his place. He went green at the sight inside and his cheeks bulged as he fought to keep down his lunch.

"You all right sir?"

"Don't ask bloody stupid questions." Pettifer undid his straps and threw them over his shoulder. "I'm fine. It's not our blood."

He batted some feathers out of the way and blew one out of his mouth. He hauled himself out of the cockpit, taking his time as he got feeling back into his arms. Concerned faces were waiting for him when he got back onto terra firma.

"Bit of a slaughterhouse isn't it?" asked Arthur.

"We flew through a bunch of sodding ducks," said Pettifer in disgust. He brushed some more feathers off his jacket but stopped when he saw he was just smearing the blood around even more. "A load of them fluttered up right in front of us. I tried to avoid them but one of our feathered brethren decided he loved the engine and tried to mate with it." He was appalled by the state of the wing. No wonder she'd flown like a brick. "At least one went through the nose." he shrugged, "maybe more."

One moment he'd been flying a perfectly good airplane, the next moment he was struggling to keep it in the air. He'd felt the thuds as the birds struck the aircraft; each hit a jolt on the yoke. Blood and bits of duck had swirled around inside the cockpit and icy cold air had rushed in through the broken nose. Feathers fluttered around in the hurricane. He had to squint as his vision dropped to a narrow piece of windscreen that was clear of mess.

"Duck for supper, is it?" asked Arthur casually.

Even Pettifer laughed at that. Now the shock and adrenalin was starting to wear off, reaction was settling in. Kittinger guided them towards the flight hut for a hot cocoa with something stronger in.

Dempster came out from under the tail and wiped his chilled hands on a rag.

"Rear frames been pulled, sir."

Burke nodded. He'd feared as much when he saw the Blenheim jolt over the rock hard ground. He sighed, more work.

"All right, let's get her wheeled back into the trees."

Later that afternoon, Locke was mooching around the woods. He watched Kittinger take the gun crews through their paces for a little while and then went for a walk. Wing had issued an alert and everything was made ready. The kites had been air tested and now they were waiting for the other shoe to drop.

His walk had brought him to the armoury hut and he went inside to get out of the cold. Two of the armourers stood by the bench, stripping down a Browning machine gun. He found Hagen sitting on an upturned ammunition box surrounded by boxes of bullets. He was shoving brass rounds into the circular magazines that fitted the turret machine guns. Each magazine held one hundred rounds and Hagen balanced it upside down on his lap as he pushed against the spring. He finished a magazine and put it on the pile by his feet before picking up another empty one and starting again.

He rummaged around the bucket of ammunition and pulled out one round. It was just like all the others apart from the red painted tip. There was a mix of bullets in the bucket. Some were tracers, some were standard rounds and some were armour piercing. He loaded a mix into the magazine, making sure every fifth round was a tracer otherwise the gunners would have no idea where their fire was going. He made the last fifteen rounds all tracer. That way, the gunner would know he was about to run out and needed to reload.

"Keeping you busy?" Locke asked. Hagen shrugged while he worked.

"Better to be doing something rather than just sitting around on my arse like the rest of them. Any idea what's for lunch?"

"Bully beef I assume. As long as it's something hot I don't really care."

The Corporal came over with a tin mug that steamed in the cold.

"Cuppa, Sir?" he asked, offering up the mug. "Powdered milk I'm afraid."

"Oh, thanks very much, Corporal."

He took an experimental sip. It was very hot and he hissed as he scalded the tip of his tongue. Hagen kept glancing at Locke as he stood there, sipping his tea. After a few minutes of this, he grew irritated.

"If you're going to hang around, make yourself useful and sit down."

He handed the younger man an empty magazine drum and pointed to another upturned box. Locke sat down and picked up some cartridges. They worked like that in silence for a few minutes. It was strangely calming and Locke filled two magazines before he spoke again.

"Fancy going to town later?" he asked.

Hagen stopped loading while he thought about that. The roads were icy and it would be hard going, but there was nothing else to do around the airfield. He was bored with cribbage and cards and out of date newspapers and it would be good to see Lorraine.

"Why not? We can but try."

He went back to loading. Click, click, click, just the sound of bullets being shoved home against the spring. Locke got into a rhythm. Ball, AP, ball, AP, tracer, ball, AP, ball, AP, tracer. To break the monotony, he occasionally went ball, ball, AP, AP, tracer. The pile of loaded magazines grew on the floor around them.

"Have you heard from, Lorraine?" Locke asked.

"No, but then I didn't expect to." Hagen picked up another empty magazine and balanced it on his knees. "She knows I can't always send word."

"Laura will be worried," said Locke, glum.

"I don't see why," Hagen murmured. "She's a big girl."

"But she's all on her own, she gets lonely."

Hagen thought about that. Laura had money, a flat of her own and all she needed to survive; but from what Locke had told him, Laura had never been truly alone. Even when she had followed Locke to France, she was fleeing from one dependency to another. She needed to grow up a bit, he thought.

Although Lorraine and Laura shared a common interest in art, they were poles apart. He saw that the first time he'd met her. Laura Locke pouted and preened like a cat, spoiled. She sat as one does in front of a mirror thinking, *'aren't I pretty?'* and expecting everyone to agree and pay court to her. If they didn't, she would huff and puff and play the helpless female for all it was worth. Hagen saw trouble ahead for Locke if he wasn't careful. Women like that were like a thoroughbred horse. They needed careful handling to keep them interested.

He thought about Lorraine then. She was no stranger to the trials life had thrown her way. There were moments when she sank into herself in quiet contemplation, but her mood could change in an instant. A word, a gesture, a kiss and she would be back in the world. Her face would light up in a smile, her eyes shining. Yes, if something happened to him, there'd be some tears, but he knew she'd be all right.

"She'll be okay," he assured the younger man, trying to sound like he meant it, telling Locke what he wanted to hear. He picked out some lint from the magazine feeder port. He blew on it and then wiped it with an oily rag. He carried on loading.

Locke looked doubtful. Only a few days before, he'd had to deal with one of Laura's moods. He'd come to the flat, buoyed by a good day's work, only to have it pricked by her petulance.

"But you didn't let me know you were okay yesterday," she had said, lips pouting. Irritation and then anger crossed his face.

"I can't just come round when you feel like it, Laura," he'd said, his voice spiky. Sensing his anger, she slid off the couch with a sibilant hiss of silk. She crossed the room and put her arms around his shoulders, fingers clasped behind his neck. She stood on tiptoe and fixed him with her blue eyes.

"I'm sorry darling, but I miss you so much."

She held his gaze for a moment and then flounced around the room. He watched her stand on tiptoe in her bare feet, pirouetting like a dancer. She trailed a finger along the top of the sofa as she danced.

"It's *so* boring. The weathers *positively* dreadful and you've got the car. What's a girl to do?"

It was like listening to a child. He reigned in his temper while she sulked the rest of the afternoon away. Nothing he did seemed to please her and in the end he'd been glad when Hagen had knocked on the door. He didn't talk about it during the drive back to the airfield, what would be the point? He just stared out the window and stewed while Hagen drove.

He felt a little selfish. He liked that she was close by, but some days he just wished she would disappear. Her being around provided a welcome escape from the basic life at the airfield, but he couldn't just come and go as he pleased. She didn't seem to understand that.

Once the balloon went up for real, there'd be little time to see his wife, regardless of what she wanted or expected. He thought about their walk along the river. Better to remember the good times, he thought.

As the light started to go, the squadron was stood down. Wing decided the Germans weren't invading today and a collective sigh went up in tents, huts and down at dispersal. The hours had ticked by and they'd been winding themselves up like the spring of a watch, waiting for the word that would send them into action. When they were stood down, the tension released itself in different ways for different men.

For some, the tension manifested itself in a burst of aggression. Borrowing some Enfield rifles from the armoury, Pettifer and a few others went to the far side of the woods. They carried boxes of empty bottles and tins from the cookhouse with them. They set the bottles up on a broken down stone wall and blazed off clip after clip, turning the glass bottles into a glittering mosaic of fragments. They took it in turns to throw the empty cans into the air and try and drill them before they hit the ground. They laughed hysterically as the tension ebbed away, firing their guns like schoolboys playing cowboys and Indians.

The rest went to the mess, played loud music on the gramophone and started drinking. All of them mentally reset their clocks until the next time they'd be asked to screw up the courage for a new day.

1.24 – Attend The List

Two hours after they were stood down, Saundby turned up in a staff car. He pulled into the main gate as Hagen and Locke were going the other way in the Mathis. He came into the mess to a cacophony of noise and chaos as bodies spilled on the floor. One man rode piggyback on the other while holding a broom pole like a lance. He held a rolled up jumper as a shield in his other hand. They charged up and down the hut at each other, ducking to avoid the rafters in the ceiling. Dane steered the Air Commodore towards the makeshift bar and pressed a drink into his hand.

"The men seem in good spirits," he commented.

"Youthful high spirits, Sir."

Dane explained the rules above the general noise and clamour as the game progressed.

"Everyone gets three lances and goes up and down the hut against each other. You get one point for a hit, two if you manage to knock the other man off his horse."

Pendleton went flying as the pole caught him dead on. He crashed to the floor with his navigator Morton underneath him.

"And the head?" Saundby asked.

"Ah, well that's off limits, but accidents do happen occasionally," Dane said with a grin. Pendleton picked himself up and smoothed his hair back down. He had a wild look about him and he dragged Morton off the floor.

"Come on Mort. We've got one lance left."

Morton dutifully bent over and Pendleton leaped onto his back, eager to get back into the game. They staggered back to the starting point and Pendleton grabbed hold of another broom pole.

"The lack of action is starting to get to them I think," commented Dane. Saundby grunted at the observation.

"Well, it's a waiting game..?" He arched an eyebrow at the intelligence officer, searching for his name.

"Dane, Sir. Wallis Dane, formerly of Kings College amongst other places."

"A reservist, eh?" commented Saundby, noting the little Brass VR's on Dane's lapels. Dane quirked a smile.

"For my sins." He ran his forefinger around the top of his glass, his brow creased in thought. Finally, he spoke. "May I ask a question?"

"Of course."

"I wondered what your thoughts were about a lot of the French aircraft being obsolete?"

The question caught Saundby off guard. He'd been expecting something a little closer to home with less of a strategic sweep to it. Trust an intelligence officer to be awkward.

On paper, Saundby knew that the RAF Air Component and the French Air Force were a match for the Luftwaffe. Of course, that was on paper, the reality was something else. The Germans had organised themselves around a new concept of Blitzkrieg. Their aircraft operated closely with their ground forces, almost as airborne artillery. They'd recent combat experience as well, fighting as the Condor Legion during the Spanish Civil War.

"I don't think it will be an issue," he said dismissively. Dane's mouth twitched. "Weight of numbers, Dane; weight of numbers," he said with conviction. Sometimes, for the good of morale, reality needed to be adroitly ignored. "If they cross the line we'll swamp them before they can get a foothold. Every bomb dropped will make a difference. You'll see."

"I see, Sir. I suppose that depends on them doing what we expect them to?" he said, completely deadpan. Saundby's eyebrows shot up, unsure if Dane was being sarcastic or serious. "What I mean is, we've all bedded down and we're expecting the Germans to do the same. That's what happened in the last show." Saundby nodded in agreement. That was certainly true. The Western Front had very often been a seasonal war. "But the Germans *haven't* slowed down, have they? They've annexed the Danzig corridor while we've been sitting on our duffs."

"And what do you think we should do, Mister Dane?" asked Saundby. He finished off the beer he'd been given and looked at the leftover froth in the glass. "This is good stuff by the way."

Dane reached over the bar and hooked another bottle of beer. He took the top off and poured.

"I'd bomb the living daylights out of them. Take the fight to them and go for their airfields. If they're in winter quarters, let's get our licks in first."

"If we go over there, they might do the same to us," Saundby said with some caution. He frowned; he didn't like talking shop in the mess.

"I thought we were at war, Sir? Isn't that what one does, *attack* the enemy?"

"My god, Dane, I didn't realise you were such a firebrand," Winwright said as he joined them. Dane turned at the interruption.

"I'm only a reservist, Sir. They unbox us for hostilities, don't you know?"

Saundby laughed uproariously. Using the pause, he left Dane and led Winwright away by the arm. They sat on two rickety chairs along the back wall. Dismissed, Dane went back to the game, cheering from the sidelines. Saundby tested his weight on the chair. It creaked ominously and he wiggled, expecting it to collapse.

"Rescued them from the old barn before it collapsed," Winwright informed him. "There was all sorts of junk in there, but waste not want not." They watched as the men charged up and down the hut, taking it in turns to prod the daylights out of each other.

"What can I do for you, Sir?"

"Just a flying visit, Arthur, I wanted to come by personally and see how you are."

"I appreciate it, Sir."

"I'm going round the doors to see everyone. Damn silly cock up this afternoon. Gods knows what the Frogs were playing at. Someone gets a twitch and there's panic up and down the bloody line. Sorry your chaps had to be put through that but we can't take any chances."

The call had gone out from Headquarters after a German artillery barrage along the Siegfried Line. Fearing this was the start of a German advance, the French had jerked into action. While he was boiling at the balls up, Saundby was secretly pleased at how the Wing had coped. He felt it was a fair test of what was to come.

"Now; about your bird strike?"

Winwright told him the story. He pointed out Pettifer across the room who was at that moment, the horse element of the latest jousting pair careering along the hut.

"Lucky boy. We all need a slice of luck like that."

They shared a look and both of them remembered an ugly accident in Malta when a member of their flight had ploughed through a flock of seagulls. He was coming in to land at Luqa and piled it in from fifty feet. His kite looked like it had been dug out of a King Kong footprint and carved a ditch six feet deep.

"You've had a lot of luck recently?" Saundby said.

"Sir?"

"Bird strikes, friendly fire."

Winwright looked grim. Friendly fire was still a sticking point for him. His squadron wasn't anything special though. They weren't the only unit to have been jumped by friendly fighters, but it still rankled.

"We all get our share, Sir."

"Hmmm maybe." Saundby brooded over his beer. He moved the glass in small circles, making the brown liquid swirl. In some ways, Saundby believed crews made their own luck. Some just had more of it than others. The thing was coping when it turned. He wasn't a fatalist, but he'd been a flier long enough to know that sometimes, even if you did everything right, it was out of your control.

"Your man who walked it in a few days ago; didn't he do that recce job for the navy when you first arrived?"

"That's right, Sir."

"A lucky boy indeed." Saundby grunted. "Write him up, I'll see he gets something."

"You think so?"

"Happens he deserves it. Shot up twice, walks home *and* there was that recce job over Germany too. Give the boys something to cheer about. A story for the folks back home."

Winwright thought about that. First a mention in dispatches, now a decoration, Chandler was sailing under a lucky star indeed.

"All right, Sir. I'll sort it out."

"Good."

Saundby finished his beer and got up to go. A roar went up from the crowd and they saw Dane take centre stage, charging around on Kittinger's back. Rolled up blankets were tied to his chest and arms and he howled at the top of his voice.

"Rum chap, your, Dane."

Winwright looked askance at Saundby, a measuring glance. Just like the old days, his mind leapt about, never staying fixed on one thing for long.

"He's just as crazy as all the other Intelligence Officers I've known," replied Winwright. "They ask awkward questions, they play devil's advocate. I think they must be bred especially."

"Now I've got some good news for you."

Saundby rarely gave out good news. Winwright often found that what Saundby considered good news didn't always match everyone else's viewpoint. He also used it to soften the blow for something else. They exited the hut and Winwright escorted him to his staff car. They walked slowly. The older man linked his hands behind his back and puffed his chest out. He kept his voice low as he walked.

"HQ doesn't think much will happen now until the New Year. Start handing out some leave passes, but not everyone at once for god's sake. Keep some of the chaps back just in case something does happen."

"That'll please the boys. A week at home should do the trick."

They paused by one of the Bofors gun pits. Saundby kicked at a sandbag

"I wish the blasted weather would clear," he muttered.

"The forecast isn't very good, I'm afraid."

"I know, I've seen it. Frost, snow, ice. It's going to be a hard winter, Arthur. Keep the chaps occupied as much as you can."

"We're trying, Sir. It's hard when there's not much flying."

"I don't suppose cross country runs, ground lectures and clearing snow will be very popular, but do your best. I'm not sure if any more concert parties are coming, but keep your calendar clear. The Frogs are throwing some kind of New Year's ball not far from here at one of their airfields. We have been cordially invited to attend. Pick a few crews and bring yourself along. I'll lay some transport on."

They got to the staff car and the driver opened the door. Saundby paused as he was getting in, one hand on the roof.

"One more thing." *Here it comes*, thought Winwright, the bit of bad news he was really here to deliver. It was Saundby's way. He'd always been like this.

"The Battles have been taking a hammering the last few weeks. Jerries chopping them down left and right, so in their infinite wisdom, the Air Ministry has decided to switch them over to night bombing."

There was a pause as the enormity of the bombshell became clear. The wing had two Battle squadrons and one Blenheim squadron for offensive operations. They were supposed to work together to support an advance. The Air Ministry's decision had just cut their fighting power by two thirds.

"More work for us," muttered Winwright. He wondered what other missives Saundby had up his sleeve. They were already pulling double duty with the recce flights. Now they were going to have to pick up the slack for the Battle crews as well. He wondered what Bainbridge would make of this decision.

"I'm sorry, but there it is. Goodnight, Arthur."

"Goodnight, Sir."

Message delivered, Saundby got into the car. Winwright saluted and stood watching while it drove off, its headlamps barely lighting the way. He strolled back to the hut, thinking hard about the Battle units and what it would mean for them all. He started mentally composing Chandler's commendation as he went inside. The din hit him as he opened the door.

The game was in full swing, with A Flight just one point ahead of B Flight. The final match up was Chandler against Farmer. The combatants got ready and Chandler balanced on Morgan's back. A pint of beer was shoved in front of him and he guzzled it down. At least half of it missed his mouth and went down his Navigator's neck. Morgan howled in complaint until someone shoved a pint under his nose as well.

Farmer clambered onto Arthur and it looked ludicrous. Six feet of barrel chested man was perched on top of a scrawny navigator who drunkenly swayed back and forth from the load. He took a few steps forwards and creaked under the weight. There was little chance of him getting beyond a trot.

"Come on horsey," said Chandler. He tugged on Morgan's ears, making clicking noises, patting him on the rump.

"I'm warning you," said Morgan, hitching Chandler further up his back. A hand pinched his face. "Thabs dy bose." The hand disappeared and he tried to keep a firm grip on Chandler's legs as he shifted the weight around. Mitchell pointed down the hut, telling Morgan to make sure he went the right way.

"That way, Morg. Up and down, old chap."

"Bugger off!" he roared, "I know where I'm going."

He wobbled to the starting point. He was wearing his Sidcot flying suit and had jammed jumpers down the front. White and lumpy, he looked like the Michelin Man from the tyre adverts. Chandler was handed a broom pole and he gripped his rolled up uniform jacket firmly in his left hand. He waved the pole around, experimenting with his aim.

The combatants lined up at either end, facing each other. Arthur looked like he was about to buckle, his knees knocked and he was going red in the face from the effort.

Pendleton raised his right arm, a handkerchief theatrically gripped between thumb and forefinger. He looked left and right, dropped the hanky and they were off.

With a roar, Farmer headed for Chandler. He leaned forwards, aiming along the pole, lining it up on Chandler's chest. He would accept nothing more than dumping him on his backside. He jabbed Arthur in the side with his heels. The struggling navigator stumbled forwards, trying to build up some speed.

The poles wobbled as they went down the hut, each step making it harder to keep it under control. Farmer lunged for Chandler as they passed each other and missed, the pole going over his shoulder. Chandler hit, catching him on the arm. Farmer snarled in anger as they went back down the hut to get ready for the second run. One- nil.

The next attempt was a tie. Both of them hit each other a glancing blow on the chest. Two-one. Farmers temper was bubbling. He shot Chandler a venomous look as they got ready for the final time.

"I'm going to get that bastard," he spat. Arthur groaned inwardly. It was only a game. He couldn't understand Farmers need to make such things personal. He bowed under the weight as Farmer got onto his back for the final time.

He wobbled down the hut, leaning forwards to gain speed, his feet slapping the floorboards. The pole hovered above his head and he looked at it, watching it settle down as Farmer got it under control. Just before the clash, he straightened up, throwing off Farmers aim. The pole went up to the ceiling and connected with the rafters. Farmer went backwards and landed in a heap on the floor. Down and out.

There was a loud cheer and Chandler was snatched off Morgan's back. They sang *'For He's A Jolly Good Fellow'* as they paraded him around the hut on their shoulders, the conquering hero.

1.25 – If You Go Down To The Woods Today

In the dead of night, a select few walked the perimeter while the remainder slept. Even though France was a friendly nation, there was still the need for security. Rumours abounded of spies and wretched fifth columnists. There was also the more mundane possibility of petty pilfering.

Living in the field, units brought with them a massive amount of stores, tools, ammunition, fuel, bombs and food. All of it was there to tempt anyone willing to take the chance. Barbed wire was set up around the perimeter and the men had to take it in turns to guard it around the clock.

A hut had been turned into a guardhouse of sorts. An NCO, four men and Chandler sat on upturned ammunition boxes around a stove. A kettle was on top ready to brew up some more tea while they watched time go glacially by.

Chandler would have let them play cards to pass the time, but the Adjutant had a nasty habit of turning up to do some spot checks. Kittinger had already caught one man dozing on the job and put him on a charge. The rumour was he prowled round trying to catch someone out.

Chandler hadn't figured Kittinger out yet. No one could argue his achievements. The medal ribbons on his chest were testament to that, even though he remained tight lipped about how he'd got them. Chandler had seen him chew some erks out over their work standards but he had also seen him go to bat for the men against some bullying SP's. The man was all spiky with rough edges.

Coming through training, the Adjutant at Chandler's OCU had been like a mother hen. He'd seen to their needs and looked after them. Kittinger was more like one of the drill Sergeants back at the depot. He needed someone to soften him up a bit, Chandler mused.

He yawned and rubbed his hands up and down his face. His eyes felt gritty and he blinked fast as he worked his jaw. He was tired and knew it but it was hours until dawn and the end of his stint. He stretched and stood up, stamping his feet as he did so. Fastening his holster around his waist, he made for the door.

"I'm going to do the rounds," he announced. A few laps around the track might help wake him up.

Outside, the air was crisp, the cold stinging his cheeks. He spent a few minutes breathing deeply, letting the lethargy from the warm hut wash away. Shoving his hands into his pockets, he stamped off towards the gun posts to make sure the men were awake.

He found the two erks in the Lewis gun pit by the huts to be reasonably happy. The gun pit and sandbags afforded them some protection from the light breeze. They were taking it in turns to man the gun and had a few blankets draped around their shoulders to help them keep warm.

Looping back around the outer edge of the wood, Chandler moved the sentries around. Too long in one spot made men bored, so he swapped their positions to keep them interested.

He was walking to the next post when a strange noise made him stop. He was on the eastern edge of the wood where the land fell away down some steep banking to a little stream. Coils of barbed wire glistened with frost in the moonlight. He looked around slowly but there was nothing obvious.

The sentry behind him coughed, their voice carrying on the breeze. They hacked and coughed some more. Chandler's face pinched in distaste at the wretched sound of the man sniffing and spitting. He strained to listen to the night sounds, his ears adjusting to the quiet. There was the light babble of the water, lapping at the bank. His boots crunched on the frosty ground as he moved his feet. He wiggled his toes and rubbed his hands. He winced at the cold. He reckoned they were in for a hard winter in the months ahead.

He was about to move on when he heard the strange sound again. The hairs on his neck stood on end and he glanced to his right. The sentry was still in the same place, huddling inside his greatcoat. The sound had come from behind him and Chandler turned on his heel and peered in the gloom of the trees. He heard it again; a sort of snuffling and he could hear something moving around.

The tents and huts were in the trees on the other side of the dispersal so that ruled out some kind of casual wanderer. Besides, it was that cold it was unlikely anyone would be out for a casual stroll at this time of night. Chandler rubbed his chin. Something wasn't right here and he crept over to the sentry, trying to keep low. He put his hand on the sentry's shoulder. The Corporal started and Chandler motioned for the man to follow him.

"There's something screwy going on here, Corporal. Follow me."

Chandler led the way as they edged back into the trees and stopped by a low lying bush. He crouched down, resting against a thick trunk while he listened. In the quiet, every little sound was amplified. His pulse, the wind through the leaves, even his breathing boomed in his ears. They waited like that for a few minutes, ears straining.

"Are you sure, sir?" asked the Corporal, teeth chattering.

An old timer, the Corporal peered at the glowing hands of his wristwatch in the dark. Ten more minutes and his stint would be over and he could head back to the warm hut. He had little interest in crawling around the woods humouring young officers that jumped at shadows. He'd been stood on sentry duty for nearly an hour and not heard a thing.

Five more minutes went by and a worm of doubt began to gnaw on Chandler. He felt stupid crouching there, seeing nothing, but then his ears perked up. He glanced sideways at the Corporal, who nodded quickly, his eyes wide like saucers. He'd heard it too, an odd snuffling and slithering sound.

Chandler shifted left slightly and tried to see where it was coming from. Whatever it was, was keeping very low to the ground, crawling through the undergrowth amongst the trees. He could see leaves moving in the gloom and he heard a faint voice, hissing.

"Ça y est, il regarde autour."

It meant nothing to Chandler, languages weren't his thing. Clearly, someone was somewhere they shouldn't be. The voice had come from further

145

back in the trees, some distance from the snuffling noise he'd heard, so there were at least two of them. Chandler's lip curled. The fuel dump was that way; it was probably thieves out for petrol.

"I'll take the man in front, Corporal. You cover the other with your rifle."

The older man nodded dumbly. The snuffling got closer. He slowly slid the Lee Enfield rifle off his shoulder and moved the safety catch forwards with his thumb. Chandler's mouth was dry. He was a pilot. He should be up in an aircraft, not about to fight on the ground in a freezing cold wood.

The first man was crawling around their tree trunk when Chandler burst from cover. The Corporal stood up and levelled his rifle at a small Frenchman about ten yards away. He wore a dark blue work shirt and pants and was crouching forwards, his hands on his knees. Staring down the barrel of the rifle, the man suddenly stood very tall, arms above his head, screaming, "Non! Non!" as he did so.

A high pitched squealing came from the right and Chandler was rolling around on the ground, struggling with his man. The screaming became shrill. It increased in volume while the pilot continued to splutter and struggled to contain the body that was writhing under him. The other Frenchman made to intervene until the muzzle of the rifle was pressed into his chest.

"Don't you bloody move!" shouted the Corporal. The man started babbling, his hands pressed to his head, weeping in distress.

"S'il vous plaît, Monsieur. Ne pas lui faire de mal. Elle est mon cochon, mon bébé . Ne pas lui faire du mal, Monsieur. Mon cochon, mon pauvre bébé."

He was still weeping when Kittinger, the Sergeant and two other sentries came pounding through the trees to see what all the noise was about. Petrified, the Frenchman dropped to his knees, hands clasped tight to his chest as he prayed. He rocked back and forth, his voice shaking, almost incoherent.

Chandler was still rolling around on the floor until helping hands rendered assistance. Hair and uniform in disarray, he got to his feet, exhausted from his efforts. Hunting amongst the undergrowth, he found his peaked cap and jammed it back on his head.

"They got past the wire somehow," he reported to Kittinger. "We caught them coming back from the fuel dump."

Kittinger flicked on a torch and stifled a laugh as the identity of Chandler's man was revealed.

"A pig? Oh my." Valerie smiled at the thought of the scene.

"A very valuable pig apparently," said Winwright in some amusement. "A truffle pig, in fact."

Far from being petrol thieves caught in the act, Chandler had been struggling with a panicked female pig. The poor thing had taken some time to be calmed by the distressed Frenchman. He produced an apple and some carrots from a pocket for the frightened animal and soothed it by stroking its back.

Marched to the flight hut, the man had stood in the middle of the floor, chastened at being caught. It didn't take long to establish that he was no thief or saboteur. His big beefy hands wrung his faded cap as he told his tale.

He was a truffler who had taken great exception to the fact that one of his favoured hunting grounds had been handed over to the RAF. Never one to be bound by rules, he'd decided that no barbed wire was going to stop him.

Finding a weak spot in the perimeter, he had sneaked into the woods and gone back to work. He was on his way back when Chandler heard the pig rooting amongst the undergrowth.

Amused, Valerie threw back his head and had a good belly laugh while he poured himself some more wine. Winwright had arrived in the middle of lunch. Crumbs on the cheese board were the remaining evidence of a good meal.

"And what did you do with him?" he asked the Englishman.

"Nothing too drastic, I assure you. We confiscated his truffles and told him if we found him in the woods again we'd eat his pig." Winwright lit a cigarette and dropped the match in the ashtray on the desk. He wrinkled his nose at the sulphurous smell. "He got quite upset about that."

Told of his pig's possible fate if there were any further transgressions, the man had become almost inconsolable. He'd shaken his fists at them, his passion stirred at their barbarity. His eyes burned in defiance as he poured threats of harm on them if anyone harmed his pig. The curious pair was led to the main gate and shown the road. They'd walked off into the dark, the man shuffling along, his loyal truffle pig following behind on its lead.

No names had been mentioned but Valerie had a fairly good idea who'd been caught last night. The man had made no secret of his irritation at the arrival of the RAF and the disruption their coming had caused.

"I presume you are wanting me to pass the word, as they say?" he asked. Winwright nodded.

"Would you?" asked Winwright in relief. The last thing he wanted to do was shoot someone out hunting for truffles.

1.26 – The Coming Of The King

The winter of 1939 was the worst in forty five years. In England, snow fell in quantity not seen for a generation. Roads became clogged and freezing fog covered the land while everyone hunkered from the cold. The newsreels made it look like fun. Children shot down hills on their sledges, trains battered through drifts on the track with snow ploughs.

In reality, schools closed, pipes burst, homes were flooded and froze as the temperatures continued to drop. Isolated villages were cut off and people tried to cope as best they could. The army was called in to help throughout the countryside, rescuing sheep and people on higher ground.

In France, the sodden ground of Flanders fields had frozen hard. Snow fell and banked up in deep drifts. Cold winds knifed across the land. At Bois Fontaine men shivered in tents and dreamed of warm baths and a cosy log fire. In the dark, they prayed to the gods to bring spring as soon as possible.

In early December, King George VI braved the cold and crossed the Channel in company with the Duke of Gloucester to visit the BEF in the field. The press pack swarmed like bees around a honeypot at the news. Reporting on the King talking to the troops was an easy sell and all of them wanted a piece of the action.

Rather than have a horde of reporters follow the King around, they divvyed up who went where. Cullen pulled Douai out of the hat. The King would inspect ground personnel there on the 6th December. Cullen had to look up Doaui on a map and found it was a French airfield east of Lens.

Cullen was glad he allowed himself plenty of time to get to Douai with a photographer. The night before, a sudden thaw had set in and the rain began again. Snow had turned to slush and the frozen fields turned back into a quagmire. Navigating the soggy roads in his tiny car, he arrived at Douai. He flashed his pass to the Provosts at the gate and was ushered onto the base.

A keen Flight Lieutenant pointed out where the inspection would take place and Cullen decided where he should stand. In front of the hangars was a large tarmac apron. A Warrant Officer was busy pacing out the parade. He looked like a tailors dummy with his razor sharp creases in his uniform. His boots were buffed to a deep glossy black while his brass buttons glinted in the daylight.

Just before three, trucks started delivering a selection of personnel. The Warrant Officer had them form up in ranks of three. Once he was happy everyone knew what they were doing, they were dismissed until it was time to parade. They gathered in the open hangars to shelter from the breeze while they waited.

Cullen got the itinerary from a harassed Flying Officer who was rushing around. The plan was for the men to form up at half past three in their formation. The King would arrive at four, inspect them and say a few words before moving on to his next destination. It was all pretty standard stuff, but Cullen noticed a certain frisson in the air. The King was coming!

Cullen knew that servicemen had little patience when politicians or senior officers inspected them. Formal parades were something you suffered with a certain amount of patience. It was a different matter when the King came to see you. It was the King who they swore allegiance to when they joined the service. A King coming down from on high to talk to his men was appreciated more than any other dignitary.

Cullen was kicking his heels sharing a cigarette with some of the men when he saw a blue staff car come barrelling across the grass of the airfield. It was coming on at a fair lick, mud spraying up from the wheels as the driver poured on the coals. The car bounded onto the tarmac and screeched to a halt. The rear door opened and a Group Captain shot out and shouted, "On Parade! The King is here!"

Cullen checked his watch, it was twenty past three. He looked around. A few airmen regarded the Group Captain with mild amusement. They had tons of time yet before the parade. Cullen kept looking between the senior officer by the staff car and the hundreds of airmen.

The Group Captain shouted again. This time he pointed to a distant convoy of cars coming around the administrative buildings near the main gate. The leading staff car had a larger than usual flag fluttering from its pennant. Airmen, NCO's and officers looked from each other, to the cavalcade, to the Group Captain and back again. The penny dropped and the air was rent by the sound of officers and NCO's calling the men to get on parade.

This was priceless, there'd been a cockup somewhere and Cullen had a front row seat. The units took up their positions. The markers went first and the rest of the men dressed off them in turn, three ranks deep. In mere moments, order emerged out of the chaos.

There was a clamour of commands. Feet stamped, timings were called out and one thousand men were arrayed at ease in open square formation. Shoes gleamed, brass buttons glinted in the afternoon light. Cullen checked his watch again; it was twenty five past three.

The staff car screeched off and the Group Captain headed over to the edge of the formation. About thirty seconds went by and then the King's car appeared and came to a stop. A soldier jumped out of the front passenger seat and opened the rear door smartly. The King emerged in a Field Marshals uniform. The parade came to attention. A thousand boots stamped on the ground. Trumpeters played the fanfare and their brassy sound bounced off the sides of the hangars.

There was a long pause as the King saluted in reply, his eyes roaming over the formation, picking out details. His arm dropped and people relaxed as he smiled. For the men on the parade square, it was as if they were having their own private moment with the King. He stopped occasionally and shared a few words with individuals as he went along the ranks.

Cullen surreptitiously tacked himself onto the back of the pack of dignitaries. The King completed his inspection and went back round to the Warrant Officer. Salutes were exchanged. His Majesty was shown towards a Nissen hut for a cup of tea. Cullen heard the King ask the Group Captain about driving across the grass. Cullen smiled. It was like a naughty schoolboy being caught by the beak. It was wonderful stuff, but there was not a hope in hell the censor would let it be printed. It was a shame, it was a smashing story.

In the hut, he discovered that the inspection of the 4th Division had been cut short. Some bright spark had paraded the men in a field that could have doubled as a quagmire. Cullen may not have been a military man, but even he knew that making thousands of soldiers parade in conditions like that was a stupid idea. Slipping and sliding in mud was not very dignified for a King. It was all very unfortunate that the weather had done its best to sabotage a lot of hard work.

After finishing his tea and biscuit, the King took advantage of being ahead of schedule to go back outside and talk to the men. Cullen was pleased to see him do that. It was something special to share experiences and talk to them, bridging the gap between royalty and the common man.

The King was whisked off for a tour of the Maginot Line while the men got back on the trucks to be returned to their respective units. Cullen returned to Rheims to write his story.

The piece he put in was quite tame. It mentioned nothing of the chaos but the censor approved the bit about the King talking to the men by the trucks. While he'd been drafting his copy in his room, the photographer had looked round the door with an envelope. He'd developed his prints and gave Cullen some shots of the staff car careering across the grass and the Group Captain standing on the tarmac pointing towards the cavalcade. Cullen loved it. He wrote some notes about what had happened and put them in his personal scrap book for his memoirs. Maybe one day he would be able to write about it.

1.27 – Joyeux Noel

Two days after the King returned to England, a succession of dignitaries followed. The Prime Minister put in an appearance and his visit was a much more informal affair. Eschewing formal parades, Chamberlain set a brisk pace, inspecting gun positions and doing the rounds of units in the field. He visited a number of French villages and gave speeches in the street. He extolled the virtues of the entente cordiale between France and England. Cullen was amongst the press pack following as the great man posed for photographs. Children yelled, *'Papa Chamberlain'*.

At Villeneuve airfield, Chamberlain watched a demonstration of bombing by Fairey Battles. At Mourmelon he spent a great deal of time examining a Dornier 17 which had been brought down. As he went back to England, he told the press his tour had been great fun.

Falcon Squadron missed most of the fuss of all these comings and goings. With the going on the roads so difficult, no dignitaries came to see them at Bois Fontaine. They were disappointed to miss their chance to be in a Pathé newsreel, by they didn't miss the nonsense that went hand in hand with a glitzy parade.

A week before Christmas, a detachment of soldiers turned up unannounced to man the Bofors guns. Kittinger had a busy morning finding spare tents to house them. He went into town in the afternoon to haggle with Valerie's deputy for extra supplies to feed and keep them warm. Their arrival caused a bit of a stir. Having some brown jobs around became a talking point, but the men soon settled in to life at Bois Fontaine.

With Christmas fast approaching, it was hard to keep the men's minds focused. Naturally, their thoughts turned to home and family and Winwright spent the morning signing leave forms. Sending men on leave sounded easy, but it involved a lot of paperwork. Each man needed a leave pass, a travel voucher and other pieces of paper and it all had to be signed, stamped and authorised in the appropriate places.

Once that was done, Winwright settled down in the tiny cubbyhole that passed as his office. He nursed a bottle of red Valerie had given him with the squadron's operations book in his lap. 1939 was drawing to a close and it had been a mixed year for the squadron. There didn't seem to be much on the positive side of the scorecard. No bombs had been dropped in anger and aside from a few recce trips; they had little to show for their efforts. Gardner poked his nose round the office door. Winwright waved him in and Gardner slid inside swiftly to keep the cold out.

"Ready to go, Sir?"

"Yes, Alan. You know what you're doing?"

"I'll be all right, Sir. We can hold the fort until you get back, I think."

Winwright left last minute instructions as he piled his luggage into the green Citroen. He still had to pick up something for the kids on the way home. Gardner got in the driver's seat; he was going to drop Winwright off at Rheims.

"The rest of the chaps get off okay?"

"Yes, Sir. The first batch went off a little while ago."

Winwright offered his hand and Burke shook it warmly.

"Merry Christmas, Sir. Take care."

Half of each flight and some of the ground staff were given seven days' leave. Once away from the field, they scattered to the four winds. Winwright went home to his little house in a Lincolnshire village near to RAF Allenby. Using his key, he caught Margaret up to her elbows in flour, bent over a rolling pin. The children were at a friend's house and he gathered her into his arms, holding her close.

"Arthur, you are beastly for not telling me you were coming," she said between kisses.

"Sorry darling; thought I'd surprise you and the kids." Laughing, he lifted her up despite her protests and twirled her around the kitchen. They stopped under some mistletoe hung above the back door. "Merry Christmas, Margaret."

He went to collect his children from their friends, to their delight. James rode on his shoulders while William skipped alongside him, gazing up at his father, giddy with excitement. Dinner was ready when they got home and he sat at his own table. Homemade paper chains hung over the fireplace.

Here, surrounded by his family, he was very much reminded of dinner at Valerie's. He told them about his friend as they ate. After dinner they retired to the living room and Margaret put on the radio in time for the evening news.

After a few minutes, he turned it off. He was on leave and the war could wait for a few days. Settling down on the carpet, he tugged out some board games from the corner and played with his sons. Margaret watched from her armchair while she knitted a scarf.

The Locke's went south and kept going until they came across a bustling town not far from the Swiss border. They secured a room at the hotel and settled down, continuing their honeymoon. Down south, RAF uniforms were thin on the ground. Laura was delighted at the attention they got walking down the main street.

Life was less serious here. The nearest German was miles away and down south, the blackout was something that was only paid lip service. The towns and villages were a blaze of light and noise.

After the first day, he changed into mufti and they went walking in the hills. He took his camera and snapped off a few shots in the valley. He found a beautiful spot which was right out of a picture postcard, a ford in the river with a gorgeous waterfall as a backdrop.

While her husband was off walking, Laura found shops stocking an abundance of cosmetics. She spent a glorious morning browsing as she stocked up on perfume and lipstick. She blew a small fortune on a beautiful winter coat in Sapphire blue with fur trimmed cuffs and collar. She rounded off the day with a visit to the salon to get her hair done in a smart bob that framed her face.

In the evenings they enjoyed the local night life, such as it was. They went to the cinema one night. The film was in French but they weren't there for the film. Near to the hotel was a cosy bar which had a band and a small dance floor. They listened to the music for a while before dancing close together amongst the press of bodies.

Christmas Day was noisy. In the gloom of war, this was one day for cares to be set aside and to enjoy the moment. What was most fun; were the little things. The hotel burned a Yule Log in the fireplace in the lobby. A nativity scene occupied an area by the main stairs.

Locke had found some time to do shopping of his own. He presented Laura with a delicate diamond necklace of white gold with matching earrings. She gave him some practical things, a scarf, a hip flask with brandy in and some new leather gauntlets.

Their first Christmas together as man and wife was roast turkey with chestnut stuffing and all the trimmings. The gravy was wonderful and Locke tucked in. He'd not had food like this since leaving home. They'd chosen their hotel well.

Lorraine hung off Hagen's arm as they walked down the Parisian street. Locke had been good enough to drop them at a train station on their drive south. They'd caught the next train at Arras and squeezed into a carriage filled with a cross section of French society. Soldiers on leave rubbed shoulders with travelling salesmen and mothers soothing tired children. He found a space in the overhead rack for their suitcase and then stood most of the way, holding hands with Lorraine who found a small corner to sit down. Their fingers did the talking while the train covered the miles to Paris.

Pulling in at the Gare Du Nord, she was all smiles as they exited the station and took a cab across town. Hagen was pleased to see her so happy. Her eyes lit up and she kept pointing out the window, telling him about places as they passed.

He shifted his grip on the suitcase as they walked and took in some of the details around him. The taxi had dropped them at the corner of the Rue Édouard Vaillant and Lorraine had led him down the street. She steered him towards a four storey building, little different from the ones around it. A lumpy woman in wrinkled stockings and wrapped in a threadbare robe sat knitting on a rickety chair outside the entrance. She turned rheumy eyes on them as they approached. Her face broke into a toothless grin and she stood up, arms outstretched in welcome. Lorraine hugged her and then stepped back and gestured towards him.

"Joyeux Noël madame Ferraud. Voius êtes si bonne mine. Puis-je présenter Lieutenant d'aviation Mark Hagen."

He stood a little taller and stumbled through a greeting, a little shy in front of someone who had known Lorraine since she was a little girl. The old woman held open the door for him and they went inside. He was about to go into the lift when the old woman waved a finger and pointed up, miming that the lift was broken. He nodded his understanding and followed Lorraine up the stairs. He kept his eyes on her slim ankles as she told him they were headed to the fourth floor.

When they made it to the top of the stairs, he took a few moments to compose himself. Her father's apartment was to the left of the landing at the end of a gloomy corridor. Lorraine checked her makeup in a compact mirror. She refreshed her lipstick before snapping the lid shut and putting it back into her handbag. She straightened her hat and flashed him a smile as she knocked on the door. He gulped as she used her key to open it.

"Bonjour Papa!" she said as she crossed the threshold.

Kittinger tucked the shotgun under his arm as he worked his way across the field. The snow was up to his knees in places and it was heavy going. He took big steps to make progress. It was a cloudy day and the light was poor. Grey clouds on the horizon promised more snow to come. A breeze cut over the ground and light powder swirled into the air. The icy crystals sparkled in the weak sunlight.

Unlike most of them, he'd not gone home on leave. He'd stopped going a long time ago. Sometimes he went to see his Aunt in Dorset, other times he went wherever the mood took him. Now, he took advantage of a chance meeting to pass the Christmas period. The constant visits to haggle with Valerie's right hand man had turned into a friendship of sorts. It was further strengthened when it turned out he was the owner of the estate next to the airfield. At a loose end, Kittinger accepted the invitation to come to the estate and help with their rabbit problem.

He spotted a cluster of them lounging in the middle of the next field. He peered over the low stone wall. There were at least three of the little buggers, maybe more. One of them was digging in the snow, chucking divots of white behind. Kittinger fished around in a pocket and loaded the shotgun automatically, keeping his eyes on the rabbits. There was a nice plump one in the middle and he slid the shotgun over the wall as quietly as he could.

He drew a bead on the group and let fly. Two booms split the silence and crows scattered into the sky from a nearby tree. Kittinger picked up two rabbits and tied their feet together. He looked up for a moment as he heard a Mercury engine start up in the distance. That wasn't his worry today. He hooked the rabbits over the bag to add to his tally. Five rabbits wasn't bad going for morning's work.

He headed back to the estate, taking the long way round. He skirted the frozen lake and went towards the stable block at the back of the house. He found her brushing the horses as he expected. She gave him a wave as he came striding through the gate and he waved back in return. Changing course, he went over to her.

She was putting great energy into brushing a chestnut brown mare. She had a brush in each hand and alternated each stroke. Her face was a mask of concentration as she worked her way around its flank.

Kittinger hung the bag from a hook by the door and leaned the shotgun against the frame after making sure it was clear. Hooking his thumbs through his trouser belt loops, he leaned against the wall and watched her while she worked.

Her name was Hortense and she was Monsieur Moreau's sister. A widow, she lived with her brother and kept house for him. She was short, but trim. Her dark hair was tied back with a ribbon. She was wearing jodhpurs and he enjoyed the view, following the line of her legs upwards. Blushing at the attention, she moved round to the other side of the horse and glanced at him, her violet eyes crinkled in good humour.

"Did you have a good day?" she asked as she did every day, her accent making his pulse surge.

"Not bad. How was your ride?" he asked in return, as he did every day. He crossed the short distance to the horse and stroked the Chestnut mare along her ribs, moving his hand over the thick fur to the back and along the spine. Their hands touched briefly and she started at the contact. He held her hand for a moment, her skin cool before taking one of the brushes from her and working it back and forth.

They worked like that for a few minutes, neither talking. When they finished, Kittinger mopped the floor while she put the horse back into its stall. She made sure it had food and fresh water before putting the blanket on.

They walked up to the house together, crossing the frozen yard. He grabbed her hand as she slipped. She stood, rubbing her knee while she held onto him for support.

"Careful," he warned, his tone full of concern that she was all right.

"Sorry."

"Lean on me," he said, crooking his right arm for her.

She took a firm grip, her riding boots skidding on the slick surface until they got into the house. He went into the kitchen and put the day's catch on the table. Hortense went upstairs to change from her riding clothes. When she came back down, she found him hard at work with a knife on the rabbits.

He'd already slit the belly and gutted the animal. He cut off the paws and feet and eased the pelt back. Taking a firm grip, he pulled the pelt over the head and laid it back on the chopping board. With one stroke, he decapitated it and pushed the skin off to one side.

He glanced up from his work and saw she'd changed into a cream silk blouse with a dark red skirt that ended just below the knee. She perched next to him on a tall stool, the small heels of her flat shoes balanced on the middle rung. Her elbows were balanced on her knees and she rested her chin on her hands.

She watched quietly while he jointed the rabbit into portions. He washed the pieces and then placed them into a cast iron pot. Wiping his hands on a cloth, he was just about to start chopping up vegetables when she clapped her hands, laughing.

"Enough. That's my job and you know it."

"I *can* cook, you know," he said in protest.

"I'm sure you can, but while you are in this house, Michael, you're our guest. Away." She shooed him away from the table and took over.

He sat watching her as she worked. Her fingers moved quickly, holding the carrots while she chopped them, the knife a blur as it moved up and down.

"You do that very well," he said. She blushed and kept her attention on the chopping board.

"I've had *lots* of practice."

She filled the pot with some water, seasoned it and then scraped the vegetables from the chopping board in. She finished with a knob of butter before putting the lid on and sliding it into the stove.

He handed her a glass of wine as she turned, wiping her hands with the cloth. She smiled with warmth when she took it from him. Their fingers touched again and she looked at him over the wine glasses. He fixed her eyes with his own, brown looking into violet. They stood like that for a few minutes, the only noise the clock ticking on the wall.

Kittinger was a man transfixed. He stared at her heart shaped face, the thin aquiline nose, the amused dimple that appeared on her cheek when she smiled. The spell was broken when her brother shuffled into the kitchen, nose buried in a newspaper. They turned away from each other, Kittinger making himself busy with the shotgun, Hortense fiddling with the oven.

Claude sat down at the big table and spread the newspaper in front of him. His face darkened as he read. He gestured angrily at an article and appealed for Kittinger's opinion. Kittinger put the shotgun down and went round to the other side of the table. He tried to focus on what Claude was saying but found his eyes kept straying away from the newspaper.

Claude gestured angrily and stabbed his finger at a photograph of Maurice Thorez. He was the leader of the PCF, the French Communist party. A rotund, dark haired figure, Thorez was raising his fist in defiance towards the camera.

"Incroyable! This man,! This...this...this; traitor to France!"

"Calm down, Claude, you shouldn't excite yourself so," Hortense cautioned in her smooth contralto. Claude fumed as he carried on reading. Kittinger waited while Claude paraphrased the article.

"Imperialist war mongering, the party stands on the side of peace and protests unwarranted aggression."

Finally, it was too much. He gathered up the newspaper in his hands and screwed it into a ball, throwing it towards the fireplace. Hortense clicked her tongue in annoyance and gathered it up from the floor.

"Cochon, merde!" He spat the words in hate, breathing hard. Shoving off from the table, he went to the larder and rummaged amongst the shelves. He came out with a plate covered by a piece of muslin and a small baguette.

He got as far as cutting a piece of cheese before a small hand slapped his wrist and scolded him. His protests fell on deaf ears and he was hustled out of the kitchen, casting a plaintive look back at Kittinger. Eyes twinkling, Hortense went back over to the stove looking well pleased with herself.

Picking up the shotgun, Kittinger made for the door. There were things to do before dinner. He had to clean the shotgun, get a bath and get changed. Hortense watched him cross the room out of the corner of her eye.

As he put his hand on the door, he turned, mouth half open. He cleared his throat, the sound loud in the large kitchen. She looked up from her cooking and transfixed him again with her violet eyes. Her expression was open, expectant, waiting for him to speak. His jaw moved but no sound came out. The pause lengthened and then his nerve failed him and he left the kitchen having said nothing. Humming to herself, Hortense returned to her cooking.

Pettifer sat perched on the edge of a hard chair in his Aunt's drawing room. He kept his back straight and did not slouch. Long forgotten strictures continued to shape his behaviour.

Every year, for as long as he could remember, he had endured Christmas with his family. Even after he'd joined up, he always managed to snatch a few days around the festive season to attend the morbid gatherings that passed as the Christmas holiday in his family.

The house was cold, almost as cold as the weather outside, but Pettifer didn't notice. The harsh weather in France had hardened him. A clock on a side table ticked; the sound echoing in the room. He cast a bored eye over the things that were so familiar to him. The side tables were covered in photo frames and trinkets and woe betide whoever moved them. He remembered one summer visit when he'd shown a rare flash of rebellion and moved items around. His pants had been hot for a week after that little stunt but it had been worth it.

His Aunt Agatha handed him a cup and saucer and he held it steady as she poured. He watched, fascinated as her hands shook and she tried to keep the spout over his cup without spilling anything. He said 'when' as the tea reached the top and then repeated himself. Aunt Agatha was notoriously deaf and it always needed to be said twice for her to hear it.

The teapot went back on the sideboard and he was presented with a two tiered cake stand covered in small pastries and sandwiches. He made his selection and then she moved on, offering the pastries to Aunt Augustine and then his mother.

His mother cleared her throat as she always did before speaking and leaned forwards .

"Is it very difficult in France, dear? I do worry so."

"It's fine mother," he replied with forced cheerfulness.

"I expect you'll be home soon. We all hoped the war would have been over by Christmas. Oh, I do hope it isn't like the last time."

"Did you get the woollen underwear we sent you?" asked Aunt Augustine. Pettifer bit his tongue and answered in the affirmative, counting the hours until the torture was over.

The house was quiet. It was late and the only noise was the ticking of the clocks in the various rooms. He listened to the howl of the wind whipping round the house, probing for a weak spot. A shutter in the stables block banged back and forth but there was no way he was going out there to fix it. Snow had fallen in abundance and the white stuff was piled up around the windows and doors of the house.

In the library, candles on a side table cast a small pool of light in the dark. In the gloom he could just make out the bookshelves on one wall. On the other, there were little glints of light reflected off the gilt picture frame. The chaise longue creaked as he shifted his legs and pulled the blanket up.

He knew he should really get his packing done, but there would be time in the morning, he decided. He liked this period of the evening before going to bed. He had the house to himself and he liked the quiet. Claude was a good man but he could be a little intense sometimes. His passions ran hot, which was both good and bad. It was this passion that had sparked their conversations when he was trying to organise food and supplies.

Claude had been bending over his newspaper as usual when Kittinger had made a comment on the lead article. That had started a spirited debate in his pokey little office, their voices bouncing off the walls while they argued. Since then, Kittinger had to see Claude every time the squadron needed something and the debates had continued where they left off.

Claude enjoyed their conversations. In a small town, you saw the same old faces and Kittinger was a fresh viewpoint that lifted his mood. Just before the Christmas break, Kittinger had come hunting for more braziers, coal and extra food for the newly arrived army detachment. Wing had given him short shrift for more winter clothing, but remembering his promise to Burke, he had gone ferreting for what he could get.

While they enjoyed their spirited discussions, Claude guarded his resources as jealously as the RAF's own supply chain. Kittinger had swept into his office expecting a battle. Instead, he'd walked straight into a pair of violet eyes and a disarming smile that turned him into a stuttering fool. Hortense had come to take her brother to lunch. As Claude was missing, she took Kittinger instead. Claude found them later at a cafe across from the town hall. Over coffee, at his sisters' urging, he'd invited Kittinger to stay for his Christmas leave. He'd also grudgingly agreed to the delivery of extra food and coal.

This last week had been Kittinger's first family Christmas in years. Christmas Day itself had been a relaxed affair. He went for a walk in the morning, letting the biting cold invigorate him before returning to the warm house. There was a light lunch and then he joined his hosts in the drawing room. Claude had got a blazing fire going and the room was decorated with paper chains.

"Joyeux Noel," said Claude with gusto, embracing him and kissing him on each cheek in European fashion. His cheeks were red and he was merry from a good cognac.

"Merry Christmas, Michael," said Hortense, her eyes smiling, her voice husky. He had kissed her gently on the cheek, a little hesitant, and she laughed as she held up some mistletoe above his head. She closed her eyes and pursed her lips and he took the kiss he'd been wanting for the last five days. He was enveloped by the fragrance of her perfume and he lightly put his hands upon her trim waist as he kissed her. Her hands gripped his forearms and pulled him closer as the blood hammered in his ears.

They shared an intense look as he broke the contact and she held onto his hand as he pulled away. He was conscious that Claude was right there but he needn't have worried. His host was merrily warming his backside on the fire and drinking his cognac.

They settled down for the afternoon. Claude read a political treatise and muttered to himself as he marked passages in pencil. Kittinger and Hortense played cards. She had set up the card table away from the fire and they played Quinze, a variation of Blackjack. The player and dealer had to get as close to fifteen as possible rather than twenty one. Play was slow as they shared lingering looks over the cards at each other. More than once she'd sought out his hand under the table.

They played for an hour until it was time to get dinner sorted out. He joined her later, picking his moment to slide unnoticed out of the drawing room. They stood next to each other in the kitchen, hips and shoulders bumping as they peeled and chopped vegetables in comfortable silence. She showed him how to make a terrine, using the rabbit he'd caught and some wild mushrooms from the woods. Kittinger's mouth watered as she cooked shallots in melted butter before adding wine that she let simmer.

She mixed minced rabbit in a bowl with nutmeg, egg, salt and pepper and added the shallots and wine and lemon. She stretched rashers of bacon in a terrine tin and then put the meat mixture inside before folding the bacon over the top. She had a pan ready with hot water and she gently lowered the tin into it, making sure the water came up about halfway. Using a cloth to protect her hands from the heat, she put the pan into the oven and slammed the door shut.

"There, all done for tonight," she announced proudly. He responded by coming up to her and putting his hands on her waist. She didn't object as he pulled her close and looked up at him, her violet eyes going wide. She tilted her mouth up and he kissed her, one hand coming up to stroke her hair, his thumb rubbing her cheek. Her skin was soft and he traced down her cheek, down her neck. She leaned against him and put her arms around him.

He was falling fast and he could feel her warmth, her lean body against his. She buried her face into his chest and he ran his fingers through her hair, his head feeling very light.

Giggling, she leaned back and looked at him with an impish smile on her face. She took his hand and pulled him towards the door outside. He shrugged on his greatcoat and put the big collar up. He wrapped a scarf around his neck and shoved a woolly hat on his head. Hortense put on a dark purple coat, the colour of liquorice, with the cuffs and hood trimmed in black fur.

They walked across the yard, Kittinger slightly ahead, breaking up the snow for her. Outside, he offered his arm and she took it, holding onto him. They didn't walk far, the snow was too deep, but Kittinger didn't mind, just being next to her was enough for him. On the way back, they stopped in the stable block and Kittinger pulled her into one of the stalls and kissed her again.

Afterwards, he sorted through his swirling thoughts. *Come to France and fall in love.* If someone had told him this would happen a few months ago, he would have sneered at them.

Love didn't feature in his life. Aside from a slight diversion in 1916, it never had. It had been pummelled out of him in the churned up fields of Ypres and the skies over the Somme. He'd seen enough death and destruction to last a lifetime and it had shocked him to the core.

War was not glorious; it was dirty, horrific and brutal. He had seen fliers far better than him shot to pieces in a second. Skill had nothing to do with it. At Ypres, he had been charging across no man's land with his platoon. In the next moment, a random shell had landed in the middle of them and cut his men down like a scythe cutting through wheat. There was no such thing as being fair in war, you just kept piling up the odds in your favour until you could kick the shit out of the enemy. Kittinger turned himself into a killing machine to survive. Killers didn't love or woo, they had nothing left to spare after the killing.

When he came home after the war, he got himself quickly posted abroad. He didn't want to see the depressing towns with the depressing people who'd seen a whole generation wiped out. He ran in the opposite direction, shutting himself down. He immersed himself in travel, seeking out places untouched by war and destruction. It took him a long while to find himself again and make peace with his demons.

Even when his flying days were over, he was still part of the mechanism of war. It was all he had left. He looked after his squadrons, saw to their needs and kept them operating. He was the friendly ear when required, the whip when the CO needed him to be. Now, a long forgotten part of him had stirred from its hiding place. Here he was, making a fool of himself in his middle age. The two halves of him warred inside while he ate his dinner with Hortense beside him.

Christmas in his youth had been nothing like this. There was garlic soup with chunks of crusty bread. They had the rabbit terrine, a truffle omelette, roasted capon, roast potatoes, peas, green beans and carrots slathered in butter. Turkey with chestnut stuffing took centre stage. Dessert was small chocolate candies wrapped in shiny paper.

The day drew to a close with presents. Kittinger was quite humbled when Claude had presented him with a superb pair of leather boots. They reminded him of the old style officer boots he'd worn in the first war. They were a perfect fit, supple in the upper with support for his ankles. He was quite embarrassed handing over his gifts, which suddenly seemed wholly inadequate to him.

His fears were unfounded. Claude was almost overawed by his gift, a folio of political thought authored by Napoleon III. Kittinger had found it one afternoon shoved inside a tatty book at the back of a bookshop in Béthenville. Claude reverently held the yellowed papers as he looked at the densely printed text on each page.

Finding something for Hortense had proven to be more difficult. He never pretended to be an expert on women. Jewellery was too intimate and he knew nothing about make up. He spent an agonising few hours in various boutiques until one of the ladies in a store took mercy on him. She showed him a few things that caught his imagination.

Unwrapping the tissue paper, her eyes lit up when she felt the silk on her hands. She held up a scarlet silk scarf but there were other things too. There was a bottle of the perfume she usually wore and a range of powders that made up the mystery of female make up rituals.

Finally, Hortense and Claude retired to their beds, leaving him in the library. His brain kept firing on all cylinders as he thought about the day. He kept coming back to a pair of violet eyes and dark hair.

He started when the door moved. For a moment, he thought it was a draught, then her hand appeared around the door and she came inside, her finger to her lips. He sat bolt upright, every sense tuned. She had her coat over her shoulders, her night dress on underneath. Her bare feet padded across the floor as she sat next to him.

"Hortense?"

"I'm sorry for disturbing you, Michael."

"It's okay. I wasn't sleeping." He sat straighter and pulled up his knees in front of him, resting his arms on them. "I've been thinking."

Her mouth quirked in a smile and she leaned towards him. She put her own arms on his knees, their faces close to one another, noses almost touching.

"That sounds mysterious. What have you been thinking about?"

"Lots of things."

He shrugged. His eyes searched the oval of her face. Her thick dark brown hair hung down in curly strands, her skin pale as milk. Her cheeks dimpled when she smiled. He thought she was very beautiful.

"Won't your brother object to you being alone like this with me?" He pointed to the ceiling. She burst into fits of giggles.

"Claude? It will take a lot to wake him up, not after all the Cognac he's had today. No, he will rise late and complain of a sore head and scold anyone who cares to listen that we should not have let him drink so much."

She kissed his fingers and then ran her hand through his hair. He stroked her hair in return, rolling the tresses through his fingers.

"I need to thank you," he said quietly, sure that every word could be heard upstairs.

"What for?"

"I'm only here because of you." Her fingers stopped moving. "It's the first time I've felt alive for a very long time."

"I'm glad, Michael."

The clock ticked in the quiet, its metronome regularity falling in time with the beat of his pulse. To fill the silence, he asked a question that had intrigued him.

"Why did you come back to France?"

She looked through him, her eyes distant with memory.

"It's no great mystery," she said, her voice very matter of fact. "My husband died and my family needed me. There was nothing else to keep me in England, so I came home."

"And that's all?"

She fixed him then with a piercing gaze, a challenge there. "Need there be anything more?" she asked him, her voice proud.

"Don't you want-"

"What?" she said sharply. He started and she softened her question. "Want what, Michael?"

There was a moment's pause as he rallied his thoughts. Her eyes glinted with hidden steel and his regard for her swirled and roiled within him. He looked down and plucked at the blanket across his knees.

"Don't you want to get married again?"

As soon as he asked the question, he was afraid of the answer she could give. She cocked her head, intrigued. She could see the struggle within him. He was like a drowning man trying to reach the surface, searching for something to cling on to.

"I would get married again; to the right man," she said simply. "But he would have to be a very special man indeed," she teased, smiling at him, willing him to look at her. His jaw tensed up and she could see the muscles in his cheeks working.

"I've found that being in love is like walking along a cliff," she told him. He looked up then, his heart thudding in his ears. "You walk along the edge, and down below lies oblivion. It's dark down there and lonely on your own. And it's over the edge you must go."

He was deathly still, his eyes wide as he listened. His nostrils flared as he breathed slowly; in, out, in, out, long slow shuddering breaths, the sound like waves along the shore.

"You seem to have thought about it a lot," he whispered.

"I've had lots of time," she shrugged.

"Love is very hard."

"The good things always are," she shot back quickly. "If it was easy, everyone would do it."

He looked at her carefully, but there was no teasing now. Her eyes were glinting pools, completely open. She wanted him, but he needed her far more and that scared him. It meant opening himself up and the doors to his soul were very rusty indeed. Her analogy about the cliff was right though. He was teetering on the edge; he had been teetering all week. He feared the jump, feared being hurt, but wanted to make the jump all the same.

"Being in love-" his mouth was suddenly dry.

She squeezed his hand, her feelings written clearly on her face.

"It's easier when someone is holding your hand and you take that jump together," she breathed, holding his gaze as he nodded slowly, swallowing hard. He felt a coward for not saying something but he was undone. His mind cast around for something to say, anything. He noticed goosebumps on her arms. He caught her off guard as he moved suddenly, feeling her feet.

"God, you're like ice, here." He lifted his blanket and shifted over to the side of the chaise longue, giving her room. She snuggled next to him, her right hand on his chest. He covered them both with the blanket and held her, his right arm making a warm line along her back.

"You're leaving tomorrow?" she said quietly.

"I know. But I won't be far away, Hortense," he reassured her.

"But it won't be the same," she countered.

"No, I suppose not, but then I don't think I'd change anything." He smiled ruefully and plucked at the blanket again. "I'll not forget this time with you."

"Truly Michael?" she asked, suddenly afraid that it was all just words. "Promise me you'll be careful?"

He grinned and laughed; the noise rumbling through his chest.

"Promise me," she insisted.

"Is that my first order?" he enquired with a little humour.

"Promise me."

He thought about it for a moment, then took that leap and jumped.

"I promise," he said. "I promise, my darling." She looked up at him then.

"Darling?"

"If you'll let me."

Her response was to lift herself up and kiss him, putting all her hopes and happiness into it.

So strange it is when it comes at last, he thought. He held her close in the darkness and listened to the sound of the wind outside.

1.28 – Leftovers

The first Christmas of the war had come and gone. This was the mythical milestone most thought would never be reached. People had clung to the hope that it would all be over and the troops would be home in time for the festive season. The government debated whether extra spending should be discouraged. The Chancellor, Sir John Simon, insisted that money should not be wasted in time of war. Some MPs maintained that business as usual was good for morale. Few people took notice of these concerns in any case. Everyone was determined to enjoy the festive season. Hotels were fully booked, as were restaurants.

For many families, the traditional get together had been marked by an absent chair or two. Some sons were overseas in the armed services. Hundreds of thousands of city children had been evacuated from their homes and sent to live in the country.

Like everyone else, Falcon Squadron celebrated the close of the festive season. The first batch of personnel had returned from leave and the rest went off home. Winwright returned from his leave refreshed. Even a few days at home had restored his spirits, a reminder of what they were all fighting for. He dumped his gear and toured the field, seeing that Gardener had done his best to keep things ticking along. Mounds of white abounded where the men had been attacking the snow with shovels around dispersal.

He spent a day wading through the usual admin that never seemed to stop. The weather may have been bad, but paperwork waited for no man. Half of it was the usual Air Ministry bumpf that he pitched into the confidential waste basket to be burned. SP's had written up three men for having scruffy uniforms in town. Those went in the bin as well.

The aircrew who had come back on leave lolled around the mess. Over the last few weeks the hut had been spruced up. A few pinups were on the wall, a Christmas tree was in the corner, draped in strands of tin foil. Coloured paper chains hung from each window and the rafters.

Everyone had brought back newspapers and magazines with them, so there was plenty of reading material. Ralph Marchland was sat hunched over a table having a stab at The Times crossword. He filled in a few boxes, then muttered and used an eraser to rub out his answer. He nibbled on a nail while he pondered the clue. Arthur peered over his shoulder.

"Timbuktu." he said.

"What?"

"Five across. A metaphor for far and distant lands under French colonial rule, eight letters; Timbuktu." Frowning, Marchland filled it out.

"You're welcome," said Arthur. Marchland ignored him and carried on staring at the newspaper, willing for the answers to come.

"Renege," suggested Arthur. He pointed to seven across and Marchland rapped him on the knuckles with the pencil.

"Thanks, but I'd rather finish it myself."

"Just trying to help."

"But I don't need it."

"Your funeral," said Arthur, "but you might want to change ten down. You don't spell eviscerate with two S's, because I've never heard of a train station called Sharing Cross before. That's e-v-i-s-c-e-r-a-t-e; one S."

He dodged out of the way as Marchland reached for him and missed.

"Now, now, children." scolded Osbourne from behind his paper. The pages flicked down and he scowled at them.

"He started it." said Marchland, pointing with his pencil. Arthur blew a raspberry and picked up another newspaper. He ignored the front page and flipped it round. He spent a few minutes leering over the Jane strip. The eponymous heroine had shed her dress as was usual and was parading around with naught but a tea towel, her faithful Dachshund Fritz at her heels. Calming himself, he turned to the back of the paper and thumbed through the sports pages. He scanned the articles and then chucked it back on the table.

"Depressing. No horse racing because of the weather. No FA Cup, no national football league, just some local games, boring."

He meandered over to the Christmas tree and pulled on some of the branches, making it sway. He grazed on the magazines but there was nothing he fancied. Going over to a metal cake tin, he levered the top off and peered inside.

Someone's mother had sent a heavy fruit cake. He prodded it experimentally with a finger, feeling the icing give. He wrinkled his nose at the smell of the marzipan. He cut himself a big slice and took a plate. It was a slab of dark, moist cake peppered with dried fruit. A thick line of yellow marzipan along the outside was covered by white icing. He started picking the raisins out and putting them on the plate. He nibbled on a glace cherry while he rummaged around the slice, hunting for them. The slice started to resemble a pile of fragments.

"Steady on," said Osbourne. "Divnae waste it."

"I hate raisins," replied Arthur. He dropped one by accident and watched it hit the floor and bounce under an armchair.

"Then why cut yourself a slice?"

"Because I happen to love fruit cake. My mother doesn't use raisins in hers." He squeezed some of the fragments together into a lump and stuffed it into his mouth. He chewed happily. Apart from the raisins, it was a good cake, tangy, with bits of lemon peel and a firm sponge.

Osbourne scowled, so Arthur pinched a raisin between thumb and forefinger and flicked it at him. The first one dropped short, unnoticed. He flicked another and it hit Osbourne's newspaper. Osbourne ignored him. Another one came sailing over, then another. The corners of the newspaper shook and Osbourne's knuckles went white. The fifth raisin got the reaction Arthur wanted.

The newspaper flew into the air. With a roar, Osbourne was out of his seat, rushing at Arthur, but he was too late. Arthur shovelled the rest of the fragments into his mouth before flicking the plate of stray raisins at the rampaging Scot. Osbourne flinched as they flew at his face and that second's pause gave Arthur the chance to escape his clutches. He went out of the door to the hut like a rocket, Osbourne fast on his heels.

Ashton was walking towards the mess, feet thumping on the duck boards. Arthur nearly collided with him as he rounded the corner of the hut, heading towards the woods. Osbourne was close behind, hands flailing to grab him. Ashton stepped to one side as the vaudeville act went past.

"Hullo, Sir. Bye, Sir." said Arthur, gabbling like a machine gun as he flicked off a casual salute on his way by.

Back in the hut, Marchland slammed the door shut and resumed his crossword. He spelled out Malacca on his fingers and filled in the squares. Happy with that, he leaned back and lit a cigarette. He watched the smoke drift lazily to the ceiling.

"I heard an ugly rumour doing the rounds the other day," he announced to the whole room.

"Why ugly?" asked Mitchell. He turned a blasé eye towards Marchland.

"What?"

"Why does it have to be ugly? Can't rumours ever be pretty? Why do they always have to be ugly? Can't we have a beautiful rumour for once?"

"Such as?"

"Ooh, I dunno. How about the wars over, we can all be home in time for Christmas?"

"As I was saying," Marchland said, rolling his eyes at the interruption. "A little bird told me we're going to be switched over to night bombing."

That got their attention. Faces paled at the prospect of taking off in the dark. Scrabbling around in the dead of night was a horrifying prospect.

"Says who?" asked his navigator, Alexander. Marchland tapped the side of his finger.

"A trusted source," he said with smug superiority.

"Poppycock." came a voice from the back of the room.

"They can't do that." wailed Morgan, his voice quivering in horror. "We aren't trained to navigate at night."

The room erupted in mirth.

"That won't make much difference anyway," said Alexander. He patted Morgan on the shoulder. "You can't navigate in the daytime, can you ducks?" Morgan brushed his hand off, his face sour at the dig.

"Birds don't fly at night; I don't see why I should," he said.

"Lord no." said Timber Woods, agreeing with him. He'd drawn his knees up to his chin, his arms hugging his legs. The thought of having to feel his way around the skies of Europe in the dark made him feel physically sick.

"Owls do." said a lone voice. Faces turned towards Pendleton. He was standing by the Christmas Tree, nibbling on a slice of cake.

"Go away, Pendleton," said Marchland in irritation. He'd taken an instant dislike to the brash new money since they rode the truck to the squadron together that day as replacements. "If you're so keen to be an owl, then bugger off and leave the rest of us alone."

Pendleton's lip curled at the sound of Marchland's voice. It was full of refined pronunciations, off sounding like orf; the clipped voice of aristocracy. He approached Marchland, plate held in one hand, the other holding some cake.

"I was just saying–"

"Saying what?" interrupted Ashton as he opened the door, his South African accent a complete contrast to the other voices in the room. He stamped his feet, getting the snow off. Marchland hooked a finger over his shoulder.

"Pendleton would like to spend his millions becoming an owl."

"Is it true we're training to bomb at night?" asked Morgan, his voice plaintive. Ashtons eyebrow arched up in genuine surprise. He wondered where they'd heard that. He was one of the few who knew it was only the Battle squadrons who were being switched over to night bombing.

"First I've heard." he said offhand, his voice casual.

Confused faces stared back at him.

"Pukka gen?" said Marchland, doubt writ large on his face. That was not what his friend at Wing had told him.

"From the heart. It beats me how these rumours get started anyway. You're like a bunch of old women in a knitting circle, gossiping amongst yourselves." He stood there, hands on hips, casting an eye over them all. He straightened. "My God, you're like a herd of wildebeest, fat and waiting to be killed. Disgusting!"

He wrenched open the door and pointed outside. Freezing air rushed in, hungrily exploring the corners of the hut. Big flakes of snow blew inside.

"Outside," he ordered. "Come on, the CO wants everyone clearing snow to keep the roads open."

"Us, use shovels?" said Marchland. Ashton's mouth pulled into a thin line, unimpressed at how precious they were being. He pointed again.

"Yes, you lot. Now get out there and put your backs into it!" He used his boot to encourage a few tardy souls to move faster as they shambled past him.

The calendar rolled round to the final night of 1939 and people the world over helped put the year to bed. Bottles were opened and resolutions were made and Europe remained at war. Poland had been crushed under the heel of the Nazis and the Russians. The giant chess game went on while governments and generals moved counters around the map. The common man looked to himself and what tomorrow would bring.

Hapless sentries stood in their trenches on either side of the border staring into the night. They rubbed their hands to keep warm and stamped their feet as they waited for their stint to end. Occasionally someone would fire a flare and the dark would turn a lurid red, shadows moving as it crossed the sky. They would peer into no mans land for a few minutes and then go back to walking their beat.

At the airfield, they were getting ready for the New Year's party the French were throwing. Chandler came breezing into his tent, to find Pettifer sitting on the edge of Morgan's camp bed looking into a small square of mirror with a chipped corner.

"Very smooth," said Chandler as Pettifer put the finishing touches to his uniform. His shoes were gleaming, the uniform clean and pressed.

"Good leave?" asked Chandler to fill the silence.

"Bloody awful. The trains were a shambles. I lost at least two days going to and from." Pettifer neglected to mention his Aunts and the family gathering.

"Spare a thought for, Osbourne. I heard he only got two days at home."

"More fool him for living in jock land then." said Pettifer absently. He tugged his tunic down and examined it for lint or fluff. It was his number one uniform and he had dug it out from his suitcase. "How did you do?"

"Not bad, got back okay. You know what Christmas is like." They shared a look and painted a false smile on their faces.

When he returned home, Chandler found he was a changed man. Standing in his room looking at the bed and his things, he felt remote and distant, like that was a former life. He'd grown up in the last six months and become his own man. Some things though, never changed.

His father dealt in vegetables and was up to his eyes in Ministry of Food directives regarding rationing. His mother fussed about him as always, saying he needed feeding up. They asked him questions over the dinner table, but what could he say? The food was awful, the living conditions were horrendous, he'd nearly been killed by his own side twice.

They wouldn't have understood so he fed them the standard lines. There had been a wizard prang, the squadron was a smashing bunch of blokes, the food was good. He told them a highly sanitized version of how he got his mention in dispatches and left it at that.

Morgan stuck his head through the flap of the tent.

"We're off; transports pulling in."

They grabbed their caps and walked through the woods. They gingerly picked their way on the frost covered duck boards.

"Keep your eyes open tonight, Morg. We mustn't miss the chance of meeting a girl."

"I wonder if we're looking in the wrong place," said Morgan.

"What makes you say that?"

"You should see the dolls that Hagen and Kittinger have brought with them." He shrugged. "Beats me how they managed to meet someone like that."

1.29 – First Foot

The French had done their best with the hangar. They'd turned a large slab sided utilitarian space into something a little more welcoming. Multicoloured bunting hung from the roof and a banner with *Bonne année et bonne santé* painted in large black letters was strung from one side to the other.

Netting held up an enormous number of balloons. A wooden platform had been built at one end in front of three high winged Amiot 143 bombers. Spotlights hung in the rafters. A bar had been built along one wall and tables draped in white cloths covered the concrete floor. Maroon material had been hung like curtains in front of the sliding hangar doors to cut down on the draught. Paraffin heaters did their best to warm the air but the majority of the warmth came from the crowd that filled the space.

The hangar was awash with uniforms. RAF blue mixed with the darker blue of the French air force. The brown uniforms of the BEF contrasted sharply with the light blue of the French army. Everyone rubbed shoulders with local dignitaries.

Some of the Battle boys had set up shop at the bar and surrounding tables. Hagen threaded his way through them. He held his loaded tray high to stop grasping fingers liberating any of the bottles and glasses balanced on it. He adroitly dodged a glassy eyed Pilot Officer going the other way and carefully put the tray down at his table. He handed out the glasses of champagne and held his glass up.

"A toast."

He glanced at each of them in turn. Lorraine was all smiles, eyes shining. Her hair was swept up and piled on her head. Her maroon silk dress was off the shoulder with plenty of décolletage on display. Laura clung onto Locke's arm, giggling at one of his jokes and Hortense and Kittinger had eyes only for each other. Hagen grinned into his glass; anyone would think they were teenagers rather than forty somethings.

"We've all ended the year very differently to how we started it. To the New Year and new beginnings."

They echoed his words and drank the champagne. Hagen topped up their glasses and sat down next to Lorraine, her leg pressing firmly against his.

The band struck up a racy dance number and Laura sprang from her chair, tugging on Locke's sleeve. "Come on darling, I want to dance," she announced.

Locke managed a muffled protest before giving in and getting dragged along. Lorraine took Hagen's offered hand and joined them. Hortense watched them go before tilting her head to one side as she fixed Kittinger with a look. She jerked her head towards the dance floor, her cheeks dimpling. Steeling his nerve, Kittinger pushed off from the table and stood up. He bowed theatrically and held out his hand.

Winwright watched them cross the hangar to the dance floor. He was pleased he'd allowed the ladies to come. He still had his concerns about them being a distraction, but he was not so churlish that he would begrudge the couples their happiness. When the balloon went up for real, then he hoped that good sense would prevail. Until then, female company, particularly on this night, was welcome.

Saundby had been as good as his word and arranged transport to the New Years party. He had arrived in a staff car with three Bedford trucks to pick them up at six. It had taken an hour to get there along icy roads. They drove onto the airfield and pulled up outside the large hangar. Before they'd gone inside he reminded them of the behaviour he expected from King's officers and then suddenly stopped himself. He was starting to sound like a doddering old schoolmaster.

Saundby nodded politely at an observation made by the French station commander and then turned to Winwright.

"I don't see your man, Dane here tonight?"

"No, Sir. He's off on leave."

"Quite a bit of fire and brimstone in him I thought."

"I was rather amazed as well. He's normally a quiet retiring type." Winwright nodded a hello to Bainbridge and indicated a spare chair next to him. "I just think the waiting is getting to everyone."

Saundby grunted.

"We'll have all the action you can handle and more once the weather improves, Arthur. Be careful what you wish for." He left the sentence unfinished as he stood and shook hands with the blonde Squadron Leader. "My dear, Bainbridge, we were just talking about the big push."

Bainbridge snorted in amusement. "Not with my aircraft you won't. Nothings flown for two weeks. I doubt I could even get one engine started at the moment."

"We aren't much better," admitted Winwright gloomily. For the last two nights, he'd had groups of groundcrew running up the engines for ten or fifteen minutes at a time to stop them completely freezing.

Bainbridge introduced his Adjutant to Saundby and then headed for the bar. He was still cold from the drive over and needed warming up.

"I almost ordered a load of snowshoes," Saundby said, half serious. "It has been colder. We had minus twenty five here while you were away. I've never seen anything like it."

The young bloods were gathered round two tables towards the back. Bottles were piled up. Pendleton gave some of them an experimental shake, checking to see if there was any drink left. He found one which still had champagne inside and poured it into his glass.

"I heard an interesting story earlier. One of the Battle boys was telling me about it," he announced as general conversation. No one offered an alternative, so he continued. "Apparently they got shot at coming back from the Siegfried Line." He set the scene with his hands, moving them through the air like birds' wings. "There they were, minding their own business; no harm to anyone, when crack went a gun." He clapped his hands together. "Off went a bit of the Battles tail."

"Not surprised," said Padgett. "The Frogs shoot first and ask questions afterwards." He belched and quaffed the rest of his champagne.

"Anyway," said Pendleton, warming to his theme. "The pilot landed in a field nearby, flagged down a spot of transport and went back to the AA site. The officer came up to him, and the pilot said, *"I'm awfully sorry to bother you, but are you in charge of this gun site?"* and the officer said *'yes'*, so the pilot said *"All right, you can hold this for me."* and dotted him on the nose." He was laughing hard as he spoke; getting it out in fits and starts. He banged the table with his hand, tears streaming down his face.

"Boring," said Arthur, yawning. "Someone told me that story already and it wasn't a Battle, it was a Wellington flying near Norwich."

"Over Manchester you mean," said Osbourne. "*And* it was a Hampden-."

"-A Whitley," Woods corrected him.

"Hampden."

"Whitley." They started arguing the merits of which aircraft it was before Pendleton cut across them all and banged his fist on the table.

"Well it's my story and *I* say it *was* a Battle," he said in a huff, annoyed at having his thunder taken.

Padgett leaned across the table, his chin resting on his arms. He rolled an empty bottle backwards and forwards, watching the dregs swirl inside. He was bored. They couldn't drink to excess under the beady eye of the Air Commodore and he wasn't much interested in women at the moment.

He'd thrown his own girl over during his Christmas leave and he didn't want to get entangled with someone else. Her father had thrown a pre Christmas soiree. Going into the back yard for some fresh air, he'd caught her locking lips with a guy in the dark. The man had one hand on her waist while the other roamed up and down her back. She'd been like a deer caught in headlights as he caught them *In Flagrante Delicto*. He didn't even wait to hear her stuttering apology. He just turned on his heel, and brushed past her mother and out the front door. She tried calling the following day but he ignored her excuses.

Into the quiet loomed a party of RAF pilots. At their head was a black haired Flying Officer with blue eyes and a handlebar moustache. He placed two beefy hands on the back of Padgett's chair and yanked it backwards. Padgett yelped at the sudden interruption and his arms flailed as he tried to keep his balance. Handlebar looked down at him and shook his head in pity, tutting Padgett's sudden panic.

"You lot owe us five pounds," he announced, looking around the tables. Someone blew a raspberry and collectively they got to their feet. Handlebar let go of Padgett's chair and it slammed back onto the floor. Padgett shot to his feet, his face colouring. Handlebar looked him up and down. Even right side up he was unimpressed.

"Be a dear and bugger off old chap."

"Something we can do for you?" Mitchell asked. As one of the senior men of the squadron, he felt it was his place to save face and speak up.

"I'm Ian Drake, from the Lysander squadron on the other side of town," said Handlebar. "The last time we bumped into you lot in town at that club, there was some mayhem involving a broken mirror." He nodded to his cronies, "We're here to collect."

"Balls," said Mitchell. "If you broke a mirror, it's nothing to do with us."

Everyone else chorused agreement while they bent some thought onto the event described. A lot of the night was a drunken haze but Mitchell did have vague recollections of a bottle being lofted. They'd been having a rather spirited discussion over the merits of the Lysander at the time. Drake's face split into a grin. He flipped round the chair he was holding and sat down, leaning against the back of it. Negotiations had begun.

Chandler sat with Pettifer and Morgan over a bottle of wine. Morgan attacked a cheese board with a knife and put a wedge of something smelly on a cracker. He munched through it and then had another.

"I thought I'd left gits like Farmer behind at school," said Pettifer. He'd been quite pleased to come back from leave to find that Farmer had already left. The man had been a bear with a sore head lately and it was wearing having to put up with his mood swings. A two week break was good for his mood.

"I had considered going to Ashton about it a few times," admitted Chandler.

"So why didn't you?" asked Pettifer, intrigued at the revelation.

"Because it would be like telling tales." Chandler folded his arms and leaned over the table. "For whatever reason, Farmer's taken a distinct dislike to us and I don't think running to Ashton is going to solve the problem." He broke off a chunk from a block of Roquefort and chewed on it while he ordered his thoughts. "If I ask Ashton for help, it'll seem weak. I know exactly what he'll say. If I can't handle Farmer on my own, then what else will I be unable to handle? No, Ashton is out of the question."

"The problem with, Farmer," Morgan said round a mouthful of cheese, "is that he's a shit."

"He's stiff necked," said Pettifer. He ruminated on the problem. Bullied most of his life, Pettifer had learned to be patient. School had been an ordeal rather than a pleasure and he preferred to let his actions do the talking. He knew people looked at him and saw a weedy physical specimen, but that hadn't stopped him being one of the best cricketers at school.

Chandler had proven he was a cool customer more than once. His mention in dispatches was well deserved and maybe that was it. Maybe Farmer actually felt threatened by them. By all accounts, he was considered top dog until Pettifer had arrived. Now he'd been embarrassed by Chandler during the bombing exercise faux pas.

Maybe things would improve when they got back into the air. Boredom tended to turn people inwards, giving their anxieties room to breathe. Action was a great leveller and the New Year provided everyone with the chance of a fresh start.

"He wouldn't be so bad if he didn't have his little posse hanging off his every word."

"My dear, Morgan," said Pettifer theatrically. "If there is one thing I've learned over the years, it is that there are leaders and there are followers. Preddy and Arthur are followers. I doubt they've ever had an original thought in their heads. If they weren't following, Farmer, it would be someone else. No, they're nothing without him."

"Take him down a peg or two then," said Morgan with a sudden flash of brilliance.

"I've already done that if you remember," said Chandler, moodily remembering the bombing exercise. "Make a fool of him in front of people and it just makes him worse."

"So we suffer in the meantime? That's just marvellous. Why don't we just kick him in the balls," said Morgan. All the pussy footing around bothered him. He saw the issue in far simpler black and white shades.

"It won't solve things," argued Pettifer.

"No," agreed Morgan, "but it'll make me feel better. I'll hold him down while you deliver the coup de grace and we'll all be happier." He tried a piece of gooey brie, scraping his knife over the cracker, trying to smooth it out before eating it. "He's such a Neanderthal anyway he'll probably enjoy it."

Marchland was across the hangar making progress with one of the nurses. She was a pretty little thing, petite with wonderful blue eyes and brown hair. She'd not been a nurse very long; just a year, but she enjoyed it. Now France was at war, she thought it even more important to be doing her bit.

Taking his arm, they walked towards the exit. A white jacketed Steward stood behind a table. Marchland handed over a ticket stub and the man retrieved his greatcoat and her black coat from a table along the back wall. They walked outside and gasped at the change in temperature.

Drake got up from the chair and smoothed his jacket down. Mitchell snatched two pound notes from Padgett and then handed them over to Drake. He took them and shoved them into his pocket.

"A pleasure doing business with you gentlemen." He gave them a mocking two fingered salute and bowed from the waist like he'd seen the French do. "Good evening."

The Lysander pilots walked off, laughing amongst themselves. If looks could kill, they would have all collapsed in a heap.

Negotiations had been going well until Padgett had let slip that he had thrown a bottle during the argument in the hotel. After that, it was a losing battle. Drake had driven a hard bargain but came down to two pounds as recompense for the damage. As soon as Drake was out of sight, Mitchell rounded on Padgett and cuffed him over the back of the head.

"Silly sod," said Arthur.

"Hey," he protested. "It was my money, I didn't see you contributing." He rubbed his head where Mitchell had clipped him. "Anyway, fairs, fair. He could have dropped us right in it with the CO but he didn't."

"Because they'd be in as much trouble with their own CO as we would be, you dunce. Even if we did throw the bottle and broke the mirror, I wasn't going to admit it to them."

Padgett's face screwed up in thought while he considered that. Then his face dropped and his mouth formed a silent 'oh'.

"Bad luck's started already, old boy," said Arthur. He clipped Padgett across the head. "Apparently you get seven years bad luck breaking a mirror, you know." He swung his hand again but Padgett grabbed his wrist, murder in his eyes. Pendleton clipped him instead, then Osbourne, then Woods. All of a sudden, he was in the middle of flailing arms and hands.

He was fighting them off until Arthur swept his feet out from under him and he went down like a sack of spuds. Shoes started kicking and he rolled onto his hands and knees, head tucked down as he crawled under the table. He made for a gap among the legs and crawled fast, coming up unnoticed on the other side. Covered in dust and dirt from the floor, he made a beeline for the bar and took the first stool he could find. Ordering a drink he lit a cigarette, his blood boiling.

Bored after ganging up on Padgett, Arthur went wandering around the hangar. Pendleton, his navigator, Morton and Alexander joined him. They hovered on the fringe, watching the patterns of people moving in the hangar. Most were stood around drinking and talking shop. Couples danced to the music of the band and Arthur saw Kittinger dancing with his French girl.

They went round the back of the stage and stood looking at the French bombers. Big, boxy and ugly, they weren't very inspiring to look at. The corrugated metal skin and fixed undercarriage made it look like something out of the ark. Up front was a glazed nose like their own Blenheim, but here the similarities ended.

"Wonderful isn't she?" said a voice behind them. They turned to see a young officer in his dark blue uniform with two yellow stripes on the arm. His shirt was undone at the neck and his tie loose. He had a wine glass in one hand and a yellow Gauloise in the other. His face was flushed and he staggered ever so slightly from one too many drinks. He walked up to them, blowing smoke towards the ceiling.

"Yours?" asked Pendleton.

"Non. Mine is in a hangar on the other side of the field. This one is the Colonel's." He jammed the cigarette between his lips and held out his left hand. "I'm Lieutenant, Girard."

They did the introductions, all the while looking at the bomber. Girard chuckled to himself and looked down, crushing the cigarette beneath his heel.

"I know what you're thinking; she's not much to look at."

Arthur and Pendleton shared a look. *Would it pay to be brutally honest?* Alexander spoke first, "Well I wouldn't say-"

"-non, it is good to tell the truth. She is ugly, yes? But she can take a lot of punishment, you know."

He pointed out the main features to them; the glazed nose, the gondola that ran the length of most of the fuselage. There were gun positions covering below as well as behind, but it was crude, not at all refined like the Blenheim. Pendleton got down on his haunches and looked under the gondola. He pointed to the racks on the wings outboard of the engines.

"How many bombs does it carry?"

Girard got down next to Pendleton and brushed some blonde hair out of his eyes.

"We carry some internally in the bomb bay, some in the wing racks. Sixteen hundred kilograms all together. She has a crew of five and a top speed of nearly three hundred kilometres an hour." Girard said the last with some pride.

They turned a hair at that but Girard missed it, he was lighting another cigarette. Arthur did the calculations in his head. Three hundred kilometres an hour was barley one hundred ninety mile per hour. The Blenheim did forty more than that straight up and the German fighters did another hundred above that. Girard may as well be flying a world war one kite for all the chance it stood. Modern fighters would go streaming past the Frenchies like they were standing still.

Arthur noted the defensive armament. There was one gun up front in the nose, one in a turret on top and one in the back of the gondola underneath. That wasn't much for such a large aircraft.

"You don't have many guns," he said, pointing at the nose. "Wouldn't speed be better?"

Girard shook his head. "Not if we fly in a good formation, mon amis." He put the wine glass down and then used his hands to demonstrate. He held them out flat, the left slightly in front of the right. "We fly together, yes? Nice and tight." He pulled his hands closer together, the thumbs tucked in next to each other. "It gives us a good field of defensive fire." He pointed to each gunnery position in turn. "We look after each other. We position ourselves so things overlap. The Germans won't dare to touch us."

Girard's voice was full of confidence but Arthur said nothing. He'd heard that before more than once in the last few months and he'd seen the results. He shivered, a sense of doom suddenly rushing over him.

"I'm going for a fag," he announced. "Gimme a fag will you?" Pendleton patted his pockets, found a packet and upended it over his open palm. No cigarettes appeared.

"Sorry, I'm out."

Before anyone else could offer, Girard handed him a Gauloise and Arthur took it gingerly. He knew they were strong, but it paid to be diplomatic. He was going to use his matches, but Pendleton offered his lighter.

Finished looking at the Amiot, they went outside and Girard joined them. They huddled by the corner of the hangar near the concrete apron out front. Their feet crunched on compacted snow as they walked in slow circles. Arthur glanced at the sky. The cloud cover was heavy, but here and there he caught little glimpses of the stars twinkling.

A woman's voice drifted on the breeze and he saw a couple a short distance away. They were chatting to a sentry standing next to a bomber. A few other people were strolling around, taking a breather from the party inside. The couple were coming back towards them and Arthur recognised Marchland. He waved an arm but Marchland ignored him, listening to the girl.

"Get your number dry," Alexander shouted to his pilot.

"Up yours," said Marchland in response.

Grinning, Arthur turned around and Girard held up another cigarette. He lit it off Arthurs and shivered; the cold seeping into his bones. He checked his watch; it was one minute to midnight. The book was closing on 1939 and old father time would be ushering in 1940.

The band had stopped playing. A Colonel stood swaying on the stage in front of the microphone and waved his arms, calling for quiet. He glanced at his watch and held up his right hand, forefinger extended. He dropped it, like a starter does at a race and the drummer in the band bashed his drums, once a second, counting down.

Kittinger held Hortense in his arms. It had been a good evening and he was glad they'd come. Bumping around in the dark in the back of the truck had been a chore but it had been worth it. Besides, it felt good to show off a bit. He knew some of the chaps saw him as a grumpy old sod. It had been good seeing the shock on their faces when Hortense turned up.

"Happy New Year darling," he said as he kissed her.

Locke meshed hands with his wife. It was good having her here. Their first New Years together, this was something special to remember. Laura counted down and turned to him when she got to five, her eyes shining with happiness.

The bloods were on their feet, their glasses raised high. They shouted out the numbers loudly along with everyone else. Many clapped and Osbourne put two fingers in his mouth and whistled loudly.

Winwright stood next to Saundby. He called the numbers in time with the beat of the drum, but his mind was elsewhere. This was another New Year he was away from home and he thought about his wife and children. The boys would be tucked up in bed and Margaret would be with her parents. They'd be huddled round the radio no doubt, glasses of port and sherry in hands, ready to toast the New Year.

He remembered the first New Year after they were married. He'd been Duty Officer that night and no amount of pleading or trading could get him out of it. He got home at two, the house in darkness except for one small light in the parlour. He found her asleep in her armchair, feet tucked up underneath her while she did some sewing, doing make work to stay awake.

As he crept towards her, the floorboard had creaked and she'd stirred. He'd held up a silver sixpence and she'd smiled when she saw him. It wouldn' do for the first foot to arrive without an offering for the house to bring prosperity and good fortune. It must have worked; James had come along that September in 1933.

Arthur could hear the noise from inside and they were making their way back to the party when he stopped, one ear cocked to listen. He tried to filter the voices out and for a moment he thought he could hear the thrum of aero engines somewhere when the world came apart around them.

The explosion was bright in the darkness. The shockwave punched him in the chest, knocking the air out of his lungs. He was flung across the hard ground, landing heavily, his head pounding. Clods of earth landed around him and shrapnel pinged off the nearby aircraft. One Amiot span round, peppered with shrapnel. Another bomb skewered it and it flew to pieces as its own tanks touched off.

Arthur might have blacked out, he wasn't sure. When he opened his eyes again, the sky was lit up with fire and he could feel the heat on his face. He hauled himself up into a sitting position, his body screeching in protest. His shoulder was numb and he worked his left arm, praying to god it wasn't broken.

Somewhere in the distance, a searchlight turned on, piercing the sky with a beam of light. He wiped the dirt off his face and worked his jaw. His ears hurt and everything seemed to come from far away. Pendleton pulled on his arm, his bad one, and he tried to push him off, but Pendleton was far stronger. He swayed but Pendleton kept a firm grip to stop him from falling.

"All right?" he asked. "Are you all right?" He kept asking until Arthur nodded.

Once he was sure that Arthur could look after himself, Pendleton searched the dark, the moving shadows playing tricks on him. He found Morton and Alexander lying in a heap twenty yards away. They'd been much closer to the explosion and the shockwave had flung them around like rag dolls. He bent down to check for a pulse but he already knew they were dead. Morton's legs lay at an odd angle and his eyes were glassy, staring off into the distance unblinking. Alexander was the same, his face pulled into a rictus of a smile. Blood trickled from his ears.

Girard lay nearby. There wasn't a mark on him but he was dead too. His blonde hair was smoothed back from his forehead and he lay on his side, cheek pressed against the ground. The blast had blown his dark uniform jacket off and left him in his shirt and trousers. His uniform cap was a short distance away. Pendleton picked it up, and placed it over the Frenchman's face.

For a moment, the searchlight caught one of the attackers in its beam. Pendleton saw the blue underside of a Heinkel bomber with the black and white crosses on the wings. He stood there, shaking his fist at the sky until he heard the screaming and ran towards the hangar.

Everyone started cheering when the Colonel got to one and the band struck up a cheery tune. He stood on the stage waving his hands when the first bomb went off. It went straight through the roof, slicing into the cockpit of the bomber behind the stage. Those standing nearest didn't stand a chance. Shrapnel flew in all directions and shredded the band. The Colonel was dismembered, bits of him flying across the dance floor.

People dived to the ground, hugging their arms around their heads. The roof of the hangar caved in above the bombers and sheets of corrugated steel knifed into them. Petrol spilled from the aircraft and exploded, blowing out the back wall of the hangar.

A second bomb hit alongside the hangar, peppering the walls with shrapnel. A number of people were scythed down instantly. A Lieutenant had his leg lopped off below the knee as neatly as a carving knife dismembers a roast chicken. He fell, clutching the stump as blood gushed around his fingers. Men and women screamed as the lights flickered, went out and then came on again. The ropes holding the netting up were cut and balloons tumbled to the ground, adding to the confusion.

Winwright fought his way through the milling crowd, looking for his men. Mitchell picked himself up off the floor, brushing dust off his uniform. His temple was bleeding and he dabbed a handkerchief to a cut. He spat to get his mouth working again and shouted out names. As the shock wore off, they started answering him.

Locke lay across Laura, his hands over her head as the earth shook from more explosions outside. She trembled underneath him, scared, frightened. It seemed like an age, but once the earth stopped shaking, he cautiously lifted his head. Laura tried to move as well and he shushed her, telling her to stay where she was. The hangar was ablaze at one end, smoke billowing through the holes in the roof. Metal screeched as another panel of steel came crashing down.

He helped her up and she buried her face in his chest, the sobs shuddering through her. He held her close, soothing her as best as he could. He steered her over to a table and righted a chair that had fallen over. He checked her over. He couldn't see any blood. Her dress was torn on the left shoulder, a scrap of material kept her modesty intact. He moved his hands down her legs. There were no broken bones. She had a graze to her left knee and that was all. He noticed one of her shoes was missing and he found it under another table.

The air was filled with the noise of screaming and wailing as the wounded cried out for help. The nurses amongst the crowd got down to the grisly task of sorting the dying from those that could be saved.

Marchland opened his eyes to pain, undulating waves of pain that lanced through him. He could feel great heat off to his left and his fogged brain told him something was on fire. He groggily sat up and tried to stand. He was surprised when his legs refused to obey him. He was going to lay back and wait for the medics to arrive when a stockinged foot caught his eye off to the right. *Chantelle!*

His head turned oh so slowly, and peered in the dark. His vision was blurry and the flickering shadows confused him. She lay on the ground five feet away, her back to him. He called her name but she didn't respond. With his legs not cooperating, he dragged himself over to her. His hands dug into the snow and he paused a moment to rub some on his face. That woke him up and he gasped as the cold wiped the fog from his brain.

His hand caught her sleeve and summoning his strength he pulled her towards him. He gritted his teeth as pain shot down his arms and his stomach churned. Eyes wet with tears, he wrapped his arms around her and held her close.

He heard the clanging of the bells as the ambulances pulled up outside the hangar. They would get to him in a minute. He laid his head on the snow and struggled to keep his eyes open. He felt very tired. His legs had gone numb but he just thought it was the cold. He never imagined for one second that he was actually badly hurt. He couldn't have been more wrong. A nasty saw toothed scrap of shrapnel had sliced deep into his right thigh and nicked his femoral artery.

An orderly found them together ten minutes later. There was nothing he could do for either of them. The girl had been killed outright by a jagged piece of steel to the chest that had cleaved her heart in two. Marchland had bled out. The snow around him was stained crimson, a smeared trail showing where he had dragged himself towards her.

Pettifer came across Chandler face down at the edge of the dance floor. Bits of debris covered him and he had a nasty gash to the scalp. A woman came over and took charge. She pulled Chandler up to a sitting position. She looked at his head and told Pettifer to keep the pressure on. She rushed off. People more seriously injured needed her help.

Hortense and Lorraine mucked in straight away. Alongside Kittinger and Hagen, they started pulling casualties away from the stage. They dragged them to the back of the hangar as far from the fire as possible. Kittinger was grim as he rolled one young girl over to find half her face missing. Shrapnel had ripped off her jaw and her chest was covered in blood. Glassy green eyes stared back at him until he closed them and moved on to the next person.

He helped Hagen lift an officer with a broken leg. The bone showed through the skin and the ripped material was wet with blood. The man screamed every time they moved, his lower leg flapping like a clock pendulum. He passed out after a few steps and they laid him down next to the growing number of casualties.

After twenty minutes, white coated orderlies from the airfield hospital turned up. Order came from chaos and everyone was moved out of the hangar. The more serious casualties were whisked off to the hospital. Some of the nurses went with them, hands keeping the pressure on wounds.

Those that were left were hustled over to the Mess. The cookhouse staff were roused from their beds to lay on hot drinks and nibbles to settle jangling nerves. With a blanket around his shoulders, Chandler sat down on the steps outside. He had a crackerjack of a headache and a nurse had wrapped a bandage tightly around his head.

He sipped his tea as he watched the blazing hangar a short distance away. Firemen were working hard to get the blaze under control but it was a losing battle. By morning, it would be a burnt out shell. Bomb craters peppered the grass, scarring the perfect white of the snow. A row of fires marked where some bombers had been caught by a stick of bombs.

"What a night," Morgan said as he sat down next to him. Chandler stayed silent. He had nothing to say. Tonight had been another sharp reminder that it didn't matter what you did, if your number was up, it was up. This was his third close shave and he wondered how many more lives he had left. He glanced at his watch. It was twenty to two.

"Happy New Year," he said.

1940

2.1 – Waving The Flag

There were better ways to start the New Year. For the next few days, the squadron was subdued. Taking casualties in action was one thing; they knew the risks and accepted them. Being pilots, they lived with death every time they strapped on a parachute and took to the skies. It rubbed very raw indeed to lose men at a party.

Coming back from the French airfield in the wee small hours, feelings were running high. Most of them wanted to load up the aircraft and go bomb the nearest German positions they could find. It was just as well perhaps that the Blenheims were stuck on the ground, snowbound.

All of a sudden, Winwright heard no complaints when he called for the airfield to be cleared. For the next few days they went to it with a will like men possessed. Whenever snow fell, they were out almost as soon as it stopped. They attacked the white stuff with shovels and whatever tools they had to hand. When the other half of the squadron came back off leave, they couldn't believe it when they saw their fellows out with shovels in the freezing cold. Their amazement ended as soon as they found out what had happened. They went straight to their billets, got changed and were back, working alongside them.

The funerals came and went. Everyone was in their best blue again and this time there was no laughing from Preddy and Arthur in the pews. Even Morgan stood quiet and solemn while the Chaplain went through his interminable ritual. It wasn't so funny anymore. It took the gravediggers hours to hack into the frozen ground and make holes deep enough for the coffins. The rifle party fired into the air and they left Marchland and Morton and Alexander alongside their fellows.

By the middle of January, the fires of anger cooled. There were no more bombings and aside from that raid, the front remained static. No troops moved into battle and no airplanes came over dropping bombs. The hurts turned to aches and aches turned to pains. The squadron licked its wounds and bided its time.

In the middle of all this, Marchland, Morton and Alexander's replacements arrived. Sergeant aircrew, they were billeted in a large tent together while the Squadron got used to the new arrivals. They sat in a corner of the mess feeling very self conscious at the ring of silence around them. They retired early, saying it had been a long day, but Chandler thought he knew better. He'd hardly been welcomed with open arms himself so he wanted to extend an olive branch. He caught up with them half way to the woods.

"Wait up chaps."

They stopped walking and looked over their shoulders. They started to salute when he got closer.

"Don't bother with that nonsense," he told them. "I just wanted to make sure you knew the way. It's not so easy in the dark if you aren't used to it."

"Well, thanks, I suppose, sir," said the Sergeant pilot.

"No problem. Peter, isn't it?"

"Yessir."

Chandler shook his hand.

"I'm Charles, Chandler."

"Peter Andrews."

Andrews looked barely old enough to shave. Dark hair capped a square face with drawn cheeks and a pale clammy palor. Short and pigeon chested, he was a total contrast to his navigator, Michael Jones.

"Tubby, they call me, sir," he said in his west country drawl. Chandler could see why. Jones was big and Chandler wondered how he would fit through the escape hatch. Moon faced with a broad smile, Jones had one of those irrepressible personalities that always took the positive from a situation.

The last Sergeant was Neville Chambers. Gaunt and serious, he was a little older at twenty four. From the RAF Reserve he was finding the thought of being on the front line more than a little daunting. A week ago he had been a wireless instructor with a cosy Nissen hut as his billet.

"Don't worry about the lads. They're not a bad bunch but they can be a bit standoffish at first."

The three new arrivals shared a look.

"If you say so," mumbled Chambers.

"It's just the way it's all happened is what I'm trying to say."

"Bomb wasn't it?" asked Andrews. Chandler took his cap off and pointed to the back of his head. The gash was still a bit red. "Where I got my souvenir," he said, very matter of fact. "Jerry brought the house down at New Year, literally." He smiled. He could laugh about it now, but it hadn't been so funny at the time.

Arthur moved the blackout curtain ever so slightly and watched the four of them disappear into the woods. His lip curled at the thought of Chandler trying to ingratiate himself with the new arrivals. He sat down in a particularly worn looking armchair and picked up a pack of cards. He started riffling them before dealing out a game of solitaire on the low table in front of him.

"Greenhorns," he muttered. A middling pilot himself, he had lofty views when it came to pilots and what they should be. For him, being a pilot was a matter of class as well as training.

"Oh, I agree whole heartedly, old boy," echoed Preddy. He had his feet up while he looked through a copy of The Daily Mirror. "Lowers the tone somewhat, don't you think?"

Arthur peered at the board he'd laid out. He moved an eight onto the seven and then turned a new card over.

"Can the man fly? I mean seriously, can he fly?" He looked at the faces around him. He tapped the embroidered wings on his tunic. "He's got wings on his chest but–"

"How many hours would you say?" asked Preddy. He shrugged, who knew how many hours they were getting these days at the conversion units?

"Fifteen hours?" Arthur pondered aloud. He moved the ace of clubs to one side and put the two and three of clubs on top of it. "That's the going rate, isn't it? At least, that's what it was during the last war."

"I give them a week," said Preddy.

"Maybe not even that," said Arthur, agreeing with him.

Osbourne laughed. It was a cackling rough laugh that cut through them and made them wince. Sitting across from Preddy; he folded his newspaper and dumped it on the table, scattering Arthur's cards.

"Just listen to yourselves," he said, visibly disgusted.

"Yes," said Pendleton in agreement, coming alongside him. "One of them is replacing Mort. He was a good chap and I dare say they are as well."

Preddy turned a superior look on the new money. He'd been expecting Pendleton to speak up and stick his oar in, defending the new men.

"Like attracts like, is that it? If you want him in your crew, you're perfectly welcome to him," he said, his tone indicating he considered this discussion was over.

Pendleton took one step forward, his hackles rising. "Why you pumped up popinjay." Osbourne put a warning hand on his wrist and that small contact took the fire out of him. There were some things simply not worth arguing about. Arthur and Preddy were a precious pair and ignorant to boot. He walked off, quietly fuming.

Oblivious to it all, Arthur cocked his head as a headline in Osbourne's paper caught his eye. He snatched it up from the table and sat up straight as he read down the page.

"Talking of breeding, some harpies have been handing out white feathers to chaps who aren't in uniform." He smoothed out the newspaper. "Listen to this in the Daily Mirror; *It has been reported that nitwit girls are reviving the infamous 'white feather' campaign of the last war. Rumours reach us from Doncaster to the effect that certain female louts are insulting male workers in or out of reserved occupations."*

"We suppose we mustn't suggest that the workers should promptly retaliate by boxing the ears of these you know what's. The sickly stench of powder and cheap paint might cling to the honest smacking hand." He slammed the newspaper back onto the table.

"Bloody cheek," said Preddy, nostrils flaring in indignation as he took the newspaper off Arthur and read the article for himself.

"Bloody good job none of them tried it with me," said Padgett. "I'd have paddled their self righteous little behinds. I remember my father telling me about this from the last show. "

"It's a damn disgrace is what it is," said Pendleton, his temper rising again. "Who do they think they are, putting white feathers on people? Who appointed *them* judge and jury?" Snobbery from the likes of Preddy and Arthur offended him but he could deal with that. Warped patriotism that insulted brave men angered him more. "They should be doing their bit, waving flags. Don't they know there's a war on?"

On the 14th January they got their chance for pomp and ceremony when Air Vice Marshal Playfair came to visit. Saundby, a brace of staff officers and a few reporters turned up in a bunch of staff cars as well. The aircraft were drawn up in a neat line outside of their bays in the trees. The squadron had spent the previous evening doing their best to get their uniforms up to snuff.

Playfair took one look at them drawn up in their crews and told them to gather round. While he liked a bit of bull and gloss, he was just as eager to get inside and get a hot drink out of the cold. He kept his speech short before moving onto the main event. To everyone's surprise, he called Chandler forwards. Nervous, Chandler wove through the group and stopped in front of the Air Vice Marshal. He gave a crisp salute and Playfair pulled an official citation from his pocket wrapped around a box. He unfolded the paper and read from it aloud.

"This officer has performed sterling service in the last few months. Already mentioned in dispatches, he has pressed on regardless in every mission for which he has been selected. He exemplifies what it means to be an officer in the finest traditions of the service. It is with great pleasure that I present him with the Distinguished Flying Cross."

He took the medal from its box and pinned it to Chandler's tunic while the squadron cheered. Caps went into the air as a photographer took a picture. The press took more photographs as Saundby and then Winwright shook his hand. Chandler found himself the centre of attention as his fellows swarmed around him.

Winwright took Playfair on a tour of the airfield. Kittinger took Chandler and his crew to their Blenheim. Cullen walked with them while the photographer snapped a few photos.

When he'd found out that Playfair was coming to the squadron he'd made sure he was invited along. With so little action the last few months, it was becoming harder to write stories that engaged the public imagination. The French General Gamelin had recently been quoted, saying he might consider an offensive in 1941. It looked like they were in for the long haul.

The coffee shops and hotels in Rheims where the reporters hung out were awash with gossip and theories. Most argued that it would be a defensive war and that made for poor copy. With so little to stir their interest, they were playing Boule and Monopoly and cards to pass the time.

Cullen was always looking to make the conflict more personal, to try and put a human face on the war. In Chandler he thought he had found a good subject. Young and fresh faced, he photographed well and Cullen knew he would be an easy sell to his editor for the front page. He made notes as Chandler answered his questions.

The lack of action was not the only impediment to a good story. In times of war, the censor had the final say on what could be published. Cullen had permission to roam far and wide and write his stories, but he still had to submit them via the censor. Cullen knew of a BBC reporter writing good copy on a 73 squadron pilot called Kain. After the censors were done with it, Kain had been reduced to a twenty one year old New Zealander at some anonymous squadron. It was frustrating. Past wars had shown that people needed heroes. People needed to feel they were a part of the war to be motivated to work long hours in the factories.

Chandler told him about his recce flight over Germany and Cullen wrote pages of notes. He liked the way Chandler described the little details. The idea of a lone aircraft ranging over Germany, with the odds stacked against them, would make a good centrepiece.

He talked to the other aircrew and then wandered amongst the aircraft. The men were well muffled against the cold. A parcel from the Women's Institute had arrived with extra scarves and balaclavas and gloves to help keep them warm.

He was impressed they had managed to maintain the Blenheims in these conditions. Trolley accs had been fitted with runners so they could be dragged over the snow. The same went for the bomb trolleys and Kittinger had the men bomb up an aircraft to show him how it was done. As he watched a GP bomb being winched into the bomb bay, Cullen asked Kittinger about his own experiences.

"How are you coping with the weather?"

"Oh, not bad," Kittinger said offhand as he watched the groundcrew, looking for mistakes. He could have said more but he kept his own opinion reigned in. Having lived through the hell of the trenches, nothing could ever compare after that. He pointed to a Blenheim in the next bay instead.

His efforts with Wing had finally borne fruit. Around the port engine and undercarriage beneath was a canvas tent. The tents afforded the men some cover from the biting wind. Inside the tents was a paraffin heater to provide some comfort. The men buttoned up the cowling, packed the tent away and then fitted a canvas hood to the end of one propeller blade. A rope was attached to the canvas hood. The men started pulling on the rope, tugging hard to make the prop spin round. Cullen hadn't seen that before.

"What are they doing there?" he asked, pointing.

"Turning the engine over. With the intense cold it's been tough to keep the engines in good condition." That was a fairly large understatement. Even with draining off the oil and warming it over heaters, the Mercury engines had been difficult to start after being in the cold all night. Turning the propeller helped circulate the oil. It looked simple but could still hold dangers for the careless.

Only a few days before, one of the erks had nearly been killed when they flicked the propeller prior to start up. The engine had backfired and the prop had slammed him to the ground. Thankfully he got nothing more than a bump on the head, but it was a reminder to take care even on the most mundane of tasks. Kittinger changed the subject.

"Of course there's not been much flying. Once the weather clears, then we'll see the shooting start."

"You sound very sure of that."

"Simple human nature, Mr Cullen." Kittinger watched the groundcrew position another bomb underneath the Blenheim. He put a finger up to his mouth and tapped his fingertip off his teeth. "You can't put two armies next to each other without something happening."

Cullen blinked, waiting for Kittinger to elaborate, but that was it. He looked at his notes on the page. It was a little dry, a little glib.

"How would you say this compares to the Great War?"

There was a long pause. Cullen was just about to ask his question again when Kittinger spoke.

"It's a different kind of war now. We used to fly over in penny packets, drop the bombs and race back to the lines. We never thought of things on a strategic level then."

The photographer snapped off a few shots of the erks bombing up. He moved from left to right on his haunches, hunting for a good angle to make a better photograph.

"Of course there's always going to be the need to support front line operations, but it's the long reach of the bomber that can help win this war."

Cullen scribbled some more notes as he walked back to the visiting dignitaries. He saw plenty of potential for a story back home if he could get it past the censor. Men in the field; struggling to cope with the harsh weather while ready to strike at the enemy. He felt a story and pictures would show the public the hardships the fighting men were going through.

He saw Playfair and his entourage making their way back to the cars. The tour was over. As Playfiar made ready to leave, Cullen managed a few moments with Winwright.

"Thank you for your time, Wing Commander."

"My pleasure, I was pleased to see your previous article although we weren't named exactly."

Cullen gave him a wan smile.

"The censors at work, I'm afraid."

"Did you get what you came for?"

"I think so." Cullen waved his notebook. "I prefer to see things for myself."

"And where to now?"

"Wherever the stories are. It's hard work waving the flag."

Winwright shook his hand.

"Then I wish you well. Until the next time, Mr Cullen."

2.2 – Hard Knocks

The first explosion engulfed the stage. Men ran screaming, their backs on fire, their hair alight. They dropped to the floor, convulsing as the world came apart around them. More explosions went off and the walls and roof shivered from the force of the blast. Sheets of metal twisted like paper and fell down on them. She woke up screaming, hands failing in front of her. Her fingers clawed the air. Her eyes were wide, her voice hoarse.

Locke snapped awake next to her, his heart hammering. It took him a few moments to realise the world wasn't about to end and he was in his own bed. He grabbed her wrists and shook her, saying her name, trying to snap her out of it. She turned blank eyes on him and stared right through him. Her scream turned into a high keening and he shook her hard. Her head jerked like a rag doll until finally the sound died out.

"Laura?" He gently brushed the hair from her face. "Laura?" She whimpered and turned from him, burying her face into the pillow. Her body was wracked by sobs, her cries muffled. It took a while for her to regain her composure.

He glanced at the small travel clock by the side of the bed. The hands glowed in the dark and showed half past three. He lay back down beside her with a heavy sigh. It had been more than two weeks since the air raid and every night, she woke in the early hours from the terrors of her subconscious. In the daytime she was withdrawn and distant from him. She'd lost weight; her cheekbones were more prominent on her face, giving her a gaunt, sharp look.

He slid out of bed and went to the small kitchenette in the flat. He groped his way in the dark. The window was closed but neither of them had drawn the curtains and he didn't want to bother with the blackout. He lit the stove and put a pan of water on. He had a cigarette while he waited for it to boil.

He saw her lying on the bed, silhouetted against the moonlight. He was at a loss at what to do. They'd all been scared that night, but she had taken it far worse. One night he'd asked her what bothered her but she said nothing. Outwardly she seemed fine, she was just bottling it up inside and wouldn't talk to him.

He had another cigarette as he stood barefoot in his briefs as the water began to bubble. There was a phrase for this sort of thing on the squadron. They called it, 'twitch'' or 'the shakes'. You hung around someone like that and two things could happen. It could rub off on you and you got the chop, or the CO would pack them off quick smart before anyone else got affected. Hagen had the shakes for a while but he seemed to have got past it since he was with Lorraine.

Locke didn't have the luxury of choice. She wasn't some officer who could be transferred out of the way. He was married to Laura, for better or worse, so the vows went. He just never imagined that the 'or worse' part would rear its head so soon.

He made two cups of tea and padded back into the bedroom. He put one by her bedside, one by his and slid into bed beside her. She was shivering and she nestled in close to him.

"I'm sorry, Alex."

"Hey, don't be silly," he said, trying to reassure her. "You're not the only one who dreams, you know, Laura."

She turned slowly and faced him. He could just make out her face in the dark, her brow, her nose limned by the moonlight. Her eyes were hidden, dark and mysterious, but he could the see the wet of the tears on her cheek.

"I'm sorry, it's just I start thinking about what happened, how close those bombs were. The noise, the smell!" her voice rose in volume, an edge of hysteria creeping back in.

"Let it go, Laura. It does no good bottling it up like that."

"We were nearly killed!"

"But we weren't," he finished for her. He sighed. He had very little idea of what else to say to her. He wasn't very good at this sort of thing. The silence was broken periodically by Laura's snivelling in the dark. The minutes ticked by while he thought about what to say next. His mind ran along very practical lines. It was the only way he could rationalise it

"Could you do anything about it?" he asked quietly.

"No, but-"

"-then why worry about it?" Laura went quiet while she tried to figure it out. Locke took her lack of response to mean he could continue. "Do you worry about getting run over by a car?"

She sat up and faced him, her face confused. She wiped the tears from her eyes. Here she was having nightmares about dying and he was asking her about bloody cars!

"No, of course, I don't worry about being run over by a car." She shot him a moody look. Her eyes narrowed in suspicion, the thought growing that he was playing with her. "Why?"

"Because there isn't much chance of it happening," he said. "This is no different," he said with intensity, willing her to believe him. "In fact, come to think of it, there's even less chance of a bomb hitting you than getting hit by a car."

Laura was about to shout at him for being ridiculous when she actually listened to what he'd said. Her mouth dropped open and she sat back.

"I never thought of it like that."

He got up from the bed again and stood by the window. He leaned against the frame, his forehead touching the cold glass.

"How do you think I get up every day?" he asked, talking as much for himself as for her. "An engine could conk out on take-off. Turbulence could flip us onto our back. I could stall in on landing. Flak could get us. A Jerry fighter could tear us to shreds. There's one hundred and one different ways I could get killed flying." He thumped his right hand against the glass as his voice cracked. He'd just bared his soul, the fears that played on his mind and he felt foolish. "If I worried about that lot I'd never even get into an aircraft again."

Laura looked at him, as he stood with his back to her. He bunched his hands and rested his knuckles on the windowsill. She was entirely ignorant when it came to flying. To her, they were things that went up, came down and took you places around the world. She'd fallen in love with the glamour of it all; being an RAF pilot's wife. The dangerous elements never even entered her head. She swallowed hard.

"Then how do you-"

"-go up every day?" He turned round and shrugged. "Training, I suppose." He sat down on the bed and picked up his tea, it had cooled and he made a face as he sipped it. "It's other things too. It's like not worrying about getting hit by a car. I can either lock myself away and worry about all the things that *might* happen, or I can just get on with it."

He carried on sipping the tea and looked at the clouds moving across the sky. Maybe things would clear up today and they might actually get some flying in.

He thought about the hangar, the explosion. It had all happened so fast. One moment they were celebrating the New Year, the next they were running for their lives. He didn't actually remember the explosion, but the noise would stay with him forever. He felt it as much as he heard it, the force knocking the air from his lungs, vibrating his chest. The smoke had been choking and the heat from the flames was terrific, worse than any bonfire night. Through it all, his only concern had been for Laura, keeping her safe.

He would be lying if he denied thinking about it himself. That was the closest he had come personally to death, but he had seen death before. During his flying training more than one pupil had run into a hill or crashed on landing. This was different, more immediate. Shivering, he got back under the covers and embraced her.

She kissed him then, hard. Her teeth bumped against his as she pressed herself to him, feeling his cold skin, warming him with her hands. She sobbed again, emotion overwhelming her. It was a mixture of feelings, the thought of nearly being killed, the thought of losing him, of being on her own; she hated that the most. She clung to him like someone drowning clings to a rock.

"I'm sorry," she whispered.

"It's all right my love," he said, his voice gentle. His thumb stroked her cheek, wiping away the damp of her tears. "Just try and think of it like that. It'll help, I know it will. You'll see. Just give it a try, will you do that for me?" She nodded and he held her close. "Good girl."

Hagen sat quite happily at the top of a step ladder humming to himself. His legs dangled and he had a pot of paint gripped between his thighs. He carefully filled in the black outline he'd already put on the nose of the Blenheim. Dip, brush, dip, brush. Gradually, the picture took shape, a long legged skeleton holding a brown staff striding along the side of the nose. The word 'CHARON' was next to it, painted in red and outlined in black.

Hagen's engine fitter came out of the canvas tent surrounding the starboard engine and looked up at him. He wore a balaclava on his head and a red and white scarf wound around his neck. He stamped his feet to get some feeling back into them. He pointed at the word.

"What's that then, Sir?"

"Charon?" Hagen asked and the fitter nodded. He painted in some ribs. "Do you know about the gods of ancient Greece, Bailey?"

"You mean, Zeus, Poseidon, lightning bolts, things like that, sir?"

"That's right. You see, the Greeks didn't believe in heaven or hell as we know them. They believed that you had a soul, but when you died, that soul went to the underworld for eternity."

"Heathens." Bailey muttered.

"That would be *one* viewpoint." Hagen agreed, not wanting to cause offense. "Certainly they saw death as a continuation but with no real form, or purpose."

"And this," Bailey pointed, "Charon." Hagen winced as Bailey pronounced it as 'car-on' "Was a god of the dead then?"

"Not quite a god." Hagen went on to explain the Greek understanding of life and death. How Hades, the brother of Zeus ruled the underworld and Hermes would lead souls down to Charon, the ferryman. They would give him a coin for their passage and he would guide them across the river Styx.

Bailey paid rapt attention. School had never been as interesting as this and he was rather sorry when Hagen finished talking. He was about to ask another question but excused himself when Hagen's navigator, Jones turned up with Pendergast.

Jones stood with his arms folded while Hagen carried on painting. He didn't think much of the subject matter himself. If there was going to be something painted on their aircraft why not something humorous or sexy?

"Bit macabre isn't it?" he commented. Hagen shrugged and dipped the brush into the pot, he added another rib.

"If you say so."

"The ferryman of the dead, that's a little morbid," said Pendergast. Hagen stopped painting and looked down at them.

"We drop bombs for a living. How morbid can you get? We deal in death and help people shuffle off their mortal coil." He turned back to his painting. "I happen to think its highly fitting."

"Who said we could paint the kites?" asked Jones.

"No one."

Jones and Pendergast shared a look and then glanced over their shoulders, seeing who else was around.

"I can't imagine what the CO will say when he sees that."

"I think he knows already," said Hagen. "Kitty saw it earlier and didn't say a word."

"Kitty?"

"Kittinger. He's been as mellow as a pussy cat since he met his French girl."

They loved it. Word soon spread and after that Kittinger was often called Kitty, although never to his face.

Winwright saw Hagen's handiwork for himself later that day. He stood for a few moments, looking at the skeletal figure and then walked off. What he thought of it as a piece of art remained a mystery, but he made his feelings clear amongst the men. No one was reprimanded, the nose art was not removed, but no other aircraft were painted either.

Not long after the paint had dried, the field shook to the sound of Mercury engines starting up. The weather had cleared enough for Winwright to order the squadron up for a formation exercise. Skills got rusty if they weren't maintained and his men had spent too long on the ground the last few weeks.

They took off in sections and formed up into flights as they circled the field. Once they were all up, Winwright set course south, looking for clearer skies.

They climbed through grey muck that clung to the wings and waited for the sun to put in an appearance. At eight thousand feet they burst into sunshine and blinked furiously as their cockpits were bathed in light. A carpet of cloud spread as far as the eye could see and they continued climbing, passing twelve thousand.

At fifteen thousand, Winwright levelled off and asked his gunner how they were all doing back there. Assured there were no aircraft missing, he had them open out, B Flight going off to starboard. A Flight formed up on him. Ashton was to his left, Pettifer to the right. Winwright avoided Arras like the plague. There had been enough instances of losing aircraft to friendly fire already. Even so, the French AA gunners thought they would have a go anyway, but their aim was awful. Black puffs trailed behind them.

The gunners scanned all around them, tense and nervous. After Chandlers experiences, the merest hint of a fighter in the sky and they were going to fill it full of lead.

Beyond Bapaume, the cloud base cleared and the frozen landscape opened up below them. Winwright's navigator picked up a pinpoint and saw Amiens in the distance. After Arras, they kept even further away.

Once there were no clouds for a French fighter to hide behind, Winwright put them through their paces. He pushed them hard and then started naming individual aircraft to drop out of the formation. He got them to close the gaps and adjust their formation in response.

Once he was happy they could cope with sudden changes, he did it again, but this time he mixed the Flights and the Sections up. Flying with someone you were familiar with in your Section and Flight might not always happen. He wanted to see how they coped with a stranger flying close. This was not as tight and he lashed them repeatedly to sort themselves out.

Chandler focused intently as he bounced in turbulent air off Farmer's starboard wing. Farmer wasn't as smooth as Pettifer or Ashton or even Locke. Farmer's flying was like his temperament, aggressive. Chandler found himself having to juggle the throttles more to keep position. Suddenly, this was no longer so enjoyable. Flying alongside Locke he'd been able to come in very close, tucking his port wingtip into the gap between the other aircraft's wing and tail.

He'd got so good at it, it was almost a game. On one formation turn, Locke had looked back at him from the cockpit and waved him to get nearer. Taking it as a dare, Chandler had edged in closer, holding position through the turn. Sat in the nose, Morgan had been frozen in fear. His eyes had been fixed on the wingtip bobbing about only a few feet from his canopy. Chandler's whole world shrank to the gap between his wing and Locke's fuselage. When Locke's aircraft bounced on an air pocket, Chandler was making corrections with the yoke and pedals, riding the controls to keep it precise. Coming out of the turn, Chandler slid back out, opening up the gap between them.

"You maniac!" Morgan had shouted over the intercom. Chandler had just laughed, exhilarated by the challenge.

Considering they'd done virtually no flying for over a month, Winwright was more than satisfied. As the weather improved, there would be plenty of time for more practice in due course. Wing had made arrangements for them to make use of some of the French bombing ranges and he wanted to test their navigation too.

Taking a big loop to the east of Arras, they headed back to Bois Fontaine. The erks were out in force to see them in upon their return. Each Blenheim touched down, trundling along the hard frozen ground and then turned off to be seen into their bays.

A Flight came in first and then B Flight broke into the circuit, thundering the length of the field in their vics. They peeled off at five second intervals and then circled round, lining up to land.

Andrews was at the back of the stream, nerves jangling a little. This was his first landing under the beady eye of the CO and watched by everyone on the squadron. He knew some of them thought he lacked enough flying experience but the only way to stop the gossip was to show them he could do it. Fifteen hours of accumulated flying time wasn't much on the Blenheim but he thought he'd flown good formation today. He had kept nice and tight on the leader and there had been very few corrections by the CO.

He went through his landing routine, repeating it in his head as he worked. *Hydraulic selector to the down position, undercarriage to the down position, close the throttles slowly to let the airspeed drift down towards one hundred indicated and make sure the mixture was set to normal.*

He felt the controls stiffen as the wheels poked into the air and he peered over the nose, keeping lined up on the runway. His wingman was turning off ahead of him and he had a clear run. He gripped the yoke tightly, using small inputs to keep the wings level when he first noticed something felt wrong. The nose kept dragging to the left and he was using more rudder than normal to keep lined up. He risked a quick glance at the throttles, wondering if one was closed more than the other, but they were fine.

All eyes were on Andrews landing as he came in. He was shaping up nicely. Burke stood next to Kittinger as they watched him land. It had been good to see the squadron go up together. After all the weeks of inactivity the men had something to keep them occupied.

Andrews speed was good, the flaps came down and then the wheels. Burke was just about to turn around and get things organised when he saw the port mainwheel had not locked down. It hung at a drunken angle and stayed there. The bomber edged left and headed towards them. Burke shouted out a warning but he was far too late. Others had also seen the danger and bodies ran in all directions to get out of the way.

Andrews eyes swept the cockpit, checking the instruments in turn. The nose was still dragging but he was damned if he could see why. As he got to thirty feet he began to panic. His left hand came off the yoke and he rammed the throttles forward to the stops. On the Blenheim, that was one of the worst things you could do. Rather than give more power, petrol flooded into the engines and produced a rich cut, a momentary loss of power. Wallowing on the edge of a stall, with only his right hand on the yoke, the port wing dipped. His nose drifted off course and he headed right at Milton's Blenheim.

He sank even lower before the engines opened up. Surging forward with a burst of power, Andrews hauled back on the yoke to bank hard right. He almost got away with it.

His port wingtip caught Milton's Blenheim between the turret and the cockpit. The wing sliced through the metal like paper and broke the Blenheims back.

Burke was horrified and time seemed to slow down as he watched Andrews Blenheim nose in hard. There was a loud bang and shriek of metal as it cartwheeled across the field, bits flying off in all directions. The tail tore off, flung aside like a rag, rolling across the grass. The turret was smashed to pieces. The remains ploughed through a hut full of tarpaulins, splintering it apart like matches before slamming down and rolling to a stop.

It finished upside down, the port outer wing snapped off at the engine nacelle. The starboard wing reached to the heavens. Metal clicked and hissed as fluids leaked over the hot engines. Fuel spilled from punctured tanks and filled the air with fumes.

People started running before it even came to a halt. Chambers was crushed to a bloody pulp, mangled almost beyond recognition in his turret. Andrews was dead. He hung upside down in his straps in the twisted cockpit with his face smashed in. To everyone's amazement, Tubby Jones was found alive but unconscious twenty feet away from the wreckage lying on his back. Gentle hands carried him swiftly away.

The next moment, they ran from the mangled remains as the petrol touched off with a loud whoosh. Flames licked into the sky and hungrily crawled over the metallic corpse. Paint blistered from the heat and before the fire truck could get anywhere near it to lay down some foam, the main tanks exploded. The earth shook and what was left of Andrews Blenheim was torn apart as smoke billowed into the sky.

It took them half an hour to get the fire out. When it was over, the charred remains were dragged off the field and dumped at the edge of the wood. The bits of Milton's aircraft was put into a bay in the trees. It would be stripped for spares later.

Jones was taken to hospital to be examined. Chambers and Andrews were laid in the morgue downstairs. Unbelievably, all Jones had was a concussion and a cut to his cheek. The doctors kept him in for two days for observation. Milton and his crew also got away with it unscathed but the doctors kept them in as well, just in case.

2.3 – Picking Up The Pieces

Kittinger was bustling around the field when the sentries found him. He was chivvying on a work crew to get the holes filled in when they told him he had a visitor by the main gate. Hortense waved as she saw him looking in her direction. He watched the picks and shovels going up and down for a few more minutes before going over to see her.

She was sitting on her bicycle, one foot on the ground. She wore dark blue culottes with a white blouse and a worn brown leather jacket. She propped the bicycle against the stone wall and walked forwards, hands clasped behind her back. She gave him her best smile but he could still see the concern in her eyes. Taking her by the arm, he led her back down the lane away from prying eyes.

"I had to come, Michael," she said.

"I know."

"You could see the smoke from miles away." She looked back at the field, searching for a sign of what happened earlier. As soon as she could, she'd hopped on her bicycle to make sure he was alive. "Are you angry with me for coming?"

He looked at her then, surprise on his face.

"Good lord, no. I've just been so busy." He gave her hand an affectionate pat. "I'm sorry I didn't send a message; that was inconsiderate of me. I'm sorry, Hortense. Je t'aime ma chérie"

He glanced around quickly before kissing her on the cheek. She smiled and looped her arm through his while they strolled along. They went up the lane once and back again before she let him go. She could see he had things to do. She span the pedals as she got back on the bicycle.

"I'll see you tonight?" she asked, looking back at him.

"I'll try," he said, meaning it. She gave him a wave as she rode off, keeping to one side as a green Bentley staff car came the other way. Kittinger caught a quick glimpse of Saundby and snapped off a salute as he swept onto the field.

The Air Commodore found Winwright in his office, writing a letter to the next of kin for Jacobs and Andrews. Winwright tapped a pencil against his chin as he considered the latest draft. He crossed a line out.

"How does, 'unflinchingly did his duty for King and Country' sound?" he asked the DO in the next room as the hut door opened.

"I'd say it sounds fine," said Saundby as he parked himself in the chair on the opposite side of Winwright's desk. In the small office, his bulk dominated the space. He dumped his gloves and hat on the desk. "I'm not stopping long but I was over with the Lysander boys when I heard about what happened."

Winwright grunted and put the letter on the table. He fussily arranged the pencil so it lay parallel to the paper and then sat back in his chair. He balanced his hands on the arms, his hands steepled in front of him.

"News travels fast."

"Perhaps," Saundby agreed, "but a dirty great pall of smoke is hard to miss as well."

Winwright frowned as he looked out the window. In the gathering dark he could see the bits of Andrews Blenheim in a charred pile not far away. A few groundcrew were looking at it and he saw arms pointing at things of particular interest.

"Two dead, four in the hospital, two aircraft written off." He glanced at the letter. He crossed out a word he thought didn't fit the tone of what he was trying to say. "It could have been worse I suppose."

"Is there anything you need?" Saundby asked.

"I've already asked for replacement aircraft. Apart from that," he shrugged, what else was there to say?

"I know the weather's not been up to much," said Saundby. He lit a cigarette and dropped the match in the ashtray on the desk. "But it looks like it might clear properly in the next few days."

"Good. We need to get down to some serious training."

"I've made arrangements for some cooperation exercises with the French." Saundby scolded Winwright as he made a face, wagging a finger at him. "Now, now. I know you're not exactly bowled over by the French, but accidents do happen. A few flights with some French fighters will help settle everyone down. Also, the army are doing some kind of exercise and they've requested some aircraft to add to the atmosphere. The Wing will be lending a hand. I thought it was a good opportunity to give our chaps a chance to get more familiar with tactical bombing."

Winwright nodded his approval. While the Wings role was defined as giving support to the army on the battlefield, it was not something that had ever had much time devoted to it. Before the war, the thought of close support of troops was borne little thought. Then the Germans had rewritten the rulebook over Spain and Poland. Everyone else was now having to play catchup.

The current rumour was that the allied forces would advance into Belgium and Germany and counterattack. If they did, the Air Component could support the advance from their current fields. The problems would come as the advance progressed. They had no direct contact with the army and any operation would be dependent on whatever information they could get. This was where the Lysanders came in. Winwright expected to be seeing a lot of them once the big push came.

Winwright ran an eye briefly down the paperwork Saundby had brought with him. The exercise was scheduled for the beginning of the week. There would be a number of scenarios to fly with the Wing operating as both attacker and defender.

Winwright saw Saundby back to his car and once he'd gone, he got his own vehicle ready. He'd promised to see Valerie earlier in the week and after today's debacle, he could do with a friendly ear. He passed the word there would be no restrictions on leaving the base that evening and the mess could serve alcohol until eleven.

After her nightmare that morning, Locke had tried to tempt his wife out for a short walk before heading to the airfield but she'd refused. He'd left her curled up on the sofa listening to some mournful French music on the radio.

193

He brooded on her mood on the drive over to Bois Fontaine. She had always been prone to sulks even when they were courting, particularly if she didn't get her way. God knows he'd seen more than his share of them, but she'd changed since the New Year. All the gaiety had gone out of her; the spark had been snuffed out.

He cursed Winwright for not giving him permission to live out. Over the last few weeks, Locke and Hagen had both asked more than once. They had the Mathis and could get to and from Béthenville quite easily but Winwright had said no. While he was prepared to tolerate Locke's wife being nearby, like Burke, he wanted to keep his men near to hand.

The one concession Winwright had given was that they could do what they wanted in the evenings provided they got back before midnight. The occasional blind eye was turned if they stayed over, provided they were back for morning roll call.

Locke spent the day worrying about Laura. His head wasn't in the game and he knew it. His flying was awful and he was lashed up and down by Winwright because of it. What happened with Andrews just put a seal on the day.

As soon as Kittinger had released them for the day, Locke and Hagen had piled into the Mathis and left for town. They agreed to meet at their usual cafe and went their separate ways. Locke rushed home to his wife and found her with her feet up and hair in curlers while she read a fashion magazine. She seemed to be in a better mood and he was surprised she needed little persuasion to get ready. She disappeared into the bedroom while he surveyed the flat. It was no tidier than it had been this morning, but he was just pleased to see she'd perked up a bit.

He told her briefly what had happened while she dressed. He kept the gory details light, focusing more on the flying than on the crash and subsequent deaths. He watched her from the door while she went between her two wardrobes. He liked the way she moved, lithe and fluid like a cat. He adored her legs, supple but toned, like a dancers.

She tugged out a number of dresses, holding them in front of herself while she looked in the mirror. Five were rejected as being unsuitable and made a growing pile on the bed before she made her choice. Personally, Locke would have picked any of them, but then, he wasn't a woman. Deciding on a dress, she chased him out of the room, closed the door and got ready.

Locke left her to it and made himself some toast. He crouched down watching the small gas grill brown the bread. He flipped it over and then liberally spread some butter and marmalade on it. He was munching on a slice when she came into the living room. The toast stopped halfway to his mouth when he saw her. She gave him a little twirl.

"You like?" she asked, fluttering her eyelashes at him. He nodded and mentally devoured her while he continued chewing. She grabbed a blue scarf and wound it round her neck. "Perfect," she said, glancing in the hall mirror. "Now I'm ready."

They joined Hagen and Lorraine at their usual cafe. Hagen stood the first round and had a bottle of wine waiting for them. Sitting in a corner booth, Hagen relaxed; his arm around Lorraine's shoulders while she sat close to him. It had been a bad day.

They made small talk for a while, Lorraine keeping the conversation as light as she could. She already had the day's story from Hagen and the town was awash with gossip about the crash. Andrews wasn't the only casualty of the day. The Battle squadrons had also lost aircraft and Béthenville was buzzing with the news. A noisy bunch of Battle crews had appeared earlier, took one look inside the cafe and moved on, looking for a bar for some serious drinking.

To provide a new topic of conversation, she broke the news that she had found herself a job. Hagen was pleased. It didn't seem right her being in limbo when he wasn't around. Something to keep her occupied during the day was a good thing. He poured the last of the bottle of wine and then shook it before peering down the neck.

"I guess it's my round," said Locke, taking the hint. He got up to go to the bar and Hagen went with him, leaving the girls alone. Locke caught the attention of the man behind the bar and ordered the drinks, champagne all round and a Pernod for Lorraine.

"What a day," muttered Locke.

"We've had better, I agree."

"There but for the grace of God go I." Locke pictured the crash and winced. It was such a silly crash. One slip and a perfectly good aircraft had been turned into a twisted smoking pile of metal. Locke thought back to his conversation with Laura in the wee small hours that morning. It almost seemed prophetic somehow.

Hagen was lost in his own thoughts. There had been too much death recently, he decided, and all for nothing. He glanced at Lorraine who was in animated conversation with Laura. Locke's wife held up her wrist and something sparkled as it caught the light. That reminded him; he really needed to buy Lorraine something special that she could remember him by. He scowled at the gloomy thoughts.

She had been a tower of strength recently, picking up on his moods, being the perfect listener while he talked of his fears. The feelings that had assailed him when Wilkes had been scythed from the sky were more muted now. He still felt it would be a hard fight, but the strange thing was, he had little fear of death itself. He would just have to do the best he could and let fate decide. He just hated the idea of leaving with things left undone, of letting the side down; of leaving her. He left that last unsaid, not quite ready to declare himself. Nevertheless, the feelings for her were there and growing stronger every day.

Hagen sometimes wondered if he had any business being involved in a relationship at all. One part of him said there was no future in it. Here today, gone tomorrow. Another part of him said he should enjoy things while he could, embrace life. The positive side was still in the majority for now.

The bar man theatrically popped the cork from a bottle of champagne and then poured the Pernod for Lorraine into a shot glass. Locke gave it an experimental sniff and gagged.

"Ghastly."

"I know," Hagen agreed, coming out of his introspection. "Lorraine does try to extend my range but I think I'll stick to wine and champagne." Hagen asked for three fresh champagne flutes and leaned with his back against the bar while they were set up on a tray for him. "Laura Okay?" he asked casually.

"She's fine," said Locke, quickly; too quickly. Hagen snorted.

"Come off it. I might be a bit dim when it comes to women, but even I can see something's bothering her."

Locke played for time and poured some champagne into the fluted glasses. He watched the bubbles climb up the yellow liquid, the condensation forming on the outside. He ran a finger up the body of the glass, feeling the chill.

"You see, it's like this-"

Lorraine glanced at her man chatting freely at the bar with Locke and once again she offered up a silent prayer that he'd not been taken today. When she first heard of the crash at the airfield she had to tell herself to calm down and wait for news. It was not the first time she waited to find her man had been taken from her.

She noticed Laura staring off into the distance. Lorraine had seen that look on her face before. She sighed, sad to see her so distracted. Everyone seemed to have something on their mind lately.

"You should take, Alex to see Paris in the spring," she suggested, trying to give her something to look forward to. Laura didn't respond for a moment and she blinked, coming back to herself.

"I'm sorry, what?"

"Paris, in the spring. Mark and I stayed with my parents at Christmas, but Paris in the winter is not the same. Next time, Alexander has some leave, you should go."

Laura nodded, her face glum, not really listening. She ran a finger round the rim of her wine glass, trying to make it ring. Lorraine caught the flash of diamonds on her wrist and pointed.

"That is new?" she asked.

"This?" Laura held it up. It was a single strand of diamonds in a silver setting. The gold clasp was in the shape of a swan. "A Christmas present from, Alex. He spoiled me."

"He must love you very much."

As Laura didn't reply straight away. Lorraine looked up from admiring the bracelet to see the young woman's eyes damp, her cheeks flushed.

"I'm not so sure sometimes," Laura almost whispered in response. Lorraine was shocked.

"How can you say that? Alexander worships the ground you walk on."

Laura brooded with no easy reply. How to put into words what she was feeling? She wrung her hands, trying to find a way of saying it.

"He just seems so distant sometimes."

"Distant?" Lorraine gawked. That was the last thing she expected to hear. If that was all Laura had to worry about, then she was being very silly indeed. Lorraine knew when you married a military man; then you married the service too. Certain freedoms that seemed logical simply did not exist. One of which was being at the mercy of whatever strictures were put on your man's movements. Clearly, Laura didn't seem to understand these things very well.

"Oh, it's stupid," said Laura. "Forget I said anything."

Lorraine finished her wine, glancing at Laura over the glass. She waited for Hagen and Locke to return but they were deep in conversation at the bar, their heads close together.

"How's your knee?" she asked to kill some time.

"Healing." Laura stuck out her leg and pulled up her dress slightly, showing her left knee. There was a line of angry red across her pale skin. "I don't think it will scar. I was quite lucky really."

"Bon; that is something."

"How can you be so calm?" said Laura suddenly, her voice almost an accusation.

"I'm sorry?" asked Lorraine, slightly affronted at Laura's tone.

"Aren't you worried about what happened? The bombs, the hangar?"

"Non, should I be?" she responded, her face pinched, her voice edged in irritation, as one speaks to a naughty child. "I have seen death before."

That shut Laura up. The only people she'd ever lost had been her grandparents. But they'd died when she was two, so she had no real memory of the lingering deaths old age had imposed on them.

On New Year's Eve she'd been shown a small corner of wars reality. All those people laughing and having a good time in the hangar and then the next moment, pain, flames and death. It was all too much to think about.

While Laura wrestled with those thoughts, Lorraine wondered if losing so often, so recently, had coloured her viewpoint. When those bombs had gone off and brought the world crashing down around their ears, the nurses, even Hortense had all mucked in. They'd all helped where they could, but the one thing they all had in common was that death or dealing with death had touched their lives before. Maybe that was the answer. There was no substitute for experience after all. Sometimes she forgot she had far more life experience than Laura. She'd certainly led a less sheltered life than her at any rate. She patted the girl's hand, offering reassurance.

"I wouldn't worry, Laura. C'est la guerre." She gestured to the street outside. "Think about where we are. Towards the end of the last war, this town was largely a ruin from all the shelling and bombs and fighting. The townspeople returned to find their homes destroyed, friends and family killed or missing."

"My God, how did they deal with that?"

"They found a reason to go on." She found her own control slipping slightly as she thought about the last few years. The heartache, the glow of loving and losing, despair and then being loved again, the desolation when it was all snatched away a second time. *We all suffer a trial,* she thought to herself. *I've had mine, more than once.* She glanced at Hagen as he walked towards her, champagne flutes balanced precariously as he walked. *God, please don't let me lose him.* "It's easy to find something worth dying for, soldiers do it every day." she said. "It's harder to find something worth living for, don't you think?"

2.4 – Scissors, Paper, Stone

"Fine!" he snapped, voice strained. He looked around and then tugged one of his shirts off the back of a chair. "Fine! You do that!"

Annoyed, he pulled it on, fastening the buttons in double quick time. He fiddled around when he realized he'd fastened the buttons wrong. He started to do them again and then left it in frustration. He couldn't be bothered. He put the tie around his neck and then looked around for his uniform jacket. He found it on the floor by the window. Without waiting for a reply, he strode to the door. He scooped up his peaked cap and draped his greatcoat over his arm. Her voice stopped him just as he put a hand on the door.

"If you walk out that door-" she threatened.

"What? You'll what?" He asked her, trying to keep his temper in check.

He turned round to see her standing by the bedroom door, chest heaving. Her blonde hair was all tousled and chased off at crazy angles. Her eyes were wild with anger. She held a pillow from the bed gripped tightly in both hands.

"I'm on alert Laura. I'm in the RAF."

"I thought I'd married a *man*," she shot back, with emphasis on the last word. What could he say to that?

It had started like most arguments do, one wrong word, one more sensitive to a remark than the other and they were at each other's throats. In recent days there had been one too many of these arguments for his liking. It had been Laura that had started each one and always about the same thing, being on her own in the flat.

"You did marry a *man*, an officer and a gentleman."

"For all the good it's done *me*," she spat out, her voice pure venom.

He grunted to himself, his mouth pulled into a lopsided smile. He was growing very tired of this repeat performance. Any anger on his side had long since burned very low indeed.

"I thought you understood duty?" he said, almost challenging her. "Well, I have mine."

"To *that*! Duty to *that*!" she roared in frustration and threw the pillow at him. He didn't even bother to bat it out of the way. It hit him on the chest and dropped to the floor. "What about your loyalty to *me*; your *wife*?"

"I was an officer when we met, Laura. Nothing's changed." His voice was flat, almost emotionless. He opened the door. "There is a war on you know, it's about time you realised that."

Twenty five minutes later, the Mathis screeched up the lane, skidding to a halt at the gate. He pulled round the back of the mess hut and parked. He spent a few minutes tidying himself up before exiting the car. He headed for the tents.

Chandler saw him storming across the grass and turned back to Morgan and Griffiths checking the ready aircraft. It was their turn as the duty crew to be ready to go in fifteen minutes if a call came from Wing.

"He's back again."

"What's up with him?" asked Morgan.

"Mooning over his girl again, idiot." He pointed out a leak on the port undercarriage oleo to the erk following them with the form 700. "You wouldn't catch me doing that."

Morgan grunted. It was an open secret that Locke was having problems. He might not have gone into details, but it was pretty obvious that all was not well in Denmark. Morgan wanted none of that grief, thank you very much.

While Griffiths checked out the radio, Morgan and Chandler got into the cockpit to run up the engines. While they got settled, Chandler asked something that had been on his mind for a few weeks.

"Morg? How come you've suddenly become a whizz at the navigation?" Morgan stopped arranging his things on the navigators table and looked round the instrument panel up at his pilot. "What I mean is, you got lost about as often as we found the way. Now, all of a sudden-"

Morgan shrugged and went back to unfolding his maps. He checked his stopwatch and started sharpening some pencils.

"Honest answer? I don't know. It just all started making sense."

Chandler had to laugh. Here was Morgan, not exactly the most reliable navigator on the squadron, and all it took for him not to get lost was to be shot at. He started the engines and checked the instruments, feeling the energy vibrating through the controls. Satisfied, he shut down and got out of the aeroplane. As he signed the form 700, he looked up and saw a familiar contrail passing overhead.

"I see our friend is back." He pointed up with the pencil.

For the last few weeks, the contrail had appeared in the clear skies and flown unchallenged. It had become a bone of contention in the Mess, with a lot of verbal flak being lofted at the brylcreem boys.

"What's the point of having fighters if they can't even swat down one little recce plane?" they had groused.

Since the war had started the Germans hadn't been shy about flying reconnaissance missions of their own. In the Dornier 17, they had something capable of flying unchallenged, at least that's how it seemed to them. He shaded his eyes as he watched the interloper's progress. He must be up at least twenty thousand feet, maybe more.

"What I don't get," said Chandler, "Is that the Jerries are knocking down our chaps when we fly over Germany. 57 squadron has taken a right pasting the last few weeks. Swarms of the sods apparently. So how come we aren't doing the same thing to them?"

"Because they've got the better kit," said Morgan in response.

"Not if we had Spitfires in France. All those shiny new fighters at home and what did they send over? Hurricanes. Why aren't the Spits in France?"

"Saving them for the big push," he said. "It stands to reason, doesn't it? We don't have that many Spit squadrons. Why blow them all in the first few weeks of the war? Let Jerry make his move and then we know how we're fixed."

"The French'll probably say we're holding back," responded Morgan gloomily.

"Sod the frogs," said Chandler. "They wouldn't know pukka gen if it bit 'em on the backside. They're all bolshy commies anyway, either that or they couldn't organise a proper war to save their lives. We outnumber the bloody Jerries, don't we? We should be knocking on Hitler's door already. All the French are good for is stuffing their faces with women and wine."

Ignoring the contrail, Chandler watched as a much closer aircraft shaped up for a landing. The Lysander had spent the last few minutes circling the field but now it headed in, a slight crosswind adding a little extra challenge. It bounced once, twice and then taxied towards the huts.

Ashton watched from the door of Dane's hut as the Lysander turned around. The blast of air from its engine hammered the huts and rattled the windows until the engine was shut down. Ashton crossed the short distance from the intel hut to the flight hut. Sweeping past Anderson as OOD, he knocked once on Winwright's door and went in.

"Lysander, Sir."

"A message for us perhaps?"

Ashton shrugged. He went back outside and walked over to the Lysander. The pilot was just getting down from the cockpit. He tugged off his flying helmet as Ashton drew near and ran a gloved hand through his flattened hair. He caught a movement out of the corner of his eye and came to attention.

"Sir." Ashton returned his salute. "Flying Officer Drake; from the other side of town. Engine problem I'm afraid. We were stooging around on an exercise when we lost power. I thought it best to drop in before we fell out of the sky."

"I'll have someone look at it," Ashton replied amiably. Burke, who was in earshot, was already shouting at some bodies to make themselves useful. Once the problem had been explained, Ashton led Drake and his observer to the Mess for a hot drink and a sandwich.

Not hanging around, the groundcrew had the panels off and were tinkering with the engine. A crowd gathered as they were working on it.

"Look at it," said Padgett. "It's held together by bailing wire and matchsticks."

They looked. The Lysander would never win many prizes for being pretty, but it was solid. Designed to meet an Air Ministry specification for an army cooperation and liaison aircraft, it had a nice roomy cockpit up front. Sitting under a single high wing, the pilot had a beautiful raised viewpoint. An observer sat in the back with plenty of room as well. He had a single Vickers gas operated machine gun on a pintle mounting to ward off interested Jerries.

The wing was big, fifty feet in span, with an unusual reverse taper towards the root that gave the impression it was swept forwards. It had fully automatic slats, slotted flaps and a variable incidence tailplane to give it awesome low speed performance. The undercarriage was fixed, like something out of the ark. Each wheel was in a large faired spat that also housed the forward armament of two browning machine guns. They were still staring at it when Drake walked back towards his aircraft. He noticed the little crowd and smiled.

"Coming through, hot stuff," he called as he wove through the press of bodies. "She ready, Corporal?"

The fitter stepped back and wiped his hands on a rag as his colleague closed up the cowling.

"Just some of the plugs got oiled up, Sir. You'll be good to go now."

"Thank you." Drake spotted a familiar face amongst the assembled throng. "Mister Padgett. How are you this fine morning?"

"Fine, Sir."

"Good, good. Run into any mirrors lately?" Padgett let the comment pass.

"Are you seriously going to take off in this hairdryer?" asked Osbourne. Laughter broke out. "It looks like it might go backwards in a headwind."

Drake let them have their digs. He'd been expecting that anyway. Rather than have an argument, he decided to just show them what she could do. He knew the Lysander was not the sleekest aircraft to look at, but he wouldn't change her for the world. She could get in and out of fields little bigger than postage stamps and while she lacked a turn of speed, she could turn on a dime.

Getting into the cockpit, he asked them to clear away. The fitter plugged a trolley acc into the socket and pushed the button. The engine started with a roar, the exhaust blasting them back. A few caps were blown off and their owners went running to retrieve them.

Taxying forwards, Drake turned into the wind. He brought in full power and the Lysander went barrelling across the grass. Within fifty yards it lifted off. Their jaws hit the floor. They knew the Lysander had a good short field performance, but that was unbelievable.

Not long after the Lysander's flying visit, a footsore Hagen made it back to the airfield. He found Locke in his tent attacking a piece of wood with a penknife. A pile of shavings on the floor was testament to his hard work. "What the hell happened to you?" Hagen demanded. "Meet as normal you said. We'll drive back together you said."

Locke shot him a morose look and went back to making shavings. In his haste to get out of the flat he'd totally forgotten about picking Hagen up until he arrived back at Bois Fontaine.

Hagen could easily hazard a guess as to what had gone on, but he would much rather have heard it from Locke. He waited, and waited some more. When no explanation was forthcoming, he kicked at the pile of shavings on the floor.

"Stop mooning over your bloody wife and sort things out with her."

"Don't want to," said Locke moodily. "Best thing I can do is leave the little twit to cool off." He put the pen knife down and picked up a book from under his cot. "If I go back to have it out with her we'll just end up arguing again."

"Big mistake," said Hagen.

"Well, it's my mistake to make isn't it?" Locke replied petulantly.

"I'm just saying. Better to sort it out before it festers, that's all."

Scowling, Locke barged past him and stalked off into the woods.

"I'll bear it in mind," he shouted over his shoulder.

In town, Laura Locke was moodily walking down the Rue du Fache. She hugged herself, arms folded, hands tucked in to keep warm. She stopped

201

outside a milliner's and saw a pretty hat she liked. She went in and tried it on, canting her head at different angles to see how she looked in the mirror the assistant held up. Not sure, she tried another, a powder blue wide brimmed hat with a small crown. It matched her eyes and she bought it. They had some silk scarves as well. She spent ten minutes rummaging before settling on a flame red scarf that matched her lipstick. It was a lot of money. She didn't care, she needed something to cheer herself up.

She thought about the argument with Alex. He had no idea how she was feeling, all alone in the flat all day while he was off playing pilot. He saw things in such black and white terms. He was such a boy in many ways. She thought about when they first met.

It had seemed all so glamorous then, being on the arm of a man in uniform, a pilot. Now, here she was, stuck in a provincial little town, left alone with no idea what was going on. She couldn't understand how Alex hadn't figured out a way to get posted to Paris or somewhere else equally glamorous.

She kept walking until she went past a cafe that caught her eye. About twenty feet across, a counter was down the right wall, glass cabinets displaying a variety of pastries and confections. White china cups and plates were stacked neatly on shelves behind. Music came from a radio in the corner. A sweet smell hung in the air from the pastries. She picked a table near the window and sat down, putting her purchases on a seat next to her.

The waiter came over and she ordered coffee along with a sandwich and some fruit. It would be the first thing she'd eaten today. Someone had left a newspaper behind on the seat and she idly looked through it while she waited for her lunch to arrive.

Her French wasn't very good but the headlines were fairly clear: 'Fight the Germans, defend France'. The rest of it made little sense and she turned pages without really looking until she realised there was someone standing next to her.

Glancing up, she saw a tall man with dark hair and grey eyes. He looked like an older David Niven, right down to the thin pencil moustache. He wore a sharp blue business suit with gold cufflinks glinting at the wrist. He gestured to the newspaper in her hand.

"I'm sorry Mademoiselle, I left my newspaper behind."

Laura blushed and her heart did a small flip flop when she heard his voice; sonorous rolling vowels with a slight accent. It was like smooth caramel to her ears. She folded the newspaper and offered it to his outstretched hand, eyes wide, mouth slightly open.

"May I join you?" he asked. He pointed to the chair across from her and she managed a small nod. He sat down and clasped his hands on the tabletop in front of him.

She held out her left hand, wedding band clearly visible glinting on her ring finger. He took it and theatrically kissed her knuckles, his thin moustache just brushing her skin.

"I'm Laura Locke," she said by way of introduction.

"Pascal Dubreton," he said in return, his voice turning her knees to jelly. "I don't believe I've seen you round here before?"

"N-no," she managed to stammer. "I was taking a walk and saw the cafe." Her hands fidgeted under the table.

They sat chatting for an hour, covering a vast range of subjects. It was only afterwards that Laura realised she'd been doing most of the talking. The perfect listener, he sat nodding while she poured out the catalogue of woes. Being on her own, feeling lonely, how the war was not what she had expected it to be, it all sounded so feeble.

She liked it when he smiled. His top lip pulled back to reveal a perfect row of white teeth and his eyes were mesmerising. He had a small import business in town, he explained. He'd been having a late lunch when he forgot his paper and came back for it. She apologised for keeping him from his work but he assured her it could wait. After all, what was work in comparison to the company of a beautiful woman?

Flattered at the attention, her earlier mood was soon forgotten. He asked her what she had bought and she took great pleasure in showing him her hat. He laughed when she asked him if it made her look more like Carole Lombard. She agreed to meet him for lunch the following day and he walked her to the corner of the street before saying his goodbyes. Laura walked back to the flat smiling, she had found a friend.

2.5 – Every Dog Has His Day

It had been a good week since Andrews crash. The weather forecasts had been spot on and the clear weather had continued. The ground remained rock hard with temperatures still hovering around zero. Farmer had come to hate the teeth shattering juddering as they rumbled across the field on take off and landing.

Snow remained in piles around the field but the hard work in clearing the main areas paid dividends now. According to the gossip, a number of Battle squadrons further east were still snowed in.

Two replacement aircraft were flown in, putting them back up to full strength. No one mentioned the crash. Andrews had got the 'chop'. Like chip shop papers, he was in yesterday's news. His fate was relegated to memory to be recalled in the future purely for 'do you remember' type anecdotes.

With clearer weather had come hard work. Every morning the erks came out and ran up the aircraft. The Blenheims were an icebox inside but they all started first time. The cookhouse laid on warm porridge, bacon and eggs and toast for breakfast to keep them going.

Winwright would come out of his hut and twirl his hand above his head. There was no briefing, he'd told them what he wanted, perfection. All they had to do was follow him and keep it nice and tight. They did their best. For two hours, he tested their skills, squadron formation climbs, splitting off into sections, reforming after bomb runs. He ran them through everything they would need to fight and fly as a unit. They came back for lunch, minds buzzing from concentration.

In the afternoon, they were sent off on single navigation exercises. It had come as a welcome relief after the trials of the morning, a relaxing jaunt in the country Preddy had called it. In truth, no one really relaxed. Being shot up by friendly fighters was too fresh in their minds. They missed the security of flying as a group and spent the entire time tense and jumping at shadows.

The fighter familiarisation exercise earlier in the week had been interesting. Assembling over the French countryside, they had gone south to meet up with the fighters. Pendleton saw them first. They all nervously watched as three Morane Saulnier fighters gave them a once over before ending up on their port beam.

Farmer thought the Morane an ugly looking plane, but then, most French aircraft were pretty ugly. The Morane was stubby and blocky, not at all like the sleek lines of the Spitfire or the larger Hurricane. It could only go forty miles an hour faster on the level than a Blenheim.

Winwright and the lead French pilot had conversed in a mish mash of language to agree on a plan of action. Peeling off, the fighters disappeared into a cloud and then climbed for height. They headed east to use the sun to their advantage.

After ten minutes, some of them thought the French had done a bunk when they came screaming down out of the sky. They dived either side of the formation before standing on their tails and going back up. Reforming, they came in from behind for a much more conventional stern attack.

Gunners sat in their turrets and made machine gun noises to themselves. It was all one big ludicrous game of cowboys and Indians while the French came in from every possible angle. Occasionally, Winwright told a pilot he'd been hit and had them drop out of the formation, opening up a gap in the defences. The squadron had to adjust their positions to maintain their hedge of defensive fire.

Winwright was less amused when he dropped out of the lead position to simulate being hit and the formation went to pieces. Some of them followed him down, others pressed on. Those at the back of the squadron had to break hard to avoid a pile up and all the neat and tidy unit cohesion was lost in seconds.

The French swooped in to exploit the confusion like dogs snapping at their heels. Winwright was quite sure they would have suffered losses if that had been for real. Eventually, they got back into some kind of formation but it took a good few minutes to restore order.

The French fighters formed back up into a vic and came up alongside Winwright. They asked if he wanted another turn but Winwright sent them on their way. Nerves had been frazzled enough for one day.

The following day, there were more navigational exercises and more dummy attacks from fighters. An RAF hurricane squadron used them for target practice this time. Winwright had aircraft drop out of the exercise to see how the men would cope. It was less of a mess than the previous day's effort, but there were still a few hairy moments. Overall though, there had been visible improvement.

Feeling buoyant, Falcon squadron looked forward to the army exercise with some confidence. Their formation flying would keep them safe. Now they had to show their bombing could get the job done. There was no point fighting all the way across to a target if the bombs missed.

Bright and early, a staff car turned up and disgorged two officers before speeding off towards Béthenville. They were umpires for the coming games. They wandered around the airfield with white armbands on their sleeves while the squadron went about its daily business.

At seven thirty, these umpires gathered the crews together. In a packed room, they pointed to a map board and described the coming events. The red forces were advancing north west from Hazebrouck, attacking the blue forces around Watten. The squadron would play their part by flying over the 'front lines' to drop live bombs in a designated area. They would then defend themselves from fighter attack. Umpires on the ground watching the aerial ballet would later assess casualties.

It all sounded fun. Go to A, fly around a bit, go home. There were worse ways to pass the day. Winwright told them he wanted a lot of swank when they flew over the army. Tight formation, tight turns, good bombing. There were bigwigs to impress and Winwright had no doubt that Saundby would be there keeping tabs on their performance.

They flew over the exercise area to see men moving around like ants across the countryside. French tanks swept across the fields, leaving trails of flattened grass behind them. Red smoke and black arrowhead panels laid out on the ground indicated the field they were to bomb. They sauntered along unchallenged to drop two 250lb bombs each.

It was all an illusion, of course. They weren't rocked by flak, they weren't molested by fighters. It was all very pretty and sanitised.

After the bomb run, some sleek Dewoitine 520's swept into the attack. Farmer was much more impressed by them than the blocky Moranes. Faster and more heavily armed, the Dewoitines were brand new and only a few of them were yet in service. They fluttered around to make three passes from astern before beetling off for home.

On landing, there was an outraged howl when the umpires assessed that half the attacking force of bombers had been shot down. Incensed, Winwright had turned the air blue and spent considerable time bending the ear of the umpires to little avail.

They flew twice more that day, each time heading northwest and dropping practice bombs in support of the advance of the red forces. For the final attack, they had an escort of six Moranes that chased the Dewoitines away.

By the end of the day, the umpires had ruled that from their three sorties, half the squadron had been shot down. There was general derision of that assessment. The army officers took the relentless ribbing in good humour and they joined in the mess games with gusto just as much as everyone else.

The following morning, the umpires had enforced the casualty assessment. To add insult to injury, they ruled that both Winwright and Ashton had fallen to enemy fire. As a result, Gardner led nine aircraft in three vics into the crisp morning sky. The blue forces were counterattacking and the squadron was to 'bomb' a bridge to halt the enemy advance.

Flying at half strength, Gardner split them up into three vics to give them as much chance as possible of hitting the target. Farmer was not sure he entirely agreed with that. Flying together afforded them more protection, which he felt was an overriding priority.

They were five minutes out from the target when he saw white puffs of smoke from Gardner's starboard engine. He used a little rudder to drift right, putting some space between himself and his flight leader. Gardner's Blenheim juddered and Farmer could see he clearly had a problem. The puffs of smoke coalesced into a steady stream of smoke and he shouted up over the RT.

"Are you okay, Red Leader?"

He got a curt 'roger' in reply while Gardner fought the controls of his bomber. The Blenheim surged backwards and forwards. Finally, Gardner admitted defeat and waggled his wings.

"Move up red two. I'm losing power."

He put his nose down and dropped out of the formation. Farmer acknowledged and took up the lead position with Hagen on his left wing. Coming up to the exercise area, he could see a large cloud of smoke clinging to the ground around a bridge and a road. Men moved over the ground, pausing to stop and fire at the 'enemy'. Somewhere down there were some brass hat's and reporters watching the show. Farmer had no doubt this would all be in a newsreel at some point in the future.

He began his descent and leveled off at three thousand feet. Down in the nose, Preddy had a view of everything. At his ten o'clock was the bridge where all the action was taking place. At two o'clock there was an area of woodland with white panels pointing towards it and a thin stream of red smoke rising from the middle of the trees.

It was almost too easy. With the red smoke drifting up from the wood, Preddy knew exactly what the wind was doing. He adjusted the sight for drift and lined up on the target. Farmer kept it smooth, running them in on rails and Preddy had to make few adjustments to stay lined up.

Preddy's finger hovered over the release. Due to a peculiarity of design, there was a random wrinkle he had to take into account when dropping bombs in the Blenheim. The bomber didn't have powered bomb doors. They were kept shut by elasticated bungee cords and the doors opened by the weight of the bombs dropping against them which varied slightly on the strength of the bungee cord. Anticipating a half second delay, Preddy thumbed the release and there was a slight bounce as the 250lb bombs dropped free.

"They're away."

Farmer climbed in a gentle turn and closed the throttles slightly to give the other sections a chance to latch on behind. He orbited to the right, giving them the opportunity to cut the corner and catch up when Gardner came over the air.

"Bandits, bandits!"

"Where away, Red Leader?"

"East of your position. There's a flight of 110's wanting to play."

Farmer looked to his right and saw Gardner's solitary Blenheim heading towards them with three dots not far behind. Judging the distance, Farmer reckoned he had about thirty seconds before the 110's were on him. Gardner had no chance whatsoever on his own. There were no friendly fighters in sight, so Farmer made a spur of the moment decision. He couldn't stand idly by and watch Gardner die and it was always said the best form of defence was attack. He continued his turn and headed towards his flight leader, dragging Hagen and the other two vics with him.

On the ground, Saundby stood next to two Brigadiers and a clutch of French generals as he saw the scene unfolding through a pair of binoculars. Black smoke rose from the woods where the 250lb bombs had landed bang on the button. It was another testament to how good Winwright's training had been. One of the Battle units that had bombed earlier in the day but their formation flying was sloppy in comparison. Saundby's heart was in his mouth as he saw the lone Blenheim being chased by the 110's.

A Brigadier pointed and asked aloud, "What the devil does he think he's doing?"

"The only thing he can," replied Saundby. "He's turning to fight."

Twenty yards away, a Pathé news crew were turning their camera to capture what was going on. Cullen stood next to them. He'd just been about to leave but now he stood in rapt attention.

He saw the Blenheims open up their formation slightly, giving themselves room to move independently within the Flight. Even as they raced to the rescue, Cullen could see that the single Blenheim was in trouble. Already

207

streaming a thin white trail from one engine, he saw it stagger from repeated hits. Pieces flew off the airframe and then the first lick of flame appeared along the port wing.

The Blenheims opened fire, their guns as effective as children's catapults. Holding their course, they passed over their stricken fellow and flew straight at the marauding Huns. Cullen winced as the two formations were closing awfully fast.

"Is everyone tucked in back there?" Farmer asked Keller in his turret. Without waiting for an answer, he advanced the throttle and pulled the boost. There was a moment's pause and then his Blenheim shot forwards, engines screaming at full power. He didn't have time to be scared. Bombers simply didn't take on fighters like this, but here he was, the bit between his teeth rushing headlong towards them.

Preddy came up out of the nose and sat down next to Farmer. He leaned close and shouted to make himself heard above the engines.

"Are you crazy? We've only got one gun."

"But there's eight of us and only three of them. Huns are bullies. They don't like it when the kids in the playground stand up to them."

He hoped he was right. Gardner was doing his best, but on his own it was only a matter of time. The 110's fired, their cannons picking him apart. They shredded his tail and then walked their shells up the fuselage, peppering the port wing. Fuel streamed back from punctured tanks and then ignited.

Raging, Farmer aimed his whole aircraft right at the lead 110, a big grey bastard with a red and white shark's mouth painted on the nose. Long before he was in range, he held down the gun button on the yoke and his pathetic single wing mounted gun started to fire. Preddy flinched and clutched his navigator's bag tightly in front of himself as if that would ward off bullets.

The rest of the Flight joined in, eight streams of ball and tracer reaching forwards to the marauding 110's. Before the two formations flew through each other, the 110's broke off hard to the left. Gardner's stricken Blenheim passed underneath going the opposite direction. Farmer broke right and split the Flight in two, telling sections two and three to turn around and escort Gardner while he continued to chase the 110's.

Like a bulldog in a yard, he snapped at the heels of the German fighters to send them on their way. Once he was happy they were leaving, he turned back to rejoin the Flight. As the Germans withdrew from the field, ack ack belatedly opened up, the black puffs exploding far behind them.

No sooner had he turned around, Farmer saw Gardner's Blenheim lurch to the left, trailing a banner of flame behind it. One parachute appeared; then another.

"Come on, come on," Farmer muttered as he watched, helpless, as the bomber nosed in.

He breathed a sigh of relief as the final parachute opened, floating on the breeze. The Blenheims circled them all the way down to the ground, keeping a weather eye out in case the 110's decided to come back. Once they were safe on the ground, they turned for home, elated at the action.

It should never be said that officialdom misses every opportunity presented to it. The press loves a hero. A hero who comes to the aid of a comrade in trouble made even better news. Someone who rushes to the aid of a comrade under the noses of the brass was even more blessed.

Before they even made it back to the field, Winwright knew what had happened in the finest detail. By the time they landed, everyone was waiting to see them in. Once word came through that Gardner and his crew had been safely picked up, there were smiles all round.

Cullen drove immediately back to Rheims to file an article. He managed to get a short story through the censor that was broadcast the following evening on the BBC.

The piece de resistance came a few days later when a full page story ran in the newspapers. Sanitised, of course, it proclaimed the fighting spirit of the RAF and the lack of courage of the cowardly Germans. If the Pathé news hadn't recorded it, no one would have believed it. They'd caught it all; from Gardner's Blenheim being shot down, to Farmers' charge. They also got some footage of Gardner's crew being picked up, parachutes under their arms as Generals and Brigadiers shook their hands. It was all jolly hockey sticks and home in time for tea and medals. The folks back home must have loved it and Farmer felt a thrill of pride when he saw it in the cinema at Béthenville.

Farmer was given an immediate award of the DFC. Officially, it was from the King but the paperwork would be filed later. When the brass pinned the medal to his chest, Farmer felt so proud he was fit to burst. The respect of his peers meant a lot to him, but there was only one person's approval he really wanted, his fathers.

The son of a war hero, people often told Farmer that he should be proud of his father and he was. The family name was important to him. Farmer's for generations had been in the army, serving the country. Farmer's had fought in every major campaign for the last one hundred years going back to Waterloo. He was the first to the take to the air and he felt the weight of family history on his shoulders when he'd gone to war.

Throughout his life he'd felt a need to prove himself. As a young boy, he'd interpreted his father's indifference as disappointment. He'd expended a lot of time and effort trying to show he was worthy of the family name, to gain his father's approval.

Major Farmer had returned from the Great War in 1919, feted as a hero. His single handed attack on a cluster of German machine gun nests had earned him the Military Cross. Crawling through the mud, he had flanked them and got in close before throwing his grenades. Then he charged in, clearing each nest on his own with a pistol and a knife.

Farmer never heard from his father what actually happened. The yellowed newspaper clippings called it a heroic act. The citation framed on the wall laid out in dry verse the official version. Neither of them gave a young boy much insight into what had changed their father into a hollow shell of their former self. Vague memories of a father who smiled and played with him were replaced by a man who never smiled, his mind stuck in the horrors of the western Front. Once a year, the Major donned his uniform and his medals and stood at the cenotaph holding a wreath of poppies, his face unmoving.

Over the years, Farmer had thought a number of times about what made a hero. Books and newspapers always talked about courage in the face of fearsome odds, but that was too simplistic for him. Glory hounds like Pendleton might talk a good game, but line shooting made a man unpopular. No one was willing to follow someone like that, you were liable to get killed and all for their benefit.

He fought with the dilemma as he always did, head on. At school he had the reputation of being determined, even headstrong. At rugby, his aggression on the field gained him a reputation that gave him time to take the initiative from his opponents. In the air, he went straight at something too. This directness sometimes caused him problems. Higher rank required a certain subtlety. It was no secret he was one of the older Flight Lieutenants on the squadron for a reason.

For all his uncertainty, when the moment of crisis had come he'd not been found wanting. He hadn't hesitated, he'd balanced the odds and he had acted.

It was only later that doubts gnawed at him. What-ifs played games with his head. Those doubts resurfaced when he saw the newsreel. Sitting in the dark, seeing the action unfold in the third person, he realised how different the outcome *could* have been. Maybe that was the secret he decided in the end. Maybe worrying about the what-ifs made you hesitate at the moment when you needed to decide.

He tried putting his thoughts down on paper. He wrote a long rambling letter to his father, but in the end he had torn it up. It didn't say what he wanted. In the end, he sent the newspaper clippings in an envelope to join the other relics in the family library.

2.6 – Twilight Blues

Pettifer took another look out of the cockpit at the ground and scowled. It was still the same as it was two minutes before. A bank of cloud clung low to the undulating terrain, blanketing the land in grey clag. He made another wide circuit, hunting for a glimpse of anything that would let them get a fix. They were close to home, he knew that, but he needed to know exactly where they were. The field was on an elevated ridge west of Béthenville and he didn't relish the idea flying into the side of a hill.

The Section had set off four hours before for a simple navigation exercise. Winwright wanted them to fly to six points on a map and return. Everything had been fine until the return trip when the weather closed in. For the last thirty minutes they'd been casting around for a pinpoint. The clouds though were not the real worry. They had more than enough fuel to stay up for hours yet, it was the fading light. Pettifer reckoned they had another thirty minutes before the light went and then they would be flailing around in the dark.

"Anything, Baker?" He saw his navigator's head bobbing around up front, searching for the merest glimmer of an opening.

"I've got absolutely nothing, Sir."

Pettifer considered his options. Anderson and Pendleton were depending on him to make the right decision. He knew Béthenville was south of them, the cloud was not as thick there. The heat from the town thinned it out but they couldn't land on houses. West, there was nothing but a grey curtain as far as the eye could see. The last resort would be to pick a point, descend blind and pray they didn't fly into the ground.

"What about Merville?" he suggested out loud.

Baker played with his maps. Merville would be perfect. About ten miles north of Béthenville, it was a French airfield the Battle squadrons had taken over. The surrounding land was flat which made it a safer proposition if the worst came to the worst. The trick was going to be finding it.

Reversing his course, Pettifer headed back to Béthenville. Once they had a fix on the town, they could fly a dead reckoning course to Merville and see what happened. In the time it took them to get back to the town, the sun started to disappear beyond the horizon. The grey cloud became even more solid in the dark, odd highlights limned by the remaining light, like rolling hills. Even Béthenville was almost lost to view. The only sign of it was a thinning in the clag and a few badly blacked out windows. Thankfully, the belfry stood nice and tall amongst the black.

He circled until Baker was happy, then they headed zero one zero, feeling their way. Cruising along, they had about three minutes flying time before they were over where the airfield should be. Even before they got there,

Pettifer knew there was going to be no easy fix. The cloud was no different here as it was over Bois Fontaine so he took them back up to five thousand feet and Pettifer had Willis drop a parachute flare.

It burst into life, thousands of candle power shining bright like a tiny sun. The flare revealed nothing new and he thumped the yoke in frustration. This was one of those instances where skill, planning and preparation had absolutely no influence on the outcome.

He had Willis drop another flare and came around for another pass. Leaving the other two aircraft circling at five thousand; he dove down in a lazy spiral left wing low. The flare just made the shadows a hard, dense black.

Ten minutes passed by and there was still no change. The clouds remained thick and impenetrable, so Pettifer rejoined Anderson and Pendleton. He asked Willis to call the field and have them pass a request to Merville for some guidance. They circled while they waited. Anderson and Pendleton said nothing. What was there to say? They knew the options as well as the next man. They could bail out but they doubted if Winwright would be pleased at losing three perfectly good aircraft. As time went on, that option was becoming increasingly attractive.

They were going to drop another flare when an arrow of white flew up from the grey, arcing and then disappearing back amongst the clouds again. Two more followed it.

"I guess it's a sign," Pettifer said over the R/T. He called up Anderson and Pendleton. "I do believe that's our cue gentlemen." Baker came up out of the nose and held up a folded map. He used a shaded torch so Pettifer could see. The runway at Merville ran roughly east to west and it was pretty much flat. Another bunch of white little stars burst through the clouds. They appeared in clumps a few hundred yards apart. Pettifer checked his compass; the line of flares ran roughly parallel to the orientation of the runway.

"I do believe someone is trying to tell us something. Peel off at fifteen second intervals. Luck to us all."

Pettifer crossed himself and then gripped the yoke tight. He really didn't want to be doing this but they were out of time and this was their best chance at getting down.

He flicked on his landing and position lights and banked left, letting the nose dip below the horizon and descend. He circled round and headed in. Flares continued to pop up, making the clouds glow. He dropped the gear and the flaps and slowly let down. At seven hundred feet he nosed into the clouds, wisps of grey and white wrapping around the canopy. As they sank lower, the cockpit went very dark and Pettifer's view shrank to his instrument panel. He started looking at the instruments in a strict order.

Flying on instruments was very difficult. The mind played tricks on you. Your inner ear got scrambled. While your instruments said you were flying straight and level, you could be convinced you were diving or banking. You had to learn to fight the urge to rely on your instincts and do what the instruments told you. This was easier said than done. You could screw up in a link trainer and have another go. Doing it for real made his stomach tie itself in knots.

His eyes constantly flicked between the turn and bank indicator and the climb and dive indicators. He needed to keep level as he descended at one hundred feet a minute. Faint white glows illuminated the inside of the clouds ahead of him, so he knew he was still heading the right way.

At two hundred and fifty feet he broke into clean air. The underside of the cloud base was a swirling mass of shadows as a succession of flares were fired. Pettifer picked out the shapes of hangars and aircraft on the ground. Another bunch of flares went up in a line. Before they disappeared into the clouds he caught a quick glimpse of the runway. He was off line and to the right. He sideslipped and went straight in.

The ground rushed up to meet him and he put the Blenheim down immediately. The wheels squealed on the tarmac and they bounced twice before they were on the ground. Pettifer went the length of the runway to give the others room to land. Erks waving torches gave him something to follow. He pulled onto the grass and cut the switches. He threw off the straps as fast as he could and pulled back the escape hatch. Pendleton taxied fast behind him and turned off the runway.

Pettifer strained his eyes, peering into the gloom for Anderson. There was a roar of engines as his Blenheim flew over their heads and receded into the distance. Anderson had seen the runway too late and he opened up the throttles to come around again. They heard him circle the airfield and another bunch of flares went into the air to guide him in. Pettifer sat on the fuselage, feet dangling in the cockpit while he waited. Pendleton came across from his own aircraft while Pettifer continued to search the sky for Anderson.

"Grief, that was hairy." said Pendleton. Coming in after Pettifer had not been too bad, he had something to follow. He wouldn't have led for all the tea in China. There was the steady drone of engines as Anderson flew an abbreviated circuit, coming in fast before the light got any worse.

He cut the corner on the final turn, coming in on a long curling turn, intending to line up at the last moment. In the dark he had no idea there was a bunch of tall trees between him and the runway. At the last moment, another flare was fired and his eyes opened wide in horror as he saw the light filtered through the branches. He hauled back on the yoke and rammed the throttle forwards but it was too late.

The bomber ploughed through the trees, turning them into matchwood. The starboard wing folded like tissue paper, the nose crumpled like a tin can. Anderson had just enough time to scream before his face was smashed in.

The dark sky lit up from the explosion, an orange blossom of flame and debris. Fire raged as the tanks split and spread petrol on the grass. The gunner was miraculously thrown clear from the wreckage. They found him face down, his legs lying at an odd angle, his right arm broken. He started screaming when they picked him up and got him on the stretcher.

After reporting to Bainbridge, Petttifer beat himself up for a while. He returned to stare at the smouldering ruins while he thought about Anderson and his crew. The burden of their lives weighed heavily upon him. It had been his decision to attempt a landing. It had been his decision to go to Merville. They could have risked going south. They had the fuel to carry on looking for some clear skies but it was his impatience that led them to Merville.

He watched in mute silence as what was left of Anderson and Prentice was laid out on the grass. If they were lucky, there might be enough to fill the coffins without anything extra to make the weight up.

"Tough luck." said Pendleton, lighting a cigarette. He lofted the spent match onto the grass.

"I'm sure, Anderson will be touched by your sympathy."

Pendleton turned to look at him, his face all harsh angles from the flickering light of the fire.

"Those are the chances we take. He was a big boy, he knew the risks."

Pettifer looked at Pendleton but he saw he was totally serious, no sarcasm, no arch smile, he meant every word. This was a side to Pendleton he'd not seen before. Pendleton shrugged under the scrutiny and took a hard pull on his cigarette, looking at the end glow in the dark. Pettifer was nonplussed for an answer.

He took a last lingering look before walking over to the briefing hut to join the Battle crews. He had little appetite to spend the wee small hours staring at four blank walls in the guest accommodation block while others went to war.

He found a seat at the back of the room. Eighty feet long by thirty wide, there were two blocks of folding seats with a central aisle. A low stage was at the far end, along with a large map of France and a blackboard. The long walls were covered with French posters for the Armée de L'Air. Some wag had defaced them with little Hitler moustaches and a comb over.

Eight crews sat figuratively and literally on the edge of their seats for the CO to come walking down that central aisle. This was not their first trip, but this sense of anticipation, the edge of fear, never got any easier.

While Falcon Squadron had been training, the Battles had been flying over Germany for a while now. While it reduced the Battles vulnerability to enemy fighters, they'd experienced more accidents.

Pettifer saw the result of that before the briefing began. He spotted some people he knew, but there were also some very young faces in the room too. The old guard was gradually being replaced.

Pendleton slid in next to him and Pettifer scowled. He folded his arms and shifted slightly to give him room.

"Come to watch the show?" he asked.

"May as well, the bars closed. I'm going to sleep well tonight though. Have you seen the beds?"

"Not yet."

Pendleton was looking forward to that. It would be his first night's sleep in a warm room and cosy bed for a long time. Pendleton cleared his throat and dropped his voice, leaning in close.

"How come the Battles got a nice cosy airbase and we get a field and a bunch of trees in the middle of nowhere?"

"Beats me," Pettifer said in reply. "I was asking myself the same question."

Merville had concrete runways, big hangars and was far more suitable for the Blenheims than the field at Bois Fontaine. There was no accounting for how headquarters types thought sometimes. He wondered if a man got a lobotomy once he was posted to a command position. According to the rumour mill, a Hurricane squadron down south had taken over some swanky French chateau. They had squash courts, a billiards room, a wine cellar, even indoor plumbing.

He heard the door creak behind him and saw Bainbridge come in.

"Heads up," he said as chairs scraped the floor and everyone got to their feet.

Squadron Leader Bainbridge stood on the dais looking at the faces in front of him. He was not a superstitious man, but the Blenheim crash did not strike him as the best way to start an evening. Anderson's Blenheim was not the first aircraft those trees had claimed. He vowed that in the morning, he was personally going to take a work party armed with axes and shovels to sort them out. This time, no objection from the landowner was going to stop him from doing what he should have done months ago.

There was no surprise when their bombload was revealed to be a cargo of leaflets. The Roosevelt rules were still in effect, but Headquarters was never one for letting crews sit idle. With improving weather, it had been decreed that they should take the fight to the enemy and bomb them with leaflets; that would show the filthy hun! After dropping the bumpf they would fly on to recce some targets and take a few photographs.

Bainbridge emphasised the weather reports and adverse headwinds for the return journey. The navigators would have to be careful or they would end up all over the map on the way back for this one.

The briefing ended and chairs scraped again as Bainbridge left the room to get ready. He was flying tonight as well. As the crews filed past, Pettifer put two fingers to his temple, a mock salute and a big man with a frown stopped. His face lit up when he saw Pettifer.

"Well blow me, as I live and breathe."

"Halliday."

They shook hands warmly. Halliday's broad smile showed bright white teeth in a tanned and weathered face. Blonde straw like hair was brushed back from his forehead.

"Good to see you again, John," said Pettifer.

There were introductions all round and they stood off to one side as the other crews filed past. Halliday playfully punched Pettier in the arm.

"Fancy seeing you here," he said with a west country drawl. He threw his head back and laughed, the years falling off him.

Pettifer pointed at the map board. "Flying a leaflet raid, huh?"

"Nickel raids we call them." Halliday's face pinched in distaste. "Until they let us load up with real bombs, it's all we can do."

Halliday looked at the door and nodded. His navigator was getting impatient. Pettifer shook his hand again.

"You be careful out there, okay?"

"I always am." Halliday turned as he got to the door. "Coming to see us off?"

"Just try and stop me."

They followed Halliday and his crew out of the briefing hut and hopped onto the back of a truck. It drove them out to the flight line. Pettifer found that fate had a fickle sense of humour as the overcast had now cleared. A fresh wind had rolled in from the east and ripped the thick clouds apart to show clear skies and glittering stars under a slither of moon.

The truck stopped at each aircraft along the line and three men got down, ready to start their evenings work. Halliday's aircraft was at the end of the line. The ground crew had it ready and waiting for him.

An LAC lugged thick bundles of leaflets over in a wheelbarrow. Nosey, Pendleton took one off the pile while the erk handed the bundles up to Halliday's gunner. He angled the paper so he could see it in the moonlight. He managed a few lines before he laughed out loud.

"Oh my, this is priceless. Get this, *Warning! Great Britain to the German people. Germans, with full and deliberate intention, the government of the Reich had forced war upon Great Britain. They well knew that the consequences of their action would plunge the people into greater disaster, as the case in 1914.*" He got no further. He screwed the leaflet up into a small ball and flicked it into the dark. "Blah, blah blah, blah. Bumf. God, what a load of bilge."

"Still, it's what we've got to do," Halliday said in resignation. He checked his watch and shook Pettifer's hand. "Clear skies."

Halliday used the foot step to get onto the port wing of his Battle. He stepped gingerly towards the cockpit, the wing slick with moisture. Just before getting in, he half turned to wave goodbye and his feet went from under him. He crashed down onto the wing and rolled off, his momentum carrying him onto the concrete with a heavy thud. Everyone stood rooted to the spot; it had all happened so fast. They moved when Halliday screamed.

"Bloody hell," said Pendleton, shocked by the sudden change. Pettifer crouched down next to Halliday.

"Medic! We need a medic here!" Halliday had his eyes screwed shut as he clutched his left knee. "Can you move?"

A Corporal went running to find Squadron Leader Bainbridge. Some of the other Battles started their engines and taxied out. Pettifer stood up and eyed the Battle. He was still in his flying gear and he looked between Halliday and the plane. He was about to take a step towards it when Padgett grabbed hold of his arm.

"You're not serious, skipper?"

"Someone's got to do it," said Pettifer. Before he could put himself to the test, another pilot came hustling along out of the gloom and got aboard. An ambulance pulled up in a rush and Halliday was transferred to a stretcher and put inside.

His Battle started up with a roar. Not waiting on ceremony, it pulled out of its slot and turned right onto the taxiway. Pettifer and Pendleton watched it take off into the gathering night.

"If I didn't know any better," said Pendleton. "I'd have thought you were thinking about taking his place."

"Nearly...." He shrugged and left his answer unfinished.

"Well, good luck to them," said Pendleton. "It's a long way to go to drop a load of free toilet paper."

2.7 – Cafe Au Lait

The atmosphere in the room was tense, something not so unusual these days. Locke sat slumped on the sofa. He was flicking cards into a pot on a chair a few feet away. His wife was in the bedroom doing something with her hair. At least he thought she was. Right now, he couldn't care if she did not not.

Earlier that evening he'd dropped Hagen off in town before driving home. He'd had high hopes for the night but he was to be disappointed. He received an indifferent peck on the cheek and things went downhill from there. Laura had another one of her pouts on and all he'd done was ask her if she had a nice lunch.

He was having trouble figuring this all out. He knew she was lonely during the day but there wasn't much he could do about that. At least if they were back at RAF Allenby there would be other wives and girlfriends for her to mix with. Here, aside from Lorraine and Hortense, there was no one else, no family to talk to.

Sometimes he just wished she would disappear, it would make his life a whole lot easier. Even as he thought about it, he felt guilty, but it was true. He didn't want to fight, but the last thing he wanted to do was come home to an argument or a frosty atmosphere night after night. He'd tried to talk to her. If it was something he'd done wrong he could change, he assured her, but she had no answer to give him.

He flicked another card at the pot. It hit off the lip and skittered across the floor. It joined its friends by the curtain but couldn't be bothered to pick them up. He looked at the last card, turning it in his hands. The Jack of hearts, the knave. He remembered a bit of Lewis Carroll. *The Queen of Hearts, she made some tarts, All on a summer day: The Knave of Hearts, he stole those tarts, And took them quite away!*

The Jack, the thief, the knave. He rolled the card round and round. Something had changed but he didn't know what. He loved her, he knew that, but that wasn't really the question.

Laura looked at herself in the mirror as she applied her makeup. She just felt numb. She could hear him in the other room playing with those stupid cards of his. She dropped the makeup brush on the desk and put her head in her hands.

There was nothing to feel guilty about, but she couldn't bring herself to tell him. Maybe it was storing trouble for the future but when Alex had asked her what she'd done for lunch, she felt like she was being spied on. Pascal was just a friend, pure and simple. She kept telling herself that while she made her eyes go big and put on some eyeliner.

She had met Pascal again that afternoon. It was the third time she met him and always at the same time and the same place. She had worn another new hat for him and he was full of praise for the effort she made to look good for their lunches. This time he had taken her for a walk and they strolled along arm in arm. He paid rapt attention to her and she talked of her worries, about feeling ignored and alone. It felt good to share.

"But you're not alone, Laura." he reassured her. "You have friends, me at any rate. You are not as alone as you think you are."

"Pascal; you have no idea how happy that makes me feel," she said, meaning it. It made a change to be with someone that actually listened. She'd looked in the mirror and found herself thinking of him. His warm smile made her feel good and lifted her spirits.

She had stood outside the cafe waiting for him to show up. She looked forward to these trysts. It broke the monotony of the day being stuck in the apartment. A thrill of anticipation shot through her when she saw him round the corner in his blue pinstripe suit. She found herself wondering what he looked like under those clothes. She was blushing as he came up to her and doffed his hat before taking her hand and brushing a kiss across her knuckles.

While they walked, his hand snaked around her waist, coming to rest on her hip, his arm a warm band around her back. She did not shrug him off and leaned in to him, feeling his strength.

They talked more as they walked. He lived alone but had family living in Arras. His older brother, Georges, was a wine merchant, a widower with six children. His parents were long dead but he had an elderly aunt living in Béthenville who he took to church on Sundays.

Laura was very relaxed with him, she liked his easy going way. He was a marked contrast to her husband, who came home tense and irksome. She didn't like that. He would come stomping into the flat, asking how she was. Pascal actually listened to her. She felt she could tell him anything. There was no distance between them like there was with Alex.

He took her to a wine merchant near town and they spent a few hours sampling various wines. His palate leaned towards coarse reds but she preferred the fruity whites, something with a crisp edge to it. She bought two bottles and carried them back to the apartment in a string bag, the glass chinking against each other as she walked. He left her at the entrance to the apartment. Today she grew more bold and kissed him on the cheek, her lips leaving their brand on his skin.

"Until tomorrow," he had said.

There you see? She told herself. *Absolutely nothing to worry about. Pascal is a friend who helps me through the lonely days. LIAR,* her reflection told her. She stared herself down, making it true.

She loved Alex, she knew she did. He was the man she had given her promise to. She remembered the advice her mother had given her when she was at their house in Norfolk. They had been sitting in the morning room, her mother at her needlework and Laura trying to occupy herself with a book. Laura had been bemoaning the fact she was separated from her husband but she got little sympathy from her mother.

"Marriage is not a sprint, my love," she said without looking up from her embroidery. "It's a marathon. If you think every day will run smoothly, then you're in for a shock." At that, they both looked out the door of the morning room and saw Laura's father going into his study, pipe clenched between his teeth.

Laura's parents had married young, more of an alliance than a marriage really. Love had come later. Laura had heard the stories more than once, the raging arguments when they were first married. A dislike that had turned into respect had taken many years to nurture to fruition. She sighed. When she'd got married she promised herself that it would be different for her. Marriage for love; not for convenience.

She heard Alex rummaging around in the kitchen, going through the cupboards. A pan slammed on the stove and she listened as he made himself busy. The kettle started to whistle. Cups clinked and he came in, holding out a cup.

"Tea?"

It was his apology, in his own way, even when he had no idea what he was apologising for. She smiled and took the tea from his hand, their fingers touching.

Ashton sipped his coffee slowly. It was piping hot and he set the cup down again. He fiddled with a biscuit and then started spooning sugar into the coffee. While he loved the smell of it, he found it was too bitter for him. He needed lots of milk or cream and lots of sugar.

He watched the bustle of people going to and from the Gare du Nord while he waited for Gardner. He saw a young couple sitting two tables over from him. A French army officer who looked barely old enough to shave was consoling his girl, who was obviously having trouble saying goodbye. She was sobbing into a handkerchief and he had his arm around her shoulder, whispering encouragement and expressions of love.

"C'est la guerre." Ashton whispered to himself, lifting his cup as a salute. He breathed deeply; savouring the smell of the coffee.

It had been a good leave. Seventy two hours may not sound like much, but even a few days rest was a welcome respite.

They took a taxi from the train station. There was the usual chaos as mad French drivers careened around the traffic circles laying on the horn and waving their arms around when they failed to get their way. Gendarmes blew their whistles and waved white gauntleted arms but they were roundly ignored. They booked in to the Hotel Crillon. Built as a palace by Louis XV it had been turned into a hotel in 1907 after it was purchased from the Comte de Crillon. The Naval Ministry occupied an identical building the other side of the square.

Ashton liked it. It was at the centre of everything. The Tuileries Gardens and the Louvre were nearby, and the Rue de Rivoli had all the fashionable shops close at hand.

Their rooms were bigger than the mess hut back at the aerodrome. Tall windows looked out onto the Place de la Concorde. In the centre of the square was a giant Egyptian obelisk decorated with Hieroglyphs exalting the reign of Ramesses II. A gold leafed pyramid cap on top glinted in the sun.

During the French Revolution, King Louis XVI and Queen Marie Antoinette had been executed by guillotine in the square. Ironically, one of the architects of the Revolution, Robespierre followed them to the block a mere eighteen months later.

219

The first thing Ashton did was take a hot bath. He warmed his chilled bones, lying in the bath with the water up to his chin. He followed the bath with champagne cocktails down in the bar. At 3/6d a bottle, it would have been rude not to.

Suitably fortified, they went down the length of the Champs-Elysees, ending at the Arc de Triomphe. They spent some time looking at the names of the battles from the Revolutionary and Napoleonic wars inscribed on it. The famous ones leapt out at them of course, Austerlitz, Marengo and Ulm but even the losses like Aboukir were on there as well.

"Could you imagine marching from one end of Europe to the other, following the beat of the drums?" Ashton asked Gardner. Waterloo was not on there he noticed, nor was Trafalgar. As a boy he'd read about Wellington and his army battling the French in the Peninsular campaigns.

"Give me two engines and a pair of wings, that's what makes me happy," said Gardner in response. *March across Europe?* He was appalled at the idea.

They spent a few sombre moments looking at the tomb of the unknown soldier under the arch. They read the inscription carved into the slab, ICI REPOSE UN SOLDAT FRANÇAIS MORT POUR LA PATRIE 1914–1918.

"Here lies a French soldier who died for the fatherland 1914–1918." murmured Gardner. He thought about the carnage of the First World War. A single flame as a monument seemed inadequate somehow.

Crossing the river, they went up the Eiffel Tower, delighting in the view of the city laid out before them. Gardner was amazed at the sprawl, the neat avenues, the wide boulevards and parks. They moved on to the army museum at the Invalides. They looked at the relics of a bygone age before returning to the hotel.

They had more cocktails at the bar before pushing on for food and drinks. God alone only knew what time they poured themselves into bed. Ashton woke up the following morning with a crackerjack of a hangover. He reconvened with Gardner over breakfast to rehash the night's events. They agreed there was a club with jazz music, pretty women and cocktails but exactly where it was remained a mystery.

Invigorated after a big breakfast, they went off again, seeing the sights that Paris had to offer. They wandered around Mon Martre before getting changed at the hotel and heading to Maxims, a restaurant round the corner on the Rue Royale. They enjoyed dinner surrounded by the Art Nouveau decor and then moved onto the airman's club with some charming female company. Now they were heading back to Bois Fontaine.

Ashton looked around the station. Light flooded through the glass triumphal arch behind him and he could feel the heat on his back. It had been good to get away from living like a boy scout in tents and huts, even for a few days.

He finished the last of his coffee and waved as he saw Gardner come out of the shop. He had a kitbag slung over his shoulder while he munched on a croissant. He sat down next to Ashton and caught the eye of the waiter. They sat in silence until a cup of coffee arrived for him and Ashton got a fresh one.

"I've decided I like Paris." Gardner nodded as he tasted the coffee.

"Really, why?"

"Are you kidding?" Gardner smiled; he was in an expansive mood.

"Comfy beds, baths big enough to swim in. Bars, music, ladies." He drank some more coffee. "All the things worth fighting for."

Gardner's mood was infectious. Ashton enjoyed his enthusiasm but he couldn't help thinking of the thunderclouds on the horizon.

"Enjoy it while you can," he warned.

"You really think the shootings going to start soon?"

Ashton nodded grimly.

"Got to." He knew the reason why Winwright had given them some leave now. He wanted his flight commanders properly rested before things started for real. Everything that had happened so far was just the prologue.

"We'll be ready." said Gardner.

"I hope so. I really do."

An announcement echoed around the station, a blur of French that was unintelligible except for the name of Arras, their stop. They would get a connecting train from there back to the Squadron. Ashton fished in his pockets for a few coins and left them on the table. He picked up his suitcase.

"I guess that's our train." Gardner stepped aside and gestured towards the platforms. "Oh, after you."

Cullen shook his umbrella as he stepped into the lobby of the Lion d'Or hotel. The lashing rain had driven everyone inside and the bar was jammed. Civilians mixed with reporters and military personnel. White shirted waiters weaved through the crowd. He carried his umbrella in with him. There was no way he was putting it on the pile with all the others. He would never see it again.

He found his cronies at the far end of the bar. Clifford, a writer from Reuter's nursed a whisky. The others were enjoying the ever cheap champagne. They swapped notes for a few minutes but none of them had much to show for the day. Clifford had been following the army but got bored with battling the censor. The final straw had been when they told him to take out a reference to the moon shining down on the troops as they marched along.

"He told me that I was giving information to the enemy about when we moved our troops around," he bemoaned.

Dodds found it highly amusing until he realised that Clifford was being serious and then he just rolled his eyes in exasperation. Cullen wondered if Clifford would have any better luck getting a story past the RAF Press Office.

Dodds was a writer for the Express, his bland expression and big spectacles gave him an air of schoolboy innocence that women found appealing. When he wasn't out chasing stories, he was enjoying as much female company as he could get. Everyone knew he had a wife back home, but that was up to him. Provided he put in his stories, what he got up to off the clock was no one's business.

Another damp officer came into the bar and held up two fingers and shouted, "Deux Coupes Marianne." over the general clamour. He shouted again before anyone noticed him and he got service.

Restless for a story, Cullen cast a languid eye over the bar. There were plenty of RAF types in the room, there was bound to be someone willing to talk. He circled round, looking for a friendly face when he recognised some Battle pilots from Rheims.

Cullen motioned to join them and they made space for him. He snaffled a chair from the neighbouring table and sat down. The mood was mixed. They had lost one of their number that morning to a large force of 109s and were dissecting the action.

"I'm telling you," said a particularly soused Flight Lieutenant, "the rear gunners, bless 'em, don't stand a chance." Some of the heads nodded in agreement. "They know we can't stop them getting underneath. So they slide down." his right hand he held steady and level. His left went down in a smooth arc, coming up underneath his right. "Knock us off like bottles on a wall." He took a swig from a beer bottle.

Cullen knew the Battles had been fitted with an extra gun on the underside, but he didn't ask about it, he knew it was just a sop to morale.

"Don't you have a fighter escort?" he asked.

A Flight Sergeant snorted and reached across for some bread. He tore a hunk off the baguette, spraying bits of bread everywhere.

"Escort?" he said with contempt round a mouthful of half masticated bread. "Don't make me laugh. They've only turned up once or twice and then they bugger off. We haven't seen them since. We've had to make do on our own."

"So what *can* you do?" asked Cullen, the picture of innocence.

"Dive," said the Flight Lieutenant again. "Oh, I mean it, we could fly straight and level and get chopped to pieces, but I'd rather come home with an intact rump if you don't mind." He belched loudly then lit a cigarette. He blew a cloud of smoke in Cullen's face. A Pilot Officer sporting a DFC on his chest put an arm around the Flight Lieutenant.

"You'll have to forgive our friend here," he said, patting him on the shoulder. "Narrow escapes strain his nerves. The Battles a wonderful kite. She can take a hell of a lot of damage."

"But what about manoeuvrability?" Cullen pressed, looking for an answer. He had seen Battles thrown around the sky numerous times at the Hendon Air Pageants before the war. He wondered how it actually held up for real.

"They'll loop quite nicely, I've even managed to roll one off the top in a pinch, but they're damnably slow."

Opinion on that comment was divided roughly fifty-fifty. Cullen left them to their debate and rejoined his fellows.

All four of them had put on their newly issued gas masks and were talking to each other. It looked ridiculous, four grown men, sat at a bar with a rubberised gas mask on their faces. It was like some ENSA vaudeville act. Dodds turned to look at him. His myopic eyes blinked from behind two Perspex eyepieces. His voice had taken on a tinny far away quality like a voice on the radio. When he pulled the mask off his face, he was sweating buckets.

"God, that's awful," he gasped. He polished off a Champagne cocktail to get the rubbery taste out of his mouth. "How do soldiers bear it? I couldn't manage more than five minutes in that thing."

"Agreed." said Clifford, pulling off his own gas mask.

An order from Headquarters had gone out stating that gas masks would have to be carried at all times. Personally, Cullen thought it a waste of time. This was the modern age. Gas might have been used in the last war, but he couldn't see it happening this time round. The moral outrage that would accompany its use would doom whoever used it in the eyes of the world.

Cullen had left his gas mask in his room at the hotel, but the pouch made an excellent handy bag to carry around with him. He kept his notebook and pencils and other knick knacks in it. It saved him having to stuff his pockets with the tools of his trade.

A roar went up at the other end of the bar where some RAF aircrew had gotten onto their compatriots shoulders and were wrestling for supremacy. Some waiters were already heading in their direction to stop things before they got out of hand.

Cullen saw two trench coated types sitting by the windows looking quite sour. His first thought was they could be Special Police. He'd heard the rumours that the hotel was a hot bed of gossip and a lair for spies but it had never been shut down. Maybe it was a double bluff, he reasoned. By letting it operate, they knew where to find all the enemy agents. He had sudden visions of shadowy figures crawling around the countryside, trying to ferret out spies and fifth columnists.

There was a rumour that one of the Special Police had actually entered Gort's Chateau and stood watching the General asleep for a few moments before exiting via the window. Personally, Cullen didn't believe it. It was too farfetched even for them. However, he knew his own hotel room had been checked. More than once he had got in from a long day to find things had been moved around. It was an occupational hazard.

Clifford spread a map over the bar and they started arguing over what to do tomorrow. Dodds asked if he could double up with Cullen. He had no car of his own and he was forever latching on to someone for that day's work. Cullen had no objection, he had a thought to go north again and have a wander along the Belgian border. Maybe he could check out the progress on the expansion to the Maginot Line.

Dane saw Ashton and Gardner when they came back from their leave. He smiled as they splashed through the puddles, dodging the rain. The weather had turned that afternoon, the deluge washing away the last of the snow. Puddles formed all over the place and turned the green between the huts into a small lake.

He went back to his desk and sharpened his pencils. He trimmed each one into a sharp point and put it on the table in front of him. Corporal Beverly, his orderly, stood across from him. He worked through the pile of signals from Wing, updating the map on the back of the wall.

Dane was bracing himself for upheaval. Squadrons were being moved around wholesale from Headquarters. It would surely only be a matter of time before their own movement orders came through.

Beverley was moving pins around, shoving them into the board. Each pin was hundreds of men slaving to pack everything up and move twenty miles. Dane glanced at the map. He tapped a pencil on his teeth while he watched this ballet of movement.

It was all a waste of time of course. No doubt it could be justified militarily, but moving units around would only confuse enemy intelligence for so long. If you believed the rumours, the countryside was crawling with spies anyway. Even if it wasn't, the regular German reconnaissance flights would discover what had changed soon enough.

Information had been coming thick and fast from Headquarters recently. The tempo of operations was increasing again now that the weather was improving. Only yesterday, Wing had issued an alert and the squadron had been put on fifteen minutes standby. The crews had gathered in the mess and flight hut, poised for the order to take off. The erks had slaved to bomb up all the aircraft and then the readiness had been dropped to five minutes standby.

The sense of anticipation had been overwhelming. This was it; they were finally going to war.

The crews had dashed out and sat in their kites, waiting for the word. They waited, and they waited. They sat like that for two hours before they were stood down. It was a grumpy bunch of men that shambled back to their tents to get changed. Once again they had been brought to the brink only to have the show called off. Locke and Hagen had disappeared into town as usual but no one else could summon the energy to go anywhere.

Dane thought about Locke and Hagen. Personally, he thought Winwright was wrong about their living out. He saw no harm to it, but then he wasn't a career RAF man and he was bringing his civilian sensibilities to his job. In his opinion, anything that helped morale was good. Besides, what did Winwright think was going to happen? Even if Locke's wife hadn't followed him across the channel, you couldn't stop healthy, gregarious young men from making connections with female company.

He rubbed the bridge of his nose. He was woolgathering again and went back to work. He looked at an intel folder with the latest guesswork regarding German Luftwaffe units thought to be currently in theatre. His particular interest was in plotting where the fighter units were. For the last week or so, the Germans had been coming over in packs, getting more aggressive. They had tangled a few times with the Hurricanes and the French Escadrilles, picking fights where before they had run from them. They were no longer testing the water; they were pushing, probing for weaknesses. It was only a matter of time now before things started for real.

2.8 – A Place In The Sun

The move, when it came, was a little unusual, it was a lot further than Dane had ever expected. They received orders to go on detachment to Perpignan in the south of France. With the miserable weather forecast to last well into the New Year, Headquarters put a backup plan into effect. Squadrons would rotate to go south on detachment and get in some training while everyone else froze up north. Other squadrons had already gone, now it was their turn. Bainbridge's Battle squadron went with them and they arrived in warmer climes for two weeks of intensive training.

Like any move, the orders caused organised chaos while the kites were made ready. The aircrew were gathered in the flight hut and told them the good news. Go off to your quarters and pack for a trip. It felt like going on holiday.

Locke and Hagen had fits. With no warning of the move, they had no time to go into Béthenville and let the girls know. Besides, even if they had time, Winwright wouldn't let them go because of security. In the end, they had to settle for writing short notes and giving them to Kittinger in a rush to pass on. Locke handed over the keys to the Mathis as well. If he was going away for a while, there was no reason Laura shouldn't have the use of the car. She had bought it after all.

The squadron took off into a dark and moody sky. Wind gusted in sharp vicious flurries as Winwright led them south towards Arras. Bainbridge and his Battles orbited the town, waiting for them at twelve thousand. Bainbridge was grateful they turned up on time. The gunners around Arras were known to be twitchy. Shoot first, ask questions later was their policy. Even though he'd fired off the colours of the day more than once, he didn't want to outstay his welcome any longer than necessary.

The Battles formed up alongside the Blenheims and they were on their way. They took in the sights as they went. Paris slid by on their right. The city was wreathed in low lying cloud, but the Eiffel Tower stood tall, a spear thrusting through the sheet of white.

They flew over the palace at Fontainebleu. Winwright led them down to get a good look at the ornamental gardens surrounding the palace. They thundered over the courtyard where Napoleon had bid farewell to the Old Guard before going into exile to Elba in 1814.

The further south they went, the warmer it got. They left the tendrils of snow behind them and began to sweat in their flying clothing. Chandler had dressed for the cold and worn long johns underneath his Sidcot. He was almost swimming in his seat as the sun bathed the cockpit in heat. He shrugged off his gauntlets and wiped his palms down his legs.

After three hours flying time they came to Perpignan. The land all around was flat and there were no trees to tempt their wing tips. RAF personnel were there to see them in and they lined up outside the hangars before shutting down.

The men luxuriated in rooms with proper beds and the mess served good food for growling stomachs. They were worlds away from Bois Fontaine and their grotty little tents and camp beds. Their first evening, they were treated to a real taste of home, a roast dinner with all the trimmings and jam sponge and custard to follow. Sated and full, they retired to their beds.

Winwright and Bainbridge worked the men hard. Every day they went up in a variety of exercises. They went out to the bombing ranges and took it in turns to knock seven shades out of the targets. A friendly rivalry built up between the crews and Winwright and Bainbridge encouraged it as much as possible.

On the cross country navigation exercises, they went out singly and in Flights. Winwright made younger crews lead, wanting to push them and give them responsibility. He wanted to see who could act under stress. There was no point being a navigator if you just blindly followed the pack and then got hopelessly lost when it was your turn. Morgan maintained his record, a changed man since those days back in England. His baptism of fire had turned him into one of the squadrons' more capable navigators.

During their time away, Locke and Hagen both tried placing long distance calls but officialdom hampered their efforts. They ran head first into a measure introduced to frustrate so called Fifth Columnists. All telephone conversations had to be conducted exclusively in the French language so the operators could listen in. If the operators couldn't understand what was being said, then they had the power to disconnect or interrupt the call.

Locke managed to get through to Laura twice but it was a short call as their French was limited. They managed a few words before the operator butted in, her voice terse *'Parlez Francais, ou je coupe!'* and cut the call. Locke spent a fair amount of time remonstrating with the operator, trying to explain he was an English officer to little avail.

Hagen fared slightly better. Once he said hello, Lorraine did most of the talking, but it was a very one sided conversation. Once she was in full flow, he struggled to keep up with what was being said. Suffice to say she was very happy that he called but it was a frustrating experience.

Most days were the same. They had an early start, breakfast, and then an air test followed by two or three exercises before finishing for the day. In the evenings, they often went into Perpignan. Not far from the coast was a beautiful Mediterranean town, the old capital of the kings of Majorca.

On Palm Sunday they attended church. The Padre mumbled through the service while they stood in the pews in their dress uniforms. It was not the only service they attended in Perpignan. Unfortunately, mistakes followed them south and they lost one aircraft to an accident while the Battle squadron lost two.

Pilot Officer Odell had gone out on a solo navigation exercise and failed to return. He was listed as missing until a Gendarme called the station and reported their aircraft had slammed into a hill. There were no survivors and little to bury once the wreckage was picked over.

The Battles lost their two because of a random bit of carelessness. Forming up after dive bombing at the range, the leader in the second vic of three got too close to the lead element. Bounced around in the turbulence of their slipstream, the pilot only lost control for a moment, but it was enough.

Veering to the right, he ploughed into his wingman. The wingman's propeller chewed through his leader's wing and they fell out of the sky, locked together. The navigator and gunner of the lead aircraft managed to bail out at a perilously low altitude. One broke an ankle, the other broke his leg. The rest were killed.

The good thing to come out of the two weeks intensive training was that it gave the new men a chance to show their stuff. Back up north, they had flown so infrequently there was no way to get a handle on how good they were. For all his boasting, Pendleton showed his skill matched his mouth and the others were not far behind.

The Squadron fielded teams for football and rugby and played all comers. They ended the two weeks about even although the final result against the Battle boys was a sore point. On the final evening, they had played each other to a standstill. With the score all square, the final seconds were counting down when one of Bainbridge's Flight Commanders, took possession at the halfway line and made a break for goal. He sidestepped one tackle and then laid off a pass to the wing. He connected with a low return cross to fire the ball like a bullet past Preddy in goal just as the whistle went. The hapless referee, a Flight Lieutenant in supply was surrounded almost instantly with protesting players but he stuck to his ruling. He awarded the goal.

The Squadron was itching for a rematch but that would have to wait for another time. Their two weeks were up; they were going back up the line to Bois Fontaine.

2.9 – Whilst The Cat's Away

She sat impatiently drumming her fingers on the table while she waited. She opened her compact and checked her coiffure and makeup again. Her lipstick was just so. Perfect. Andre behind the bar caught her eye but she shook her head, no, no pastry today. A girl had to look after her figure after all.

She'd come to love this cafe after the last two weeks. It had a homely feel and she was comfortable in the surroundings. The two old men sat by the window as always, playing backgammon, wreathed in smoke as they smoked their pipes and drank their wine. There was a constant rattle of dice and click of counters as they moved the pieces around the board. This was their spot, a home away from home.

The bell above the door rang and Pascal came into the cafe. He smiled broadly as he shrugged off his trench coat and draped it over the chair across from her. He sat down, hitching his trousers slightly to stop the knees stretching. He was impeccable as always, his shirt crisp, the silk tie glossy and his hair neat and tidy.

"Good afternoon, Laura."

"Pascal."

"So what shall we talk about this afternoon?"

Andre put a small espresso cup and saucer down in front of Pascal. He nodded his thanks and took a sip. He studied the woman across the table from him. She sat very demure, very proper, her legs crossed, her back ramrod straight, shoulders back. There was that haughty toss to her chin and a gleam in her eye that he always found so stirring.

"Why don't we try something different?" she responded. "I don't feel much like talking at the moment."

He arched an eyebrow, intrigued. Her moods had been up and down lately. She had volunteered little and he did not ask. She would tell him when she was ready.

"What did you have in mind?"

In response she stood up, an impish smile on her face. She took his hand.

"Let me show you."

In the cafe, she had been confident. On the walk back to the apartment, she was nervous. By the time they went in the door, her heart was fluttering. She had been thinking about this for days, rolling it around in her head. In the intervening days her anger with Alex had cooled. Now she just felt ambivalent about it all, it just was.

After the squadron had flown away to other skies, Kittinger had come knocking. When she opened the door, he took the peaked cap off his head and the breath caught in her throat. Her first reaction was fear. When a uniformed officer came knocking at your door, it was for only one reason. It took a few seconds to register that Alex wasn't dead.

They'd sat on the sofa while Kittinger told her the boys were off on detachment for a while. Her temper rose when he was vague in his answers. Kittinger would not be drawn on how long they would be away for. She had asked, she had wheedled and pleaded with him but he had said nothing.

"Operational security," he had said. "Need to know," he told her. Even her best teary eyed look had left him unmoved. She thanked him for his visit, but as soon as she'd closed the door she flew into a rage. She felt abandoned, again. *So much for his assurances that he would look after her!* Once again she was playing second fiddle to his job and she struggled to comprehend the realities of this. Laura was used to being courted, to being the centre of attention. The thought that she was not galled her.

Alex had tried to call twice, short calls that had been cut off by the operator. That was all she'd got, no letter, not even a telegram. After she'd cooled down she went round to see Lorraine. She had no sister available in reach and the French woman was a friendly ear she could talk to.

She was surprised to find Lorraine had taken the news quite well, but then Hagen was not the first military man she had been in a relationship with. She was used to them suddenly disappearing at short notice. The note Kittinger had delivered to her was a welcome surprise and one she appreciated. It showed her Mark cared and that single sheet of paper meant more to her than a dozen roses.

Lorraine advised Laura to be calm. "These things happen, Laura," she'd said. "They'll be back soon enough. Enjoy the quiet while you can." Laura nodded but she didn't really absorb what she said.

They had different viewpoints on life entirely, different frames of reference. Laura left feeling sour; she found Lorraine's equanimity frustrating. She didn'tt even consider trying to ring her mother, she knew there would be no friendly ear there.

So she had turned to Pascal instead, and he listened. She looked forward to those lunches with him, he let her talk about anything, and piece by piece she had talked of her frustrations with Alex.

She stood there trembling in the living room until his hand covered hers. He brushed the tear away from her cheek and trailed his finger down the line of her jaw. She shut her eyes, shaking her head slightly from side to side as his hand went down her neck. He carried on across her shoulder, his thumb swirling small circles as it went.

"It's all right Laura," he whispered in her ear. "A beautiful woman like you should be worshipped." He kissed her neck. Her skin was smooth, soft. She had put on some Chanel, his favourite. He could feel her pulse hammering.

He led at first, making his movements slow but gradually she got warmed up, responding to him, moving under his hands. She groaned when he undid her blouse, his fingers moving down the inside of the silk, brushing over her bra.

She opened her eyes and looked at him, hot with desire. She wanted him and she tugged on the lapels of his jacket, pulling him towards the bedroom. They shed their clothes as they went, kicking off their shoes.

Afterwards, they lay on the bed together, exhausted from their exertions. Her arm draped over his chest; her leg over his. He stroked her back while she played with the hairs on his chest, running her fingers through the coarse hair.

She lifted her head to look at him. Her cheeks were flushed, her skin clammy and hot. She kissed him and rested her chin on his chest.

"Regardez moi," she told him, her voice light and teasing.

"What are you thinking?" he asked; his voice quiet.

"Not much. I'm just enjoying the moment."

Her left hand moved down his chest and slid under the sheet, playful. He grunted as her fingers made contact.

He moved from under her, rolling her onto her back, leaning over her. He cupped her breast in his hand, his fingers rubbing the areola, bringing the nipple to life. She gasped at the sensation and he leaned in, kissing her hard.

"Let's enjoy the moment again," he said, his voice husky and they started from the beginning.

An hour later, he sat naked on the bed, a sheet across his knees. He reached across to the bedside cabinet and picked up the cigarette from the glass ashtray. Smoke drifted up to the ceiling while he let his pulse slow down back to normal.

He shivered as the sweat cooled on his skin. It had been worth the wait. *How did the saying go?* he thought to himself, *to the victor goes the spoils.* He fluffed up the pillows and sat against the headboard so he could see her while she busied herself around the room.

He watched as she moved around naked, picking up stray items of clothing as she went. He remembered how her lithe body felt under his hands, the way she'd responded to his touch. She had been like a bitch in heat, writhing on him, her back arching in response to his thrusts, her moans of delight when they crested together.

Now spent, he let the fatigue wash over him, relaxing on the bed. He had no idea what time it was. It might be four, perhaps later. He knew he should really start making a move. If he was late, there would be questions but he didn't feel like moving just yet.

She gathered his things and began folding his clothes, draping the trousers over the end of the bed. She was exhausted but happy. For the first time in a while she felt fulfilled. Her body tingled and she could smell him on her, his scent.

She stepped into the shower to get cleaned up. The hot water invigorated her, the heat penetrating and relaxing her. She worked up a lather with the soap and rubbed herself down, running her hands up her legs, up her thighs and over her taut stomach. Rough hands ran up her back and she squealed in surprise as she turned to find him standing there. Smiling, he stepped into the bath with her and pulled the shower curtain round, gathering her into his arms.

2.10 – Walking Through Gethsemane

Bainbridge and Winwright put on a show when they got back to Béthenville. The Blenheims and Battles formed up nice and tight and thundered over the town. They came over the town square en masse, before breaking left and right. The Battles came back over in sections, followed by the Blenheims.

They'd got back in time for Easter. Colourful bunting was strung from building to building, fluttering in the breeze. People came out of the houses, shading their eyes from the sun. Others looked out of their windows. Boys ran along the streets with their arms stuck out like wings, making plane noises.

Farmer led his section lower than anyone else. Preddy had got the best bombing scores on detachment which made his crew top dog, so he felt like celebrating. In jubilant mood, he slid lower, just skimming the rooftops. Dead ahead was the town belfry. It was coming up fast. Preddy cringed as it loomed large in front of him.

Farmer pulled hard and went straight up, just scraping over the point of the steeple while his two and three split left and right. They reformed at three thousand feet and tacked back on at the rear of the formation.

"Very nice, Blue One," said Winwright. "Showy, but nice. Let's go home people."

The squadron did one pass over Bois Fontaine and the groundcrew saw them in. The crews were bouncing when they got out of the aircraft. Two weeks away in the sun had given them energy and they were pleased to be back. While Perpignan was comfortable and warm, it was far from where the action was going to be.

Things had changed a bit while they were away. The field was looking the best it had since they arrived. The erks had taken the opportunity to drag a big heavy roller up and down to help flatten out the bumps.

They stowed their gear in their tents and huts and went to the mess. Kittinger had laid out the mail and parcels that had arrived and they drank copious amounts of tea and worked their way through a pile of sandwiches. After three hours in the air, they were famished and they attacked them like a starving horde.

Mitchell had a letter from his girl, one of the dancers with an ENSA touring company. Angela had sent him a thick envelope filled with some photos and a folded poster. He whistled quietly to himself as he appreciated one of them. She had acres of leg on display as she stood with her hands on her hips, flashing a dazzling smile at the camera.

She'd used pink paper for her letter and he held it to his nose. She'd sprayed her perfume on it. Her handwriting was bold and looping, flowery he called it. He grunted when he got to page three.

"Huh, typical. She's just told me her show is going to be in Perpignan next week." He had to laugh at the irony. "We always seem to be like ships passing in the night."

But she promised him she had some free time soon and would be coming to see him. The last page had a lipstick kiss at the bottom.

"Very nice," said Preddy, looking over his shoulder. He canted his head to get a better view of the photograph. "You're still seeing her, huh?"

"Yep." Mitchell tucked the photograph into his tunic pocket. "She's got a friend," he offered.

"That pasty faced dancer from the theatre?" Preddy stuck his tongue out. Mitchell laughed.

"I presume drink is affecting your recall from that night." He hitched round in his seat to stare at Preddy. "For your information, that pasty faced dancer was five ten with milky white skin, amazing legs and chestnut red hair. For some reason she sort of liked you. I can't imagine why."

Preddy just blinked, rummaging around in his head for a memory that might match the description.

"Tell me more," he pleaded.

Mitchell pantomimed thinking about that while he folded the letter carefully around the remaining photographs. He put the bundle back in its envelope.

"Oh, go on," wheedled Preddy, now keen to be fixed up.

"I couldn't possibly inflict her on *you*. She's *just* a pasty faced dancer after all," Mitchell said with an air of superiority. He was enjoying this. He stood up, still looking at Preddy. "You'll just have to see when ENSA comes back around." He dotted him on the nose with the envelope. "Won't you?"

Chandler looked up from a week old newspaper. He was skimming; turning page after page trying to cull anything interesting. Meat rationing had started back home. The Russians had just about finished duffing up the Finns. He sat up when he read a piece on a Royal Navy Destroyer retrieving a few hundred POW's from a German freighter in Norway.

"Isn't Norway neutral?" he asked aloud. He was unsure.

"Last I heard it was," said Pettifer as he unwrapped a big metal tin covered in brown paper. "Why?"

"One of our Destroyers went into Norwegian waters and boarded a Jerry freighter. They took a load of POW's off," Chandler continued. He turned to the right page and saw a photograph of the *Altmark* aground in the Jøssingford. Pendleton took the paper out of Chandler's hands. He went down the article.

"My God, they used cutlasses," he said, "Makes them sound like pirates. I wouldn't give much for this Captain's career. The Norwegians will be livid."

"I doubt he'll have done it without instructions," said Pettifer. Pendleton passed him the paper and he put the tin box to one side for a moment. "Humph, typical," Pettifer said as he carried on reading. "The Norwegians are protesting the action."

"Won't save them," said Pendleton. He hovered over the sandwiches, pondering which to choose. "Same thing with the Belgians. I can't see anyone being able to stay on the fence this time around."

"You sound very sure," said Osbourne.

"It's just common sense. I can't see the Jerries giving a fig for neutrality. If they want it, they'll take it. People need to either piss or get off the pot."

Pettifer couldn't disagree with the judgement, however coarsely Pendleton put it.

"I say, has anyone heard about the erk who put in for a forty eight?" asked Osbourne. He felt that the conversation had become decidedly serious. He remembered the last time talk had turned political in the mess. Heads shook in answer to his question.

"No, what happened?" asked Pettifer.

"He said his wife was going to have a baby, so the CO said off you go. When he got back, the CO asked him 'is it a boy or a girl' and the erk looked at him like he was crazy and said 'don't be silly, sir. It takes *months*."

That tickled them. It was just the right thing to say to lighten the mood.

"Pass me a wedge will you?" Chandler asked.

"We've got cheese and onion, cheese and pickle and we've got Bully Beef." Pendleton's voice was muffled as he spoke round a big pickled onion he'd shoved into his mouth. He lifted the corner of a slice of bread and inspected the contents. "There might be ham as well."

"Cheese and pickle," Chandler decided. Pendleton handed one over. Chandler took an experimental bite. Whoever had made it was heavy handed. It had big slabs of cheese and lashings of pickle. He wolfed it down.

Farmer stood hovering over the gramophone, sorting through the records. Chandler had a question on his mind but he debated asking it. *Why not?* he thought, he had to try and make peace some time.

"Hey, Farmer, what was that stunt over town?" he asked, keeping his tone light.

"That's my business," said Farmer offhand. "The CO seemed to like it though."

He lifted a record sleeve that caught his attention. He studied the cover for a second. He put it back and lifted another record out of the pile. Chandler winced. He knew exactly which one Farmer would pick. For weeks he'd played little else. They'd only had a break from the wretched track when they went to Perpignan.

Satisfied with his choice, Farmer put the record on the player and kneeled down to make sure the needle went on properly. Music started blaring from the speaker, it was *'The Teddy Bears Picnic'* sung by Henry Hall. Farmer's toe started tapping to the beat.

"Why are you asking anyway?" Farmer queried, his voice dripping with contempt. "Jealous you hadn't thought of it?"

"Forget it," said Chandler. He had tried, Farmer would never change.

"Still not his favourite then?" whispered Morgan.

"Apparently so."

Pendleton passed him another cheese and pickle sandwich and Chandler ate in silence, stewing; trying to work out how to break through to Farmer. Morgan sat down next to his pilot. He started rummaging through his bundle of letters, looking at the postmarks.

"You know I've got about two month's worth of letters here." He shoved one under Chandler's nose. "I see the postal service is as efficient as always."

"Nothing new there then."

Pettifer passed around a tin of biscuits. His mother had sent them along with a long rambling letter about the family. Morgan took one and balanced it on his knee while he ate his sandwich.

Ashton grimaced as he heard the strains of *The Teddy Bears Picnic* coming from the mess hut. He was really starting to hate that song. He breezed into the flight office and knocked on the CO's door. He found Winwright looking at a table of paperwork. He was riffling through his In Tray and didn't look up when Ashton came in.

"Welcome back," said Ashton dryly, pointing to the stack of missives from Wing.

"I wouldn't be so cheerful," said Winwright. "Your pile is bigger than mine." He pointed back outside to the main room. Ashton looked out the window as the erks worked on the aircraft.

"I joined this job to fly," said Ashton ruefully.

"So did I," agreed Winwright. He signed another form and dropped it in the Out tray. He scanned the next one and he shook his head in exasperation.

"What's that?" asked Ashton.

"Report from the Provosts." Winwright scanned quickly down the page. "Security concerns."

"The boys are going to go to town later," Ashton hinted. Winwright grunted.

"Fine," he said without looking up. "Get some transport laid on and look after them. I've got to clear this little lot before I get over to Wing. Saundby wants to see me."

The Squadron headed to town in high spirits. Locke stayed for a while to be social and then slid out to see his wife. Hagen went off to see Lorraine. Ashton shepherded the rest of the men home while they sang at the top of their lungs. God alone knew what they would be like in the morning but he figured they were allowed to let their hair down occasionally.

The following morning, most of them felt like the world had fallen on them. It was Good Friday, so Winwright stood them down for the day. Those that wanted to could go to church for the morning service.

Pettifer, Chandler and Morgan joined Kittinger on a walk around Claude Moreau's land. They took pot shots at pigeons and hares as they tramped across the fields.

"Is it much further?" asked Morgan, trudging along behind them. He had his fingers jammed in his pockets, head down as he followed the pack.

"A few miles, I should think." replied Chandler. "Why?" It was a gorgeous day, crisp and fresh. "Nothing beats a long walk to build a healthy appetite, don't you think?"

He looked over his shoulder and grinned. Morgan was clearly suffering. He was learning the hard way that you should not go on a bender starting at tea time, particularly if you were drinking on an empty stomach. If he didn't move his head he felt fine, but every jolting footstep over the ploughed ground was giving him a colossal headache.

They went as far as the river at the bottom of the meadow and then walked along the path. They circled back to the house carrying a brace of hares for the pot. Kittinger put the shotguns back in the cabinet. He would clean them later. Claude came out of his study and invited Kittinger's companions to stay for dinner. He went into the kitchen to give Hortense the good news.

On Easter Sunday, Winwright sank into a comfortable armchair in Valerie's study. After a large dinner, he needed time to relax and let the food go down. Easter Sunday was a big occasion in the town and Winwright and the other units had been prevailed upon to get involved. One section of A Flight had been left on standby while the rest took part in the festivities.

In the afternoon, there was a town fete and squealing children took part in an Easter egg hunt, races and games. There was food aplenty, and the RAF put on a good show. They brought with them sacks and spoons to introduce some typical English games for the children to enjoy.

Bainbridge's men won the sack race. The Lysander pilots had an easy win during the egg and spoon race although there was some controversy that Drake had tripped up Preddy in a clash of legs on the first bend. Wide eyed children came up to them, tugging on their trousers, demanding attention. It put a more human face on these interlopers that lived among them.

Valerie had addressed the gathering in the town square, wishing the townspeople a happy Easter. For this day, the war seemed a long way away. Afterwards, Winwright had accepted Valerie's invitation to dine. Winwright was touched by the regard shown to him by Valerie and his family. Whilst he had contact with the other squadron commanders in the Wing, it was Winwright he spent the most time with.

Edith put on a fine table of several courses. The centrepiece was a rack of lamb with vegetables. She finished Winwright off with a creamy confection for pudding. The table buzzed with life as Valerie's two daughters chattered away about their day. Over the cheese course, Valerie explained he was taking his family to the Normandy coast for a week the following morning.

On hearing this news, Winwright made ready to leave but Valerie was quite relaxed. He hustled the Wing Commander through to his study. Offering him the best seat, he poured two brandies, handing one to Winwright before settling down to rest his knee.

"I have little involvement when we travel, Arthur." He gestured to the door. "Edith is an organiser and she will brook no interference." He gave the younger man a wry smile. He'd experienced a lot of arguments with Edith when they were newly married. It had been a non stop battle of dominance in the packing of bags and getting things organised. Valerie eventually learned to give in and let his wife have her way. When they travelled, he left things in Edith's capable hands and the house was all the quieter for it.

Winwright finished his Brandy and got up to put the crystal glass on the table. The newspaper headline caught his eye and he picked it up. It proclaimed the resignation of Deladier as Prime Minister of France. His reluctance to support the Finns in their war against Soviet aggression had been his downfall. As Finland had fallen, so had he, swept aside by a militant chamber led by Flandin and Laval that denounced his failure to act.

Paul Reynaud had been announced as the new Prime Minister on Good Friday. He was now the head of a wavering government that was supported by the left and hated by the right. Such upheaval was nothing new in French politics. Governments never lasted long. The constant announcements of change, sometimes two or three times in a year, had assumed almost comic status.

"All change again," Valerie grumbled.

"Is it so bad?" asked Winwright.

Valerie shot Winwright a dark look. While it may have been funny on the outside, on the inside it was slowly killing the country. Lack of stability was stalling the economy and it generated an air of apathy and militancy that frustrated reform.

"I worry for my country, Arthur." He got up and paced up and down behind his desk near the fire. "Oh, I know; the Propaganda Ministry talks of our vast armies and strong air force but the fire has gone out." He turned suddenly and slammed a fist down on the desk, steel in his eyes. "We should be attacking now! Advancing on the Boche and showing them they made a mistake in starting this war. What do we do? Gamelin sits behind the Maginot Line and talks about attacking next year."

He almost spat in contempt. Winwright was not surprised at Valerie's strength of feeling on the matter. He also understood the frustration. The French had Deladier, the English had Neville Chamberlain. He was hardly a firebrand either. His limp speeches did little to stir the people at home and the spectre of Munich and his pitiful attempts at appeasement failed to inspire confidence. Having the RAF abide by the Roosevelt rules was just one example of some very mixed up thinking as far as Winwright was concerned.

It was not all one way though. There were some in the British government agitating for more aggressive action. One of those was the First Lord of the Admiralty, Winston Churchill. Churchill was a vocal proponent of taking the fight to the Hun. He was also one of the few politicians that had stood his ground while Hitler pulled the wool over everyone else's eyes.

"Maybe now that Reynaud's in charge, we'll see some changes?" suggested Winwright.

"I doubt it," muttered Valerie. "Reynaud may have taken over but Deladier is still in the cabinet, as Minister of Defence of all things."

Valerie refilled Winwright's glass and they sat down again. They heard raised voices in another part of the house and Valerie listened for a moment. There would be arguments over how much his daughters could take and what was suitable. He was glad to be out of the way in his study. They sat in silence for a while, relaxing after such a big meal.

Winwright grew drowsy in his chair, the combination of the food, the heat; the busy day playing on him. Valerie's voice stirred him.

"The town has not stopped buzzing since you returned," he said. He swirled the brandy round in his glass, savouring the woody notes and the rich colour. "Some people thought you weren't coming back."

"But you knew better?"

Valerie smiled. He knew the military. He knew units moved, sometimes with little logic, but when the aircraft left but the groundcrew remained behind, he knew they were coming back.

"I tried telling them, but people believe what they want sometimes. Your little flying display convinced them otherwise, finally."

"I'm glad people enjoyed it. The boys enjoyed the weather down south."

"But they yearned to be back up here, yes?"

Winwright didn't respond immediately. That was a pointed question, it deserved a candid answer.

"This is where the war is," he said finally.

"Some things never change," agreed Valerie. He eased his leg and moved a pillow to give his knee more support. "It was much the same in my day."

Valerie had thought about this a lot over the years, how the cauldron of war could both repel and attract men in equal measure. There were so many reasons why men fought. Some went to war because they were genuine patriots, fighting in the defence of their country. Some just delighted in the slaughter, the carnage slaking their bloodlust. Some went because they had no choice. Conscripted into service, they went along the conveyor belt like a sheep to slaughter.

By 1916, Valerie had seen the maelstrom of the trenches devouring men and equipment like a living thing and yet he fought as hard as anyone else in his unit. Logic suggested that a sane man would say 'enough' and put an end to all the killing, but war did strange things to people.

Valerie couldn't face being labelled a coward, so he buried his fears every day and went to war instead. Part of him was ashamed that he had been a part of such lunacy, but only a small part. He was a patriot first, a soldier of France defending his country against the hated Boche, and he had done his duty.

Hagen spent the remainder of Easter Sunday with Lorraine in the park in Béthenville. They took their time, walking arm in arm, enjoying each other's company. The park was crowded. The gravel lanes had children running up and down while families enjoyed the day. A military band played in the stand, entertaining everyone with some martial music.

They sat listening for a while. Lorraine gripped his arm and held him close. Waiting for a pause in the music, he rummaged around in his pocket and dragged out a long thin box wrapped in pink paper.

"It's not much, but this is for you."

He'd wanted to get her a ring of some kind but that was something he would rather they did together. Two weeks away had made him realise how much he missed her. She pulled off the ribbon and then the wrapping paper. There was a six inch long blue velvet box inside. Opening it with trembling hands, she found a string of pearls inside. She put a hand to her mouth and her eyes glittered.

"Mark...I-" she was lost for words.

"I'd been meaning to get you something for a while." She kissed him then, hard, pouring her feelings into it. She took the pearls from the box and handed them to him, half turning for him to put them on.

"I'm sorry," he said as he fastened the gold clasp. "I should have done it sooner."

"No more talking," she said, turning to kiss him again.

They made love back at the apartment. It was urgent and quick, their movements fast, like there was no tomorrow. They loved each other as they needed one another, all consuming. Afterwards, they lay intertwined in bed. Hagen dozed, his breathing even. Lorraine looked at him, sorting things through in her head. She had missed him these last few weeks and now he was back she was happier than ever.

She opened the drawer on the bedside cabinet on her side of the bed. She pulled out the note that Kittinger had brought round two weeks ago. It was creased and the pencil was smudged, but she knew every word by heart. Some people would have just left without a word, saying they didn't have time to leave a note, but he had; that said a lot. He cared for her; she knew that, the pearls around her neck were proof of the depth of his feelings.

In the quiet of the bedroom she thought about relationships and their power. The hold they had on you, the way they shaped your life and affected your decision making. She had loved more than once. Loved and lost, as her father occasionally reminded her. She thought about what pulled people together and what pulled them apart.

She contrasted her own situation with that of Hortense and Laura. Hortense had gone through a tragedy of her own and both of them knew what it was like to have someone taken from you without warning. On the other hand, Laura seemed hell bent on tearing her marriage apart. Lorraine found herself torn over whether or not to reveal her secret.

More than once she had seen Laura in town; hanging off a man who was tall, charming and well dressed. He was clearly more than a friend. Lorraine was not naive in that regard. Having an affair was nothing unusual; people did it all the time for various reasons. She just never thought she would have this kind of responsibility thrust upon her. She had no idea how she could look at Alexander with a straight face and not give Laura away.

When Laura had come round after the squadron left, she'd watched the blonde woman pace up and down the room, as she fumed at being left behind. It was all a show of course. What she was really looking for was approval for her actions. Maybe Laura had thought her guilty secret was out. Nothing specific was said between them, but part of Lorraine wanted to ask Laura what she was playing at. Caution held her in check. If she challenged Laura she was afraid it might force the young English girl into making a rash decision she would later regret.

"Don't ask, don't tell," she thought to herself while she continued to look down at Hagen. While the squadron had been away, it had delayed the decision. Now they were back, she had to figure out what she was going to do. Setting aside exactly how she was supposed to disclose such information, even if she did say something, Locke may not believe her anyway. If Locke did believe her, that would cause even more problems.

Maybe it would be best to let the future take care of itself, she decided. If it was just a passing fancy on Laura's part, she saw no need to punish the poor girl for a momentary indiscretion. If it was not; if Laura was serious, then things would sort themselves out in time. She closed her eyes and lay down, holding Hagen close.

While Lorraine was happy with her choices, on the other side of town, Laura was agonising over hers and the situation she now found herself in. She looked at her husband across the other side of the table as he finished the meal she'd made for him. He wiped a piece of bread around the plate to mop up the white wine and garlic sauce she'd made to go with the piece of fish she had bought from the market.

He had swept into the apartment two days before, full of bonhomie, a winning smile and presents for his wife. She had stood in the hall, heart hammering, hoping to god she'd not left out anything that would betray her secret and invite questions. What had started as a dalliance, almost an act of revenge against her husband, had morphed into an addiction of sorts that she found hard to get away from. When the Blenheims and Battles had roared over town, she had been roaring to a pinnacle of her own in bed with Pascal.

When Farmer came in extra low with his section to zoom past the belfry, her groans of pleasure had transformed into a gurgle of horror. With a burst of strength she pushed Pascal away, sending him sprawling. He had dressed quickly and left while she put the apartment to rights.

She sat across from Alex with a fake smile painted on her face. Her cheeks ached as she kept up the pretence, waiting to be caught in a lie. She needn't have worried. Locke had no idea anything was wrong. The apartment was tidy, his wife was smiling, the weather was good, what more could a man want? He reached across the table and took Laura's hand, giving it a small squeeze.

She ushered him over to the sofa to relax and then set about clearing the table. He watched her as she picked up the plates and took them into the kitchen.

"God, I'm whacked," he announced out loud. He sat for another minute and then levered himself up to see what Laura was doing.

She was up to her elbows in soap suds when his hands snaked around her waist. He leaned in close and rested his chin on her shoulder. She tried not to flinch when she felt his breath on her neck.

"Missed you, wife." he said, kissing her neck and squeezing her in his arms. She dabbed some bubbles on his nose and told him to sit down. He blew the suds off in good humour and laughed as he left the kitchen.

Laura suppressed a shudder as he left her alone. She felt a sharp stab of guilt as she cleaned their plates. She'd told herself once before that Pascal was just a friend. It was her fault. The lines had become blurred. She clung to that thought, trying to convince herself that it was still the truth. She sighed and put a damp wrist to her forehead. She had no idea what she was going to do.

She wondered how she'd managed to keep up the pretence for the last two days. She had cried when Alex explained his thoughts to her. Two weeks away had given him time to think and adjust to the idea of a new perspective. He decided he had to listen more and be more patient with her. All too often, he was forgetting that she was on her own for a lot of the day. Hortense was busy, Lorraine had her job. It was fine for him; he had the squadron to keep him busy.

He tried to explain his thinking as best he could but he was perplexed when the tears rolled down her cheeks. He was blown away when she clung to him, telling him she didn't deserve him. He was pleased she appreciated his efforts. He had no idea that there was another hidden meaning wrapped in her words.

All she wanted was for him to go back to the squadron so she would have time to think. The fantasy was over. She had thrown caution to the wind the last few weeks, doing what she wanted, and now it was time to pay her dues.

2.11 – Back To Work

Winwright woke early. Back at home, a batman would have been fussing around, making him a cup of tea while he dressed. In France he'd done away with all that nonsense. In the field there was more important work to be done. Picking up his cap, he went for a walk before breakfast.

He'd stayed late at Valerie's the previous evening, enjoying his friend's company as well as his brandy. It had been a good day. After two weeks of intensive flying, it had been a good idea to let the men relax and let their hair down a bit. He was pleased with the progress of the last two weeks and there was still plenty of war left to go around.

A long winter had dulled minds as well as reactions and some training had been just what the doctor ordered. He was still convinced that tight formation flying was the answer. Bombers had to get their bombs on target to deliver the knockout blow. If they had to battle their way through a horde of fighters, then good formation and gunnery were the only things that were going to bring them back alive.

In the sunny skies of southern France their formation flying had been good, their shooting less so. Winwright couldn't really blame the gunners. Aside from Sergeant Harris, they'd only had rudimentary training and pre war there had been little opportunity to practice. He thought about what they could do about that over breakfast.

Clearly, the men needed more training, but he also thought it was an opportunity to educate. Pilots and navigators sat up front in the nose while the gunners froze in their turrets; they often seemed to forget that fact. Cold did things to a man, fatigue did too; it dulled their reactions. Hitting on a sudden idea, he went off in search of Kittinger to scrounge a cup of tea and talk it over.

Kittinger stood at the gate looking between the clipboard and the driver of a truck. For the second time he walked round to the back of the Bedford. Inside were piles of thick coats, scarfs, hats and gloves.

"I'm not signing for this lot," he said again.

"But I've got your requisition order here, sir," protested the Corporal who'd brought it. He pointed to the manifest.

"I don't disagree, but I ordered this stuff months ago when the snow was laying hereabouts deep and crisp and even." He gestured around the field. It was lush green grass and bright sunshine everywhere. "It's no good looking at me like that, Corporal. There's no point having foul weather gear when there's no foul weather."

"So what am I supposed to do?" asked the Corporal. Kittinger frowned, the man's voice had a whiny catch of protest to it which he didn't like.

"Take it back where you got it from. I don't care." He wrote *'not accepted'* on the requisition and then signed it. He handed the clipboard back to the Corporal. The truck left with a crash of gears and Kittinger gave the driver a little wave as it went. He was walking back to the flight hut shaking his head when the CO crossed his path.

"Problem Adj?"

"Nothing to worry about, sir. Just the supply system showing how good it is. Absolute bloody shambles."

"Don't worry about that, I've got an idea I'd like you to handle."

Feet pounded across the grass, arms pumped back and forth as they ran. A long line of bodies was strung out over a few hundred yards as they crossed the field. While the leaders clambered over the low stone wall, the stragglers were crossing the stile at the other end.

Flight Sergeant Davis rushed around, snapping at their heels like a bulldog. He covered twice as much ground as everyone else, all the while cajoling and shouting. He urged them on to make greater efforts with his thick Brummy accent.

"Goots and drive, sir, goots and drive. Open those legs and pick up the pace a bit. Wonderful, sir, that's grand that is."

Before Chandler could give him a scathing response, he was off up the line, shouting at someone else. Chandler stared at the man's back, trying to pace himself off him. He managed a few yards before the Sergeant hared off in his red t-shirt and black shorts.

"God, the man's a gazelle," muttered Chandler.

"Give up," wheezed Morgan. He held his side as a stitch developed behind his ribs. "You'll never catch him. Davis ran for the County before the war."

"Bugger him then."

They pounded on, their breath heaving in the morning air. Tired feet slogged through soft ground while muscles burned. Shoes splashed through the odd puddle, turning white socks brown, caking their legs in dirt and mud.

Morgan struggled alongside his pilot. His head was muzzy, still thick from the day before and his legs were tired from the walk in the fields. It had been a glorious dinner and Kittinger's girl had even conjured up some Yorkshire Puddings. He'd not seen one of those for months. His stomach growled with the memory and his mouth watered at the taste of it. He was jolted out of his reverie by Davis.

"Goots and drive, sir, goots and drive."

The man was off again, shouting at the stragglers. Morgan winced as the stitch spread down his side.

They ran across the next field and then turned the corner round the trees. They ran by the front gate. After one lap, the men were fairly spread out and Dane checked their names off on his clipboard as they went past him. He resisted offers of bribes to let them off another lap. The CO had been very clear, there was to be no cheating.

After breakfast, the men had been lined up in their ranks, pretty as a picture in their shorts and singlets. Kittinger had prowled up and down the lines under the watchful eyes of the CO.

"Flabby!" he had shouted. "Soft! Soft bodies equal soft minds. I already know you lot can't shoot. How well do you think you'll be able to fly if you can't even keep your bodies in shape? Two weeks holiday in the south of France has got you all off your game." He came back around to the front of the men and beamed.

"So you're all going for a little run. Two miles!" They groaned and he grinned with relish. "I'm glad to hear it. Seeing as you're so keen let's make it four instead. Two laps!" He held up two fingers in case anyone at the back had trouble hearing. "Flight Sergeant Davis is going to accompany you on this little stroll."

Eyes fixed on the compact man who stood off to one side. Muscles rippled under his singlet. There was a moment's silence, then Davis stepped forward and the nightmare had begun.

"Thank you Mister Kittinger. Right then, let's get started, shall we? Goots and drive, goots and drive."

On the second lap, Morgan tripped over a wall and landed in a heap on the other side. The mud cushioned his fall. He emerged from the stinking yellow puddle covered in filth. His shoes had disappeared under a thick layer of dirt that extended up to his knees. Water squelched between his toes as he ran. He wiped dirt from his face and spat to clear his mouth.

"A vast improvement," said Chandler.

"Har de har," said Morgan. He was wet through and his thighs were sore. The seams of his shorts were rubbing on his legs and the skin felt raw. "What's the point of all this?" he moaned. "I just sit and look at maps, *you* fly the plane."

At the conclusion of the second lap, they came to a ragged halt. They lay on the ground, sucking in vast lungful's of air. Morgan's mouth felt like dry carpet and his head was pounding. His thighs were burning and all he wanted now was to lay down in a bath of hot water.

Unfortunately, a warm bath was some way in the future as Davis got them to their feet and herded them to the far end of the field. Kittinger was waiting for them along with some bods from the armoury. There were four Vickers K guns set up on pintle mountings, pointing over the stone wall that marked the end of the field. In the next field, was a long deep drainage ditch about thirty yards away. Kittinger gathered the men around him.

"Glad to see you all enjoyed your little exercise." He beamed with bonhomie as he rocked back and forth on his heels. "Now to test your shooting." He pointed to the guns. "Four of you at a time will man the guns while targets will be held up on sticks for you to shoot at." He blew a whistle and sticks came into view. Shapes of aircraft were attached to the sticks. "The targets are what you see at two hundred yards. Hit them and you go top of my list."

They got to work. The staccato clatter of Vickers machine guns ripped the air apart. The targets appeared at random intervals and stayed in view for a few seconds. Drums emptied. They reloaded but before they could fire again, Kittinger shouted at them to stop.

"Miserable! Pathetic! Twenty five pushups gentlemen. Twenty five pushups every time you empty a drum without hitting a target."

He picked up a red metal fire bucket from a line of them off to one side. He upended the bucket over Preddy, who spluttered at the sudden deluge.

"No one told you to stop, Mister Preddy. Proper pushups now," he warned. "My elderly aunt could do this and she's over sixty."

Arms shaking, wrists aching, they were back on the guns, firing short bursts. Pettifer managed to clip a corner of the target but that was the only success in the first group. The next group of four went up and did little better. Those not shooting had little time to jeer at the appalling accuracy. Kittinger and Davis had them doing star jumps, sit ups and short sprints while they waited. They kept them at it non stop, anything and everything to make them tired, to make them wheeze, to make their arms tingle.

"Remember, short controlled bursts," Kittinger reminded them. "In a turret you'll be bouncing around in the slipstream."

They got better. Griffiths nailed a target dead on. Others succeeded too, but it was an effort, trying to focus on the skittering shape while your head swam with fatigue. There was a pause when new cutouts were rigged to the sticks. While they waited, Davis herded the men up and down. He split them into groups and ran a relay race to keep them occupied. A rope was produced so they could play tug of war.

Kittinger kept them at it for an hour until the sticks were shredded. They drifted off to get changed, worn out from the morning's exertions. Winwright released them for the rest of the day, but he'd made his point. They had to be able to do each other's jobs and maybe, just maybe, they'd gained a little more understanding of what the gunners had to go through back in their turrets.

2.12 – A Moment To Themselves

Hortense had found a nice spot in a glade on the other side of the manor house. It was her family's land, so it was private and there was no danger of them being interrupted. It was bordered by trees on three sides and ran downhill. In years gone by, the Moreau family had farmed this land but it had been allowed to lay fallow for a long time. The grass had grown tall in the spring. Small meadow flowers gave the local insects a place to go hunting for food.

She spread out a blanket in the lee of the trees. It was a small island surrounded by the tall grass around it. Kittinger drowsed as the sun beat down. He listened to a bird singing in the trees nearby, trying to attract a female.

He smiled as he stretched out, feeling the warmth wash over him. He stroked her hand next to his and ran his fingers up and down her arm. She moved her hand out of the way and gave him a playful slap on the wrist.

She sat up and stared off towards the manor house. She could just see the tops of the roof over the trees. She loved that house and knew every part of it but it had been awkward returning there after her husband died. Keeping house where her mother had once ruled felt strange. It had taken a while before she felt at home once more. She'd hoped that Claude would settle down but he was wedded to his work. Before she knew it, three years had drifted by and she had settled back into the lazy provincial life she remembered of her youth.

"I used to play in these meadows as a girl," she told him. There was a break in the trees and a path that led to the hill. She'd chased her dogs many times in the summers along that path when she was home from school. The wind rustled the trees and carried the sound of running aero engines with it. Kittinger stirred at the noise.

"Engine test," he mumbled. "Or an air test perhaps." He rolled over and wiped sleep from his eyes.

"It never ends, does it?" she asked him.

"No," he sighed. He looked up at her. She was sitting next to him, her legs folded under her, left hand resting on her thigh. Her right hand propped her chin up. She was wearing a white blouse with the sleeves rolled up and a knee length maroon skirt. She slipped off her sandals and stretched her legs out in front of herself, wriggling her toes in the grass.

Kittinger felt lightheaded from the sun on his face and he levered himself up, locking his elbows. He watched quietly while she combed her hair, her chestnut tresses shining. She hummed quietly to herself and he listened, content. He walked his fingers up her back and she stirred under his touch.

She swivelled round to face him and leaned in, rubbing up and down his chest. She began to unbutton his shirt, her hands following the line of his muscles under the material. She traced her fingers over the pink scars on his ribcage, the pebble dash pattern of ridged skin on his shoulder.

"My poor, Michael."

"Long time ago," he grunted. He tried to shut out the memory of the mud and carnage. The horrors were something he could never forget. He believed it was the closest you could ever come to hell on this earth. He couldn't imagine how to describe mud that stank of death and living amongst vermin while you walked around waist deep in water.

Now he was a penguin. He no longer flew and he had to stand and watch while younger men went off to war to be shot at. He felt a bit like a fifth wheel, surplus to requirements sometimes. He brooded for a while, his thoughts far away. In the Great War, he'd measured his life out in pieces. As an officer in the trenches you were living on borrowed time. He learned very quickly that no matter how prepared you were, your life could be snuffed out in a moment.

He remembered a Major in the second battalion called Anderson Smythe who had come from India. He'd likened the war to a tiger hunt. He was the best shot in the regiment but he treated the war like a game. None of it counted for anything when a shell exploded and wiped him out along with seven men from his platoon. Smythe never did get to show the Germans what a good shot he was.

Transferring to the RFC had been no safer. A new man's life span was measured in days. If the Germans didn't get you, there was plenty of other ways to die. Biplanes were flimsy things, held together with wire and canvas. If that didn't do it, the weather could take care of you quite neatly. He'd never expected to survive and see the end of it all. Now his epitaph had as much chance of reading *'Died In His Sleep.'*

He came out of his reverie to see Hortense scrutinising him, trying to divine his thoughts. Her face was shaded from the sun, a little pull to her smile that dimpled her cheek. She slowly unbuttoned her blouse and leaned over him. He caught a glimpse of pale skin, the swell of her breasts and a smattering of freckles. She got on top of him, her legs straddling his.

"Christ woman, have you no shame?" She was good enough to laugh and rested her hands either side of his head, her blouse hanging open, her breasts rubbing against his chest. "What if someone sees us?" he asked her, his voice mock outraged. Neither of them moved.

"Let them." she said, her voice husky. "It's not the first time I've done this. It probably won't be the last either."

Kittinger laughed, lines crinkling around his eyes. She was a breath of fresh air to him. A heady mix of abandon to pull him out of his shell of steel, to protect him and love him according to her mood.

"My husband told me once that I scandalised the village." Kittinger's mind raced with the possibilities. It probably wouldn't have taken much to scandalise a village in the Lake District.

"How did you manage that? Daring to wear a skirt above the knee? Making French Fancies for the village stall at the summer fete?"

"No!" she said and kissed him. They made love then, oblivious of everything around them. Afterwards, they lay spent, looking at the clouds, searching for recognisable shapes in the fluffy sky.

"What's it like being an officer's wife?" she asked him. Kittinger was stumped for a moment while he formulated an answer. Being in administration, he'd dealt with service wives often enough, it just wasn't a thought that had ever occurred to him.

Station life in England had a certain hierarchy attached to it. The chair of the wives committee tended to be the CO's wife and as Adjutant it was his job to liaise with them when there were events. Being a bachelor, they were almost another species to him. Kittinger's life revolved around the squadron, the crews and service wives. The trials and tribulations were just something he had to deal with. Hortense frowned while he told her snippets of his experiences.

"It sounds like a fete planning committee," she decided. "Lots of queen bees making a lot of noise."

"I suppose," he nodded, agreeing with her. "Some certainly make more noise than others."

"Sounds ghastly," she said.

"You'd be fine," he reassured her, then stopped, suddenly realising what he'd said. Was he ready to be married, he asked himself? Only a few months before, he'd been all alone. He'd made one jump this year, maybe he could end up taking another. Would Claude approve, he wondered? Being hospitable to him and welcoming him into his house was one thing and he'd not voiced any problem so far, but marrying his sister? He was unsure.

He gathered her into his arms and she rolled into him. She rested her chin on his shoulder, her body pressed against him. One leg draped over his and her hand walked up and down his chest.

"You'd be fine," he said again, his hand stroking her neck, twirling the wisps of hair. Hortense smiled. He'd not asked and she'd not said yes but she knew what he was thinking. He wanted to, she was sure; it would just take him a bit longer to get there, that was all.

"You know, the last time I was like this-"

Her eyes snapped open and she sat up. She looked down at him, her right hand slapping him playfully on the chest.

"Who was the woman?" she demanded peremptorily. "Who!"

"No, dash it." He blushed crimson. "I mean, just lying in a field like this." He gestured around himself, worried until her saw her impish smile. "Doesn't matter," he said, cupping her face with his hand and pulling her down for another kiss. She fell willingly and they made love again under the warm Easter sun.

2.13 – Gearing Up

When word of the German invasion of Denmark and Norwy reached Bois Fontaine, the news was taken with a mixture of dismay and anticipation. Once again, there was a feeling they had missed the boat. Last year they nearly missed going to France. Now they were here and all the action was happening elsewhere. It was hard not to feel cheated.

On the 10th April, Winwright put them on alert at fifteen minutes' standby. He was jumping the gun a bit, but if there was going to be some kind of retaliation he wanted to be ready. Besides, the men were starting to fidget with nervous energy; this gave them something to stay busy.

Late in the afternoon, Saundby did the rounds of his units, sharing what news he had. He found the crews lounging around in agitated repose. Some lay on the grass outside, eyes closed as the sun beat down. Some sat poised in armchairs, thumbing through magazines without really seeing the pages. The gramophone was playing the hated *'Teddy Bears Picnic'* but no one could be bothered to turn it off. They were shocked when Saundby had told them that Denmark had fallen.

"Six hours," said Osbourne in undisguised contempt. "My God, why bother?"

"Hardly seems worth the effort, does it?" agreed Farmer.

He was a little perturbed with the news. Poland and now Denmark had been erased from the map. Norway was struggling. Who else would suffer the same fate, he wondered. Once again, the tactics of Blitzkrieg had proven unstoppable. He almost expected to see the German tanks rolling over the hills, the air filled with the shrill scream of the Stukas coming down.

"I mean, you wouldn't even get through a good innings at Lords in six hours," said Pendleton. "What you need-" he got up from his worn armchair and mimicked a move with a cricket bat, "-is a good forward defensive stroke."

"I'm not so sure," asked Farmer. "I think I'd rather have something a bit more substantial than a piece of willow between me and a bunch of tanks."

"They had lancers in Poland," offered Osbourne.

"My point exactly," said Farmer.

"Oh," Osbourne drummed his fingers on the arms of his chair when the penny dropped. "I see what you mean. Touche."

"Anyway, you don't need a cricket bat, they've still got to get past the Maginot Line," said Pendleton.

"I suppose," said Farmer in grudging agreement. "Assuming they come crashing over the border and hurl themselves against the guns and defences." He paused to let that sink in first. That comment brought Pendleton up short. He shot Farmer a searching look, wondering if he knew something they didn't. "So far the Germans have been anything but stupid. I don't see any reason why they should stop now. You mark my words, any day now they'll come through Belgium."

"Yeah, but France isn't Denmark or Poland for that matter," argued Pendleton. "You could fly over Denmark in about half an hour full tilt. It's tiny. No wonder they folded so quickly, the Jerries just swamped them with weight of numbers. Belgium will have the same problem but they won't be on their own. As soon as old Adolf puts one foot over the border, we'll come charging to the rescue."

Farmer had to give him that but he was tired of going over and over the same old ground again. They had been doing it for hours. Suddenly tired of it all, he went outside and made a bee line for his kite. He wanted to make sure she was ready to go, all this waiting was starting to get to him.

Hagen watched the big man stalk across the grass. Farmer shouted at the waiting groundcrew and harangued them into hooking up a trolley acc so he could start her up. Soon the sound of Mercury engines being run up to full power assailed their ears. Hagen shared a look with Morgan when they heard the pop and grind that indicated a loss of power. Shaking his head, he turned back to their game of boules while Farmer tore a strip a mile wide off some hapless erk..

"One of these days he'll blow a gasket," murmured Morgan. Hagen grunted agreement while he took aim on the jack with his metal boule. He'd picked up the game from watching men in town play it on Sundays. Lorraine had explained the rules to him and he'd spent a few francs buying a set of boules to play back at the squadron.

Round the back of the mess he'd used the roller to give them a flatter playing surface. Using a dustbin lid and some whitewash, he had marked out two circles. He put them fifteen metres apart and then put a rough line in front of each circle. That was the limit of the play area. They would take it in turns, playing from each circle, or 'end'. If the jack was knocked beyond that line, then it was dead and the end was over.

He threw the boule underhand, flicking his wrist as he let it go. It sailed through the air in a high arc and bounced beyond the yellow jack before coming to a halt, the slight backspin stopping it dead.

Morgan peered at Hagen's boules gleaming under the sun. He had two lying close to the jack, one beyond, the other in front. His own lay between them off to the right, a good three feet away. Hagen's first shot had knocked it out of the way with a solid hit. He picked up his own boule and hefted it in his hand. He wiped the stainless steel with a cloth and lined up on his target.

He figured a gentle backwards stroke and a high arc and he could get his boule to run up alongside the jack. He took Hagen's place in the circle and made a few practise swings. The ball was heavy in his hand. He still wasn't used to throwing it. It was nothing like bowling in cricket. There was no run up and the boule was too big to flick with your fingers.

He made his shot, watching as it went up and down and fell short, rolling up next to Hagen's boule in front of the jack. So far, he'd scored nothing while Hagen was three up after two ends. He needed to improve if he was going to keep his shilling. Locke clapped as he rounded the corner of the hut with Ashton and walked towards them.

"Nice shot."

"I'm still learning." He stepped back and motioned to the circle, looking at Hagen. "Your turn."

"The trick," said Hagen, "is to take your time." He flicked a glance at Morgan before taking a fast shot. It whipped out on a low flat trajectory and hit Morgan's boule with a dull crack. It stopped dead, taking the place of Morgan's boule which skittered away at a forty five degree angle, coming to rest up against the hut.

"Enough, you win," said Morgan. He dug around in his pocket and flicked a coin towards Hagen.

"Another game?" Hagen asked, looking at the shilling in the palm of his hand. Morgan shook his head.

"Another time. I guess I need to practise some more."

Picking up his uniform jacket, he shrugged it on and walked back to the mess. He needed a cup of tea. Hagen appealed to the squadron leader.

"Sir?"

Ashton shook his head.

"I always subscribe to the view that a fool and his money are soon parted. I think I'll watch."

Locke picked up Morgan's final boule and tossed it between his hands as he walked towards him.

"I'll play," he said. "Same stakes?"

Hagen nodded and walked over to the boules. He roughly chucked them towards the other circle, clearing the playing area for the next round.

"Why not?"

Locke went first. He knew Hagen's aim wasn't so good at longer distances, so he pitched the jack two thirds of the way down the field, about ten metres away. His first boule bounced shallow but he had put a bit too much on it. It skipped beyond the jack, coming to rest two metres long.

"Interesting move," commented Hagen. He bent down and picked up his first boule.

"Can I ask a question, sir?" Locke said to Ashton.

"What's on your mind, Mr Locke?"

"Is this it, sir? I mean, are we going to war at last?"

Ashton didn't answer right away. He folded his arms and rubbed the pad of his thumb on his lip.

"Maybe." His expression was sombre. "If it is, have you given any consideration to your wife?"

"My wife?"

"If the shooting starts, she might have to leave in a hurry." He glanced at Hagen. "Your girl too." That stopped play momentarily. "It's just something to consider," Ashton said. "If the army advances into Belgium, we might end up moving forward in support of it. It might be best if you make some arrangements for their safety. I'd think about that."

Leaving them with that thought, he went over to the flight hut for a meeting with the CO and Saundby. He saw Gardner coming across from the line of aircraft and waved to get his attention.

Hagen's brow was creased in thought while he scrutinised his boule. He could see the clouds reflected in its hard surface and his own face was reflected back at him. Suddenly the war was not just about him.

"Have you talked about it with, Lorraine?" asked Locke.

"Not yet," Hagen walked back to the circle and tried to think about his shot. He shrugged absently. "Even if I did, I'm not sure she'd go." Locke had to agree. Lorraine was very stubborn when she wanted to be. "I'll ask her to go, but she knows her own mind." Locke was surprised that Hagen's voice was so flat.

"Ashton's right, you have to think about the future," he said firmly. Hagen was about to snap off a reply but then he caught himself. He focused on the boule and made his shot. It fell short and off to the left.

"You know, all these months I've tried to avoid thinking about next month, next year. I know I probably won't live to see the end of the war." He laughed to himself, trying to shake off dark thoughts. Every day he had to fight the urge to curl into a ball. "You know it's funny. Sometimes I catch myself thinking about the *what ifs*. Maybe in another life I would have married Lorraine." He took a kick at a pile of stones they were using to keep score. "But I don't want to put her through that pain, she's suffered enough already."

Locke could not help but snort in amusement.

"You're an ass!" he said in soft sarcasm. Hagen's face pinched in annoyance.

"I'm an ass? You're a fine one to talk," he said, stung into a response. "Look, Mark. I'm not saying the path to wedded bliss is smooth. My marriage is hardly perfect, I know that." They shared a look.

Hagen knew full well that Locke wasn't happy. He was sad his prediction in the armoury was coming true. He'd seen what Laura had been like over the last few months, how petulant she could be. More than once, Locke had come to him for advice, telling him about the pressures she was putting him under, the rows. Locke knew there was something wrong, however much she avoided telling him. He just couldn't figure out what.

"But think about this, if you *did* die, whether you're married or not, Lorraine will still be upset." Locke had seen them together. He saw the way they looked at one another. There were deep feelings there, he knew it. Hagen looked chastened.

"I didn't think of it like that," he replied.

"You said you could see yourself marrying her if it wasn't for the war. What difference does that make? When we found out we were going to France, that was the spur for Laura and me. We just didn't see any point in waiting anymore. I've no doubt we'd have got there eventually. The war just speeded things up a bit." He put a reassuring hand on Hagen's shoulder. "Go that one step further, for her as much as for you."

In the intelligence hut, Dane had read through the intel briefs Saundby had brought with him. He looked at the map spread out on the table, imagining forces moving across it like pieces on a chess board. He gathered up the map and latest briefs and strolled across the grass to the flight hut. Even from the limited information that Wing had sent him, he knew there would be no war for them today. Hitler's book, Mein Kampf, the bible of all good Nazis, warned against a war on two fronts.

Dane knew that German heavy industry was dependent on iron ore from

Sweden. Last year they had imported nearly ten million tons of the stuff. Over the winter months, the RAF had mined the Skaggerak and the Royal Navy had been playing merry hell off the Norwegian coast.

The Nazis were practical. If something stood between you and something you wanted; you took it. They had done it with the Saarland, with Austria and with Poland. Now, rather than waiting for the Norwegians to be pressured into turning against them, they had taken the simpler course. They sent their troops north to take it for themselves.

Now that Denmark had fallen, the way was clear for the Germans to advance into Norway. Narvik, Stavanger, Kristiansand and Bergen had already fallen. There were also reports of German paratroopers taking strategic locations such as airfields and bridges with little resistance. Things were looking grim.

What Dane didn't know was that this wasn't all the surprise it appeared to be. A few days before, a recce Blenheim flying over the Kiel area had spotted thousands of vehicles heading towards the port. Trucks four abreast were crawling along the autobahn towards ships and slipways that were a blaze of lights with no regard to the blackout at all.

At Rhiems, the information was scrutinised with quiet intensity. Goddard expected everyone to leap into action but there seemed to be an air of lethargy pervading the various commands. He'd spent a frustrating morning talking to a contact at the Air Ministry. While his friend saw the possibilities, to him, ships were a naval problem. He rang off with a cheery assurance that he would let the Admiralty know. Goddard eyed the telephone in shock at this devil may care attitude.

On a whim, he rang GHQ to find they weren't even aware of the troop movements. While the news was considered interesting, no one seemed bothered. If the Germans were going elsewhere, then it gave them more time to prepare in France. Goddard felt this was a mistake but there was little more he could do.

Bomber Command did in fact dispatch a raid the following day but it had little effect. Bad weather prevented follow up reconnaissance and the opportunity to catch the invasion fleet in the open was missed.

Dane entered the flight hut and dumped his maps and briefs on the table. Arrayed around him were, Saundby, Winwright, Ashton and Gardner. When he came in, Winwright nodded to the orderly and Corporal Taylor exited through the door.

"Sorry I'm late, sir."

"You're not. Have a seat."

Dane sat down next to the table and fished his reading glasses out of his top pocket. He spread the map out and looked from face to face. They were waiting for him to start.

"Based on the briefs the Air Commodore has brought over, I think I can safely say we'll not be in any danger for a while yet."

"That's a very positive statement, Mr Dane," said Saundby. "Defend it."

For a moment, Dane felt like he was back in his lecture halls at King's College. He would be stood there at the lectern, with a wall of faces looking at him, asking him questions. Some would be serious, probing for more knowledge; others would be trying to trip him up.

"If our intelligence reports are correct-" he paused for a glimmer and glanced over the top of his glasses to see Saundby nodding, lips pursed. "The Germans have just over one hundred thirty divisions in the field. Including the French army and the BEF, we have one hundred forty six divisions facing them. Victory is not certain either way." His finger traced along the border of France, from the coast next to Belgium, down to the Maginot Line. Heads strained to follow. "Fighting defensively, we are of course spread out along this line, with a larger proportion along the Belgian border. Strung out like this, the Germans can pick a time and a place of their choosing. They can concentrate their attack, but it would only be a temporary advantage before we could converge on that point."

"To invade Norway and Denmark, the Germans *must* have taken those units from somewhere. The recce Blenheims have seen nothing moving for the last week, no massing of troops along our border. Their air activity has dropped to almost nothing. Even their reconnaissance flights are down." He shuffled through the intelligence briefs that Saundby had brought from AASF headquarters. "Conservative estimates would suggest they've fielded something like eight divisions in Norway, possibly more than ten. When you include the resources they've diverted to Denmark, that's a lot of men. So I've got no doubt we're going to be next, just not today."

He put his glasses on the table and looked at Winwright, trying to gauge his thoughts. The CO narrowed his eyes as he returned Dane's gaze.

"I see," said Winwright thinly. Like everyone else, he had been shocked at how easily Denmark had fallen. He couldn't believe it when Saundby told him. Any hope the German advance could be stalled would seem to be a very remote prospect. "And what do you propose we do about that?"

"That's the big question, isn't it? I'd hit them with both barrels." Dane said matter of fact as he rubbed the lenses of his glasses on a handkerchief. Winwright stifled a grin.

"Still the firebrand I see?" said Saundby.

"Yes, sir."

"So we should attack them?"

"Without a doubt, sir. With hundreds of fighters and bombers supporting their ground offensive up north, the Luftwaffe can't possibly be in two places at once. We should be giving them a jolly good thumping while we can."

"Hear, hear," murmured Gardner.

Saundby gave them his best smile.

"Gentlemen, I'm very pleased to see such fighting spirit. I wish I could oblige you, but we're all waiting for some orders. If the Norwegians can hold out for a few days, then I can't see the government doing nothing. We can't let Norway go the same way as Poland."

Saundby thought about the conversation he had with headquarters that morning. He'd argued for an immediate attack but he was told to wait. He looked at Dane's map across the table and asked everyone to crowd around. Just because there were no orders forthcoming at the moment didn't mean there wouldn't be any.

Falcon Squadron spent the rest of the day at fifteen minute readiness, bored and listless. Once again; no war today, at least in their own backyard.

Saundby returned to Arras for an update from HQ but there was nothing new. There was no German activity in the west and the Phoney War continued.

The following day, Winwright put A Flight at thirty minutes readiness and stood down B Flight for the morning. They would swap around after lunch. Although they were stood down, they had orders not to stray too far just in case Headquarters got off sitting on its hands and did something. Runs to Béthenville were off limits at any rate, so they kept themselves busy at Bois Fontaine. A few went down the back end of the woods with some rifles. One or two went for a walk. The rest hunted up a football and had a kick around. Tunics and flying kit were dumped in piles to make makeshift goalposts and they chased the ball for a while.

Locke spent a few hours tinkering with the Mathis. He crawled over the engine, checked the plugs, the oil and then cleaned it up inside. He borrowed his fitter to double check his work. If Laura did need to go somewhere in a hurry, he wanted to make sure the car was running fine.

Winwright called Headquarters for orders but none were forthcoming. They were taking a wait and see approach. In truth, there was little they could do. AASF took its orders from Gamelin's headquarters like everyone else and the great General preferred to 'await events'.

Under a balmy afternoon sun, an Air France Potez transport pulled up outside the terminal building. A bulky high wing aircraft, it lacked the visual glamour of the newer all metal monoplane transports but it was a loyal workhorse to the airline. Cullen wiped sleep from his eyes and yawned, stretching in his seat.

Typically, big events had happened while he was elsewhere. After so many weeks of inactivity, he'd decided to chance a few days at home. He'd barely made it to his house in Chelsea when the Germans went streaming into Norway. Then he'd spent a frustrating two days trying to get a flight back to Paris. Initially, all civilian traffic was grounded as a precaution. When it was clear that nothing was going to happen immediately, normal service resumed. Even then, he had to wait as priority was given to military personnel recalled to France. On the second day, he bumped into Dodds and the pair of them debated trying to hop a ferry to Calais, but the schedules were all over the place.

Biding their time, they hung around the terminal building looking for an opportunity. It came in the afternoon when two officers failed to answer the final boarding call. Grabbing their bags, they had to run before they missed their chance.

The steward went down the cabin from the cockpit, opening the door at the rear of the aircraft. A mechanic wheeled over a set of ladders and Cullen touched down onto solid ground again. Army officers recalled in a hurry from England followed him out and made their way to the terminal building. Cullen waited for his fellow reporter to join him. Dodds had drifted over to a Dewoitine fighter outside a hangar. He was peering into the barrels of its wing mounted cannon when an airman waved a rifle at him, calling him a spy. There was a heated exchange until Dodds remembered to pull out his press pass. Mollified, the airman went back to walking around the fighters.

Passing through customs was a formality, their press pass and khaki uniforms were enough to see them through. They sat down to a late lunch in the terminal restaurant.

Over Beef Bourginon and a coarse red, Cullen skipped over the day's papers. He compared between the French daily paper Les Echos and The Times. The tone in each was generally the same. Positive action over Norway was demanded yesterday. An early filip to morale was news from Narvik and once again the Royal Navy was to the fore.

On the 10th April, a flotilla of destroyers had caught the German Navy with their pants down. With dash and elan, two destroyers had been sunk and four others were damaged. Seven freighters along with their ammunition supply ship had also been sunk. In the great scheme of things, it wasn't much, but it was enough to show that the Germans weren't getting it all their own way.

Dodds finished off his glass of wine and put the cork back in the bottle. He shoved it into the top of his bag, there was no point wasting it.

"I've got this," he said. He left payment and a generous tip on the table before they piled into the Citroen and headed for Rheims. They needed to be where the war was.

In actual fact, things were moving, albeit slowly. Although the thought of heavy casualties on the Western Front gave the French and British governments pause, both Prime Ministers and their military advisers agreed that military action was required. They were not prepared to let Norway go the way of Poland or Czechoslovakia. The big question was how they were going to do it.

A pre-emptive strike through neutral Belgium was out of the question. They were not about to do what the Germans themselves had just done to Denmark to get to the bigger prize. Decisive action was needed and if they managed to build up some momentum, it could even force the Germans to withdraw from Norway altogether.

The victory at Narvik was followed up by a hastily assembled collection of troops. The French arrived well stocked but lacked straps for their skis. British troops had no skis at all and had to stick to the roads while Norway shivered under a layer of snow. They were soon outclassed and after some early successes, were soon on the back foot with the Germans in control. Once again, the Nazi war machine was sweeping all before them.

While soldiers fought and died in the cold, rugged terrain of Norway, the forces in France basked in warm sunshine. The harsh winter was finally consigned to the history books as spring started in earnest. The countryside was suddenly a riot of colour as flowers blossomed.

After five days of being on standby, the men of Falcon Squadron were thoroughly browned off. Being on standby sounded exciting, but once you had done it for more than two days in a row, you came to view it as some kind of exotic punishment.

Being at fifteen minutes standby meant being dressed in your flying kit ready to go. You could cheat a bit and have it unfastened at the front but it didn't take long to start sweating like a pig when the sun came up. Those who thought ahead had a pack of cards or a paperback book jammed into a pocket to help pass the time.

On the morning of the fifth day, Winwright leaned out of his office window, arms resting on the sill. He went from listening for the phone, looking out at the sky and surveying his men. He could see nerves playing on some people. Some who were usually quiet were loud, others had withdrawn into themselves.

Mitchell sat with Ashton in the shade under the wing of their Blenheim. Parked in its bay in the trees, the leaves rustled as the wind passed through the branches, making them sway. Mitchell was an old hand at this sort of thing. He always carried a small folding chess board in his navigator's bag for these occasions.

The playing surface had a small hole in each white and black square that corresponded with a peg on the playing pieces. He started plugging each piece into the board while Ashton finished making a daisy chain.

"You want to be white or black?" he asked his pilot.

"I'm not bothered. You start."

Ashton draped the daisy chain over his head. It was quite a big one and went half way down his chest.

"Very fetching," commented Mitchell.

After putting the pieces in order, he swivelled round and lay on his front, his chin resting on his hands. He wiped some beads of sweat off his forehead. Even in the shade, it was getting warmer the closer it got to midday. Ashton sat across from him, lying on one side, like a Roman patrician. It would have been good to have a few slaves wafting them with fans right about now.

Mitchell moved a pawn in the middle of the board forward two squares. Ashton frowned at this opening. Mitchell had moved that pawn very quickly, with authority almost, and that was a break from the norm. He moved a black pawn in response. Mitchell countered; his move crisp. Ashton sat up and eyed his navigator with suspicion, but Mitchell focused intently on the board.

They played like that for ten minutes, silently moving the pieces around. This time it was Ashton who sat and thought between moves, Mitchell who acted quickly.

"What's come over you?" asked Ashton, trying to keep the curiosity out of his voice.

"Nothing." Mitchell shrugged and took a bishop with his knight. "I read a book or two." He put the small black playing piece into a peg hole on one side of the board. He glanced up at Ashton and smiled. "Your move."

Ashton moved a pawn to threaten the knight. Mitchell's rook took the pawn. Now his centre was open to an aggressive thrust. Ashton rubbed his chin. His brain was firing on all cylinders now as he plotted more moves ahead and considered his options. His fingers hovered over his queen.

Mitchell's breath hitched and Ashton shot him a look. He looked from the queen to his navigator. He edged his fingers closer and teased the top of the black queen.

"Heard from Angela?" Ashton asked casually, his eyes on Mitchell. Mitchell didn't bat an eyelid. Ashton moved his queen and took the offending knight, threatening the rook or a stab at the white king. Mitchell gave him a feral grin, his lips pulling back to reveal a row of uneven teeth.

"Nice try, skipper." He picked up his other knight and frowned while he considered the board. "If ENSA keeps to their schedule, I might see her next week when they get to Arras." He took Ashton's queen with the knight.

It all went downhill from there. Mitchell seemed to have had a brain storm and was playing out of his skin. In the end, Ashton was soundly beaten.

"You got me."

Ashton lay back and looked up at the sky, his arms behind his head. The clouds were moving fast, the breeze shoving them along in layered swirls. Mitchell unzipped his Sidcot and mopped his neck and face with a handkerchief from his back pocket.

"Hot."

Ashton absently nodded in agreement, but he was actually quite comfortable. The South African veldt was hotter than this by a long chalk. South America had been hot as well. The heat was nothing, but it was the English way to moan about the weather. When it was hot, people moaned wanting some rain. When it was cold or it rained or it was damp, people moaned about wanting some sun. There was no pleasing some people.

It was hard to believe the land all around had been frozen solid and covered in snow and ice only a few weeks before. Even in the shade he could feel the heat radiating from the ground. He drowsed for a few moments, listening to the sounds around him. The trees rustled and a bumblebee plied their trade, going from flower to flower.

Shouting voices carried on the breeze and Ashton rolled over and opened his eyes. Preddy had dug up a cricket bat from somewhere and was using a wooden crate as a wicket. He swung wildly as a fast ball from Farmer nearly took his head off. He remonstrated about the yorker but Farmer laughed as he scooped up the ball. He rubbed it vigorously on his Sidcot as he walked back up the pitch for another delivery.

Ashton thought back to his youth, playing cricket in the dry park by the church in a suburb of Pietermaritzburg, a city near Durban. They always played after Sunday school. Father Smit would be the umpire, encouraging them to have fun. It was just a bare patch of soil in the park, dry and dusty, but it had been fun.

One day he would go back, he promised himself. No matter how far you travelled, it was always good to go home. Even when he was flying in South America, he always knew that one day he would get a farm of his own in the land of his youth.

Ashton tried not to think about the coming maelstrom. His whole life had been leading up to this moment, it would be wrong of him to back out now. He had joined the RAF to fight for freedom against oppression. The Nazis were the Mongol horde of the twentieth century and they had to be stopped. He took off his daisy chain and started pulling off the petals.

"I die, I survive, I die, I survive," he said in his head.

He went on like that, making a small pile of white petals in the grass. When he pulled all the petals off each daisy, he discarded the stalk and moved onto the next one. He pulled off the last petal of the last daisy.

"Survive," he breathed to himself. He carefully put that last petal into his breast pocket and buttoned it closed.

256

2.14 – The Vagaries Of Life

After the initial success at Narvik, the tension slowly ratcheted up over the next two weeks. The situation in Norway deteriorated and the newsreels started to show some of the destruction. Both Namsos and Andalsnes were heavily bombed and thousands were made homeless. By the end of the month, allied forces began to pull out of Norway, slowly retreating to their starting points. The Wehrmacht chased them all the way, nipping at their heels.

As the allied efforts in Norway stalled, the familiar sight of a high flying reconnaissance aircraft appeared over the airfield once more. Dane started receiving reports that Me109s were coming over the border spoiling for a fight. 109s had rarely been seen up to this point. This sudden appearance was Dane's first sign that things were about to change and not for the better. The Hurricane squadrons were being scrambled more often and their scorecards began to fill up. Fierce combat took place in the skies of France as both sides jockeyed for position, probing each other's tactics and responses.

For the AASF, the Phoney War had been anything but. They may not have been bombing the enemy, but they were still losing crews to enemy action. The reconnaissance flights had continued and they were losing recce Blenheims at the rate of almost one a day. In the meantime, the Battles continued dropping their leaflets with little apparent effect.

The sense of anticipation was palpable. Everyone knew it was only a matter of time now before the main event kicked off. Everything was in place, the troops were ready; the weather was perfect. Now they just needed someone to give the word.

Cullen drove up and down the lines, hunting out stories that caught his attention. While everyone else did stories on soldiers in dugouts, he ran a story about a field kitchen unit, considering it a good human interest angle.

Continuing that thought, he decided to do a follow up on the RAF. He'd shown the groundcrew slaving away in the freezing cold, now he wanted to show normal squadron life in good weather. He contacted Wing HQ at Arras and was given permission to visit Bois Fontaine again. He knew Saundby had given him almost carte blanche in this regard, but it did no harm to check that he was still allowed.

Laura Locke stretched languorously on white silk sheets. Sweat dried on her skin and she fluttered a fan in her left hand, trying to generate a little bit of breeze. She was in a cool bedroom with pastel blue walls, a polished parquet floor and net curtains. Pascal's apartment was on the top floor of an apartment block and she had the benefit of a light wind coming in through the wide open windows.

Her thighs were tingling from their recent lovemaking. Her heart raced at the thought of being possessed by him, at joining with him and feeling his arms around her. She ran her right hand along his side, tracing the line of his ribs, the taut muscles moving as he rolled over. He stroked her stomach, running his fingers up to her carnelian tipped breasts. She gasped as he pinched her nipple between thumb and forefinger. He leaned in and his breath teased her skin and she luxuriated from his touch. Making love with Alex was nothing like this.

Pascal was like some kind of animal that possessed her. She had gone right over the edge in her feelings for him, giving back what he gave her. Her feelings for Alex hadn't changed. She still loved him, but it was a childish love now. He was the little boy that played with his toy aircraft and talked about cricket and giving the Germans a thrashing.

Pascal was part of the real world. He smoked, he drank; he had travelled, doing the grand tour in his younger years after university. He was a complex soul and she delighted in peeling back the layers to see what else she could discover about him. In comparison, Alex was a simple puzzle, easily solved. He wore his heart on his sleeve. Pascal could be moody and introspective, a fascination for her that she never tired of exploring.

She wondered how long it would be before the truth came out. That bothered her the most, the lies. Putting on a face for Alex was hard, but she was still trying to figure out a way for him not to be hurt. Pascal made no demands of her. He'd not insisted she leave Alex but she knew the situation would have to be resolved soon, one way or another. Perhaps the squadron would get posted somewhere she couldn't follow. Alex had told her they might advance forwards with the army when they moved. She hoped he was right. Alex could run off and have his war and she would be free to live her life how she wanted.

She thought it was ironic how events came about. As much as her marriage to Alex had been rushed, without it she would never have followed him to France. She would never have met Pascal. Thankfully, there were no children involved to complicate things further.

With the squadron on alert, Lorraine did her best to keep herself busy at the office where she worked a few hours a week. Monsieur Fache was a notaire and a very good one, handling a large number of civil cases in the town. Working under the senior clerk, she did the filing, took dictation and wrote letters. She also helped compile Monsieur Fache's notes on his cases.

It was a small office with only seven staff. She and one other girl did the filing. Two junior clerks did most of the work, while Monsieur Dupre watched everything from his desk in the corner of the main office. In the hall, the doughty receptionist Madame Legarde handled the telephones and visitors. Monsieur Fache ruled all from his opulent office. He sat in his throne like chair behind his large desk and dictated letters in his gravelly voice while she scribbled in shorthand.

The telephone rang. She let it ring while she assembled a bundle of paperwork. It carried on ringing and she leaned back in her chair to look out into the hall. Madame Legarde wasn't there. Everyone else was out to lunch. She was tempted to ignore it but it might be important. She got up from her desk and walked across the office, her heels clicking on the tiled floor.

"Good afternoon, office of Monsieur Fache, Notaire in law."

"Good afternoon," said a hesitant voice. "Would it be possible to speak to Mademoiselle Janvier?"

"Pierre?"

"Lorraine?"

She burst out laughing and smiled from ear to ear.

"My God, what are you doing, how are you?" she asked her baby brother.

"I might ask you the same question," he replied. "No letter for weeks?" he admonished.

"I know, I'm sorry. It's been so busy here." She perched on the corner of the desk and twirled the cord of the telephone in her fingers. "Shouldn't you be on alert?"

"Of course, the whole army is ready if the filthy Boche try anything. We'll murder the dogs if they dare to attack France," he said with passion.

She agreed with the sentiment but it was strange hearing her brother say it. With some sadness she realised he was no longer the little boy she'd grown up with any more. He'd become a man, just like that.

"But how are you calling?" During his entire time in the army she had never had a telephone call from him, let alone a call when she was at work.

"Special treat," he told her. "Being a staff officer has some privileges, you know." His tone changed. "That's all a secret, you understand?"

"I understand."

"You sound happy," he remarked.

"I am; oh Pierre, he proposed. Mark proposed to me and I said yes." Her voice rose in giddy excitement and she looked down at the ring on her finger. She watched the way the diamond glinted as it caught the light. She clenched her fingers together, feeling the metal band dig in, reminding her it was all real and not an illusion.

"You're engaged!" he exclaimed, voice rising in reaction. "To, to, to an Englishman!" He made the last word sound like an insult and she bristled with pride. "I haven't even met him!" he protested.

"You will," she reassured him. "You will. Oh, Pierre, you'll like him, I know you will. You must come to Béthenville on your next leave."

"I'll try; it's rather busy here at the moment."

"Pappa likes him," she said with a little bit of a pout.

"So I heard. Tell me more about him," he ordered; his tone a little peremptory. "I need to make sure he's worthy of my sister." She laughed in good humour and began to tell her brother what had happened.

Ever since the RAF had come to Béthenville, Lorraine was always amazed at how quickly the town's grapevine worked. It didn't take long to find out if they were up flying or confined to the airfield.

The first evening the squadron was put on alert that week; she went round to see Hortense. Lorraine had tried to get Laura to come with her but couldn't find her. There was no answer to knocking so she cycled across on her own.

After a coffee, she'd walked with Hortense across the meadow that separated the airfield from Claude's land to the stone wall. Hagen and Kittinger had come out to them and they stood either side of it, talking. After a while, Hagen had taken her hand and walked her a short distance away, leaving Kittinger with Hortense.

Still holding her hand, he kept stuttering and coming to a halt. She waited patiently while he gathered himself. He'd been doing a lot of thinking about what Locke had said and realised he was right. It was time to look forward, not back.

"You know, I didn't think this could be so hard," he said to her, his voice trembling. He blew out hard. He patted her hand and she could feel him trembling. Fear started to gnaw at her then, the worm of doubt stirring inside.

"I know we've not talked about the future much," he said solemnly. "In fact, we've not spoken about it at all, have we?" he smiled, his mood lightening. "And that was always enough before. But now that we come towards the end of all things, I've found that as much as it scares me, I *do* want there to be a tomorrow." He paused for a fraction and shot a nervous glance at her. "I want all those tomorrows to be with you, my lovely, Lorraine." He let go of her hand and pulled a small blue velvet box from his pocket. "I love you, will you marry me?"

He looked at her intently, his heart hammering in his ears. He'd planned something a little more grand than this; but with all these alerts, he might not get the opportunity for a while.

She put a hand to her mouth while her eyes glistened. She'd hoped he would do this one day. She looked at the box as he opened it to reveal a simple gold band with a pear shaped diamond. Taking it from the box, he slid it onto her ring finger. She grabbed his wrists and pulled him towards herself so hard he nearly lost his balance.

"I say, steady on."

"Shut up," she said between sobs of happiness. "Yes you fool, yes I'll marry you." She kissed him fiercely, holding him close, burying her face into his shoulder.

That had been three days ago. A lifetime. She was counting the minutes until the latest alert was over and he could come to her.

Hortense watched them out of the corner of her eye.

"He's going to propose," she told Kittinger, very matter of fact.

"How can you be so sure?" he asked.

"He has the look," she said, chuckling in amusement. She knew the signs; her dear John had looked the same before he proposed to her all those years ago. Hagen had the same pallid look; he was swallowing hard while he screwed up the nerve to ask.

"It's going to start soon, isn't it?" she asked Kittinger. He nodded silently, watching the younger couple further along the wall. Hagen was going to propose? He felt a stab of guilt then. All these months he'd been seeing Hortense and he'd not made up his mind. Maybe he should too. He loved her, he knew that now.

"It is. It has to. All the waiting will soon be over."

"And you'll be careful?" she asked, reminding him of his promise from Christmas. He kissed her hand.

"I'll be careful darling, as much as I can be anyway. It's not me I'm worried about, it's you."

"Me?"

"Béthenville was in the centre of the action in the last war. A lot of the town was flattened by shelling and the Germans have to know about the airfield. It's going to be dangerous-"

"-I don't care," she said fiercely, cutting across him. "I can't leave Claude, I'm all he has. Besides, I said once before I wouldn't leave you. I go where you go, Michael."

He saw the steel in her eyes and knew she wouldn't give in. If she stayed, he would worry, but if she went away, she would worry just as much about him. Together, they could at least draw on each other's strength when they had to. He nodded his acceptance and she gave him her best smile.

On 3rd May, Mark Hagen married Lorraine Janvier at a small church just outside of Béthenville. With Hortense and Valerie's help, they found a priest who was prepared to marry a good French girl of Catholic stock to a heretic Englishman.

It was a low key affair. Lorraine's brother Pierre got special leave from his unit to give his sister away. Hortense had taken Lorraine shopping and they'd found a dress of white satin with a train and some exquisite detail work. The bride was radiant as she walked down the aisle with her dark hair pinned up under a veil. Hortense was maid of honour in a burgundy dress holding a bouquet of spring flowers.

B Flight attended the service and they formed an honour guard as the happy couple came out of the church. Afterwards, there was a wedding breakfast at the Palace Hotel in town. There were speeches, one from Pierre, another from Winwright.

The CO granted a forty eight to the bride and groom and the newlyweds went to a nice hotel on the waterfront at Dunkirk. Locke loaned them the Mathis and cans clattered behind the car as it pulled away from the hotel. They made the most of their time together. They walked in the sunshine along the harbour and watched the fishing boats going about their daily business. After a pleasant lunch at a bistro, they browsed through the stalls at a market.

The only blip to the weekend was when Hagen brought up the subject of leaving for England. They'd spoken of it before but never really made a decision. Previously she'd refused to go at all, then she gave in a little bit and suggested going to Paris to stay with her parents.

Now she was Mrs Hagen, Lorraine dug her heels in, refusing to leave her husband. He admired her spirit but he was exasperated with her change of mind. Hagen was adamant. Once the shooting started; he wanted her far away and safe in England. Once things settled down again, she could always come back, *providing I'm still alive*, he thought to himself.

2.15 – Do Unto Others

On the 8th May, French Headquarters warned BAFF HQ to expect air attacks at dawn the following day. The warning was taken with a pinch of salt. There'd been a lot of these alerts lately and none of them had been right. However, it wasn't something that could just be ignored either. The warning was filtered down to the various commands.

On the 9th May, Winwright had the men on alert at dawn. The Bofors guns were manned by bleary eyed gun teams scanning the horizon. By lunchtime, the crews were stood down and the erks went back to their normal schedule of maintenance work.

Just after lunch, a dispatch rider turned up with a bundle of paperwork. Ashton was in the flight hut when he turned up and signed for it. There were two items for Winwright. He put those on the CO's desk; then took the short walk to Dane's Intel hut. He knocked on the door and Dane bid him enter. Ashton found him as always behind his table, glasses perched on his nose as he perused the maps and signals.

"I come bearing gifts," said Ashton, waving the pouch of signals. Dane nodded at Corporal Beverley, who took them from the Squadron Leader.

"Another waste of time, I suppose. It's a bind isn't it?" said Dane, commenting on the standby. Ashton had to agree.

"Sods law. If we hadn't, you could almost bet that something would have happened to catch us out. It's like waiting for the other shoe to drop."

"They're there, waiting for their moment," Dane said with certainty.

Ashton tried changing the subject, "What's the news from Norway?"

"Bad," said Dane. There was no other way to describe it. He glanced at his European map on the wall. It was all over bar the shouting really. The Norwegians were still holding out, but with the allied withdrawal, they were fighting for their lives against a resurgent German offensive.

"It's just a matter of time, I think." he said gloomily. "The Norwegians have done well but they've practically been on their own for all the help they've had."

Ashton noted the tone.

"Still regretting joining up?"

"Lord no." Dane took off his glasses and rubbed his eyes. "I wouldn't trade this for the world." He gestured to the hut around him. "University life is very insular. It's very easy to float along oblivious to everything else." He perched the glasses back on his nose and smiled. "I've felt more alive here than I have for a long time."

Ashton left Dane to his maps and arcane black magic of guessing what was going on. He strode towards the flight line when Burke intercepted him. He wiped his hands on a rag and then came to attention.

"What can I do for you, Mister Burke?"

"624 and 891 need running to the air maintenance park for overhaul, sir. I just need two crews to fly them over and they'll provide us with two spares."

"Get Chandler and Pettifer to take them," he said. Ashton had just seen them gadding about playing boules near the Mess. Their hard luck really, wrong place, wrong time. Burke sauntered off to give them the good news. To start with, they thought it was a wind up. Burke assured it wasn't and they went and got their flying kit back on.

Twenty minutes later, they swung the aircraft out of their bays and lined up for take off. Pettifer went first, Chandler following close behind. Pettifer took his time taking off. He kept his movements slow and the turns gentle. The last thing he wanted was a tired airplane breaking on him. Chandler tucked in close on his port side and Pettifer's navigator gave them a course to steer.

It was only a short hop south west. Thirty minutes flying got them to the maintenance park and they went straight in. It was a huge sprawl of hangars and open space with a variety of aircraft on the ground. Hurricanes and Battles lined up with Lysander and Blenheims in various states of repair. There were even a few Gladiators amongst the Tiger Moths.

There were a number of these maintenance depots scattered in an arc around Paris. Replacement aircraft were flown in to the depots and held there, ready and waiting to be doled out to the squadrons as required.

They taxied up to an open hangar and shut the engines down. No one came out to meet them, as Pettifer got out of the cockpit and dropped to the ground. His navigator and gunner joined him and they walked over to Chandler's aircraft.

"Nice place," observed Chandler, "although the valet service leaves something to be desired. They do know we're coming, right?"

Pettifer shrugged. That was what they'd been told. Fly to Soudge, drop off the Blenheims and pick up two replacements, a few hours at most.

A Flight Sergeant directed them to an office on the side of the hangar and they made their way over, paperwork in hand. They found a harassed Flight Lieutenant who was shouting into a field telephone. He directed them to wait while he finished his call, his voice rising in volume, a finger jammed in one ear.

"No. We ordered airscrews, AIR SCREWS, *not* aircrews! Yes, tomorrow, fine, thank you." The receiver slammed down. The scowl remained for a few seconds and then the man's face brightened. "Communications foul up." He waved a hand at the field telephone. "Reception leaves a lot to be desired."

"Quite," said Pettifer. He held up their form 700's. "Two aircraft to drop off and replace."

The Flight Lieutenant nodded and consulted a list on his desk.

"You're early," he said. "Yours should be ready in about thirty minutes or so."

With time on their hands, they traipsed out of the office and found a shady spot in the lee of the hangar. Morgan pulled out a pack of cards while Chandler produced a flask of tea. Time dragged. Morgan dozed, his head resting on his parachute pack. Pettifer went for an explore.

At the back of the hangar he found the dumped remains of a number of aircraft. Rows of Fairey Battle fuselages sat on wooden blocks, shorn of wings, tails and engines. They were being cannibalised for parts to keep others flying. The wings were piled up haphazardly nearby. Pettifer winced at the sight. The shooting hadn't even started yet and there was easily a few hundred thousand pounds worth of hardware lying on the grass.

He heard a Flight Sergeant shouting as a work party changed the engine on a Blenheim. Chains rattled as it was winched into place, inch by miserable inch. The Flight Sergeant verbally lashed them some more and Pettifer frowned at his style. It was a stark contrast to Burke's way of doing things. Burke could shout when he wanted to, but that was the point. He did it so rarely; it had far more impact when he did.

The admin Flight Lieutenant waved at Pettifer from the door of his office. Their aircraft were ready. Pettifer got Chandler and their crews up on their feet and took possession of the replacement aircraft.

Pettifer was less than impressed. Both of them had seen better days. The tail unit of one had been replaced at some point in the past. He could tell because the camouflage pattern along the fuselage didn't quite match up. The other Blenheim just looked very sorry for itself. The paintwork was tired but both cowlings were new and the paint on the control surfaces was quite fresh. Sensing Pettifer's disquiet, the admin Flight Lieutenant checked the form 700's for each of them.

"I know they don't look the best but they've had overhauls, new engines." He offered the forms over for signature. Ignoring the clipboard, Pettifer started his walk around. If he was signing for something, then he was making damn sure he knew what he was getting first. They arrived back at Bois Fontaine within the hour. As soon as they got in, the erks were fussing over them, checking them for faults.

Hagen watched Chandler and Pettifer stroll back to their hut under the trees. He stood with his hands shoved in his pockets, chin tucked into his chest while he brooded.

It had been a magical few days away with Lorraine but all too short. He made sure they had gone to a photo studio in the town and had some shots taken. They may not get another opportunity for a while and he wanted a photo to carry with him. He had her portrait in his wallet. It was a head and shoulder shot with her looking at the camera, head tilted to one side. He decided it was time for his wife to leave. His wife, he had to repeat that to himself,

"You think so?" said Locke when he told him his thoughts.

"I know so," said Hagen with conviction. "It's just a feeling I've got." Ever since he'd come back from Dunkirk with Lorraine he had a sense of foreboding. They had to get the girls away while there was still time. Locke couldn't argue with Hagen's feeling, he had it too.

"Let's go then."

They collared the CO and explained what they wanted to do. Winwright agreed, better to get them away before all hell broke loose.

"Do they know what they're doing?" asked Winwright.

"Oh yes, Laura came out from England in the first place. They'll take the car and use it to get back to the coast and get a ferry back to England. They'll go to Laura's parents' in Norfolk."

The CO gave them permission and they headed rapidly to the Mathis.

Kittinger waved them down as they were about to drive through the main gate.

"You're going to get the girls?"

"Yes," said Locke. "Probably best to do it now while we can."

"I wish Hortense had agreed to go."

Locke gave Hagen a pointed look.

"And you were worried about Lorraine being stubborn."

"I know, she's a fighter, that girl."

Kittinger thumped the roof of the car and he watched it pull away, wishing that Hortense would change her mind. This was her home, she was staying and none of his entreaties for her safety could move her.

Locke pulled up outside Lorraine's apartment building first. Hagen got out and said they'd be round in twenty minutes, thirty at the most. He'd already got Lorraine to pack up two suitcases. All she had to do was add a few last minute things and she would be ready to go. He knew she wasn't working today, but he hadn't anticipated her being out. He came into an empty apartment and fretted, wondering where she was. She came in a few minutes later, carrying a fresh warm baguette and some milk.

Her face lit up when she saw him, but it dropped when she noticed his serious expression. Unruffled, she overrode his anxieties and insisted they have some tea before they left. She cut him some bread and lathered butter onto it for him, peremptorily telling him to eat it. He wolfed his bread down but she would not be hurried and took her time, chewing slowly and sipping her tea.

Finally, they were ready to go. She changed into some practical walking shoes and put the finishing touches to her case before they left the apartment and locked the door. She had a tear in her eye as they walked down the stairs.

"Hey, we'll be back," he reassured her. He picked up the suitcases and led the way to Locke's apartment.

After parking the car, Locke pounded up the stairs, taking them two at a time. He shouted her name as he went but got no reply. He opened the door and went straight in. His first thought was that she was out, but then he heard some noises coming from the bedroom.

He froze in the doorway when he saw how Laura had been keeping herself occupied. She was naked on the bed with some man on top of her. She arched her back, her mouth open as she moaned and writhed in pleasure, legs spread wide. The man had his back to him, his attention on Laura as he thrust back and forth.

Emotion rushed through him, upset, amazement, embarrassment and then anger. Before they even realised he was there, Locke lunged forwards with a snarl and took hold of lover boy by the shoulders. He yanked back, hard.

Laura was edging towards the crest when the pleasure suddenly stopped and the weight on top of her went away. Dazed, she opened her eyes and screamed as she saw a dark shape looming over Pascal where he lay on the floor. She was about to scream again when the man turned and she saw it was her husband, it was Alex.

"Don't you dare move," Alex said, his voice vicious as he turned and kicked Pascal in the ribs twice, putting him down. He bent down and took hold of Pascal by the scruff of the neck and then ran at the wall, throwing him into the wardrobe. The door came apart and splintered into pieces.

Kicking some bits of wood out of the way, Locke maintained the pressure, not giving the man time to recover from the shock of the first blow. He grabbed an ankle and pulled it, dragging him back into the middle of the bedroom.

His head was ringing. One moment, he was enjoying sex with one of his women. The next he was being pummelled and thrown around like a rag doll. Pascal managed to roll onto his back and opened his eyes, trying to shield his face with his arms when a fist landed on his nose. He felt something give way and tasted blood.

"Bastard!" said his assailant. "Bastard." A boot crunched into his ribs and Pascal curled into a ball. He whimpered as blows rained down.

Terror froze her; she had never seen Alex like this before, his face contorted in a rictus of hate, his teeth bared. He had always been so mild. She never imagined for a second he was capable of such violence. Pascal screamed again as Alex stamped on his ankle. Laura's eyes were wide with horror as Locke gave Pascal a good hiding.

"Stay down, comprendez?" Alex spat on the prone figure and then turned towards her, his eyes wild. Terrified, she gathered the sheets around her, wailing at him not to hurt her.

"Hurt you?" He laughed. It wasn't a pleasant laugh and that chilled her. It was a low snicker, laced with contempt and anger. "You said I had no honour, that I didn't care and all the time you were shagging *that*." He pointed at Pascal when he said the last word, all of his hate and loathing put into it. "I could die up there and you're screwing for Britain!"

He whipped round and gave Pascal another punch to the face just as he was getting up. The Frenchman went down heavily again.

"Please stop," she said quietly. "Please stop, Alex."

Her use of his name gave him pause, penetrating the red mist that had descended on him. He unclenched his right hand and turned oh so slowly to look at her.

"You don't have the right to use my name. Not after that. You've killed any regard I could *possibly* have for you. You did that the day you let another man take you. You were my wife, Laura, my *wife*!" He said that last with a sob as his voice cracked.

He snapped round and turned on Pascal. Frantic, Laura screamed again but Alex didn't hit him. He got down onto his haunches; arms balanced as he looked down at her lover and said four words that hit like punches to her stomach.

"Do you want her?"

"Wha-what?" croaked Pascal between cracked lips. He ran his tongue around his mouth and could taste the coppery tang of blood. His body ached and his ankle burned like fire.

"Do. YOU. Want. HER!" said Locke, enunciating each word distinctly. "Take her then." Locke stood and strode quickly over to Laura. He pulled her right arm from under the sheet and squeezed hard and dragged her along the bed. "She's yours. She's *nothing* to me now. TAKE HER! She's yours if you want her."

Pascal avoided looking at this man's eyes. He could hear the challenge there. He shook his head slowly. This little dalliance had come to a rather violent end.

"I didn't think so," Locke said with contempt. He straightened and spotted a brown suit hung over the back of the chair in the corner. A shirt was on the floor, spotted with blood. Locke picked them up and draped them over Pascal's prone form. "Go on, get out. Find some other whore to screw."

Laura flinched at the word *whore*. Without saying a word, Pascal rolled onto his knees and slowly got to his feet. Gripping the clothing in his hands, he took small shuffling steps and left the apartment. Locke stood quietly until he heard the front door click shut.

He walked from the bedroom and hunted through the apartment for the suitcase. Without saying a word, he came back into the room and opened it. It was still packed so he took a quick look around the room and gathered a few things, dumping them on top of the clothes. He took the sponge wash bag from the bathroom and put a few bottles inside it, not caring whether they were the right things or not.

"Get dressed," he said; his voice flat and cold. He had to say it twice more before she responded. Like an automaton, she slipped some clothes on, keeping space between them while he smouldered in the corner, looking at her. She hurriedly brushed her hair and then put some shoes on.

"Alex-"

"Don't bother, Laura. I don't want to hear it. Get dressed; you're going back to England with, Lorraine. The only reason I'm letting you get in that car is because I promised, Mark I'd help him get his wife to safety. I'll not tell anyone what happened, but never speak to me again."

Choking back tears, she clutched her handbag tightly as Locke followed her outside carrying her suitcase. Raw with emotion, his mind whirled at the events of the last twenty minutes. His whole life had fallen apart in front of his eyes. Rage had been replaced by a hollow feeling inside. The violence, the outpouring of emotion had overwhelmed him. The betrayal cut the deepest. All those months of arguments and this was what she'd been doing behind his back.

The anger stoked up again and he stamped down on it hard as he went out to the car. She followed him downstairs and sat in the front passenger seat, her cheeks wet with tears. A few spots of rain pattered off the roof but he stood outside, not trusting what his reaction would be if he was in the car with her alone. He cast an eye up and down the street, his foot tapping the ground with impatience. He checked his watch. Thirty minutes at the most, Hagen had said.

It was another five minutes of waiting before Hagen appeared with his wife, carrying two suitcases. He opened the boot and slung them one after another into the car.

Lorraine got into the rear passenger seat behind the driver on the left hand side. Hagen apologised for the delay but pulled up short when Alex said nothing in response.

"Hey, you okay?"

"Sure. I just got browned off waiting for you to show up. What kept you?"

"You know women," said Hagen, missing the fixed gaze on Locke's face. "You tell them to pack light and they try to take everything."

267

"Let's go."

Locke started the engine and spared Laura one glance as he got in. She sat upright in the front passenger seat, eyes closed, shaking with silent tears. He ground his jaw as Lorraine reached forwards from the back of the car and squeezed her shoulder. He slammed the car into first gear and headed out of town back to the airfield.

They were back at Bois Fontaine twenty minutes later. It was just after three o'clock, plenty of time for them to get to the coast before the evening drew in. They got out of the car to say their goodbyes. Lorraine leaned into Hagen while he held her close, stroking her hair.

"We'll be together again," he whispered.

"I know," she sniffed, keeping herself under control, wanting to be strong for this moment. "I love you."

"I love you too. I wish we had more time, but we've got all the tomorrows to come. It'll just be for a short while," he said, trying to sound convincing. They kissed then, wanting the moment to last.

Locke stared off into the distance while Laura stood next to him. She tried taking his hand but he very slowly and deliberately shoved his hands into his pockets.

"Don't," he said; his voice almost a snarl.

"I-I'm sorry."

"Sorry it's not good enough." He paused and gathered himself. "You better get going if you want to make tonight's ferry," he said coldly, his eyes glittering with intensity.

Laura swallowed hard. There was a chasm between them that she saw no way to bridge. Time was short and she could think of nothing that would get through to him.

"Goodbye Alex, I-"

She got into the driver's side and started the engine. Hagen gave his wife a final hug and saw her to the Mathis. Lorraine wound the window down and looked at him.

"You take care."

"I will." Hagen leaned in and kissed her one last time before the car pulled away. He stood watching the road a long time after it turned right and went out of sight. Locke left him there and went for a walk through the surrounding fields. The last thing he needed right now was company while he tried to make sense of what the hell had just happened.

2.16 – From Out Of The East

Cullen groggily sipped tea from a tin mug as he sat on a rough log by a brazier by the barn. The twins were washing from an upturned tin hat and Cullen envied their energy this early in the morning. He checked his watch again. The little glowing hands told him it was 5am. He winced and rubbed his eyes, willing himself to wake up properly. He'd arrived late the previous night after getting lost on the road from Arras. He'd pulled up at the gate, not certain he was in the right place, until Ashton appeared to tell the sentry to let him in.

He'd parked his car at the back of the Mess hut and a space was found for him to lay his head. He was rudely woken at 4.30am by the clomping of boots as the aircrew shambled in to slump on armchairs, the floor, whatever space they could find. Someone threw a few extra bits of wood in the stove and poked the fire back into life.

HQ put them on four hours' notice and erks had done the rounds of the tents and huts, banging on canvas and doors to get them up.

"Standby, sir. The CO wants you up and ready in five minutes," the voice had said, before disappearing and moving on to the next one. Most of them couldn't believe it.

Cullen yawned and stretched. Lacing up his boots, he'd grabbed his notepad and pencil and gone outside. The air was chilly and the sun was creeping over the horizon, a big orange blue bowl with wisps of cloud high to the north. A few strands of mist clung to the ground here and there. His wanderings took him to the barn; coming to rest by the brazier.

He could. What he wanted was the story of the airfield coming to life in the morning. The fact they'd put on an early alert was an unexpected bonus. The Griffiths twins were the icing on the cake. One on the ground, one in the air gave him the story he needed to tie it all together. He talked to them for a while, listening to them while they described life on the farm. They had joined up together and now they were serving on the same Squadron together. A pilot joined them by the brazier and warmed his hands by the fire.

"Good morning, Mr Locke, sir," said one of the twins.

"Griffiths. Griffiths."

"Up with the owls, again," commented the young gunner in good humour. Locke nodded but his face was a mask, his jaw set. In truth, he'd barely slept. He lit a cigarette and used it hard, letting the smoke assault his lungs.

He kept thinking back over the last few months since Laura had come to Béthenville. All those rows and arguments they'd had about nothing. He remembered what she said, the little things that meant nothing then and everything now. He felt a fool. His cheeks burned for missing what seemed obvious.

"Do you think anything will happen today?" they asked him.

"I doubt it," he replied. He got up, nodded to everyone and then walked off. He wasn't in the mood to talk much.

Cullen finished his tea, flicking the dregs onto the grass. He handed back the mug and then took a photograph of the brothers getting ready. It was a good shot, with the barn behind them and a bit of ground mist.

He sauntered over to the Blenheims and watched the erks start the engines ready for air testing and a day's work. A trolley was dragged past with some yellow bombs on board. It was backed up underneath a Blenheim and the bombs were winched into the bomb bay. There was much cursing as cold hands fiddled with the bomb racks in the gloom. He took a few photographs of them at work, looking for a good angle that would make it more interesting.

Moving on he walked through the woods, following the route of the duckboards. At an intersection, a tree had a number of place names painted on bits of board, pointing in all directions. London, Paris, Berlin, Rome, New York etc, they were all there. Some wag had put a line through the signs for Copenhagen and Warsaw. He took a photograph but it was a grim joke that he knew would never get past the censor.

He followed the left fork and topped the rise, coming out at the bomb dump. A few armourers had the fiddly job of fitting the tail fins to bomb bodies. Cullen took a snap or two to show the process.

He went back through the woods and walked over to the gunpit near the entrance to the airfield. The soldiers sat in their seats, slowly panning around the horizon in a never ending circle. The loader stood ready, his hands resting on a clip of shells, ready to be inserted into the loading guides. Cullen crouched down and took two photos of them looking up at the sky. He took another shot canted at a slight angle to give it more of a dramatic edge.

He stood up and wound the camera on, checking how many shots he had left when he heard aero engines nearby. He looked up, trying to figure out where the sound was coming from, but one of the Blenheims started up and drowned it out. He turned his attention back to his camera when a hand grabbed him by the shoulder and dragged him to the ground.

"Down!" they bellowed in his ear. The ground shook and Cullen got a mouth full of soil as the concussion slammed into his chest. A dark shape rocketed past overhead and the Bofors gun cracked as it fired. The ground shook again and Cullen curled into a ball. The hand on his collar relaxed and he peeked up through slitted eyes to see Kittinger running towards a group of aircrew that spilled out of the Mess hut.

"Get to the shelters you bloody idiots. Can't you see it's an air raid!"

He turned and unslung his Lee Enfield rifle and drew a bead on another aircraft that zoomed overhead. Stood out in the open, he fired off three rounds in quick succession as chaos rained around him.

Chandler was supervising the bombing up of his aircraft when the bedlam started. His first warning was when a bomb hit in the middle of the airfield. The explosion threw up lumps of earth, dark against the yellow of the flame. He flinched as another one ploughed into the trees on the far side. The ground shook and he dropped, crawling rapidly to find shelter. He sheltered under the wing of his aircraft but thought better of it. There was no point hiding under something that was a prime target.

He ran to the back of the bay in the trees and crouched down next to a tree trunk, watching as a succession of German bombers flew overhead. He heard the sharp flat crack as the Bofors at the far end of the field opened fire. 40mm shells were hurled into the sky as fast as fresh rounds could be loaded.

Breaking from cover, Chandler shot across the open ground, his feet eating up the distance. Legs and arms pumping, he dived over the sandbags and rolled, coming to rest against boxes of Bofors ammunition.

Getting to his feet, he helped pass heavy clips of shells to the loaders. The crew worked frantically, their arms winding the training mechanism back and forth to keep the gun tracking its targets. The muzzle belched flame as it fired again.

They flinched as fire from a Junkers 88 tore up the sandbags to their left. The Bofors began tracking but it was out of range before they could draw a bead on it. Coming back around they started firing at another Ju88 that flew along the treeline. Bombs dropped from its wings and huge plumes of smoke and debris flew into the air. A shell caught it in the tail and the upper half of its rudder came apart, pieces spinning away in the slipstream. It banked hard to the left, almost standing on its wingtip as it put distance between itself and the Bofors gun.

"Hot work, sir," shouted the soldier next to him.

Chandler just nodded and carried on passing clips. He kept his head down, arms aching as he fed the gun.

Farmer spilled out of the mess at the head of the aircrews. Anger flushed through him at the temerity of the Jerries to come sneaking in at dawn. More aircraft came in and he saw a 109 break to the right as a Ju88 lined up for its bomb run.

The bombs came off the external racks and he threw himself to the ground, arms wrapped around his head. The air was knocked from his lungs as the first bomb hit behind him. The Mess hut blew apart into a thousand pieces. Two men went down, caught in the explosion. The rest of the bombs went long, exploding in the meadow beyond. Someone screamed for their mother while another voice shouted for a medic.

Farmer picked himself off the ground and ran towards the slit trenches nearby. He passed Kittinger who stood his ground, firing off round after round from his rifle at the marauding German aircraft. He pulled the Adjutant with him, not wanting to see him killed. Kittinger tried to shake him off but Farmer kept a firm grip on his arm.

They ran past a twin Lewis gun mount surrounded by sandbags. The guns pointed to the sky. The Corporal manning them lay face down while his blood soaked into the canvas. Farmer felt for a pulse while Kittinger shouldered his rifle and checked the guns. He cocked them both and then turned, drawing a bead on a Ju88 that was coming in. He fired low, the tracer passing underneath and adjusted upwards, leading the target. His next burst caught it on the nose, the glazed panels shattering and starring into pieces.

It jerked to the right to avoid his fire, giving the Bofors gunners a perfect shot. They pumped a whole clip into it as they stitched it straight up the middle. It wallowed for a moment and then dived into the ground. Its bombload

271

touched off as it hit.

Farmer rolled the dead Corporal over the sandbags to give themselves some room to move. Kittinger fired again but cursed as the Lewis guns clicked, their magazines empty. Snarling, he kicked open the box next to the mounting and tugged out two fresh magazines. He wrenched off the empty ones and reloaded.

Farmer slapped him on the shoulder and pointed at two bombers that were coming in from the right. The second of the two was slightly lower and tucked in on its leader's port wing. Kittinger swung round towards them. He started firing early, trying to lay down tracer to put them off their run.

The gunner in the nose of the leading Ju88 replied and a line of bullets kicked up the grass in front of them. Kittinger roared his defiance, oblivious to the rounds ripping into the sandbags around him.

A 250Kg bomb landed on a Blenheim at the end of the line. It reared up as its back was broken and shrapnel went pinging off into the trees. Fuel spilled from its ruptured tanks and started a fire amongst the undergrowth. Ammunition in the turret cooked off and added to the chaos.

Locke was walking through the woods when the first bombs fell. Sprinting back towards the huts, he came onto a scene right out of Dante's inferno. Flames reached into the sky and the wooden planks of the Mess hut popped and crackled as fire consumed it.

A bomb detonated behind him and he was slammed to the ground from the shockwave. His eyes fluttered open as he tried to focus on things around him. He brushed flecks of dirt and wood off his face. His right shoulder was on fire and he gasped as he tried to put weight on that arm. Something felt wrong and he rolled onto his back as the pain shot up and down his right side.

He struggled up to a sitting position, oblivious to everything going on around him. It felt like he'd been hit over the back of the head with a cricket bat. He looked left and right, wondering where his peaked cap had gone. He was still wondering when a burst of fire ripped into his back, nailing him to the grass. As his life slipped away, he had an image of blonde hair and a nice smile in his mind's eye.

The German aircraft ranged at will. More bombs landed amongst the trees, sending deadly splinters in all directions. Trees were felled, severed as neatly as if an axe had cleaved through them. Tents were flattened and huts blown apart like matchwood.

Another Blenheim was straddled by a stick of bombs. The groundcrew next to it were cut down like so much corn. There were fires everywhere and smoke drifted across the field.

Cullen hugged the ground, eyes wide, trying to look everywhere at once. He was too busy to be scared. He put his camera to his eye and started taking photos, snapping almost blindly at the action unfolding in front of him.

An erk running past him was cut down by flying shrapnel. No more than a boy, he stared into the distance with glassy eyes as his life's blood dribbled from his mouth. Cullen clicked the shutter without thinking, but almost immediately felt ashamed. The eyes had been staring right at him, almost accusing at how unfair it all was.

He saw Kittinger blazing away with the Lewis guns and crawled towards him. He kept low to the ground and his legs kicked as if he was swimming. He reached the ring of sandbags and rolled over them into the gun pit. Hot cartridge cases fell around him, some pinging off his tin hat as he shoved the camera to his eye. He focused on Kittinger as he sighted along the Lewis guns, firing on the Germans above. He managed a few more shots before Farmer roughly grabbed him and told him to drop the camera and pass the ammunition.

The 109s came in next, to finish what the Ju88's had started. Their guns chattered and bullets and cannon shells tore up the ground, chopping down men left and right as they ran from the onslaught. The fighters made two more passes; then as fast as they had come, they were gone.

It took a few minutes for everyone to realise the raid was over. The Bofors crews scanned the horizon. Winwright's head appeared over the top of one of the slit trenches. He cocked an ear but heard nothing over the crackle of burning wood. He pulled himself out of the trench and brushed the dirt off his trousers. People were starting to emerge from their hiding places, blinking like moles emerging into daylight.

Burke was running towards the Blenheim nearest to the huts. Its nose stuck out of the bay and smoke billowed from under the tarpaulin used as a roof. The aircraft was burning and four 250lb bombs sat on the grass underneath it. Groundcrew rushed to help him and one of them dragged a bomb trolley behind him.

Cullen watched as they worked like men possessed to lift each bomb into the trolley. The heat of the flames was intense and attempts were made to fight the fire. One of the fitters threw a tarpaulin over the rear fuselage but that just funnelled the flames forward.

The cockpit turned black as smoke filled the nose and billowed out of the top escape hatch. They flinched as ammunition in the turret started to explode. They managed to get three bombs away before the heat and flames and smoke drove them back.

Pettigrew pulled on Burkes arm, trying to get him away, but the older man shrugged him off. He grabbed a large piece of canvas lying on the ground. It was the remains of one of the engine tents they had used over the winter. Throwing it over his shoulders and covering his head, he raced back into the bay.

The Blenheim was well alight and it was only a matter of time before the fire reached the fuel tanks. Some groundcrew went running for buckets, but it wouldn't be enough. Burke hugged the ground and groped his way forwards as much by touch as by sight. He felt his way with his hands amongst the grass, trying not to breathe in too much. Smoke stung his eyes and he tried to pull his shirt over his mouth to give him something to breathe through.

The canvas was getting hot. He shifted underneath it, using his arms to try and keep it off his head. More smoke leaked underneath the canvas and he coughed as it stung his lungs. Eyes watering, he was about to turn back when his hand brushed something metal. It was curved and heavy. Following along its length, he felt the tail fins. The metal was hot. Ignoring the pain, he gripped it hard and yanked backwards, using his weight as leverage. It moved.

The pain was building. Digging his heels into the grass, he pushed with his legs, pulling the bomb with him. He kept it up, legs pumping, hands burning, face burning, scalp scorched. He kept going until hands gripped him under the arms and dragged him away. Someone pulled the scorched canvas off him. He sucked in glorious deep breaths of fresh air and then had a coughing spasm as his lungs tried to purge the smoke. Eyes watering, he saw the Blenheim sag as its back broke and the main tanks cooked off.

"Easy," Pettigrew told him as Burke tried to get to his feet. If he'd not seen it, he'd never have believed it. He was convinced nothing could have lived in that furnace, but he'd seen Burke rush back into the flames and achieve the impossible.

"Just lie still," he cautioned Burke, who was still coughing. "Medic!" he shouted.

"Nobody move!" shouted Winwright. "Not all of the bombs might have gone off yet. Wait while we try to clear the area."

As he said it, there was an explosion somewhere in the back of the woods off towards the bomb dump.

Winwright ran off to get on the blower to Wing. They needed to know what happened and so did he. This can't have been the only raid.

It wasn't. In fact, the Luftwaffe flew over seventy raids that morning. As the RAF and French air forces had stood ready, the enemy had come in low across the border and attacked airfields up and down the frontier. They had also attacked Belgium and managed to wipe out half the Belgian Air Force in the opening round.

Falcon Squadron had its nose bloodied. In all, the tally was four aircraft destroyed with two more damaged. Eighteen personnel had been killed including Locke and two navigators. Fifteen others had been wounded. In return, at least one Ju88 had been shot down and one 109 had been damaged.

Merville had been attacked too. One hangar had been gutted when two 500Kg bombs went through the roof. The Battles inside were destroyed. Two others had been caught at dispersal and turned into scrap. Both squadrons had suffered few casualties but the airfields remained operational.

Winwright rung Saundby for orders. Saundby rang Headquarters. They waited, then they waited some more. Despite Air Marshall Barratt's repeated requests, General Gamelin refused to countenance wide spread bombing of the attacking forces. He was fearful of an all out bombing war. He wanted his bombers to hit precise targets and he couldn't do that until he knew what was happening. Reconnaissance aircraft were duly dispatched to try and find out. The Phoney War had come to an abrupt end.

2.17 – Case Yellow

Just before the off, Adolf Hitler sent a message to his troops. After reminding them that France and Britain had repressed German ambitions for the last few centuries, he whipped them up with a final encouragement;

> *Soldiers of the Western Front, your time has come. The fight, which begins today, will determine Germany's future for the next thousand years.*

The Germans had been allowed to choose the time and the place and activated Fall Gelb, a massive operation involving one hundred thirty five divisions and over two thousand tanks. Neutrality meant nothing to the onslaught of the Nazi blitzkrieg. Army Group B bypassed the strength of the Maginot Line and swept into Belgium and Luxembourg.

Using audacity and daring, ten gliders carrying seventy eight men landed on the fortress of Eban Emael and took it in a lightning dawn raid. Using hollow charges and flamethrowers, they knocked out the blockhouses in minutes. They pinned down the garrison until reinforcements could arrive.

Thirty other gliders landed close to the canal bridges near Maastricht. This airborne spearhead preceded the armoured advance that broke through the frontier and drove west. Although the bridges in the town centre of Maastricht had been blown, the three main bridges over the Albert canal were captured intact. Belgian troops immediately counterattacked and one of the bridges was subsequently blown, but the other two remained in enemy hands.

Recce Blenheims went out to gather intelligence of the enemy movements. A large number of aircraft were spotted over The Hague. Other Blenheims made a low level recce over the Maas and Meuse rivers. One was shot down. Another made it back heavily damaged.

Recognising the danger, Belgian Fairey Battles mounted an attack on the Maas bridges. Nine aircraft went out to attack with no bomb sights and 100lb light bombs. They bravely dived through intense flak but did no damage, their bombs not even chipping the concrete.

The offensive may have been only six hours old, but already the allied High Command was making the wrong decisions. In response to the German invasion, the allies executed what was known as the Dyle plan. Convinced that he knew where the main German attack would come from, Gamelin ordered the French armies and the BEF to advance into Belgium and meet them head on.

2.18 – Poised

They stood looking at the hole in the ground. The stink of sulphur mixed with the smell of charred wood and hung in the still air. A few splinters of wood and melted patches of tarred canvas were about all that was left of the Mess hut. Some rusted distorted springs showed where one of the armchairs had been. A few scraps of newspaper fluttered around on the grass. A smoking pile of metal marked where Cullen's car had been parked out back.

Chandler picked up the twisted and deformed horn from the gramophone. Next to it was a piece of one of the records. He peered at the blackened label and could just make out *'Siegfried Line'*. He stooped down to pick up an intact record a few yards away. It was the hated *'Teddy Bears Picnic'*. He smashed it to pieces against a piece of wood.

"Oops," he said quietly. He glanced at Morgan and shrugged. "Casualty of war."

"A tragedy," agreed Morgan.

There was an explosion in the woods and Chandler flinched. In the two hours since the raid they'd lost two more men to delayed action bombs.

"Another one," muttered Morgan

"I guess we haven't found them all yet."

"Dirty Germans, using delayed action fuses."

"Not very sporting at all," Chandler agreed. "You wouldn't catch *us* doing that sort of thing."

Morgan turned as the sound of an aero engine ripped across the field. He relaxed when he realised it was one of the Blenheims being run up. The last two hours had been a strange anti climax. The urge to strike back at the enemy was strong but there had been no orders for an immediate counterattack. The Squadron had been left to pick up the pieces and put things to rights instead. There was certainly plenty of work for them.

The field was peppered with bomb craters and they got the shovels out once again. A few months ago they'd been shovelling snow, now they started filling holes. Some work parties had gone into the woods with buckets and brooms to try and put the fires out. Some army engineers arrived. They got to work marking unexploded bombs with little red flags until they could get round to defusing them.

Burke seemed to be everywhere at once. He rushed around to supervise the work and make sure it was being done to his satisfaction. His face was an angry red from the fire and his hands were blistered. One of the medical orderlies chased after him, trying to get him to stop long enough so they could bandage his hands and put some cream on his face.

Light relief was provided by Preddy and Arthur who turned up smelling worse than a rubbish tip. They'd been sat on the latrine in the woods when the raid started. When the first bombs went off, the log they were sat on shifted and dumped them unceremoniously, literally, in the shit. They were doused in buckets of water but it made no difference. Ashton pointed them towards the river with bars of soap and told them not to come back until they'd sorted themselves out.

Everyone else got to work on the kites, checking them for damage. They brushed dirt and debris off them and patched whatever holes they found. Some of the trolley accs had been destroyed. The survivors were checked to see if there were any still in working order. Pettigrew rang through to Wing to organise replacements from the aircraft parks.

The cookhouse had been straddled by incendiaries but some quick work had quenched the fires before they had a chance to take hold. Now they went to work, laying on an early lunch to calm jangling nerves.

Kittinger went over to Claude's manor house to see how the wounded were doing. Almost as soon as the raid was over Hortense had come to help. The wounded were carried on crude stretchers to the manor house and she did her best to see to their needs. An hour later, Valerie arrived with some ambulances to take the men to the local hospital. Winwright gave him a quick look around of the damage. The Mayor promised to return with some men from the town to help get the holes filled in.

Hagen was in the middle of a beef sandwich when he noticed the red Mathis parked by the perimeter wall. He almost choked on the bread when he saw it. He thought his eyes were playing tricks on him. He was seeing a car that should be waiting for a ferry at a French port somewhere.

He stomped over to the car. The closer he got, the more he was overwhelmed with a feeling of dread. He glanced over to a line of blankets in the meadow. Locke's body lay under one of them, waiting to be taken to the morgue.

As he approached the car it rocked on its suspension. He started running when he saw Lorraine get out of the driver's seat. She'd changed clothes since yesterday and was wearing a blue cotton blouse and tan slacks. He thought she looked wonderful but he was annoyed at her for coming back.

"I thought I told you to go," he said as she rushed into his arms.

"We got as far as Amiens before we turned around," she said. "She wouldn't leave." She pointed to Laura who sat in the front passenger seat. Her eyes were red and her face was puffy from too many tears. "She says she needs to make it up to Alex before she goes."

"Make it up to..." Hagen was dumbfounded. "Of all the damn fool things to come back for." He doubted if he would ever understand women. He wondered exactly what had happened between Locke and Laura that afternoon before he turned up with Lorraine. It would explain why Locke was so distant yesterday. Hagen thought Locke just missed his wife but obviously there was more to it than that.

Lorraine neglected to mention the extended argument she'd had with Laura in the car. It had started as soon as they pulled away from the airfield and carried on for hours. Wracked with guilt, the younger woman begged Lorraine to go back. When pressed for the reason why, Laura confessed to what had happened, both in the flat and in the weeks prior with Pascal.

Lorraine contained her temper. She would have upbraided her but it was obvious that Laura was close to the edge. Eventually she agreed to stop at Amiens overnight while she thought about it. It was a convenient place to break their journey and it was far enough from the border just in case something did happen. Finally, she gave in and agreed to go back when she realised that Laura would have walked back on her own if she'd said no.

"If she wants to talk to Alex, she'll have a job asking for his forgiveness," Hagen said harshly.

"Is he...flying?" she asked, hoping for the best. Hagen shook his head slowly. Lorraine nodded in understanding. She flicked a glance back to the car and Laura's expectant face.

"He's dead," Hagen said. He looked at the row of bodies in the morning sun. Flies buzzed around the blankets, wanting to feast on the glorious dead.

He glanced over at Laura. Her lips were trembling and he could see she was barely holding herself together. Best to tell it straight he thought, there was no other way to soften the blow. Lorraine took his hand as he walked towards the Mathis and shattered what little self control Laura had left. The girl held onto him through the open window of the car, sobbing her heart out as she realised it was all too late.

It took a long while for her to regain even a modicum of composure. Saying their goodbyes again, Hagen told his wife to drive for the coast fast.

"Avoid the main roads as much as you can and get to England," he told her.

Satisfied they were on the way again, he walked back to the squadron, shaking his head at the lunacy of it all. He picked up a spade and joined other members of his Flight filling in a hole.

2.19 – Get Stuck In

As soon as he heard the invasion had begun, Air Marshal Barratt was requesting orders to attack the enemy. These requests were echoed by General D'Astier of the French Air Force. The recce aircraft were reporting columns of tanks, trucks and infantry stretching back for miles. It was the target of a lifetime and their best opportunity to nip the offensive in the bud before it got started.

Sitting in his headquarters, Gamelin made no response. Over the next few hours, Barratt repeatedly asked for instructions. Eventually, he ran out of patience and took matters into his own hands. He issued orders to get his planes in the air.

Thirty two Battles went off to attack the columns advancing through Luxembourg. They got shot to pieces. With no self sealing tanks they fell prey to enemy flak. Many burned before they hit the ground. Only nineteen aircraft made it back.

Saundby sent out his aircraft. The two Battle Squadrons at Merville put up eight aircraft each and went off towards the Grand Duchy. One turned back after its undercarriage would not retract. Bainbridge led the rest of them east. In four Flights, they tucked in tight, giving their gunners a nice field of interlocking fire.

Near to Liege, 109s pounced on them from out of the sun. Three Battles went down on the first pass. The survivors held their formation but there was little they could do against cannon armed fighters. The 109s picked off two more of them before a roving Belgian Hurricane unit swooped down and drove them off. The survivors attacked a column of trucks and infantry on the Dippach-Luxembourg road. A blizzard of tracer rose up to meet them.

Bainbridge took them in low at five hundred feet. Flying through the teeth of the fire, one more Battle went in as they dropped their bombs. Streaming flame, it smashed into a row of trees. The survivors turned south to get clear, leaving columns of smoke behind them.

Ten Battles out of the starting sixteen made it back. Aside from the men lost on the raid, six others were wounded. Ambulances whisked them off to hospital on their return. Bainbridge rang Wing with his enemy sighting report to help build up a picture of what was going on.

The Blenheims went into action just after midday. Saundby gave Winwright orders to head north. While the offensive around Luxembourg appeared to be the main point of attack, there was also that sighting of an airborne landing in Belgium to deal with. They had no intel on the target, only an approximate location near Rotterdam by the docks. Saundby sent them to sort it out.

Gardner led six aircraft to sweep the area around The Hague. He led them northeast until they got to Ghent and then turned towards the sea. He wanted to go up the coast and run in from the estuary, using the open water to avoid any flak.

As they flew over the countryside, they saw the roads choked with columns of civilians. Heading away from the fighting, heads snapped up as they flew over. Men and women watched bombers rush towards the sound of the guns.

After fifty minutes, Gardner saw Rotterdam on the horizon at his two o'clock. He rocked his wings and took his Flight down. Dropping to one thousand feet, he let the speed build up in the dive. When they went into the attack, he would go even lower. The bombs had eleven second fuses, giving them plenty of time to drop and get clear before they went off.

"Second section, follow us in," he ordered.

Farmer cut his throttle slightly and let the gap between himself and the leading element open up. Milton and Arthur flew formation on him. He checked the sky anxiously, searching it in quarters.

At the Hook, Gardner turned right and followed the river inland. For centuries, Rotterdam had been the gateway to Europe. The port serviced trade from all over the world and the Dutch East India Company had seen goods flood in from its trading empire. All the way along the south side of the river were docks and slipways with a number of ships tied up alongside.

Waalhaven airfield was in the middle of this and Gardner slid to the right, flying over the warehouse complex to the west. No defensive fire had come their way yet and he hoped it stayed that way. Plumes of smoke were dead ahead and he peered through the canopy, trying to pick out targets on the ground.

Waalhaven was a large airfield with a complex of hangars and admin buildings on the east side. Some of the buildings were ablaze and thick columns of smoke pumped into the air. Gardner could see a number of smashed aircraft and there were bomb craters all over the place. Between the craters he spotted at least ten Ju52 trimotor transports and some trucks.

Gardner told them to pick their targets and went in. He lined up on a pair of Ju52's in the middle of the field. In the nose, Andrews got ready. They shot across the field and he glanced at the bomb release panel, checking his settings. Gardner went lower, skimming two hundred feet. He smiled as he saw men running in all directions, pointing as they spotted him for the first time.

Andrews hit the bomb release and Gardner felt the bombs go. He held the nose down, sinking even lower as he flashed over the transports. His gunner gave them a squirt as they went past. There was a cloud of dust as the bombs sliced into the ground around the aircraft. Seconds later, the bombs went off. One Ju52 was lifted bodily into the air, surrounded by flame as it broke apart.

Quad mounted 37mm guns opened up and tracers as big as cricket balls shot towards them but they were too late. There were more explosions as the other aircraft unloaded their bombs and headed out.

Milton was on Gardner's starboard wing and had just dropped his load when he was hit. The yoke jumped in his hands as explosive rounds wrecked the port engine. The Blenheim crabbed at the sudden loss of power and he struggled to hold it. The rudder pedals bucked under his feet as more fire shredded the tail surfaces.

He hauled back on the yoke and cursed as the starboard engine lost power as well. He tried to get some height but the heart had gone out of her. He could barely maintain altitude and he knew the only direction he was going was down. He picked out a piece of clear ground between two burning hangars and slammed her down hard on the concrete.

There was a shower of sparks as the Blenheim slithered along on its belly. Milton was thrown hard against his straps. He crossed his arms over his chest as he rode the bucking bronco to a halt. It was suddenly quiet after the roar of the Mercury engines for the last hour. He got a thumbs up from his navigator and then hauled back the escape hatch above his head.

He just had time to fire a flare gun at the leaking petrol before German soldiers levelled their rifles at him. He raised his hands and put them on his head as he watched the rest of the Flight get chased off by AA fire. The soldiers took him away as the fire took hold and incinerated what was left of his Blenheim.

Climbing away from Waalhaven, they were circling over the open countryside south of the city when Arthur was hit. A burst of shells hammered into his tail and jolted the controls.

At seven hundred feet, Arthur felt the controls go slack. The nose went down and there was nothing he could do to stop her going in. He made his peace with god and closed his eyes as he slammed into the ground. The engines were still screaming at full power as the nose crumpled on impact. The fuel tanks split and P-Popsie tore herself apart in an explosion that left a gaping crater in the embankment.

Farmer had no idea his friend had gone in but Osbourne did. On the port side, he looked over and watched in morbid fascination as he saw Arthur's Blenheim stagger under the impact of the enemy fire. He saw the tailplane shred, pieces fluttering away in the slipstream. He followed her all the way in. There were no chutes and he winced as it folded like tin foil when it hit the ground.

His curiosity cost him as he levelled off. He was a good few hundred feet out of position from where he should have been. Pulling the boost button, he fed in some rudder to catch up when the enemy fighters came in. All on his own; he was an easy target.

His gunner was looking the wrong way when the pair of 109s closed in and fired. Still staring at the ground where Arthur's Blenheim was burning, he was perplexed when he felt a thump on his back. He fell forwards, smashing his mouth on the rear sight of his Vickers machine gun.

Head reeling, he saw the 109s zoom past and break hard to the right. They circled round and shaped up for another pass, their yellow noses bright under the noon sun. He paled when he saw the streak of red flowing down his chest.

"I'm hit," he managed to get out weakly as he sagged in the turret, the pain hitting him hard.

Osbourne glanced over his shoulder but couldn't see anything. What he would give for a rear view mirror right about now. He knew they'd been hit. He'd felt the rounds go home, the shudder through his seat. Farmer was still too far away and he could hardly ask for his section leader to wait for him. He'd been careless and now he would be lucky to come out of this alive. He already had the boost button pulled as far as it would go, but he willed the Blenheim to give him more speed.

"Timber, tell me when to break." he told his navigator. Woods unfolded his lanky frame and squirmed up to the cockpit, looking back out the starboard window. He caught a glimpse of light reflecting on metal and then lost it as they slid further astern.

In his turret, Jacobs was doing his best to keep his gun tracking on the fighters as they came in. He was growing faint from the pain that threatened to overwhelm him.

"Get ready to break," he called, his tongue thick in his mouth. He spat blood and ran his tongue along his front teeth, searching for damage. The 109s closed in. "Break right!" he yelled.

Osbourne tugged the yoke right and stamped on the right rudder pedal, using it to turn tighter. The Blenheim reared up onto its starboard wingtip, the nose passing through the horizon. Almost immediately, he tugged left and fed in left rudder to reverse his turn. He flinched as the 109s flashed past in a blur of blue and grey. He felt as much as heard the *tik-tik-tik* as more bullets went home.

Pain lanced through him as he felt a sledgehammer on his right thigh. The Blenheim jolted as his feet slipped off the rudder pedals. Biting down on his lip, he used his right hand to ease his leg and get his foot back on the pedal. Pulling the scarf from around his neck, he pressed it to his thigh and almost screamed at the pain.

Eyes watering, he levelled off and raced to reach Farmer. The flight reversed their course slightly. They turned left to give him the chance to cut the corner and get in under the protection of their guns. Farmer slid in on Gardner's right wing and Osbourne slotted in behind, making up a diamond of four aircraft.

The 109s took one look at this and broke off, looking for easier pickings. Osbourne glanced right to see Woods slumped forward, blood streaming down his neck and a hole in the canopy the size of his fist. Air whistled in through the hole and the rushing air chilled his cheeks.

Wrestling with the controls, Osbourne grabbed Woods by his collar and hauled him back to a sitting position. Woods head lolled on his shoulders, flopping from side to side as the Blenheim undulated in the air. Osbourne felt a worm of horror stir in his stomach. It was a good hour back to Bois Fontaine; he wondered how long he would last.

Gardner was angry with himself. A single pass over the target and he'd lost two aircraft and had another damaged. It seemed a high price to pay for seven or eight transports and a few hangars gutted by fire. He turned on a course to home and took what was left of his Flight down, using the terrain to his advantage.

The flight back was uneventful. They saw more civilians on the roads and some French units heading in the opposite direction. After the first group of infantry opened fire on them, Gardner took it back up to five thousand feet to stay out of their way. There was no point getting shot down by their gallant allies.

They gathered round Dane and his clipboard. They felt wrung out. They'd taken off two hours before and come back ten years older. Sandwiches were handed out with mugs of tea. They were ravenous, combat used up a lot of energy.

Gardener had just seen Osbourne and his crew off in an ambulance. When he saw him, Gardner was stunned that Osbourne had made it back. The right leg of his Sidcot flying suit was stained dark red and he was deathly pale when he was lifted onto a stretcher. He'd made a hard landing, bouncing twice before getting down. The cockpit looked like a slaughterhouse. Blood from Woods head wound was everywhere and the turret was a mess.

He was also surprised Farmer had managed to walk away from his landing. The big man had slammed down his Blenheim hard, keeping it down with sheer force of will while he stood it on its undercarriage. He'd taxied to his bay with aggressive bursts of power.

Dane looked expectantly from face to face, waiting for someone to kick off. He wanted to get this over with before A Flight came back. They had gone off an hour after B Flight to have a pop at some targets in Luxembourg. He pulled the top off his fountain pen and scribbled the date on the top of the paper.

"Anyone care to start?" he asked.

"Wizard prang," said Preddy half heartedly, the humour falling a little flat.

"Nothing for the scorecard?"

Farmer's mouth did a little moue at the remark. His shoulders were hunched, tense. His anger flared at Dane's casual way of phrasing things. Scorecards indeed, he made it all sound like an afternoon at the cricket ground.

Dane tapped his pen on his clipboard, impatient. The men shifted uncomfortably on their feet and waited for someone to take the lead.

"I saw six Junkers up in flames, one hangar looked a bit worse for wear," said Gardner, finally. "Anyone else?"

"We got at least two ourselves," said Preddy. "That's direct from Keller. We laid our stick of four down the northern side."

"It was a bit hard to tell," said Hagen, he picked another sandwich off the plate and sniffed it, eyeing what was between the two bits of bread. He pulled out a bit of onion and flicked it on the grass. "I was too busy dodging the flak."

Dane kept a running total on the page. Even allowing for double counting, that was a low number to trade for two aircraft and three crews. He looked off across the field and frowned. The holes had already been filled in and were now just scars on the grass. If you sprinkled round some grass seed and waited a few weeks you'd never have known what had happened this morning.

The wrecked aircraft were still in their bays. On balance, it looked like they had come out of this about even. He waited for more information as teachers do. If you were teaching a class and someone started talking over you, you waited until they stopped and let you go on. You made the silence work in your favour. Here, the silence was deafening. He tried a different tack.

"How would you evaluate the target? What aircraft were on the field? What types?" Here, he did slightly better.

"It was filled with Ju52's, maybe fifteen of them?" offered Hagen. "At least ten anyway." He put a good face on it. More aircraft on the ground meant they'd attacked a worthwhile target and not just thrown their bombs away for nothing. "There were some trucks round a few of them so it looks like we caught them unloading," he added. "I thought I saw a few liaison aircraft by the admin buildings. There were four hangars on the east side of the field, I think. Two were on fire when we came in so someone had already given them a bit of a drubbing."

"There was extensive damage to the field," agreed Preddy. "There were quite a few bomb craters. I saw some wrecked aircraft, but I don't know what type they were though."

"What about, Milton and, Arthur?"

"I saw Milton go down." said Farmer, contributing for the first time. "He caught a packet from the AA on the eastern edge of the field as we pulled away. I saw him pancake it in by the hangars. I don't know if he got out but he'll be in the bag if he did."

Dane wrote furiously, trying to get the detail down word for word. "And, Arthur?" he asked, looking over his spectacles.

Farmer looked off over Dane's shoulder, his cheek pulling in a twitch.

"He's had it," said Gardner. "He went in nose first, no chutes. Osbourne saw it all."

"I saw it too," said Keller. Farmer glared at his gunner and the lad paled under the baleful glare of his pilot. "They shot his tail off; he had no chance at that height."

They had no chance at this height. The flak and small arms fire was murderous. Pettifer hunkered down in his seat as he hung off Ashton's starboard wing. At one thousand feet a storm of bullets was lacing the air in front of them. Every soldier with a rifle was contributing to the maelstrom they were flying through.

"Left a bit," said Padgett. "Left." his voice quivered and Pettifer could hardly blame him. If he was scared, Padgett must have been terrified up front in the nose. At least flying the aircraft, Pettifer had something to occupy himself. All Padgett could do was lie down in the nose, look through the bomb sight and hang on until it was all over. Pettifer's navigator had been killed in the raid that morning. As Locke had also died, Pettifer had taken over his crew to make up the numbers.

Padgett had the best seat in the house. He felt like a god flying over the fires of hell as they spat brimstone up at him, trying to drag him into the pit. He kept focused through the bombsight, trying to line up on a row of trucks parked at the side of the road. He could see soldiers in grey uniforms running from the cabs as the Blenheim bore down on them. The bomber rocked as a string of shells exploded off the starboard wing. One went off in front of them and they raced through a black, evil smelling cloud with flame at its centre. Bits of shrapnel pinged off the nose.

Wide eyed, he peered through the sight. Just a little bit longer and they would be away. He gripped the bomb release and poised his thumb on the button. Two more seconds and he let them go.

"Bombs gone!" he shouted, his voice high and pinched over the intercom.

The four bombs dropped from their racks towards the ground. The first one clipped the road next to the trucks. It tore up the tarmac and sprayed chunks of rock and dirt in all directions. The fuel tanks on two Hanomag trucks were torn open by hot shrapnel and detonated. The rest of the bombs walked down the line of trucks, ripping them apart.

Other bombs landed in the field next to the trucks, catching a unit of infantry in the open. Bodies tumbled like skittles, shoved around by the shockwaves. One bomb took out a fuel tanker parked on the road. A fireball reached for the sky and then spat burning fuel onto the trees, turning men into human torches.

A Flight had got lucky. Flying east, they'd come across an armoured column supported by infantry, on the move in open countryside. Ashton had led his six aircraft straight into the attack. Flak filled the sky and he gripped the yoke tighter as he fought his bucking aircraft to keep it under control.

Never for a second did he imagine it would be like this. The defensive fire was intense. It was a solid wall and they were having to fly straight through it to drop their bombs. He looked ahead. There were lines of infantry and vehicles as far as the eye could see. There was no way he could fly over that and expect to live through it. He saw a dense wood off to the right and went for it, trading height for speed in an effort to get away from the flak and bullets. The rest of the Flight followed him.

None of them got away scot free. Chandler's starboard engine was running a little rough after a flak burst went off underneath the nacelle. Griffiths reported they were trailing a thin ribbon of dark smoke and Chandler kept a weather eye on the cylinder head temperatures. He really needed to back off the throttles but didn't dare until they were clear.

Pendleton's navigator, Neville Chambers, had flinched when shrapnel smashed the clear view panel in the nose right in front of him. He went back to his maps and found them in disarray. There was a ragged hole in his navigator's table and a corresponding gash in the underside where a bullet had blown straight through.

He came up into the cockpit to find Pendleton fighting the controls. Pendleton had the yoke hard over and was doing all he could to keep the wings level. Their gunner reported there was a gaping hole in the port wing. A panel was twisted up into the airstream causing an enormous amount of drag on one side. Pendleton had full right rudder on just to keep the nose pointed straight.

"Need a hand skip?"

"Piece of cake," Pendleton said through clenched teeth and then laughed at the ridiculousness of it all. His leg had gone dead and he winced as he tried to rub some life back into it.

The last Blenheim was flown by Flight Sergeant Sutherland. It was the worst aircraft on the squadron. He was the youngest, least experienced pilot so he was given her to fly. There was no point wasting a good aircraft on a new man. Twenty one years old, he was fresh out of OCU and only had thirty hours in the Blenheim. He'd only joined the squadron after they came back from the

South of France the month before.

His navigator was seven years older but it could have been a lifetime. Peter Ormond smoked a pipe, had a moustache and sounded like his father, so Sutherland called him Pop. Ormond didn't mind. He was married with two children, so he was used to it. His gunner Garfield, was not much younger and he was married with a son as well. Sutherland had not even had sex yet and here he was in charge of six tons of aircraft and two other lives.

That thought sobered him as they were diving into the fire and he used that to keep calm. They were relying on him to get them home and he needed to focus to avoid mistakes. He swung in closer to Pendleton as the flight reformed back into sections in vic.

Climbing away to the south, Ashton took them to six thousand feet and levelled off on a course for Bois Fontaine. He wiped the sweat out of his eyes and shivered involuntarily as reaction set in. Out of the danger zone, he backed off the throttles, giving the engines a chance to rest.

"Bandits, god, hordes of the swine! Three o'clock level!" The voice rang in his ears and Ashton snapped his head to the right. Coming out of some pretty fluffy clouds was a swarm of Me109s heading in the opposite direction.

His hand hovered over the throttles while he watched the 109s blithely continue on. Either they'd not seen them or they were out of ammunition. The fighters went on their merry way and Ashton counted his lucky stars.

The day was far from over but Falcon Squadron needed a pause to gather themselves together. They'd started the day with eighteen aircraft. Four were smoking ruins at Bois Fontaine. Two more were smouldering in little pieces in Belgium. Of the remaining twelve, all of them had varying forms of damage.

Winwright had orders to go back to Rotterdam and make an attack on the transports on the beach at The Hague. It was his turn to go to war. He picked five crews and got Burke to ready the six least damaged aircraft and put them on the line. Chandler, Hagen, Sutherland, Nugent and Ashwood got ready to go back out. Winwright gathered them together.

"All right chaps. No mucking about, we'll go straight north, head out over the ocean and come in from the sea. That should cut down the chances of running into any fighters. Then we head back out the same way. Any questions?" No one said anything. "Right, then let's go." He put on his flying helmet as he walked towards his aircraft, T-Tommy. "Hagen, you lead two section and take Sutherland and Chandler as your two and three."

Before the blare of the engines droned out all sound, he sat on the lip of the escape hatch above his seat and looked around. For a moment he thought of home, his wife and his children. He patted his pocket to make sure he had their photographs with him and then strapped in. He started up and taxied out.

They went in fast. Winwright had no intention of waiting around. He separated his unit out and had them go in from line astern. He descended in a curving dive, keeping the target at his ten o'clock as he passed through one thousand feet. At five hundred he thundered in. The tide was out and there were Ju52's all over the flat sand.

He fired his wing gun, using the rudder to move the nose left and right, spraying the beach. He dropped the bombs in trail, one after the other, and then held the nose down. He ran the length of the beach to give his gunner a chance to spray the transport aircraft on their way past. Each aircraft added to the mayhem.

The second section attacked further up the beach. Plumes of sand went into the air with each explosion. One transport had its back broken as a bomb sliced straight through it. When the bomb went off underneath, it fell into the crater, like a hangman's drop. Another was straddled by two bombs and flipped onto its back. They left seven JU52's burning or destroyed and headed west, engines screaming.

The only mishap was when Ashwood caught a seagull on the nose and blood and gore smeared itself over the canopy. He spent the return flight peeking through a bloody mess, struggling to keep position on his leader.

The Battles at Merville went out again at three. Bainbridge led his men again. This time his orders were a little more precise. As the day had worn on, the recce information began to firm up the guesswork and conjecture. He looked at the orders in his hand as he conducted an impromptu briefing under the wing of his aircraft.

Despatch two half sections, each squadron to attack enemy mechanised column between Luxembourg and Dippach. Town must be avoided. Position and troops as notified but special care to be taken if target not found as indicated. Position of our most advanced troops is at a point 3½ miles south of Dippach and another group at Mont St Martin, 10 miles SW of Dippach.

Bainbridge put up four aircraft as did the other squadron, and they headed off straight away. He kept low, while the other Flight of four went up to three thousand feet.

He found the target as briefed and went into the attack. He dropped his bombs on the road but he was so busy dodging machine gun fire he couldn't see the result of his efforts. The bombs of the second Battle undershot and took out a small barn by the side of the road.

The third caught a packet on its run in. Its fuel tanks were holed and almost instantly it burst into flames. Its pilot put it down fast in a field. It ploughed through some hedges and came to rest in some gorse bushes next to an infantry unit. Scorched and wounded, the crew scrambled from the burning aircraft and were captured.

The last Battle pressed home the attack, bombing two mobile flak guns to pieces. The port petrol tank was holed but didn't ignite and it streamed glycol as it exited the target zone. Crippled by the intense ground fire, they struggled to cross the lines before force landing near a French infantry unit.

Bainbridge got back to Merville with twenty new bullet holes in his fuselage and four holes in the canopy. After two attacks he'd lost five aircraft, almost a third of his strength. He was starting to have serious doubts about attacking at low level in the face of the murderous crossfire the Germans were able to put up. They seemed to have a gun behind every tree to fire on him.

The other Flight fared little better. Intending to use friendly airspace as much as possible, they flew over the French lines only to discover the Germans had overrun the friendly positions. They came under a hail of fire while they flew straight and level. One gunner was killed and another wounded before they managed to duck out of the way.

They laid their bombs at the crossroads and scored direct hits on trucks and half tracks. Keeping low, they made a sharp turn to the left and skimmed the tops of the trees to make good their escape. All of them were damaged and the erks would have a busy night getting them serviceable for the morning.

2.20 – Taking Stock

The sun was just starting to go down and Winwright felt a million years old. Every movement was an effort and it was old eyes that stared out of his face after the trials of the day. He found Burke chivvying the men to more effort.

"Are we on top line?" asked Winwright.

Burke snapped to attention and saluted the CO. Winwright indicated for him to carry on and he relaxed. Burke was a sight. His eyebrows had been scorched off, his face was a very angry red and his hands were wrapped in bandages.

"I'll be able to give you nine right now, sir." He pointed at two others further down the line. "914 needs an engine change and 856 has a pulled stern frame." He pointed in the other direction. "858 needs some panels on the wing fixing and the flaps will need checking out. We've got the spares; it'll just take a while to sort it out. That'll give us twelve for the morning. Mr Pettigrew says we'll have some replacements coming tomorrow."

Winwright nodded. They only had fourteen crews anyway. He left Burke to it and went back to the flight hut. Ashton and Gardner were in there with Dane. All of them looked tired and they turned a bleary eye on him as he came in the door. He tried to summon an encouraging smile but gave it up as a bad job.

The reporter sat at the back of the hut, notebook in his lap, head resting against the wall. His khaki battledress hung open. There was a tear on his right shoulder and dirt streaked his face. Cullen's eyes snapped open when Winwright came in. He watched the CO sink onto an upturned wooden ammunition box and gratefully sip the mug of tea Gardner handed him.

"We'll have twelve for the morning," he reported.

"I'll let Wing know," said Kittinger. "God knows what tomorrow will bring."

"Hopefully things will settle down as the picture becomes clearer," said Ashton. So far it had been a mobile war and that was always hard to plan for. "Dane?"

The lecturer straightened his shoulders and pushed the spectacles up his nose. He clutched his clipboard to his chest and tried to put a positive spin on things.

"I'm afraid there's not much to tell at the moment, sir. It's all rather up in the air. Clearly, the Germans have launched a major offensive. They've advanced into Belgium and Luxembourg and are sweeping towards the French border. There's been no reported movement against the Maginot Line. No surprise, but Jerry seems to have left that alone entirely. Elements of the BEF and French divisions have started advancing into Belgium. I would expect us to start flying raids to support that tomorrow."

"What about the other RAF units?" asked Ashton.

"Quite a few got caught by the raids this morning. Some of the French fields took a drubbing as well." Dane frowned and glanced at his clipboard. "The information's a bit patchy though. I did manage to get through to Merville. The fields operational, but they lost about the same number of aircraft we did."

"And no sign that tomorrow is going to be any different," said Gardner gloomily.

"I agree," said Winwright over his tea. He gestured with the mug outside. "Tomorrow could be more of the same so I want the crews up at 4 a.m and the Bofors guns manned and ready just in case."

"It might be a good idea to rig up something under the trees," suggested Ashton. He looked at the walls of the hut and noted the broken glass of the windows and the holes in the wood from near misses. "This huts got to be on borrowed time if they come back for another raid in the morning."

Dane wrote that down on the clipboard. "I'll get Burke to add it to his list of things to do," he said.

"Anything else?" asked Winwright, his voice weary.

"Just some letters, sir?" said Kittinger quietly.

"Letters?"

"To next of kin, you asked me to remind you earlier."

Winwright frowned and nodded as he remembered. The hut was quiet while they watched him. Kittinger cleared his throat and it was loud in the silence. Winwright drummed his fingers on the mug of tea. He watched the liquid ripple in time with his fingers hitting the outside of the mug. Putting pen to paper was the last thing on his mind right now. Summoning platitudes about sacrifice and duty didn't come easily to him and he'd written enough of those letters over the last few months. He swigged his tea and eyed the reporter.

"Did you get the story you were looking for Mister Cullen?"

Cullen grunted and hunched over, his arms resting on his knees. He gripped the notepad hard, the pages creasing slightly.

"Everything and more."

He lifted his head and looked at each of them in turn. He thought about the raids, seeing the aircraft come back with holes in. He thought about the bloody clothing, the dead and the wounded. "I never imagined it would be anything like that."

Winwright gave him a grim smile.

"I don't think we did either. Where do you go next?"

"Rheims?" he pondered aloud. "First I have to get to Arras, then perhaps I'll follow the army into Belgium. I don't know how I'll get there though. My car got blown to pieces this morning."

"We might be able to help you out there. Mike, can you rustle up some transport for Mr Cullen to get to town?"

Kittinger nodded and went to the door. Cullen levered himself up. He shouldered his camera case and shoved the notepad into his breast pocket. He turned and held out his hand to Winwright.

"I wish you good luck tomorrow, sir."

"Thank you. Write us well," said Winwright quietly.

Nodding to them all, Cullen left the hut, closing the door quickly behind him.

Fifteen miles from Bois Fontaine, Osbourne jerked awake from a fitful sleep. The ride in the ambulance had been a jolting toboggan ride along the country roads. It was a very stop start affair as the ambulance forced its way through the growing lines of civilians walking west. Osbourne felt every jolt through his leg, strings of fire shooting up and down his thigh. He felt weak as a kitten as he lay there.

The ambulance squealed to a halt and the doors were flung open. The stretchers underneath him were pulled out first. When it was his turn, he was carried into a large country house. Sheets hung from the windows with big red crosses hastily painted on them.

When they put the stretcher down, he sat up and looked around. He was in a large room with high ceilings and a musty air tinged with the tang of blood and antiseptic. A pile of white dustsheets were in one corner.

The air was filled with a hubbub of voices, some shrieking in distress. He was surrounded by other wounded men on stretchers. A medical orderly was going from man to man, seeing to their needs. There was no sign of Woods or Dodds in the room. He waved a hand to get the orderlies' attention.

"Hullo, a brylcreem boy."

He came over and knelt next to the Scot. He glanced at his tag and made a note of his injuries. He put a hand on Osbourne's leg and glanced at the wound, making sure his dressing was tight. "You'll be all right lad. It went right through." He held up a packet of cigarettes.

"Thanks." Osbourne took one and stuck it between his lips. "I'm gasping." The orderly struck a match and held it until the cigarette was lit. Osbourne blew a cloud of smoke up to the ceiling. He hitched on the stretcher and gasped as his body reminded him it was not in the best of shape. The orderly clicked his tongue and helped him lie back down.

"You need to be careful and not open that wound up."

"Are there any other aircrew here?" Osbourne asked. "My crew should be here with me."

"I don't know." The orderly pulled out a pad from his breast pocket. "I'll have to find out. Quite a few of you came in all at once."

Osbourne gave him the names and the man went off to find out.

The erks worked through the evening and into the night to get the aircraft ready for the morning. The torn wing panels on Pendleton's Blenheim were removed. The upper panel was peppered like a colander. Pendleton had been lucky. A 37mm shell had gone straight through and exploded a second too late otherwise it would have blown the wing off.

The men worked in the half light of torches and inspection lamps under canvas. Knuckles were skinned on sharp edges as they put things to rights. A lot of the damage was superficial but it was the volume of it. Ribs and panels were inspected for damage. Here and there, rivets had popped from the strain of the day's exertions. Patches were riveted over holes, engines were checked, plugs changed and oil drained.

Chandler's Blenheim needed its starboard engine replacing. The flak burst had wrecked the underside of the exhaust collector ring and connecting pipes. An engine was taken from one of the wrecks. Waste not want not as Pettigrew said.

Up till now, he'd been content to leave Burke to the day to day work. He was a firm believer in letting good NCO's sort things out. Looking over their shoulders just produced resentment and a bad atmosphere. Now he stepped forwards and mucked in with his men. They were amazed when he took his tunic off, rolled up his sleeves and stood alongside them, pulling on the chains to help change Chandler's engine.

It was past eleven before they called it a night. They would have worked longer, but even Pettigrew had to give in to reality. The men had been working all day. Tired hands made mistakes and it was going to be another early start on the morrow. Better to let them finish and get some rest.

Hagen lay on his camp bed, hands behind his head. His boots were at the end of the bed but he was still dressed in his flying kit. He was too tired to change. He looked up through the ragged hole in the canvas roof of the tent at the stars overhead. After the chaos of the day, the night was a welcome reprieve, but even now he could hear the constant rumble in the distance. To his surprise, he'd survived the first day. Some of the others hadn't made it, Locke among them, but he closed off that part of his mind. They'd got the chop, he was still alive, that was all that mattered for now, all the consideration he could spare.

His Blenheim was a little the worse for wear but she had got him through. His only worry now was Lorraine and Laura. It had been a blow to think they were safe and then have them turn up at the airfield. He hoped they'd been able to make good time and get away from all the upheaval.

Exactly what Laura had to confess bothered him. He'd not asked and she'd not told him, but he could guess. Locke was dead, there seemed little point in discussing it further. There were far more important things to worry about anyway. He shifted on his bed and fell asleep.

At that precise moment, the Mathis was twenty miles north of Rouen pulled over on the side of a country road. The bonnet was up and Lorraine was nonplussed while she pointed a torch inside. She knew nothing about engines. One moment they'd been driving along and the next, it had come to a sputtering stop.

Their day hadn't gone well. After they left Béthenville for the second time, they'd headed back towards Amiens, retracing their steps. They'd tried going towards Arras but the stream of civilians on the road had increased with each passing mile. They ground to a halt at Souchez, stuck behind a horse and cart while people trudged past them, heads bowed.

They sat there for half an hour before she decided to turn off onto a side road. Arras was not their final destination. If they couldn't get to it, they would just go around it. The narrow country lanes were free of civilian traffic but the going was slow. They drove through a number of deserted hamlets but had to stop at Manin when an abandoned cart was blocking the road. It took them twenty minutes to push it out of the way. More than once they had to retrace their steps when the route took them south.

Eventually, they got back onto a main road at Frevent and drove towards Abbeville. The final straw came when the car coasted to a halt outside Saint-

Riquier. There was a few minutes of frustration before the penny dropped when she realised they'd simply run out of petrol. She had been so distracted she never thought to check the gauge. She blessed Locke and Hagen's foresight that they had thought to put two petrol tins in the boot.

Her rage knew no bounds when she discovered that someone had stolen the tins. It must have been when they were stationary near Arras. She fumed for a few minutes, calling the refugees every name under the sun until she calmed down again. They had no other choice, they had to find some more petrol if they were going to go any further.

Laura was next to useless. She'd been crying almost nonstop since they left Bois Fontaine and she was no use now. Lorraine had to shout at her to get her to do anything. In the end, she left Laura in the car and walked towards Abbeville. She found a small garage after twenty minutes.

It was a typical small garage that you found in the countryside. Some rusting enamel signs were attached to the walls. The Michelin logo was painted on one side of the building. In the yard, a single petrol pump stood outside. Two buckets of sand were next to it. The wooden double doors were closed, the red paint cracked and peeling. There was not a soul in sight.

She banged on the door, shouting for help. No one stirred. She banged again. She walked round the back of the house. The kitchen door was locked. She put her hands on the dusty windows and tried to peer inside. She saw lunch laid on a table, cheese and biscuits on plates, a tea pot and cups. A chair lay on the floor.

She walked back around the front and had another look. She tried the pump but nothing came out of the nozzle. It probably needed turning on somewhere inside the garage she reasoned. Lorraine went rummaging amongst the grass for a large stone and went back to the double doors.

She glanced once more left and right and then brought the stone down on the padlock and chain keeping the doors closed. Lorraine hit it again and again until the padlock broke and fell loose. She waited a few minutes but no one came to challenge her, so she opened the doors slightly. In the gloom she could see a blue Citroen covered by a dust sheet. It was up on jacks and the front wheels were missing.

There was shelving down one wall covered in tools, parts and boxes of junk. The smell of oil was strong and the floor was gritty underfoot. She had no idea what she was looking for to make the pump work. She crouched down and rummaged amongst containers piled by the door. Two of them gurgled when she gave them a shake. She took the lids off and sniffed. One of them stank of petrol. She put the lid back on and walked outside. She was about to walk off when guilt took hold. Muttering to herself, she went back inside and left some francs on the side of the shelves. Carrying the tin, she walked back to the car.

Back on the road again, they drove into Abbeville. The town was a lot calmer here. Shops were open as normal and they found a garage to buy some more petrol. Lorraine had an argument when the proprietor tried to charge her twice as much as he should have done. She spent five minutes calling him a bloodsucker before getting back in the car and heading towards the coast.

Fifty minutes later, the car stopped for the final time. Lorraine had no idea why. Nothing happened when she turned the key and they were in the middle of nowhere with night closing in. She got the blanket out of the boot and got into the back of the car with Laura and tried to go to sleep.

Kittinger was perched on the edge of a chair in Hortense's kitchen. She knelt in front of him with a bowl of warm water. A green bottle of antiseptic and some cotton wool balls were next to them on the table. Sounds of movement came from other rooms in the house and Kittinger looked towards the door. There was a *tsk* of admonition from Hortense as he jerked his head back from her hand. She took a firm grip of his chin and moved his head back so he was facing her.

"Sorry."

Her mouth quirked in amusement and she stole a kiss from him.

"Keep still," she told him. She dabbed the cotton wool bud against the bottle of antiseptic and brushed it against his cheek. He hissed as the antiseptic stung. She shushed him and dabbed again at his cheek, pushing firmly against the skin. She wiped the dried blood away and dropped the bud into the bowl. Wisps of red swirled in the water.

Finished with his cheek, she moved onto his hands. The skin on the knuckles was broken and she began cleaning them up. He watched her as she worked precisely, her hands deftly moving the cotton gently over his knuckles. He could smell her perfume and he closed his eyes for a moment, letting the fragrance surround him. It made a change from the smell of smoke and oil ingrained into his shirt and uniform jacket.

"You're sure the men can stay here?" he asked while she worked. "Won't Claude object?"

"My brother is in town, cowering in case a stray bomb hits the house instead of the airfield," she said, her voice hot with anger. Kittinger opened his eyes, surprised to see her so moved. "This is my house too." She finished swabbing his hands. "There, finished." She stood up, dropping the cotton bud into the bowl. She clapped her hands, pleased with the standard of her work. "So. I decided. The men can stay." There was the sound of boots clomping around upstairs and she looked up at the ceiling. "It sounds like they're getting settled up there."

"I still wish you'd reconsider going somewhere safe, darling. Claude could be right, you know." He looked around the kitchen, at the beams in the ceiling, the big windows that overlooked the courtyard. "One bomb could flatten this place."

"Whatever happens, happens," she said serenely. Kittinger remained unconvinced. While no bombs had gone amiss this time, there was no certainty they would be so accurate next time.

She crossed to the wine rack on the sideboard of her Welsh Dresser. She had brought it back to France with her after her husband died. She picked out a bottle and took it back to the table, looking at her man as she walked towards him. She could see the strain in him. His shoulders were tight and his eyes overly bright, fine lines showing at their corners.

He'd not told her about the raid but she'd heard about it from some of the men when they came in trailing their kit bags behind them. The image of him standing in the open roaring his defiance at the enemy like some demon frightened her. He'd promised her he would stay safe, but she knew he wouldn't sit on the sidelines when his men needed him. It was the essence of who he was.

They retired to the drawing room and Hortense dimmed the oil lamp on the side table as they walked past. He sank into the armchair by the fire and she sat on his lap, arms around his shoulders, legs crossed at the ankle. She rested her chin on his head and closed her eyes, blotting out distant rumbles.

A voice laughed in the next room. Kittinger thought it sounded like Satterley, one of the fitters, and he heard the hiss of the radio as the volume went up and down. Kittinger recognised Chamberlain's voice as the thin warble from the speakers became stronger. "-are being tested already. And you, and I, must rally behind our new leader, and with our united strength, and with unshakable courage, fight and work until this wild beast, which has sprung out of his lair upon us, has been finally disarmed and overthrown."

The volume dropped so the rest was a dull muffle. Kittinger stirred slightly and Hortense hugged him closer, kissing him on the head. *So the wet blanket had done the decent thing and resigned at last*, he thought. He'd not heard the name of who had replaced him, but anyone must surely be better than Chamberlain.

Chandler, Morgan, Pettifer and a few of the others were clustered around a small fire in the woods. A tarpaulin had been stretched between the trees to provide some cover from above. They sat on logs and talked in hushed tones, discussing the events of the day.

Pettifer thought about sleep but his mind was running a million miles an hour. Good men had died today. Others had been wounded, but was there anything that could be learned from it all, he wondered. He glanced at the faces around him. Chandler was staring into the fire but his mind was elsewhere. Morgan sat across from him next to Pendleton and Chambers.

Pendleton was recounting his tale of making it back on a wing and a prayer. Pettifer had to tip his hat to him. There weren't many people on the squadron who could have brought his aircraft back. Pendleton had always boasted about being a good pilot. Now he'd shown it was no idle boast.

Pendleton stretched his right leg out in front of him and rubbed his knee. The muscles were cramping up and his leg still spasmed uncontrollably.

"God knows what'll happen tomorrow," he said.

"I'll settle for a nice little easy target," said Chandler.

"I'm just surprised we didn't lose more today," said Pendleton, stretching his leg. It was still trembling even now. "We should have." He could picture the scene in his mind's eye as he tried to thread a way through the wall of fire that had been reaching for him. The damn flak had been thick enough to walk on. How all six aircraft had come out the other side had been a complete mystery to him.

"I'm not altogether convinced bumbling along at one thousand is a good idea," he murmured. "Everyone can see us up there and take pot shots at us." He used his hands to demonstrate the point, holding them flat up at shoulder height before zooming them down towards the ground. "We come beetling along in a shallow dive flying nice and level all the way." He thought about that bombing run over the trucks and infantry. "Why not get down *really* low, say less than five hundred, lower even? We tail fuse the bombs and we can get in and out before they can spot us or even draw a bead on us."

They thought about that for a moment, considering the possibilities. Chandler remembered flying over the beaches later in the day. Winwright had led them out of the south west on the deck with the sun behind them. They had all the advantages on their side. Against the infantry and the tanks, they'd just rolled in from altitude and the Germans had seen them coming from a mile away.

"Coming in low like that would make it difficult to see the target," said Pettifer. He tried to imagine scrubbing around on the deck. You would be just as likely to wrap yourself around a tree or crash into a hill while they went sniffing among the grass.

"Can't use the bombsight either," Morgan finished for him. Chambers rumbled agreement. Below one thousand feet, the Mark IX sight was next to useless.

"I'm not saying there wouldn't be times we could do that," said Pettifer, "but I don't think we could risk it for some unplanned target." He advanced his own theory. "I think we got lucky today because we didn't see any fighters. Our formation flying was a shambles. We've *got* to keep it tight. If we give ourselves interlocking fields of fire, the fighters will think twice about playing with us."

"Oh, come on," protested Chandler. "Parade ground formation flying over the target will just make things easier for the flak." He shuddered at the thought of it. Running along on rails when the flak was coming up at you would certainly make life interesting. It would be short; but interesting.

"You can't have it both ways," said Morgan, backing up his pilot. "If you insist on tight formation flying, that's just going to make us sitting ducks."

"I wouldn't worry about the flak," Pettifer assured them, trying to allay their fears. "They put up an enormous amount of stuff at us today and we did okay. Didn't we?"

"We got lucky?" queried Morgan, filling the silence. Pettifer snorted in response.

"There's no such thing," he said.

"You're forgetting B flight's run over the airfield," Pendleton reminded him.

"That's different," Pettifer shot back immediately. "Those were proper gun emplacements. I don't care what colour their uniforms are. Soldiers can't shoot for toffee and you know that. I'll bet you ninety five percent of everything they shot at us exploded behind us."

"That still leaves five percent and we still got hit," said Chambers. He recalled the hole in his navigator's table. He'd pulled out a fragment of metal about two inches long embedded in his log book.

"Law of averages," said Pettifer, his tone dismissive. "If you fling enough scrap and rubbish into the air you're bound to get pranged eventually." He spread his hands wide and appealed to their common sense. "Look, it's our job to drop bombs and get them on the target, right?" Heads nodded. "There's no point flying all the way there if we couldn't hit a barn door once we arrived."

Chandler wasn't convinced. Neither was Pendleton. Pettifer was right; that was their bread and butter. They had to get the bombs on the target. It was a long way from their serene practice in the south of France all those weeks ago.

2.21 – More Of The Same

The 11th May 1940 continued pretty much as the 10th had done. The Germans kept the initiative and they used it. They advanced at great speed across Holland, streaking past Apeldoorn and Arnhem towards Utrecht. Around Rotterdam, the paratroops controlled the city and surrounding region.

The situation in Maastricht rapidly deteriorated. The Germans had held the Veldweselt and Vroenhoven bridges. Spanning the River Meuse and the Albert Canal, they were the gateway to western Belgium. Soldiers, vehicles, guns and tanks streamed across the bridges.

In the face of coordinated all arms warfare, there was little the Belgian army could do. Stukas fell out of the sky, their sirens screaming as they planted their bombs on target. They were the airborne artillery preceding the armoured fist. The Germans advanced on Tongres as the defences crumbled. The Belgians withdrew to a new position on the river Gette while they waited for the allied units to come up.

Now that they had focused the allied attention firmly on Belgium, the Germans unleashed the next stage of Fall Gelb. French military thinking held that the woods of the Ardennes around Sedan were too dense for tactical operations. As a consequence, the area was only lightly defended. Army Group A proved them wrong, advancing through the forest with tanks and trucks.

Within a few hours, the lead elements of the Wehrmacht were pushing hard against reserve units. They scythed through the lines and found the biggest impediment to rapid progress were the traffic jams on the poor quality road network. Forty one thousand vehicles were backing up over the border into Germany as they tried to cram down four routes of march.

At first, the French didn't believe it. Reports of tanks and trucks were put down to garbled communications. Reservists weren't line soldiers. They had to be inflating their estimates of the enemy strength. Perhaps this was a feint to draw off soldiers from the main front. Only later did it begin to dawn on them that something more was happening.

At AASF HQ the staff were still smarting from their losses of the previous day. Nearly forty aircraft had been lost yesterday and those that'd got back had all been damaged. Going out on the prowl had cost them dearly. This time they wanted solid information and the recce Blenheims were sent out sniffing for trouble.

While the RAF units waited on the ground, the Luftwaffe came over again. There were raids up and down the line and Falcon Squadron got it again. They'd been up since 4a.m twiddling their thumbs, waiting for orders when the Ju88's came in from the east. The first warning was when a stick of bombs landed short and exploded on the northern part of the airfield. The second stick walked across the perimeter. The stone wall where Winwright and Goddard had walked all those months ago was blown to bits. Stones and huge clods of earth were flung into the air.

The Ju88's were bombing from height, sailing serenely along in a sky of rich purple chased with streaks of blue and yellow as the sun came up. The Bofors guns flung defiance at their attackers. They elevated their barrels to the maximum and opened fire.

Everyone else ran for the slit trenches. Men cowered, hands cupped over their ears, as they heard the whistle of the bombs coming down. The air was thick as they packed tightly in this narrow ditch in the earth. Farmer locked eyes with Preddy and tensed as the ground shook again. One bomb in the wrong place could wipe out the whole Squadron.

A massive cloud of dust flew up as a 500kg bomb exploded amongst the trees. Balls of red, green and blue shot into the sky as the crackle of firecrackers ripped through the air. They had front row seats to a free fireworks display as their pyrotechnic stores blew up. Fires started all over the place as the powerful magnesium flares ignited.

The barn they'd been using for accommodation all winter was next to go. A bomb landed in the courtyard and the sturdy doors of the barn were perforated by flying shrapnel. The next bomb went through the roof. The stone walls blew out and the structure collapsed in on itself. The upper gallery folded and a sturdy barn that had stood for over a hundred years was a smoking pile of stone.

The Bofors gun nearest the gate rocked on its mounting as a bomb exploded close by. Two of the crew were scythed down, ripped apart by shrapnel. One of the loaders took the seat of a gunner to keep the gun operational.

It wasn't all one way. A Ju88 headed east, its engine trailing a thick ribbon of smoke, but it was small consolation. Their bombs expended, they broke off and headed home. Clouds of smoke obscured the field. A kaleidoscopic catherine wheel of colour blazed amongst the trees as the flares burned. Men rushed off with buckets of sand and shovels to stop any fire from reaching the fuel dump or the armoury stores.

For all the noise and mayhem, only one Blenheim was destroyed. At the end of the line, it had been unlucky. Caught between two bombs, it had been torn apart. Some of the others were damaged, undoing the hard work of the ground crews the night before.

Hauling himself out of the slit trench, Farmer threw his peaked cap at the retreating bombers.

"Bastards!" he shouted, venting his fear and frustration as they flew off back towards their lines. He shielded his eyes and stared up into the sky. The 88's were disappearing in the distance, tiny little black specks against the blue. In and out fast, with no losses. It was enough to make you feel sick.

Other people began emerging from the slit trenches. Preddy joined his pilot, surveying the craters on the ground.

"Lumme, the mice have been at it."

They walked over to the nearest crater and peered over the edge. The stench of sulphur was strong and in the centre, the bent fins of a bomb stuck out of the ground. Preddy threw some pebbles at it.

"Get away from there!" Kittinger stomped over to them and almost dragged Preddy back from the crater. "Bloody idiots!" He looked at the bomb then pushed them both back a good ten yards. "Make yourselves useful."

He pointed to the slit trenches over by the Bofors gun. The trench had partially collapsed and buried some of the erks. Helping hands were pulling them out one by one. Covered in dirt, they looked like miners fresh from the coal face. Preddy baulked at the prospect of physical labour.

"And get my hands dirty? Whatever next," he said in falsetto. Kittinger glared and they started walking. "More holes to fill in," muttered Preddy. "I had a bellyful of shifting all that snow."

"Stop complaining," Farmer handed him a shovel. "It builds your muscles up." Preddy slung the shovel over his shoulder, almost taking Farmer's head off.

Pettigrew did a count of serviceable aircraft and went over to the flight hut. The door was hanging off its hinges and he squeezed through the gap. The hut was a mess inside. Blast had shattered the windows and there were bits of glass scattered everywhere. He picked up the squadron diary and record books from the floor, flicking slithers of glass off the pages. He dumped them on the table and righted a few chairs before he went into Winwright's office.

The CO was stood with one foot resting on his chair. He had a handset glued to his ear, his shoulder keeping it in place while he flicked bits of broken glass out of the window frame.

"Hello? Hello? Yes, I'm still here, sir. That's twice we've been hit now. It's not good enough, sir. A couple of Bofors guns and a Lewis are not enough to defend the airfield. We need more guns if you want us to stay open for business." Winwright rolled his eyes at Pettigrew as he stood watching him, arms folded.

"Hello?" He banged the handset twice on the desk and listened hard. "That's right. They waltzed over and bombed us to hell, the fields U/S at the moment." His face pinched as his head bobbed. "Yes, sir. I'll bear that in mind." Winwright bit his lip and stared blue murder down the telephone. "How many will I have for operations?" he repeated the question he'd been asked. He paused and shot a look at Pettigrew. The engineering officer held up eight fingers. Winwright's face turned a shade darker.

"Eight, sir. Yes, eight. The bombs knocked us about a bit." He pulled the handset away from his ear for a moment when the volume went up a few notches. "Sir, I've got the crews. That's not the problem; it's going to take a while to get the field into some kind of shape for us to take off. Yes, I've got every available man out filling holes. Will we get some replacement aircraft?"

They said their goodbyes and it was only with great self control that Winwright was able to put the handset back into its cradle.

"Bloody idiots!" He shoved his hands in his pockets and came up with a pack of cigarettes. Pettigrew struck a match and Winwright leaned over to light it.

"That was Wing." He blew cigarette smoke at the window and watched as wisps swirled around the frame. "They were a bit miffed we got pranged." He pinched the bridge of his nose and snickered. "114 Squadron got caught on the ground as well."

"How bad?" asked Pettigrew with some concern. There weren't many

Blenheim squadrons in France. If the Germans were specifically going after them, it would seriously damage their striking power. Winwright's face was grim.

"Bad enough. Some Flying Pencils came in at low level and straddled the fuel dump on the first pass. Then the cheeky sods came back and shot them up. Wiped out the aircraft, god knows how many casualties they've got."

Pettigrew whistled under his breath.

"We got off pretty lightly then."

"I suppose." Winwright looked at the chaos outside. "I was *advised* that it might help dispersing the aircraft a bit better so it didn't happen again."

Pettigrew choked when he realised Winwright was serious. Words failed him. Here they were dodging bombs and bullets while they were getting second guessed by some wallah flying a desk. It was outrageous.

"It'll be a few hours at least before we can get the field clear, sir. There's some UXB's and a hell of a lot of holes to fill in." The Germans had done well for a mornings work. One Blenheim squadron wiped out and their own planes grounded. "How did the Battles do?"

"Better than us. The Jerries had a stab but the fields operational." Winwright picked his cap up off the table and knocked glass onto the floor. "Come on, let's go and get things organised."

While the Squadron licked its wounds, Osbourne was drifting in and out of consciousness at the casualty clearing station. In the early hours of the morning he'd been placed on the top of a table in what had been the buildings kitchen. There, a surgeon got stuck into his thigh, working fast, carving and cutting like one would a Sunday roast. He was stitched up and dumped on a ward by the orderlies. The wound hurt like hell and a nurse forced him to drink some foul tasting concoction that made him retch.

When he came to, it was late afternoon and Timber Woods was lying in a bed next to him, his head swathed in bandages. His feet hung over the edge of the bed, it being too short for his lanky frame. His skin was clammy and pale and he sat up against the wall, the pillow behind his head. Woods held a blanket up around his chest as his teeth chattered.

"Christ, the dead walk among us," murmured Osbourne.

Woods slowly turned his head towards the Scots accent and did his best to smile.

"As I live and breathe," he said through gritted teeth. He shuddered again, the tremor rippling through him. "Do you know, if I squint, I can see three of you."

"You look; like I feel," said Osbourne, trying to keep his tone light. Woods looked awful, like death warmed up.

"I wonder how the squadron's getting on?" asked Woods.

"I haven't got a clue," said Osbourne. "I tried asking earlier, but no one seems to know what's happening."

Woods turned his head but didn't have a direct view out of the window. It seemed to be a bright day outside, but all he could see was a glimpse of some trees.

"What's going to happen to us?"

"God knows." He winced as his leg reminded him it was still there. He sucked in air through his teeth as the pain brought tears to his eyes. "Stick us on a truck back to England I suppose."

"Fantastic," said Woods in exasperation. "All those months of waiting and we're going to miss the show."

Lorraine came into view down the road. Laura leaned out of the window and watched her as she walked. The older woman's shoulders were tense and she was stiff as she got nearer.

"No luck?" asked Laura, even though she could guess the answer.

"Non." Lorraine cursed in French and opened the driver's door on the left side. She took the lid off the flask and drank the cold tea that was left.

It had been a wasted morning. Waking up shivering with a stiff neck, they had eaten sparingly. They'd not brought much food with them as they'd expected to be in England by now. They shared a stale croissant and Laura found some mints in her purse. Lorraine had gone in search of some help but found no one to assist them. The car still wouldn't start and the nearest town was miles away.

At nine, while she'd been waiting for Lorraine to come back, Laura saw a refugee on the road. A man was pushing a large pram loaded to the brim with bundles of bedding and suitcases. A woman walked alongside him, holding the hand of a small child. The child was crying, a teddy bear clutched in their other hand. It was only afterwards that Laura realised she could have asked the man if he could fix the car. She tried asking a few people after that but they ignored her, locked in their own misery and interests.

Laura wasn't very different. While she waited for Lorraine to come back, she wallowed in her own morass of self pity. She'd tried not to think about Alex but was failing miserably. His last words flayed her and she fought back tears while she sat alone in the car.

Lorraine put the flask on the back seat and then with little hope, she turned the key in the ignition one last time. Silence. She pulled the key out with a snarl and threw it out the window. She went round the back of the car and opened the boot. Her suitcases hit the grass verge, closely followed by her shoulder bag. Laura's case followed after that.

"Come on," she said. "We're walking. I refuse to hang around like some helpless woman, waiting for a man to save me." Laura looked horrified at the prospect.

"But it's early yet. Someone may come along."

"And they might not," Lorraine finished for her. "We could be sitting here for hours. Let's go." She rummaged around in her shoulder bag and pulled out a cardigan. Then she consolidated the two suitcases down to one, leaving what she didn't absolutely need. She had made her decision; she wasn't going to argue with Laura any more. Either she could come with her or she would leave her here.

Laura cast a final plaintive look up and down the road and then sighed. The skies were bright and clear. Even the weather had turned against her. If it was raining, she might have been able to make a case to wait it out. She righted her case and took out a pair of flat shoes. Just as she was about to close the lid, Lorraine opened it again and sorted through the contents. She held up some glass bottles.

"Do you really want to carry those?"

"I can't throw my perfume away." Laura hurriedly took the bottles off her and put them back in the case. Alex had given her these. There was no chance she was throwing these away. Lorraine just shrugged and stood up.

"You're carrying it."

Without further debate, she shifted the strap on her shoulder and started walking. Laura tested the weight of the case and followed, leaving the car behind her.

While the girls walked west, the Merville Battles headed east. After the morning raid, they'd sent up two Sections of three before lunchtime. Their success had been mixed. Six aircraft had gone up. One had aborted early due to an engine fault and only three of the other five had returned. Lunch was a rushed sandwich out at dispersal while they got ready to go out again.

A column of trucks had been spotted near St Vith, so off they went again. Simpson led his vic of three aircraft at nine thousand feet. Flying over Charleroi, he dipped his wing slightly and looked north. In the distance were the battlefields of Waterloo and Quatre Bras, where Napoleon had been seen off by Wellington.

Their orders were to attack at St Vith but Simpson was going to go for the first worthwhile target he saw. The reconnaissance information was hours old, the trucks could be anywhere by now.

After another fifteen minutes, he started paying more attention. He glanced left and right; looking for tell tale clouds of dust on the ground, a sure sign that vehicles were on the move.

He was still looking down when the 109s fell on them. The first burst killed his gunner and navigator. The petrol tank behind his seat was holed and the fumes stung his eyes. Another burst holed the glycol tank and there was a fizzing sound as the vital coolant leaked out. He pulled his goggles down and pulled back the hood. The roar of the slipstream assaulted his ears as he stuck his head out and the rush of air battered his face.

He jettisoned his bombs and headed for the deck. Petrol sloshed around his boots. The engine temperature shot up and the first lick of flame appeared under the cowling. The cockpit began to fill with smoke and burning petrol poured along the floor under his seat. Heat from the flames threatened to stifle him. The heat was playing up the back of his legs when he undid his harness and jumped.

No sooner had he pulled the ripcord before he was falling through the trees, branches tugging at his clothing. There was an explosion as the Battle ploughed into the wood, a funeral pyre for his crew. He jerked to a stop, dangling from a tree, no more than ten feet from the ground. Bracing himself, he released the harness. Pain shot up his ankles as he landed heavily. He lay in agony for a few minutes rubbing his legs.

He was surprised to find the trousers of his flying suit were scorched and in tatters. He hissed when he gingerly touched the inflamed skin underneath. Finding a long stick, he started hobbling west, away from the sound of the guns.

Winwright managed to get the squadron into action at 4.30pm. There had been a delay while they waited for an army unit to deal with the unexploded bombs that dotted the field. It took another three hours to sort out the burning pyro stores and fill the holes in. By then, three replacement aircraft and two new crews had arrived. By mid afternoon, they had fourteen aircraft on the line.

Ashton took up six aircraft. Four came back after plastering a column of infantry and tanks. Coming in low to dodge the flak, their sticks of bombs blasted the Panzers as they crossed a bridge. Taunton took a burst to the stomach over the target. His strength failing, he clawed for height as his engines began to die to give his crew a chance to bail out. As his senses slipped away, his Blenheim dived and ploughed into a section of infantry hiding behind a stone wall.

Ashwood caught a packet over the target but managed to nurse the engines until he was south of Wavre. He belly landed in a field, coming to rest amongst green stems of corn. The Flight circled once to make sure he was okay. They had a long walk back.

At Wing HQ in Arras, Saundby stood staring at a map, grim faced. If yesterday had been a poor start, today was even worse. Even when they did find the German units, their contribution had done little to slow the advance. The issue would be decided on the ground but things were not going well. As fast as orders were issued for units to take up defensive positions, the Germans had already passed that location. He looked at the signal from AASF HQ clasped tightly in his left hand. Obviously, Air Marshall Barratt had something in mind.

Stand all squadrons down. Have all aircraft on standby from 4am, morning of the 12th. Await instructions.

At dusk, Barratt issued his battle orders. The Maastricht bridges remained in enemy hands and it was clear something would have to be done about that. Tomorrow would require a maximum effort.

2.22 – Once More Unto The Breach Dear Friends

The 12th May dawned bright and early but there was no rude awakening by German marauders. Roused at 3am anyway, the squadron was up and nervous. They jumped at noises and expected a clutch of bombers to come screaming in at any moment. They ate breakfast on the hoof while the aircraft were warmed up.

At six, orders came through from Wing. Nine aircraft were required to attack troop concentrations around Maastricht. An attack would be going in on the bridges themselves and their raid would provide a distraction. Gardner would lead and the briefing was short. They chewed on bully beef sandwiches and sipped tea from tin mugs while Gardner outlined his plan.

They would go in at five thousand feet and bomb in vics of three at ten second intervals. That height might vary once they got over the target, depending on the cloud cover. After the last few days of action, Gardner was convinced that low levels attacks were just too costly. He figured bombing from medium height would ensure a measure of accuracy while keeping them out of reach of the light flak.

The new replacements hung at the back of the briefing, a mix of excitement and nerves. They'd come straight from England, and spent three days travelling to get here. A ferry flight had dumped them in the middle of chaos in Paris. Then they'd jammed themselves in the back of an army truck to be taken up the line. Gardner put them on his wing and told them to keep close. They nodded, mute, their eyes like saucers.

Winwright walked among the men, encouraging them where he could. They went out to the aircraft to get ready. They were tired but their tails were up.

Chandler and his crew were a typical example. Their eyes were gritty from fatigue. Worn out, they struggled to summon the energy to go to the stream to bathe. They smelt like a bonfire. Their flying clothes were thick with the aroma of flame and smoke from the previous day's action. For all of that, they remained in a buoyant mood.

While he walked around the Blenheim, Chandler thought about the coming flight. He'd always imagined their attacks would be a clear cut process, with specific objectives and detailed briefings. The reality had proven very different. Maybe today was the day that things changed. So far they'd been reacting to the German moves. Now the allied armies were starting to reach their defensive positions, the Wehrmacht would have to react to them for a change.

"Sprung rivets here, Corporal," Chandler said, indicating a small panel near the tail. "Of course, it doesn't matter much with a bullet hole right next to it." He wiggled his little finger in the hole and it went in as far as the knuckle.

The erk noted the damage on the form 700. They'd fix it if the aircraft got back.

Pendleton was giving his Blenheim a thorough going over. Under the port wing, he ran his hand over the replacement panel that had been riveted into place. The square of metal had a layer of flat red primer slapped on it that contrasted sharply with the normal sky underside colour. He crossed himself and tapped the panel with his knuckles. Chamberlain stared at him when he stood back up.

"What?" Pendleton asked his navigator.

"You suddenly got religion? Hold the front page."

"Very funny, PM." He shrugged and looked a little sheepish as he stepped up onto the wing. "I don't suppose it hurts. I'll take any edge I can get if it helps."

At eight, Gardner fired a green flare across the field and the nine aircraft started their engines. Kittinger stood by the flight hut, his Lee Enfield rifle leaning against the wall. He watched them taxi out in groups of three, ready to take off. Winwright joined him.

"I hope we have a better day today."

"Of course we will," Kittinger reassured him. "The Jerries have had it all their own way. Now it's our turn to get some licks in."

The engine note of Gardner's Blenheim changed as it thundered across the field, rocking slightly as it rolled over the recently filled earth. Gardner let it run, gaining as much speed as he could before pulling back on the yoke and clawing into the air. The wheels came up and he levelled off before starting a lazy turn to the right. He would circle the field, letting the rest of the squadron form up on him as they took off.

"Was it a good idea to send the replacements?" asked Kittinger. In the first war, some men had come and gone before they could even unpack their kit.

"Better they go up in a group to gain some experience." replied Winwright. He chucked the dregs of his tea onto the grass. He remembered a similar conversation with Valerie in the graveyard last October. Then, it had been himself with all the doubts and Valerie the wise old sage.

Now, he was the one making the hard decisions, sending young men out whether they were ready or not. He would have preferred to give them time to settle in, but he didn't have that luxury. If he'd sent them out singly he may as well just slit their throats to save the aircraft for somebody else to use. At least this way, they had a fighting chance.

The next Blenheim accelerated down the field and Winwright watched it with a critical eye. One of the replacements, Flight Sergeant Harding was at the controls. From Harrogate, Harding had told Winwright he was twenty five but he looked younger, his cherubic face adorned with a broad grin and friendly eyes. He looked like a teenager in his flying suit and forage cap.

The Blenheim pulled up sharply into the air and Winwright winced as it shuddered on the edge of a stall. Harding had his tongue clamped between his teeth as he worked the controls, overcorrecting. He could feel the stall juddering through the airframe, the flutter in the yoke. He held the nose level and swore, waiting for the engines to recover and provide some extra airspeed.

He raised the undercarriage and relaxed as the speed built up. He shared a weak smile with his navigator, Ambleside who sat next to him, maps clutched tightly to his chest.

"Piece of cake," Harding said to reassure him.

Winwright watched Archer, the other replacement follow along behind. He was much smoother in his handling of the aircraft, lifting off with no fuss at all. Winwright looked at Kittinger.

"It might not hurt to ring Wing and chase up some more replacement aircraft and crews."

"Yessir." He was just about to go into the hut when Winwright asked a question.

"Any word on, Ashwood?"

"Not yet, sir, but, Mister Ashton said they landed okay and started walking before they left them."

He watched them take off before going into the hut.

Burke managed to get nearly two hours of work out of the groundcrews before their efforts slowly trickled to a halt. Their eyes kept drifting to the northern horizon as they twirled screwdrivers and wielded spanners. Finally, all pretence was dropped and they stood in clumps, waiting.

Kittinger was no exception. He used a cigarette hard as he wandered up and down the line, his rifle slung over his shoulder. He checked his watch again and pulled up alongside Burke.

"Shouldn't be long now."

"No, sir."

Burke wondered how much work would be waiting for them this time. The men had been slaving for days to keep the kites in the air. It was ironic really. All the work to keep the Blenheims in tip top condition during the most horrendous winter on record and two days of action had undone all that effort. He cocked his head as a faint rumble came to his ears. He stepped round Kittinger and shielded his eyes against the sun. The sound got stronger. They were back

"Look sharp!" he shouted at the men. "Get ready to see them in."

The men scrambled to get ready and then waited, and then they waited some more. One of them shouted and pointed as the first Blenheim came into view.

A second one followed. Both of them were streaming thin wisps of smoke. There was a hushed silence as they came straight in. Both of them were shot to pieces, control surfaces tattered, airframes holed. They touched down and taxied up with a quick burst of power.

Chandler and Hagen were home. Both crews had somehow got away scot free although the same couldn't be said for their aircraft. Hagen's gunner, Guillroy hobbled out of his turret with a graze to his thigh. The skeleton nose art sported a number of holes and both Blenheims would need work before they would be flyable again.

Five minutes later, a third Blenheim came over in even worse shape. One engine trailed a thick stream of smoke with the prop feathered. Oil streaked back from the cowling. There was a large hole in the nose and the canopy was starred. As it shaped up to land it was clear it wasn't going to be pretty. The port undercarriage leg hung down at a drunken angle under the shattered engine.

Burke peered at the fuselage and saw its code letter, 'Q-Queenie', Mister Nugent. He was a good lad, twenty two, dark haired with an easy West Country manner. The struggling aircraft lowered itself down gently as Nugent used lots of rudder to counter the dead engine.

The starboard engine turned into a whisk as the prop tips touched the grass. Burke nodded in approval as the Blenheim slid to a halt, steam rising from the good engine. Engines and propellers could be replaced but it was harder to fix an aircraft when a pilot thumped it down like a brick and bent everything.

Men started running as it slid to a halt. The top hatch shoved back and Nugent appeared, shouting for a doctor. Willing hands helped Pendergast out of the nose. His right arm hung limp and his flying suit was covered in blood. He was deathly pale as he was stretchered away for the MO to take a look.

Nugent staggered back, looking at his crumpled Blenheim. He dragged off his flying helmet as he circled round, his eyes searching without seeing. Ashton put a steadying hand on his shoulder and that seemed to do the trick. Nugent focused on the older man, coming back to himself.

"Steady on, old man," said Ashton quietly.

He shared a look with the orderly who gently took Nugent by the arm and walked him towards the MO's tent. Dane stood next to Burke, hugging his clipboard, lips pursed in concern. There was hushed bemusement amongst the men. An erk asked the question they were all thinking.

"Lumme, where's the rest then?"

"I think that's it, lad," whispered Burke quietly in response, his face sombre.

The story, such as it was came out in pieces from the survivors as Dane, Ashton and Winwright stood quietly listening. They took turns telling their stories. Dane wrote furiously, his pen covering the page in reams of notes. They talked quickly, still coming down from their adrenalin rush as their minds replayed events. Their eyes gleamed with intensity as they brought forth one detail after another.

During the briefing, Gardner had stressed the need to press on regardless. He'd also warned them to watch out for friendly aircraft. They would not be the only squadron going in today.

"Sounds like a cattle market," Pendleton had said, and that had raised a laugh. After the battering of the last few days, they were itching to get in some licks of their own.

They'd weaved in and out of the patchy cloud cover as they approached Maastricht from the west. The fighter cover they'd been promised failed to show but Hagen was far from surprised. Little else in this war had been going according to plan so far. Why should the escort be any different? Heads swivelled in all directions as Maastricht loomed on the horizon. It was Hagen's gunner that spotted the 109s first.

Coming up from behind at ten thousand feet, they hovered like vultures circling a carcass in the desert. Two Sections of four broke off and dived on two lonely Battles a few miles away running parallel to their course. Hagen didn't get a chance to see what happened to them as the rest of the fighters swarmed the nine Blenheims like bees around a honeypot. He had no idea how many times they attacked. He lost count after the sixth pass and his world shrank to one of personal survival.

Making coordinated attacks to split their defensive fire, the 109s nipped at the edges of their formation as they probed for weaknesses. Keeping together, Gardner led them through the final turn in the run up to the target.

The first to fall was Pendleton. A fast slashing attack from the rear quarter took out his starboard engine and his stricken Blenheim began to fall behind. He pulled the boost for extra power and shoved the throttle forward to the stop, but that wasn't enough to keep pace with the rest. He could have jettisoned his bombs, but Gardner's words from the briefing rang in his ears. He pressed on.

As his Blenheim fell further behind, he was easy pickings. A pair of 109s came in low from astern. The element leader pulled up from underneath and opened fire at fifty yards, skewering Pendleton from nose to tail.

Metal sparkled as rounds tore through the thin skin and tore apart the crew. Chambers was busy firing at the 109s to port when he was hit. A cannon shell took off his left thumb. He stared in bewilderment at the stump as a line of bullets tore through his stomach. He slumped over his gun, screaming in pain. He was nineteen. He wouldn't see twenty.

Bullets ripped into Pendleton's back. The 7.92mm rounds made no distinction between old and new money, class or education. The bomber reared up as he slumped in his seat, the yoke pulled into his stomach. The remaining engine thrashed the air before the Blenheim dived for the ground with a dead hand at the controls.

Next to go was Chandler's wingman, Dudley. The first burst punctured his wing tanks. The second turned his Blenheim into a flaming torch. It took about two seconds for Dudley to make his mind up. He tried the controls, felt nothing there and reached for the escape hatch.

He just had time to tell his crew to bail out before he undid his straps and went over the side. Pulling himself into a tight ball, he tumbled end over end while the slipstream battered him. He felt the whoosh as the tailplane brushed overhead and then he was clear. A moment later, the outer tank exploded and blew the port wing off. What was left of his aircraft fell out of the sky, turning nose over tail as it span faster and faster.

"Oh balls!" Dudley muttered and pulled the ripcord. So much for counting to three, or was it five? There was a hollow thud, like a sail banging in the wind, the straps tightened and suddenly he was no longer falling.

The snarl of machine guns was all around him and he watched helplessly as the 109s ripped into the squadron. He saw Chandler's number two torn apart. One moment Gleason was tucked in nice and neat on his port wing, the next, pieces of him were falling to the ground wrapped in flames.

Chandler's cockpit was bathed in orange light as he fought the controls through the shockwave of the explosion. He pushed forward on the yoke and discovered he was on his own. With Dudley and now Gleason down, he felt naked. He slid over and tucked in a little behind and a little below Gardner, keeping to the clear air. Morgan peered over the lip of the canopy and looked behind them.

They were now tail end Charlie while the fighters circled round for another pass. Hagen and Nugent doggedly clung on off to their left. He didn't rate their chances very highly.

Chandler's lips pulled thin. The conversation in the woods came back to haunt him. Pettifer had argued for tight formation flying to get the bombs on target and keep the fighters away. He would have gladly swapped places with him at this moment so he could prove his point. Some escort fighters would have been nice right about now.

Gardner's gunner kept up a running commentary of what was going on behind. Three down and not one enemy fighter had been shot down in return. He tried a few gentle weaving turns. They flitted in and out of the tops of the wispy clouds for cover but every time they broke into the clear, the fighters were there waiting for them.

Hagen dropped his element back a little below and behind Gardner. Chandler took the opportunity to slot in on Hagen's left wing to form a new vic of three from the two shattered sections. They charged madly on, firing back at the fighters as they came diving in, guns blazing.

"Keep calling out those fighters, Griffiths!" Chandler snarled. Griffiths didn't waste his time with a reply. Now a veteran, he fired short efficient bursts, conserving his ammunition as much as he could. There was a dead click as his Vickers gun fell silent. He tore off the magazine, dropping it between his feet. He slapped another one on with practised ease and pulled back the charging handle.

A 109 had edged in closer while his gun was silent, wanting to make certain of a kill. Griffiths gave him a burst, the tracer whipping over his wing. Startled, the pilot broke off.

"Cheeky sod!" said Griffiths, giving him another burst to send him on his way. He scanned the sky again and clicked on his RT. "Two coming in at ten o'clock skipper."

He swung his turret round and sighted along his machine gun. He laid off to the right to allow for the slipstream and tracked the fighters through their approach. He fired the same time the leader did.

Hits sparkled on the cowling of the 109 and then the engine let go. A gout of flame shot back from the exhaust and then a huge gob of oil plastered the canopy. The 109 snap rolled onto its back and dived, its pilot blind and his engine losing power. Griffiths watched as the second fighter broke off to shepherd its leader down.

"I got one! I got one!" he exclaimed over the R/T.

"Great," said Chandler. He'd felt the thump as some shots went home somewhere behind him. "Hit 'em again."

He gritted his teeth. That last hit had affected the controls. They felt soft and he fed in some trim to keep the nose level.

For a moment, he spared a thought for the replacements. If he was scared, the new boys must be absolutely terrified. Here they were, their first time up and they were in the biggest swarm of fighters Chandler had ever seen. He tried to remember how he'd felt on that first mission all those months ago and couldn't manage it.

They were hit again and he could feel as much as hear the hits. One round went through the nose in front of Morgan's face and he pressed himself lower in this flying coffin. He eyed the escape hatch on the floor and licked his lips, his mouth dry. While Chandler and Griffiths were occupied, he could only lay there and watch the chaos around him. More tracer flashed by and flailed Gardner's aircraft in front of him. Bits of fabric fluttered off his rudder in the slipstream and Morgan saw the exposed ribs glinting in the sun.

All of a sudden, the 109s sheered away and the sky was empty apart from six battered Blenheims sailing along. Before they could catch their breath, the sky turned black from flak. Gardner rode over one explosion and then took them down. He pushed the yoke forward and told his observer to get ready.

Peering down his bombsight, Rafferty reeled off the directions thick and fast. The ground was alive with the flashes of every calibre of gun you could think of. He tried adjusting for drift but it was difficult. Clearly, the forecast winds were off, you only had to see the clouds moving to realise that. The flak bursts were also being pushed around by a stiff breeze. Rafferty did his best but when he pushed the bomb release he knew it would be a miracle if the bombs went anywhere near the target.

The bombs were just starting to spill from their bomb bay when Gardner's luck ran out. An 88mm shell burst directly underneath him and lifted the Blenheim up like it had been grabbed by the gods. Shrapnel tore through the fuselage. The main spar let go, the port wing folded and the Blenheim lanced towards the ground.

The rest of them dropped their loads. With the sudden loss of Gardner, Harding and Archer flying in the number two and three spots had no idea what to do. For a moment, the formation wallowed on through the blizzard of fire, leaderless. Hagen slid into the lead position and turned away, diving for the deck. The rest of them followed hot on his tail.

Archer caught a packet on the way out. A burst of flak tore into the wing tanks and he went down fast, a blazing pyre. Chandler saw one parachute drift clear before it slammed into the ground.

The 109s came in again as they battled clear of the flak. They swarmed the Blenheims from all sides. Chandler clung desperately to Hagen's wing in despair as the 109s moved in to deliver the coup de grace. The German fighters had swatted them from the sky like flies and he saw no way of stopping them now. Two Sections came in from dead ahead and Chandler steeled himself for the hail of bullets that would flay them to pieces; but they never came.

Before they could fire, the 109s sheered off to the left and climbed hard. Griffiths whooped loudly as he saw a group of Hurricanes dive headlong into battle. Distracted, the 109s left them alone and the Blenheims didn't need telling twice. Hagen took them low, leaving a trail of broken bombers behind them, their black funeral pyres darkening the sky.

The formation limped for home. As they passed Mons, Harding's Blenheim decided it had done enough for the day and the engines packed up. The cylinder head temperatures went through the roof and the only way after that was down. Harding stretched the descent as long as he could but made a hash of his landing. Misjudging his approach, he ploughed through a thick hedgerow that ripped the undercart off. The bomber slithered to a halt in the adjoining field. They would have a long walk home.

Exhausted faces stared at Dane as he finished writing down the tale. He read back some of his notes, his brow creased in concentration. Having heard the story, he dare not ask them to delve back into the nightmare and repeat anything. He wanted to make sure he had it down right.

No one said anything to fill the awkward silence. Chandler and Morgan were wrung out from the morning's slaughter. Nugent stared at the floor. Hagen just stood there, grim faced. Once again, everyone around him had suffered but he'd made it home without a scratch. It didn't seem possible. He'd winced at the number of bullet holes around his cockpit. The painting of Charon almost seemed like a joke now.

Winwright shot a glance at Ashton. Ashton shook his head and stared into the distance. The questions he wanted to ask could wait until later.

"Get some lunch chaps," Winwright said wearily. "We might have to go up again, so take the chance to get some food. You did well today."

They shambled from the hut, their feet dragging as the fatigue began to hit home. Chandler and Morgan sat under a tree mechanically munching some sandwiches, not caring in the least what was in them. Hagen went to his tent and lay down. He took out a photograph of Lorraine from his wallet and stared at it, wishing she was near.

After they'd gone, Winwright looked at Dane and Ashton. Six out of nine crews gone, and for what? None of them had seen if their bombs had hit anything useful, they were too busy trying to stay alive. Their attack was supposed to have been a diversion for the attack on the bridges, but Winwright was struggling to see that they'd managed to accomplish anything at all. It had been a massacre and it had all been for nothing.

"Get me Wing," he said quietly.

2.23 – Shell Shock

The Squadron was ordered to put up six aircraft to attack Maastricht again. Winwright had an angry conversation with Wing, pointing out he didn't have six aircraft to send. He refused to put up less than that. The last few days had shown him just how vulnerable they were to fighters without any escort of their own.

He looked out of the window of his battered office to see feverish activity amongst the trees. The squadron was in a pitiful state. He had three serviceable aircraft and two more that needed work. It wasn't much to fight a war with. Three more were due to be ferried in but even then they were down to what he considered the absolute minimum for operations.

Supplies were an issue too. The last few days of effort had eaten into their aviation fuel stores and they were almost out of pyrotechnics. Bainbridge was sending over some fuel from Merville to help out but it had yet to arrive. Wing had promised some more for the following morning but Winwright would believe that when he saw it. Nothing else had gone right so far. There was no reason to suppose that would either.

Aside from a lack of aircraft, the ranks of the squadron had also been decimated. Winwright scowled when he caught a glimpse of the crew list on the wall from the corner of his eye. There were lines through a lot of those names; too many names really.

With Gardner gone, B Flight was leaderless again. Faced with choosing either Farmer or Hagen, Winwright felt the big man might just fit the bill. Farmer could be a bit of a prig sometimes, but he was a good pilot, aggressive. Maybe that was what they needed right about now.

Spirits were lifted a little at lunchtime when Ashwood returned with his crew. They hopped out of a passing army truck and wearily walked down the road to the field. They had got lucky. After pancaking in the corn field the day before, they'd come across a French infantry unit heading in the right direction. Ashwood felt a lot safer surrounded by blue clad infantryman armed to the teeth when the sound of the guns wasn't far behind.

They spent a few hours huddled in a wood. None of them slept much that night. The constant booming of the guns was a reminder that the war was not far away. At three in the morning, the French moved out, heading east to take up a new defensive position. According to the scraps of conversation the crew overheard, the Germans were only a few miles away. They took to the roads again and walked the rest of the night, making do with an apple and a bit of baguette for breakfast.

They cadged a lift when an artillery unit drove past. They hopped a ride on the last truck and left the front line behind. Seeing the war on the ground convinced Ashwood that flying was the way to go. Scrubbing around, marching, dodging bullets amongst the mud and muck was not for him.

Ashwood managed to get back to his tent and kick his boots off before he slumped onto the bed. He was asleep before his head hit the pillow.

Saundby spoke to Winwright at three. Winwright made it very clear he wanted a fighter escort the next time the squadron went up. Saundby couldn't really disagree with the request. Down south, the Hurricane Squadron's were doing their damndest to support the Battles and the Blenheims. Up north, the promised support from the fighter units had been sorely lacking.

It had been a costly day all round. The bridges had to be destroyed but the allied efforts to drop the spans had borne little fruit. One had been badly damaged, the other was possibly damaged; maybe.

Courage had not been lacking, but raw courage was not enough. The Germans had been given too much time to prepare their defence and the allied bombers had paid the price. The Maastricht bridges had become the eye of a hurricane, consuming everything that was sent against them. 12 Squadron had put up nine aircraft and come back with one and most of the other squadrons had fared little better. The Germans continued to advance on all fronts and now there was word they were attacking towards Sedan.

Tomorrow would bring no let up. Even now, requests to support units were starting to come in and there were more targets than aircraft available. The Wing staff were working the list down into some kind of order of priority but it was like trying to plug the leaks in a dam by just using your fingers. 2 Group based in England had been helping as well the last few days, but it just wasn't going to be enough.

Saundby's force had already been bled dry and there was no indication that things were slowing down. The BEF would be expecting support on the morrow as they dug in on the Dyle Line. He had perhaps half his Wing left to support them and even that was a false statistic. With only eight Blenheims available, most of the Wings striking force was made up of Fairey Battles. His review of the casualty figures from the other Wings had shown just how vulnerable they were and he'd blanched at the losses.

Barret was already making noises about switching the Battles exclusively to night bombing to try and stem their losses. Saundby understood the reason why, but it didn't help with his immediate problems.

Hortense saw him walking up the drive as the light started to go. Although he'd dropped by the house briefly in the middle of the afternoon, he didn't come back until he'd put things in order with the Squadron. The replacement aircraft were being checked out and the remaining planes were being made ready for the morning. Work parties offloaded the supplies that had arrived around six.

The aircrews were too shocked by the day's losses to do much. No one had the energy or the motivation to go to town. Mostly, they gathered in small groups in their tents, nursing bottles of beer or wine they'd stored. Now everyone had something to do, he could take a moment for himself.

He looked up and saw her standing there by the door. She was in her nightdress with a shawl thrown across her shoulders. Her hair hung loose around her neck. Even with no makeup on, she still stole his heart. She summoned a smile as he kissed her. She'd not seen him so tired before but said nothing. His shoulders sagged and it wasn't just from the weight of the rifle.

She steered him into the kitchen and he sank into a chair. It was the first time he'd stopped all day. Hortense sat next to him, sipping a mug of coffee while he asked about her day. She told him what she'd been up to but she watched him closely, seeing the tension in every part of him.

With the wounded shipped off to a military hospital, she had spent the day starting to put the house to rights. Some things would need to be replaced, but the men in general had been quite tidy, considering. She had no doubt that Claude would fume over the sheets she'd torn up to make bandages, but it needed to be done.

She'd seen the planes take off in the morning but she avoided asking about that. She didn't have to; she'd been tidying one of the upstairs bedrooms when the remaining three came back. The window gave her a good view of one end of the airfield when they landed. She stopped what she was doing and looked out, waiting for the rest to return. It took her a while to realise they weren't coming back.

"I can't stay long," he said softly.

She nodded silently. She knew he had to go, but she didn't move. She wanted this to last for as long as possible.

He stared at the fire while thoughts rolled around his head. There was something he needed to say, he just wondered how he could say it. Fear gnawed at him while he worked it through in his head. At the field, he was the person people looked to. They expected him to know what to do, to be organised. If only they knew, he thought to himself.

Hortense had become the most precious thing in his world, but he knew they had been very lucky after all those raids on the field. Aside from a few broken panes, the house was fine. All it would take would be a few stray bombs and it would become a burnt out shell.

"I worry about you, you know," he whispered. "This house is spitting distance from the field." She stayed quiet, reluctant to answer. He continued. "I know you made me promise to stay safe, but I can't help being worried about you too."

She stirred then and shifted slightly, raising her head to look at him.

"I'll be fine, Michael," she said, trying to reassure him. He kissed her forehead and wrapped his arms around her.

"I hope so. I hope so."

The last rays of the sun were slipping away over the horizon when she opened the front door. Faint sounds of banging came from the direction of the field. He stood on the threshold. She couldn't see his face in the dark.

"If this all goes wrong, is there somewhere you could go?" he asked bleakly. She nodded, noticing his tone of voice.

"Nothing's going to happen, Michael." He stared at her, willing her to reassure him. "I have an aunt in La Rochelle," she said. Satisfied with that, he nodded slightly.

"If things don't improve in the next few days, it might be a good idea," he said. "It might get a bit hot around here."

"If it's hot for me, then it's too hot for you also," she shot back. "You made me a promise," she reminded him.

"I know," he said, almost in resignation. He could see this was not one of those arguments he was going to win. She knew his concerns but he knew that short of tying her up, she wouldn't be going anywhere.

"I love you," he told her.

She smiled and stood on tiptoe to kiss him goodnight.

"I love you too."

Lorraine leaned over the railing at the stern, watching the water churn up in the ship's wake. Seagulls wheeled around the ferry, skimming the surface, looking for pickings. She watched a truck loaded with children creep slowly along the quayside. Two military trucks followed that, their drivers leaning on their horns, which made not the slightest bit of difference. The roads were stiff with traffic. It seemed like all roads ended at the docks in Le Havre. Soldiers rubbed shoulders with civilians, women and children crying in distress. Everyone wanted the same thing, a boat out of France.

Lorraine was glum as she saw her homeland receding behind them. She had been so busy the last few days she had never really thought about leaving France for England. Back there on the shore was her family, her life and her husband. She almost felt like a coward for running away like this.

Despite all the obstacles thrown in their way, they'd made it. They had crammed on board the ferry with all the other desperate refugees. Laura stood next to her, still clutching that silly suitcase filled with her bottles of perfume. In another hour or two the war would be far behind them and they would be safe in England.

After they'd left Rouen, they'd hopped a ride on a bus, but after a few miles it had gotten stuck in traffic at a crossroads. They'd waited patiently expecting it to restart, but after an hour, Lorraine had grown tired of waiting. She felt vulnerable, sitting on a bus like this, stationary.

The rumour in Rouen was that Nazi fighters had been strafing civilian traffic. Lorraine had no idea if that was true but the stories sounded real enough. At the side of the road they'd come across some burnt out vehicles, but that could have been anything. Even so, it would have been foolish to take the chance.

She let her feet do the talking and set off towards Le Havre, walking the rest of the day. Laura trailed along behind her, still stubbornly dragging her suitcase. By cutting across fields and avoiding the roads choked with refugee traffic, they made good progress, but they were still many miles short of Le Havre when it grew dark. Laura found an abandoned barn and they slept amongst the hay in the loft. They made Le Havre late in the afternoon the following day. The closer they got to the port; the crowds on the road grew larger so that even the short cuts were jammed with people. It was seven in the evening before they made it to the docks.

They got lucky. While the crowds milled around the ticket office for the ferry, Lorraine went straight to the dock and collared one of the crew. There was a rapid flurry of conversation, some money changed hands and they got their spot on the rail.

On the way out of the harbour, a British destroyer was their escort. The bow carved through the blue green water as it sailed along, its mast raked back. Small and nimble, it almost glided across the water, straining to get up to speed. They watched as it drew ahead of the ferry, the white ensign fluttering at the masthead.

Laura opened her suitcase. She rummaged around inside the contents and then stood up, holding a bottle of perfume in her hand. She leaned over the rail and held the neck between thumb and forefinger. She waited for a moment and then let it go, craning her neck to watch it tumble into the water. The splash was swallowed by the ships wake.

"What did you do that for?" asked Lorraine. It seemed a little strange after Laura had struggled to carry that case all the way from Béthenville.

"An offering," Laura said sadly. She looked up and Lorraine could see tears glinting in her eyes. "I ruined everything," she said, sniffing. "I've been very stupid." Lorraine handed her a handkerchief. She blew her nose.

Lying on hammocks below deck were Osbourne and Woods. After surgery, they'd been packed in like cattle on a hospital train. The ride had been hell. While he was awake, Osbourne's ears were assaulted by the screams and wailing from the other casualties. Hour after hour he'd tried to keep out the noise to keep his sanity. They were supposed to go to a field hospital but got delayed somewhere. They spent several hours in a siding looking out the carriage window at a bunch of goods trucks. Eventually, the train started moving again. They were rerouted and came into Le Havre after fifteen hours of pure torture.

Transferred on to some trucks, they were shipped off to the docks and taken to the destroyer. Once the ship started moving, Osbourne gripped the mattress tight, wet with fear. He stared at the ceiling in this floating steel box and glanced nervously at the lifebelt that had been fastened around his chest. After a while, he sat up and unfastened the ribbon ties, chucking it on the floor. If the ship was hit and went down, there was no chance he would ever make it to the top deck. For starters, he didn't know the way; secondly, his leg would never carry him the distance.

2.24 – The Door Swings Both Ways

The war was going badly for the allied forces. After taking up defensive positions in Belgium, the BEF was coming under increasing pressure to its front. Even though their government had already surrendered, the decimated Belgian forces desperately fought on alongside them.

The French 7th army had shortened their line and pulled back towards Bergen-Op-Zoom. The cries for air support were loud and many, especially when a German tank force threatened to cut them off. Under pressure to assist, Saundby held his Blenheims in reserve and sent the Battles off in support. This time, they had all the advantages. Fighters covered them in and they had the room to pick their spot. The flak was light here. With the tanks up front as the spearhead of the advance, the supporting units hadn't caught up yet.

They swept in and bombs rained down amongst the Panzers. Tanks exploded left and right. One was blown across the road and ended upside down in the river. A company of infantry was torn to pieces and scattered across the grass. Bainbridge smiled in grim satisfaction as he surveyed the damage.

At Bois Fontaine, two more replacement aircraft came in and the mechanics used the lull to patch up the other aircraft. The crews were on edge. Whenever a car or truck came down the road, they craned their necks to see if it made the turn up the lane. Preddy joked that they should find the field telephone lines and cut them so they could get a break. No one took him up on the offer.

No orders had landed by lunchtime and they began to relax slightly. Even a few hours' rest was a welcome respite after the chaos of the last three days. The cook house put out soup and sandwiches for lunch. They sipped it from tin mugs under the trees. It was basic food but it felt like a feast.

Tank columns were rumoured to be trying to hook round the flank. Saundby wasn't willing to risk his slender resources on a fairytale so he ordered an armed reconnaissance. Ashton sent Pettifer and Chandler to take a look. Chandler found little of worth but just about everyone on the ground shot at him anyway, allied and German. Pettifer drew a blank as well.

Saundby kept his aircraft on a tight leash. He could have sent them up on the prowl but he thought it was better to give them a chance to recover. They'd got away with no casualties in the morning. Saundby thought it prudent not to push their luck any further. After the mess around the Maastricht bridges, he knew there was another advance coming. He wanted to keep the Wing ready for that.

On the evening of the 12th May, three armoured Corps had pushed through the supposedly impassable Ardennes forest. Columns of tanks had gathered along the river, ready to strike. On the 13th, they attacked. Over two thousand tanks supported by massed aerial bombing advanced on the Meuse. Here was Blitzkrieg at its finest, an all arms affair with each unit aware of its place and what it had to do.

French units wilted under the heavy air attack. Their spirit broken and they fled, carrying other units along with them. Morale seemed was on the verge of collapse. Units behind the lines fled when they heard that German tanks had gotten around their flank. Before even a single enemy tank had crossed the river, there were gaps in the defensive line for them to drive through.

General Erwin Rommel's 7th Division made the first crossing north of Sedan at Dinant, smashing past concrete pillboxes and defensive strongpoints. Engineers started building pontoon bridges to get their tanks across the river to support the advance. Soldiers were amazed to see their divisional commander up to his waist in water, helping to move heavy baulks of timber. By the end of the day, they were across and securing their bridgehead.

General Guderian, the great proponent of rapid mobile warfare, led his three divisions to force two other crossings near Sedan. Pontoon bridges were put in place and the tanks rumbled across the water. All night, the Germans reinforced their positions on the western bank and consolidated. They were across, now they had to hold it.

By the late evening, the seriousness of the situation started to become apparent. This was no spoiling attack, but an assault in force, with power behind it. General Billotte of the 1st Army Group urged strongly for an immediate air attack on the bridgehead. Already under serious pressure to the north, he now had the Germans in strength on his right, threatening to cut him off from the 2nd Army.

There was consternation at Air Component Headquarters at the news. Most of the AASF airfields were around Rheims. Some of them were only fifteen minutes flying time from Sedan and were now under immediate threat. At the time they were being requested to attack the enemy bridgehead, they also had to consider the possibility of evacuation if there was a breakthrough.

The focus was shifting from the Belgian front to a wooded area on the Meuse River. Once again, action along the Meuse would dictate the shape of the offensive.

2.25 – Forty Pieces Of Silver

Just after midnight on the 14th, Saundby received orders to ignore his target priorities and put up nine aircraft to attack pontoon bridges around Dinant. The rest of his units were to be put on standby. Just after the new orders went out, another dispatch rider arrived and those instructions were cancelled too.

Word had come in that the French had successfully counterattacked and destroyed the bridges. New orders arrived requesting an attack as soon as light permitted. Nine Battles would attack transport at Charleville-Mezieres. A fighter escort was promised. At 3am, the orders were amended again. The number of aircraft required was reduced from nine to six.

Saundby watched his Wing staff update positions on the map as snippets of intelligence came in. It was like trying to assemble a giant jigsaw puzzle with bits missing. The Germans had attacked along a fifty mile front and already made significant gains. Squadron Leader Embery, Saundby's staff officer, read the latest signal.

"What happened to keeping the Battles back for night attacks!" he asked aloud, a little perplexed.

"I don't know," said Saundby, a little glum. At least coming in from the west at dawn, they would be attacking from the dark. That might give the vulnerable Battles some chance.

After the fiasco at Maastricht, Saundby planned this next raid with meticulous care. He didn't want a repeat of the losses the Wing had suffered on the 12th. He found out who'd been tasked to provide fighter cover and put a personal call through to the commander of the French Escadrille.

Bainbridge took off at 5am as the first rays of light were creeping over the horizon. He was pleasantly surprised when the promised escort turned up and they headed east. No 109s put in an appearance for which he was grateful. He'd come to dread those yellow noses.

At Charleville they found their target north of the town crawling with activity. Here, the river looped back on itself and a stub of land stuck out like a thumb. The water glittered like molten gold, catching the low angle of the morning sun. In the middle of the river was a spit of land about two hundred yards long. Pontoon bridges crossed over it on both sides. Bainbridge could see troops streaming over them like an army of ants.

Diving from four thousand feet, they dropped 250lb bombs on time delay fuses. All three bridges were hit and two were destroyed. The other was damaged but still there as the Battles turned for home.

Winwright put the squadron on standby at 4am after Wing asked for an armed reconnaissance to report on enemy troop movements near Deville. It took him a fast half second to decide and he sent for Chandler. A little bleary eyed and still rumpled from sleep, Chandler came in to the CO's office. He knew something was up when he saw Dane and Ashton were in there with him.

"I've got a job for you," Winwright said with no preamble. Chandler's mood turned sour as he guessed what was coming. "It's another recce job." Dane watched Chandler carefully. The lad's eyes glittered with intensity, his mouth fixed in a grim rictus of a smile.

"A Lysander spotted a force of enemy tanks and infantry around Deville," Winwright said, he pointed it out on the map. "We also need you to take a look around Charleville-Mezieres. The bridges there are being attacked this morning but we'll need an assessment of how successful that is and what the trooop concentrations are like. The French army are screaming for help, but Wing won't commit us-"

"-without knowing where they are first." Chandler finished for him.

Now Chandler really felt ill. He rubbed his eyes, they felt gritty. His stomach was doing flip flops on him at the thought of going up alone once more. He was just tired enough to be a little belligerent.

"Why me?" he asked sullenly.

"Because I said so," Ashton rapped sharply, speaking for the first time. "This isn't a democracy, Chandler. You've done recce jobs before. I know you'll press on and get it done and you've got the experience to make it count."

Chandler nodded quiet acceptance. He glanced out the window. It was going to be another clear day. He could feel it. There wouldn't be much to hide behind out there.

"I'll go and get ready," he said in resignation. This was a far cry from that first day when he was sent up to recce along the coast for a German Cruiser. He'd just been an ignorant boy then. He knew the risks now. He knew he could be picked off far too easily by a stray fighter as easy as winking.

He swung by the cookhouse and got them to make him some sandwiches and a couple of flasks of tea. If Winwright wanted them up immediately, that meant no time for breakfast. They'd have to eat on the hoof this morning. After getting his crew together, he took off just after 4.30am loaded with two 250lb bombs so he could attack if a target presented itself.

The sky was starting to lighten and the deep black had given way to hints of mauve and blue as he climbed away. The land below was dark but flashes on the horizon kept going off like fireworks on bonfire night as the fighting continued.

He levelled off at 8,000 feet and headed east. Morgan was studying his maps intently when he noticed his pencils kept rolling back and forth across his navigation table.

"Problem, skipper?" he asked.

"We're fine, Morg, you just worry about your maps. The last thing I want to do today is end up in the wrong place."

Chandler tried to keep his response light, but Morgan heard the underlying tension there. He leaned back for a moment and watched Chandler as he flew. He was making big corrections on the controls, holding on too tight, his face a mask of concentration.

"Coming up to the turn, skipper," Morgan said on the intercom. Chandler nodded and took up the new heading automatically.

As they got closer to the Ardennes, a ground haze clung to the trees, wiping out details. Visibility began to reduce and Chandler was forced to descend to see anything. He came down to 5,000 feet and dodged in and out of some wisps of cloud.

On the road leading from Deville he saw heavy troop movements in the woods. Light flak started to reach for him and he took the Blenheim back up and changed his course. The flak stopped so he let down again after a few miles. The closer he got to Charleville the more troops he saw. Machine gun nests were being constructed along the roadside.

Emerging into a clear patch of air, flak fired at them. Chandler stamped on the rudder pedal to get out of the way. He came around and then dived, jinking left and right to throw the flak off. They made one pass over Charleville-Mezieres. Once was enough. He saw the results of the morning raid and noted the feverish activity to put the damaged pontoon bridge to rights. On the south side of town, he could see that the two road bridges were still intact.

He reversed his course and followed the road leading to Hirson. Not long after as he passed over a small village, the Germans had gotten themselves into a bit of a mess. A tank had rammed a truck at a crossroads and the traffic was backed up behind the log jam.

Chandler put his Blenheim into a shallow dive and dropped his load on the crossroads. Coming from the east, the Germans weren't expecting him. The first they knew, explosions were going off around them, turning the young day as bright as the sun.

They got away clean without a shot being fired. Morgan made a note of some tanks under the trees and marked their position on his map as they continued to head west.

Back at Headquarters the situation was deteriorating. The planned French counter attack had stalled before it even got started. An attack by the 2nd Army had run head first into the German 10th Panzer division on the Stonne Plateau. To the west, the French 6th Army was now engaged with lead elements of the 1st and 2nd Panzer Divisions.

Like a door slowly opening, a crack was developing between the French lines. If the Germans could exploit it further, they could sweep down the middle and cut the allied forces in two.

Barratt knew he didn't have enough aircraft to force a result at Sedan on his own. He requested a combined effort with the French Air Force, which was agreed. It was decided they would send in four waves of bombers with heavy fighter escort to attack the bridgehead.

Saundby was mulling over target lists when he was told Air Vice Marshall Barratt wanted to speak to him personally. Saundby looked up from his work in surprise. He'd made an almost standard request for more replacements only an hour ago. That wasn't something that would warrant a call from Barratt. Saundby took the call at his desk. Embery sat across from him, his lap full of recce photographs.

"Saundby here, sir."

"Saundby," boomed Barratts voice. "There's a strike order coming through to you now but I wanted to emphasise the seriousness of the situation we have facing us."

"I understand, sir," Saundby said; his voice cautious. Barratt continued.

"I know you've got target priorities along the Dyle Line that you've already had to delay but this is more important. I may even go so far as to say that the importance of the next few hours may decide the whole campaign."

Saundby sat up a little straighter. Embery saw the change in demeanour and wondered what was being said.

"I want you to send everything you have against the German advance in Sedan. The exact details will be in the signal. The Hun has made some gains and they're now threatening a breakthrough in that sector. The French don't have much on the ground to stop them."

Saundby glanced at the large scale map of France on his office wall. He could almost picture great columns of German tanks pouring through the gap in the line and fanning out across France.

"What's the situation now, sir?"

"Confused, to say the least. The French say they're holding the line but they're also asking for all available aircraft to bomb the advancing German columns. I leave you to draw your own conclusions." Saundby grimaced, hearing Barratt loud and clear. "Throw everything you have into the attack."

"Even the Battles?" Saundby said in concern. Sending the Battles up at first light was a little different to attacking in broad daylight.

"Even the Battles," Barratt repeated, although it pained him to say it. "We have to mass enough strength to deliver a knockout blow."

"But, sir-"

"I'm aware of the risks, Saundby," Barratt said, cutting him off. "But there it is. We have to flood their defences with numbers. I don't want a repeat of Maastricht."

"No, sir."

"Good. Plan your attack for the afternoon."

The line was cut and Saundby carefully replaced the handset into its cradle. As he did so, one of the clerks knocked on the door and came in with a signal clutched in their hand.

"Sorry to bother you, sir, more strike orders from HQ."

Saundby had to read it twice before it sunk in. He was directed to make further attacks on the bridges at Charleville-Mezieres. The signal called for a maximum effort with a second raid at tea time. French bombers would attack the same targets while he was rearming for the second strike.

Saundby eyed the timetable carefully. In all, there would be four waves of raids planned for that afternoon to try and saturate the enemy defences. He sat at his desk, feeling hollow. Saying nothing, he handed the signal to Embery. Embery's eyebrows shot up.

"This will take some coordinating."

"I know." Saundby picked up a pencil from the top of his desk and gripped it tightly as he stared off into the distance.

"Surely the situation can't be that bad, sir?"

"Evidently, HQ thinks so, Embery." He glanced up to see Embery's face wracked with concern. "Maximum effort, John. If we can stall the Germans here, we gain a breathing space to regroup. If we save the Battles for later, there may not *be* a later. How many can we put up?" he asked.

323

"Bainbridge can put up eight. The other squadron's a little low, five, maybe six."

"And Winwright?"

"He had some replacements yesterday, at least ten, perhaps twelve."

Saundby nodded grimly. It was all starting to run away from them. All the plans made last winter about supporting an advance, torn to shreds.

"Signal Merville and Bois Fontaine and tell them to get cracking to make the kites ready. HQ wants to schedule the first wave for 2pm."

As Embery left the office, Saundby leaned against the desk with his eyes closed. It was going to be Maastricht all over again. He could feel it in his bones.

2.26 – Today's Fox

Winwright used the morning lull to get the remaining aircraft ready for action. Harding and Hunter had turned up on the back of a white horse. Footsore and tired, they'd found it wandering along a country road, so it only seemed fair to appropriate it. Winwright's only concern now was Chandler and his crew.

They'd still not returned from their recce and were long past the point of no return. Dane rang around a few airfields and army units but it was proving difficult. It was a large front; he could easily have come down in the countryside somewhere. Just when they were beginning to write him off, a French liaison officer at Wing rang to say that Chandler and his crew were unhurt.

An hour later, a battered military Citroen drove up to the guard at the gate. Chandler got out, rubbing his back. He dragged his parachute harness out of the boot and slung it over his shoulder. The Citroen went off with a swirl of dust and exhaust fumes. Chandler didn't bother to say goodbye to the driver. Face like thunder, he stomped over to the flight hut, Morgan and Griffiths dutifully following along behind. He dumped his gear on the floor and perched on a stool, shoulders hunched. Ashton appeared at the door to Winwright's office nursing a mug of tea.

"Tough day?" he had asked as casually as he could. Chandler shot him a look.

"Sod the French and sod the Jerries." He swivelled on the stool and kicked out at his parachute. "And if one of our gallant allies from the Armée de L'Air decides to pay us a visit, then I'm not holding myself responsible for what happens."

As he finished talking, Morgan and Griffiths piled their parachutes on the grass outside and shambled into the room. Griffiths looked exhausted while Morgan glanced at Ashton.

"Have you told him?"

"I hadn't got to that part yet," said Chandler.

Ashton walked over and put the kettle on the stove.

"We figured something had happened when you were overdue, but none of the local spotters had seen anything. The French only let us know they were bringing you across an hour ago." He stirred the water with a spoon and tapped the lid twice. The orderly Corporal brought over some tin mugs and set them up on the desk.

There was a pause while they waited for the kettle to boil. Morgan watched the flames jump in the grate and listened to the water as it bubbled in time with his temper. Ashton noticed Chandler's hands unconsciously clench and unclench but said nothing. He wrapped a rag around the handle to pour out three mugs of tea, adding milk. He handed the mugs round. Chandler sipped his carefully.

"What happened?" enquired Ashton, judging that the time was right.

"You'll laugh when you hear it; it's a corker this is. We were on our way back from Charleville but leaking fuel. One of the last bursts of flak had caught the wing tanks. We were never going to make it back, so Morgan gave us a steer to the nearest airfield." He flicked his fingers, trying to think of the name.

"Doaui," Morgan reminded him.

"Doaui. Anyway, we were coming straight in on final approach. I was taking my time because the flaps wouldn't come down when a bloody Morane shot us up. We had wheels down and everything."

He shuddered as he remembered the bullets thudding into the thin metal skin. Chandler had been able to keep the wings level but that was about it. The Blenheim hit hard, bounced once, twice and then ran to a halt, leaking fuel over the runway. They were out before it had even stopped moving in case it brewed up.

A Citroen came speeding across the grass to them followed by an ambulance and a fire tender. It was all Chandler could do to keep himself from flattening the French Captain who got out of the car to see how they were.

"I'm telling you, we have to do something about our little French brothers. We need to parade a Blenheim under their noses again so they know what one looks like. This is the *second,* no!" he corrected himself, "the *third* time they've done this to me."

Ashton gave a wry smile at the understatement. He could hear the strain in Chandler's voice. Pettifer came through the door whistling away quite happily as he polished an apple on his chest. He took in the little scene in a fast second, caught Ashton's slight shake of the head and did an abrupt about face.

"Did you see much?" Ashton asked.

"We got a peek over the front and I got some pretty good shots with a camera." Morgan tugged out a crumpled up map from inside his Sidcot and unfolded it on the table. He used a pencil to point out specific features. "We saw a build up of armour heading west away from Charleville. It's crawling with infantry around there." Ashton made some notes as Morgan carried on talking. "I figure there was at least another Division on the way. We dropped some bombs, caused a bit of mayhem"

"Then we sprinted for home," finished Chandler.

"You chaps look like you could do with some food," said Ashton.

"Better make it fast," said Winwright, joining the conversation as he came out of his office. "We take off in an hour and I need my best pilots out there."

It was a simple remark but one that had the desired effect. Shoulders went back, heads lifted a little higher.

"All right, sir," said Chandler. "We'll give it a go." Nodding his thanks, Winwright watched them wearily leave the hut to hunt up some food, their nerves still on edge.

Ashton went back into the CO's office. Winwright was deep in conversation with Dane going over intelligence reports and maps. Ashton handed over Morgan's notepad to Dane who started flicking through the pages.

"A French fighter jumped them; *again.*"

Winwright scowled and shoved his pipe between his teeth, clamping down hard on the stem.

"Bloody French. How could they miss the coloured roundels?"

"Maybe they thought he was a Dornier?" Dane offered, trying to be generous. Ashton didn't dignify that remark with a response.

"It's happening too often," said Winwright shortly. "We can't afford to lose a single aircraft." His voice was edged in anger. They'd already been knocked back for extra replacement aircraft. The last thing they needed was to lose any more from stupid accidents or mistakes. Ashton put Morgan's map down on the table and explained the results of the reconnaissance.

Dane went to update Wing while Ashton and Winwright left to get the crews together. As they walked across the field, they could hear the thump of heavy guns in the distance. One or two groundcrew looked nervously towards the horizon and Ashton noted that the gun pits paid a little more attention to the sky. Kittinger was prowling round keeping them on their toes.

They found Chandler down by the aircraft talking with the erks while Burke was supervising the bombing up. Morgan and Griffiths were flat out on the grass under the shade of some trees. Winwright waved for his pilots to come over.

Under the lee of the nearest Blenheim, Winwright spread out Morgan's map and went through his briefing. A light breeze ruffled through the trees behind them and the sun beat down. It was a nice day with clear skies and good visibility for miles, perfect fighter weather. He would have preferred more broken clouds as cover but they had a job to do.

He looked at each of his pilots. Chandler and Pettifer, serious and all business. Naisby was smiling, still too fresh to regard it as anything other than a game. Nugent was crouched over the map while he listened attentively. Winwright would lead the first element, Ashton the second, Farmer the third.

"We'll go in at 8,000 feet. High enough to dodge the light stuff but still low enough for some good bombing. Keep it nice and tight, we'll have fighters to escort us in," he told the assembled crews.

There was little reaction to that. They'd heard this more than once before. Preddy was tempted to blow a raspberry but Ashton was looking right at him.

Winwright laid out a new map on the ground in front of them. He put two stones down north and south of the town. The Meuse wrapped around Charleville like a coil of rope. There were three key road bridges that would allow traffic to cross from the east to the west bank. Chandler's recce confirmed there were still two bridges standing as well as the pontoon bridges at Montcy-Notre Dame.

"I've spoken with Squadron Leaders Bainbridge and Chancellor at Merville. They're going to attack the pontoon bridges here to the east." He indicated the position on the map. Necks craned to see where he indicated. "That leaves us these road bridges over the river here. We will attack in our elements but we'll have to play it by ear once we know what we have to deal with. French bomber squadrons are going to attack after us and mop up what we miss. Be careful on your bomb runs," he emphasised with them. "We have to succeed against this target at all costs. Questions?" No one spoke. "Then let's go."

Chandler watched as the last bomb was winched up into the bay.

Chewing on a crust, he settled himself in the cockpit and made sure everything was set how he liked it. He raised the seat slightly and then tried the rudder pedals. Satisfied with the movement, he started the engines while Morgan sorted out his maps and instruments in the nose. Griffiths checked the radio and then his turret. None of them said anything about that morning.

Griffiths hands shook as he thought about scrambling out of their Blenheim. The first time he'd bailed out, Chandler had managed to hold the bomber straight and level. Escaping from the tail wasn't easy. You had to get out from the turret, twist through a small gap, clip on your parachute, open the hatch and jump.

Griffiths was tall, probably too tall for the Blenheim, and he found getting in and out difficult enough at the best of times. When the Blenheim had gone in hard his mouth went dry. He'd panicked when his harness got caught on the turret and he lost precious seconds freeing himself before he was able to make his fingers work.

Nugent's Blenheim failed to start. Burke went running down the line to demand action while the erks worked double quick time to figure out the problem.

Chandler fretted at the delay. He watched his engine temperatures rise as they waited. His back hurt from the hard landing and his eye and cheeks still throbbed after headbutting the yoke. He was surprised his hands could be so steady on the controls. Finally, a green flare arced across the field. He waved an arm out of the side window and the chocks were tugged clear.

The first element pulled out; then Ashton's Blenheim swung out of the line in a wide circle. Chandler held his aircraft on the brakes and then let them go as he inched the throttles forward, taking up position on Ashton's port side. Pettifer was on his right. Nugent and Hagen lined up behind Farmer in the third element.

Once the CO had taken off, Ashton waited a moment more and then opened up the throttles. Chandler waited a few seconds before following after him.

"Here we go again," he muttered.

Burke stood with his hands in the pockets of his coveralls as he watched them go. He wondered how many would return this time.

The Battles and the Blenheims headed towards Charleville-Mezieres independently. They'd talked about going in as one group, but decided it was better to attack separately. That way, if any one formation was caught by flak or fighters, the other might still get through. The plan had been to take off at 3pm but Winwright was delayed ten minutes by Nugent's problem.

Mercifully, their escorts were waiting for them and took up position ahead of the Battles, sweeping the way clear on the way to the target. As they got closer, Bainbridge closed the throttle slightly to open up a gap between his formation and that of Chancellor. When they were half a mile or so ahead, he started to drift down, heading in for the bridges.

He picked up his target soon enough. He saw one of the pontoon bridges had been repaired. Engineers were in the process of putting a third bridge across the river. Plumes of smoke drifted up from the fields around the town, tell tale signs that the first French wave had met with stiff resistance. He kept watching the sky for enemy fighters.

The flak started to come up, black blots dirtying the sky. He told his men to open up their formation but warned them to close up fast if enemy fighters put in an appearance.

Chancellor and his five Battles went in first. He led his men down in a steep dive. The flak intensified. Lines of tracer reached up and hunted the bombers. Bainbridge watched helplessly as they were picked off one after another.

The tail end Battle blew up, a bright flare. A second nosed straight into the river. The three survivors pulled out of their dive and Bainbridge saw the splashes as the bombs sliced into the water around the bridges. Then there was one explosion, two, three, four. Debris blew into the air. Smoke and dust flew up, obscuring the target. As they pulled out of their dive, flak claimed a third victim. It ploughed into a house on the river bank and burned. The surviving two Battles headed north, trying to outrun the flak.

Bainbridge watched events unfold with both pride and dismay. The amount of guns around the bridges was terrifying. It was far heavier than it had been that morning. It looked like the Germans had put every anti aircraft gun they had around the bridges. The sky turned black with explosions but Chancellor and his men had pressed home their attacks with unbelievable courage. Now it was his squadron's turn to run the gauntlet of defences.

Still some way from the bridge, 109s started to appear. Hurricanes did their best but they were hopelessly outnumbered. The first one to fall was Macy, a bright faced twenty four year old from Sheffield. There was a massive bang up front and oil spattered over his canopy. He bailed out with his crew at two thousand feet, landing in a field outside of town.

Rather than wait to be picked off, Bainbridge led his flight down in a steep spiral to keep their tail clear. They levelled off at five hundred feet and raced towards the bridges. The fighters followed them down but broke off when the flak closed in, leaving the Battles to the blizzard of the guns.

The smoke from Chancellor's attack cleared. Bainbridge saw one Pontoon bridge drifting downriver. That left two more to take out.

Flak exploded under his nose and his Battle roared through a chain of black puffs, tendrils of smoke swirling off the wingtips. A piece of shrapnel starred the canopy. Bainbridge had seen nothing like it. He glanced over his shoulders and saw his other aircraft still tucked in close. Simpson was on his left, Fanshaw on his right.

They flashed over a battery of 37mm flak guns and the gunners traversed like mad, trying to keep the bombers in their sights. The German gunners couldn't believe it. They'd been expecting massed formations of aircraft to knock down the bridges. Coming over piecemeal like this, it allowed them to concentrate their fire on each group. It was like swatting flies.

The Battles opened out their formation, giving themselves room to manoeuvre. A tree passed between Bainbridge and Simpson and he went even lower. He would only pull up at the last moment, he decided, using the terrain as much as possible to mask his approach. His men followed him, dodging left and right to avoid the lines of tracer that reached up for them.

The closer they got, the worse it became and finally their luck ran out. One man down already, the second Section was caught by a string of 20mm shells as big as cricket balls. Three sawed off Wright's tail. He ploughed a furrow into the ground, before his bombs exploded.

Bainbridge passed under some telegraph wires and then screamed over rooftops at fifty feet. Simpson followed close behind but reacted too late and wrapped himself around a pylon. His starboard wing sheared off and the nose pitched up before he went in.

Down to three aircraft, Bainbridge charged on. He angled left to avoid a tall poplar tree and the Section went straight over a battery of guns in a grassy park. Every gun was pointed in the air and perforated the Fairey Battles. Bainbridge's navigator, doubled over, screaming as he clutched his stomach. His gunner arched his back, arms flailing as bullets shredded his spine. He collapsed over his gun, blood gushing from his mouth.

Bainrbridge's feet jerked on the pedals as bullets smashed into his legs. The nose dipped and he fought back waves of pain as he hauled back on the stick, coaxing the bomber into a climb. His stomach burned and he knew he had very little time left. He was committed now.

"Just a few more minutes," he murmured. He shoved the throttle forward, the lever slippery in his hand. His vision narrowed to the target in front of him. He could see the line of the river. The water glowed almost silver under the sun, like a halo. He saw the little dots of men and trucks driving over the bridge. He aimed his whole aircraft at the bridge, picking a pontoon with a tank on as his target.

Darkness flickered at the edge of his vision. Objects telescoped in front of him. He saw a man sat on the commander's cupola in the turret of the tank. They were pointing at him, gesturing madly. Bainbridge smiled as he bore in, flame streaming out from under the cowling. His eyes closed and his hands went slack on the spade grip. The nose dipped and his Battle plunged into the water fifty yards short of the pontoon he'd been aiming for. A huge plume of water went up as his bombs exploded and drenched the tank.

A flak burst claimed Simpson. He was still snarling when shells walked up the fuselage and blew up the fuel tanks. The port wing tore off and his Battle buried itself by the side of the river. Spooked by the slaughter in front of them, the remaining aircraft broke off their attack. Before they could come back in again from a different direction, the fighters took care of him.

Mansell tried to coax his crippled aircraft along but it was no use. Hot Glycol was blowing all over him, scalding his face. He could feel the controls going limp and he tried to find somewhere to put the Battle down. As they went in, he aimed between two trees. The wings ripped off and the fuselage shot through the gap, coming to a halt against a stone wall. That was how the Germans found him, calmly sat on the wreckage having a cigarette. When he was finished, he was marched into captivity.

2.27 – Fingers In The Dam

Ten minutes behind Bainbridge, Winwright saw none of this. If he had, he might have changed his attack plan. Instead, he came on in the same old style. Everyone was tucked in nice and neat. Three elements of three, each element formated on the leader. Above them was their escort, nine Morane 406 fighters. Even with the escorts, they still felt vulnerable and they constantly craned their necks, watching for trouble.

As they made their final turn for the target, the 109s appeared. Twelve of them came in from four o'clock, circling around to attack from the rear. Winwright looked over his shoulder when he heard the warning. The sun was over there. They were taking their time to come in for a perfect bounce. He glanced up at the French fighters. They were serenely sailing along, seemingly oblivious.

Winwright's gunner kept up the commentary. The 109s were now passing six o'clock and getting closer. Finally, the Moranes reacted. They scattered left and right. Six going to port, three breaking hard to starboard. Engines screaming they climbed to meet the Germans head on.

"Buster, buster," called Winwright. He waited a second and advanced the throttles, pouring on the coals. His aircraft surged forwards, the extra power giving him a few more knots of airspeed.

The 109s blew past the Moranes. They weren't interested in them, they wanted the bombers. They would get one free attack before the French could come back around and intervene. Lining up on the rear of the formation, the leader ordered his men to pick their targets. In a rough line, they opened fire, lashing the Blenheims.

Nugent's ailerons were shot away and his Blenheim started to go down in a lazy spiral. He tried to correct by juggling the throttles and stamping hard on the rudder but couldn't get her back.

He waited two seconds for his navigator to drop clear before bailing out himself. Floating down on the end of his parachute he watched the Blenheim pick up speed as it dived. No third parachute appeared before it slammed into the ground far below.

He landed on top of a French infantry unit. There was a moment's confusion when he was hauled to his feet and bayonets were shoved under his nose. He gabbled fast in a mish mash of French and English until a Lieutenant took control. He was hustled to a company command post in the rear. While a truck carried him south, he watched the skies to the north.

Nugent was the only one to fall on the first pass, although all the others sustained damage. Winwright spat blood from his mouth and held a hand to his forehead as the stench of burnt wiring stung his nostrils. Half his cockpit instruments were smashed but the engines sounded okay so he pressed on.

Hagen saw the strikes go in on Winwright's aircraft even as his own was hit. There was a brief chatter of machine gun fire from the turret, then Guilroy's replacement gave a terse, "I'm hit!" and went silent. A 109 whipped between them and the CO to the right. Seconds later, a grey and green Morane chased after it.

Hagen's face was a mask of concentration as he battled to keep tucked in on Winwright's wing. Coming up from the nose, his navigator, Jones looked back down the fuselage. Their gunner was slumped in his turret. Without even thinking about it, he shook off his parachute harness and then crawled over the main spar. Wind whistled through holes in the metal skin as he crawled in the gloom of the fuselage.

Jones pulled Andrews down from the turret. The boy was spark out, he was pale and his skin was wet and clammy. No blood was visible but Andrews was wearing a thick Irvin jacket so it was hard to tell. Jones dragged the youngster to the main spar and left him propped up before going back to the turret.

He had to blink a few times to let his eyes adjust, suddenly going from dark to light. He rotated the turret left and right and found everything was still working. Aircraft were milling around all over the place. The Moranes were mixing it up with the 109s, doing their best to keep them off the Blenheims.

Jones fired at a 109 that was coming from dead astern. He only managed a few shots before the gun went click. Ammunition pans were scattered over the floor but he found a full one and slapped it on. The yellow nose was much closer and Jones opened fire the same time the fighter did.

Balls of tracer seemed to come right at him and he felt an almighty blow to the right side of his temple. Putting up a hand, he expected it to come back red with blood. His head was pounding and it felt like his ear had been shot off. He felt gingerly to find a gaping hole in his flying helmet where the earpiece had been. Flushed with relief, Jones carried on working the turret and fired at any 109 that came too near.

The Moranes did their best but they were outclassed. Underpowered and under armed, they took the fight to the Germans to try and give the Blenheims the breathing space they needed to make their attack. One Morane chased a 109 and fired as he closed to point blank range, his 20mm cannon sawing through the 109s tail. Before he could celebrate the victory, two more 109s skewered him in a crossfire. The French pilot died as his aircraft came apart around him.

Winwright took the corrections from Willis as they came up to the target. The road bridge was a short one but it was packed with traffic heading south. Infantry were visible spreading out across the countryside.

Flak came up at them in a storm. It was heavy stuff too. Winwright predicted some 88's were mixed in amongst the lighter guns they were expecting. Hagen gritted his teeth as he saw the wall of flak. It was no worse than it had been around Maastricht but now he knew just what it could do.

Willis had no problem correcting for drift as he looked through his bomb sight. Burning buildings in the town were putting up plumes of smoke that allowed him to judge the wind. He tried to ignore the large number of burning aircraft littering the countryside.

The flak intensified. Winwright barrelled through a stinking sulphurous shell burst. Willis cringed when a fragment smashed one of the nose panels.

As the crosshairs drifted over the bridge, Willis waited one more second and then hit the bomb release. The Blenheim leapt up as the bombs fell out of the bay. Winwright clung to his course for ten more seconds to give the rest of the squadron a chance to drop their loads.

Sutherland was on the CO's starboard side when there was an almighty crash and he was blown almost upside down. He fought the controls, getting the Blenheim back onto an even keel to find he was quite alone. The almighty bang had been Winwright. One moment he was there, the next, a big orange ball of burning fuel took his place. Farmer went right; Ashton went left, taking their elements with them to avoid the debris. Sutherland could only see one other Blenheim in the sky, so he headed straight for it.

"Fighters coming in fast astern, skipper!" Garfield called from his turret.

Sutherland poured on the coals, dropping the nose to gain some speed. The port engine was vibrating and he shot a glance left. Part of the cowling had been blown off. A two foot jet of blue flame shot out of the head of one of the cylinders. There were holes all over the wing and a six inch gash was torn in the floor of the cockpit to his right. The windscreen was smashed and he hitched over in his seat to get a better forward view.

Hagen's cockpit had lit up with the flash of the explosion and he also had to fight to keep his bomber under control. Farmer's element was off to his left so he angled towards them. He wouldn't last five seconds on his own. As he joined up, Sutherland slid in next to him.

Ashton, Chandler and Pettifer were racing to form back up when the 109s fell on them. Pettifer took the brunt of the first pass. His bomber lurched under the battering. The port engine burst into flame as sparks glittered over the wings. Cannon rounds pinned Pettifer into his seat as they lashed down the fuselage.

The bomber lurched, reared up and then rolled over onto its back, the dive steepening rapidly. The gunner kept on firing all the way down. No one bailed out before it ploughed into the ground.

Ashton pulled in alongside Hagen as Farmer took the whole formation down to the ground. The 109s followed them and Farmer saw their death written there until the Moranes saved them.

The four surviving escorts dashed back into the fray. The 109s were so intent on the kill that the Moranes got a free shot, destroying two and damaging two more before the Germans realised they were there. The 109s sheared off to get themselves out of trouble.

Although he never lived to see it, Willis' aim had been bang on. The gods had been smiling and his four 250lb bombs hit the bridge dead centre. The span came apart, spilling trucks and tanks and men into the river below. The rest of the squadron's bombs fell like rain upon the bridge.

French infantry watched the carnage from the ridge overlooking the town. Standing next to a Char B heavy tank was Cullen. While other reporters had followed the action north, he'd gone east, smelling a story. There had been spoiling attacks on the Maginot Line and he wanted to see it for himself.

333

Begging a lift with an army unit, he was on his way there when the Germans attacked at Sedan.

He stood there, pencil and pad in hand as he watched one allied bomber after another get blown out of the sky. The wrecks littered the countryside around the town and he counted at least twenty plumes of smoke. He'd already seen the Battles get chopped down, now he saw the nine Blenheims come in. He watched the 109s make their attack. He flinched when the leading Blenheim blew up, pieces of it tumbling to the ground. He tracked the bombs down and saw them hit the bridge.

Another Blenheim took the death plunge. Flame poured out of its port engine and wrapped around the wing. Cullen made another mark on the pad as he kept a running tally. Thirty one.

He'd already seen the Potez and Amiot bombers of the Armee de L'Air get slaughtered not an hour before. Now the same thing was happening to the RAF. There was no glory, no chivalry like the old films, no knights of the air.

"Murder, it's pure bloody murder," he murmured.

"C'est la guerre," agreed the Captain stood next to him.

Cullen turned away, sick to his stomach. They had done it, the bridges had been blown but the cost was too horrible to contemplate.

The guns fell silent as the remaining Blenheims fled. They trailed smoke behind them while the surviving Moranes escorted them home. The gun crews relaxed, taking the opportunity of the lull to clean their weapons before another attack began. If things carried on like this, the war would be over in a matter of weeks. It was too easy, like shooting fish in a barrel.

They'd decimated the French bombers first, now the British had their turn for the same result. Over thirty aircraft had been shot down in exchange for some bridges and a few tanks. They were unconcerned. The pontoon bridges would be replaced in a matter of hours and the advance would continue unimpeded.

The survivors limped back to Bois Fontaine. The airfield had been bombed again while they'd been away. They gingerly picked their way around the craters and taxied into their bays. Two tents smouldered where the fires had been put out.

After shutting the engines down, Hagen sat in his cockpit feeling numb. Once again, everyone around him had been cut down and he'd sailed through unscathed. That was another of his lives gone. He joined the others around Dane as he stood with his ever present clipboard. Giving them all a winning smile, he stood waiting to hear their reports.

"Who wants to kick off the score?" he asked cheerfully.

Hagen pinched the bridge of his nose for a second. He shared a look with Ashton and shook his head. The man had just no idea, none at all.

"We got the bridges," said Ashton flatly. "The CO led us in and Willis was bang on the money. The Battles got the rest. The pontoon bridges on the north side of town are gone as well."

"And what about Nugent?"

"I saw him bail out," said Farmer, his voice gruff. "I saw at least one chute."

"I saw two," said Naisby quietly.

"They bailed out well before the bomb run. There's a good chance they'll have been picked up," said Ashton. He lit a cigarette and used it hard.

"The CO?"

They shifted uneasily on their feet. Dane looked from face to face. No one could meet his eye. It was like trying to get blood from a stone.

"Blew up. He just bloody blew up," said Hagen. The flash was still imprinted on his eyelids. "I was right alongside him when he blew." He shuddered. "Bits everywhere. Same with Pettifer. They just chopped him down. It was a slaughter."

"But you're sure you got the bridges?" pressed Dane.

Chins lifted and every face looked at him. Dane shrank slightly under their stares and for the first time he felt the wall that separated him from them. He might be a part of the squadron, but he could never truly share their world. He was a penguin, a flightless bird and that was all he would ever be.

"I just hope it was bloody worth it," said Ashton sourly.

Saundby waited in his office for the results. He sat perched on the edge of his chair, his elbows balanced on the edge of the desk. When he heard a telephone ring in the office outside, he tensed. His ashtray was filled with the stubs of cigarettes. He lit another and wrung his hands. Time ticked by. There was a light knock at the door and Embery came in. He waved a folder.

"Reports just in, sir."

Saundby held out his hand and Embery silently passed over the folder. He put it on the top of the desk. He squared it so that it was parallel to the edge of the table, two inches in. His eyes focused on the green leather of the table top. His hand reached for the corner of the folder and then went back to his lap. He couldn't bear to open it. He looked up and turned bleak eyes on Embery.

"What's the count?"

Embery suddenly found something very interesting on the floor.

"Ten. Ten got back, sir." Saundby flinched like he'd been physically slapped. "Six Blenheims and four Battles. There's more." Saundby's head came back up, braced for the worst. "Winright, Bainbridge and Chancellor bought it as well."

The clock ticked. Saundby stared at the folder. Finally he sighed and stood up. Walking to the map on the wall, he looked at it without really seeing. Twelve aircraft, thirty six men, gone, just like that and no telling how many wounded.

"And the bridges?" he got out, his voice cracking.

"It looks like they got them all, sir."

"What about Sedan?"

"We've not heard anything yet, but the French have taken an awful pasting too. Sir, do you still want to schedule the next wave? Sir?"

Saundby continued to stare at the wall.

"Thank you, Embery."

Embery remained in the middle of the office for a moment but Saundby said nothing more. Embery left the room so he never saw the silent tears rolling down Saundby's face.

At AASF headquarters, Barratt stared at the casualty figures on his desk.

Ninety three aircraft dispatched, fifty lost and many more unserviceable due to battle damage. Over fifty percent losses. It was probably the worst casualty rate the RAF had ever suffered.

Barratt had thrown his aircraft into the breach to try and stem the tide, but he was no Henry V and this was no Battle of Agincourt. It had been a slaughter and he was the architect of that. If his planes went in low, the flak got them. If they went in high, the Messerschmitt's were waiting for them.

Reports said they'd got the bridges and they'd bombed numerous targets on the roads around Sedan, but that wasn't going to stop the Germans. It was up to the French army to do their part now.

As the extent of the casualties became known, the French postponed the third bombing wave. At AASF Headquarters, Barratt pondered his choices. He was damned if he did and damned if he didn't. They needed to keep the pressure on the Germans to support any counter attacks, but at the current rate of attrition, his units would be wiped out by the end of the day. He had no choice, he cancelled the fourth wave.

2.28 – Bitter Ashes

Chandler wound his way through the crush with two bottles of wine in his hands. He barged a soldier out of the way and slumped heavily into an empty chair at the table.

"Plonk, red, for the drinking of."

He handed a bottle over to Farmer and they started pouring out wine to the assembled throng. Crumbs littered the table where they had demolished a block of pate and sticks of bread. A waiter put more bread on the table and they began nibbling again.

Ashton had warned them not to get too plastered. Every indication was that they would be on again in the morning but they knew that already. They also had the good sense to reign in the drinking. No one wanted to fly with a hangover. Once everyone had been served, Farmer held up his glass and there was a momentary hush amongst the hubbub in the bar.

"Absent friends," he said quietly. He emptied his glass in one go and sat back down. Chandler polished off his glass and waited for more wine to be delivered. He folded his arms and slumped onto the table, resting his chin on top.

The mood was subdued. The losses of the last few days still rubbed raw. Farmer suddenly smiled and nodded when a random fragment of memory popped into his head.

"I was just remembering what Osbourne said about 109s being money for jam," he said.

"Didn't he get that wrong," said Preddy.

"We got a lot of things wrong," replied Morgan gloomily. Naisby just blinked rapidly and listened. This was all past history for him. He was the baby, the newcomer.

"I miss that great lump," Farmer said.

"Yeah, but *he* was smart," said Preddy. "He got himself a blighty wound as my old dad used to say."

Sutherland held up his hand and said sotto voce "Please, sir. Can I have one too?" They laughed at that. Maybe it wasn't such a bad idea. Sutherland draped his leg on the table, shoving plates out of the way with his foot. He pulled up his trouser leg. "Just a small one," he said. "See?" He pointed to the meaty part of his calf. "Right there."

They beat at him with their peaked caps.

"Who says you get to go first!"

"Get down."

"Lunatic."

Laughing, Sutherland raised his arm and clicked his fingers in the air.

"Garcon! Vino!"

When one of the waiters vaguely looked in his direction, Sutherland demanded food and drink. There was a wild air in the bar that evening. The booms of the guns were closer. People imagined the end of the world was coming. Champagne and wine was being sold at rock bottom prices. The singer on stage was belting out something slow and sexy, but it was just background noise. The squadron had already seen the edge of hell, so this was nothing.

There were less soldiers in the bar than usual. They'd all gone to the front, but it was as busy as ever. A few young women went from man to man, their eyes scared, looking for a protector.

A striking brunette draped herself over Naisby. Social niceties seemed to count for little this evening. There was no idle chit chat, no come hither or lingering gaze. She perched on a stool behind him and put an arm around his shoulders. She whispered something in French while her fragrance wafted over him. He blushed to the tips of his ears and tried to engage her in conversation. His pidgin French was embarrassing but she was prepared to make allowances.

Naisby found her eyes hypnotic. Everyone else found her curves hypnotic. She ran a hand along his arm. Her touch was like electricity and the hairs on his arm stood on end. His brain shorted out. There was a stirring down below but he was finding it hard to articulate it into words. Everyone else watched intently as this boy had paradise offered on a plate but seemed unable to pull it off. The wait was excruciating.

Preddy finally ran out of patience. He grabbed hold of the girl around her trim waist and lifted her off the stool. She screamed in anger and began kicking back with her high heels. He dropped her, clutching his shins.

"Bugger off!" he said, brushing her away. Her eyes narrowed and her mouth pulled thin.

"Cochon," she hissed, before moving on.

It had all happened so fast, Naisby just watched it happen. Now he suddenly woke up.

"I say-"

"Not suitable," Preddy said; very matter of fact. "Not suitable at all. I saved you. You should be thanking me."

Naisby half stood, sat down, stood up again and hovered like an idiot. He was still trying to figure out what to do. He sat back down, looking confused.

"That's awfully hard on a chap, you know," he said finally.

"You wouldn't know what to do anyway," said Preddy dismissively.

"I would too," pouted Naisby. He gave her pert behind a wistful glance as she sashayed off through the crowd. He liked the way the seam of the silk stockings went up her legs, but it was too late now. For a moment he contemplated going after her.

"No, no, no! *This* bit," Preddy held up his little finger. "Goes in *this* bit." He made a circle with his other thumb and forefinger and then jabbed his little finger through the gap. "It's really quite simple."

Naisby smiled and nodded.

"Silly me, I've been doing it wrong all these years and never realised."

His attention was diverted when a waiter walked past with a loaded tray. He appropriated two bottles of something and put them on the table. The waiter objected and reached over to get them back. Sutherland grabbed his tie and pulled it down, hard.

"Ah, ah," said Preddy, waving an admonishing finger. "Non, no, no, no." He leaned over and flicked the waiter on the nose and then beat him over the head with the knobby end of a bread stick. "No taking food from a table. That's exceptionally bad manners."

The waiter yelped and kept trying to stand back up. Sutherland pulled on his tie again and jerked him up and down like a jack in the box.

"Stop, stop, stop," said Farmer. "Stop! The man's starting to change colour."

Sutherland kept firm hold of the tie and turned his head slowly to look at Farmer. The waiter was going red in the face. Sutherland paused a few more seconds, waiting for the right moment and as the Waiter pulled back, he let go. The man toppled back and spilled on the floor.

"Can't hold his drink," he said. He took the bread stick off Preddy and sprinkled crumbs over the waiter's head. "Ashes to ashes, dust to dust," he muttered. The waiter rolled over onto his knees and crawled off, brushing crumbs out of his hair.

Naisby's navigator, Padgett came back from the mens loos. They all looked at him and beamed; the picture of innocence.

"What'd I miss?"

He was pelted with bits of bread and told to sit down.

"More drink!" they shouted.

Chandler leaned back and stretched. His back was still hurting after his rough landing earlier in the day. He rubbed his cheek, trying to massage some feeling back into it. A gorgeous shiner had come up on his left eye over the intervening hours, stark against the pale skin. He took a chunk of bread off the table and chewed rhythmically, in time with his thoughts.

"I wonder how the Battles got on?" asked Naisby innocently. He totally missed the look some of the others gave him. It was bad form to be talking shop like that. Although he'd flown during the day's raid, they still considered Naisby wet behind the ears, not quite as worthy as them.

"I'm not sure I want to know," muttered Farmer severely, trying to kill the conversation.

"We weren't the only ones who had a bad day," observed Preddy.

Chandler banged the empty bottle of wine on the table. He stood up and put on his peaked cap, tilting it forward over his eyes.

"Come on boys, this is getting too glum. Drink up and let's find some life."

There was a rumble of agreement. Some francs were thrown onto the table and they left the bar. The Maitre'd approached them as they crossed the lobby, his face like thunder. He was about to speak but one glower from Farmer was enough to make him think twice.

They ambled out of the bar and went hunting for somewhere else to drink. Chandler ended up walking next to Farmer. Straight away he was on his guard. Farmer's mood had been spiky since Arthur had died, but since then, so many more of the squadron had gone west, it hardly seemed justified.

"Give it another hour?" suggested Farmer, trying to make conversation. Chandler shrugged, uncertain.

"If you like."

"I do like," Farmer paused. "Glory boy."

Chandler shot him a look to see that the big man was smiling.

"Farmer, I swear-"

"You did pretty good today," he said matter of fact. Chandler was so surprised to hear the praise he didn't know what to say at first.

"Well, thank you," he said finally.

They carried on walking. Farmer whistled a little, badly off tune. The only consolation is that it wasn't *The Teddy Bears Picnic*.

"I hated you for a while, you know," Farmer said suddenly, his voice stiff.

"I don't see why."

"Neither did I at first. Then you got that DFC." He tapped Chandler's chest. "It just made things worse."

Chandler glanced down at the white and purple ribbon on his left breast. It was such a little thing to cause so much grief.

"We've both got one now," he pointed out.

"Makes us even then."

"Everyone should get one of these after what we've been through the last few days."

"I suppose," agreed Farmer, nodding. "They were better than both of us," he said gruffly.

"Why say it now?" Chandler asked.

"To clear the air? Maybe because we won't be here tomorrow and it just seemed right to say something while I had the chance?" Farmer held out a hand towards Chandler. Chandler grasped it and shook his hand.

Ashton walked down the corridor and stopped at the door. He waited a moment and then knocked. There was a curt *'enter'* and he went in. It was dark, the windows were closed, the curtains were drawn for the blackout and the main light was off. Valerie sat at his desk, surrounded by a pool of light from his desk lamp. He looked up and smiled.

"Squadron Leader, this is a pleasant surprise." He gestured to the chair in front of his desk. "Take a seat please."

"I'm sorry to bother you, sir. I called at your home but your wife said you were here."

"At home, it would be nothing but interruptions. I needed some peace and quiet tonight." Valerie smiled and gestured around the room. "So I came here."

"I can understand that. Its days like today I miss the veldt." He could instantly picture the wide vistas of home, the orange glow of the sun as it went down; the way dust swirled and filtered the light. "People need moments of solitude."

He'd needed some time to himself that afternoon but a moment was all he could spare. With Winwright gone, he was senior and until anyone from Wing told him otherwise, he was now in charge of the Squadron. Pettigrew had come in looking pained, particularly when he said he could only put up four aircraft for tomorrow.

"Four?"

"363 needs an engine change. Yours has holes in the main spar so I'm not sure about that yet and Chandler's needs an engine change and a raft of other things. The fuel tanks need patching-"

"I didn't ask for a shopping list!" he had said, terse.

"You asked." Pettigrew shrugged, looking a little offended. "All the rest are going to need work. The lads have been working for twenty four hours solid, sir."

Ashton sighed.

"I know. I've already asked for some more replacements but there's no guarantee we'll get them. Do your best, George."

Pettigrew cracked him a tired smile as he left.

"Always."

Ashton sat down and mulled over the crew lists. Right now, he had more aircrew than aircraft. They had to get those replacements otherwise there wasn't much else they were going to be able to do.

His eyes caught a signal on Winwright's desk. His desk now, he reminded himself. He glanced at it and his brow creased. His lip curled by the time he got to the end. It had come from the Air Ministry.

> *Please convey to the pilots and crews of the AASF, my congratulations and admiration of how they have carried out the tasks allotted to them under intense pressure of this German advance. Their determination and fortitude have earned unstinting praise from our allies and reflect the greatest credit on the service and Britain's commitment to the coming conflict.*

Ashton felt the anger bubbling up. He screwed the letter up into a small ball and threw it across the room. There was no way he was going to read that out to the crews; they would laugh him out of the room.

Valerie watched Ashton quietly. He recognised that look from a long time ago. It was happening again.

"You have some bad news?"

Ashton fiddled with his peaked cap, twirling it in his hands.

"I don't suppose there's any easy way to say this. Wing Commander Winwright is-"

"Is gone, yes?" Ashton nodded. Valerie sat back and glanced at a wall covered in black and white photographs in their frames. All of them were of pilots in flying gear stood near their aircraft. "I thought it was something like that."

The room was silent. Valerie rested his elbow on the edge of his desk and rested his chin on his hand. He sat like that for a few minutes until he finally cleared his throat.

"Is there any hope?"

Ashton shook his head.

"None, I'm afraid."

Valerie reached for the glass of wine on his desk. He cradled it in his lap for a while and then toasted the photos on the wall before finishing the wine off. Still looking at the wall, he asked Ashton a question he would have asked Winwright.

"Will we stop them?"

Ashton took his time answering.

"I don't think so. There's just not enough of us."

Valerie suddenly sat up and rummaged amongst the paperwork on his desk. He found what he was looking for and waved it in front of Ashton. It was a newspaper with *'Churchill'* written in bold black type.

"I was reading the words of your new Prime Minister, Winston Churchill. Blood, toil, tears and sweat. That's what he says it will take to achieve victory."

"Churchills a bit of a firebrand sometimes," Ashton said stiffly.

Valerie thought that perhaps they needed a bit more vim right now. French politicians had been very good at making noise for years but achieving very little. What was required was someone with some fire. Maybe Churchill was going to be that man.

"It will be different this time, I think. They won't be content to just beat us. The Boche have never forgiven us after Versailles."

Ashton grunted.

"We'll do our best, sir."

"Then my prayers go with you, Squadron Leader."

While the crews were in town, Kittinger started getting the personal effects of the missing, killed and injured together. He'd already done the CO's kit and was working his way down the list. He ducked into Pettifer's hut with Burke following behind to lend a hand.

Pettifer had shared a hut with Milton, Archer and Pendleton over the winter. Since Sunday he had been in the hut on his own. That Sunday evening he'd helped Kittinger help pack his comrades' kit. Looking around the room, they took stock. What they saw chilled them somewhat.

Pettifer's bedding was all rolled up. His valise was packed. A few personal items were out on a makeshift table made from ammo boxes, but apart from that, everything he had was ready to go. Three envelopes were leaning against a travel clock. Burke looked at Kittinger.

"How did he know?"

Kittinger gave a small shrug of the shoulders.

"People just know sometimes." He picked up the valise and undid the clasp. He opened the bag and peered inside. Just because Kittinger had packed it, didn't mean there wasn't something in there his family wouldn't want to see. "Hullo, what's this?" he said. He reached into the bag and pulled out a picture frame. Burke stood at his shoulder and looked at it.

It was a photograph of all the squadron's pilots with Winwright in the centre, his arms crossed. They were stood in front of a Blenheim.

"I've not seen this before," said Burke. He took the photograph in his hands and peered at it.

"The CO had it taken the day we arrived in France. I didn't realise Pettifer had a print made." Kittinger had seen the photo on the CO's desk in his office numerous times before.

Pettifer had made one change to the photograph. He'd blotted out the face of every pilot the squadron had lost since arriving in France. It was a grim sight. Of the squadron's original eighteen pilots and Winwright, there were only five of them left.

2.29 – One Fine Day

They had a subdued breakfast in the woods under canvas the following morning. There was bacon, eggs, porridge, tons of toast and fresh butter and jam for those who felt like it. Chandler was ravenous, having missed lunch the day before. Farmer on the other hand just picked at his food, which was unusual for him. He kept one eye on the sky and one ear cocked listening for aero engines. The last few days had got to him a little and he was more than prepared to admit it.

Six months before, the squadron had flown to France to be a part of the great adventure before it was all over. They'd gone through one of the worst winters on record and now, less than half of them were still around. Flak and fighters were not particular; they'd gobbled them up without preference or mercy.

They were still eating when two new pilots arrived. Chandler glanced at them briefly over a steaming bowl of porridge. They looked like they'd walked in from some sort of fashion show. Their uniforms were clean; the straps of their gas mask bags were hung neatly across their chest. They looked very out of place amongst the rest of them sitting around in their flying gear.

"Pull up a pew," he said, kicking over an ammo box with a flying boot. He finished the porridge and moved onto a bacon sandwich. He spread butter on the bread and then rearranged the bacon so it didn't peak out from the ends of the slices. The newcomers sat down.

"Thanks, that's decent of you," one of them said, holding out a hand. "I'm Purvis."

Chandler shook it, his fingers greasy with butter. He wiped them afterwards on the leg of his flying suit. Purvis looked at his hand in distaste. He pulled a handkerchief out of his pocket and wiped his hand. No one else had spoken.

Purvis eyed the pilot; he assumed it was a pilot, sitting next to him. There was stubble on his cheeks; his eyes were hollow with fatigue. His flying suit looked like it was ready to be cut into rags. There were scorch marks, grease marks and general dirt all over the fabric. Bacon fat dribbled down Chandler's chin and he wiped his sleeve across his face. He reached over for a bottle of sauce but couldn't reach far enough. Purvis leaned forwards and handed him the bottle.

"Thank you."

Balancing the sandwich on his lap, Chandler removed the top slice of bread. He carefully banged the bottom of the bottle, encouraging the tomato sauce to dribble out all over the bacon. Putting it back together, he bit into it with relish.

"Are you a red or brown man?" Chandler asked Purvis around mouthfuls.

"I'm sorry?"

"Sauce; on bacon. Tomato or Daddies sauce?"

Purvis took a moment to think about it.

"Daddies sauce," he decided.

"And I thought there was some hope for you," said Chandler, his voice edged in genuine disappointment. He turned his attention on the second replacement. "How about you, mister?"

"Croft. Peter Croft," he replied, his voice a little nervous. "Tomato sauce for me, I think."

"You think, or you know?" Chandler challenged.

"I know."

"Good. We're all tomato men in A Flight."

Farmer examined the two pilots over his mug of tea. Croft looked like he should still be in school. His skin was soft and pink like a baby's. He had light downy blonde hair on his cheeks and very fine hair on his head. His forage cap looked like it was two sizes too big for him. Slight in build, he reminded Farmer of Pettifer but he shut that memory down before it had a chance to float to the surface.

Purvis was older, maybe twenty three and built more solidly. He was short and compact and looked like a rugby player or a boxer. He certainly had the ears for it. Mangled cauliflower ears had been haphazardly attached to his head. Thick black hair was combed over the top of them.

"Purvis, Croft," called Kittinger. The two newcomers snapped their eyes right towards the Adjutant. Kittinger hooked a thumb over his shoulder. "The CO will see you now."

Purvis and Croft stood up, collected their bags and followed Kittinger to the flight hut. They nodded goodbye but the frosty response stopped them saying anything else.

"Did we look as keen as that?" asked Preddy.

"I'm not sure. I don't remember," replied Farmer.

Croft and Purvis walked behind Kittinger. Both of them noticed Kittinger was carrying a rifle. They'd wanted action, now it looked like they were going to get it. Kittinger wheeled the replacements in. They dropped their bags and flicked off a crisp salute. They waited patiently for Ashton to speak.

"Gentlemen, welcome. It's been a turbulent time here recently, but I hope we can make you comfortable. It's going to be a busy day today, so get your gear and find Flight Lieutenant Farmer; I've got a job for you."

They almost floated out the door. Croft was bursting with pride at being given an assignment so soon. Purvis was a little more reserved in his reaction. Ashton shared an amused look with Dane.

"Does Farmer know you've got him shepherding some greenhorns round?" the academic asked.

"Not yet, but we've got to collect those replacement aircraft and I can't spare any of the other lads right now."

He turned his attention back to the map and listened as Dane outlined the latest news from Wing.

Farmer was less than thrilled when he was told he'd be taking the two new men as passengers to the depot park near Saint-Riquier. He said nothing on the trip out. After they picked up the two new Blenheims, he curtly told them to stick to him like glue for the flight back.

While he was gone, Ashton led four aircraft and hunted for enemy tank columns on the other side of the line. They didn't see any Panzers, but they did find a motorized column on the move. Going in from 9,000 feet, they laid their bombs on the target, causing mayhem amongst the infantry. The crews loved it, no flak and no fighters bothered them.

They eagerly gathered round Dane as they gave their battle reports. Dane was just pleased to be writing down positives for once without any negatives attached. He gave them a rousing well done and sent them off for lunch.

Ashton had Pettigrew turn the Blenheims around fast and they took off again within the hour. He led again but changed out the remaining crews to give everyone a fair roll of the dice.

Once more, they went out and got back intact. This time there was some flak, but apart from a few minor holes, no one was injured. The Germans must have had the day off as no fighters were seen at all. No one complained at the change.

Farmer returned with the two spares close to dusk. There had been innumerable delays at the depot and it was an angry Farmer that led the flight back. Purvis and Croft had been nervous. They had no crew, no navigator and were on their own. They kept close to Farmer's wing in fear of losing him as the sky darkened. They had no idea where Bois Fontaine was. If they lost Farmer, they'd be lucky to find the aerodrome at all. As soon as they arrived, the erks started getting them ready for the morning.

The pilots sat around laughing and joking about their day. This time, Purvis and Croft were included in the banter. Chandler talked to Croft about their instructors at the OCU. They'd gone through the same unit only months apart.

Purvis was more of an old hand. He'd come from a Blenheim Squadron in 2 Group and volunteered to come over to France. That gained him instant respect. He gained further approval when he fished out two bottles of whisky from his kit bag and passed them round.

Ashton watched the activity from his office window in the gathering dusk. He mused on how little it took to raise the men's spirits. The Squadron's tail was back up and the crews were laughing and joking again, which was a good sign.

Only one day had gone by without casualties, but it had been a good day. Ashton reached into the bottom drawer of the desk and pulled out a half full bottle of whisky. He poured out a measure and held the glass up in salute before drinking it. Everyone had gone out and everyone had made it home. That was reason enough to celebrate.

2.30 – House Of Cards

The confused situation around Sedan crystallised. By Thursday, just six days since the campaign had started, the Germans had broken through. They had bowled over the French army and were already well on their way to Paris. With the front sundered apart, the German Panzer divisions fanned out, hooking round the flank of the 9th army. French units began falling back to reform the line. The door, hinging at Sedan had swung open. In twenty four hours, Rommel's 7th Division smashed through the lines and advanced thirty miles. Utilising speed and mobility, they caught a motorised infantry Division bivouacking for the night and cut them to pieces.

The breakthrough revealed the weaknesses of the allied command structure. Sluggish, slow to respond at the best of times, this sudden advance left it reeling. General Gamelin had set up his headquarters in the Chateau of Vincennes. A pretty Royal fortress, Mata Hari had been executed there in 1917. It had no radio contact with the outside world and Gamelin relied on regular dispatches like some 18th Century commander.

He started issuing orders to units, urging a counterattack. By the time those orders went out, the units either no longer existed, had surrendered or retreated. German forces advanced quicker than the maps could be updated. Rather than accepting that he was at fault, Gamelin believed he had been betrayed. He caused more chaos by sacking some of his commanders.

Defeatism started to waft along the corridors of power. The stench pervaded every department, going all the way to the top. The French Prime Minister Paul Reynaud called Churchill telling him 'we have been defeated, we are beaten; we have lost the battle'. The French commander's floundered like headless chickens. While Gamelin and the government steeled themselves for an attack on Paris, Rommel and Guderian turned right and headed for the sea.

Now only a few miles from the front, the BAFF had to pull back. At the moment they needed to be attacking the Germans, they had to pack up and move to the secondary airfields prepared the previous year. The move was a costly one. Having already suffered heavy losses in equipment, unserviceable aircraft had to be left behind. Stores were blown up, runways were mined. Nothing was to be left for the Germans to make use of. Convoys of trucks carried the groundcrews to their new airfields to carry on the fight.

Even while they relocated, the Battles went out night bombing, but the effect was like pelting a blazing fire with snowballs. It was a David and Golaith struggle, but this time there was no lucky shot that would fell the giant. Barratt's only consolation was that the night flying reduced the casualties amongst his Battle crews.

Further north, Saundby's wing continued to fight. By night, the Battles went out, by day, the Blenheims. Flying in support of the beleaguered BEF forces, they bombed targets along the Scheldt River. Harding was shot down again, this time bailing out but was back by tea time. Naisby went down in flames over his target, a pontoon bridge ringed by flak guns. Croft and Purvis survived their baptism of fire and flew five times in two days.

While the BAFF reorganised, 2 Group flew sorties from the UK in support to cover the gap. They paid a high price. 82 Squadron lost eleven out of twelve in one raid. The cracks were starting to show.

2.31 – Do What You Can

It was Saturday, the eighth day since the German offensive began. The morning started like the others; an early stand to in case of an air raid, then the groundcrew carried on repairs and servicing of the aircraft. A civilian truck dropped off bundles of fresh bread and the men had tea and sandwiches at ten.

Dane was walking away from the cookhouse munching on a sandwich when he saw the dispatch rider going towards the flight hut. He'd heard the motorbike come snarling down the lane and wondered what it was doing here. The rider was walking fast and already reaching into his satchel for the paperwork. He kept looking over his shoulder at the sound of heavy guns in the distance and quickened his pace. Dane considered that. The noise had become so frequent in the last few days he'd almost blanked them out, but they did sound louder today. He ambled over to the hut to see what was going on. Ashton handed him two signals as he walked into the hut. Farmer walked in behind him, his large frame filling the door.

"Are we on?" he asked.

"We're on," said Dane, reading down the page. It was all there; target; times, numbers.

"Get the boys ready," said Ashton. "Twenty minutes."

Farmer nodded curtly and started shouting for the crews to get ready. Burke shouted "Two Six!"

The erks started organising to get bombs from the dump. A small tractor puttered off with the bomb trolleys attached. A bowser went down the line topping off the tanks. The air split with thunder as the engines were run up and the machines made ready. Ashton signed for the orders on a small clipboard the dispatch rider handed him.

"Anything else you can tell us?" he asked the Corporal.

"Blooming chaos everywhere, sir. There's loads of refugees on the roads. The Jerries are only thirty miles from Arras, the last I heard, but that was two hours ago. Gawd knows where they are now."

There was another loud explosion and the Corporal flinched. While he was on his motorbike, the sound of the engine drowned out the guns. He took the clipboard from Ashton, saluted and left rapidly.

Ashton read the other signal. It was a warning to be ready to move at short notice. The exact location was yet to be decided. That depended on how successful the French counterattacks were in the Sedan sector and how well the Dyle Line held. He folded it up and put it in his top pocket. He turned his attention to Dane.

He was looking at the map on the wall. He found Le Cateau easily enough. Curious, Dane checked the scale legend on the map and then hunted out a ruler. He measured the distance. Only fifty miles away, this would be a very quick raid indeed. It also explained why the guns sounded louder this morning.

"And so?" asked Ashton.

"There are reports of troops and transport at Le Cateau. We've been asked to put up six aircraft and attack as soon as possible. Bomb them, or a bridge or a road. Anything to stop the advance. Height etc at our discretion. Maximum bomb load."

Ashton grunted.

"They'll get what we have." Just last night, Burke had told him they were running low on 250lb HE bombs. No new supplies had arrived despite requests, so they would have to use a mix of 40lb and 20lb bombs in containers to supplement the 250's. "I see we'll have an escort," he commented, glancing at the top sheet.

"Yes. You're supposed to rendezvous over Douai and they'll cover you in."

Pettigrew came into the hut. He rubbed his oily hands on a bit of cotton waste and wiped his forehead. He left a dark streak behind.

"I can give you six, sir."

"Six is fine. We've only got seven crews anyway." Ashton picked up his parachute harness. "For what we are about to receive," he said as he made for the door.

Ashton led with Chandler and Purvis. Farmer had Hagen and Sutherland. Croft watched them go with some envy. At eleven they were over Doaui. Ashton circled the town to the west. A twitchy AA battery had lofted a few shells up at them and he had no wish to provoke them further. After two circuits, he checked his watch. No fighters had shown up. He gave them five more minutes but no fighters put in an appearance. He decided to push on. His navigator gave him his course and Ashton set off. Not long after, they were at Le Cateau.

It was a small town west of a large forested region, lying on the Cambrai to La Capelle road. A junction led roughly south to Saint Quentin. There had been a battle here early in the Great War, where the British troops had fought during the retreat from Mons.

An important road junction, it was one of the main routes of advance for the German thrust and the defences had been prepared accordingly. The flak rose to meet them as they came into range. The intensity was nearly as bad as it had been over Maastricht only six days before.

Not wanting to make themselves a target, Ashton took the Squadron down immediately. He pulled the boost and let the Blenheim go down at a fair old lick. It felt like he was on a fairground ride. His stomach clenched as they went down. Tracer came up to meet them, strings of bright lights that got faster and faster as they whipped past.

Ashton could see mechanised transport going down the main street of the town. Rather than bomb the tanks, he had an idea. He altered course slightly and ordered the Flight into line astern. Farmer broke off as instructed and went to starboard. Once there was enough separation, he angled back and converged on the centre of town from a different direction. He would cross the target just after Ashton and rejoin with him after the drop.

Mitchell peered down the sight. Rather than go straight down the street,

Ashton intended to cut across at an angle. He told Mitchell what he wanted. Dead ahead he could see the main street. Troops packed the cobbles alongside the tanks. Either side were houses and shops. One house at the end was burning. He lined up on it and watched it grow closer.

The German gunners hesitated for a moment. Two groups were coming in from two different directions at the same time. They split their fire between them, which was exactly what Ashton wanted.

A criss cross of tracer reached up towards him. Mitchell dropped his bombs one after the other.

"They're away!" he shouted.

Ashton angled to port; Hagen and Chandler following close behind. Farmer flashed over the same point a few seconds later at 1,200 feet after releasing his bombs. He formed up behind them.

Each aircraft dropped two 250lb bombs and eight 40lb bombs. They straddled the street, bursting among the houses either side of the tanks and infantry. The burning building split apart. Bricks flew everywhere as it collapsed onto the road.

Griffiths looked back out of his turret and shouted for joy as plumes of smoke and flame went up. Two more houses collapsed as the other bombs went in. When the dust settled, the road was blocked. The wreckage of bricks and broken vehicles would need to be cleared before anyone could use that road again.

On the way out, both elements took hits. One moment, Sutherland was tucked in nice and neat on Farmer's starboard side, the next he nosed in, the Mercury engines going full belt. The Blenheim blew up as it dug a hole in the French countryside. Chandler caught a burst in his starboard engine and began to lose power. Ten minutes from home, he started to lag behind but he managed to nurse the Blenheim back to Bois Fontaine.

An admiring crowd gathered round as he shut the engines down. Most of the cowling had been shot away and thick oil streaked back over the wing. There were holes in the flaps and strips of canvas hung down from his elevators.

Pettigrew and Burke got to work surveying the damage. They'd become all too familiar with this sort of thing in the last few days. The engine change was easy enough, the rest would take a bit longer to fix.

Dane gathered everyone round and went through his questions, the nature of the target, had they hit it, what was the opposition like, anything else of note. Standard stuff.

"How would you evaluate the forces on the ground?" he asked.

"Loads," Said Hagen.

"Lots," echoed Chandler, their tone teasing. One thing nobody had seen was any appreciable mass of French troops to stop the Germans.

"I reckon there was at least a Brigade getting ready to pass through La Cateau," offered Morgan. "There was dust of columns of vehicles on the horizon to the east. I think there was a Battalion of infantry in the town itself, a company or so of tanks and a load of trucks."

"Defences?" Everyone grimaced.

"Heavy," said Purvis, his tone level. "The Germans are serious about keeping the advance moving. Everything from 20mm upwards around the town."

"88's?" queried Dane, pushing his spectacles up his nose.

"I'd say no," said Farmer. "Everything else though; including the kitchen sink."

"Better than Maastricht."

"We still lost, Sutherland though," said Ashton.

"It couldn't be helped," said Purvis, "but we could have lost a lot more."

Heads nodded in agreement.

"Will Sutherland make it back?" Dane asked; his tone neutral. He knew Sutherland was missing but no one had mentioned what had happened to him yet.

"Not a chance," said Ashton. "Straight in from low level. It'd be a miracle if there was enough left to fill a thimble."

Dane blinked rapidly and then scribbled a note on his clipboard.

"Any fighters?"

"Not this time," Farmer informed him. "Good job too really considering our escort never showed up." He lit a cigarette and glanced at Chandler. "What happened to you?"

"Flak coming off the target. No big deal."

Dane promised to raise the issue about the escort with Wing but Chandler rolled his eyes. He knew how much good that would do.

"Alright chaps," said Ashton. "Get some lunch and relax until we find out what's going to happen next. Off you trot."

He watched them go, their mood quite buoyant despite losing Sutherland. Dane went back to his small hut, amending some details to his report as he walked. Ashton caught up to him.

"Not bad," Dane congratulated him. "Another target hit."

"It still doesn't feel like we're making a difference though," Ashton grumbled a little.

"That'll come," said Dane. "The French are due to put in another counterattack shortly.

"I hope so." He paused to let Dane through the door first. "If we don't stop them soon we'll get cut off."

"That's right." Dane pointed to his wall map. "They're driving for the sea." Ashton looked at the arrows showing where the Germans were reported to be. That information had to be at least twenty four hours old, maybe more.

Griffiths found his brother's arms deep in an engine. He picked up a spanner from the tool box and tapped it against the collector ring. His brother's head appeared above the cowling.

"Hullo, Mark. You alright?"

"Yes.

"I brought lunch." Griffiths held up a flask and a greaseproof paper bag.

"Gimme a minute. Burke'll have my guts if I don't get this engine fixed."

He tightened up a fitting and then got down. Oil was smeared all over his arms and fingers.

"What have we got?"

"Tea and a wedge."

"Grand." He fished in the bag and pulled out a thick cut bully beef sandwich. Martin poured the tea into two tin mugs he'd brought with him. They sat on the grass, letting the sun warm them. Flies buzzed around while the guns continued to boom in the distance.

Mark Griffiths envied his brother sometimes. Here he was, earth bound, while his brother was out taking the fight to the Jerries. If he had his way, he'd be up there too, but he suffered from chronic air sickness. So his brother flew, while he remained on the ground.

He nudged Martin when he saw Kittinger walking across the field. He wasn't exactly sneaking, but he was spending a lot of time looking over his shoulder while he made for the stone wall beyond the huts.

"He's going to meet, Miss Hortense," Mark said. Martin grinned. Since she'd thrown open her house to the wounded those first few days, the squadron had a soft spot for Hortense. Everyone knew she and Kittinger were an item.

They ate in silence, enjoying the sun and the sounds around them. They were a long way from home but sitting like this for a while got them back to the nature that they loved. Martin threw a few pieces of bread for the birds to take and they watched as a Starling hopped down and pecked at it.

Another dispatch rider came onto the airfield. They watched as he was directed to the flight hut and went tearing across the grass and went running inside. They shared a look. No one moved like that unless he had some bad news. It looked like the squadron would be going up again shortly. Mark handed his brother the tin mug and went back to work. They may need this Blenheim sooner than he thought.

On the other side of the field, Kittinger stood at the stone wall with Hortense having lunch. She'd brought a basket and spread a small white and blue chequered table cloth over the flat stones of the wall. An opened bottle of Bordeuax peaked out from the basket. They held hands over the wall.

"Will you come over tonight?" she asked, as usual.

"If I can," he replied, as usual. It had become their routine these last few days and she looked forward to these moments. They'd meet for lunch if they could and he would spend a few hours at the house in the evening.

"I saw only five come back this time," she said quietly.

"Yes, we lost Sutherland." He gave her hand a squeeze. "Bought it. Nice chap." He was not sure if she'd ever met him. "Good batsman for the county. Played a sterling hook shot by all accounts," he said, as if that answered all further questions.

She gave him a wan smile. Typical English understatement. Three young boys had been killed and the fact that the pilot had been good at cricket was considered explanation enough.

He stared off into the distance for a moment, his eyes far away while he thought about the jobs waiting for him. He had three more sets of kit to pack up now, letters to draft for the CO, bomb and munition supplies to chase up, flares to replenish, fuel, the list went on.

They both saw the motorbike going across the grass. Kittinger saw the urgency in the rider immediately, the set of his shoulders, the questing eye, looking for someone in charge. He picked up his rifle.

"I have to go."

"I know. I know you'll be busy, so I think I'll go to town for a while. I need a few things. I'll see you tonight, Michael."

He leaned over the wall and she kissed him, hard. Her hands grabbed the front of his tunic and pulled him closer. He surrendered, holding the kiss for as long as he could.

"I love you," he whispered, and Hortense thrilled at hearing him say that.

"Je'taime," she replied and smiled.

He stepped back and picked up his rifle. He was the Adjutant again as he turned away.

2.32 – Take What You Can

The Squadron returned a little after two. The target had been a concentration of armour around Rethel, north of Rheims. Ashton came straight in. As he touched down, the props windmilled to a stop and he came to rest far back up the field, out of fuel.

His tanks had been holed by flak over the target and he'd expected to burst into flame any second. When he didn't brew up, he'd nursed his Blenheim carefully to make it back. He'd watched the fuel gauges like a hawk, watching them go down steadily as the fuel poured out of the tanks. They were nudging empty as he came over the field. Just as the wheels kissed the grass, the engines cut and Ashton had let her run, just amazed he'd made it back at all. He leaned back in his seat and let out a sigh of relief. Mitchell gave a whoop of joy.

"Blooming marvellous skipper. I thought we were going to have to step out for a moment."

"So did I," Ashton admitted. "So did I."

One by one, the rest of them landed. Farmer's port engine was spewing out smoke. Croft had to blow the undercarriage down with the emergency cartridge because his hydraulics were shot out. Touch and go this time, but they'd made it all back again.

Ashton took his time walking back while some ground crew rushed out with the small tractor to tow his Blenheim to the trees. Kittinger met him halfway. Ashton had seen him coming, eating up the distance with his big strides, his shoulders taut, his face a picture.

"I'm glad you're back, sir."

"So am I Adj. Problem?" he asked, noticing how on edge Kittinger was.

"Not now you're here, no."

He pointed over to dispersal where Ashton could see a number of army uniforms milling about.

"What's the fuss?"

"A bunch of engineers turned up about twenty minutes ago with orders to blow the field immediately. That's the fuss, sir."

"Blow the-"

"Blow the field. I told him the Squadron was out on a raid and you were due back any time. It was all I could do to make him wait. He's very keen to get the job done."

"I'll bet he is. Any orders from Wing about this?" Ashton asked.

"Nothing I'm afraid. The field telephones are out so there's no direct contact and there's been no dispatch rider since this morning."

So it's finally come to this, Ashton thought. First the initial assault, then the breakthrough, now the retreat. It's what he'd feared was going to happen after seeing the state of affairs from above. The Germans were advancing everywhere and nothing would be able to stop them. He felt a little like King Canute, trying and failing to keep the waves back.

"Billy, take the debrief. I'll have a word with the brown jobs."

"Righto boss."

Mitchell angled left towards the crews and waved his arms, beckoning them to come towards him.

Ashton dumped his parachute harness by the door and then sagged onto the chair in his office. He didn't ask the Captain to sit. He glanced around the office for a fast half second and then turned his attention to the soldier.

"So, what can I do for you, Captain?"

"Matthews, sir, Royal Engineers. I have orders to blow the airfield and its facilities."

"I see." Ashton steepled his fingers in front of him, elbows perched on the desk. Matthews continued.

"You need to get your men loaded onto trucks and get them away. I'll destroy all your stores and mine the field to prevent the enemy from using it."

Ashton bristled at being so bluntly told his business, particularly when there'd been little notice to get organised. Wing had only warned them this morning about a potential move. Pettigrew knocked on the frame and poked his head through the door.

"Four serviceable, sir. 361 probably needs an engine change, yours is a bit leaky and 374 has hydraulic problems. Everyone else just has holes to patch."

"How long for those three?"

Pettigrew shrugged.

"A few hours. I'll know more once we get the cowlings off on Farmer's. The rest just need their tanks topping off."

Ashton turned back to Matthews.

"There you go, Captain. It'll be a few hours at least before we'll be ready to go."

"I'm afraid that runs counter to my orders, sir. I'd already have been getting to work if your man here hadn't persuaded me to wait until you returned."

"Then that poses something of a dilemma." Ashton rose to his feet as his anger began to build. He bunched his hands and leaned over the desk towards this Captain who was so peremptorily telling him what to do. "This is a bomber squadron of the Royal Air Force." His voice started to rise in volume. "This is *my* airfield and I'm not about to up and leave just because you tell me to. If we leave now when the aircraft aren't ready, we may as well run up the white flag right now!"

Matthews didn't flinch as he went onto the counterattack.

"For your information, the Germans have taken Amiens. That's forty miles away! They may even be closer by now. You don't have hours."

Ashton looked out of the window and sighed. Forty miles. Even allowing for a slow rate of advance, the Germans could be here any moment. Matthews was right. It was time to go. He shouted for Burke out the broken window. Burke came hustling across the grass.

"Sir?"

"We're packing up. Drop everything, get the four that are serviceable

355

ready to go and find Mr Pettigrew."

"Sir!" Burke saluted. He turned on his heel and dashed off to get things moving. Ashton glanced back at Matthews.

"Fair enough?"

The young army Captain smiled.

"Fair enough."

Ashton was sorting through the desk when Pettigrew came into the hut. He issued instructions fast. They were to leave the stores and the dumps to the Engineers, but he wanted the trucks loaded with as many spares as they could in the time available. Pettigrew asked how long he had.

"Twenty minutes? Thirty? Don't bother refuelling. We've got more than enough for a short trip. Bomb up each aircraft and then get the boys into the trucks. Make your way to Saint Omer, that's where we're headed."

It seemed like the obvious choice. Saint Omer was a depot park and was directly away from Arras by at least twenty miles. It would do until he was able to make contact with Wing.

He dumped all his confidential paperwork into the waste basket and then carried it outside. He lit a match and then watched impassively as flames licked at the paper.

Elsewhere, personnel were running in different directions. Dane and his orderly were piling confidential information on the floor in the Intel hut. A soldier started pouring petrol all over it. Dane left clutching the squadron diary and records books. The soldier flicked a match into the hut. It went up with a massive whoosh, orange flame roaring out of the doorway, lapping around the overhanging roof. The soldier moved onto the flight hut, lugging two petrol cans. He started throwing petrol around inside.

"Wait," said Ashton. He went back into the small office and recovered the photograph of the squadron in its frame from the desk. He left the soldier to it and went to get his personal gear together.

Kittinger rushed around, getting the transport organised. Nine trucks were serviceable but two others failed to start, so he had them hooked up to another one by a tow rope. Erks started chucking boxes of spares and tools into the backs of the trucks. The bowser was topped off from the fuel dump and then parked next to the trucks ready to go.

Time was ticking and Kittinger kept glancing over to the engineers as they went about their work. The Bofors guns were spiked. A pin was pulled and a grenade was pushed down the barrel. A few seconds later there was a clang and the barrel ballooned. Smoke drifted out of the muzzle. The ready lockers with the ammunition in them would be blown up later.

Thick columns of smoke rose into the sky as the remaining huts were torched. Wood crackled and there were tinkling sounds as the glass in the windows fractured from the heat.

Chandler looked at the spread of personal items in his tent. He rolled his uniform up and shoved it into his kit bag. Shoes went on top. Everything else just got thrown in, followed by his sponge bag. That scene was repeated all over the field.

The aircrews gathered back at the aircraft while people scurried around. Ashton broke the bad news to those who would be left on the ground. Himself, Hagen, Chandler and Farmer would fly the four serviceable aircraft. They stowed their personal gear in the planes while the rest of them traipsed over to the trucks.

Griffiths hunted out his brother and found him chucking tool kits into the back of a Bedford. He gave him a hand. They lifted a hydraulic jack up together.

"I'll be off soon, Mark."

"I know."

"You be careful, okay?"

His twin brother flashed him a confident smile.

"Always. Besides, we'll have, Mr Kittinger and, Burke looking after us. We'll be alright."

They embraced and then went their separate ways.

As final preparations were made, it suddenly occurred to Kittinger that Hortense wasn't at the house. For the first time in his career he found himself torn between duty and personal desire. The men were looking to him to look after them, but he needed to make sure that Hortense was safe too.

He scribbled a quick note and then grabbed LAC Griffiths as he was going past with a spanner set. He told him to take the note to the house and pin it to the front door. There was no time to spare to go searching for her in Béthenville. He had no idea where she'd gone. As Griffiths was about to go, Kittinger said one more thing. Griffiths had never seen him so serious.

"If you see her at the house, tell her we're heading out and she needs to follow as soon as she can. The Germans aren't far away; she needs to get out of here."

At half past three, Matthews decided he'd waited long enough. He'd allowed himself to be persuaded into waiting far longer than he dared. He tapped his watch and pointedly looked at Kittinger. Distracted, Kittinger kept looking off to a big house visible in the distance and Matthews had to shout to get his attention. Kittinger nodded in understanding and found Ashton by the trucks talking to the men.

"It's time to go lads. No one could have worked harder, but it seems that events have overtaken us. Keep together on the road and for god's sake, no one gets lost all right? I'll see you all at Saint Omer."

He left them in Burke's hands. Kittinger and Pettigrew did a count to make sure there were no missing strays.

Two erks stood by each aircraft, waiting to help with the start up. Matthews stood by the nearest Blenheim, his brown uniform at odds with the RAF blue.

"Once you've gone, we'll mine the field and start the demolition work." Ashton extended his hand. Matthews ignored it.

"Thank you, Captain."

"I'll be reporting this."

Ashton almost laughed in his face. The whole world was collapsing around them and he was more worried about the regulations.

"You do that."

Just before he got into the Blenheim he took a last look around. He could hear soldiers in the woods causing mayhem. The huts were well ablaze, the skeletal remains blackened and charred. The Bofors guns pointed crazily to the sky.

The rest of the squadron watched the four Blenheims take off. As they headed north west, the men boarded the trucks. They stopped when the first of many explosions started to sound behind them.

The three U/S Blenheims were blown up first. Petrol had been poured over the wings and inside the fuselage. One grenade in the cockpit and that was that. Their backs broke and they burned fast, their noses pointed to the sky.

Kittinger couldn't bear to see any more. He got into the leading truck. Pettigrew got in with him and Burke chose a truck in the middle. Allowing for refugee traffic, he reckoned it would take an hour, maybe two to cover the distance. The Blenheims should be waiting for them when they arrived.

The trucks pulled out and hit the main road, turning right to hit the Auchel to Therouanne road. Kittinger's heart was heavy in his chest. He was leaving Hortense behind and there was no way of knowing when she would be following on or if she was safe.

Martin Griffiths was driving the last truck in the line. He waited for his turn, while each one drove off. The last two Bedford's in front of him moved off gingerly, the second one being pulled along on a tow rope. Griffiths dipped the clutch and engaged first to follow. He drove down the lane and then slowed up as he approached the junction, giving the one on tow plenty of room. While he waited, he looked to his left and saw a woman on a bicycle frantically waving at them as the trucks drove off. He pulled on the handbrake when he realised who it was.

"Come on Griffiths, what's the problem?" said LAC Cooper, who was in the passenger seat next to him.

"Don't worry," Griffiths reassured him. "We'll hardly get lost." He pointed out the windscreen. "Its bright daylight and we've only got twenty miles to go."

"You heard the CO. We're *supposed* to stay together," replied Cooper, fretting.

"Wait," Griffiths said. He turned the key in the ignition and the engine stopped. He got down from the cab and watched the woman on the bicycle get closer.

"Mark!" protested Cooper.

"Just a minute," he said shortly over his shoulder.

The bicycle soon closed the distance and Griffiths saw he'd been right. It was Mrs Allison. He waved a hand and she pulled up next to him. Her face was flushed from the exertion of cycling at speed.

"What's going on?" she asked, speaking quickly in concern. "Where are you all going?" She looked beyond Griffiths while the Engineers continued their work. There was a loud bang on the other side of the wood when the fuel dump was put to the torch. Smoke billowed out of the trees.

"We're moving out, ma'am."

"Are you coming back?"

"I don't think so, ma'am."

"Where?"

Griffiths hesitated, but the Adjutant had told him to say that she was to follow them. She could only do that if she knew where to go. He passed the message.

Hortense looked towards her house and then over her shoulder towards Béthenville. She'd been shopping when the rumours started that the Germans were within a few miles of the town. Then an army truck had gone speeding through the square, shouting that the Boche were hot on their heels.

"Tell him, I'll follow as quick as I can." She span the pedals and pointed the handlebars towards the road.

"On that?" Griffiths was surprised by her response.

"I'll make it," she said with determination.

He looked a little dubious.

"Mark, come on!" Cooper leaned out of the cab and pointed up the road. The rest of the convoy had disappeared round a bend. Griffiths made a snap decision.

"Get in," he told her. "Get in," he repeated. He banged on the side of the truck. A head appeared from under the canvas.

"Wassup?"

"Tubby, give me a hand getting this bike in."

The disembodied head disappeared for a moment and then a portly erk dropped down off the tailgate. He grabbed the bike and shoved it up to waiting hands in the truck.

"Come on, ma'am."

She hesitated a moment longer and then let Griffiths help her into the cab. Clothes could be bought. She had money in her pocket and she could always come back when things settled down again.

"Thank you."

"It's nothing ma'am. Just helping out."

Griffiths settled himself behind the wheel and turned the key in the ignition. It was a little cramped in there, but it wouldn't be for long. He just wondered what Burke would do to him when he found out what he'd done.

He floored it and soon caught up with the rest of the trucks. They made a good steady twenty miles an hour for a short while, eating up the distance. Things bogged down when they passed through the village of Therouanne. Three roads converged in this small hamlet and the squadron's trucks ran into the middle of a mish mash of army units, refugees and foot traffic. Griffith's truck stopped short of the village.

Strung out along half a mile, they inched forwards while people swarmed past the truck. Either side of the road was a drainage ditch and there was no room to turn around and try a different route. Griffiths wound the window down and leaned out, trying to see how far the blockage went up the road. One or two men spat on the truck as they walked by, shouting abuse. Griffiths ignored them.

"Ignorant blighters," said Cooper. "Pardon, ma'am."

"It's all right. They lost everything; I suppose they have to blame someone."

"Blame the Germans then, not us," said Cooper. "Oi!" he shouted as someone kicked the front wheel on his side. He leaned over and mashed on the horn.

"I told you," said Griffiths. "No one touches that but me."

A gap opened up so Griffiths edged forward a few yards. He crawled slowly, hoping that he could catch up to the truck in front, which was a good few hundred yards ahead. A British soldier jumped up onto the running board and hung off the driver's door.

"You got any room in the back chum?"

"I might."

"There's four of us. We got separated from our unit days ago."

Griffiths looked at him hard. He certainly smelled like he had been roughing it for a while. One epaulette was torn off his battledress. He hooked a thumb over his shoulder.

"Get in. You might have to budge up a bit."

"Thanks mate." Griffiths watched him in his mirror as he gestured across the road and then clambered into the truck. The truck wobbled a little as they got in.

Gradually they moved forwards, moving into the town. Some civilian trucks came out of a side street and forced their way in front. Griffiths shook his fist as his view ahead was blocked. They kept moving slowly. Griffiths felt nervous, hemmed in like this on all sides.

As they got to the crossroads, there was some debate in the cab as to which way to go. Both signs said Saint Omer. One turned right, the other straight ahead. None of the squadron's other trucks was in sight.

"Blessed if I know which way to go."

Hortense leaned over Cooper and asked the foot traffic if they had seen a convoy of trucks. There was a lot of Gallic shrugging. One military truck looked much like another.

Griffiths elected to go straight on. If they'd chosen the wrong route, they could always meet the Squadron when they got to the airfield. They passed slowly through the town. It had taken over an hour to go a few miles.

The refugees outside stopped them moving again. Griffiths turned off the engine. It was just burning up petrol sitting there doing nothing. Besides, the engine was running hot and this was not one of the better trucks.

While they waited, Hortense asked about Kittinger. She only saw one side of him; she took the opportunity to ask what he was like on the Squadron. Cooper caught Griffith's eye and imperceptibly shook his head.

"He's okay ma'am," Griffiths said, keeping it neutral.

"Hortense, please," she corrected him. "At the very least call me Mrs Allison. Ma'am makes me sound ancient."

"He can be a terror at times." Griffiths grinned. He remembered what Kittinger had been like during that first raid on the airfield, standing in the open, shouting his defiance. "But he looks after us. He's good with the men."

She smiled, pleased.

People started moving more quickly around the truck and Cooper hitched in his seat to get a better look outside. He opened the door and hung off it to look back down the road. People were starting to panic. Voices were getting louder.

"Can't see a blessed thing," he said. "Something's upset them but I don't know what."

A few seconds later, they realised what it was. People started pointing up. A woman screamed. Children were crying. One girl stood at the roadside wailing. She'd lost her grip on her mother's hand and been left behind. People started to panic. The old and infirm were shoved aside. If they fell, they didn't rise again.

Cooper shouted at people to get out of the way. Griffiths started the truck and leaned on the horn. He gunned the engine as a warning and then edged forwards. Someone pushed against the door. He made sure it was locked.

"C'mon, move, move," he muttered. Neither of them saw Hortense almost shrink inside the cab, hugging herself close. An AA gun on the other side of town started firing, the deep thud adding to the general clamour. There was more pointing, then the crowds scattered off the road, taking cover in the ditches.

Griffiths took the opportunity to floor the throttle and the truck leapt forwards, gathering speed. Cooper looked back. What he saw chilled him to the bone. Stukas were falling out of the sky. He heard the keening sound of the sirens as they dived down.

The leading Stuka pulled out of its dive, releasing a bomb from its belly. The bomb speared into the road ahead of them. Dirt flew into the air, lit from inside by a blossoming ball of orange. The truck rocked from the shockwave. Griffiths stamped on the brakes. The truck slid ten yards before it came to a halt.

"Out. Out fast!" He thumped on the cab's back wall and shouted, "Out, everyone out!" He tried the door handle but it didn't budge. He was a moment remembering that he'd locked it. He opened the door and almost fell onto the road.

"Out! Get out!" He looked up as the next Stuka came down. "Move!" Bodies started spilling out of the truck. The stray soldiers came out, tumbling for the ditches. Tubby Jones was next, followed by Maguire, then the rest.

Griffiths helped Hortense out of the cab and pushed her towards the ditch. He was making sure the truck was clear when the second Stuka dropped its load. He turned to run when the bomb landed next to the truck.

The explosion lifted the truck and moved it sideways. Griffiths was blown off his feet and across the road. He landed in the field beyond the ditch and landed in a heap amongst some rocks. The truck brewed up next. Flame consumed the canvas and started on the tyres.

Three more Stukas released their bombs. The ground shook in quick succession. Hortense crouched in the bottom of the ditch, burying her head in her hands. This was terrifying. When the airfield had been bombed, it was somehow remote, something she watched from her window. In the middle of it, she screamed, wanting it to end.

The AA guns boomed in reply. One Stuka was hit, a lucky shot that smashed into the cockpit. With a dead hand on the stick, it went straight down and buried itself in the ground.

It went on. More bombs rained down. The sirens wailed during the dive. People screamed. Some ran, unable to take the noise any longer. A few got away; others were cut down by flying shrapnel.

After dropping their bombs, the Stukas came back down to strafe the road. A bus, two Citroen town cars and two carts towed by horses were shot to pieces, the machine guns tearing them apart. Men and women flattened themselves on the ground. Bullets tore up the grass around them. The Stukas came down again and again, raking everything in sight. Anything that moved received special attention.

Heat from the burning truck intensified as some of the cans of petrol in the back burst. Blazing petrol leaked onto the road. Cooper grabbed Hortense roughly by the shoulder and lifted her out of the ditch.

"Quickly!" he shouted.

Eyes wide in terror, she ran first one way, then another, the grass pulling at her shoes. Something hit her in the back and she fell to the ground, unconscious.

Finally, it was over. The noise of aero engines receded and people cautiously peered out from behind protective hands. They started breathing again. Slowly, they picked themselves up and blinked, hardly daring to believe they were still alive amongst the carnage.

Cooper started rounding up the men. The four soldiers they'd picked up in town had disappeared. They found Griffiths in the field. His head had been smashed in against a rock. His eyes were wide open. Hortense was lying on her side a few yards away.

She moaned in pain when he rolled her onto her back. The right sleeve of her jacket was torn and the material was red with blood. A bullet had hit her arm and she had taken a bash to the head. The skin on her temple was already starting to swell and purple with bruising. He shouted for a bandage and Tubby Jones managed to produce one from the first aid kit he'd salvaged out of the truck. Cooper rummaged amongst his memory for some first aid basics. He put pressure on the wound and then wadded up some gauze to put over the gash before wrapping the bandage around her arm.

People from the houses were rushing out to help those the Stukas had gunned down. Two little girls lay face down in the dirt. They were still holding hands when they were gently lifted up together. Cooper turned away, sickened.

They carried Hortense back into town and searched for a Doctor. Cooper found a nurse who directed him to take her to the village hall. Some casualties had already been taken there and were laid on blankets on the parquet floor. They found a place for her and laid her down. Medics rushed around, overwhelmed with the number of casualties.

"I'll stay with her," Cooper told Jones. "You guys get to Saint Omer and I'll follow on as soon as I can."

Jones glanced at Hortense. She was very pale and Cooper mopped her brow with a handkerchief.

"I'd rather stay."

"Come on Tubby, someone's got to show some good sense. I'll stay until I know she's okay; then I'll hoof it along the road."

Jones blew out hard, his cheeks ballooning while he decided what to do. He clapped Cooper on the shoulder.

"See you later."

2.33 – The Sweepings

The four Blenheims circled the depot near Saint Omer. It was west of the town, a very large field with clusters of aircraft dotted around the perimeter. Even here, Ashton could see that the Luftwaffe had made their presence felt. The grass was dotted with bomb craters and some huts were burned out shells. After landing, he taxied towards some Blenheims already on the ground. A group of ground crew in boiler suits stood watching them.

As the engines windmilled to a stop, an RAF Flight Lieutenant came out of a hut by a slit trench. He shaded his eyes as he looked up at Ashton's aircraft. Ashton sat on the lintel of the cockpit and looked down. He tugged off his flying helmet and ruffled his hair.

"Good morning," said the officer. He waited while Ashton got down from the Blenheim. Ashton shrugged off his parachute harness and gave it to Mitchell.

"Get the boys together, would you?" Mitchell nodded and started rounding up the crews.

Ashton unbuttoned his Sidcot flying suit and the officer caught a glimpse of Squadron Leader rings. He snapped to attention and saluted. Mildly amused, Ashton returned the salute.

"Good morning. Squadron Leader, Ashton, from Bois Fontaine."

The Flight Lieutenant blinked in surprise. He glanced at the paper on his clipboard. He lifted the top sheet and then looked up, confused.

"Flight Lieutenant, Towers, sir. I'm afraid I don't have you down on my list, sir."

"List?"

"To pick up replacements. I'm afraid I don't have any Blenheims available."

Ashton clicked his tongue in annoyance.

"We're not here for replacement aircraft. We were moved to continue operations." There was a pregnant pause. "You've got no idea of what I'm talking about, do you?"

"I'm very sorry, but I've had no word about this at all."

Ashton pinched the bridge of his nose.

"Right then." He started walking towards the hut. "Let's go and sort this out. Follow me," he said over his shoulder.

Towers was left behind for a moment before he scurried to follow. The men stood around, expectant faces turned towards him when he returned ten minutes later.

"Shambles, total bloody shambles," Ashton raged.

"Problem?" asked Mitchell, deadpan.

"God knows. No one has a clue what's going on. We've got no idea where Wing is. Can't raise them; or HQ either. Shambles," he said again. Mitchell snorted.

"Doesn't surprise me. It's been a total mess so far. Why should this be any different?"

Ashton hooked a thumb over his shoulder.

"All they have contact with is some Divisional HQ for the army. They're trying to find out where HQ has gone." He watched as a bowser went to each aircraft and topped up the tanks. The depot erks were stood looking at the aircraft. A Warrant Officer asked Mitchell where the form 700's were.

"Sorry. In transit. Our gear should be arriving soon."

The Warrant Officer sucked on his teeth. His brow wrinkled in disapproval.

"Irregular, sir. Most irregular. We're supposed to have the forms to go with the airplane if you're going to do anything to it."

"I do appreciate that. We did leave Bois Fontaine in a bit of a hurry. There is a war on."

With grudging reluctance, the Warrant Officer nodded his head.

"We'll do our best, sir."

Mitchell watched as they serviced the planes. Their best was slow. It was all done properly but there was no sense of urgency about them at all. Mitchell found himself comparing them to their own groundcrew. Burke would have had it all done by now. He supposed this was the difference between a front line squadron and a depot unit.

"So what do we do, boss?" Mitchell asked.

"We find a target to hit and keep on going unless I hear otherwise."

While they waited for things to sort themselves out, the crews gathered on the grass by their aircraft. Their stomachs were grumbling and they rummaged amongst their pockets for anything to eat. Preddy found two chocolate bars in his flying suit.

Some of them dozed. Morgan produced a pack of cards and got a game of brag going. He quickly lost a week's pay to Mitchell and loaned a pound off Chandler. The way Chandler saw it, he'd either get paid back soon enough, or they'd go down together, in which case it didn't matter. His pilot glanced over his shoulder as he lost another hand.

"I tell you what, Morg. Why don't you just *give* him the money? It would be the same thing."

"Aw skipper, where's the fun in that?" Morgan picked up a new hand as Mitchell took a turn at dealing. He rearranged the cards so they were all neat and tidy. He won the next three hands but they were all keeping a weather eye on the rest of the field.

"How long before the trucks turn up do you think?" asked Griffiths aloud. He rolled onto his back and draped his forage cap over his face.

"They'll probably get lost," said Farmer. "They're lucky they didn't have Morg map reading."

"Hey!" said Morgan in protest. "That's not fair. I haven't got lost for weeks now." He shouted in glee as he won another hand off Mitchell. Coins changed hands. "One more like that and I've won my money back."

"Beginners luck," said Mitchell, scooping up the cards. He shuffled the deck but had to start again as he spilled some of the cards on the grass.

"The trucks might be a while," said Chandler. He pulled at a large dandelion and started tugging the yellow petals off one by one. "You saw the crowds on the road. They've got to get through that lot to get here."

"I suppose," replied Griffiths, his voice muffled from under his cap.

"You wouldn't see it happening at home, I tell you that for nothing," said Preddy. He chucked a shilling onto the pile and looked at his cards again.

"Wouldn't see what?" asked Chandler, although he had a fair idea what Preddy was going to say.

"The panicking hordes. It's just not something a decent Englishman would do."

"Oh lord, this again." Mitchell rolled his eyes. Even Chandler groaned. Preddy was like a stuck record that just kept on going.

"I must admit," said Chandler, throwing Preddy a bone, "I've not exactly been impressed by our froggy friends this past week."

"It's not been good, has it?" murmured Mitchell. "Four shillings, blind," he said, announcing a bet. "All those tanks we saw on the newsreels-"

"-Blown into tiny pieces by the Stukas." Preddy tore up a handful of grass and then let the bits fall to the ground. "The BEF'll stop 'em." Farmer grunted in doubt.

"They better pull their fingers out then. The Jerries are coming on like an express train." There was a general murmur of agreement on that score. Morgan chucked some more money in to match Mitchell's bet.

Bored by the discussion, Hagen went for a stroll amongst the wrecks. He walked past a row of damaged Battle fuselages, slender metal tubes shorn of their tailplanes. A Queen Mary trailer was parked nearby, ready to go out and recover another wreck. He looked at all the code letters on the fuselages. JC was 150 Squadron. Over there was a 218 Squadron Battle, coded HA. He leaned against a 103 squadron wreck. The skin was peppered by shrapnel and the perspex was smashed. Suddenly moody, he tugged out the photo of Lorraine he had inside his wallet.

Two hours later, the convoy of trucks turned up from Bois Fontaine. Kittinger got down from the cab of the leading truck, frazzled from the stress of the journey. He left Burke and Pettigrew to sort the men into some kind of order while he hunted out the CO.

He found Ashton in the hut, hunched over a field telephone. He was scribbling some notes down on a piece of paper. The handset was clamped between his head and his shoulder while his free hand held a smoking cigarette which he used regularly. He nodded as Kittinger came in.

"I think if you give us an hour, we'll be able to do something about it, sir." He nodded. "Yes, sir. Not at all. We'll do our best. Yes, goodbye, goodbye."

He straightened, smiling to himself. Kittinger stood watching him. There was an air of weary resignation about him he'd not seen before.

"I'm sorry we're late, sir. It's a bit more difficult coming by road than it is by air."

"It's all right Adj. Get the boys working on the kites. We'll be going up soon."

"Yessir."

The depot's Warrant Officer collared Burke over the Form 700's. Irritated over such pettifogging, Burke had them retrieved from the second truck.

Pettigrew stood looking at a pile of aircraft debris and winced. There were all sorts, just piled up as scrap. A stack of wings were on the ground next to what was left of a Lysander. He beckoned over Flight Lieutenant Towers and pointed to two Mk IV Blenheims that seemed intact.

"What about those?"

"Sorry, sir. Both are U/S I'm afraid."

"What for?"

"One of them had its main spar holed by some 20mm. The other one needs an overhaul."

"I see. Thank you." Nodding to himself, he walked off looking thoughtful.

It didn't take the men long to make the aircraft ready. The depot staff had already serviced them but there was no way Burke was sending them off without checking the work himself first. Now all they had to do was find some bombs for any more raids. After this trip they were out and there were none to be had at the depot.

During all this, someone finally noticed that they were a truck short. Kittinger did a count and cursed, berating himself for missing that kind of detail. He knew Griffiths and Cooper's truck was not the most reliable one in the squadron, but there was little time to worry about it now. If they'd broken down, Saint Omer was a short walk and there was still plenty of daylight left for them to arrive. He assumed they would turn up at some point. Once the aircraft were away, he would go out in one of the trucks to look for them.

The crews were just heading over to Ashton's aircraft to be briefed when a Fairey Battle came into view and circled the depot. The engine was misfiring badly and it wasn't long before it landed and taxied up to the Blenheims. The crews gathered round in interest as they noticed the code letters on the fuselage. It was one of the Battles from Merville. The pilot looked surprised when he saw a load of faces turned in his direction. He waved when he recognised who they were.

"It's all right, sir," said Mitchell. "It's Smith. We were at 105 together for a short while."

"What are you doing here?" Ashton asked the new arrival. Smith got down from the Battle and took his gloves off as he walked round the wing towards them.

"I might ask you the same question. Hullo, Billy." He shook hands with Mitchell and then snapped off a salute to Ashton. "Sir."

"The army told me you all left Merville hours ago."

Smith nodded. The radiator of his Merlin engine cracked and pinged as it started to cool behind him.

"That's right, sir, the Squadron did, but I had a duff engine. The bitch wouldn't start." He slapped the leading edge of the wing with his gloves. "So they left and I was to follow on when I could. Then when I did get away it was playing up again. I didn't fancy crossing the channel like that, so I put in here to get it looked at first."

"Cross the channel?"

"We were told the Wings being reformed back in England. I'm heading to Lympne."

"No one told us," said Mitchell.

"The ground staff left to be ferried back, where was it?" he asked his navigator who had got out and was stretching his legs on the ground.

"Boulogne, Calais? Something like that," he replied. He stamped his feet and did some knee bends.

"At least you had some notice of the move," said Ashton.

"Not much." Smith replied in annoyance. They'd been compelled to leave behind five perfectly good aircraft due to a lack of spares. If they'd had the time, they could have taken them with them. Now the Jerries got to play with them instead. "We just got told to drop everything and head out."

"I suppose that answers one question," said Ashton as he scratched the back of his head. "No wonder we couldn't find Wing, they're not here."

He left Smith to get his Battle sorted out and gathered his crews together for a briefing.

"What are we going to do, sir?" asked Hagen, speaking for everyone there. They'd all heard what Smith had said.

"We might not have any orders but we're committed to this attack. I made a promise and I'm not going to let the army down now. When we get back," Hagen noted he said when, not if. "It'll be too late to do anything more today." Ashton rubbed his chin in thought. "First thing in the morning, if we can't make contact with HQ, then off to England it is. We go and the groundcrew set off to get the ferry home."

"You're the boss."

It was a quick briefing. He talked them through the attack. They would take a direct route out and back towards Arras. The situation was fluid and they would have to react to what they saw on the ground. There was a buzz of excitement when Ashton informed them they would be supporting a British advance against the German army. It was an armoured attack with infantry support and the BEF needed their help. This time it would be low level all the way there and back with only a loose formation for protection.

Feeling positive that he was actually doing something amongst all the chaos, Ashton climbed into the cockpit. Mitchell was in the nose as always arranging his maps and pencils.

"Ready, Billy?"

"As I ever will be."

Smiling, Ashton went through the start up sequence and thrilled as he always did when the engine burst into life.

2.34 – Lost

Kittinger was about to round up a driver to start hunting for the missing truck when Jones and the others turned up, footsore and hungry. Kittinger was pleased they'd made it for about one minute. He was upset when he found out Griffiths had been killed. He lost his composure when he was told about Hortense.

Fury gripped him. He went through the full gamut of emotions, one after another crashing over him. Anger, rage, worry, anguish, loss. Without waiting, he rushed to the nearest truck. With a roar of the engine he raced off down the road to find her.

He sped along the road, weaving to avoid potholes and bumps. Driving like a maniac, the truck quickly ate up the distance until he came up to one corner just a bit too fast. Jamming on the brakes, the Bedford slid into a wall and nearly went down the embankment into a ditch. While the sweat cooled on his back, Kittinger got down from the cab to inspect the damage. The front left wing was a bit mangled but nothing underneath seemed to be damaged.

He backed up a few feet on the road. There was a rending sound as metal pulled against stone. The wing was looking very sorry for itself but the tyre seemed to be all right. While he checked for damage, he had the chance to calm down. Racing to find Hortense would be no good if he killed himself doing it. When he set off again, he took more care, slowing down on the bends and paying more attention to the road ahead.

Not long afterwards, he came across Cooper, who was resolutely walking in the opposite direction. He pulled up next to him and told him to get in. Cooper was grateful for the lift. He'd not expected anyone to come looking for him. Kittinger soon corrected him. He asked how Hortense was and Cooper told him as much as he could.

"And you're certain she was alive when you left her?" Kittinger asked; his voice peremptory.

"Absolutely. She'd been hit in the arm and she had a bump on the head, but it wasn't that serious. I'm sure of that."

Kittinger remained doubtful. What did Cooper know about combat wounds? Kittinger had seen more than his fair share of those over the years.

"Do you know if they were going to be moved anywhere?"

"I'm not sure, sir. A few people were being carted off in ambulances straight away; then they started talking about moving some people in cars and stuff. I have no idea what actually happened in the end."

Kittinger stewed silently the rest of the way back to the village. Cooper directed him to the centre of town and they parked in front of a fountain outside a cafe. He got down from the truck and looked around.

The town had not changed in the intervening time since he'd started walking. There was still a number of refugees milling around, carrying the bundles of their belongings. One family hurried past with a child's pram piled high. The man walked quickly, one hand pushing the pram, the other keeping the bundles balanced as it bobbled over the cobbles.

Cooper pointed out the village hall and they walked across the street. Poking his head inside, Cooper found the hall to be empty. There was blood on the entrance steps and smears of red on the parquet floor inside. An old man in blue dungarees, dirty shirt and flat cap was pushing a mop around. Back and forth he went, shoving it through sticky pools of blood.

"Hello?" Kittinger called out. The old man continued mopping. Kittinger cleared his throat and said, "Excusez-moi."

The old man stopped and glanced at him.

"Messieurs?"

Kittinger tried explaining he was looking for an injured woman, but he may as well have been speaking Greek for all the cooperation he got. Eyeing him with some disdain, the old man went back to his work.

Kittinger's ears went red and his hands gripped the stock of his rifle, the knuckles going white. He strode across the hall. There was a sign indicating there was an office there. He tracked through some blood and the old man objected as his boots left bloody prints on the part he'd just cleaned.

Kittinger wrenched open the door of the office to find it empty. Turning, his eyes a little wild, he was about to say something impolitic and unbecoming a King's officer when a voice came from the heavens.

"Can I help you?"

The voice was heavily accented but it was English. Cooper and Kittinger looked up. A face looked down at them from a high window in the far wall, above the exit.

"I'm looking for someone, two people actually." Kittinger told him.

"Just a moment."

The face disappeared and they heard feet coming down a wooden staircase. A portly man, perhaps in his fifties with smart suit trousers and a white shirt stood in the doorway. His black hair was slicked back and a little moustache was perched on his top lip.

"You'll pardon me Monsieur; I was in the upstairs office to stay out of the way while the cleaning was going on." He motioned to the door and Kittinger joined him. "Now, what can I do for you?"

"My unit was passing through when the Germans attacked earlier. I lost some people."

"Ah," the man nodded in understanding. He nodded sagely to himself. Without another word, he went out into the square and they followed him. Outside, the man breathed deeply.

"You'll forgive me, the air in there." He made a waving dismissive gesture with his left hand and coughed lightly. "You were saying."

Kittinger did his best to reign in his patience.

"One of my men and a woman were brought to the village hall this afternoon after the air attack. The man was killed. He would have been in RAF uniform. The woman was a civilian."

"That's right," said Cooper. "She was pretty, a brunette, wearing a blue jacket and a floral print dress if that's any help."

369

It was not. The man nodded in understanding but there had been a lot of women injured that day. One more in a blue jacket was neither here or there as far as he was concerned.

He circled round the back of the village hall to where the dead had been laid out. A number of bodies were there, wrapped in blankets. He gestured to the mounds. A few of them were quite small, Cooper noticed.

"Your man will be here somewhere. I'll find out exactly where in a moment."

"And the woman?"

The man shrugged; his jowls moving as he tilted his head to one side.

"Everyone who survived was taken to hospitals in the local area. How bad was her wound?"

"I'm told it was just the arm."

"That's right," said Cooper.

"Ah, bon, then she'll have been taken to a hospital." Kittinger almost cried in relief. "I have the records in my office." They walked back into the village hall and went up the narrow stairs. A large room was up in the eaves. The ceiling was low but a window let in plenty of light. The man sat down at the table and turned to a journal of some kind open at a page.

"Town records," he explained. He produced a pair of pince nez from a breast pocket. He peered down his nose as he looked at a list of names written in a tight, small hand. "What was the lady's name?"

"Hortense Allison, or she may be listed as Hortense Moreau." Kittinger's heart was thumping in his chest and he offered up a silent prayer to whoever might be listening.

"Here we are. Allison, yes."

"Fantastic, where did she go?"

"I don't know." Kittinger's face fell. The man carried on talking quickly. "You must understand, ambulances came from all over. There were so many casualties when the Boche attacked the refugees on the road. A lot of people were taken in private cars. I'm afraid I don't know where she went."

All the pent up frustration went out of Kittinger when he heard that. There was no point making demands of this man. He scribbled the locations and names of the hospitals on a piece of paper.

Thanking him profusely, they returned to the truck. Kittinger felt limp as he turned the key in the ignition. The thought that Hortense was in some strange hospital, on her own, made him ill. As they set off, they asked where some of the hospitals were. A local pointed them towards two of them. They dropped in on the way back to Saint Omer but Hortense was not at either of them.

2.35 – Bread And Circuses

They went into action a little after 4pm. Heading south east, they passed over Béthenville. Ashton rocked his wings as the houses flashed underneath. Some people waved but there were more on the roads out of town heading west.

Hitting the open countryside he dropped down, skimming over the green fields. Spread out as they were, everyone kept an eye out for fighters of any kind. There was plenty of smoke on the horizon to tell them they were heading in the right direction.

On the ground they caught glimpses of British infantry advancing. At the forefront of the advance were British Matilda tanks. Designed to escort infantry troops in the attack, they had excellent armour protection and a 2lb gun capable of carving any German tank apart like a can opener.

Spirits rose. For over a week, the squadron had taken a shellacking in the face of the German advance. Now they were dishing it out. Closing within sight of Arras, explosions tore up the ground. Artillery was shelling something but it wasn't clear if it was theirs or the enemies. Ashton got a little height so he could see better.

There were fields of wheat subdivided by hedgerows. He could see the lanes tanks had made rolling over the crop. Two Matildas were smoking and burnt out, their guns pointing to the sky. Around them were a number of German wrecks, trucks and tanks that had been caught broadside on, easy meat for the Matildas.

The remainder of the British tanks had forced through the bushes into the next field. He saw explosions ahead as they exchanged fire with anti-tank guns dug in at the front of a thin wood.

It was a colourful light show as the German shells skidded off the front glacis plates of the Matilda. One Pak gun blew apart, and then a Matilda ground to a halt as one of its tracks was shot away.

"Here we go," Ashton murmured to himself. He clicked in the R/T. "Okay chaps. Follow me to the left. We're going to attack the guns and give those tankers a hand."

He eased the Blenheim into a steady turn to port until he was running parallel to the wood a mile or so ahead. Once he thought he had gone far enough, he reversed his course to the right, putting the skinny wood dead ahead of him.

He eased the throttles forward and then held it straight and level while the other three aircraft followed him in line astern. No flak came up to meet them.

"All yours, Billy," he said on the R/T. Mitchell smiled as he hunched over his bombsight. It was a perfect day. There was next to no ground wind, no haze and no rain, nothing that could put him off.

The target was coming up and he saw a gout of flame come out of the barrel of a German Pak gun. He used that as his aiming point. He asked Ashton to make a slight adjustment and the Blenheim rocked as his pilot nudged the nose left with a deft use of the rudder. Mitchell counted down, four, three, two, one, He salvoed the bombs in one go. Two 250lb HE and twelve 20lb bombs spilled out of the bay and rained down on the unlucky Germans below.

Two Pak 36 guns were blown to pieces, the crews torn to bloody shreds. One 250 landed on a trailer of shells and the explosion was quite spectacular. The rest of the squadron dropped on target and laid waste to the battery. More guns and trucks exploded. The morale of one crew broke. Under threat of tanks from the front and bombing from above, they ran, screaming their heads off as they careered through the trees.

Bursting from cover, they bumped into some nervous infantry behind them. A Corporal took one look and that was all he needed. He dropped his rifle and started running too. Some of his platoon followed suit. The Matildas swept either side of the wood and fired on the infantry. Their Besa machine guns added to the confusion. Infantry were scythed down in heaps.

A Panzer II turned off the road and opened fire with its main armament. 20mm rounds spattered off the turret of the nearest Matilda. Its driver used the tracks to help train the main gun onto the target and it returned fire. Its first shot went wide but the second caught the Panzer II in the engine bay. It came to a shuddering halt and brewed up immediately. A Panzer III appeared but its main armament had no luck either and it fired off smoke cartridges to cover its withdrawal.

The Matildas pushed on. Artillery fire landed amongst them. Two brewed up, their crews spilling out of the hatches writhing burning parodies of men.

Ashton circled above and spotted a column of infantry marching up the road towards the British position. He looked around. The sky was clear. There were no clouds to hide behind and no flak was coming up to meet them. The bit between his teeth, he shoved the yoke forward, pulled the boost and dived on them.

Surprised by his sudden movement, there was a few seconds' pause and then the other three Blenheims followed him down. They spread out and converged on the hapless infantry. Ashton opened up early with his single wing gun. He watched the tracer arc out ahead of him. Some rounds skidded and shot off at crazy angles.

He pulled back on the yoke and walked his fire up the road, working the rudder to spray bullets left and right. Some infantry gallantly stood to return fire but most hit the deck and tried to find something hard to hide behind.

The rest of them followed suit and tore into the grey green ranks, venting a week's worth of frustration against an enemy they could see and shoot at. The turret gunners joined in as they passed over the troops, firing until they emptied the pan. Nimble fingers quickly reloaded and carried on shooting until they were out of range.

Finally satisfied, Ashton turned for Saint Omer. He went up to one thousand feet and called in the others. Well practised now, they smoothly slotted in on his wing and kept it tight.

They were whooping in delight as they got down from the aircraft and made their way over for debriefing. Kittinger had managed to evict Towers from his office so Dane could debrief the men properly.

There were plenty of positives on the scorecard this time. Guns destroyed and enemy units attacked. Dane wrote furiously as he called in each crew for their report. Farmer's crew went last.

"How many enemy tanks did you see?"

"At least eight or nine," said Preddy. Up front in the nose of Farmer's Blenheim he had a good view throughout. "Our tanks were having them for breakfast."

"How many wrecks?" Dane pushed his glasses back up his nose and flexed his fingers; they were a bit sore from so much writing.

"About five or six of ours," said Farmer. "Say, the same number of theirs. Plenty of smoke though, it might have been more."

Dane added the number to the tally he'd been keeping on a scrap piece of paper. Releasing Farmer's crew, he totted up the numbers before going out to find Ashton. Allowing for active imaginations, it was still a fairly respectable score.

"Not bad," he said to Ashton. "At least a battery of guns taken care of and some infantry as well."

"I just wish there had been more of that the last few days," Ashton breathed. Dane checked his wrist watch.

"I'll put a call through to Division; no doubt they'll want to know the position of the troops you all saw. Bad luck about Griffiths," he said.

Ashton nodded in agreement and left Dane to it. It had been a good end to a reasonably stressful day. No more losses. Maybe taking things one day at a time was the answer he pondered.

He walked over to where he saw Farmer and Chandler talking in animated fashion. Chandler was using his hands to describe a move to Croft.

"What's the word on tomorrow, boss?" asked Farmer.

"Have to wait and see on that one. Still trying to get things organised."

"What about tonight?"

"I've managed to prevail on Mr Matthews to provide some rations from his store." Ashton didn't bother to tell them it had been like getting blood from a stone. In the end, Matthew's hands had been metaphorically prised off some tins of bully beef and some loaves of bread. Supplemented with what they had brought away from Béthenville, it would make for a spartan evening meal.

"Oh well," said Croft. "I suppose it's better than nothing."

Chandler and Farmer had other ideas.

"Will it be okay if we snag a truck and head to town?"

Ashton saw their look and smelt a rat. He shook his head; they weren't at Béthenville anymore.

"Not tonight. I don't want anyone going too far, just in case. Head to one of the hamlets and see if you can get some bread," he suggested, "And eggs, the essentials. But no further."

Chandler and Farmer got together a foraging party. As the truck pulled out, Ashton waved them down. Farmer leaned out of the window.

"No boozing!" he warned. Farmer looked back, his face the picture of innocence. Ashton watched the truck as it left on its adventure.

"Excuse me, sir," asked a voice.

"Yes, Croft?"

"What about quarters, sir?"

"Quarters?"

"Somewhere to sleep, sir? We left all the tents behind at Béthenville, sir."

Ashton pointed to their four Blenheims and then to the other aircraft dotted around.

"There's no harm in roughing it, Mr Croft." He thought about the times he used to sleep out in the open on the veldt of his boyhood. He patted Croft on the stomach. "It toughens you up a bit."

Chandler glanced at Griffiths out of the corner of his eye while he drove. He'd told the young lad he needed him up front so he could map read, but he really wanted to keep an eye on him. He didn't want to leave the poor lad on his own tonight. When Burke had broken the news that his twin brother was dead there'd been virtually no reaction at all. Even now, Griffiths just sat there, unnervingly calm. He leaned back against his seat and kept his hands in his pockets.

"Let's try down here," Chandler suggested. He turned down a lane that looked the same as any other to Griffiths. Chandler had spotted a sign post on the grass verge on the other side of the road. The sign was missing, but the post had been left in place. Half a mile down the lane they came to a farm.

"Told you," Chandler said proudly. He got down from the cab and strode across the yard. He took no more than two steps when he got the fright of his life. A big dog came barrelling out of the barn, barking and snarling. There was no chain visible and Chandler legged it back to the truck. He got in and managed to slam the door before the animal could sink its teeth into him.

"Go away!" he shouted. "Wretched beast!" The Alsatian, stood on its hind legs, its front paws skittering against the door of the truck. "Wretched creature, bugger off! Can't you sort it out, Griffiths?"

"Me, sir? I don't think so. Remember what happened last time?"

A door opened and a man came out of the main house. He whistled and the dog dropped back down onto all fours. Giving a final grunt, it scampered towards the man. It circled his legs while he walked towards them. He made waving gestures, telling them to go back. Chandler smiled at him as he approached.

Farmer dropped down from the truck and walked round the cab. He eyed the dog nervously while he raised his hand in greeting.

"Bonjour, Monsieur. Um...vino, plonk?"

Chandler groaned. The farmer looked insulted.

"Good grief," said Chandler. "All these months in France and you can't even order properly." He addressed himself to the farmer. "Pardon Monsieur, je voudrais a cheter quelques bouteilles de vin s'il vous plait."

Hearing his mother tongue, the farmer became more amenable. They talked and the farmer took them to the barn. He lifted some hay and showed them rows of wine bottles.

"He doesn't want the Germans getting them," explained Chandler. As he said, *'German'*, the farmer spat on the floor.

"How much does he want?"

"Five francs a bottle."

Farmers eyebrows shot up.

"Five? The stuff must be paint stripper. Tell him four each and we'll take the lot."

Chandler replied in rapid French.

"He said we have a deal."

Money changed hands and they went back to the truck. Chandler looked in the mirror while they turned around. The stupid dog was running around in the yard and the last thing he wanted Griffiths to do was run it over.

They were going at a steady clip on the way back when Chandler suddenly shouted at Griffiths to stop. Griffiths hit the brakes. The truck slid to a halt and Farmer nearly went through the windscreen.

"Bloody clot!" he said, rubbing his forehead. "What's going on?"

He fished out a handkerchief and held it up to his nose. It came away red with blood. Griffiths looked where Chandler pointed and smiled. There were loads of chickens in the next field. He got down from the truck and started running after them.

"Well don't just stand there!" he shouted. "That's our dinner wandering around out there!"

Ashton walked around the men, listening to the gossip. It was a warm evening so no one felt the lack of tents very badly. There was a cheer when Chandler and Farmer came back in the truck.

"Dinner is served." shouted Chandler, chickens held aloft in his hands. Their necks flopped left and right after having been expertly wrenched by Griffiths. Someone got a fire going while the chickens were plucked and skewered and held over the flames. While the chickens had been getting plucked, Kittinger returned with Cooper in the Bedford. Cooper joined the erks but Kittinger shunned company and went to Matthew's office.

He sat in a chair and didn't bother lighting a lamp. He sat in the gathering dusk, trying to marshal his thoughts. His hands shook as he pulled out the list of hospitals from his tunic pocket and stared at it. For the first time in his life he felt lost. He reached for the field telephone.

The bottles of wine were passed around while they waited for the chickens to cook. Chandler nearly choked when he took his first swig. Farmer hadn't been kidding.

"God, that's strong." He coughed as it stung his throat.

"I don't care," said Hagen. "I'll drink it." He took the bottle off Chandler and tried it himself. He had a coughing fit and his eyes watered. He handed the bottle over. Farmer tried an experimental taste and made a show of swishing it around his mouth.

"You know, I think it's rather good. Robust, rustic, I think the term is?" He drank some more. Pettigrew came over to Ashton and offered a chicken leg.

"Eat up, sir."

"I hate to ask where you got them from," said Ashton, tucking in.

"Wandering around, sir," said Chandler. He saw Ashton's doubting look. "Scouts honour. Honest. They must have escaped from some farm."

Ashton said nothing more. He was at heart, a practical man. If he'd seen

375

the chickens, he would have done the same thing. After all, if they'd not taken them, someone else would have

"I was looking over those two U/S Blenheims earlier," Pettigrew said, pointing towards the parked aircraft, using the chicken leg for emphasis. "I reckon I could have one of those running again if I let the lads loose on it."

Ashton licked his fingers. He went over to the fire and pulled off another piece of chicken. He took a bite out of a carcass while he thought about that.

"Seems a shame to let it go to waste," he said.

"The other one could actually fly, but the main spar's a huge question mark. I don't think I'd like to sling it around and put it under any stress, but all it needs is some fuel."

Ashton nodded.

"Once we know what's happening, I'll talk to Matthews in the morning."

"Thank you, sir. There is one more thing?"

"Yes?"

Pettigrew hesitated. He stared off to the other side of the field and then looked down at the ground. He shrugged and cleared his throat.

"I was wondering if you could look in on Kittinger."

"What's up with him?"

Pettigrew swallowed hard. If Ashton didn't know better, he would have said Pettigrew was embarrassed.

"Spit it out, George."

"He's mooning over his popsy."

Ashton nodded in understanding. He'd heard the story earlier.

"I'll have a word with him."

Ashton snagged half a chicken and a bottle of wine and wandered over to Matthew's office. As he got closer, he heard Kittinger's voice shouting inside the hut.

"Someone must have some to spare. Fine. Fi-yes, thank you. Yes, I'll be here. Call if you have any luck."

Ashton knocked on the door and opened it. He brandished the chicken and the wine as an offering.

"Food?"

"Thank you, sir, but I'm not very hungry."

Kittinger rubbed his temples and leaned back in his seat. His eyes were sunken, strained. Ashton thought he looked tired. Up till now, Kittinger and Burke had been the tower of strength hauling the men up by their boot straps. Even they had their limits, it seemed.

"Everyone has to eat, Adj."

Nodding reluctantly, Kittinger took the chicken from him and Ashton put the wine bottle on the table. He gestured to the field telephone.

"Not interrupting anything, am I?"

Kittinger sat up a little straighter.

"No, sir. Of course not." He shoved a pad across the table. A number of names had been crossed out. "I've been trying to find some bombs for us tomorrow."

Ashton's interest quickened.

"Any luck?"

"Not so far. I've rung some of the French airfields, but no joy I'm afraid.

There are none at the depot and the army can't help."

"Keep trying. A bomber squadron is not much use without bombs."

"No, sir," Kittinger said, grim faced. Ashton tapped the table. He looked at the pad, playing for time.

"Adj?"

"Sir?"

Ashton wondered why it was so hard to ask such a simple thing.

"Do you want to take a truck back to Béthenville?" he asked. Kittinger looked up in surprise. "Mrs Allison may be there, you know."

"No, it's all right, sir. The line's been cut. I can't contact her brother. I've rung a few hospitals but I've no idea where she is."

He pointed to the crumpled list he'd been given in Therouanne. In between trying to find some bombs for the squadron, he'd called quite a few of them. None of them could provide any information as to where she was. There were two left to try, but he was almost tempted not to call them. He didn't think he could face hearing *'non'* anymore.

Kittinger almost laughed out loud at the memory of Hortense begging him to be careful. After everything he'd been through this last week, he'd been far from careful and he knew it. He had come through it all without a scratch and yet the woman he loved was lying in some hospital, god alone knew where. Feeling awkward, Ashton patted him on the shoulder.

"If you need to talk, Adj, you know where to come?"

"Thank you, sir." Sniffing, the older man sat straighter and rubbed his hand across his eyes. "I'd best call some more units, see if I can scare up a few bombs."

Ten miles away, Hortense was asleep in the spare bed of Therouannes Doctor. After Cooper had left, the town doctor had cleaned her wound, stitched it and dressed it. The wound itself wasn't very serious. The bullet had gone straight through but she had lost a fair amount of blood. The doctor gave her a painkiller and that, in combination with the pain and the blood loss, had knocked her out.

It was only a mild wound, not something worth cluttering up a hospital place for. The Doctor had two men take her to his house. Immediately installing her in the spare room, his wife made a fuss of her while he remained in the town hall to see to other casualties. When she woke in the morning, he would find out where she was from and see if he could get in touch with her family.

2.36 – The Last Gasp

Ashton woke early. He rolled onto his back and stared at the underside of his Blenheims port wing. There was a light breeze running across the grass and it looked like it was going to be another lovely clear day. He yawned as he sat up and scratched. He felt the rasp of some bristle on his chin as he rubbed his face. His mouth felt dry.

He found Griffiths sitting by one of the fires from the previous night. He was poking the ashes with a stick and blowing on them, encouraging them to glow. He added some sticks and got down onto his hands and knees, blowing harder. Some tendrils of smoke drifted up and Griffiths added some more wood. Soon enough, he had a roaring fire going and Ashton sat in front of it.

He watched quietly while Griffiths went through his morning ritual. He washed in cold water in his upturned steel helmet. The cold woke him up and he dabbed his face dry on a small hand towel. Ashton looked at him as he shaved. Griffiths did it blind, without a mirror, and he rubbed his skin as he worked, figuring out where he had shaved and where he had not. He dipped the razor into the water and rinsed the head regularly to keep it clean. Ashton watched for some kind of reaction as he worked. The boy went through the motions but his eyes were dead inside. When he'd seen him before, there had always been a sparkle of life in his face. Now it was fixed, lifeless.

Ashton walked back to his Blenheim to find Mitchell was still snoring away. Ashton nudged him with his boot. Mitchell's head lolled from side to side so Ashton nudged him again until he woke up.

"Good morning."

"Morning." Mitchell turned a bleary eye to his wrist watch. "Christ, it's five am."

"Like I said, morning."

Leaving Mitchell to rise in his own time, Ashton walked amongst his men, seeing them get ready for the day. No one seemed the worse for wear after sleeping in the open anyway.

By six, everyone was up and laughing and chatting to each other. Ashton assembled the squadron staff; Burke, Kittinger, Pettigrew, Dane. They drank from mugs of tea and smoked cigarettes while they stood in the open.

"I don't think I can ever tell you all how proud I am about this Squadron. We've faced some heavy odds but still managed to get the job done. There are some Squadrons that would have collapsed under the strain, of that I have no doubt."

He looked down as his foot brushed against a small rock in the grass. He pushed it with the toe of his boot, driving it into the soil.

"Unfortunately, we find ourselves in a strange situation. No contact with Headquarters, no way to get replacements and no bombs. So the question is;

what we do now." They waited in silence. "Is there any chance the situation might improve, Dane?"

The Intelligence Officer looked up in surprise that he'd been asked first. He shrugged.

"Anything is possible, sir. If the counter attacks around Arras are successful, then maybe we can hold the Germans from making any more gains." He squatted on his haunches and used a stick to describe a notional map. "At the moment, the Germans have a salient of advance that leads nowhere and they're surrounded on all sides by us and the French army. Concerted counter attacks *should* be able to cut them off."

"I sense a, *but* coming," said Pettigrew. Dane grinned.

"The last solid information I had yesterday evening was that the Germans were skirting round Arras and still driving hard for the coast. They may have already reached it. If they have, then it's us who are cut off from the rest of France."

Ashton's mouth pulled thin with frustration. The battle was entering its most crucial phase and here they were out of touch, out of the chain of command completely.

"Any luck raising Wing or HQ this morning?"

Kittinger shook his head. He looked exhausted. His eyes were red rimmed from lack of sleep.

"No, sir. No one's got a clue what's going on. If what Smith told us yesterday *is* right, then Wing will be setting up back in England wondering where the hell we are. The Colonel I spoke to at the Divisional headquarters seemed to think the BAFF HQ had pulled back from Rheims but he didn't know where."

"So we're on our own?" said Pettigrew.

"It would appear that way," said Ashton. "You're very quiet, Mister Burke."

"I've not got much to say, sir. My mother always said if you've not got anything to say, don't try and fill a gap."

"Do you still intend to fly back to England?" asked Dane. Ashton drank the last of his tea and flicked the dregs onto the grass.

"I don't see that we have any other choice. We've got to reform the squadron, get new aircraft and get back in the fight."

"How soon do you want to get away, sir?" asked Burke.

"In the next hour?" Ashton pondered. There were no bombs to load and the trucks were ready to go practically. Once they managed to prise some petrol out of Matthews, there was nothing to keep them at Saint Omer. "Then you chaps head for the coast and get the next ferry."

"So that's it then?" said Pettigrew, his voice grim.

"For now," Ashton agreed with sombre finality.

The meeting broke up, each of them getting the men organised. Ashton sought out Matthews. He found him in a hangar tasking out the day's work schedule with his work crews.

"We'll be pushing off shortly. I just wanted to ask for some petrol to get us away."

"I'll see to it, sir," Matthews replied readily. In truth, he was glad to see them go. They'd brought disruption to his ordered little world. The quicker things got back to normal, the happier he would be.

The squadron was ready in short order. After packing up yesterday at Bois Fontaine, there was little left to do. The kites were run up and the engines were kept ticking over while Ashton did the final rounds. Burke was waiting for him by his Blenheim. He shook Burke's hand warmly.

"Thanks for everything."

"Good luck, sir. We'll see you soon enough."

"Just don't fall overboard on the way back."

Chandler watched as Ashton taxied out fast. There was very little breeze. The wind sock barely twitched so they could take off practically straight ahead. Ashton's Blenheim gained speed and the tail came up. With no bombs on board, it almost leapt into the air. Ashton held it level while the wheels and flaps started to come up.

As he cleared the perimeter of the field, he was just going to port in a gentle level turn when his Blenheim blew up. There was a massive fireball as the petrol exploded. Chandler watched in horror as the engines buried themselves in a field and what was left of the fuselage tumbled to the ground.

They were all still frozen in shock when a 110 shot across the field. It was so low its propeller tips almost skimmed the grass. The guns in the nose flashed and tracer stitched lines in the ground, puffs of dirt flying into the air. People ran in all directions as one of the Bedford's brewed up.

Chandler unhooked his harness and scrambled to get out of the Blenheim. In the air, he had a chance. On the ground, stationary, he had none. Morgan followed hot on his heels and they ran for a pile of wooden crates to hide behind.

A Vickers machine gun fired at another 110 that wheeled right overhead. Chandler peered over the crate and saw Griffiths was still in his turret, blazing away.

"The young fool, he'll get himself killed," said Chandler. He started to stand up to run back to the Blenheim when Morgan grabbed him by the scruff of his neck and dragged him back.

"Watch it!" he shouted. Chandler banged his chin off the corner of the crate and fell back, slightly dazed as bullets tore into the ground around them.

After the 110's first pass, Hagen was tempted to try for a take off, but another flight wheeled in behind the first group and he changed his mind. He ran from the Blenheim just in time as a burst of cannon fire tore his bomber apart. A line of bullets chased him across the grass. He flung himself behind some oil drums. He shook his fist as a 110 roared overhead.

"Bastard!"

There were no AA guns at the depot. Being in the rear echelon, it had been decided by a clerk at HQ that they didn't need any. The 110's had free reign to shoot up whatever they fancied.

Bombs landed in the hangar. The roof collapsed and crushed the three Battles and ten ground crew inside. Matthew's office went up next. Maintenance records went skyward along with his desk and ink well.

Again and again the shark mouthed 110's roamed over the field, their guns dealing out death and destruction. Fireballs blossomed into the sky. Tents burned, stores burned. Men were cut down like wheat in a field.

Kittinger went charging across some open ground and slid down next to an inert Tubby Jones. Grabbing hold, he slung him over his shoulder and staggered under the weight as he carried him to safety.

Two bombs exploded and clods of earth were thrown into the air. Pettigrew was scythed down along with three other erks as they ran for some slit trenches. Burke cringed as cannon rounds thudded into the ground next to his head. He squirmed across the grass until he reached a pile of sandbags. Cooper landed in a heap next to him. He lay on his back, his eyes wide while blood trickled out of his mouth.

Some of the men found refuge amongst the broken airframes stacked on the grass. Bullets tore into the thin aluminium skins and screams mixed with the noise of snarling engines and explosions.

As quickly as it had begun, the mayhem stopped. The 110's cleared out and quiet descended. Chandler stood up from behind the crates to survey a scene of utter destruction. The hangar was burning. Hagen's Blenheim was a wreck. The undercarriage had collapsed. It lay at a drunken angle, its starboard wingtip resting on the ground.

Scraps of paper drifted across the grass. Chandler stooped to pick up a piece that fluttered past his feet. It was a form 700 for a Battle. He looked over to the row of fuselages and heard shouts for help. He ran over and started pulling casualties from amongst the carnage.

Croft was dead. He'd been shot in the back while trying to retrieve his personal effects from one of the burning trucks. A number of erks sported wounds but for all the mayhem, the damage was mainly material. None of their trucks had survived. Parked next to each other, they had made a juicy fat target for the 110's. Once the first one brewed up, the rest quickly succumbed to flame and bullet.

Miraculously, two of the squadrons Blenheims were intact. They were checked for damage but aside from a few new holes, nothing major was wrong.

With Ashton gone, Farmer found everyone looking to him to make the decisions. As the most senior surviving member of the squadron's aircrew, the mantle fell to him to pick up. Taking command, he saw no need to change Ashton's intentions. With only two aircraft left, there was nothing they could do here. Issuing final instructions, Farmer and Chandler started up their bombers again. Hagen and Purvis' crews squeezed in with them and the aircraft moved off.

Burke stood next to Kittinger and watched as they took off and headed north, towards the coast. They remained watching until the Blenheims were out of sight, climbing into some fluffy clouds at about three thousand feet.

"Time to go," said Kittinger darkly. Shifting the sling of the rifle on his shoulder he turned to the men. "Listen in lads, here's what we're going to do. Leave your gear. Take only what you can carry. Make sure you all have your tin hats. We're going for a stroll."

He let his gaze range over the men in front of him. Some of them looked scared. Others were grim faced, determined. He nodded. They were no different to the lads he'd led in the last war. It was time to head home but he was leaving his heart behind him.

Burke led the way, the men following behind in double file. Some of them walked heads down; some had their shoulders back, pride driving them. Dane shuffled along in the middle, his shoes already starting to pinch. Kittinger brought up the rear, counting off the men as they walked past him. He looked back at the trashed field, taking one last look at the smoking Blenheims.

"Next time," he muttered before turning and following his men.

THE END

Author's Note

This novel came about after reading an article about the fall of France in an aviation magazine. It relayed the fact that a particular Blenheim squadron had deployed to France in September 1939, and after tens days of Blitzkrieg in May 1940, they had lost 18 out of 21 crews. What was even more shocking was that this figure didn't even include the replacement crews who had also been lost during that period!

I was very struck by that figure. I tried to imagine how it must have felt to be in that squadron and to lose people you had known for years in the blink of an eye. I started some research and reading the accounts of survivors was even more chilling than the original article. Before May 1940, it may have been a 'Phoney War' according to the press but the bomber units suffered regular casualties to enemy action. Time and again I was gripped by stories of amazing bravery and a press on spirit. A lot of the units endured some pretty dreadful living conditions in France. The winter of 1939/40 was one of the worst on record so using that as a setting for my characters was an easy decision.

Many events throughout the novel were inspired by real episodes. There was no shortage of material to draw upon. It's true; a Blenheim did accidentally take off bombed up with live ordinance during a bombing exercise. I merely adapted the circumstances slightly to fit my story. The details I recount about the German offensive are also as accurate as I could make them based on the sources I was using. Aside from that, I have done my best to use period language and provide a period flavour to set the scene as a backdrop for my characters.

Bethenville as a place does not exist; neither does Bois Fontaine, but Merville did. It was a French Air Force airfield north of Bethune, I just had the RAF borrow it. The war correspondent Cullen was loosely based on the well known BBC correspondent Charles Gardner. Air Vice Marhsal Victor Goddard's personal Memoir about his time in France in the AASF provided the episode where Cullen witnessed the staff car bowling across the grass to beat the King to the parade ground and call the troops to order.

Some people might question why I have called the unit 'Falcon Squadron' rather than assign it a number. The simple fact is that at this period of the war, a lot of the higher numbers that would come into use later were nowhere close to being activated. For quite a while I contemplated bringing a squadrons reformation date forward and I dabbled with using 120 Squadron for that purpose. I have no wish to cause offence to veterans of such units so borrowing their number, even for a novel was something I decided not to do, hence 'Falcon Squadron' was born. Incidentally 120 Squadron's crest is described as 'standing on a demi-terrestrial globe, a Falcon close.'

While writing the novel, I have been fortunate to have had invaluable input from The Blenheim Society based at Duxford in Cambridgeshire.